Sing to Me
of Dreams

Books by Kathryn Lynn Davis

Too Deep for Tears
Child of Awe
Sing to Me of Dreams

Published by POCKET BOOKS

Sing to Me
of Dreams

KATHRYN LYNN DAVIS

POCKET BOOKS

New York   London   Toronto   Sydney   Tokyo   Singapore

POCKET BOOKS, a division of Simon & Schuster Inc.
1230 Avenue of the Americas, New York, NY 10020

Copyright © 1990 by Kathryn Lynn Davis

Davis, Kathryn Lynn.
    Sing to me of dreams / Kathryn Lynn Davis.
        p.   cm.
    ISBN 0-671-68313-6 : $19.95
    I. Title.
    PS3554.A934924S56   1990
    813'.54—dc20

First Pocket Books hardcover printing November 1990

10 9 8 7 6 5 4 3 2 1

POCKET and colophon are registered trademarks of
Simon & Schuster Inc.

Printed in the U.S.A.

DEDICATION

Always—

To my husband Michael,
who recognized and understood
the creative madness,
and helped me to accept and survive it.

And to Jillian Gardner,
who turned anger into inspiration,
friendship into trust,
and, most important, wished me
success *and* peace of mind.

ACKNOWLEDGMENTS

From the beginning, *Sing to Me of Dreams* has taken its own time, created its own detours and transformed itself through impulses that astonished and bewildered me. Writing this novel has been the most turbulent and satisfying, frightening and exhilarating experience of my life. As always, I would not have persevered without the support and enthusiasm of my friends and family. I wish to express my profound gratitude to these people:

For their help in the inevitable struggle to choose a title, I want to thank Chris Krummenacher, Bill and Jeff Odien and Virginia Magnuson Odien, who have more than once gone above and beyond the call of friendship. Also Camille Guerin-Gonzales, who read Indian poetry and wisdom with me while we searched for the true heart of the story. And Chris and Victor Sandoval who, after hours of frustration, came up at last with the title that eventually became *Sing to Me of Dreams*.

My mother Ann Davis, Kathy Bolyanatz, Marcella Waggoner, Jill Gardner and my husband Michael, all of whom read the manuscript and were moved, yet whose honest criticism I value more than praise that does not come from the heart.

ACKNOWLEDGMENTS

⁂ My sister Annie James, whose early excitement touched me deeply and inspired me when I might otherwise have despaired.

⁂ Merle Hausladen, who listened well and helped illuminate, through *my* eyes, the personal turmoil that so closely echoed the conflicts in the novel.

⁂ My agent, Andrea Cirillo, who has a very rare faith in me, and an even rarer ability to articulate that faith when I most need to hear it.

⁂ My editor, Linda Marrow, whose dedication is extraordinary, and whose patience, perception and intuition strengthened both the book and my belief in myself.

⁂ Finally, and especially, my publisher, Irwyn Applebaum, who had the wit and sensitivity to make me laugh at a lingering doubt, and so begin to conquer it.

Semper F.I.

Prologue

―――――――◖◗―――――――

Vancouver Island, British Columbia
1861

The child was born on a night of moon and thunder and a wind that sang high, sweet and clear, naming this a night of miracles. The clouds rumbled with rain that never fell and the grasses whispered the secrets of the night, the sighing, singing secrets of the darkness and the stars.

Koleili lay propped on her elbows, waiting, her hair a blue-black fall of water on the cattail mat. She was young and fragile, though oddly unafraid as she felt the uncanny stillness that had settled where the Many Waters flowed—the hush of the spirits' breath withheld, as if they too were waiting. The fear, which had shadowed and made dim the sun since she learned of the child growing within her, had left when the first pain ripped through her dark-skinned body. Now nothing moved but the distant wind and the baby, flailing in darkness, fighting its way toward the soft, beguiling light.

The People crouched outside the hut of woven mats, silent, expectant, for they felt the chill of magic in the air. They tapped their drums gently, rhythmically, reverently. Hawilquolas, who held sacred the creatures of the earth, he who would call himself father of the child, prayed to the sunrise, the beginning of all beauty, light and life. He prayed that Koleili would prosper and the child be strong and safe.

Koleili turned in the golden light, hands on her swollen belly, weary from the ebb and flow of pain, thinking of the Stranger who had given her this child. An impalpable presence drifted about her shoulders, flickered in the light of a single torch, shone in the eyes of the midwives, chief among whom was Kwiaha, who had the gift of *siwan*—the little magic. She it was who muttered words of power, who blew eagle-down from her callused palm, who painted with red ocher in the sand. She it was who stroked Koleili's belly and sang softly, crooning,

> Come easy to this world,
>   little spirit.
> Come from the secret waters of your exile
>   to the Many Flowing Waters of the Earth,
>   which welcome you and bless you.
> Come to me,
> Come easy,
> Come.

Kwiaha's daughter knelt beside her, rubbing Koleili's body with oil, gripping her hand when the pain was blinding. She crouched, poised and ready when the child began to come. Outside, among the tall and fragrant trees, the air stirred with a promise while a shadow fell upon the moon and the Thunder raged.

The girl-child came so quickly that the women were without speech. Before they splashed her with sacred water to wake her sleeping, unborn soul, she opened her mouth and smoke came from between her lips to fill the hut with a soft blue light.

Sweat-soaked and astonished, Koleili froze while Kwiaha and her daughter knelt, for they heard the sighing of the earth and the singing of waters which before had been stilled and silent. The midwives saw the child, who should have been frail and unable to hold herself upright, turn on her stomach, lift her head, and look at them with eyes the color of an Island lake—clear, ageless and wise.

Around the hut the sacred wolves—spirits of revered ancestors—made a circle, an impenetrable circle through which none could come or go. The sleek silver wolves claimed the girl-child theirs with a howl that split the Thunder and swept the shadow from the moon.

The white-breasted owls on the roof hooted; Koleili heard the mournful cry and whispered, "My child will be a Dreamer." Raven circled, dipped low over the hut, and Hawilquolas said, "The child will be a Dancer." Thunderbird moved through the heavens, roaring his power, and Kwiaha murmured, "The child will be a Healer."

The clouds sank low and the mist rose to meet them while the child opened her mouth and the three women gasped, enchanted, transfixed. The baby's voice, which should have been harsh and full of fury at her birth, flowed like water, like the silvery music of the birds.

Outside the People murmured songs of gratitude and worship. The earth had spoken in a rush of gilded waters, the sky in the clouds of thunder rimmed with moonlight, and the animals, each in his own voice and time. Thus was she born and blessed, the Child, the Prophet, who would bring the People to thrive among the Many Flowing Waters on the Island of the Raven in the light of the misted sun.

So it was promised, so it had come to be.

PART I

TANU

———⊶◆⊷———

Vancouver Island, British Columbia

Chapter

1

1876

She whom the People called Tanu, in awe and gratitude and not a little fear, lay awake, dreaming. In her dream, she saw the soot-blackened walls of the Longhouse, the sturdy cedar planks—unbent by rain or wind or cold sea air—that kept out the dark, cloudy night. In her hazy, half-dreamed dream, she smelled the damp mustiness of the house that rose above her into darkness, had risen so for many suns and many generations.

Four days ago Tanu had left the small, scattered huts of the summer village, where the People had been working since spring to catch and prepare salmon and game, berries, roots and leaves. These they had smoked and dried so there would be food when winter came. The summer storage containers had been filled to overflowing, so Tanu had offered to bring the food to the People's winter home, to store it safely in the low dug-out room of the Longhouse until it was needed.

Now she lay isolated by a curtain of smoke so fine it was invisible, except when a breeze rippled past, and the lines of the Longhouse wavered and grew dim. The looms and their carved spindle whorls stood empty, abandoned until winter captured the People within these moss-chinked cedar walls. The ridgeposts, with their carved likenesses of cougar, bear and deer, stood tall and strong, and cast shadows that breathed life into the fine old cedar, so that Tanu felt the power of their guardian spirits all around her.

She brushed the long black hair away from her face, yet still she felt on her cheeks the breath of her People, the memory of their voices, tinged with unusual excitement. There were many unspoken things that eddied in the air of the summer camp—plans and expectations which they did not share with Tanu. She was bewildered by their silence, unused to feeling such confusion. She had come here to be alone, to know again the aged Longhouse, because she felt unsettled, certain that change was coming to the Salish village. She was full of trepidation, yet oddly excited. She had had to get away, to be alone to think and dream in private. The People had let her go without protest. She was Tanu and none would have dared to stop her.

She lay alone on the wooden sleeping platform that circled the huge room, and into her dream came Colchoté, the companion of her childhood, his gaze unreadable.

That was strange; always she had read so easily the thoughts of others. And this was Colchoté—her friend, her brother. His father, Hawilquolas, had treated Tanu like a daughter, had, indeed, given her her first name. Colchoté's grandfather, Tseikami, had become her teacher, since her mother's parents were long dead. They had become her family— Hawilquolas, Tseikami, her mother Koleili, and Colchoté. She knew him well—his hawk nose, square face and wide, round eyes and open expression, as if he had no secrets he would not share.

She turned restlessly, crossed her arms over her chest, remembering with poignant clarity a day five summers earlier. She had just seen the passing of ten winters and was supposed to have been sorting herbs and roots—drying, boiling, putting them in pouches for the shaman's medicine bag. But the azure sky had called her, and the pounding sea on the sand. She had been unable to resist. She had crept away to an abandoned bay covered with patterned driftwood, sheltered by high rocks on either side.

She had barely arrived when she felt someone watching. She looked up, startled, at Colchoté, who was contemplating her intently. "I thought you would be here," he murmured. "It is where you find escape when you wish to be alone."

"If you know that, then why have you come?" Tanu challenged.

"Because I too wanted to be alone." He spoke as if there were no contradiction in that statement.

Perhaps, after all, there was not, she mused. She was surprised to find she did not mind his presence. She had grown with him from childhood as brother and sister grow—side by side and step by step. She was comfortable with him, at ease. "I come because of the driftwood. I like to draw the patterns in the sand."

He nodded. "Show me."

Tanu and Colchoté spent much of the day examining wood, tracing drawings in the sand, trying to make powder of the darker wood to give their pictures color and tone.

Tanu touched the patterns reverently, smiling. "I think the rituals of the People, made visible, would look like this. Here"—she swept her arm in a broad gesture to indicate the crescent beach—"in the wood, the colors, the textures, is magic which fades and shifts and darkens, but does not really change. It comforts me because it is dependable."

Colchoté, who had seen only thirteen summers, was mesmerized by the melody of Tanu's voice, the sweetness of her smile. Yet in the back of his mind he heard the insistent, incessant rush of the sea. "Dependable like the tides?" he asked, turning outward, toward the wind-whipped ocean.

Tanu's green eyes widened as she followed his astonished gaze. Like Colchoté, she had become absorbed in the details of the tiny beach. Like him, she had forgotten the sun that moved across the sky, drawing in its golden wake the changing tides. Now the waves crashed upon the beaten sand, swirling about their ankles in white sprays of foam.

They realized at the same moment that the entrance to the beach was blocked by the sea, given power and fury by a mighty wind. They were trapped inside the moon-shaped curve of rock with the water creeping closer as the tide moved inexorably toward them.

They stared at each other, flushed with embarrassment and shame. They had been irresponsible, foolish to forget something so elemental, one of the most constant of the cycles of Nature which shaped their lives. Tanu, blessed by the spirits, she who knew so well Nature's moods and powers, had failed to remember the first lesson she had learned on the Island of her birth.

"We must return over the rocks," she said sheepishly, peering at the rugged barrier they must climb hand over hand. "And soon, before the waves surround us."

"This way!" Colchoté shouted with sudden exuberance. "Come!" He grasped her hand and they fled to the base of the rocks.

They began to climb the jagged boulders—battered by a rising wind that tugged and pushed and threw them off their course, drenched by the turbulent sea that erupted furiously, leaving the rocks slippery and difficult to cling to. The wind snarled, whipping their hair into their mouths, carrying their shouts of reassurance into the furious slate-gray sea.

They did not speak as they sought handholds and indentations for their feet, but were aware every moment of each other's presence. Colchoté sensed when Tanu lost her grip, and he grasped her ankles firmly until she regained her balance. Once, she felt a breath of chilly air and reached down just in time to take his hand and hold him steady while he climbed up beside her. The wind was bitter, the waves slashing and full of power, but the two struggled together against the raging tide, without hesitation, without fear.

When they reached the crest of the rock barrier, they stopped to glance back. The waves crashed violently against the jagged rocks, and the sea spewed upward, reaching for its victims. But they had moved beyond its power; it sprayed scattered foam ineffectually at their feet. At the same instant, they looked at each other and smiled, exhilarated by the danger they had escaped, the madness of the wind-tossed sea they had defeated. "Do not ever forget this moment or this victory," Colchoté shouted above the wind.

"I will not forget," Tanu cried, elated. She knew, even then, that had she been alone, the sense of wonder would have been pale and soon forgotten. The victory was so sweet, so full of power, because they had won it together.

As they began to descend, Colchoté lost his footing and slid down and down, clawing at the pitted rock as he fell. Tanu found him on a jutting shelf, bruised and cut, examining his foot. It was torn deep near the ankle, bleeding freely. She took her things from the pouch at her side, cleaned, medicated and sewed shut the wound, bandaging it in soft pounded cedarbark.

Now they had to reach the sand. They wrapped their arms about each other's waists with Colchoté's bad foot between them. Using their three good legs, they climbed awkwardly down the twisted rock path. Colchoté's body was pressed to Tanu's side and she felt unaccountably safe, dry and warm despite the precarious angle of the rocks and the cold, wet wind on her skin.

Slowly, limping together, they made their way back to the village where the People, having discovered their loss, waited anxiously. Tanu and Colchoté arrived bruised, cut and dirty, their clothing torn, their hair in hopeless tangles.

Colchoté calmly faced his grandfather, his father and Tanu's mother. All were scowling, yet he leaned casually on an alder stick and told them, "I was on the curved beach looking for driftwood when I tripped and hurt my foot. I could not walk far among the piles of rotting wood. Tanu sensed my danger, heard me call. When she saw the tide was coming in, she came over the rocks and bound my foot, then helped me climb back in spite of the vicious wind and the incoming sea. I am grateful to her."

Tanu stared at him, stunned. She saw at once that the others believed him. She met Colchoté's eyes, full of secret laughter which scoffed at the damage to his pride because she, a girl of ten summers, had saved him. Everyone knew she was skilled in healing, after all. His sparkling eyes told her it had been worth the price. He would defend her, even with a lie, to protect the day they had shared. She had always cared for him, but in that instant she was overwhelmed by an affection deeper than she had ever known.

But that had been five summers past. The last time she had seen him, Colchoté's eyes had been clouded, impenetrable. He had raised a hand to stop Tanu from asking what troubled him. Now, alone in the Longhouse, a feeling of loss overcame her. Where had her old friend gone that she could not follow?

In her waking dream, she stared into the dying summer fire and could not look away. The smoke drifted toward an opening in the ceiling, laced with sparks like brief stars carried on an imperceptible breath of air. The wood splintered, sparks flew, and a single flame shot upward, flickering— brilliant yellow against dim gray. It hovered in the moist summer air, then glimmered beyond the cedar walls to the forest that rose green and splendid into the sky.

Lying still, unmoving, Tanu followed the wavering light through trees and bracken and sweet-scented pine to a clearing where the reeds grew tall at the edge of a pond. The flame paused among the cattails, where it fluttered, revealing a battered upright stone. Below the timeworn stone the yellow fire became a glowing burst of light that caught the motion of water through reeds and reflected it back—bright green and golden in Tanu's eyes.

Slowly, as slowly as the flames had risen from the hot red stones, the glow faded and the scent of trees became a memory and the walls grew once more tall and strong.

Tanu shifted, freed from the power of the light. Her heartbeat raced; it never ceased to do so when she had the visions which, to her, had become promises of things to come. She thought of gray-haired Tseikami, Head Winter Dancer and shaman of the small Salish village that was Tanu's home. He had taught her to seek the symbols in her visions, to find the gift or warning they foretold, but she could not understand the yellow flame, the stone, the incandescent light upon the water.

Chapter

2

Sheltered by darkness, by clouds that circled in the black night sky, Tanu left the Longhouse and crouched on the rocks to watch the dawn. She worshipped the sunrise—the beginning, the source of all that was new and clean and pure. Not like the sunset—an ending, a song of sadness, of things undone, unsaid, unfinished.

Tanu sat on a boulder, looking across the sea, where dawn lay in a lilac veil over water and island and the far shore, lost in purple mist. She watched, silent and alone where the Many Waters met, absorbing the stillness, the soft lap of the sea on the rocks beneath, the air that touched her face and her loose black braid with tiny beads of colored light.

The People said there were ghosts about in the few fleeting moments between dawn and morning, but they did not frighten Tanu.

A bird appeared from out of the drifting mist, flitted back and forth in a flurry of bright wings. Tanu watched it fly away, then return to hover before her. She frowned when she noticed its bright yellow coat. A flicker. Then it came to her, clear and vivid—the dream she had dreamed last night before she slept. Tanu was mesmerized by the furious motion of the flicker's wings. "What is it you want of me, Little Brother?"

In the bird's tiny eyes she saw light and movement and knowledge. The flicker was a fluttering pulse of wings that lingered, flew forward, and then back until Tanu followed. Lightly, she moved over the rocks to the damp, cool earth of the forest, where the bracken made a soft carpet among rotting logs, tumbled boulders and trailing vines of twinflower and kinnikinnick.

Tanu felt the softness beneath her feet and welcomed it, as she welcomed the sound of the river—nearby but beyond her sight—as she welcomed the chatter of squirrels and rabbits and raccoons. She heard gulls crying overhead, saw red-breasted nuthatches watching from the branches of cedar, spruce and fir.

But today she did not pause to enjoy the woven greenery. The flicker was in a hurry. She ran, her shredded cedarbark skirt rustling against her bare legs as she followed the flutter of wings that matched the rhythm of her pulse. She bit her lip when the flicker disappeared into a grove of paper birch.

Tanu ducked among the swaying trees. The whitish bark peeled in shreds from the circle of tall, thin trunks. She peered into the moving shadows, saw the flicker pause, descend, and rise above a circle of reeds and cattails. The bird waited until she came to kneel among the waving grass, then, with a last shake of its wings, the flicker was gone.

Tanu saw, through the shifting green and brown, the color of old gray stone. She parted the reeds to discover a mound and above it a crumbling marker. "A Stranger's grave." The words fell into the silence of the shaded copse like lightning into a calm blue sea. They reminded her of the Stranger's blood that flowed in her own veins.

Her mother, Koleili, was full Salish, and the People had accepted Tanu as one of them long since, so she did not often think of her father. He was a man Koleili had met on a trading expedition. She had spent several nights in his tent, and when the village had finished its business with the trappers, Koleili had left the Stranger behind.

Tanu did not know his name, nor did she wish to. The Salish were her People and this her heritage; it flowed in her blood more strongly than the memory of her mother's dream. "Why did you bring me here, Little Brother?" she asked the missing flicker. The wind answered, "There are reasons for all things if you seek them well."

Tanu felt the rush of air on her skin and was ashamed of her doubts. She leaned forward to examine the grave more closely. There was a cross carved into the stone and the letters *IHS*. "Stranger's words," she muttered. Below these mysterious letters were the Salish signs that stood for Wananat, a Native name, and one of her own ancestors. Tanu wondered why he should be buried here, alone and with the cross of the Strangers above him.

The words of a song drifted by on the breeze, ruffling the reeds with its passing.

Repose toi, mon âme,
en ce dernier asile. . . .

It was only a fragment of something she had heard before, but never understood. She did not know where she had learned the song. On days when she was alone, it came to her—and went—without a trace. The light shimmered over the pond, which she loved, in its very stillness, above the constant motion of river or sea. She shifted her weight and her hand touched something round and cool that caught a shaft of light and glowed so brightly that she could not see.

She remembered the flash of light from her dream. She picked up the stone which had made the sunlight blaze. It was scattered with yellow specks in a green that was deep and clear all at once. Caught forever in the stone was a perfect piece of fern. The clear film over green, the fern floating inside, was like a puddle, rich with patterns and plants that circled beneath still water.

Tanu sat back on her heels, cradling the stone in her palm. She had collected such stones for many years. To her they were gifts from the spirits who aided her in hunting and healing, in weaving and in magic. But this one—this one lay heavily in her hand, though it was small. She knew that it was more than just a gift; it was a sign. She touched it reverently, felt its cool, lustrous surface with her fingertips. She was puzzled and distressed.

A rustling of leaves intruded on her thoughts. Tanu stiffened, looked up, suddenly alert. She peered into the trees and saw a shadow take on shape and substance. "Kitkuni?"

The other girl came forward, dappled with light, amused by the astonishment on her friend's face. "Your eyes betray you," Kitkuni said. "For a moment you thought I was a ghost."

Though she spoke airily, Tanu saw the strain in Kitkuni's face. Her almond eyes were obsidian dark, the nostrils of her slim nose flared with tension. She was bruised and dirty, her dark brown skin scratched raw in several places, her feet bleeding. "Why have you come, and so carelessly?" It was a full sun on foot from the summer camp to the Longhouse.

Kitkuni grimaced, looking down at her body. Her cedarbark top was askew, the panels of her skirt torn and ragged. "I traveled all night to find you."

Tanu's sun-browned face lost some of its color. "Alone?"

"I know the path well. I have traveled it many times, as have you. I did not fear to lose my way."

Tanu's apprehension returned, fierce and bright. "Yet you hurried so the bushes tore at you and the branches scratched your face. Let me treat your bruises. I have dried woodfern root in my pouch."

Kitkuni brushed her friend's concern aside. Restless, she wandered the tiny glen. "They do not hurt. Leave them be."

"But—"

Kitkuni whirled, smiling her uninhibited smile. With her fine high cheekbones and softly rounded chin, she was beautiful just then. "But I have not had time to bathe today. The water would ease my aches without your medicines."

Reluctantly, Tanu nodded. She was profoundly troubled by her friend's lightning moods, which echoed the disquiet of the People over the last several suns. Whatever change was coming, she sensed it had found her at last. But she did not wish to speak the thought aloud. She thought of her daily bath, and longed, all at once, for the touch of the water on her skin. "Yes, let us go to the river." She must be patient, she reminded herself. Patient and calm, or Kitkuni might flee.

Linking arms with her friend, Kitkuni moved toward the sound of the water.

Tanu wondered, as she often did, at the other girl's unaffected pleasure in her company, so unlike the respectful reticence of the other Salish. "How is it that we became friends?" she asked, startling even herself.

Kitkuni grinned, then frowned thoughtfully. "Because I grew weary of baby's games when I was six summers, and began to look for a companion. My sister Yeyi was too small, my cousin Twana the only other girl near my age. Even at seven summers, she gazed too often at herself in still ponds. So I looked to you."

"You were not afraid?"

"Of the powers of She Who Is Blessed?" Kitkuni considered, brow furrowed. "Not really. Perhaps because I inherited *siwan*, the little magic, from my grandmother." Kitkuni did charms and chants that could help make a difficult birth easier or a difficult hunt more successful. "Your magic did not frighten me; it intrigued me."

Tanu knew her friend well enough to guess there was something more. "And?" she prompted. "What do you hesitate to add?"

With false bravado, Kitkuni tossed her head. "It sounds vain to say it aloud." Her feigned courage failed her and a flush crept up her cheeks. "I thought you were too serious, that you did not know how to have fun. I wanted to show you, to be the only one who dared." She looked away. "You know I alone would admit such a thing," she added anxiously, the last word drawn out in a silent question.

Tanu was surprised, but only for a moment. She had been much alone before Kitkuni. "I am glad that you dared."

They had reached the riverbank, where Kitkuni's toes sank into soothing mud; she wriggled them with pleasure. She took the bone clip from her top, made of pounded cedarbark, which the People made by beating the bark into a soft and supple cloth. It felt loose and did not bind, but cradled the girls' breasts gently, left their limbs free among the pliable strips of their skirts. Kitkuni let her top fall onto the bracken at her feet. She untied the cedar twine and dropped her skirt unselfconsciously. "Hawilquolas was glad of my daring too, I think. He wanted you to have a friend. Someone besides Colchoté."

Tanu had burrowed into a thicket to gather some leaves of the mock orange, but Kitkuni's pronouncement brought her up short. Something in her friend's tone reminded Tanu of Colchoté's strange behavior, his shrouded but watching eyes. "Why would Hawilquolas wish to keep us apart?"

Kitkuni took a long time to answer. "There are reasons."

Tanu could not think of any. She could only remember the kindness Hawilquolas had shown her since her childhood. But more than that, he had bestowed upon Tanu and her mother all the status his family and his name could give. He was *Siem*, Head Man, and his protection had kept Koleili and her daughter safe and honored when they might have been despised.

Tanu had been illegitimate, the seed of a Stranger. The People would have cast out Koleili and her baby. But at the child's birth, Hawilquolas had behaved like a father who awaits his firstborn, avoiding the forbidden things and burying the placenta with great ceremony. When it was time to choose a name, he had distributed many blankets and gifts, and thereby given Tanu a name which none could speak against.

A rush of cold water struck her in the face, and she nearly fell backward into the bracken.

"Will you sit dreaming on the bank all day?"

Tanu smiled and shook the water away. "I am busy." She was using a large stone to pound the mock orange leaves into a froth for soap. The violent motion eased her frustration at Kitkuni's behavior and her own growing trepidation. Something was troubling her friend deeply; that she could not hide. "Besides, dreaming is sometimes pleasant."

"But not with the odor of smoke still upon you." Kitkuni wrinkled her nose in distaste.

Tanu gave up and discarded her clothes, diving into the river, sliding over the stones and soft silt on the bottom. She let the water take her where it would before she rose and broke off branches of cedar to scour away the grime and odors of the night, to purify herself.

Kitkuni sighed with pleasure as she lathered her body with fragrant soap, then ducked her hair under the water and lathered it too. At last, she floated languidly on the surface.

When Tanu rose, the water streamed over her slender body. She was taller and finer boned than the Salish; Kitkuni was certain her friend's waist became slimmer by the day, her hips more rounded, her breasts fuller.

"We are not the same as we once were," Kitkuni murmured with regret. "I would like to say I had not noticed the change, but how can I when my own body betrays me?"

Tanu was surprised by her friend's vehemence. "You are a woman now. Your body is more graceful and full of promise."

Kitkuni looked away, but not before Tanu saw the anguish that she could not form in words. "What is it, *Ladaila?*" She called her friend the affectionate nickname for a little girl.

Kitkuni smiled wistfully, wishing she could hold the nickname close, and so cling to her childhood for one more day. "Our ancestors pounded their chests with flat stones to keep themselves from growing here." Kitkuni pointed at her swelling breasts. "Perhaps they were wiser than we."

Tanu looked down at her body, which had become unfamiliar to her. "I do not think they were wise. You cannot change what is to be."

Kitkuni smiled sadly. "So they will tell you, your grandfather and grandmother as you listen to their stories. But I wonder if they are always right." Before Tanu could answer, Kitkuni reached out with a wet finger to trace the lines of her friend's face—the subtly curved cheeks, less prominent than her Salish relatives, her lips, softly defined rather than broad and flat, her eyebrows arced above arresting green eyes. "But you do not need to fear. You are stronger than they. I envy your eyes that see so much, and your face, which is like no other."

"Do not envy what came from the blood of a Stranger," Tanu cried, genuinely distressed. Then she saw that Kitkuni's eyes were veiled by heavy lids and guessed that her friend was trying to distract her once more.

The leaves shifted overhead, a warbler cried out, hidden by the greenery, and the pulse of the river grew strong and loud. "Tell me," Tanu said. Her voice held a command that even Kitkuni could not disobey.

"My father has had visitors from another village. Chatik's family has been asking about me—my age and accomplishments and whether my family would welcome him as son-in-law. My father has answered kindly. Chatik and his relatives will come in half a moon to ask for me as wife. That is why I traveled all night. I had to know you had not changed."

Tanu laid her palms on Kitkuni's shoulders while the water lapped around them, calming, tranquil. She fought the chill that threatened to engulf her. Kitkuni would be married, in another village, lost. Carefully, keeping her voice steady, Tanu spoke. "Not toward you, my friend. Such a thing will never come to be." Her face was patterned by light filtered through the leaves. "Do you hear?"

Kitkuni looked into familiar eyes, full of affection. She smiled in relief. "I hear."

The girls did not speak as they let the water slide down their naked bodies into the bracken at their feet. Each was lost in her own troubling thoughts. Slowly, when the cool drops lay on shoulders and backs and the soft curve of hips, they took hemlock branches and brushed the last of the water away, soothed by the pungent smell, the caress of needles against their clean skin. In silence they dressed and found their way to a pair of fallen boulders, where they sat side by side.

"I am afraid," Kitkuni said at last. She had never before spoken those words. "Afraid of the stranger they have chosen for me, afraid of leaving my family and friends, afraid of losing all that is sacred. The other villages are not like ours. They have not clung to the old laws, the old stories, the old songs. Their songs are new and harsh, and I do not wish to listen." She covered her ears with her hands, though the only sound was the call of the breeze, the murmur of water, the whisper of leaves. In her head were other songs, not so lovely or familiar.

Tanu did not know what to say. For the first time in her life she was struck silent by another's pain. *I am losing my only friend,* she thought. *I cannot bear it.* She wrapped her arms tightly around her knees and shivered. She was ill with the thought of grief to come.

Kitkuni swung her feet outward and back, biting her lip. Her eyes held a curiosity she could not hide. "And yet," she said tentatively, "sometimes I wonder what it is like to be truly a woman. To have a man touch your skin with his callused hands, to feel him push the hair from your brow and kiss your mouth softly. What must it be like to feel those things, to have your body learn new songs?"

Once again, Tanu had no answer. Perplexed, she glanced sideways at her friend. She knew other women did not speak of such things. Kitkuni was daring to express her thoughts aloud. Today she dared to say much she had not said before.

"I wonder." Kitkuni tilted her head so her damp hair fell down her back and the speckled light moved across her face. "I do not wish to wonder, but I do. I think sometimes I will make myself crazy because I cannot decide."

The wind cried, a long, low sigh, and Tanu raised her head, listening. She sniffed the air and caught a whiff of salt and fury and moist, dark earth. "*Stokam*, the spirit of the storm, is calling. We must go back."

Kitkuni sighed, brushed the twigs and leaves from her skirt.

Tanu touched her arm. "I do not know how to help you."

"You were here, and I found you. That is all I ask."

The lump in Tanu's throat told her that no matter what Kitkuni said, she had not done enough.

Chapter

3

Just after dawn, the two girls left the hidden ocean inlet where the Longhouse stood to make their journey down the inland waterways that would lead them back to the sea, to the bay and the summer village. The cedar canoe slid out of cool green woods into long, flat stretches of earth, surrounded and invaded by shallow sluggish rivers.

Tanu and Kitkuni spoke little, for their thoughts circled about the marriage, the change that was coming to each, the friendship that was doomed now by the choices of their elders. These things neither wished to speak aloud, to make what was only imagination real.

All too aware of her silent friend beside her, Tanu watched the swaying grasses—undulating seas of endless gold and green—the cattail and reeds that crowded the wide, meandering river, the clouds reflected in still ponds beyond the marshy riverbanks.

She turned her face to the sky until the fragrance of the sun rose on her body, then faded as the mist crept in to float upon the water. Before the sun had made its full path across the sky, they reached the bluff where, through tangled branches of oak, arbutus and dogwood, they caught glimpses of the ocean, framed by twisted, contorted wood.

Guiding the canoe with care, the girls turned down the fast-flowing river that emptied below them into the sea. Here the Many Waters came together—still and raging, lapping gently, whipped sometimes by wind, sometimes lulled clear and calm by the motionless pure air.

"Home!" Kitkuni called as the canoe edged past the rocks on which sun-browned children climbed with their baskets full of mussels. The huts of seven families made a rough semicircle on the smooth sand, and the blue smoke of fires rose lazily in the afternoon air, curling around the flight of gulls that cried along the beach.

Here the People came each spring and summer to be nearer the fishing and the plentiful beds of shellfish. The tide was low and the women, baskets hung from stout ropes about their heads, dug with pointed sticks for clams and other shellfish. Water and sand dripped from the baskets down their backs; a breeze made them shiver, then shake the cold away.

As the girls turned the canoe upside down beside the others and exchanged greetings with the villagers, Tanu caught sight of her mother, seated cross-legged outside their hut, piles of steamed clams before her. Tanu smiled with relief as much as pleasure. Always, the sight of Koleili's face brought a profound sense of calm, as if Tanu had released a deep, tense breath. Yet she was never aware until then that she had been holding her breath at all.

Kitkuni slipped away to join her own mother and her sister Yeyi, who both glanced away, flushing, as Tanu passed. She noticed their dirty faces, their arms and legs stained mossgreen, but was thinking only of her mother.

Koleili was busy stringing steamed clams on cedar threads. Many strings already hung over alderwood fires, where the smoke rose from the fragrant wood, flavoring the clams and drying them all at once.

"My Mother!" Tanu cried.

Koleili looked up, her black eyes full of pleasure. There was a serenity in her smile, a tranquillity in her hut that made no demands on her only child. "So you have returned at last." She smiled and patted the cattail mat beside her. "I hope you found what you were seeking."

Kneeling, Tanu took a moment to admire her mother's face, framed by the wings of her shiny, oiled hair. Her cheekbones were rounded, not high and sharp, her features softened by the hand of The Changer before her birth. Or so Tanu liked to think. Koleili's eyes were veiled, though wide and dark, her lips curved in a smile that spoke of dreams which nourished her more than the food she ate. "It is good to be home—"

Tanu broke off when she finally noticed how many of the women were dirty and stained, how they turned from her in shame as they passed. "What has happened?" she asked Koleili.

With a sidelong glance at the disheveled women, her mother said, "We have a Trickster in the village. Two nights past, he replaced a whole drying table full of blackberry molds with bitter yew berries." She followed her daughter's curious gaze and added, "The women found the berries mold by mold, hidden in the forest. Only now have they recovered all that were taken."

"But why do they look away?"

Koleili shrugged. "Perhaps because they think the Trickster was telling them they had too much pride in the work of their hands. They sang songs of triumph the night before the berries disappeared. They are ashamed, though they laughed as they hunted through the vines and bracken."

Tanu smiled. Her People had always been able to laugh at their own weakness. It was one of the things that had helped them survive. "Have you guessed who the Trickster is?"

"I have wondered if it is Colchoté's cousin Wahan. He watched with such amusement while the women tore at their hair and cried out. He has come to think he is very wise."

When Tanu only nodded absently, leaning back on her elbows, Koleili squinted at her daughter. The sun flared behind her, blurring the image of her face. "You are weary from your journey. I will make you some fir needle tea."

"It is not the journey that tires me, but the thought of Kitkuni's marriage."

"Ah." Koleili let out her breath in a rush. "I guessed that she had gone to you. It must have been difficult to hear such news." She was glad at least that the girls had been alone.

"It was not easy. And before she came, I had a dream."

"So you have been doubly tested." Sensing her daughter's need to talk of something besides the loss of her friend, Koleili said, "How often have I warned that your dreams tire you more than the work of everyday?"

"It does not seem so to me." But that was not entirely true. Tanu's body ached; her hands would not move quickly, and her eyelids felt heavy and gritty.

Koleili saw the girl's pallor with a mother's eyes. She leaned close to murmur, "*Ladaila*, remember that for others you see the truth, not always for yourself."

Before Tanu could answer, Koleili ducked inside the hut, found a small basket, and filled it with water from a sea lion's bladder. She went to the fire and drew out some stones, washed them clean of ashes, and, with greenwood tongs, dropped the hot stones into the basket of clear water.

While she took two cedar cups and placed the dried leaves of coltsfoot in the bottom, Tanu remembered the stone she had found and removed it from her pouch. Carefully, she placed it beside the others she had collected over the years. They lay in a semicircle, where she could see them each time she entered or left the hut.

The cooking stones grew cold and Koleili replaced them with hot ones until the water boiled and she poured it into the cups.

As Tanu drank the tea flavored with honey from their small precious store, the smell of the sea surrounded her and the cool ocean air touched her cheeks, restoring some of her strength.

The sun was sinking into the sea, painting the sky vibrant red and purple when the last shadow of the day fell across the two women. Hawilquolas stood above them with a string of mink and marten he had obviously just trapped. "It is good you have returned," he said to Tanu, his eyes full of warmth.

He dropped the string of animals beside Koleili. He smiled at her and she smiled back in unspoken understanding. She took the string and placed it inside the hut until she was ready to cure the pelts. Hawilquolas had not spoken to her, yet he had done her great honor by giving her the animals to prepare.

From the next hut, the women looked on with envy, which they quickly hid behind a smile.

Tanu knew they were wondering why Hawilquolas continued to give Koleili the honors of a wife, when she had refused to marry him. He brought her his game and fish, sharing the meat, taking the bones and carcass for himself, leaving her the hide for curing, the rest for cooking and the practical chores of a woman. Yet he rarely spoke to her, nor she to him. In silence they grew more like husband and wife daily, except in one respect.

Intrigued, Tanu watched Hawilquolas go. There were many questions she had never dared ask before. But the knowledge of Kitkuni's approaching marriage made her bold. "Why does he care for us so well? Why has he made this choice?"

Koleili considered carefully. "He has been married twice before, the second time to my sister. When she died, as had his first wife, he offered to take me in marriage. It is right that a man should marry the sister of his dead wife."

"But you refused."

"Yes," her mother answered. "At first Hawilquolas acted out of an obligation to my sister's spirit. I do not know when the obligation became a pleasure, only that his heart softened toward us. He gave us the status of his family freely. Later, when your power began to grow, *we* gave *him* status of a different kind. It is good, and we are content, Hawilquolas and I."

Tanu toyed with her sacred stones, remembering Kitkuni's desire to know the touch of a man's hands upon her body. Did other women feel the same? "Do you never want more than the food he provides and the protection he offers?"

Koleili's eyes were blank. "More?"

Swallowing dryly, Tanu asked, "Do you not wish for someone to hold you?"

For an instant her mother hesitated. "I hold someone in memory. A man with gentle hands who cannot become too familiar, whose image cannot be tarnished by knowing it too well."

It was the first time Koleili had spoken of the Stranger who was Tanu's father. She tried to hide her thoughts of him, but her daughter knew the past was always with her. Yet surely Koleili cared for Hawilquolas in her own way. Tanu herself thanked The Changer every day for the gift of Hawilquolas' affection and more than that, his respect.

Before she could press her mother further, Kitkuni's father, Alteo, knelt before her. His brown, wind-burned face was full of anxiety, suppressed energy, an unusual excitement. "I would ask a favor," he said, head bowed.

Tanu sat up straighter. "I will grant it if I can."

Alteo's black eyes were full of hope mixed with sadness; it gleamed there like a flame in a round, dark cave. "My daughter has told you that Chatik and his people will come in sixteen suns to ask for her in marriage. I would know if the marriage is propitious."

Tanu was surprised by his question. The People often asked advice, shared their worries and their burdens, seeking her practical wisdom and compassion. But Alteo had asked for the power of a shaman. "You should ask Tseikami, the shaman. His dreams are more powerful than mine," she said.

Tseikami of the striking pure white hair and face criss-crossed by many wrinkles had been watching, had seen Alteo approach Tanu. Now the shaman crouched nearby. "Alteo came to me first, and I told him my dreams for this marriage are good. But I would know what *your* spirits say." His heavy-lidded eyes gave him a shuttered look; his face was closed, full of secrets, a face whose sharp lines had been smoothed by age.

Tanu began to object, but Tseikami opened his eyes and held her with his riveting gaze. A moment before he had been an enigma, but now he had uncovered his secrets and his power. His obsidian eyes hypnotized, drew her into the web of the shaman's will. He did not wish her to question him. Tanu nodded imperceptibly and turned back to Alteo. "I will ask for a dream," she said, praying silently that her spirits were stronger than her sorrow over losing a friend.

— 24 —

Chapter

— 4 —

That night the Salish ate well—steamed clams, scallops, mussels and roasted fern roots, and red huckleberries to leave a sweet taste in their mouths. Each family ate at their own fire before their own hut. As darkness fell, the sound of the soft sea ran over stones and shells while cool evening mist wrapped itself about the moon.

Tanu ate in companionable silence with Koleili. The tranquillity of her mother's fire had crept in, veiling Tanu's thoughts of Kitkuni and the stranger who would be her husband. Now she did not wish to disturb the fragile peace. But the pull of other eyes made her look up to find Colchoté watching. He sat cross-legged before his father's hut; his smile welcomed her home, told her that he had missed her. Now his thoughts were not hidden away. He was the friend that she remembered. She was warmed by the twinkle in his wide black eyes that reminded her of the day long ago which they had shared. It was a secret between them—those rare moments in the tumult of sand and sea and wind.

But she turned from Colchoté instinctively when she heard a soft whimper; a baby cried nearby. Enis, the child's mother, was part of the circle of firelight. The baby lay in its cradle of cedar and animal skins, suspended from a rough alder frame, safe but unhappy.

Tanu rose abruptly. A call of pain from one of her village was more than just a sound; it was to her an obligation. But this burden she carried gladly. She made no sound as she crossed the sandy earth and lifted the baby from its cradle. Curls of pounded bark fell away; curls that had warmed the tiny squirming infant and kept her dry.

Tanu trembled with anticipation as she held the girl-child close and murmured, "You are not well tonight, Kwahtie." She touched the child's forehead, clammy and cool, and listened to the pulse of her tiny, throbbing heart. Kwahtie had stopped crying to gaze at Tanu curiously.

Reaching into her otterskin pouch full of dried herbs, roots, leaves and bulbs for healing, Tanu found some young leaves of deerfern. She chewed them to mush and with her fingertip, slipped them into the baby's mouth. "That should ease your rumbling insides," she whispered. Kwahtie smiled, and her eyes disappeared in her round chubby face.

Tanu held her closer, absorbed the delicate fragrance of soft skin, soothing oil and thimbleberry soap. The baby put her chubby arms around Tanu's neck. Tanu felt a lump in her throat. She found a bit of buckskin in her pouch and wiped the child's damp forehead.

Kwahtie snuggled her soft head contentedly in the hollow of Tanu's throat. Tanu closed her eyes, every nerve aware of the precious burden she held, the poignant pleasure of the weight that lay easily in her arms. She breathed slowly, afraid to disturb the fragile moment. "You must sleep, little one, and let the leaves do their work." Softly, she murmured:

> Let sleep come easy, moon of brightness.
> Let it bring rest.
> Let it bring rest.

The baby closed her eyes, lulled by the sound of Tanu's melodic voice, so different from the guttural voices of her People. Tanu glanced up to see that Enis, so recently a mother, had left her place in the circle and was listening raptly. Her angular face, with its high cheekbones, softly flattened nose and round yet pointed chin, was suffused with an expression that had become familiar to Tanu—a sense of trust and affection just edged with alarm.

Reluctantly, Tanu gave up the sleeping child. "She will be happier if you hold her tonight. Her stomach is not easy, but I have given her deerfern. She should rest easily now."

Enis cradled her daughter, then reached into the small basket at her waist. She withdrew a small pink stone and held it in her palm. "Take this." She dropped her head, ashamed. "I did not know Kwahtie was ill, but thought her restless. I thank you."

Tanu smiled and accepted the woman's gift, though not as precious as her grateful smile. Nor as the moment when she had held the baby in her arms. But to turn away the stone would be to hurt Enis' pride. "I am grateful." She went to place it beside the others—the fern caught in still green water, the dark gray streaked with blue, the black with silver specks like frozen stars. Each was beautiful, each unique and precious.

Enis followed, brushed her hand over the sacred stones, eyes closed, lips moving in a silent prayer.

Then she was gone, a part of the shifting light of many fires. Tanu looked after her and saw Hawilquolas and Colchoté frowning, their heads bent together, speaking intently. Colchoté motioned wildly with his hand, grew still as his father spoke, making a single gesture of refusal. Colchoté stared at Tanu, the flames reflected in his unblinking eyes.

The feeling of impending change welled up in her throat, and she shivered as she joined Koleili and the others, who had begun to drift toward the big fire in the center, toward the comfort of many voices, a circle unbroken, a past they all shared.

Colchoté, pale with anger, Hawilquolas, stiff and silent, and Tseikami, with his secret eyes, were the last to come.

Tanu leaned close to the flames. The smell of smoke filled her nostrils and the sound of smoke songs filled her head.

"It is a lovely night," Hawilquolas said. "On such a night let us turn from our worries and frustration"—he glanced significantly at his son—"and listen instead to a story of our past, kept sacred by our voices." He turned to Colchoté. "A story of the Child born of Raven and Thunderbird, Owl and Wolf, born of powers beyond our knowledge or control."

Tanu bowed her head.

"Yes," the People called, looking expectantly at Colchoté. He was a natural Storyteller, so easily did he beguile them with the power of his voice.

Colchoté did not look at Tanu now. Shoulders tense, he glared at the earth. *You cannot have everything you wish for*, his father had said. *This you should know.* Hawilquolas was right, but that did nothing to ease his frustration. He picked up a drum and began to strike it. Down and down and down and down. Each stroke dissipated a little of his anger.

"It was long ago, before the rising of many suns, the changing of many moons," he began in a deep, guttural voice. "The People were hungry in those unfriendly days, for the summer had given up few elk or deer or bear. The flowers and grasses had bloomed sparsely, so by autumn the storage room lay empty.

"Then white stars fell to cover the earth in the bitter mantle of winter's cape. The People traveled the rivers at night with torches, praying for deer to come down from the hills seeking water, but the hunters came back weary, chilled, with hands as empty as when they had begun.

—— 27 ——

"Until one day the Child spoke, she with eyes of wisdom and the voice of silver birds. 'I have dreamed,' she said, 'and my dreams were good. I will take three hunters and when we return our hands shall be full.'"

Colchoté leaned into the firelight and his black hair fell over his cheeks, emphasizing his square chin and hawk-like nose. "The Child stood in the canoe while the moon fell upon the white snow. With her torch held high, she watched the shadows, the moonbeams that made paths of radiance on the water. She listened to the whispering breeze, to the birds that sang out, leading her, guiding her.

"All at once, she motioned for the canoe to stop. The moon struck the hunters blind and dumb, but the Child saw where the snow had been beaten into the earth, where the moonlight disappeared in the brown mud of the bank, where the golden-brown eyes of a great buck gleamed. *Ah-tush*, the deer, was far away, so she sang to him softly.

> 'Come, *Soqwa*, Little Brother.
> Come, and the spirits will bless you,
> For we are cold and empty.
> Come.'

Tanu shivered when she saw that Colchoté was lost in the story. To him it was a legend sprung from ancient, swirling mists, not something that had happened in his own village nine winters past. But Colchoté was not alone; the others too had fallen into a vision of a wondrous event many hundreds of years old. They clung to it and nourished it, for it nourished them and made them strong. But sometimes it frightened Tanu, this fierce belief.

"*Ah-tush* came to the water's edge, where the hunters could see his magnificent body, his regal antlers, touched by torchlight. One hunter took aim, but another stopped him. 'He came to her. It is her right and obligation.' The Child whispered her gratitude to the deer, and though she was but six summers, she lifted the bow of a mighty hunter and fired.

"*Ah-tush* fell to its knees with an arrow in its throat. Silent with awe, the hunters floated the great buck back to the Longhouse, where they lifted it from the water, which fell in shining rivulets, darkened by its rich, red blood.

"When the hunters shouted in triumph, the women came, singing prayers of thanks. With their shell knives they cut deep into the deer's soft belly, then fell back in disbelief and fearful worship. For the giant buck that lay before them, a promise of food and warmth, with antlers that reached to the sky, was not a buck at all, but a fine, fallen doe."

Colchoté struck his palms against the drum, building the rhythm with the sound of his voice, until the heart of the People beat in time with his, their breath came with his breath, and they were drawn into his powerful, feverish smoke dreams.

"The People stared; each saw and was struck dumb at the sight of a doe with antlers that denied her sex and made her more than it was possible to be—a miracle. They knew, in that moment, the name of the Child they had dared to call by no name, for fear it would not be enough. In moonlight and starlight, in hunger or plenty, in the light of day or the shadows of night, they called her their savior and their Queen."

"They called her Tanu, their Queen," the People repeated, faces golden in the firelight. "They revered her as they revered the animals, the trees and waters, the paths their ancestors had walked for many suns and many generations."

Tanu shook her head to bring herself back to the reality of damp sand beneath her feet. She watched as the People began to chant, and Hawilquolas slipped away from the light. He stood where the night lay calm and mist-filled on the gently lapping sea. He did not turn when she joined him, but breathed in the darkness, the scent of salt and moist clean air and distant, fragrant pine.

She regarded with affection his square face and hawk nose, so like his son's, the strong chin and steady gaze which made the People trust him. "You are worried," she said.

He did not deny it. "Chatik's family is strong and wealthy. They seek this marriage for the status of Kitkuni's family name. Because they have much, they will bring many gifts to the marriage feast."

Tanu heard what he said and also what he did not say. Kitkuni's family was not wealthy. They could not possibly provide enough gifts to match the groom's. Their pride, the pride of the whole village, would be damaged by such a failure. "It has been a fruitful summer. The salmon have swum by the hundreds into our nets, the deer have fallen to our bows and clubs. The berries have been so many that we could not pick enough, the mink and marten and beaver have given us many pelts. Just last week, Colchoté finished two beautiful canoes, and we have blankets and baskets woven by our hands last winter."

Hawilquolas nodded thoughtfully. "If each of us gives Kitkuni's family a few of the gifts they will offer the groom, there will be more than enough. As for the feast itself, there is plenty. We will feed Chatik so much he will not be able to rise from his pile of blankets."

In spite of herself, Tanu smiled at the image. "That way none will bear the burden alone." Except for Kitkuni and each loved one she left behind. Such grief could not be shared.

For a long time, Tanu stood silent, achingly aware of the beauty of the night, the song of the waves on beaten sand, the fragile touch of a hushed sea breeze. When at last she spoke, her voice melded with these quiescent songs. "While I was at the Longhouse, a dream took me to a sacred place."

Hawilquolas, who loved the ocean and the night and she who stood beside him, said softly, "And what might this place be, and where, that it touched you so strongly?"

"In a clearing where white birches grow in a circle, where sunlight falls through leaves on a stone of gray. The name of Wananat is carved onto that stone. Was he not your ancestor?"

Hawilquolas sighed, for Tanu had conjured the place where his grandfather had been laid into the cool, damp ground. "He was Tseikami's father."

"Why does he lie in a Stranger's grave with a Stranger's words on the stone?" Tanu knew he was not easy with her questions, but she also knew he would answer. He had never denied her the knowledge she sought.

The hunter sank to the sand and Tanu sat beside him. Her arm lay against his, her shoulder to his shoulder, and though the air was chilly, his skin was warm.

"It was before so many Strangers came to the Island, for they feared the wildness of our country and our People."

He turned in the faint moonlight. "Wananat was a great hunter, but he could not fight a wildcat who fell upon him one day when he was alone. A Stranger killed the wildcat and took my grandfather to a house of logs, where he treated his wounds.

"As Wananat healed, the Stranger, who was also a priest, taught him the language and rituals of the pale-skinned people. When my grandfather had grown strong enough, he gave the priest the knowledge of Salish language and rituals. With these gifts, they exchanged a new understanding and became great friends."

Tanu tilted her head, listening. Some words whispered past, soft and ghostlike in the stillness.

> *Repose toi, mon âme,*
> *en ce dernier asile. . . .*

She wondered if they had come, somehow, from Hawilquolas, but knew he had not spoken.

"The priest showed my grandfather the secrets of his heart, and Wananat was hungry for such knowledge. He wished to understand the world of the Strangers that was not like our own."

"Did he never return to the village of his birth?"

"Always he returned to his People. But he could not forget what he had learned. He remembered the priest crying out in horror when he heard that we kept slaves, as the People have always done. To ease his friend, Wananat set free the captives of our village. It did not break the sacred laws or threaten the power of his spirits. That is why, even now, our village does not hold slaves as our brothers do."

Tanu was troubled. "Why have you never spoken of him before? It seems he was wise and protected what was sacred, yet you offer his spirit only silence."

Sighing deeply, Hawilquolas gazed at the gossamer net enveloping the moon. "Because he tried to live in two worlds, but it only caused him pain, for such a thing is impossible.

"When my grandfather was dying, he called his son Tseikami to him. 'I have honored the sacred laws of my People and listened always to the voices of my spirits,' he said. 'I know I will walk the paths of my ancestors when my *seli*, my soul, leaves the shell of my body. But my friend is full of fear for my spirit, which I know is safe and cared for. Because he is afraid, I would ease his heart by allowing him to bury me in the manner of his religion. It will not hurt me, for the spirits will surely understand. And it will ease my friend's troubled soul. This last kindness I can do for the man who gave me back my life. And thus it shall be done.'"

"So," Hawilquolas finished quietly, "it was done as he wished, but the People mourned. We did not want more suffering; that is partly why we have chosen to avoid the Strangers, to preserve all that is sacred, to keep it pure, unaltered. That is why we live in a solitude of our own choosing."

Tanu often thanked the spirits for that solitude; she had long understood that the Strangers were a threat to all that she believed. Wananat, who now lay dead, had taught his son and grandson that hard lesson; Tanu had always known it in her heart.

As season followed season, she had seen more and more of the Strangers' ships, the guns they carried and the animals they rode. Unlike the other Salish, her village did not trade with trappers and miners and farmers for metal knives or guns or the dull gray blankets that were easier to make than woven dog- and goat-wool blankets. Nor did they trade for the drink that made the Strangers into madmen and the People into strangers.

Hawilquolas looked at Tanu, who sat beside him, head to head, though he was the tallest among the Salish. Her body was graceful, soft and rounded; her hair fell thick and luxuriant about her shoulders, emphasizing her brown skin and startling green eyes. Even her features were delicate, her lips shaped and curved, her eyebrows finely arched. These things made her different and mysterious to her People, fragile and vulnerable to him.

He felt the silence heavy around him and knew that he must ask what he did not wish to know. At this moment the Strangers lay between them like unseen ghosts. To let the moment pass would be to watch the ghosts fly free until they settled, as they would one day, a shadow on Tanu's soul. He took her chin in his hand. "Have you never thought that the two worlds of my grandfather are also in your blood? That someday you will face them both and have to choose as he did?"

Tanu shook her head violently. "I have chosen, long ago and for always. And so it will be." Yet beneath her certainty, the sound of her voice, whose power could move the People to tears or to frenzy, was the rustle of wind that brought those unfamiliar singing words. She thought of the waking dream, of Wananat and his priest, the letters carved by Strangers' hands, the yellow-green stone touched by radiant sunlight.

The rush of the waves grew loud in Tanu's ears, and the moisture closed around her so she could not breathe. "There is a future I do not seek, but which will come to be just the same." Each word was an effort, an agony, a cry for help.

"What was meant to be will come to be," Hawilquolas agreed, but his chest ached and the words felt dry and bitter in his throat.

Chapter

5

Dawn crept slowly out of night while Tanu crouched on the rocks above
the beach. She was wrapped in ribbons of lilac mist that drifted in friendly
whispers against her cheeks. The islands were surrounded by clouds; only
the tops of mountains appeared dimly, floating far above the endless
motion of the sea.

A stillness settled inside Tanu, calmed her questions and her worries.
Alone with the light of dawn around her, she found a moment of serenity,
a poignant pleasure in a beauty so fine and fleeting and new. Each day the
world was reborn in tenuous bands of color, in dim, translucent light, in
silence and the first soft hint of sound.

Shaking the dew from her hair, she climbed down, the texture of
the rocks pressed into her bare feet. A shrouded shape in the half-
darkness became Colchoté standing alone, watching her approach.
He seemed always to be watching her of late. His silent yet fervent appraisal confused and upset her. It had nothing to do with the friendship
of their childhood, the secrets they had shared, the easy laughter. He
was drifting away, yet somehow drawing closer, and she did not understand.

She was relieved to hear Kitkuni calling. "Tanu!" Kitkuni held up two
berry baskets. "The feast is but two days away and we need blueberries

and red huckleberries." She tossed one basket in the air and Tanu caught it awkwardly.

She realized then that she was weary, not only because she had worked hard for the past twelve suns to help prepare for the marriage feast. The time had passed too quickly; each dawn brought Kitkuni's departure nearer. Tanu was painfully aware of how much things were changing, not only for her friend, but for herself. Her days were haunted by Colchoté's watching eyes, her nights by the dead Wananat, who drifted through her dreams, whispering the words that followed her even into sleep.

> *Repose toi, mon âme,*
> *en ce dernier asile. . . .*

Tanu was happy to escape her ghosts, even for an hour, and did not hesitate when Kitkuni turned to leave the village behind. She was vaguely aware that the People watched her covertly, expectantly. But she did not know what they waited for.

Kitkuni saw her confusion. "They are thinking of the Trickster and the fishing nets."

Tanu smiled at the memory. The young men had caught more than enough salmon for the winter and the huge wedding feast, but they had not been satisfied and had decided to go out again and again. Thinking them too greedy, the Trickster had woven their nets into a hopeless tangle with spears and hemlock branches. When they realized the other villagers were greatly amused, the young men had been forced to laugh at the joke on them and give up plans to fish the full waters. "But what has that to do with me?" Tanu asked.

The dogs barked and nipped at the girls' heels as they lost themselves in the thick foliage of the woods, the muted light, tinted green and golden, the comforting fragrance of earth and pine and morning dew.

Kitkuni ducked beneath a cedar branch, deftly avoided a patch of nettles. "They whisper that you are the Trickster."

"Have they not seen how Colchoté's cousin Wahan stands apart, laughing at the other young men? How smug and superior are his smiles? My mother says he laughed at the women too."

Kitkuni shrugged. "Perhaps. But still they call you Trickster."

"Why are they so certain?"

"Because," her friend explained, "you are She Who Is Blessed, who teaches the People so much."

Staring into the green filtered light, Tanu was inexplicably uncomfortable. "I have not yet learned to teach with laughter."

"You teach with gentleness and affection. That is what they expect from you, what they need."

Tanu swallowed with difficulty, unbearably touched by Kitkuni's sensitivity, her offer of comfort. All at once, Tanu ached with grief. She could not endure the knowledge of her friend's going. "I will miss you so much."

Kitkuni's throat felt tight and she blinked back sudden tears. Never had Tanu revealed such human frailty, the pain that glowed, undisguised, in her eyes. Kitkuni was paralyzed by this glimpse into Tanu's heart, which made her own pain flare like hot fingers of fire. She did what others had always done when they could not meet Tanu's gaze—she fled. "We cannot waste the day standing. We will not be allowed another." She pointed. "There is a hidden bed of berries where the others will not find us."

For a long moment, Tanu struggled to regain control. Her hands shook as she forced the grief down deep. She understood Kitkuni's fear, but understanding did not stop the hurt.

She swung her basket, focusing on the breath of air that stirred her skirt. "You are tired already of being the center of attention?" Her voice was soft but clear. She paused to admire a huge fir, scarred by ridges and fissures of aged bark.

Kitkuni looked back, a glimmer of mischief in her eyes. "I would not mind so much if they did not *talk* so. Their mouths are as nimble as their fingers. They speak of Chatik's family and the gifts he will bring and how well I will look and how sad it must be for my mother to lose me. I think she will be happy to see me go. Then she will have peace again."

She stopped abruptly. "Tell me once more of your dream. Tell me you are certain." She quivered with suppressed energy, her cheeks flushed, then drained and pale.

"The spirits came easily," Tanu said reassuringly. She had fasted all day, then burrowed into the woods to find a stream where the moss was deep and green and damp. She had curled up for the night with the song of the water in her ears. The stream had whispered, murmured, bewitched her until she slept.

"I dreamed of the sunrise again and again—the new beginning, the time of purity and opportunity. Such dreams are good, auspicious." Not once during that night, cradled and protected by the forest she loved, had she seen the sun set. Reluctantly, she murmured, "The marriage was meant to be."

Kitkuni let her breath out in a rush. "I was only thinking—but no, I was not thinking at all. I no longer know what I do." Without warning, she ran ahead, plunging through the woods like a wounded animal, laughing when she stumbled. She tripped once, rolling down a hillock into a tangle of twinflowers. Undaunted, she jumped up to challenge Tanu. "Let us climb those two tall firs, as we did when we were children, racing to see who will reach the top first."

Distressed by Kitkuni's odd behavior, Tanu wanted to protest, but her friend did not wait for an answer. She dropped her basket and grasped the thick trunk of a tree.

When Tanu saw Kitkuni was determined, she tossed away her own basket and began to climb the branches of the spreading fir. In spite of herself, she was soon caught in the excitement of the competition. Kitkuni was skillful, but Tanu was as good; they had spent many hours of childhood scraping their bare legs on rough bark, curling their toes into fragrant needles.

Tanu leapt onto a thin branch that swayed with her weight. She gripped the trunk tighter, her arms in a circle that did not quite meet. When she had caught her breath, she looked over to see that Kitkuni was above her, laughing down.

"You have grown old and stiff and wary," Kitkuni gasped. "I will be up and down again before you reach the top."

"You are too sure of yourself," Tanu replied. With a deep breath, she started up again. The scent of fir was strong; the sun danced through parted leaves, making patterns of light on the rich, dark earth; the birds sang in the branches overhead. The moment enchanted her, seduced her. She felt weightless, elated as she climbed step by step into the endless sky.

She moved faster, higher, exhilarated by the contest and the wind in her hair. It bore her up and lifted her beyond the everyday to the world of the spirits that lived in the trees.

The two girls reached the top at the same moment. They hung, swaying on the narrow crowns. Their laughter rose on the wind and circled the cloud-laden sky. Despite the cool morning, Tanu's skin was filmed with sweat and pieces of bark and fir needles clung in her hair. Her hands were brown with dust, her knees bruised and raw, but she did not care.

Kitkuni turned her face toward the sun and smiled, relaxed and radiant. Her almond eyes shone, her hair flew in the breeze, caressing her fine cheekbones and graceful neck, arched in pleasure against the white-blue of billowed clouds.

Tanu held her breath, mesmerized by the beauty of her friend's face, by the stillness yet sense of exuberance that shone in her eyes. Suddenly, Kitkuni turned.

"Now down!" she shouted into the sky.

In a blur of motion, she disappeared into the concealing branches. Tanu followed, sliding and finding her footholds through sheer luck, for hair and sweat were in her eyes. She was panting by the time her feet touched the bracken, but Kitkuni was there before her, leaning against the tree, laughing. "It has been too long," she said when she could find her breath.

"Yes," Tanu agreed, unable to resist her friend's laughter. "We have grown old and dull."

Kitkuni nodded, then she was off again. "We must bathe," she called back over her shoulder. "They cannot see us like this. They would be jealous of our pleasure."

The last words faded into the cool darkness and Tanu followed her friend, the berry baskets forgotten. "You must be ghost-struck," she shouted. "You are crazy with daring." She stopped when she reached the rushing water. Unlike the stream where she had sought her dream, this river thrashed and roared over shelves of flat brown stone that jutted out, each different, each carved and ridged by years of wind and water. The intrusions of stone sliced the river, sent it racing toward a deep hollow where the raging water calmed and spun in circles touched with glancing light that smoldered on the surface.

Tanu was deeply moved by the power of this place. Though she had seen it many times, she always paused, one foot on wet stone, to know it again. Such power could not be remembered or carried inside her. Each time she had to feel it anew.

A loud splash broke her reverie. She leaned out to see her friend's naked body beneath the surface of clear, circling water.

With a pleased sigh, Tanu tossed her skirt and cedar wrap aside and slipped into the chilly river. Kitkuni floated for a moment, disappeared beneath the water, rose and dove and rose again. Tanu stood unmoving, her toes buried in silt, enjoying the swirl of the water around her, yet troubled by Kitkuni. She darted and shouted and splashed like a child who had been kept from play for too long. The peace, the inner radiance, had gone from her face. Now she laughed too sharply and her eyes glittered, dark and wild.

"My friend," Tanu said softly, "come sit and listen to the whisper of the breeze. Listen and let your heart beat slowly."

Kitkuni did not seem to hear. She dove beneath the water, eyes closed, arms out before her, and headed directly for the rocks that jutted, flat and dangerous, above the water. Tanu gasped and plunged forward. Grasping her friend around the waist, she tugged with all her strength. Kitkuni's head broke the surface just beyond the huge flat rock.

Kitkuni coughed, stared at the jagged edge of stone, leaned weakly against her friend. She gripped her shoulders, arms crossed, as if the simple gesture could protect her from herself. "I did not see it," she choked out at last. "I did not even look."

Tanu guided her toward a flat rock, where they sprawled side by side, palms on the rough, patterned stone.

Kitkuni began to shake. Her eyes, dazed and clouded, filled with tears. "I am afraid," she said. "Sometimes I am so afraid that I think I will scream with the trembling inside me. I cannot bear it. I do not want to go."

Tanu slid her arms around Kitkuni and held her. For a while she said nothing, just pressed her cheek against her friend's and let the tears flow over her cool skin.

"You know you do not speak the truth when you say you do not want to go. Last night you were so full of excitement that you sang it out for the village to hear." Tanu forgot her own desire to keep Kitkuni near; her friend needed her wisdom, not envy or the woven bonds of friendship.

"But now—" Kitkuni began.

"Now you feel panic because your life will change. Everything will be new and unfamiliar. But I have heard only good of Chatik's family. They are wealthy, they live in ease, and your groom's father is known to be a good man, a man with courage and wisdom. He will take care of you."

"I wonder if you really believe that, or if you know it is what I need to hear." Kitkuni reached for a spray of white foam, then added softly, "They will choose a new name for me."

Tanu was startled, though she should have known. They would give her friend the name of her adulthood, the third name she had borne—first her nickname at birth, then her gifted name, Kitkuni. "It is time that you grow into a new name. You have earned that right." Tanu spoke calmly, but her heart ached. All that was familiar and safe would be taken from her friend. In a single night she would become a stranger.

Frowning, Tanu tried to imagine leaving her People and her village. She gazed at the stone-carved river, the trees that rose into silver-blue clouds. Painfully, she breathed in cool, damp air. It was too much to lose. These woods and Many Waters flowed in her blood like the song of the loon.

Pushing her thoughts aside, Tanu said gently, "Do not grieve so. It is hard enough to lose you. I could not bear to lose you to misery." She talked on in the lilting voice her People loved. She did not stop to think what to say; she trusted the spirits to give her the right words.

Kitkuni had been rigid beside her; soon her muscles began to melt. The sound of Tanu's voice dissipated her fears, made them pale and unreal.

She was sorry she had turned from the sight of her friend's pain. Tanu would never turn from *her*, would never think to leave her standing alone with her grief like a carved mask on her face.

Kitkuni was overwhelmed by sadness. Soon she would not hear Tanu's voice, or lean on her shoulder while she made all things but the wind seem unimportant. "I am lucky to call you friend."

"And I," Tanu answered in a voice like a song that did not reveal her sorrow or the depth of her regret.

Chapter

6

Eventually, the girls found a patch of berries and picked enough to half fill their baskets. In silence, they returned to the village and the smell of the sea.

As she came into the clearing, Tanu saw that Hawilquolas sat before her hut, deep in conversation with Koleili. She could not see her mother's face, but Hawilquolas looked grave. Tanu stopped, unwilling to interrupt. The two spoke together so rarely. Curiosity smoldered, but she would have to wait.

Kitkuni's mother, Shaula, appeared unexpectedly in the girls' path. "My Daughter," she cried in relief, "and Tanu. How glad I am to see you. Yeyi is not well—"

"I will go to her," Tanu said quickly. It would give Koleili and Hawilquolas time. Besides, Kitkuni's younger sister, The Laughing One, was a favorite in the village. Tanu would be happy to see her, to turn her thoughts to someone else's worry.

Yeyi lay on a cattail mat, staring at the light that fell in patches through the ceiling. She looked dazed, uncertain, like her sister. "Yeyi," Tanu whispered, "may I sit beside you?"

Yeyi smiled and her eyes disappeared in wrinkles of soft brown flesh.

Her face was round and full; she had never lost her baby fat. Usually, she sparkled with laughter and good humor. "I hoped you would visit."

"Your mother says you are not well."

Yeyi was comforted by the sight of Tanu's face, the sound of her voice, so like the soothing murmur of a stream. "My head aches with the noise that echoes in my ears—their laughter, their planning and their counting, endless counting."

Tanu nodded. "You are caught in a whirlwind that is not your own and cannot catch your breath." She took the girl's head in her lap and smoothed back her hair. Tanu rubbed Yeyi's temples, then laid her palms on the girl's pale cheeks.

Yeyi grinned in spite of herself. "Tseikami would sing and dance the evil spirits out."

"I do not think the spirits are evil. I think they are spirits of smoke that will dissolve in the light of day."

Yeyi did not answer. The soothing motion of Tanu's hands was making her drowsy.

"There is something else that troubles you."

The girl knew she could not deny it, not to Tanu, who would feel her lie. "It is such a tiny thing, a selfish thing. I do not like to say—"

"Say it to me. I will understand."

Yeyi sighed. "I have outgrown my ceremonial tunic, and my mother has no elk or deerskin to make another. I will shame my family on the day of my sister's marriage feast."

Closing her eyes, Tanu considered. This was no small matter. Everyone must honor the groom and his family. To wear simple clothes would not be respectful. Yet Yeyi could not easily borrow a tunic. She was bigger than the other girls; her whole body was soft and rounded. "I will think of a way. Do not worry, *Ladaila.* Only rest." As soon as the words had left her mouth, Tanu regretted them. How could she possibly help, when there were no proper skins with which to make a ceremonial dress? There were only bits and pieces, and even she had not the power to make them more than what they were.

Yeyi realized her headache had eased, the noise had begun to fade. Tanu had promised to find a solution, and Tanu never broke her word. "I am better." She touched the older girl's hand, then quickly released it, afraid of holding on too long.

Tanu smiled and, inexplicably, wanted to weep.

* * *

— 41 —

Koleili sat in her tiny hut, staring at shadows, listening for voices that might tell her what to do. The sun pricked the thatching overhead, making tiny points of light in the gloom, touching briefly shelves of beads and clothing and cooking boxes. A narrow beam glanced off Koleili's hands clasped tightly in her lap, revealing a knuckle, raw from work, a vein, close to the skin and finely blue.

Such little things could not distract her. Hawilquolas had told her his worries; they lay heavy on her shoulders. Her back was not strong enough to carry such a load. She was powerless to change what others had decided long ago.

She had always been powerless, since her childhood when she had coveted the handmade dolls of other girls and had not asked for one of her own. That was why, one cool summer night, she had given herself to a man named Nicolas, given in to his warmth, to the pleasure and the wonder he had offered.

Koleili was smaller than most big-boned Salish women, more fragile. She wondered if it was because half her spirit lived in a formless past where a man with green eyes had held her in the darkness. She had never left behind the fear born in that sweet, beguiling darkness; it had left a cloud upon her heart that dimmed and reshaped her will.

Hawilquolas had kept her safe afterward, and ever since, in silence and in tenderness. But even he had been powerless to stop the spirits who had touched Tanu and changed her life. Koleili sighed because she had no solace to offer, no strength to fight for what she knew in her heart Tanu deserved to have.

If only she would come back and—

Koleili raised her head sharply. No. She prayed for the comfort of the girl's presence, but Tanu must not see the thoughts that drifted like stale smoke through the air. She must not know how much Koleili needed the sight and sound of her daughter to make her believe that the spirits were kind.

There had never been much she could offer Tanu, for whom gifts of unimaginable worth seemed to fall from the sky with the rain. Koleili was an ordinary woman with an extraordinary child; the only gift she could give Tanu was the knowledge that there was one who loved her simply, and asked for nothing in return.

Koleili had pretended to be strong, untouched by sadness or ghosts or fear, to give the girl relief from the needs of the People, which were deep and never-ending. But her only real strength was her ability to make her daughter believe this lie.

Koleili wanted to weep, but she could not. For Tanu's sake she must keep the sadness hidden where light or tenderness or compassion could neither reach nor ease it. This gift, this unspoken vow, Koleili made willingly for the joy Tanu had given from the moment of her noisy birth.

Koleili turned when she heard footsteps and saw her daughter crouch in the doorway.

"Why are you inside?" Tanu asked. "The air is fresh and the sky clear and blue."

Koleili drew a deep breath to steady herself. "I wanted the darkness for a little." She met her daughter's gaze. "But now we must talk. Let us walk along the beach, where the sea will tell us stories as we go."

Tanu sensed her mother's distress and knew it had come from Hawilquolas, who had spoken so fiercely. She moved to let Koleili out into the sunlight. Her mother paused, blinking as though she had never before seen the strait and its islands that floated serene on the gray-blue sea.

Mother and daughter started for the shore, the sand warm against their bare feet. The tide was coming in as they followed the curve of beach around battered rocks and scattered pieces of driftwood.

Koleili found that, after all, the words were harder to speak than she had imagined. She closed her eyes, felt the burning sun, and murmured, "Colchoté has said—" She broke off, fluttering her hands in the air. "He has said he wishes to make you his wife. He sent his father to ask if we were willing."

Tanu was stunned. Her face flushed hot before the color drained away. q(5)Abruptly, she sat on the sand, legs crossed. Koleili joined her, but Tanu could not meet her mother's eyes.

She did not know why she was so surprised. She had seen Colchoté watching, but somehow she had not thought of this. She leaned on her hands, pressing down until bits of shells made their marks on her palms. She felt a vague and formless sense of pleasure, but it was swept away by the chaos of other emotions. "I never thought to be a wife," she said at last.

"Why not? You are a woman long since. You are sworn to no one." Koleili tried to hold back the unwise words, but nevertheless, they came tumbling out.

"It is not for such a thing that I was trained."

Koleili tried and failed to quell the rush of anger that turned her brown cheeks red. "Why should you not be like other women? You have a right to the same happiness. To lie beside a man, to know there is someone to keep you safe, to hold his child in your arms and feel its warmth and breath and life."

Digging her hands deeper into the dry sand, Tanu struck the damp earth beneath. "I am happy as I am."

Koleili knew her daughter believed what she said. But for all the teaching of the elders, Tanu had led a sheltered life. There was a happiness far greater than she could imagine. A joy so exquisite, so glorious and painful that a woman who had known it could never be the same. Koleili had felt it once; she knew its onus and its power.

Tanu did not suspect that such feelings existed. But someday she would discover this truth for herself. And then what? Koleili asked the sky with its wisps of trailing clouds.

Hands shaking, Tanu drew her shining hair over her shoulder. Deliberately, she began to make a braid. Inside, turmoil raged—hope, doubt, pleasure, and, most of all, dread. Yet Tseikami had taught her to be strong, to fight her own demons so she need never live in fear. "Hawilquolas is not willing." She was surprised at the pain those few words cost her.

Brow furrowed, Koleili hesitated. "He is not certain such a union would be wise."

"But you think he is wrong?"

"I know he is right." Koleili contemplated the smooth cobalt surface of the sea. "And Tseikami agrees. He says you have a duty to the People that marriage would destroy."

"*Any* marriage," Tanu murmured half to herself. Just now she had begun to understand.

"It seems so." Koleili dug her hands into the sand and it clung, sliding bits of shell under the nails until her fingers ached. "I wish—I would want for you to have someone. Not to be so much alone."

"But I am never alone. Always the People are with me, around me, inside me."

Koleili's eyes filled with tears that blurred the outlines of the islands like morning mist. "It is different to sleep in someone's house, to share his mornings and his nights."

"Yet you have no one." Tanu spoke the words she must speak, but they did not ease her agitation, her sense that she had lost something before she ever found it.

Koleili touched her daughter's cheek—the softly curved cheek above finely shaped lips that spoke of other blood and other worlds. Tanu's warm brown skin and thick black hair were of the People, but what of her heart? "I have told you, I hold a memory so vivid that it does not ever fade. And I have Hawilquolas. What we share is not what others have, but I value it greatly." Soft sea foam crept about their ankles and away. "But that does not matter. It is not my decision."

"Of course it is your decision."

Brushing a stray hair from Tanu's forehead, Koleili smiled sadly. "Speak to Hawilquolas," she said. "He will await you after we have eaten." Koleili was ashamed by her sense of relief. She had done what she must. Now Hawilquolas would take back the burden. If only, she thought, looking into the deep green of her daughter's knowing eyes, he could lift Tanu's burden as easily.

Chapter
7

Later, as the sun sank gloriously into the sea, Tanu sat at her mother's fire, her salmon and quail, roots and greens untouched. Hunger had left her. There was too much to think about. Just twelve suns past she had been happy, but now the earth had shifted beneath her feet. Colchoté's unwavering gaze reminded her how far. She could feel the tension in his body from across the firelit clearing. Her mouth grew dry and her palms damp.

Hawilquolas saw how his son stared unblinking over sand and fire and smoke. He leaned forward and Tseikami spoke. Colchoté turned, though they did not rebuke or command him. It was not their way to force obedience upon the People. Instead, they simply drew him into the circle of their low-pitched voices.

Tanu sighed with relief touched with an unfamiliar longing. The shock of Colchoté's offer had begun to fade, but her distress had grown as the sun inched toward the sea. She knew what was right—Tseikami in his shaman's wisdom had taught her that—but she was not certain that she wanted what was right. Tonight she could think only of holding Kwahtie, the grasp of her tiny hands, the softness of her baby skin. *You have a right to lie beside a man, to know there is someone to keep you safe, to hold his child in your arms and feel its warmth and breath and life.*

Tanu gasped and her hands tightened into fists full of sand. All at once she wanted desperately to have those things—a man to hold close to her heart, a husband to confide in. A family, a child of her blood—and Colchoté's. Such a child would be a blessing, such a husband a priceless gift.

She was vaguely aware of a disturbance—the hissing of tongues, gasps of astonishment, an unnatural flicker of firelight. She looked up to see Kitkuni's cousin Twana dancing around the center fire in a new elkskin tunic.

"Is it not beautiful?" Twana cried, showing off the intricate design of beads and shells that glittered like stars in the radiance of the fire.

The women frowned angrily but did not speak. To dress so for a summer evening was inappropriate, and Twana's behavior boastful. None would criticize her, but many were displeased.

"I finished the beading two suns past," Koleili confided to her daughter. "But I did not think she would do this."

The air crackled with tension until Tanu stood and an expectant hush fell over the clearing. "Such a beautiful tunic would look well on Yeyi at her sister's marriage feast. Each of us has given to Kitkuni's family. Have you, Twana?" She spoke softly, without censure, but Twana understood.

Yeyi flushed with pleasure and sent Tanu a look of gratitude. She could never have asked such a favor for herself.

Twana stiffened. "It is *my* tunic. *My* father worked hard to kill the elk who bore it!" She did not realize how harsh her voice sounded until she heard the dismayed gasp of the women. "I mean," she added more calmly, "the tunic would not fit Yeyi."

"Perhaps you are right. It would not fit." Tanu's voice was low with anger. She had to struggle to keep silent. She had seen the stricken look on Yeyi's face.

A specter loomed above Tanu in the firelight. Tseikami, the shaman, her teacher, crouched beside her. He opened wide his heavy-lidded eyes, luminous with secrets that held her immobile. "You know the precious gifts you have been given—you and no other. Do not be like Twana and risk losing them."

Before she could respond, he was gone, an apparition made fleeting by the light of many flames. In the stillness left behind, she understood his warning; she must not think only of herself. But Tseikami, of all men, should have known that she had never even *learned* how to be selfish.

One by one, the People gathered around the center fire. They were restless, thinking of the feast that was now nearer by a sun. They turned expectantly to Hawilquolas, threw logs onto the flames until they roared, blazing, into the sky.

"Give us a story," Enis called, competing with the snarl and crackle of the flames.

Hawilquolas saw Tanu approach and turned to his son. "Give them their story. Tanu and I must speak together."

Reluctantly, Colchoté took up a drum and began to beat out a slow, deliberate rhythm. His heart was heavy, for he sensed his father would turn Tanu away from him. But he did not protest, did not look up when he heard her whisper past. He knew the sound of her, the fragrance of her body, the rhythm of her footsteps as she walked along the shore.

His heartbeat slow and labored, Colchoté let the firelight take him as the sound of Tanu faded and only the snap of the flames remained. "It happened in a time long past," he began, "before the rising of many suns and the changing of many moons, when the People were tormented by a huge golden cougar and a great shaggy grizzly. The two animals attacked the People, scarred and killed many, stole their food and left them to bleed and starve.

"The strong hunters met with the Head Man to decide what must be done. Among them came the young Queen. 'I have dreamed and my dreams were good,' she said. 'We will go together to seek the enemies of our People who will become our friends.'

"The hunters wondered at her courage but did not dare to show their fear, doubted her dream but did not dare to speak their disbelief. At her command, they took a canoe and the Queen stood in the bow as they traveled a long and twisted river. They had not gone far when the cougar appeared, poised and ready to pounce. One hunter raised his bow and shot an arrow, two, then three, but all flew wide and landed in the bark of the gnarled oak where the cougar crouched.

"'In my dream I sang and the cougar fled,' the Queen said, unafraid. She met the animal's threatening golden eyes and sang in her sweet, hypnotic voice,

> 'Leave us in peace, O cruel one;
> We will not punish you for your greed.
> Go to the stream and drink,
> For the water is sweeter than our blood,
> Which is bitter now with anger.'

"'We will come and go like spirits,' she added, 'like summer rain, and we will never harm you. This I swear.' The hunters stared while the cougar uncoiled his body and slipped away into the trees.

"When he was gone, the canoe slid through the rushing water until the river was blocked by the shaggy grizzly bear, his long teeth bared and gleaming. A second hunter shot an arrow at the mighty bear's heart, then another and another. But the three arrows went wild, flew into the sky, and disappeared inside a heavy gray cloud.

"The men sat motionless, astonished, but the Queen knelt, saying, 'In my dream, I sang to him and he let us go on our way.' She looked into the grizzly's small brown eyes without fear.

> 'Do not roar of your power,
> For the spirits have greater power;
> Their touch would send you bleeding
> To the soft green forest earth.
> Let us pass and we will give you peace,
> If you still your slashing blood-stained paws.'

" 'We will come and go like spirits, like summer rain, and we will never harm you. This I swear.' The bear leaned forward, listening, and he seemed to understand, for he turned and lumbered off into the forest."

The People beat their own drums, celebrating with the motion of their hands the victories of their Queen. Colchoté moved with the pulsing rhythm, carried by it into the power of ancient, living memory. Face flushed and hands aching, he fell into his own seductive dream.

"The hunters turned back toward their village and the mist drifted over them, beaded on their glowing skin. And from that day, the cougar and the grizzly became the friends and protectors of the People. So it was promised. So it has come to be."

The Salish nodded, pounding their drums. To them the story was a promise, a charm against evil. It spoke of what had been, what was to be, of promises made and kept and cherished, of the spirit power of Tanu, their Queen, who walked now, a distant figure on the empty beach.

To the sound of the drums, Tanu walked beside Hawilquolas. The thrumming faded gradually into the lap of the sea, but her pulse, erratic and wild with her distress, throbbed loudly in her ears. When Hawilquolas did not speak, Tanu spoke for him.

"My mother says she cannot decide if Colchoté will have me for his wife. Why should this be so?"

Hawilquolas walked, hands clasped behind his back, the water surging around his ankles. His head was bent forward, but whether deep in thought or to hide his expression, Tanu could not guess. When he spoke, his voice was gentle.

"We talked, Koleili and I, and know it is our right, our duty to make this choice for you. But you are not an ordinary girl. You are wise where others are foolish, thoughtful where others are careless, selfless where others think of their own happiness. We believe you should decide."

Tanu gasped when the water closed over her feet, splashed up the naked calves of her legs. To be given such an honor, to be allowed to choose her own fate, was more than she would ever have asked. It was a gift whose value she could not express.

Impulsively, she reached out to touch Hawilquolas' arm, and he rested his hand on hers. She did not speak; there was no need. The pounding of drums grew louder, rising above the waves.

"I think you must have questions." Hawilquolas cleared his throat. "You have wondered why I do not take another wife to share my house. Why I am content with Koleili, whose hands have never touched mine."

Tanu was surprised he understood so well. She knew such things were not easy to speak of. "I have wondered."

With a sigh that whispered inside a retreating wave, he said carefully, "I have had two wives. I held them close and watched their faces change with the light of morning and the soft darkness of night. I knew their smiles, their sadness and the dreams of their hearts. And then I lost them." He stopped for a moment, unable to continue.

"I do not seek that kind of pain again. Twice I have borne it. Twice I have been strong. Twice I have pushed my memories away and refused to see them hovering in the gloom that followed me sun and moon. It is enough."

His voice was rough with a grief that left Tanu helpless. Why had she never guessed that he hid such sorrow beneath his mask of wisdom? It was part of her task to sense such things, to find such pain and try to heal it. But Hawilquolas had held his sorrow too close to his heart.

She had forced him to name his grief; now she must make him forget. "I have heard that men need to hold a woman in a certain way, to release the forces inside them that words cannot touch." She swallowed dryly, knowing the question was dangerous, knowing too that she must have the answer.

Hawilquolas narrowed his eyes, seeking the dim path of moonlight on the water. "There is such a need," he said at last, "which drives men to take wives. But when this need is unfulfilled, a man becomes stronger, for he triumphs over the weakness of his body."

"Are you not lonely, then?" Her own fierce longing for a family, born in the ashes of her mother's fire, made her feel alone and empty. How could Hawilquolas bear such torment?

"There is a difference," he replied, "between loneliness and solitude. Loneliness eats away at your spirit and your soul; it weakens you with self-pity and the ache of empty nights and days. But solitude gives time for contemplation, for quiet and calm. Solitude can make a man stronger, for it can make him wise. Besides, I have many friends, and the People all around me."

Tanu gazed up at him, trying to believe. Even in the darkness, he could see the outline of her face, made uncommon by the blood of her father. "We do not need to marry, only to fulfill the tasks the spirits have set for us. That must be our goal and our dedication."

Tanu was not satisfied. "What you say may be true, but it has nothing to do with Colchoté and me. You have answered every question but one. Why do you not wish me to marry your son?"

Hawilquolas was stunned by her grim determination. "I have told you—"

"You have told me only part of the truth. How can I believe if you are not honest? Always before you have spoken freely."

The Head Man looked away. He should have guessed that she would hear the things he did not say. He spoke deliberately, choosing his words with care. "It is a matter of pride, you see. My son has many spirit helpers, but none as great as yours. To take a wife with more power than your own—" He broke off. "If Colchoté made such a choice, the People would think him a fool. They would call me a fool for letting it happen."

Tanu paled. "No one would ever dare call you a fool."

Hawilquolas grasped her shoulders in hands gone rigid. "If I act like a fool, they will call me a fool. The Trickster would hang the mask of a magpie on my house. Only so long as I am wise will they respect me. For you this is also true." He tightened his grip until she winced.

"You must believe me, Tanu. You have grown so used to being right that you do not remember what it is to be wrong. The People believe in you because you give them cause. If you gave them cause to doubt you, they would do so. Believe this if you believe no other word I speak tonight. No Head Man lives forever, no shaman, not even a Queen."

Tanu shivered at a sudden chill. She had asked for honesty and now she tasted its bitterness on her tongue and in her heart.

Chapter
—◄ 8 ►—

Tanu crept around dark shapes against golden firelight. She was shaking, cold, bewildered—she who should have been so wise. Her thoughts were in turmoil; the sight of Colchoté's gentle face became Hawilquolas' mask of thunder when he told her one day she would die. Koleili's unspoken sadness mingled with Tanu's hunger for the warmth of a human touch. Colchoté's silent plea echoed with the warnings of her elders, and Kitkuni's fear and excitement and madness.

She thought of Colchoté, her friend, her brother. The desire to live beside him, to have his child, had not diminished. But Hawilquolas' warning sounded harshly above the ripple of the stream. *The People would think him a fool.* Could she do such a thing to Colchoté, even if he himself had asked?

You know the precious gifts you have been given—you and no other. Do not risk losing them.

Tanu walked blindly, not knowing where she went. Tseikami was right. She could not turn her back on the spirits that made her strong. But it was hard to know this, so hard that she walked through the night, until at last, near dawn, she knelt in the wet moss beside a stream.

Seeking solace, she bent over the clear, cold water. In this slow-running stream, the branches of a tree had formed a circle from bank to bank; the water around it flowed but the water within was still. She gazed into the uneven circle, saw the ferns that floated beneath the surface, the striated and gnarled wood, the thick moss that disguised the branches of a long-dead tree. The circle was beautiful and full of life, though all within it lived no more. She saw in that green water the image of her face, surrounded by sunlight. For a moment, Colchoté's face hovered beside her—his square jaw and hawk nose, so strong, so like his father's—then, just as quickly, faded into shadow.

Her heart heavy with sadness, she turned toward home.

She came into the clearing and saw Colchoté waiting near the red-gray embers of his father's fire. She did not know if he had stood all night as he did now, staring toward the tangled woods. She knew only that the sight of his face, so dearly familiar, sent a sharp pain through her chest. He stood alone with the light of dawn like a gauze cape about his shoulders.

At last Tanu stood face-to-face with the brother of her childhood. For a moment, her breath refused to come.

Colchoté did not speak. He stared into her eyes, and his heart stopped its thunderous beat. He had known he wanted her, but not how much. The glimpse of her soul through her compelling green eyes told him that—and more.

"My Brother," Tanu said gently in a voice as strong as the stone of the Island hillsides, "do not ask of me that which I cannot give. I would not wish to hurt you, ever."

For an instant, Colchoté could not respond. Then, with a great effort of will, he nodded stiffly. Somehow he had known that this would be her answer to a question he could never ask. His face, which had always been so open, was now sharp and angular, his round eyes narrowed, unreadable.

Tanu ached at the pain that tightened Colchoté's mouth into a rigid smile. She must leave him alone with his sorrow. For a man such things were secret, hidden, a matter of deep pride. She ached to comfort him, but turned reluctantly away. She had not known it would hurt so much to see his false smile, the rigid posture of his body, the blank expression that saved his dignity.

She had not known it would hurt so much to leave him in silence, without a single gentle word.

"Tanu."

Her name hung, whispered on the morning air. She turned, saw Colchoté raise his hand. Just once, he motioned toward him. Eyes black as caverns carved from tortured stone, he held up his hands, palms outward, in the sign of eternal friendship.

Tanu's eyes burned, but she was not allowed the luxury of tears. She knew how much that gesture had cost him. She raised her own hands and pressed her palms to his.

Colchoté stiffened at the unexpected warmth. Without thought, he laced his fingers with hers.

Tanu was stunned by her reaction, the way her fingers twined naturally with his. Never had a man touched her like this, awakening her body to feelings so strange, so alluring that she could not pull away. Her power left her, and her wisdom and her spirits. She realized in that instant what it was to be a woman.

She had not known it at the ceremony after the first flow of her blood, when they had called her woman. Nor had she guessed when Kitkuni spoke of her curiosity and the need for a man's touch. She had not felt it, even as she wondered at Colchoté's fervent, demanding gaze, even as Koleili told her of a happiness she could not understand.

With her palms against Colchoté's, her fingers bound with his, a need long slumbering began to stir. No one had ever taught her this. They had talked of the spirits, of wisdom, of dreams and the knowledge of her ancestors. Not once had they spoken of the hunger of her body. Now she had to learn it for herself.

In that moment of illumination, she understood the pleasure she could know, a yearning for the touch of other hands upon her skin, the urgent desire in her blood. She knew all these things, and knew, as well, that she could never claim them. She discovered the stirring promise of her body and gave it up forever, all in an instant.

Colchoté savored one moment more of the exquisite pressure of her fingers twined with his, then let her go. "I release your hands and release my dreams, for the two are one," he said.

Dazed and grieving and cold beyond words at the loss of his warmth, Tanu tried to speak, but Colchoté had already turned away. He would never know how much he had given, how much he had taken away. These things she would keep locked inside her. Like the secret of her power, she would never speak the words aloud or let them glimmer in her eyes. So many things were hidden in the safe places inside her, but none as poignant or as painful as this.

Chapter

9

Though the rest of the village slept, her mother was waiting when Tanu finally entered the hut. Koleili took one look at her daughter's face and offered the cup of tea she had prepared.

Stunned and aching, Tanu shook her head, but Koleili held the cup to her daughter's lips until she drank. The girl tried to cradle the warm cedar in her palms, but her hands began to shake. "I will hold it for you," Koleili whispered.

Tanu wondered why that simple kindness should make her pain grow sharper, her body weaker. She did not resist when her mother said, "You must rest." Gently, Koleili drew her daughter's head into her lap and brushed the tangled hair from her forehead. Her fingers circled Tanu's temples in a soothing motion, urging the girl to close her eyes.

"You have decided," Koleili said at last, "that you will take no man for husband."

"I have decided," Tanu murmured.

"And you have told Colchoté." Even in the cadence of her spoken words, Koleili shared her daughter's anguish at hurting her childhood friend. But it was more than that. She had seen the painful knowledge in Tanu's eyes. Her daughter had begun to learn of the joy that came from the hunger of her body, the sweet fulfillment of that hunger that would never be hers.

Koleili wanted to weep for Tanu's loss. She rested her palm on the girl's forehead, running her fingertips over the taut muscles at the back of her daughter's neck. Koleili bent low so her hair brushed Tanu's cheeks; she wanted her daughter to feel her nearness, believe in it. "You have done what you must, *Ladaila*. Try not to grieve." The words were meaningless, but must be spoken, though Koleili wanted to rail at the jealousy of the spirits that would keep her daughter apart and alone, except from their impalpable touch.

"But it has never been so difficult before." Tanu lay motionless, paralyzed by the grief that turned to bleakness, a loneliness so deep it filled her body, escaped with her labored breath. No one had taught her how it felt to be a woman; no one could teach her now how to turn away the pain.

Her mother's fingers circled, vaguely comforting, like the brush of her unbound hair on Tanu's face. She breathed in the fragrance of hemlock—a scent known, familiar, loved. Gradually, as the warm tea soothed her, as weariness dulled her thoughts, as her mother's touch reassured her, Tanu slept.

By the time she awoke, the entire village was busy preparing for the arrival of the groom's family the following day. The women left the clearing to gather what they would need—the last of the fresh berries, great piles of firewood, many stones to line the cooking pits for Kitkuni's marriage feast.

The men had collected poles hewn of alder and yew, along with lightweight cedar planks and cattail mats. They spent the day building a temporary structure in which the marriage ritual would take place. They had chosen a flat spot just outside the woods, where they raised a long frame of poles over which they placed planks and mats to enclose the makeshift house.

It was midafternoon when the People returned to ready the food for final preparation, dig the pits, and get out their ceremonial clothes to see that they did not need repair. Tanu had struggled all day to suppress her agitation, though she paused more than once to stare blankly at the sea. Koleili had given her a few hours of rest, but when she woke, the anguish had risen like a restless serpent inside her. The confusion of new feelings and longings she could not yet understand made her clumsy and disoriented.

The sky seemed to echo her thoughts; the blue had been consumed by heavy gray clouds that rumbled ominously, sinking lower as the sun moved through the treetops. *Stokam*, the storm spirit, cried out her silent torment.

After hours in the woods, Tanu was relieved to sit in the hut, in the restful quiet of hushed shadows. She was decorating a cedarbark dress for Yeyi, though it was not the tunic the girl should have. How could she disappoint The Laughing One, who trusted her completely? She had not been able to bear Yeyi's pain, had tried to soothe it without thinking. Tanu raged inside. It seemed her world was crumbling at her feet.

When she was finished, she reached for her own ceremonial tunic on the low shelf where the clothing was stored. She was surprised to find fine elkskin. She took it out and unfolded it.

"What is this?" she cried at the sight of long leggings covered with intricate shell patterns, with the feathers of eagles and the down of geese. She sat back on her heels, stared uncomprehending at the garments in her hands. They belonged to Tseikami; this was his sacred ceremonial costume.

Gradually, she became aware of other cries and shouts. Carrying the leggings, she stepped into the clearing and saw that half the village stood gaping at clothing that was not their own.

"The Trickster has struck again," Enis shouted in dismay. "Now we must sort these as well as everything else that must be done."

Automatically, Tanu spoke soothingly. "We will make it right."

"It is hopeless!" Kitkuni's mother cried.

"Why did the Trickster choose such a time?" Alteo demanded. "Colchoté's cousin Wahan has been given Hawilquolas' clothes and the other hunters cannot even guess whose garments they have."

Despite her distress, Tanu had to smile in admiration. The Trickster had chosen carefully. All knew Tseikami was training Tanu to follow in his footsteps, and she held his clothes in her hands. Wahan, who thought himself so wise, who had made no secret of his wish to be Head Man, had Hawilquolas' leggings and ceremonial hat.

A boy pranced up, grinning with delight. He was only seven summers, always pretending to be a great hunter and fisherman. He was impatient with being a child and could not wait to grow up. He held in his chubby brown hands the clothing of Old Uncle, the oldest man in the tribe.

Suddenly a shriek pierced the moisture-laden air as lightning pierced a black night sky. "Someone has taken my new tunic!" Twana's eyes were filled with tears, her face dark with anger. "Who would dare do this?" She carried the tunic Old Grandmother had worn for many years.

"Where is my tunic?" Twana demanded of Tanu, as if she would certainly know the answer.

At a roar of thunder, Tanu turned toward Kitkuni's hut, where Yeyi stood, a tunic draped reverently over her arms. She gazed with longing at the fine elkskin, the intricate bead- and shellwork. Her round face glowed as Tanu approached.

"I did not know where it came from," Yeyi said regretfully.

"That must be mine!" Twana cried in triumph. She looked closer and frowned. "This is not the right design. It has all been changed." She held it up, her face as thunderous as the clouds overhead. "And look! Someone has added panels to the sides. It is too big for me now."

Tanu crossed her hands over her chest to hold her delighted laughter in. The rest of the village had gathered to glance knowingly at Tanu, touch her lightly on the shoulder in approbation. She did not have time now to explain that she was not responsible. They would not believe her anyway. "Perhaps then you can allow Yeyi to wear it after all, since you can no longer say it will not fit her."

Twana gasped and the rage climbed from her blood into her face, making her brown cheeks red. Then she heard the chuckles around her, saw the approving nods of the villagers. Swallowing the anger that threatened to choke her, she realized she was trapped. She could not take her garment back without appearing ungracious or worse. She wanted to scream, beat the ground with her bare feet, but everyone was watching and waiting.

"I am sorry," Yeyi began. "I did not mean—"

"You must not apologize," Tanu said. "You did not do this."

With a forced smile, Twana handed the tunic back to Yeyi. "It is yours now. I could not wear it anyway. It must be meant for you to have it."

A cheer rose from the People, and Yeyi took the tunic in disbelief. She did not wish to humiliate Twana further by voicing her own pleasure. "I thank you from the heart," she said. "You are generous indeed." She could not hide a smile that made her eyes disappear in soft wrinkles and brought dimples to her cheeks.

"Yes," Tanu agreed in a voice that carried to everyone in the village. "The Trickster has brought out the good in both Twana and Yeyi." Because she could no longer choke back her laughter, she turned away. It was then that she saw a figure in a cedarbark cape and hat hovering at the edge of the clearing.

She knew, as certainly as she knew her mother's face, that this was the Trickster, waiting to see the trouble he had caused, to enjoy it from afar. Her curiosity was so strong that she could not deny it. Without a word, she slipped past the huts toward the huddled figure.

The Trickster saw her and turned to flee. Tanu followed, making her way easily over the sandy boulders. At that moment, the clouds could bear their burden no longer and the rain burst free with a roar.

Tanu did not mind. Her attention was on the fleeing figure, covered from head to toe by cape and hat, who darted in and out, trying to confuse her. Moving swiftly, Tanu got closer, but the rain pelted the rocks and it was difficult to grip the slippery surface with her toes.

She slowed just enough to keep from falling. It was more and more difficult to see through the rain, which fell in heavy sheets that blurred the outlines of the woods. Once beneath the trees, she breathed a sigh of relief; the leaves held back most of the moisture which dripped through vivid green needles. With a new surge of energy, mud clinging to her feet, she darted after the figure who was always just out of reach.

Tanu ducked beneath low branches, brushed water from her eyes, untangled her feet from reaching vines. She would not give up. Nothing mattered but the chase, the prey who fled, sheltered by rain, trying to lose himself in the sanctuary of the forest.

When the path twisted upward abruptly, exposing her once more to heavy rain, Tanu ducked her head and ran on, breathing painfully, her side aching from exertion. She could barely see through the downpour, but it did not matter. Now and then she caught a glimpse of the running figure.

Gasping, she paused and noticed the Trickster had also stopped to lean against a gnarled oak. The cedarbark cape blended into the color of the rough bark, but even through the falling rain, Tanu was not fooled. She decided it was time to guide the Trickster's hand.

She sprang forward, forcing the figure off his chosen path, blocking the easy escape through the woods and driving him into the hills—damp, green and slippery with rain. Smiling despite the twinge in her side and her rasping breath, Tanu pushed the matted hair from her face and jumped from rock to rock, like the mountain goats that played here when the rain did not come to ruin their games.

The Trickster moved with agility, heading obstinately upward, stopping often to catch his breath or grasp his side. It would not be long now, Tanu knew. Then she saw it—the wall of stone that rose out of the muddy earth.

The land fell off to one side, the rock wall blocked the other, and Tanu herself followed the last route of escape. The Trickster turned and turned again, the cape swirling out, flinging raindrops into the streaming air. When he realized he was trapped, he faced Tanu, choking and gasping, but determined.

A sound disturbed her, pricked at her ears, then faded into wind and rain. Tanu did not pause to wonder. She had almost caught the Trickster;

only a rocky stretch of ground lay between them. She stopped, bent in pain, one eye on the figure who stood motionless. Then she recognized the sound that rose above the violent noise of the storm. It was laughter—high, clear and pure—full of pleasure and power and triumph.

Tanu could not resist the lure of that pure sound. Her mirth came spilling out and she doubled up with the full, rich laughter she had held so long inside.

Suddenly she froze. The Trickster's voice was as high as her own—a woman's laughter. Too stunned to move, she watched in astonishment as the figure raised its head and removed the conical hat to reveal Kitkuni's grinning face.

Tanu was dazed by the sight of that face, dripping with rain, flushed with exertion, luminous in the silver-streaked light. Images flitted through her mind: Kitkuni, scratched and bruised, saying she had traveled all night; Kitkuni watching the men stare in dismay at the tangled nets; Kitkuni gazing thoughtfully at Twana as she twirled about the fire in her fine new tunic.

"Is it not wonderful?" her friend cried.

Tanu shook herself out of a dream. "I do not understand."

Kitkuni breathed raggedly, but even through the rain, her almond eyes were radiant. "I thought you understood everything, this most of all. I had to do it, to prove that I could."

Tanu could not help but share her friend's exuberance, her secret delight. "You did not want the others to know?"

"I know," Kitkuni shouted through the rising wind. "That is all that matters."

Overwhelmed by admiration that took her voice away, Tanu trembled, not from cold or wet or weariness, but from awe and deep respect. "You have dared much," she said, though it was not enough.

Kitkuni laughed again, a sound so pure it coiled itself around Tanu's fast-beating heart.

"I would dare anything! It was my last chance to live in danger, to risk all and yet keep all, to make them remember after I have gone. Tomorrow I marry. Tonight I am still free."

Kitkuni raised her arms to the sky, turned her face up into the rain. It was as if, with that single gesture, she reached out to grasp the world in her open arms, to absorb it through the raindrops on her skin. There was nothing she could not do, no force of Nature that could defeat her. Her courage and exhilaration vibrated through Tanu's body, a promise and an agony all at once. *Tonight I am still free.* But tomorrow—

"Do not!" Kitkuni exclaimed. "There will never be another moment like this one. Not for you or for me. Do not destroy it with your thoughts of the future. There is no future. There is only you and me and our friendship and the glorious rain. We are alone in all the world and everything you see is ours."

She smiled, her cheeks wet with rain and tears, and Tanu smiled with her, and wept and exulted.

Chapter

10

In the morning, after the women lined huge cooking pits with skunk cabbage leaves, they crouched before Tanu's collection of stones. Eyes closed, they touched the smooth surfaces to wish for luck and happiness for Kitkuni and her groom.

Koleili was filling a basket with fresh-washed berries, but her eyes were on her daughter. "You are different today. Something has changed you."

Smiling mysteriously, Tanu nodded.

m"I saw you run toward the woods. It looked as though a spirit had possessed you and sent you flying into the storm."

"I *was* possessed," her daughter replied. Her smile did not falter, though this was her friend's marriage day. Hands busy with herbs and roots, she gazed inward, transfixed by the image of a luminous laughing face against a wall of stone. She would never forget the sound of Kitkuni's laughter or her exaltation as she raised her hands into the pouring silver rain.

Koleili was uneasy. She did not understand this sudden change. Just yesterday she had felt her daughter's pain as sharply as a shooting flame. Yet how could she regret that Tanu was smiling again? Let the girl have her secret pleasures; she had earned the right to more than she would ever find.

The clouds from last night's storm hovered, gray and heavy in the distant sky, when the canoes of the visitors appeared. The islands, made ethereal by a sea of pale blue mist, seemed to float on woven wisps of air that cloaked the water, hiding the canoes until they were near the shore.

The groom's father and the Head Man rode in front, standing on planks balanced across two canoes. Even from the shore, the villagers could see that the narrow boats were heavy with gifts.

The beating of drums rolled in with the waves, skimming over the water, echoing up to the sky. The Salish listened to the slow, rumbling beat, but did not raise their heads. It was part of the ritual.

Through the gossamer threads of her thoughts, the fragile lacework of her memories, Tanu heard the drums and rattles. Only then, for the first time, did she know in her heart that it was real. Kitkuni, friend of fire and water and sacred stone, was going. Tanu had not let herself believe until the music swelled and she could no longer deny it.

Waiting in the shelter built the day before, Kitkuni's family also heard the drums. Her father, Alteo, rose to bar the door—a cattail mat held by two forked yew poles. He laid a third pole into the forks, across the center of the door, in the traditional signal of the unattainable. In a silence that pulsed with the absence of sound, with unspoken hope and anxiety, Kitkuni's family sat, their breath drifting on the hushed air.

Concealed behind cattail mats, Kitkuni was motionless—cold with trepidation, wild with expectation. They had given her rose hips to chew to make her breath sweet, bathed her with hemlock bows, rubbed her body with bedstraw to give it a perfume-like fragrance. She wore her ceremonial tunic, a deerskin decorated with rows of small wooden ornaments and shells and buttons of sliced deer antler. She wore fine sinews strung with shells around her ankles, and about her head a fur-trimmed headband. Yet she sat alone behind her screens, where none could see or smell or touch her.

While the village watched covertly, Chatik's relatives made their way to the marriage house. The shaman, Kwanasa, who wore a cape of otter skins, with eagle feathers fixed to the mink band on his head, placed his hand on the barred door. He spoke long and passionately of Chatik's virtues, the virtues of his future bride, the wisdom of uniting the two families. When he stepped back, another took his place.

Tanu did not listen. She knew the speeches would go on for hours. The groom had brought many to speak on his behalf. Each would attempt to convince Alteo to unbar the door, though all knew it was only a matter of time before he did so. The pride of both families demanded that the ritual be played out.

Koleili saw her daughter change, saw her smile fade, her radiance dim. "You are grieving again," she said quietly.

"I have lost my friends, both Colchoté and Kitkuni."

"You sound as if you have no other. Every member of this village is your friend. They would give all they have for you."

Tanu met her mother's probing gaze. "Not one of them would splash water in my face and swim away laughing. Only Kitkuni."

Pensively, Koleili considered. "I think it is not the loss of your friend that fills you with such sorrow. You have known from the beginning that someday she would marry. I think you are mourning the loss of your childhood."

"I never had a childhood. They took it from me long ago," Tanu cried. She was shocked by the bitterness in her voice. She had not even suspected it was there.

"But Kitkuni gave it back to you."

Tanu stared at the floating blue islands, but did not see them. In her ears were the speeches of the groom's family, in her heart the realization that when Kitkuni left, she would take with her the only carefree hours Tanu had ever known. Faithfully, she had honored the traditions of her People, but now they seemed empty, without substance. It was a game, this pretense played out for pride and pride alone.

Yet the speeches continued. Finally, Alteo removed the bar so the groom's family could enter. Chatik sat just inside the door. While Kwanasa spoke, Kitkuni's family became rigid and aloof, as was the custom. They could not appear to be convinced too easily. Eventually, the groom's relatives left to eat and rest.

Desperate behind her wall of woven grass, Kitkuni peeked out to see Chatik sitting alone. No one spoke to him or offered him food or water. He must prove his patience and wait. Kitkuni admired his chiseled features, but was wary of his square, jutting chin.

When she bit back a scream of impatience, Alteo rose and went to bring in the men of his village. He nodded to Hawilquolas, who raised Chatik from his cramped position and led him to a pile of blankets in the center of the room.

Chatik's relatives stood on one side, Kitkuni's on the other. While Hawilquolas brought Chatik forward, Kwanasa took Kitkuni's hand and guided her to a pile of blankets opposite. At last the wedding gifts were exchanged—carved paddles, fishing nets, baskets, blankets and carved cedar bowls.

Kitkuni's father raised his hand and silence fell.

"I accept these gifts for the hand of my daughter, as you have accepted mine for the hand of Chatik. We are one family now. *Chah-ma-dah.* Always, it is the custom for all time."

Thus Kitkuni was married.

Everyone cheered. The time had come for the long-awaited feast. Bride and groom went first and the others followed, to sit on mats already laid out. The women brought platters of salmon, sizzled by the fire on sticks, of clams, fish, herbs and roots boiled together in a canoe, of mussels, oysters and scallops, of quail, geese and widgeon. Last came the deer roasted in a pit, flavored with fern and camas and salal leaves.

Everyone ate until they groaned with the weight of the food in their bellies. The village was proud of the feast it had provided. But now it was time for the *Tsakwetan,* the cleansing ceremony for bride and groom which would purify their marriage.

The Salish knelt when Tseikami appeared in ceremonial leggings and cape, carrying the antlers that were sacred to his People. As he placed the antlers on a shelf covered with mink, the dancers began to appear around the fire, singing, swinging deerhoof rattles, swaying to the beat of drums that rose in the falling night like many voices full of thunder.

Tseikami stood before Kitkuni, Kwanasa before Chatik. "By joining together in marriage, each of you has become a new person and earned the right to a new name," Tseikami intoned. Kwanasa put his hand on Chatik's head. "You are a man now, a great hunter, as great as your grandfather, who killed three sea lions in one summer and fed three villages for many suns and moons. I call you now by his name, Toke, and so you shall be known, by this name and no other."

Then Tseikami raised his hands. "You, Kitkuni, are a woman now, with the power of *siwan,* the little magic which made your grandmother respected in our village. You, who share her wisdom and her laughter, share also her name. I call you now Kwiaha, and so you shall be known, by this name and no other."

He waited for the drums to grow quiet. "The *junai,* the songmaster, Colchoté, comes to sing the marriage prayer."

Colchoté raised his wooden rattle, and the drums beat softly while the People struck sticks one upon the other. When night pulsed with the rhythm, Colchoté began to sing.

> Now for you there is no rain,
> For one is shelter to the other.
> Now for you there is no night,
> For one is light to the other.
> Now for you nothing is sharp or bitter,
> For the bitterness is taken

By one for the other.
It is that way from now on
From now on.
Now there is comfort.
Now there is no loneliness.
Now forever—forever, there is no loneliness.
Tee-Mant-Quit-See!
This is the way it is!

"*Tee-Mant-Quit-See!*" the People sang.

"*Chah-ma-dah!*" Colchoté cried. "Always. It is the custom for all time."

"*Chah-ma-dah!*" the People answered.

In her elkskin tunic, Yeyi sat beside the bride and groom, her round, dimpled face alight with pleasure. Tanu examined the intricate pattern of shells on elkskin and thought how hard Kitkuni must have worked to change the design and add the side sections so quickly. She must have sat all night bent over a fire—alone, perhaps smiling to herself.

She was smiling now, but it was the smile of a stranger. Kitkuni had slipped away, given up her spirit and become Kwiaha. Rigid with dignity, she was no longer herself, but her husband's wife. Yesterday she would have dared anything; now she sat docile and expressionless. Inwardly, Tanu wept.

The dancers, turned to shadows, demons, exalted beings, revolved to the music that coursed through their blood like fire, burning away their inhibitions. The cadence echoed from earth to sky, filling the night. The dancers sang, their words indistinct, lost in frenzied movement, in the shaking of rattles, in the overwhelming resonance of the beating of the drums.

The dancing and music drew the People together, touched some primitive need, a rhythm so deeply buried that they felt it only when song and chant enveloped them. In the pulsing, primal beat, they heard the voices of the past—the magic, the spirits, the greatness that had once been theirs.

In a trance, the People of Tanu's village rose one by one to touch the magnificent sacred antlers textured with down.

The shaman Kwanasa stood beside Tseikami, watching, astonished as a young girl lifted the antlers and tied them on her head.

Tseikami smiled when Tanu began to dance, burdened by the antlers. She wore her ceremonial tunic, decorated with buttons of bone, shells of abalone and clam, with beaver teeth, goose down and eagle feathers. She wore a necklace of cougar and bear claws, a jingling anklet of scallop shells, deerhoof rattles about her knees and ankles that created a gentle, pulsing sound. Her headband was rich sea-otter fur, with the sign of a deer carved in bone at the center.

Kwanasa stared. "You allow her to wear the antlers?"

Tseikami opened heavy-lidded eyes. A moment before they had been veiled, but now they glowed. The angles of his face were reborn in the firelight. "She is Tanu, who brought them to us. It was she who killed the doe who bore them."

"The doe with antlers!" Kwanasa was dazed. "I have heard of such an animal, but I did not believe." He peered into the firelight, trying to see Tanu's face, but the light flickered madly and she moved in fragments of brilliant color. "This is She Who Is Blessed?"

Tseikami nodded. "She is our Queen." He recognized the moment when Tanu was taken by the spirit, when she began to move, not to her own measured beat, but to the beat of the drums and the call of the flames. She flung out her arms to embrace the fire, the People, and the night beyond.

Kwanasa was mesmerized. Tanu was air and earth, water and fire all in one sweeping gesture flowing from itself into itself, from the night into the dawn, from the water to the waiting thirsty land. She turned and the light struck her clear green eyes. The shaman gasped. "She is not of the People."

Tseikami raised a gnarled hand. "She is of the People and more than the People. She is all things in one body, nourished by the flow of many bloods. She is our savior and our miracle. She is herself. It is all we ask of her."

The spirit rose within her and Tanu sang, her voice golden, unbearably sweet. She brought tears to the People's eyes, made them hear the voices of mist on the water, the falling of rain, the sighing of trees. "By all that is sacred, I dance. For all that is sacred, I sing!

"Blazing golden fingers,
Luminous dancing flickers,
Come.

Touch my cold hand—shaking, shivering.
Reach my still heart—waiting, fluttering.

Smoldering orange fingers,
Shimmering fiery flickers,
Come.
Surround me."

She was lost, transported to a place where flame and song and drum were one compelling pulse. It flared within her, brought a joy so exquisite it made her weightless, freed her. The spirits held her heartbeat gently while they sent her body twirling.

She forgot Kitkuni, the anguish and exaltation of that moment in the rain. She forgot Yeyi in her new elkskin tunic, Koleili with the memories in her eyes, Colchoté, with his hands that could not hold her. All she knew, in that moment when the earth fell away, was the sound of night and wind and sea that whispered in her head until she cried out, damp with sweat and gasping for breath, in a song so pure no other could hear it.

She wanted nothing, needed nothing more than this.

She dipped her head and when she raised it, she was staring into Kitkuni's beloved face. Kitkuni, now Kwiaha, wore her new name uncomfortably, like an unfamiliar cloak, heavy and too warm on this balmy summer night. Yet her face was familiar; Tanu knew the slim nose, the gently rounded chin, even the smile on lips turned stiff with smiling. But it was Kitkuni's almond eyes that caught Tanu and held her.

Behind the thin veneer of her solemn acquiescence glimmered the real Kitkuni, the memory of the Trickster, vibrant and irrevocable, that she would carry with her always. Bowing before the bride, Tanu dropped in her lap a small, smooth stone, silver speckled with black. A sacred stone, a final, priceless gift to the friend who had left her behind.

Kitkuni smiled, cupped the stone in her hands, and looked away. When she glanced back, Kwiaha had returned, distant, unknowable. It hurt too much, just now, to remember. Protectively, she gathered the cloak of her new name about her.

Tanu stepped back. For an instant, the past lay between them like a wisp of silver down that floated on the firelight—hovering, incandescent— then drifted away into the warm, dark summer night.

Chapter

—◄ 11 ►—

The fire burned low and the voices of the People were subdued. The bride and groom had gone, and with them the men of Chatik's village. The food had been eaten, the songs sung, the rituals fulfilled. The excitement, the pulse that had made their hearts beat fast, had faded. There was no need to hurry anymore. All had been completed.

The breeze wafted lazily through the late summer night, bringing the scent of fir and spruce mingled with salty ocean air. The Salish lounged by the fire with the touch of the sea on their skin, the fragrance of the woods in their hair.

"Chatik told me there is to be a Gathering," Wahan muttered, to fill the silence.

"A Gathering?" Colchoté sat up straighter, his eyes bright with interest for the first time in many days. "When?"

"Not during the next moon, but at the crescent moon to follow. It is to be held near Nanaimo, not so very far away."

The People began to murmur among themselves. There had not been a Gathering for some time, though not long since, trappers had organized yearly rendezvous with Salish and traders. Now that the Strangers had forts and towns on the Island and across the strait, there was no need to meet in the wilderness.

"A Gathering," Koleili murmured, gazing into the last glowing coals of the fire. The mist had begun to creep in; through drifts of white, her face was softened, blurred as if Youth had once more touched her with kindness.

Tanu stiffened, disturbed by the look on her mother's face, the haze that formed a meshwork barrier between mother and daughter. She knew what Koleili was thinking. She had met her Stranger at a Gathering sixteen summers past. Tanu's palms felt damp with fear, though she could not say why.

"I think we should go," Colchoté declared. "We have worked hard these past six moons to earn a few days of rest. And we have much to trade. There are many more furs than we need, more dried salmon than we could eat in three winters." If his voice was too brittle, his desire too fierce, no one asked why. Now everyone was talking at once.

"I would like to go. It has been long since we met with others, even the nearby villages."

"It is time we went into the world beyond the Many Waters."

"I say with Colchoté."

Excitement filled the air—the impatience of men too long held back from their natural desire to roam. In their efforts to avoid the Strangers, the People had traveled within certain boundaries for many years. Rarely did they hear unknown voices. The marriage had reminded them what it was like to gossip with strangers, to share food and drink, stories and songs.

"Is this journey wise?" Tseikami asked, glancing at Tanu.

His hypnotic voice stopped the chatter. The villagers turned from their queen, gasped, and covered their mouths.

Tanu was not aware of her People's distress, nor would she have understood it had she seen it. A chill crawled up her spine and her body was suddenly cold and rigid. The fire, which a moment before had been smoldering ashes, burned so bright in her eyes that its white heat radiated outward, turning the world frozen and silent, as it was in the snowbound heart of winter.

"We thought selfishly. We should not go." Colchoté's words fell into the unnatural stillness as a log falls into red-hot coals, scattering sparks and fragments of fire.

The others nodded with regret.

"We cannot know what we should do unless we ask the spirits," the shaman declared. His gaze was fixed on Tanu, motionless and pale in the circle of dark faces.

"Then you must tell us," Koleili said. "Ask for a dream."

Tseikami shook his head. "It is Tanu who must dream for you. If her spirits tell us to go, then so it shall be."

Startled from her waking vision, Tanu gaped at him. Had he sensed the dread that held her in its freezing grasp? She realized everyone was watching expectantly. "I say no!" she cried, then added more gently, "I do not think it is time for such a journey."

"How can you be sure?" Koleili asked wistfully.

Tanu heard the thread of hope in her mother's voice. "I do not think it is time," she repeated stubbornly.

Frowning, Hawilquolas leaned forward. "It is not like you to decide before you ask the spirits."

"Are you forgetting she is *siawa*, clairvoyant?" Kitkuni's mother, Shaula, whispered. She knew Tanu well and had never seen the girl so pale or heard her speak so tonelessly.

"I have not forgotten," Hawilquolas replied. "But to be *siawa* is not enough. She must ask for a dream. Perhaps, after all, it *is* time for this journey."

Koleili was alarmed by the blanched color of her daughter's skin, the muddy green of her eyes. She wanted to tell Tseikami he was wrong, but his wide obsidian gaze stopped the words in her throat. He had not spoken on a whim. He understood the demons he was calling forth.

Leaning close to the fading heat of the fire, Tanu fought to free herself from the radiant white light. As it left her, disappeared into the glowing wood from which it had sprung, it sucked the chill from her body and she found that she could breathe again. A wisp of smoke curled upward; in that impalpable gray haze, she heard a song. *Repose toi, mon âme, en ce dernier asile.* "I will ask for a dream," she murmured. "Then we will know." The People sighed with relief and rose, drifting away from the circle and the decision that must be made.

When the others had gone, Tanu sat alone, while Koleili approached Tseikami. "Why are you so certain this must be my daughter's dream?" she whispered so Tanu would not hear.

Tseikami surveyed the stars, shrouded by a thin film of clouds. "It must be her dream because it is her fear. You saw how the others looked at her. Even they know."

"But she does not," Koleili said, half to herself.

"I think for the first time, she does not see what is before her," the shaman murmured. "Each of us must take a long, treacherous journey if we are to know our own hearts, as well as the hearts of others. It is time for Tanu's journey to begin."

"It will not be easy for her."

"If it were, the journey would teach her nothing." Tseikami sighed. "My dreams have spoken often of her great and blessed power. She must be ready when that power bursts full-blown into her hands. Besides, I am growing old. The People must become accustomed to putting their faith in her."

Tseikami's hair was white with the proof of his trials, his face lined with the burdens he had carried. When he looked at Tanu, young and strong, her limbs elastic, her eyes bright, he saw the rising sun. When he caught his own face in a circle of still water, he saw the sun set. In the end, it sank behind the horizon and did not rise again.

"What are you saying?" Tanu asked suddenly out of the darkness where the fire had been.

"Only that it is time to face your fear and see it for what it really is," Tseikami told her.

Tanu was full of unnameable dread. She closed her eyes and tried to listen to the sea, but the shaman's warning whispered in the lap and swell of the waves.

Koleili watched the girl's shifting expressions, saw the struggle for understanding which had shaped Tanu's life. Deliberately, she turned to Tseikami. "If her journey begins, is it not time to find another name? She was not given one at her first blood flow, and now that she will not marry—"

The shaman smiled. "How can she grow into another name when she is already a Queen?"

Koleili had no answer but the sorrow in her heart.

Three suns later, Tanu took a one-man canoe and headed for the lake a day's journey from the sea.

"Why so far?" Koleili demanded. She felt helpless as her daughter slipped further away with the passage of each moon; she could not hold her, yet she could not bear to let her go.

"This dream must come from the deepest water, the voices which speak only when the need is strong." *It is time to face your fear and see it for what it really is.*

She did not tell Koleili those words tormented her, that she was running from herself, from the pain that had come at the dying fire and had not left her since. She had little food in the pouch at her waist—she must fast to make herself pure—but she carried the sacred stones.

Koleili took her daughter's face in her hands. "It is that great a question, this trip to the Gathering?"

"It is that great." Tanu spoke cautiously to disguise the sense of urgency that drove her, making her hands tremble. She must calm the frantic demons who would not let her rest.

"Then I will ask you no more. Go and do what must be done."

Tanu grasped her mother's hand. "I will miss you."
"And I you, My Daughter."

Tanu knelt against the yew plank that stretched from side to side of her graceful canoe. The boat was long and low, the bow skillfully carved and formed to cut through the water. She used her leaf-shaped paddle to speed her progress toward the refuge of the woods. Once there, she inhaled the aroma of rich, damp earth. It was so still that each breath was a prayer, each beat of her heart the cadence of a song. Her violent pulse slowed.

As the sun began to set, the trees grew close around her—red alder, graceful spreading maple, birch and oak and arbutus, and the silver-green limbs of the cedar. The mist curled through the treetops, dyed russet-red by the sun, before it drifted toward the tangled undergrowth.

It was dark when Tanu stepped from her canoe and dragged the boat to safety high up on the lake shore. She was thirsty, hungry and tired, but that was as it should be. The spirits came more easily at such times.

Her back against a solid oak, she took the stones from her pouch. One by one, she pressed them to her cheek, remembering with her fingers the beauty of each—the stripe of blue like a lightning bolt through rough gray, the earth-red with an indentation just big enough for her thumb, the brown flecked with gold, and the yellow-green with a piece of fern caught in the polished surface.

She held this stone in her hand, tightly, so her fingers ached with the strain. The turbulence raged inside her, unchecked. Her lips were dry and her throat raw, but she did not drink. Instead, she focused on the waves that caressed the shore, the call of night birds and chattering animals, and somewhere, far away, the cry of a wolf.

Eyes closed, she opened her mind to images that flitted in brilliant bursts of color across her lids. Then it came to her again. *Repose toi, mon âme, en ce dernier asile.* It haunted her, that little fragment. The colors seemed to answer its meter, spin to its mystifying, elegant words.

Tanu began to walk. When she was in motion, the webs of confusion cleared; she could feel the earth beneath her feet, the swing of her arms against her sides, the sound of her own breathing. She looked to the sky and asked the stars for help, begged the spirits to come clear away her desperation and anger.

She stopped with the water sucking gently at her feet. Anger? Where had the thought come from? But she knew the answer; it had come from her own heart. She had not known it was there until the word gave a name to the feeling.

Untying her skirt and top, she dropped them on the sand and answered the call of the lake. The water closed around her—cold, clear, intimately familiar. It caressed her naked body while she ducked beneath glimmering blue-black waves. She shook her head so her hair flowed out behind her like seaweed.

Her chilled skin tingled with exhilaration. It had been too long since she had given up her will to the power of the lake in moonlight. She dove down and down. The breath was ready to burst from her lungs, and her vision grew blurred. She rose, exploding from the water in a shower of white-blue sparks.

Tanu swam until her arms ached and her head was light with hunger and exhaustion. She found herself on the beach, though she did not remember how she had come to be there. She lay listening to the seductive pulse of waves on the shore. And threaded through that pulse, a gossamer filament of music. *Repose toi, mon âme, en ce dernier asile.*

Tanu stumbled to her feet, fell back to her knees, and propped herself up with shaking arms. With an effort of will, she rose and made her way to the gnarled garry oak, where she collapsed. She could not sleep; she must deprive herself of that luxury too if she wanted a true dream.

The next day she walked, weak with hunger, exhausted from her confrontation with the lake the night before. She swam again at dusk, the ghosts all around her in the tall trees. She dove, came crashing upward, dove and rose again until her mind was webbed with the woven mist out of which vision was born.

On the third night, as darkness fell, Tanu swam naked to the heart of the lake, trembling with the weakness of her muscles, pursued by voices that spun inside her head. Struggling against her lightheaded exhaustion, she dove and rose, dove and rose.

The water began to roil around her, and Tanu heard the rumble of *Stokam*, the storm spirit, as the wind raced across, whipping the lake into madness. The water spat and snarled like a beast gone mad. Her hair was tangled in the violent motion of the waves, in the rain that fell so furiously she could no longer tell it from the turbulence of the water. The rain fed the lake and the lake fed the rain; they became one raging force, one silver-blue-black whirlpool of fury.

Tanu was tossed about until the storm lifted her to the shore and left her, gasping for breath, knowing nothing but the churning, seething water. She crawled along the sodden ground, seeking the tree where she had rested. Blindly she clung to earth that crumbled in her hand, roots that jutted upward, fallen branches, anything with weight and substance and reality.

She reached the base of the gnarled oak and pressed her face into the creviced bark, etching the patterns of hundreds of years into her wet brown skin. She slipped painfully to the ground, and so, fell asleep.

She dreamed, and in her dream the mist drifted from above, rose from below, swirled about and softened the harsh outline of a deep river gorge. Out of the mist came voices, laughter that laced itself among the drifts of white. A delicate mesh of sound and moisture stirred above the clearing.

Through that tissue of mist and human laughter, a hand appeared and the round brown shape of a smiling face. Another hand grasped the first, another face emerged, then another and another. The web of mist was torn, sent spinning into the sky.

The People twirled, hands linked—mother to child, husband to wife, child to grandfather to sister to brother to aunt and to uncle. All were laughing, playing dancing games at the edge of the gorge. They sang, each family its own song, and circled and did not look at the edge that lay so near their dancing feet.

A sound rose in the scattered mist and billowed, whirling, toward the People. The song of the North Wind, the chilling wind, the dangerous wind. Tanu cried out in warning and fear, but the People did not notice.

When the North Wind reached them, full of power and fury, they lifted their faces, raised their hands, and felt its chilly rage, reveled in its strength and fierceness. Hands high, they moved away from the gorge and the turbulent water below. They laughed and their faces were full of joy.

In her dream Tanu drifted to the gorge and looked down past the clinging mist, the striated stone, the spray that rose from the rushing water. A body struggled, tossed by churning foam. She watched in horror as the body turned and she saw her own face in the seething river.

She awoke to the fall of gentle rain. Beside her was a small puddle. She stared into it, mesmerized by her reflection. Remembering the joyful faces of her dream, she saw her own face, twisted with worry, darkened with dread. Not for the People, who were happy and free, but for herself.

It is time to face your fear and see it for what it really is. She wanted to look away, but Tseikami's warning kept her frozen, staring. She saw her fear so clearly that it made her gasp, grip her elbows, fold inward on herself.

She shivered when the light of dawn trailed through the sky, tinting the mist that lay on the water, tender as a kiss. She ate some boiled camas roots, her first food in days, and took a sip of water. One by one, she collected her stones, stored them carefully in her otterskin pouch, and began the long trip home, where her mother waited.

When she returned to the clearing by the sea, several of the People turned to glance at her curiously. Their eyes, bright with expectation, spoke of their eagerness to know her dream, but none would ask unless she chose to tell them. She turned away, flushed with shame.

Koleili was not among the other women. Tanu went to her hut and found her mother in the doorway, watching the evening games, her face in shadow. "You are safe!" Koleili cried.

"Did you doubt it?" Tanu's turmoil increased and she braided her fingers to hide their trembling. Koleili had always known that the spirits protected her daughter. Why then did her mother's cheeks burn with two bright spots of color? Where was the tranquillity that usually shone in her face, lay gently about her shoulders?

Tanu sank to the sand, yearning for the solace of her mother's presence, knowing that such comfort would come easily no more. "If we go to the Gathering, and he is there, will you go away with him?" She did not know she was going to say it; the feeling of her dream, the isolation and loneliness spoke for her. "I have lost Kitkuni and Colchoté. I could not bear to lose you too," she whispered brokenly.

Koleili stiffened, as shocked by Tanu's question as she was by her appearance. Her daughter's hair was tangled with dust and leaves, her clothes torn, her face a dirt-streaked mask that did not disguise her fear. Pale and shaken, Koleili sent a fervent prayer to the spirits who had woven the false image of her strength. *Let it not unravel now, when I most need it about me.* Slowly, with great trepidation, she spoke. "Is that why you did not wish us to go?"

Tanu stared at the sandy soil, scattered with fragments of shell and dried seaweed. "I think it is the reason." She was too ashamed to meet her mother's eyes. "I do not deserve the trust of my People."

"Why? Because you are human?" Koleili demanded. "That is not an evil but a blessing. You cannot silence your human voice any more than you can silence the voices of the spirits." Her daughter shivered uncontrollably and Koleili forced her anger down. She found a cedarbark blanket, wrapped it around Tanu's shoulders, and murmured, "You must rest. Eat and drink, and when you are ready, tell me of your dream."

Tanu grasped Koleili's hand. "Will you tell him about me?"

There was a moment's hesitation. "No, my daughter. I will protect you from that at least."

Wearily, Tanu chewed on some dried venison and drank a sip or two of water. "I dreamed that the People live on without me, that I cannot take away their pleasure because *I* am afraid. I have not the power to protect them. I can guide them but I cannot live their lives."

Koleili smiled sadly. Her daughter had dreamed a mother's nightmare. It was time to set her children free.

Tanu did not see the smile. "But it was not for them that I was afraid. It was for myself." The words came hard; she had been selfish, and worse, she had been deaf to her own voices.

With another desperate prayer, Koleili took her daughter's hand. "You are afraid because you think if I touch this man again, I will never let go. You think I cannot resist the untarnished image of my dream."

She paused while Tanu sat unmoving—fearful and waiting.

Koleili continued, dropping her words like tiny pebbles into a pattern on the sand. "You see, My Daughter, I could have gone with him long ago, when my love was bright and new. He asked me, but it was not what I wished. I could not leave behind my People and their history. I could not leave Hawilquolas."

Tanu looked up, astonished. "But you never said—"

"We agreed without words, Hawilquolas and I." Koleili gazed at her fingers, curled around her daughter's. "I would not marry him because of what I was, what I had done.

"I have been selfish. I sheltered one man's seed in my body, yet took another man's protection—the food he offered and the friendship others would have denied me, but for him. I never repaid him for what he gave so freely. I have never given him enough." Her head was bent, heavy with guilt.

"He told me he does not want a woman to lie beside him."

Koleili smiled crookedly. "That was not what I meant." She searched for the right words. "There is an intimacy that has nothing to do with the joining of bodies—to care for someone, share his sorrows and complaints and also his happiness, to know him well enough to sense his pain and ease it before he asks. There is a comfort between people who know each other well, who need no tricks, no pretenses, no barriers. That I could have shared with Hawilquolas. I could have given him more, but I was afraid. Because of that, I know he has been lonely."

Tanu tried to concentrate, but her skin was cool, her face hot with the storm inside her. "He told me he treasures his solitude. And he seems well content."

"When those who love you want you to be happy, it is easy to make them believe it is so. They wish so much to see contentment instead of sorrow, happiness instead of pain. It is not difficult to let them see only what they wish to see."

"You also seem content," Tanu managed to whisper. It was more than a statement; it was a plea.

Koleili considered carefully. "Perhaps that is because I learned a lesson many moons ago. Before your birth, I was made to live separate from the others. No one spoke to me. I did not know how I would survive and care for you without the respect or friendship of my People. I was consumed by a fear so great it was all I could see or feel or taste. It colored everything; the sky turned ugly yellow and the trees were dull and brown.

"Then Hawilquolas chose to act as your father. He fulfilled the rituals of birth as if I were his wife. He held a naming ceremony, gave out blankets and carved cedar bowls and beautiful shells so no one could say you had not earned the right to your name. The People took me back. And when you began to show your power, they forgot how you had been conceived. Because of Hawilquolas, they made themselves forget. They did not even remember that once they had made me feel the fear."

She did not say, nor would she, that the fear had never left her. She also did not name the hope that had taken root beside that fear the moment the Gathering was mentioned. It was a foolish hope, she knew—that Nicolas might be there. It had been sixteen summers. He probably did not remember. Or perhaps he was on the mainland or in the East or back in France. She knew these things, but the knowledge could not kill her hope; no more than fifteen years of kindness had killed her fear.

Koleili gathered her courage in cupped hands and lifted Tanu's chin. "Hear me, My Daughter. You are my family and my future. I would never leave you for the pleasure of a gentle touch." She paused. "I do not know if your father will be at the Gathering. You speak of him calmly, call him 'he,' like a stranger. Are you not curious? Do you not wish to see him?"

Tanu sat up, rigid and regal. "To me he *is* a Stranger, one who caused you great pain." She saw Koleili was about to object, but she shook her head. "I do not know this man. Hawilquolas is my father in all but blood. The Salish are my family."

Oddly, Koleili understood. It was this same instinct that had made her leave Nicolas behind so many years ago. But it would not be easy for Tanu to keep her eyes tight closed much longer, to preserve the precarious balance that had given her life order. This trip would be difficult for her daughter, a trial of endurance, and Tanu did not even see it. "You need to learn about the world beyond ours," Koleili suggested gently. "It will give you more—"

"I already have so much," Tanu interrupted. "To want more would be greedy. To ask for more would only bring pain."

And what, Koleili wondered, would Tanu's stubborn blindness bring?

Chapter

12

The clearing chosen for the Gathering was crowded with men and snorting horses, with tents, shacks and lean-tos. The smell of manure and unwashed bodies mingled with the reek of the Strangers' drink. Smoke from many fires and pipes made a haze that rose from the ground to the sky. Each man carried a gun or knife or both; the weapons gleamed in worn leather belts. The clink of money, the sound of harsh laughter, the growl of low, guttural voices were the songs of this place.

Tanu came forward tentatively, she who had always moved with pride. She was vaguely aware that the men of her village moved with her, protectively. She sensed their excitement in the shifting of their bodies, covered in the knee-length woven capes that kept away the chill of autumn. She saw how they looked about with interest, yet they did not leave her.

As they approached the center of the clearing, Tanu shrank back from the raucous noise, the unpleasant smells, the feeling of chaos. More than one trapper had noticed her, gaped openly at her burnished face. The Salish understood her distress and moved closer. Tanu was grateful for their presence.

Soon, however, the excitement, the action and laughter began to lure the men away. They moved barefoot over ground stamped to mud by rain and the hooves of many horses, passed tents pitched at irregular angles, with tears in the canvas and forked branches for ridgepoles. They breathed in the steam of snorting horses, the odor of men in dirty plaid shirts and worn jeans with beards like abandoned bird nests and long, greasy hair. Finally only Colchoté and Hawilquolas remained.

"Come, it is safe here," Hawilquolas whispered. He tried to lead Tanu toward the area where the women of their village were setting up lean-tos and building a fire.

Tanu smiled. "I do not feel in danger, only—" She tried to find the right word.

"Overwhelmed?" Colchoté offered. He held a string of furs, and Tanu sensed he was eager to barter them. Yet he seemed reluctant to leave her.

"If I am overwhelmed at first," she said quietly, "it does not mean I am afraid. I will become accustomed soon enough. Go, trade your furs before it is too late."

Colchoté hesitated, but his father nodded slightly and the young man turned to go.

"Why—?" Tanu began. She stopped when Hawilquolas frowned. She saw that he was watching Koleili, who had wandered to a secluded clearing blocked from the others' view by a row of birches. She had been kneeling, a basket on her hip, collecting ferns and roots to roast for dinner. But her hair fell unbound down her back, and she did not seem intent on her work. She gazed into the distance, forgetting the basket at her side.

There was a quality of stillness about her, of waiting ill-concealed. Tanu was transfixed and grieved by the sight of her mother alone with her basket and her fearful hope.

There was a shout and a man appeared in the clearing. He moved forward slowly—uncertain, restrained. A light-skinned Stranger. Koleili dropped her basket and rose. The two stood in silence, asking questions with their eyes.

Koleili said something, took a step forward, a tripping little step that a young girl might take going to the stream to wade. So this was he—the man her mother had chosen not to forget. Tanu bit her lip until it bled. He would not remember. Koleili had been young the last time he saw her, young and eager and foolishly vulnerable. Now she was a woman with the burden of many years upon her.

Hawilquolas made a noise deep in his throat. Like Tanu, he watched Koleili—the recognition, the moment of remembered joy she could not hide. Tanu fought back tears. Though she had said she did not care to see the man who had given her life, she looked more closely. He was not tall, nor particularly handsome, but strong and well-built, with red-brown hair and green eyes. He moved forward to take Koleili's outstretched hands.

Tanu was stunned by the anger that shook her as the man twined his fingers with her mother's. She touched Hawilquolas for reassurance and he tucked her arm in his.

The man spoke rapidly and Hawilquolas nodded. "He speaks Salish. I see how he forms the words with care. I wondered how they spoke together." His tone was bemused, perplexed; he could not quite believe what he saw.

The man drew Koleili close and kissed her. Tanu gasped, but Hawilquolas did not move.

"I told you," he said, smiling grimly, "I do not seek that kind of pain again. This man is a dream. He will disappear with the morning mist. But I will stay. Our friendship will endure. I know this here." He put his hand on his heart.

The man dropped Koleili's hands. She leaned forward, speaking quietly; he bowed his head to listen. Their bodies were relaxed, at ease, isolated by a fine web of comfort, tranquillity and affection whose invisible threads bound them together.

There is an intimacy that has nothing to do with the joining of bodies.

Hawilquolas stiffened and Tanu felt through his tightening fingers an anguish that shocked her with its power.

I could have given him more.

"I must help Colchoté with the bartering. He is clever, but not quite clever enough." He spoke with a harshness that rang false, then turned away abruptly.

He seems content.

But was he? Koleili's trust in a Stranger had hurt Hawilquolas deeply. More deeply than their passionate kiss.

When those who love you want you to be happy, it is easy to make them believe it is so.

Tanu wanted to go after the father of her heart, but she did not. This kind of pain she could not heal.

She jumped when his hand landed heavy on her shoulder. He turned her to face him. "You will be all right."

It was half-statement, half-question, and the intensity of his gaze disturbed her. But perhaps he understood that she too was hurt. "I will."

Hawilquolas hovered, unconvinced, but eventually released her and went to join Colchoté. Tanu watched him, frowning.

By the time she turned back to the clearing, Koleili and the man had disappeared. She hesitated, thought to go after them, changed her mind. Then the choice was taken from her. Kitkuni's mother and sister wove their way through the confusion of animals and tents and sprawled bodies to where Tanu stood alone.

"Come, you must see what the women have brought to trade," Yeyi cried eagerly. "There are so many beautiful things."

Confused by the anger and unwanted curiosity she felt toward the Stranger, upset by her mother's response, Tanu followed Yeyi blindly. She was glad for the girl's excited chatter; it gave her time to calm her stormy thoughts.

"I have never seen such things," Yeyi continued, round face glowing, "such colors and dyes and so many different beads. I could stare at them from sun to moon and never have enough."

She had obviously recovered her high spirits since her sister's marriage. She could barely contain her exuberance, though her mother shook her head in mock dismay. Shaula was as happy as the others that Yeyi was smiling once more.

"Look!" the girl exclaimed, drawing Tanu into a circle of women who sat cross-legged around a small fire. "They have shells like I have never seen, so delicate and beautiful. And the baskets—" She stopped, out of breath.

The beads laid out in low baskets were beautiful, in many brilliant colors; the shells were intriguing in their windswept designs. Tanu frowned when she saw a basket pushed out of the way, as if it were not for trade. She knew that basket. Yeyi had worked on it all winter, pounding the bark, splitting the threads, weaving the tight, careful strands. She had used bear grass and dark cherry bark to work the intricate design of V's for the waves of a lake, the diagonal zigzagging lines for the power of lightning. She had been proud of her work, had sworn never to part with it.

"Why do they have your basket?" Tanu demanded.

Yeyi grinned. "I traded it."

"But why?"

"Because." The girl was blithely unconcerned.

"For what?"

Smiling broadly, Yeyi took something out of the twilled basket at her waist. "For this." She beamed and held out a beautiful black stone. It was not hard like obsidian, but cool and smooth. In the center, the stone had formed around the edges of a perfect white feather.

"It is wonderful," Tanu murmured in awe. "I have not seen another like it."

"That is why I wanted it," Yeyi shouted, unable to hold in her excitement anymore. "As a gift for you." Beneath the glow in her eyes was wariness, the fear that Tanu might reject her gift. "Do you like it?" she asked shyly.

For a long moment, Tanu could not speak. She was deeply touched, as much by the hope, delight and fear mingled on Yeyi's face as by the unique stone in her hand. "It is one of the finest gifts I have ever received. I will keep it always."

Yeyi grinned, content, and the three women turned away. Staring avidly at the strange sights, they wandered back to their own shelter. The fire blazed brightly, in contrast to the dreary sky. The smell of roasting fish drifted lazily upward.

Tanu saw that Koleili had returned, her basket full of ferns and roots. She had not gone away with the man after all. Her daughter's heart lifted with relief, but her anger lay smoldering inside. She was startled by the heat of that anger, which had come to her first on the shore of the lake. She had known how Koleili felt about this man. Why had she been so surprised to see them together? "My Mother," she said in acknowledgment.

"My Daughter," Koleili responded. She sensed Tanu's unease in the rigid posture of her body, the fine-drawn lines of her face. "You saw him?" she whispered low.

"I saw."

"He is here," Koleili said. "He remembers."

Tanu's anger softened at the sight of her mother's face, flushed with delight. Yet suddenly she felt danger very near. She was ill with fear and could not watch Koleili's pleasure.

"See what I have found?" Yeyi cried, pointing to the stone.

The other women admired Tanu's treasure, touched it hesitantly. As Tanu helped prepare the meal, glad for something to do, she was aware that, like the men, the women watched her, waiting. Their wariness only increased her discomfort.

They sat nearby, one on each side and one behind, as if to keep someone or something away. Could it be the man who was her father? Tanu looked into Koleili's face and knew that there was something more, some secret, unexpressed anxiety.

The men returned, hungry and elated. The sound and motion, chatter and exchange of coins fueled their excitement. Already they had traded many of their furs and blankets. After the meal, people crowded laughing around the fires. Strangers sat beside Salish, everyone talking and shouting at once.

One man, who had drunk too much, spoke louder than the others. "I heard tell of a mission school them English have started outside Victoria. Them missionaries is so generous they want to teach you Indians for free. Teach you how to talk right, in English, and how to dress and act too. They's lookin' hard for Indians to fill that school. Give you all a better life, damned if they won't!'' His heavy beard moved up and down as he chewed his tobacco, and his cheeks were flushed with the warmth of the fire, the whiskey, delight at his own suggestion. He looked around expectantly, perplexed when the Salish stared at him in stony or amused silence.

The silence lengthened, grew uncomfortable. To break the tension, someone cried, "It's time to exchange stories!"

A trapper cried, "Let's hear about She Who Is Blessed."

There were grunts of acknowledgment and approval. Even the Strangers had heard of the Queen and her magic. The People looked to Colchoté and he nodded. "I will speak."

"It was in a time long past," he said, tapping his drum, "when the magic of the spirits came to earth in bursts of color."

He gazed at the firelit faces, the ragged, bearded men with guns shoved into their belts, the women of the People, to whom the men crept close and promised many things, the Salish men, some shaking with the power of the Strangers' drink, some holding knives that gleamed silver and deadly. But many faces were turned to him, many heads tilted, listening.

"One night in a Longhouse of cedar, with ridgepoles carved in the likeness of bear and cougar and deer, the little Queen slept. She dreamed, and in her dream the smoke rose from the fire, gray as the sleek gray wolf, fine as the blue morning mist. The smoke filled the room with a haze that transformed what was ordinary into what was rare, what was plain into what was beautiful, what was false into what was true."

Tanu shifted uncomfortably on her cattail mat. Colchoté's face was lit from within; the story had taken him over. To him it was magic—precious and beyond his reach. She looked at the others and they too were enthralled, caught up in the cadence of the words, believing. She stared at her fingers, longer and more graceful than those of her village, curled them inward so her knuckles turned white and her short nails bit into her skin.

"In her dream the smoke transformed itself into Raven, wings spread wide, beak open in laughter. Then came the serpent, made of sparks and mist, undulating in brilliant color, and finally Thunderbird, who sucked the smoke into himself, and the stars and the chill of the night."

Colchoté paused and People and Strangers held their breath.

"The Queen awoke to find the Longhouse full of smoke-dreams and smoke-shadows. The shaman was dancing a silent dance, singing a silent song over her body, half lost in sleep. He called on the power of the spirits to enter her, to lift her up into his tall, distorted shadow.

"She Who Is Blessed wished to refuse, for she did not want the burden of his magic and his power. She did not want to turn inward to the voices of her soul, but outward to the trees and skies and waters that she loved. But when she tried to speak, no sound would come.

"When she saw the shaman's spirits coming toward her in the firelight, she found these words. 'Why do you not choose the Head Man's son? He is strong and unafraid and wise. He would follow willingly in your footsteps toward the stars.' And the shaman answered, 'Because he is not you. You alone have been chosen and blessed. Look and you will see.'

"She gazed around and saw that all were sleeping, undisturbed by dreams or spirits or drifting smoke. She bowed her head, ashamed, and the shaman named her to succeed him. When she had taken the spirits inside her and the power shone from her eyes and the knowledge glowed on her young face, the shaman collapsed onto the floor.

"Then she understood. He was ill, the old shaman who had won the People's trust. Only another shaman could save him. Had she turned the magic away, he would have died beside her.

"She worked all night in the smoke-veiled room. She pounded roots and boiled herbs, washed the shaman's body and sang her songs. By morning, when the dawn light filtered through the smoke like sunlight through the forest, he fell into sleep.

"The People arose and saw that he was healed. They sang for joy. They thanked the spirits and their Queen, who had not been afraid to embrace the terrible power of the spirits. She was wise enough, brave enough, strong enough to keep them safe. So it was then, so it is now. Always and forever."

His voice faded, and in the hush that followed, cold fear took Tanu in its grasp. She tried to force it back to the bottom of the lake, where she had whirled in the arms of the raging black water. Colchoté's story had touched a nerve that made her tremble. Out of the fire came the radiant white cold that obliterated laughter and warmth and the sounds of the People. She might as well have been alone.

Yet the Salish pressed close; she knew they were there, in darkness and firelight, to keep her safe. But the fear, colder and stronger than their presence, began to choke her.

Later, when most slept, Koleili raised her head, listening. Reassured by the regular breathing all around, she slipped from under her cedar blanket and crept out of the makeshift lean-to.

Tanu watched but did not move. Her anger flared hot, tangled with her fear. She knew Koleili was going to the man. She wanted to shout in rage, to pound the earth, to weep for the woman who had lived on a dream, dreamed of a shadow for so long.

She lay rigid, unblinking. Earlier the noise had droned in her ears and she had wished for silence. Now the stillness was unbearable. Too restless to close her eyes, she crept into the chilly night. She stepped over men sprawled in the mud, half-naked, one arm thrown casually over a Salish woman. She held her breath against the smell of whiskey and stale smoke and sweat-soaked bodies.

Quickly, she made her way to the edge of the camp; the woods beckoned. All day the People had been nearby—so close that she could feel the heat of their skin, the rising of their breath. Now she wanted only her own warmth, her own breath.

She walked, absorbing the night air, the smell of autumn that had already changed the feeling of the darkness. Soon it would be winter and the People would move back to the Longhouse and begin their winter work.

She looked forward to the crisp cold weather; its promise was clean and pure compared to the fetid air around her. She stopped abruptly when she heard a thread of sound, hardly more than a whisper. *Repose toi, mon âme . . .*

Tanu's body grew cold, for this time the words did not float on the air or ripple through the water. This time they were real. She stood, arms clasped tight across her chest, shivering. Against her will and every vibrant instinct, she moved toward a small, rumpled tent. Inside a man was singing.

> *Repose toi, mon âme,*
> *en ce dernier asile.*
> *Ainsi qu'un voyageur*
> *qui, le coeur plein d'espoir,*
> *S'ássied avant d'entrer,*
> *aux portes de la ville,*
> *Et respire un moment l'air embaumé du soir.*

Tanu held her breath.

"Your song is lovely, Nicolas. What does it mean?"

Koleili. Tanu covered her ears. She did not wish to give this man a name. The man who sang the words that had haunted her since childhood. The man who was her father. For the first time she thought the words clearly—her father. She began to tremble, to shake uncontrollably.

"It means,

"Rest thou my soul, be patient;
here lies thy goal before thee,
And like a Pilgrim worn,
yet with heart free from care,
Pause at the open gate,
while peace comes over thee.
And breathe for a while the evening air."

Tanu clenched her teeth to keep them from chattering and turned to flee. But she could not flee the knowledge that echoed in her head like thunder. She had known his voice before Koleili spoke, because it was her own—deeper with the rumble of a man's strength—but her own voice just the same.

She knew the Stranger's song, had always known it, since before her time of remembering. It was in her blood, as this bearded Stranger was in her blood, and always had been.

She found a spreading maple and was ill beneath it, ill and wretched with the song ringing in her ears. *Repose toi, mon âme, en ce dernier asile.* Rest thou my soul, be patient; here lies thy goal before thee.

No! she wanted to scream. No! She was Salish; her heart was Salish and her visions and the spirits who guided her hand. Her thoughts and her traditions and her past belonged to the People, not to a man she had never seen, whose blood had tainted hers before she was born.

She was of the People, but her white blood had its own voice—a song she had always known inside, where her other secrets lay hidden. She wanted to deny the song, erase it from her memory, but it would not go. Her voice, which was part of her sacred power, the soothing sweetness that mesmerized and healed and calmed the People, had come from a Stranger. As had her height and her green, compelling eyes. So many of the things revered had come, not from the Salish, but from the Frenchman, man of her mother's dreams and memories.

They had protected her—Koleili and Hawilquolas and Tseikami—so she need never know. Now she understood why they had hovered near, as if they could keep her from harm if they never left her alone. But they could keep her safe no more. Somehow they had known it, while she had been stubbornly, frighteningly blind.

It is time to face your fear and see it for what it really is. Only now did she open her eyes and see what had brought the chill to her blood. It was her own image, half white, half Salish. Her own face, which she had never seen before. She had refused to do so. *It is time,* Tseikami had said. *It is time.*

The shaman had taught her to deal with hardship, never to hide or turn away. Now his teaching would not set her free. Tonight, huddled beneath a maple, with the bark scratching her shoulders and fallen leaves in her hair, she was forced, at last, to listen to the call of her white blood.

The sound was harsh, discordant, and it broke the ragged rhythm of her heart.

Chapter

⟫— 13 —⟪

As the Salish returned from the Gathering, Tanu sat in the canoe, staring into a clouded autumn sky. She was numb inside, though the chilly air nipped at her fingers, nose and cheeks. She did not speak; her throat was blocked by bile.

She was aware that the People were always near. For a while, the children sat beside her, exclaiming with delight over everything they saw, trying to make her laugh. Tanu smiled wanly, but her laughter had dried up like autumn leaves in winter wind.

Sometimes Colchoté walked along the bank beside the canoe, naming the goods they were bringing home—the ceremonial bearskin, the tools, elkskins and deerskins, new fishing nets. He spoke of the unseasonal chill; winter had swept in before autumn was over. It was unsettling after the summer of abundance and fine weather.

Tanu heard but did not understand. She was enveloped in a dark, chilling private torment. Not for a moment did the Salish leave her alone with her painful thoughts. They were there, talking to her shadow, telling her without words—with a touch, a smile, a look of compassion—of their trust and their affection. *There is an intimacy that has nothing to do with the joining of bodies.* Tanu held the words in her mind, like a talisman to ward off evil. She was overwhelmed with gratitude for her People.

She shifted on her seat, aching and uncomfortable. She could just see the back of her mother's head. She had watched as the sun moved through the sky and Koleili's head drooped forward. It broke Tanu's heart—the bare back of her mother's neck bent in grief for her daughter's misery. Tanu would have liked to speak of her turmoil and pain, but her wound was too fresh, too raw.

"Look!" Yeyi cried. Sitting at Tanu's feet, she rocked with the motion of the narrow boat, her hair in a loose plait, her new abalone earrings jingling. "See the red maple leaf?"

The canoe lay still for a moment while some tangled roots were dragged from the river and Tanu saw that the long branch of a maple hung over the water. A perfect leaf, still wet with drops of dew fringed in ice, quivered on its fragile twig. Light gathered in the droplets, splintered into rainbows fragmented by lacy ice. The small red leaf with its gift of colored light touched Tanu's cheek. When the canoe began to move again, the drops scattered and the light was flung into the air.

Tanu reached up to catch a drop on her finger, but she was not quick enough. She closed her eyes against the pain while Yeyi's voice talked on.

When the Salish arrived at their summer village, they saw that those who had stayed behind had begun to pack the belongings in each hut.

"The North Wind, harbinger of winter, comes early," Tseikami said in greeting. His heavy-lidded eyes were nearly closed, revealing nothing. "We must make our way to the Longhouse, where we will be safe and warm."

The men emptied the canoes, laying bundles of goods on the beach, and tried to talk over the excited voices of the women. Tanu stood alone, her arms hanging loosely at her sides. She looked helpless, without purpose, as she never had before.

When Tseikami started toward her, the People moved aside. Swiftly, they turned to the packing the shaman had begun. Only Koleili and Hawilquolas did not join the others. Instinctively, they moved closer until they stood shoulder to shoulder, as if to hold each other up against some great and terrible wind.

When Tseikami put his hands on Tanu's shoulders, she stiffened. He had never touched her before. The wind whipped around them, fierce and bitter, and she wondered if the dread she felt was the chill of winter after all.

Tseikami waited patiently for her to meet his eyes. He knew it was not easy; he alone could see the truth that she concealed from others. When at last she looked up, the shaman struggled to hide his distress. He was stunned by her pallor, the emptiness in her eyes. "You have seen your fear and come to know it well."

Tanu nodded. Her tongue was heavy and dry, her body numb. She could not yet put into words what she had learned in the cold, dark night outside the circle of sleeping Strangers.

"You are in turmoil." The shaman's face was creased with wrinkles, his white hair so fine that the wind lifted it like a feather which has no weight to keep it on the earth. But his eyes were alert and keenly perceptive. "You have lost the stillness inside from which your strength and wisdom flow."

Tanu tried to look away but failed. His eyes held her captive as his hands could not.

"I am not of the People," she gasped.

Tseikami shook his head. "You were born among us, blessed among us, came to womanhood among us. Each of us would gladly give you our lives." He pointed to the villagers, who watched in concern. "Have we not proven as much? Your blood is mixed, but in our eyes you are Salish."

"In *my* eyes is the truth. They are the eyes of a Stranger."

"They are the eyes of a Queen. It is your *seli*, your soul, that matters. Nothing has changed except that you have understood the truth at last. Now you must learn to accept it. You must carry no doubts in your heart. They will weaken you and we need you strong and wise and whole." He paused, then added darkly, "Winter comes early and wild to the Island. I fear it is an ill omen, that worse is yet to come. You must go to the woods to seek your peace, to restore the stillness that is necessary in a leader of our People, necessary as well to healing your tortured heart. I would give you that stillness in my hand if I could, but you must find it for yourself, just as you found the truth."

"I cannot leave the People to pack alone. They need me. I am strong and young." Tanu did not say she was afraid to go into the woods that had always been her refuge. Afraid they would no longer welcome her, that the peace she sought had disappeared forever in the few words of a foreign song.

"Then stay and help us prepare for the journey to the Longhouse. When we are ready, we will go, and you will leave us, find your own way through the forest to the healing places. You must have solitude to restore the balance inside. Hear me, Tanu. When you return, we will be there for you. We will be waiting."

By the time the sun was once more overhead, the canoes and baskets were loaded, the mats removed from the frames of the huts, which the Salish would leave until spring, when they returned to the summer village.

Tanu was helping Kitkuni's parents when she noticed Yeyi sitting on a boulder. The girl was trembling and looked exhausted. Her round face seemed pinched and pale.

"You work too hard," Tanu told her. "You must rest."

"I will sit here until the canoes are ready," Yeyi said meekly. She would not have dared argue with Tanu, even if she had the energy to do so.

When everything was done, the People found places in the canoes or on the paths along the river. Some would ride and some would walk, switching places regularly so everyone found a chance to rest. Tanu stood beside Koleili, who was contemplating the cobalt sea, made luminous by the sunlight.

"I will rejoin you soon," Tanu said softly. She wanted to say more, but did not know how.

"I will be waiting."

There was a moment of awkward silence, then Tanu touched her mother's cheek. Koleili smiled sadly. Before she could speak, the girl was gone, a blur against the trees and then a memory.

With a sigh of regret, Koleili found a place in the last canoe.

Tanu lost herself in the forest, in the confusion of green and gold, rust and yellow leaves, shaken by the wind into a weave of dancing colors. She tried to concentrate on the filtered light, but her mind was restless, her emotions still raw. Since childhood she had known who she was and where she was going. All at once she felt adrift, without direction.

There was no pattern, no certainty anymore. The rituals she had cherished belonged to another life, when her faith had been strong— unchallenged and unbending.

She went unerringly to the rock-carved river, where she and Kitkuni had last bathed together. She lay naked on a rock, face to the sky. The stone was rough beneath her, ridged and uncomfortable. Clouds covered the sun, and shadows moved over her face, her chest, her hands, which lay palms up, open and vulnerable. She absorbed the light and shadow through her skin, the heat and cold of the autumn sky. This she could understand; it was elemental, real and tangible. This had not changed.

Later she sat in the water, braced between two rocks. The river rushed around her in a furious cascade, leaving her shivering, her body cramped with cold. When her teeth began to chatter, she grasped the small drum slung around her shoulder. She held it beneath the water and struck it violently. The beat was muffled, yet amplified by the river, but she knew intimately the cadence that vibrated inside her.

She sang the songs of her childhood, of work and prayer and celebration. She sought desperately the music and meter that had given her life substance, magic, power. She sought the rush of primitive elation she had felt as she sang or prayed or beat the drum—the intoxicating rhythm that entered and became her as she danced around the fire.

Her long black hair was lifted by the wind while the breeze caressed her neck, reminding her of the soul she had lost, the pulse of her life in river and wind and the gold-tinted light of the forest. She must stop the gnawing pain and doubt which made a poison in her blood.

Tanu sat motionless while the sun moved across the sky, the river raged around her, washing her clean, carrying the poison away, little by little.

At night she rolled herself in her cedarbark blanket. She had not slept for many days, but tonight exhaustion overtook her. She fell and fell and fell until night and stars and river became the whirlpool of her dreams.

Tanu awoke and sat up, instantly alert. She listened, but heard only the cry of the gulls and the red-breasted nuthatch above the surging river. The chill was in her blood, sending icy tendrils of fear through her body.

She laid out her stones, running her fingertips over blue lightning in shattered gray, rich earth brown, smooth black that enfolded a white feather. Last of all, she picked up the fern frozen in stone, like a still place in a sluggish stream. She remembered the day she had found it, the crumbling stone and the letters *IHS*. She thought of Wananat, who had lived between two worlds and left his People grieving. *Have you never thought that the two worlds of my grandfather are also in your blood?*

Tanu gripped the stone so tightly that she gasped with pain and comprehension. This was a message, a link with one who had also suffered this bitter confusion. Her ancestor had known her sorrow and understood.

She wanted to go to the clearing ringed by paper birch; she sensed that there she would find peace. But something held her back—a call, an anguish greater than her own despair. She sat unmoving, eyes closed, waiting.

The sun had begun to sink toward the sea when she heard a distant cry. She cocked her head as the sound grew louder, echoing through the trees. "Tanu! Where are you? Tanu!"

"Here!" she cried. "I am here." She did not move for fear of missing the one who called to her in agitation. There were too many paths, too many trees, too many ferns and bushes. She moved away from the roar of the river, called out again and again. "Here! I am here."

Her name exploded in the evening air. "Tanu! We need you."

Colchoté's cousin. Her heart began to beat erratically; her skin was clammy and cold. Something was very wrong.

Wahan burst through the trees, pushing branches aside, his arms cut and scratched, his chiseled face both flushed with exertion and deathly pale.

When he saw Tanu, he groaned and placed his hands on his knees, bending down to catch his rasping breath. She waited, frozen to stillness by the gray cast of his skin.

"We—" he choked out, "need"—he gasped and ducked his head so the hair fell over his ashen face—"you."

"What has happened?" Tanu spoke steadily, though her pulse raced with fear.

"Yeyi is very ill. You must come." He raised his head, his eyes wild. "There may be others too."

"I come," Tanu said. "You drink and rest for a time until your heart beats slowly. Then follow."

He nodded and she was gone, crushing ferns and leaves beneath her feet. She saw only the path before her, the memory of Yeyi's face as she sat on the boulder, pale and weary.

The sun had nearly set when Tanu reached the clearing where the winter dwelling stood. She paused outside to catch her breath, afraid of what she would find. But she had no time for fear. With a fervent prayer, she stepped inside.

The Longhouse was dim and strangely hushed. Everyone was gathered around the central fire, except Yeyi's parents, Alteo and Shaula, who hovered beside an area separated by hanging mats. When they saw Tanu, they cried out. She crossed the packed dirt floor to part the mats without a sound.

Yeyi lay on the platform, dishes of whale oil burning at the corners of her pallet. Her face was flushed with fever, her skin filmed in sweat. The front of her body was covered in a pink-red rash and she shivered uncontrollably. By the way she swallowed, grimacing, Tanu guessed her throat was raw with pain.

The cold feeling of dread, the spreading tentacles of fear, became a living, breathing weight in Tanu's body. The People gathered outside the mats, waiting. How could she tell them what she had known from the instant she saw the rash, the ring of pallor around Yeyi's lips, the delirium in her eyes?

To be certain, she coaxed the girl to open her mouth and saw her coated tongue and the inflamed bumps underneath. She had seen it before in a nearby village, where Tseikami had taken her once. He had told her this was scarlet fever, the Red Sweating Sickness. The poison was already deep in Yeyi's blood.

It was too late.

Tanu saw the faces of the Salish all around her, expectant, hopeful, full of fear and yet a profound trust.

"Yeyi has been ghost-struck," Enis whispered, afraid to disturb the spirit that had entered the girl's body. "The ghost must be sent away."

"You will help her," Alteo said with confidence.

Only then did Tanu feel the full burden of their faith. She thought she could not stand beneath its weight. The carved ridgepoles—cougar, bear and deer—seemed to watch, waiting with the others, their shadows at her feet. "Where is Tseikami?" she managed to ask. "I would speak with him."

"Gone," Yeyi's mother, Shaula, said bitterly. "He packed his rattles, his clothes, and left us. He will not be back."

Somehow Tanu remained standing, though her legs shook and her vision blurred. Tseikami had fled; he had guessed Yeyi was lost and that others would follow. *Winter comes early and wild to the Island. I fear it is an ill omen and that worse is yet to come.* He had left her alone, to treat the Salish as best she could and watch them, slowly, die before her eyes. *Hear me. When you return we will be there for you. We will be waiting.*

Tseikami had lied. And worse than that, he had left her a burden no grown man could carry without breaking, let alone a girl of fifteen summers. *We need you strong and wise and whole,* the shaman had said. Had he known even then?

Colchoté came to stand beside the Queen. "I will not forgive my grandfather for what he has done. I would have you know that I am here and I will stay. You will need our help. What can we do?"

Tortured by the hope and relief in Shaula's eyes, Tanu was grateful for Colchoté's broad shadow which fell across her own. He was strong; he would not break. His gaze was full of compassion, not expectation. His presence gave her the courage to kneel beside Yeyi and touch her burning forehead. "I will need the seeds of red cedar for her fever," she said, "and the buds of lodgepole pine to ease her throat, some skunk cabbage root for the ache in her head, and spirea seeds."

She did not say these last were for the others, to stop the sickness from spreading, but they knew. There was a gasp of horror. "I will need a fire always burning and baskets to boil down the seeds and roots. I will do what I can."

"And we will do what we can." Hawilquolas stood beside Colchoté with Koleili behind them. Tanu thought she saw anger in her mother's eyes, but Koleili turned away, instructing the women, while Hawilquolas spoke to the men. These three alone seemed to understand the futility of the task before her, the price Tanu would have to pay.

"She makes miracles," Shaula said. "None has more spirits than she. Our Queen will do what Tseikami feared to do."

"Tanu." The voice was Yeyi's—dry and brittle, like bent brown grass when the summer sun shines too harshly. She grasped Tanu's hand. "I am glad you are here. Now I can rest." Smiling, she closed her fever-bright eyes.

Chapter

14

The Longhouse was bitter with the smell of boiling herbs, pounded leaves and oil that burned in shallow dishes at the corners of many pallets. The acrid odor filled the air like a malignant haze. The reek of sweating bodies mingled with the other smells of sickness until the air itself was unclean.

The People spoke in whispers, wrapped in gloom like evening mist, without the color or beauty of that fine-spun violet gauze. They were afraid to arouse the spirits who huddled, waiting, in corners where no torchlight fell.

Tanu's stones lay in a semicircle near the center fire. The Salish rubbed them, sang mumbled prayers, and pleaded with the spirits through these precious stones, to lift the darkness that consumed them.

Beside the stones were the sacred antlers. Hawilquolas and Colchoté had brought them to Tanu with great ceremony as she sat beside the fire that could not warm her on the night of her return. "These antlers which we revere have been in Tseikami's care for many years," Hawilquolas had said solemnly. "Yet it was you who brought them to us, you who holds the spirit power which has kept us safe. The time has come to return to you what you alone made sacred."

mThe People had murmured agreement, reminded, as Hawilquolas intended, of Tanu's great power. Now the Salish touched the antlers as they touched the stones—to reassure themselves that there was still magic enough to protect them.

Hour by endless hour, Colchoté told them stories, tried to keep their eyes from the pallets of the sick, their minds from the fear that spiraled through herb-scented, smoke-filled haze, poisoning the heavy air.

Yeyi had only been the first to succumb. Before long Shaula had fallen ill, and then a young boy. The Red Sweating Sickness had taken Old Grandmother's frail body in its grip, and she had no strength to fight it. Enis and her husband were also ill, and Hawilquolas had stumbled in, weak and burning with fever.

Tanu knelt over Yeyi, who slipped in and out of delirium. Tanu herself felt light-headed. She had not slept in three nights; even when she sat alone, she could not rest. The things she saw behind her lids were too frightening and too real.

She finished bathing Yeyi, then turned to her mother. The ring of white around Shaula's mouth was more pronounced today and her fever had risen, despite Tanu's infusions. She took a basket of cool water and touched the soft bark to Shaula's skin, made rough and dry by fever. Shaula groaned and opened her eyes. She tried to smile, but her raw throat made her wince. Wordlessly, she touched Tanu's hand, pressing the cool bark against her rash.

Tanu swallowed dryly. She ached with sympathy for her People's pain, for the trust with which they looked to her, for her own impotence and fear. She might have run like Tseikami, but could not. Instead, she worked—filling buckets with fresh water, bathing fevered foreheads, rubbing salve into burning rashes. But it was not enough. It would never be enough.

What if she should fall sick? Who would nurse the others then? Already there were more than she could care for by herself. Those who were well helped by preparing herbs and roots and fern leaves, but she would not let them near the sick; she would not risk their catching the fever.

That is why she froze in horror when she saw Koleili near the mats around Hawilquolas' bed. Her mother had worked beside her for the past few days, bringing fresh water, laying out pounded bark, measuring boiled herbs, and pouring the infusion into little cedar cups. Tanu saw the weariness that turned her mother's skin gray, but Koleili would not stop. She was trying, Tanu guessed, to prove her dedication to her daughter.

Oddly, Tanu had forgotten her anger at her mother's need for one man's touch. It did not seem important anymore. She worked beside Koleili, grateful for her mother's perseverance long after the others had fallen asleep in exhaustion.

Until now Koleili had taken care not to approach the sick. But she moved purposely toward Hawilquolas with a basket of water, a cup and some pounded bark. Tanu gripped Shaula's hand for a moment, reassuringly, then rose and went to her mother.

"You must not go in," Tanu said softly, so the others would not hear. "It is neither wise nor safe."

Koleili smiled wanly. "I intend to care for him, My Daughter, as a wife cares for her ailing husband."

Tanu understood, but still she shook her head. If Koleili's hands had been free, she would have touched her daughter's pale, drawn cheek. "I have given him little enough in the past." She did not say she was weak with fear, trembling from head to toe. She did not say she was a coward, but she knew it in her heart. She was not strong and selfless, like Tanu. But she could not turn from Hawilquolas now. He would not have turned away from her. "At least I can give him this."

"Your life?" Tanu covered her mouth, appalled.

"If the spirits choose," Koleili replied with a serenity she did not feel. "He has given *us* his strength, generosity, affection, his forgiveness often enough. Perhaps it is not too late to make up for my selfishness."

Tanu wanted to argue, to plead, to forbid. But she was haunted by the image of Hawilquolas' pain when Koleili had whispered secrets to the Stranger.

Nor would she forget the look on the Head Man's face when Koleili parted the mats and he saw her.

"I have fresh water," Koleili said, "and the herbs and roots Tanu has prepared. I will cool your fever and see that you swallow the infusion as you should." The flames that burned at the corners of his pallet did not touch her shadowed face. She put down her basket and sat on the edge of the sleeping platform. Gently, she took Hawilquolas' hand.

"You are too warm." She lifted his palm to her cheek. "I will hold it against my cool skin until the warmth leaves you."

Hawilquolas could not disguise his pleasure and relief. "So, my wife," he murmured with difficulty, "you are here."

Tanu bit her lip at the endearment. He understood the risk to Koleili, the debt that she felt honor-bound to pay. He did not argue; he was too weak with fever and pain. By taking his hand, she had told him as he had once told her, that he was not alone, abandoned, friendless. He thanked her now, as always, without speaking.

It struck Tanu for the first time how much—in silence—they had shared over the years.

Hawilquolas gazed at Koleili with a look of such tenderness and benevolence that Tanu had to turn away, her eyes burning with unshed tears. She could not weep. She had to work, to bury her feelings in caring for the sick, trying to make them comfortable if she could not make them well.

Tanu was nearly asleep when she heard Yeyi call. She pushed the hair from her eyes and rose.

Kitkuni's sister lay awkwardly, her lower body toward the wall, her flushed face dripping in sweat. For the moment, her black eyes were clear.

Tanu knelt to hear her croaking whisper.

"My hands are so hot. I want to dip them in the stream."

"The stream is far. I cannot take you there today. But I have something you can hold, something cool and smooth that will ease your discomfort." She took from her pouch the stone Yeyi had given her a few suns past. Gently, she laid it in the girl's hand and Yeyi closed her fingers around it.

"You kept it with you," she managed to gasp. Her eyes shone with tears of gratitude that Tanu had thought her gift so precious. "I will keep it here." She placed it over her heart. "When my soul leaves me, it will curl into this stone and you will carry it away. Thus you will have me near you always."

Tanu opened her mouth to say that Yeyi would not die, that her soul would stay until she had known all that life could teach her. But the lie would not come. Yeyi stared up at her with trust—a trust that she could not betray. She had made a false promise once to ease this girl's pain; she would not do it again. "Yes" was the only response Tanu could offer.

Yeyi smiled, though it was more of a grimace twisted by pain. Then she said, each word forced through her raw, red throat, "They blame you for not freeing us from the evil spirits that fill this house. It is easier to say *you* are weak than to believe the Changer is so cruel that he would let this happen. If I believe in you, I must doubt him. Tell me what to do." Gingerly, she touched the stone that lay above her heart.

Tanu placed her hand over Yeyi's on the stone. "Believe what will give you peace, *Ladaila*." Her eyes were the color of a deep green lake when a storm was near. Her gaze did not falter.

Yeyi nodded, then cried out, surprised by a spasm of pain. When it passed, her eyes were glassy and she writhed on the uncomfortable platform, sweat running from her body and soaking the mat beneath.

Glancing up in desperation, Tanu found Colchoté waiting. He had sensed the crisis and come to lend his strength. "The root must be prepared," she said. The root which was burned when death was near, to lure the spirits close, to ask for their guidance on the soul's journey into the sky.

"No!" Enis cried. "You cannot give up so soon." She was pale and gaunt, like the people who gathered at Yeyi's side, calling Colchoté back. To bring the root would be to admit there was no hope. And they could not release their hope. If they did, what would they cling to?

"Would you deny Yeyi the gift of the root because you are afraid?" Colchoté asked firmly.

Enis fell silent.

"It will be soon," Tanu added softly.

Colchoté turned without a word. There was no word for the terrible fear that haunted him day and night, followed him into dreams and stilled the comfort of his songs. He knew, as Tanu knew, that hope had mingled with the smoke and wafted upward, charred and battered, into the autumn sky. He dreaded the moment when she called for the root as she knelt at Hawilquolas' side, for he had seen the sickness burrow deep inside his father, eating slowly at his spirit.

Mechanically, Colchoté found the death root in the dug-out cellar, pounded it in a cedar bowl and brought it, burning, to Yeyi's bedside.

For several hours the girl would let no one touch her, knew no one's face, spoke no one's name. The sweet fragrance of the death root drifted over and about her, a fine, thin trail of scent that clung bitterly in Tanu's nostrils.

Yeyi tossed and turned, moaning at demons with flame-sharp tongues. Then her eyes opened in astonishment, as if she had glimpsed a secret so dazzling that it broke through her fever and illness. Quietly, staring at a vision no one else could see, she lay while her soul slipped gently away.

Tanu knelt beside Shaula, eyes damp with unshed tears. "You must get some sleep."

"But my Yeyi. I must care for my Yeyi." She has half delirious and tried to rise, though her body screamed in protest and sweat broke out across her forehead.

"Yeyi does not need you now." Tanu spoke guardedly, but the words were an agony, and her grief for The Laughing One, silent now and cold, throbbed within her—a constant, gnawing sorrow.

Shaula went pale beneath her flushed skin. "Yeyi's soul is gone? You could not help her?" She stared in blank astonishment, eyes wide with disbelief.

"The sickness had progressed too far." Tanu's words sounded empty, as empty as Shaula's gaze.

Disbelief turned to disillusion, a disappointment so bitter that Tanu tasted the bile in her own throat. "You could not help her." Shaula's face became rigid, unfamiliar. "You said you would help her. You promised." She wept without tears, rocking, leaving marks on her skin where she gripped it with claw-like fingers. "You could not help her. You could not help her."

The words became a chant, a litany, a denial. Shaula stared through Tanu; she did not exist. She was no more than a ghost. In her torment, Shaula did not think of the red, raw skin of Tanu's hands, which had not been idle for five suns, the cast of weariness on her eyes, which had not closed while she fought this hopeless battle for her People. All Shaula knew was that her child was dead. Tanu had let her die.

Tanu closed her eyes. This was why Tseikami had fled, before the People lost faith in his healing power, closed their hearts against him. In the back of her mind, she had known this moment would come. But to know was not the same as seeing the disillusionment in Shaula's eyes, watching her draw inside herself, become a stranger and an enemy. *You have grown so used to being right, you do not remember what it is to be wrong*, Hawilquolas had told her once. But she had not believed him.

She glanced up when a shadow fell upon her and she saw Alteo, his face closed and unforgiving. Behind him were the others, staring at her in disbelief and more—a terror that rose from the darkest place inside them, where all they could not understand lay hidden. She had failed them. Where were her miracles now?

Tanu stood rigid while the People hovered, waiting—for reassurance? An explanation? A plea for forgiveness? A sign that the spirits had not left them alone and undefended?

Tanu could give them none of these. One by one the faces she had known all her life became, like Shaula's, the masks of strangers. *The People believe in you because you give them cause. If you gave them cause to doubt you, they would do so.*

She flinched, grasping her elbows protectively across her chest. The earth had shifted beneath her feet, leaving a gaping void where fragrant ferns and soft, rich earth had been before. She was falling into darkness, too weak and tired to fight her own despair. The People moved away, but she felt their grief around her like a frigid, piercing wind. They moaned and tore at their hair, mourning her as much as Yeyi. Their Queen was dead; she had left them behind.

Her hands were clammy with sweat. This was only the beginning. There would be other deaths. Other souls rising with the smoke into the sky, other eyes, accusing, wild with fear. Other voices, other chants that reviled her and despised her.

Believe this, Hawilquolas had warned. *No Head Man lives forever, no shaman, not even a Queen.* She covered her ears, but the warning echoed in her head, and with it, Shaula's chant of grief and loss and desperate fear. For the first time in all the days of her living, Tanu felt helpless and utterly alone.

Chapter

15

The smell of herbs and sickness mingled with the cries of the mourners. The bodies of Yeyi, Old Grandmother, Old Uncle, and Enis' baby, Kwahtie—whose sickness Enis had hidden, hoping it would pass—had been placed facing east and washed. The dead were bound head on knees, as they had lain inside their mothers' wombs. So would they rest forever in their small cedar chests.

The mourners wailed and tore their hair while outside the splitting of wood announced that the coffins were being made. Colchoté had taken on this task—to lead the others when their own strength failed them. There was no time to take the dead to the island where the Salish graveyard lay hidden among tall firs, so the men built a low scaffold outside and placed the chests there until they could be moved to the cool green island. Tanu thought of that island, isolated, quiet, stirred only by passing winds and the fall of gentle rain, and fleetingly envied the dead their peaceful rest. mColchoté sang as he worked and the People stopped to listen.

> Many have left us
> To dance with the clouds.
> Their eyes glow like stars;
> Their voices still speak
> Through the high, whistling wind.

The odor of charred blankets and clothing drifted through the Longhouse. A huge bonfire blazed to burn the possessions of the dead. Once the bodies were raised on the scaffold, the People bathed with cedar branches to purify themselves. Cedar was burned over the sleeping platform where the dead had lain, to chase away evil spirits that might hover in the unclean air.

Yet the smell of death lingered. Tanu was smoke-stained, her eyes unfocused, her body aching with despair and weariness. The turbulence inside her never ceased, like the rush and fury of the river that had carved away the stone. *You have lost the stillness inside from which your strength and wisdom flow,* Tseikami had told her before he fled.

It had been many days since she had closed her eyes and slept. Though the People would not meet her gaze, though they avoided the place where her sacred stones lay, they did not stop her from treating the sick.

Awkwardly, she knelt beside Wahan, who had slowly begun to respond. Although he was very ill, he had not become delirious, and Tanu dared to hope that he, at least, would live. She felt movement, saw Alteo pass behind her, his face turned away, the taste of his aversion acrid in the air.

Tanu's hands shook and the hot infusion spilled on her leg. She bit her lip, trembling uncontrollably with sudden, seething anger. How much more could she give them? Had she not risked everything to save those who would not meet her eyes? She struggled to contain a rage so blazing that it took her sight.

She began to breathe slowly, forced the trembling to cease, closing her eyes against the hot white light. Anger brought weakness and that she could not afford. Yet the fury was inside her, a smoldering coal that would not cease to burn, no matter how deeply she buried it.

Tanu turned resolutely to Twana, who had also fallen ill. But she had been drinking the infusion of spirea and did not seem as affected as the others. She too would recover.

Even Shaula's wild-eyed delirium had passed. Kitkuni's mother, who had lost her faith when Yeyi died, had decided to fight for her own life after all. She tossed and turned, racked by grief as well as illness. Alteo cared for her; Shaula had turned from Tanu, and the girl had felt a stab of pain that stopped her breath.

Hawilquolas was not improving, though Tanu and Koleili worked tirelessly to break the fever that held him in its grip. His face, once brown and tough as leather, was pale, the skin dry and fragile, marked by deep lines of pain. Colchoté looked upon his father, concealing his grief, but Tanu felt his sorrow. She touched his hand in empathy; it was all she had to give him now.

She knelt beside Hawilquolas, speechless. She could not bear to lose him. She could not. Nor could Koleili. Her mother's eyes were glazed and there was about her a frightening air of melancholy. Koleili had lost hope; her face spoke without words of the emptiness inside her.

Mother and daughter had only a few moments alone together, when Tanu held Koleili's work-roughened hand, its knuckles raw. Once the girl rested her head on her mother's shoulder, seeking the peace Koleili had once offered. But it was different now; too much suffering lay between them. They parted, afraid of the violent feelings their closeness might set free.

To keep from thinking, Tanu worked frantically. She was applying a poultice to Twana's rash when she felt a hand on her shoulder. Koleili stood rigid and murmured, "Come."

Her daughter swallowed convulsively. She rose in a trance, picked up the death root, and moved toward the corner where Hawilquolas lay. Tanu was shaking and cold. So very cold.

Colchoté saw the bowl in her hands and his face turned gray. She ached for him, who had worked tirelessly and yet must lose the one he held most dear.

Tanu felt her knees give way. She was chilled to the bone, weak with hunger and exhaustion and her private, tortured grief. She could no longer pretend to be strong, that she walked on solid earth and not above an abyss of raging darkness that grew wider each time the sun moved in the sky.

Hawilquolas, father of her weakened heart, lay dying. She could see it in his eyes—already focused on a dim and distant vision—in his face, so pale it seemed the color had seeped away in his fevered sweat. His muscles were lax, his arms limp at his sides. He had given up the fight.

When he saw the expression on Tanu's face, he lifted his hand painfully and she rested her cheek against it. "Do not grieve for me, My Daughter. Like my grandfather, I know where I am going. I seek the comfort of trees and whispering grass and flowing waters. The world of our ancestors is beautiful and full of peace. My time has come to enter that world and I am glad."

Hawilquolas struggled to speak, and she hurt for him who had always been so strong. "Hush," she murmured.

Koleili lit the death root, and its fragrance wafted through air heavy with smoke and illness, bitter with grief. The sweet scent of the root spiraled upward, a silent plea to the spirits.

Closing his eyes, the dying man drew power from the fragrance. "There is something I must say. The People shun you because they have ceased to believe. They call you Queen no more. Do you not see what that means? They have freed you at last. Be grateful you need no longer carry the burden of their faith upon your shoulders. Do not throw that freedom away. Use it to find your own heart, your own peace. If you swear you will do this thing, I will close my eyes and rest in the soft light just above me. It waits to take me in."

Tanu tried to find her voice, but words would not rise through her swollen throat. The scent of the death root curled and drifted, making a fine woven web in the air. "I swear it," she said, though the voice was not her own.

Hawilquolas dropped his hand and sighed. His face was gray with the effort of speaking, and his body sagged, as if he had drawn from it the last of his strength. "Where is my son?" he asked in a hoarse whisper. "And Koleili?"

They bent above him. "We are here. We are with you. We will not go."

Hawilquolas smiled and closed his eyes, content.

Only then did Koleili give in to the sickness that had stalked her body from sun to sun. She fell, flushed and fevered, to the floor at her husband's side.

On the night of the fading moon, when the wind lay still on the roof of the Longhouse, when the animals made no sound and the sea was motionless, like a mirror which reflected only darkness, Tanu sat on the floor beside her mother's pallet. At the corners of the mat burned dishes of oil that cast wavering shadows over Koleili's pallid face.

Tanu crouched, a bowl of herbs in her hands, tears flowing inward, adding to the poison of her grief. Her hair brushed the pallet where Koleili lay, lips dry and cracked, an ugly rash on her chest. She crossed her arms tightly to keep away the pain.

But the pain would not go. Seven suns had risen and set since Hawilquolas died. The others had survived under Tanu's vigilant care. The People had begun to touch her stones again, to kneel by the sacred antlers and sing. But Koleili did not hear their songs. She closed her eyes to the firelit Longhouse, looked beyond it to a vision of her own.

Tanu had fought to ease Koleili's fever, to soothe her throat, to kill the infection and make her mother sleep.

Now she sat idle, watching the labored rhythm of Koleili's breath, the flutter of her blue-veined lids. The scent of herbs and burning oil rose acrid in the musty air. But the herbs were useless against a spirit that had chosen not to fight.

Tanu cried out in mute agony. The weight of her sorrow was unyielding stone. There was nothing more she could do for her mother. Nothing but watch and wait and plead to the moon, which had also lost its power.

She sniffed, brow furrowed, as a curl of smoke wafted about her shoulders. She knew that smell. It was the death root. Colchoté had set it aflame—the harbinger of grief and loss that smelled so sweet, unbearably sweet.

She did not move, did not dare break the line of her unwavering gaze, which called her mother back. She had lost so much already. Surely the spirits would not demand this of her too. They could not be so cruel.

Koleili began to writhe, to call out meaningless words and muttered agonies. "Nicolas!" she cried, and smiled.

Tanu took her mother's hands, though her own were shaking. Even near death, Koleili held close the memory of he who had brought her to this moment, this pain, this night without a dawn.

At her daughter's touch, Koleili came to herself. She saw Tanu's face, distorted by the unkind light of the fires. "You think I am a fool for remembering him with kindness." With difficulty, she reached up.

Tanu bent so her mother's dry, hot palm caressed her cheek. "I will never forget the look in his eyes when he held me, the gentleness of his hands when he made me a woman." She paused, cheeks flushed, sweat forming on her brow. "He gave me a gift beyond price that has not faded or lost its mystery. He gave you to me, Tanu, and it was enough." Her grasping fingers were weak and frail. "I only wish it had been enough for you."

Cold and numb, Tanu stared into the bowl of useless herbs. "He made *me* a Stranger. He poisoned my blood." The thought had not come to her for days. She had almost forgotten, yet the memory was there, as sharp and bitter as the night when she had opened wide her tight-closed eyes.

Koleili gathered her strength and drew her daughter closer. "The *People* made you a Stranger by making you a Queen."

Tanu blinked in astonishment. "They honored me."

Koleili fell back, gasping, to catch her breath.

"Do not speak again. You are stealing your strength to give it to me."

"It is what I have always done. It is my duty and my promise. You say they honored you. By placing on your shoulders the weight of their problems, their illnesses, their doubts? It is true that they loved you. But they asked so much of you. You are only human, Tanu, but they did not tell you that. To them you are a spirit, a powerful shaman, but you were not born to be a spirit. You deserve a husband, children, happiness.

"You will never find them here. You can never be simply Tanu, because Tanu is Queen." The last words were whispers, shadows. "Please," Koleili added, so softly that Tanu had to put her ear to her mother's lips. "Go from here. By all that is sacred I ask this of you." Her face was gray with the effort of speaking. She closed her eyes.

"Do not leave me," Tanu murmured.

"I am happy to go. It is my time."

Tanu gripped her mother's hand tighter and shook her head.

"You must learn to let go," Koleili said in short gasps. "Do not hold me here when I wish to fly free."

"But I need you." It was the only time in her life she would speak those words. "I need your serenity, the tranquillity of your house."

Outside, the wind uncurled itself from the roof and rose into the night sky, calling, calling the spirits to join on its ride above the tall green trees.

Koleili moved her head painfully, in denial. "Do you not yet see that we create our own peace and our own sorrow? You, who are strong, must make your own choices."

The four flames guttered, went out, flared to vivid life while the fragrance of the death root fell about Koleili's body like a warm blanket. She smiled, took the blanket around her, and the light which made it glow, and before Tanu could call out, her spirit had answered the distant cry of the soaring wind.

Chapter

16

Tanu moved in a dream through the days that followed, alone, yet surrounded by the voices of the People. She had moaned and wailed and pulled her hair, seen her mother buried in the box above the ground. But these things had not touched her grief, which was too raw and painful to look upon. She closed her eyes and heart to the frenzied churning of feelings she could neither control nor understand. She was overwhelmed by doubt and guilt and feverish sorrow that would not let her rest.

She sat by her fire, staring blankly into the flames, aware of the dirt floor on which she sat, the odor of burning cedar, the musty smell of the Longhouse. She felt the cold air of winter on her face, heard the howl of the wind, the sound of icy falling rain. Yet to her these things were not real.

One night she found she could not rise. Her head fell forward and she had no power to lift it. She gasped, deeply chilled despite the dancing flames, overwhelmed by exhaustion, desperation, sorrow. She fell forward into darkness, into silence and a night that defied the rising sun.

She knew the light came and went, the darkness deepened and faded, but the days had no meaning for her. She was too weak, too wretched to note their passing. She heard voices, distant but full of power and pain.

"Has the sickness taken her?"

"Will she die like the others?"

"No, it is not the sickness." Colchoté. Dear, familiar Colchoté. "She has tended you, fought for you, given her own strength to keep you well. But her body has grown weak and fragile. The spirits knew she would not rest, so they took the choice from her. They have wrapped her in their silence, where she has a chance to heal."

There was concern in the voices, not hatred and derision, but Tanu could not respond. She tried to speak, but her throat was choked with unshed tears and the voices grew dim, forgotten in the turbulence of her dreams. Dreams of light and color, darkness and shadow, pattern and chaos that whirled in her head until she quivered, nauseated and confused.

Vaguely, she sensed that people knelt beside her, touched her forehead, left water or tea or softened food. She was too tired to eat or drink, did not want her People's help, did not deserve it. She had failed them. Even in her delirium she knew that much, and it broke her heart.

As she began, slowly, to awaken, she heard voices, bodies moving, the swish of cedarbark and the snapping of flames. She saw the small offerings the People had left while she slept—tiny stones, fragrant hemlock bows, a brilliant red leaf. The Salish circled her fire less warily, but would not meet her eyes. Yet she felt them reaching out to her, to the shaman she had been, the dream they had dreamed before sorrow made them wake.

She shivered violently. Nothing was real but the smoothness of her stones, which held her captivated, spellbound. One she had found on a Stranger's grave; one Yeyi had given her at the Gathering. Leaf in stone, feather in stone, a Stranger's grave and a dying girl's gift, touched now with her spirit. What did they mean? *There is a future I do not seek, but which will come to be*, she had told Hawilquolas long ago. And he had replied, *It will come to be as it was meant to be.*

Tanu drifted in and out of consciousness. She saw the Stranger's school of which the trapper had spoken, saw long, barren halls that echoed with the absence of voices, rows of beds empty and rigid, made pure by crisp white sheets that could not chase the chill from the room.

She dreamed of running through the trees while ferns brushed her legs and cradled her feet, of plunging into flowing water, feeling it rush over her face, her chest, her soiled and aching body. She dreamed of sitting on a boulder to watch the dawn. She dreamed of peace and stillness and the beguiling beauty of her Island, her home.

She awoke abruptly to a touch on her bent head. Tanu sat up, stiff and weary, to find a woman crouched beside her. Startled, she could not find the name to call this stranger whom she had known all her life. She watched the figure through a fine, impenetrable mist; her body seemed to waver, as if it might dissolve into the air.

"Colchoté sent me to bring you food. He says you have not eaten in many days and will make yourself ill."

A name stirred faintly. Enis. Staring at dried ferns and camas roots, Tanu heard the remembered voice of Enis' husband.

Strange, the hunter had muttered, *that the sickness did not come to Tanu. Perhaps her Stranger's blood protects her.* Colchoté had risen, pale and angry. *You would not have dared say such a thing if Hawilquolas lived. You will not do so again. She has given us all she has, withholding nothing. You must pay for this insult to Tanu with a gift.*

The next morning she had found near her fire a blanket Enis had woven the previous winter. No one had spoken such thoughts aloud again. But the sound of the words lingered.

Yet Colchoté had sent Enis to Tanu's side. She looked up to see that he was near, watching protectively. Listlessly, she reached for the food. When her hand brushed Enis' she felt a current and dropped the roots, taking the young woman's palm between her own. The haze of gloom retreated for an instant. Tanu was startled by the touch of another hand, the warmth of skin made dry and rough by too much work and too much sorrow. She expected Enis to pull away, but she seemed frozen.

"Do not let your anguish break you," Tanu said. "For there will be another child. Already it moves within you."

Enis gasped and her eyes filled with tears. She was afraid to believe what she wanted so desperately to be true.

Her uncertainty sent a sharp pain through Tanu's shroud of numbness. "I speak the truth. I tell you only to give you comfort while you grieve for the child whose soul has left us."

Eyes swollen with weeping, face blotched and pale, Enis trembled as she tried to wipe a dry tear from her cheek. She opened her mouth but no sound came; there were no words for the grief in her eyes, the questions, the dread, the first flicker of hope she had felt in many days. Quickly, before her tears could start again, she fled.

Tanu watched her go, and grief rose within her, cold and brittle as thin ice on a winter pond.

Enis ran to Colchoté. By unspoken consensus he had been named Head Man, now that Hawilquolas was dead. It was not because he was his father's son; this title came from ability, not blood. It was because Colchoté was a fine hunter, master of song, a winter dancer. He was thoughtful, never spoke in anger, listened and advised well. He had earned the honor of becoming *Siem* by starting to rebuild what had fallen around him.

Enis knelt, poured out her guilt because she had hidden Kwahtie's illness until it was too late. She had killed her own child. Tanu guessed without hearing what she said; she knew Enis' heart, could see her pain reflected in the motions of her hands, the unnatural glitter in her eyes.

Colchoté nodded, soothing her with his voice and his compassion. Enis' tears ceased and her hands grew still. Tanu saw her old friend speak. "If Tanu has said there is a child, you must believe her. She would not give you false hope." Enis looked at the Head Man with gratitude, glanced quickly at Tanu, then slipped away.

Tanu's mouth tasted bitter. She gasped when she realized the bitterness was envy. Before the sickness had struck, Enis would have come to her for comfort, would not have doubted the promise of her Queen. Tanu had never envied anyone; she had had no cause. She was shocked at her own weakness, more shocked at her wounded vanity.

Over the years, she realized in horror, she had begun to believe the People's stories. She had come to treasure the myth they had created, and now that myth was shattered; it lay in fragments on the earth and the bare feet of the People walked upon it, pushing it deeper and deeper into the soil. Tanu felt as if some vital part of her had been burned away.

She had not been living a life, but a dream. Now, for the first time, she looked reality in the face; like a child staring directly at the sun, she was made blind. Only when the People stopped believing could she awaken from her dream. Their faith had been a powerful herb that had cushioned her, kept her safe, made her move and speak and sing in a trance. She had been hypnotized, mesmerized by the beat of their drums, which had always echoed the beat of her heart. But their faith had turned to bitter ashes and the herb had left her blood. Now, at last, the spell was broken.

She was alone as she had never thought to be—lost, without direction. She could not see the future of which Hawilquolas and Koleili had spoken—a future she could no longer imagine, in which she could not believe. She was bereft, filled with unbearable loneliness and pain.

She saw Shaula and Alteo draw closer as they mourned, Enis and her husband hold each other while the sorrow of their loss pulsed between them. The families came together, but Tanu's hearth remained empty. She had not known how much she would miss her mother's voice, her face, the graceful motions of her hands. The world had become hollow, without meaning.

What was it Koleili had said? *You deserve a husband, children, happiness.* Tanu yearned fiercely for a family of her own—the contented knowledge that a man lay beside her, the warm touch of human breath on her cold cheeks, the feel of a baby wriggling in her arms.

She felt a strong pull toward the woods, beautiful even in the hush of falling winter. The murky gloom of the Longhouse was oppressive, so she rose, taking her stones, and went outside. She did not look from side to side, but only forward, following the voice that called her from among the trees. Tanu did not choose to go; she was compelled.

She was not surprised when she came to the small clearing surrounded by paper birches. She had known one day she would return to kneel at the grave of her ancestor.

Have you never thought that the two worlds of my grandfather are also in your blood? That someday you will face them both and have to choose, as he did? Somehow that day, which she had never thought to see, had come upon her and she could not turn away.

Tanu took out the stone she had found here when the sun struck it with brilliance. The fern beneath clear water, caught there for all time. What did it mean? Even now she did not understand. She reached out tentatively to trace the letters *IHS*. They told her nothing.

She turned to the pond which had begun to freeze at the edges; the green water was tipped with white. She tried to sing, but the songs would not come. No voices spoke from water or swaying leaves. Tanu felt that her soul had been torn from her body. She could not hear the rhythms of the things that she most loved. The spirits had left her. Only the storm inside remained—constant, fierce, incomprehensible. She did not know how to make order from the chaos, though she prayed day and night for a moment of peace.

Do you not yet see that we create our own peace and our own sorrow? You, who are strong, must make your own choices. Tanu gazed into the water and saw a rippled image. Her face was the same, but she stared into the eyes of a stranger. How could she choose when she did not know what lay before her? *There is a future I do not seek. . . .*

Abruptly, she rose, the stone clutched in her hand, and started toward home. She had found no answers, but her questions grew stronger, more urgent with each breath.

She stopped on the hill above the Longhouse. The People milled about aimlessly, hugging their cedarbark capes close to keep out the chill. It broke Tanu's heart to see how pale and drawn the Salish had become. Her eyes grew damp with sympathy for Shaula, who glanced about, looking for the daughter she would never see again, for Enis, carrying her cradle as if Kwahtie slept inside. Tanu bit her lip to keep from crying out.

Yet the People seemed to hear her. They turned, one by one, to smile tentatively. Enis met Tanu's gaze and touched her stomach with reverence. Finally, every face was turned upward, calling Tanu back, welcoming her without words, but warily, with the shield of their distrust before them.

She hovered, uncertain, wanting desperately to move among them, to feel again the comfort of their affection. Then she felt a hand on her arm and Colchoté stood beside her, smiling—a smile she knew well and had longed for often. Because he had caught her unaware, she gave voice to the guilt that had racked her waking and sleeping, through fireglow and darkness. "I should not have let them go to the Gathering."

Colchoté considered, brow furrowed. He had aged since their return to the Longhouse. His grief for his father was etched into every line of his brown, weathered face. His eyes were dull, his shoulders bent with the burden of leadership. Tanu understood, but did not offer sympathy; he would not have accepted it. "But you said your dream was good."

She twined her fingers together tightly, painfully. "I knew something was wrong. I had a premonition."

"Why did you not say so?" He spoke softly, without accusation. He sat and drew her down beside him.

"I was confused by my own fear. I did not understand the warnings of the spirits. Some were for me alone, but I never thought—" She stopped, eyes closed against the light which had grown cruel and bright. "I failed them because I did not listen. Yet at the Gathering they protected me, gave everything they had—love, faith, loyalty, compassion and kindness. In return I gave them death and grief and destroyed their faith."

She did not know why she was telling him these things, except that Colchoté was her friend, her brother, the only one who had not turned from her. "My own doubts made me weak. If I had overcome them, conquered the poison in my blood—"

"The poison was in *their* blood, not yours."

She shook her head. "I could not hear my spirits, but only the voice of the Stranger, my own voice. Perhaps I did not do all I could for the sick. My confusion made me unwise. If I had been strong and whole, I might have saved them."

"Do you not think it false pride to believe you alone could cure a sickness that our bodies have not learned to fight? Even you do not have such power."

Tanu opened her mouth to object, but he was right. She had been arrogant to assume she could stop the Red Sweating Sickness from striking, that she could protect her People from all harm. She had grown vain, and in her vanity, blind.

Colchoté picked up a stone, waiting, and let it fall. The sound startled Tanu, and she stared at him in disbelief. Had he guessed that there were illnesses whose spirits were too strong for any shaman? She had long known it; there were things beyond the Salish's understanding, their power to control. "How did you know?" she asked quietly.

"I saw your face when you first looked upon Yeyi and recognized her illness. You knew then she was past your help."

The color drained from Tanu's cheeks. She'd believed she hid her thoughts, her fears, so well. It was part of her duty; to bear the burden of knowledge that would break the backs of her People. Yet Colchoté had guessed.

He reached out to cover her hand with his. "You have not lost your power to hide your doubts. I was watching closely. It was a flicker of fear, gone in an instant. No one else saw."

She had forgotten how well he knew her, how easily he guessed her thoughts. The friend of her childhood had come back to her. Her smile was bittersweet.

"You knew you could not save the sick. There was no magic which you lacked, no skill, no evil spirits guiding your hand. It is your grief that makes you speak so."

His wisdom, the soft meter of his voice, made her defenses crumble and she fought to rebuild them. She was not ready to face her grief. She did not have the strength. Yet she wanted so much to turn her palm upward and link her fingers with his, to absorb his warmth and vitality.

Colchoté felt the clammy coolness of her skin, the trembling of her fingers against the soft earth. "You do not have to bear your burdens alone. Let me carry them with you." *I would give you that stillness in my hand if I could, but you must find it for yourself.*

Futilely, Tanu brushed at the cobwebs that clouded her thoughts. She tried to break through her protective veil, but the veil was too finely woven, too tough and indestructible.

When she did not answer, he drew a deep breath. The touch of her hand was a torment he did not wish to live without, the sound of her voice a pleasure so acute that it splintered his calm assurance. "In the days before the sickness, I would have sung to Koleili:

> I have watched your daughter often
> Kneel beside the pure and sacred streams.
> Will you let me kneel beside her,
> See our faces reflected always, one upon the other?"

Tanu blinked back tears. Colchoté had offered what she wanted most in the world. But she was not worthy. She stiffened, yet did not draw her hand away. "I told you—" she began weakly. "I thought we had agreed—"

"Things are different now," he said.

What he did not say, at least aloud, was that Tanu was no longer Queen. He was Head Man now; his strength had grown with her weakness. He had defended her, nourished her until, little by little, the Salish had found the first glimmerings of their lost faith. Gently, firmly, kindly, he had reminded them that she was blessed. Tanu's magic was not gone, only tarnished. But it would not be the same again. She had broken the hearts and hopes of her People; such wounds did not ever heal completely.

More than anything that had gone before, Colchoté's simple statement gave shape and color to her pain. With four little words, he had stripped her of her power, her identity, her illusions. She whom the People called Tanu had died in the epidemic as surely as Yeyi, Hawilquolas and Koleili.

She felt a wrenching inside, a tearing apart of the cloak that had numbed her so she could go on. She had lost too much, suffered too much, wept in silence for too long. The tears broke free, and years of regal dignity crumbled into dust.

Tanu gasped at the unbearable pain that filled her body and spilled onto her cheeks. She wept, broken and defeated, as Colchoté drew her into his arms. She had no strength to fight the binding circle of those arms, the heat of his body, the pulse of his beating heart. She gripped him desperately, reaching for comfort, pleading for peace and rest and the music she had lost.

Her body shook with violent sobs. For too many years she had been repressed, subdued, restrained; now all the pain came rushing out while she choked and clutched Colchoté tighter.

When she had wept herself dry and empty and cold, when she was drained, for a time, of her wrenching sorrow, she turned her blotched, swollen face toward the sun. She did not want him to see the evidence of her weakness, though his chest ran with her tears. She forced herself to breathe evenly and turned. Colchoté looked away, back rigid, shoulders straight. She sensed a tension in his body that had nothing to do with physical pain. Tanu touched his back with a not quite steady hand.

He turned sharply, surprised into responding before he could hide his thoughts. Tanu saw the look in his eyes—the shock, the disbelief, the fear.

He had told her things were different, implied her spirits were no longer as strong as his own. But when he saw her sorrow, he had revealed his secret doubt. To him she was still Queen, protected by her magic, which would never let her weep. *It is true that they loved you. But they asked so much of you. You are only human, Tanu, but they did not tell you that.* "I am no different from you," she cried. She felt a rush of bitterness, an echo of anger, quickly denied, that had flared white-hot within her once before. "I hurt and grieve as you do. Did you think I do not feel the pain of loss? I am not a spirit; I am a woman."

Colchoté struggled to regain control, while doubt and surprise, fear and denial shone in his obsidian eyes. "This I know," he said at last.

"You know it somewhere inside, but there is another place where you do *not* believe that I am simply one of the People."

"I believe—" he began half-heartedly.

Tanu shook her head. Colchoté was trying to protect her with a lie, as he had done once before, but this time he would not succeed, because now she knew the truth. Once more she forced her anger down; he, of all men, did not deserve it. "You try to believe. You want to believe. But you have listened to the stories for too long. Like me, you came to believe in those stories, in the mist-woven girl who lived only in your legends."

He sat up, suddenly angry himself. "I am not a fool. I was *there* on the magic night of your birth. I saw you kill a buck when you were only six summers."

"Then you know that I leaned against Hawilquolas, that he held the bow and guided my hand."

"Yes," he agreed. "I saw the animal die to save us. I saw the antlers and the doe's soft underbelly—a doe that should have been a buck. I saw you stop the cougar and the bear from striking. I saw you cure Tseikami. I was there, remember?"

You can never be simply Tanu, because Tanu is Queen. She could tell him the spirits had gone, but Colchoté would not believe her. In his eyes was the too bright image of a phantom touched by magic. Her tears, a sign of weakness, had appalled him. No matter how tightly he held her, what soft words he whispered, he could not change that single fact.

The People made you a Stranger, by making you a Queen. Never had Tanu wanted to undo the miracles that had become the myths of her People. But now she wished them gone; their weight had grown too heavy. *The People have freed you. Be grateful that you need no longer carry the burden of their faith.*

Colchoté saw her slipping away, hurtling into darkness, where he could never reach her. He could not let her go. He had lost his grandfather through cowardice, his father through proud death. To lose Tanu as well— His head began to pound. "I need you so much."

Tears dampened Tanu's eyes. It had cost him a great deal to ignore his pride and admit such a need. She fought for control, touched his cheek, rested her palm on his red-brown skin. "You do not need me, Colchoté. You are strong."

Before he could object, before he could trample his dignity in the dust at their feet, she stopped him. A moment ago, he had held her as she wept;

now it was he who needed comfort. "I do not mean as hunter or fisherman or master of song or winter dancer. I mean inside, where your heart beats powerfully and your soul lives, free of guilt or failure or evil. You are strong enough to make these People a family again."

Colchoté drew his regained pride around him and sat up taller, his face unreadable. "But the spirits have chosen you."

Tanu pulled her knees to her chin and locked her arms around them. Only thus could she hold her splintering soul together. "Once, perhaps, they chose me, but they have left me now. Whatever purpose they had for me has come to pass." She heard the words she spoke and the meaning beneath them. *Please,* Koleili had cried on her deathbed, *go from here.*

In the memory of her mother's voice she heard the call of her future. Tanu knew, in that instant, that Hawilquolas had been right. *Do not throw that freedom away. Use it to find your own heart, your own peace.* The spirits had spoken through his beloved voice. She could feel them inside her, guiding her away from the People she loved. Her spirits had returned in the instant when she first began to realize she must go.

She pressed her hands to the searing pain in her chest. She could not bear another parting. She could not. The darkness was closing around her, tight and black and cold. Yet her voices cried out that it was time. "I cannot," she said at last, so quietly that Colchoté leaned close and saw the torment in her eyes—her green, compelling Stranger's eyes.

Without thinking, without hesitation, without wisdom or prudence, he took her face in his hands. Slowly, he lowered his head and kissed her tenderly.

His gentleness gave her comfort, a rush of heat for the chill that had settled in her bones. Colchoté's warm lips moved against hers, while his breath touched her softly and his hands held her safe. She knew he was fighting a battle he could not win, though he tried to pretend there was only desire between them. She wanted him to hold her, to make her forget her duty and the voices of the spirits, but it was not her choice.

She was painfully, exquisitely, aware of his hair as it brushed her cheek, the enticing pressure of his lips on hers. But she could not let him give her peace. She was guided by other forces, just as she always had been.

Though Colchoté held her close, she sensed he was not with her. The song of his spirit had drifted away, while he fought to bring it back with the heat of his lips on hers. He wanted her; he cared for her, but he could not have her. He would make her his wife, but would not let himself near enough to touch her beating heart. The songs of her spirits were loud in his ears and they wove around her a fine tissue of silence. Colchoté could touch her face, but his fingers would never meet her skin; he would cling to air—clear, empty air that held her apart from him as certainly as a wall of sturdy cedar planks.

Tanu gripped his wrists, drew his hands away from her face. "I must go," she said. The truth hovered, written on the air, too clear for him to ignore, too strong for him to fight.

Slowly, in a daze, Colchoté backed away and set her free.

Chapter

17

That night Colchoté dreamed of a dawn without the sun. He moved in darkness, praying for the light to break through blue and lilac mist. He wandered familiar paths crossed by familiar vines, but could not find his way, though he had walked these woods since the first steps of his childhood.

This was not the darkness he had come to know, which brought no fear, but only velvet shadows and the song of nightbirds in the trees. This was a darkness no light could break, so deep that the woods, once a refuge, became a place of danger.

For hours he turned and stumbled, until he saw the golden eyes of a cougar, felt the animal's hot breath as it crouched on the drooping branch of a garry oak.

Colchoté was not afraid, for the cougar was the protector of his People. But this one growled low in its throat and the sound rumbled through its quivering body. The animal trembled with eagerness to pounce. Colchoté stood frozen with astonishment. The fear would come later, when his heart began to beat again.

Then he heard the rustle of branches and saw a grizzly rear up, claws extended, mouth open in a snarl of rage. The blood began to flow again through his body. With it came the realization that death hovered before him and behind, in two animals whose spirits he had trusted. The magic had once held them back, but the magic had disappeared with the sun.

Colchoté raised his hands to ward off the attack of two growling beasts; he had no weapon, and his faith had betrayed him. He was lost, but he would not fall without a fight.

The cougar sprang, rising majestically. For an instant it was poised in the air, legs extended, tail curved forward, a beautiful golden creature that might have been carved from living cedar. Then the bear lunged, but his lumbering progress was stopped in mid-stride, where he swayed, death in his eyes, his claws just short of Colchoté's face.

Colchoté awoke in a cold sweat and drew his cedar blanket tighter. But the dream would not leave him, or the fear, though he saw that he lay safely in the Longhouse with the glowing coals of his fire nearby. His heart pounded, his breath came in short bursts, as if he had been running many miles for many suns.

Gradually, the familiar flickering shadows began to soothe him. It had only been a dream. But he believed in dreams. So he lay quiet, wondering.

It came to him slowly that something was wrong. The air he breathed was too thin; some vital essence had been taken away. He sat up abruptly, pushing the blanket to the floor. Colchoté blinked at the circles of fire near the sleeping platform, the huddled forms without faces or voices, but only the weight of their slumbering bodies.

The sound of their breathing should have reassured him, but the hush was so deep that he heard nothing, felt nothing but a chilling despair. It was as if someone had crept in while he slept and stolen the beating heart of the village, which had grown labored and slow with grief, but had pulsed and nourished his People just the same.

Now the pulse had ceased. Colchoté shivered. When he saw something in the center of the room, his uneasiness took on shape and substance, became fear—cold and bitter.

The dark shape was a stump, used sometimes for an altar. Tonight it had been made sacred. It was covered with the ceremonial bearskin. On the soft fur lay the antlers, barely visible in the dim light from low-burning fires. There were branches of hemlock, cedar and pine left like offerings, like unspoken prayers at the foot of the makeshift altar.

Colchoté could not breathe. He stood, shoulders braced against a fierce, cold wind. Yet nothing moved. Even the smoke ceased stirring and Colchoté's heart ceased beating.

He turned, knowing what he would find. Tanu's fire had died out; for the first time since she had come to Longhouse as a baby, the wood, turned to ashes and coals, had grown cold. The red glow of warmth and life had fled, and with them had gone Tanu. Her clothing, stored above the platform, was no longer visible, nor was her herb pouch or her winter cape.

Tanu had left the Salish and would not return. He knew because of the gift she had left behind. To the People the antlers were beyond value, a symbol of the magic that had kept them safe, the blessings that had come to them from the day of Tanu's birth. The simple altar held the tangible evidence of their power and their strength and wealth.

This Tanu had left, no doubt with the hope that the magic would go on. Perhaps that was the purpose of the fragrant branches, the offered prayers—a plea to the spirits to remain behind, to keep her People well and free and happy.

What, then, had she taken with her? What magic to protect herself, a Salish girl alone in a world she could not understand?

Colchoté saw that her stones, which had lain near the fire, were missing. She had not gone unprotected; the stones were her own private magic. The thought made him want to weep.

Tanu was gone. He was alone. But he had no time to grieve. She had told him what he must do. He must rebuild all that had been lost in the sickness that had taken not just lives, but also hope and joy and the People's belief in the future.

Colchoté knelt before the altar Tanu had made with such care. He touched the soft down of the antlers, traced the curve of one graceful prong. He prayed then, when the full impact of his loss struck him and his throat grew tight and dry and raw. Tanu, friend of his heart, child of miracles, woman of wisdom, was gone, and he would see her face no more.

Awkwardly, he rose, like an old man whose joints had grown stiff with the winter chill. He returned to his fire and stared into the glowing remnants. He was cold, but did nothing to cover his nakedness. He was hurting, but did nothing to ease his pain.

Then he saw it, pushed among the other rocks that circled the fire—a small gray stone with a lightning stroke of blue through its heart. One last gift from Tanu, and like her, hidden, tossed among the ordinary stones like a fine otter skin among pelts of the lynx. So cleverly had she placed it that he might not have noticed it for a sun, or a moon, or the changing of sun and moon.

But that was what she intended, he thought. That one day, when her scent had faded from this place, when the memory of the People had grown dim and vague with time, when the stories told around the fire grew more and more fantastic—on that day, he would place a cedar log in the flames and notice the streak of blue among dusty black and gray. He would know that she had been there, she was real, she had taken the time to say good-bye without words, without tears, without anger, but tenderly, silently, just as she had lived among them for the seasons of her life. She had given all she had, all she held sacred, all she loved. With a pocket full of small round stones, she had chosen to make her life new.

He could grieve, he could tremble at the emptiness she left behind, but he could not blame her or curse her or call her back. He could only wish her well, wish for her all she had once given others, wish her the stillness in her heart that she had never found, yet never ceased to seek.

Chapter

18

1879

The missionaries gave her the name Sally Fisher, but she thought it harsh and pretended she could not say it properly. Instead, she pronounced it Saylah. The other Salish followed her lead until even to the Strangers she became Saylah.

She had learned quickly in the missionary school to refer to the Strangers as Whites, to call them Sir and Ma'am, smiling inwardly when she learned what the titles meant.

The missionaries had worked hard to teach the Indians to forget their past, to discard their traditions and their faith and replace them with the rules, language and religion of the Whites. Saylah had listened intently, studied with a dedication that stunned Indians and Whites alike. She wanted to know everything about the alien world that had invaded the Island. Her ignorance was her weakness, and she intended to be strong, resilient as sapling birches that bent double in the wind, then sprang back, leaves quivering, toward the sunlight.

She had asked questions at first about a Frenchman named Nicolas, a trapper who worked the Island and the land across the strait, though she told herself she did not care if the answers ever came. But the questions haunted her, and she continued to ask until she learned from an itinerant preacher that such a man had died in a mining accident on the Fraser River.

Saylah had nodded, her face pale but expressionless, then slipped away to sit beside the stream where the song of water filled her ears, and within that song, a voice.

> *Repose toi, mon âme,*
> *en ce dernier asile.*

Even now she could hear the sound of a Stranger's voice that might have been her own.

> Rest thou my soul, be patient;
> Here lies thy goal before thee.

She could not say she grieved for him. She had never known him except through her mother's dreams. But it was because of him, in part, that she had come here. *You have faced the truth and understood it. Now you must learn to accept it.* She had arrived at the school to try and follow Tseikami's advice. In the end he had been a coward, but he had always been wise.

She asked no questions about the People she had left behind. Her grief was too deep and chilling, the pain too devastating, the loneliness too bleak. To think of these things was to risk madness. So she forced those voices into the silence where she hid her pain, even from her own knowledge or sight. She made herself forget, turned her thoughts, her dedication, her obsession to other things.

For three years she had stayed at the missionary school, drowning out the persistent voices of her past by working night and day until she fell into bed exhausted. She was weary in her soul, for the singing waters called her, and the birds in the arbutus tree outside her window, and the whispering grass from the myths of her childhood.

The Whites did not believe in those voices, in the mystical life of the woods where the Salish ancestors walked. Sometimes the voices spoke a warning in Saylah's dreams—premonitions that made the Whites uneasy. Pagan, they called her, and grew rigid in her presence, for she knew things, spoke truths that her youth and her history should have made beyond her grasp.

She was not really alive in those long, narrow halls. Tanu had died with her People; their loss of faith had destroyed her as surely as their dreams had created her. The school, the Strangers who now shaped her days, did not bring her back to life. She hovered in limbo, floating in a stillness that enwrapped her like a quilt of woven clouds, holding her apart from the world outside, sheltering her from the pain inside. She was not idle for a moment. Always she was preparing, waiting—but for what?

When the walls of the school grew close and tight around her, she fled to the forest, where she took out her sacred stones and let the songs enfold her. She rose often when night lay upon the silent, shadowed halls and went to a nearby hillside, where she waited for dawn. She breathed air untainted by the strictures of the missionaries, and watched woven bands of lilac rise into the mist, into the clouds, into the sky.

In those rare and fleeting moments, her wounded heart beat stronger and her loneliness subsided, just a little. When the mist touched her face with the colors of dawn, she went back, in a dream, to the home of her childhood—to the beating of drums and stories of smoke and fire.

Then Koleili's face floated before her, and Hawilquolas' and Kitkuni's as she laughed into the fierce, roiling storm. In those moments of dawn, and only then, the memories brought no sorrow, no bitter regret, but only solace and the comfort of the life she had once known.

She had come to the school because of her dream. After she left the People, after the desolation of her loss and grief had spilled itself into the rushing river, where she sat and beat her lonely drum, the dream had come again—of the hallways and the empty beds. But this time there was light in the grayness and she saw the books which she could not call by name, for she had never seen one before, but she knew, in that part of her which understood such secrets, that she must go. There were things she must learn, was driven to learn, though the force that drove her never found its own voice.

For three years, she had lived among other Salish girls. She learned to pretend she had forgotten her heritage and her power, learned to speak the language of the Whites, to read their books and understand their kind of knowledge, which was not of the senses, but of the written word. She learned of a religion that restrained and forbid and punished with a world beneath the earth, where people burned forever for their sins.

Yet she did not turn from her past completely. She could not bear to let it go. Instead, she preserved it the only way she knew how. As she learned to write, she began to recount the rituals and stories of her People; with pen and ink, she made permanent and unchanging the mysteries that had enchanted her from her first moment of understanding.

Saylah worked hard and learned quickly, sensing that a time would come when all she knew would become necessary. She did not know where she was going, only that she must go. She had learned long since to listen to her instincts, that to turn them aside or pretend they did not call was to invite disaster.

So, she thought to herself one night as she lay curled in the lumpy bed with the rough muslin sheets pulled to her chin, *the time has come at last.* The next day, she would leave this place. Mrs. Wilson had told her that afternoon that a family with a ranch nearby needed a girl to help them. The owner was ill and his wife and son could not keep up with all that must be done. Saylah had begun to object, until Mrs. Wilson spoke the name Richard James Ivy.

Without knowing why, Saylah had tilted her head, listening to a distant voice that bid her go. She had curtsied properly in her gray wool skirt that still felt rough and unnatural in her hands, and said she would obey.

She shifted on the thin mattress of straw and down, unable to close her eyes. The oil lamp beside her bed burned low, but when she saw moonlight drifting through the parted curtains, she turned the lamp out and let the night in.

With the soft silver light on her face, she fell asleep at last. In the pale stillness, she dreamed the dream that had haunted her since she'd left her home.

She was wading in deep water—not the rivers of her childhood or the lake of her visions or the sea, where the waves break in endless sprays of white. The water lapped about her gently, whispering songs of comfort. The light fell through the moving leaves to glimmer on the surface, like stars that had fallen from the black night sky.

She laid her hands on the moving stars and felt the motion of the water, barely perceptible on her open palms. She smiled. From far away she heard a sound and raised her head. The voice was distant and muted, and it called a name she could not hear. The sound rose on the breeze, rippled through the leaves, skimmed over the water that caressed Saylah's bare skin, but still she could not understand the name and what it meant.

She awakened, as she always did, uneasy and restless. In her long nightgown, she listened, but no sound disturbed the silence, no shadow the light that filtered through the dusty windowpane.

"Saylah?"

She propped herself on her elbow as Sarah Williams' face came out of darkness into moonlight. Saylah motioned the girl closer. Sarah, who had once been Kwaya, sat on the edge of the bed, feet curled beneath her.

"I could not sleep, thinking of you leaving us tomorrow. How will we go on without you?"

Sarah's distress touched Saylah, who had missed the faces of her People, their questions, their affection. She had felt empty and useless until the other girls began to come to ask advice, to weep out their loneliness, their fears, their doubts. She had also helped them with their English, which they found more difficult to learn than she.

Saylah welcomed the girls; their trust and affection soothed the taste of bitter loss, and she gave them what no one else cared to—a sense of family.

"Saylah?" Sarah whispered. She did not wish to be discovered, to see the harsh light of a paraffin lamp flicker along the walls, on the face of the matron, disgruntled that her rest had been disturbed, furious that another rule had been broken. "You look strange tonight. As if you do not see me."

Saylah shook away her thoughts. "Of course I see you." The girl was trembling, but whether because of the inadequate heat of the fires or her own emotion, Saylah could not tell. She wrapped her blanket around Sarah, and they sat with the warmth uniting them against the night, the cold precision of rigid metal beds.

Sarah rested her head on Saylah's shoulder. "What will we do when you are gone? Who will listen to our problems and teach us our English verbs?"

"Who will show us the places in the woods where the missionaries cannot find us?" Betty Hardy added, climbing up beside Sarah.

She was followed by Barbara and Susie and Jane, who found empty places on the bed without asking. They knew they would be welcome. Saylah had never sent them away.

"I can't bear it," Jane cried breathlessly. She was given to melodrama and heartfelt sighs. "It will never be the same again." Tears glistened in her black eyes, and her hair was wildly disheveled, as if she had tossed and turned for hours.

"You will bear it," Saylah murmured. The girls' expressions of dismay and sadness warmed her. They would miss her when she went. She closed her ears when a distant voice warned that she had not grown away from her vanity or her pride.

She had left her village and come to the Strangers because she knew she would suffer. Because of her pride, which had grown so great, she felt the need to punish herself, to know without a doubt that she was only human. She had come to learn humility.

But the girls clung to her, gave her comfort, and she knew she made their burdens less heavy, their sorrow less painful. Tonight, with their dark heads all around her, she realized she had learned nothing of humility. They needed her and it made her happy. "You will study hard so you can return to your families and show them what you have learned. You will be too busy to grieve over one girl who has gone away."

Five heads of untamed hair shook violently. Before they could protest further, Saylah whispered, "Jane, won't you tell us a story, one more before I go away? It is your turn, I think. Betty told one last night and Sarah the night before."

Jane bit her trembling lip and looked, for a moment, as if she would not be distracted. But the storytelling had become a comforting ritual that reminded her of home, and she could not resist the chance to bring back the sound of her People and the rhythm of their voices.

"I will tell of the daughter of the People who came to know the magic of Sea Otter beneath the deep green sea."

The girls nodded and settled in to listen to the powerful cadence of their childhoods, silenced, but still flowing in their blood. Because they had no drums, they tapped out the rhythm on the clean white sheets.

Saylah watched the girls, and her throat grew tight with tenderness and regret. She knew she had the strength to leave them; she had left a family far more precious and survived. But with each parting, she left a little more of her spirit behind.

The girls moved closer, arms locked about one another's waists with Saylah in the center, holding them upright, absorbing their warmth and giving it back, made sweeter and stronger by her will. They sat that way, unmoving, until the moonlight faded and the darkness fell around them.

Morning came at last, warm and clear. With her bag in one hand and her reticule over her arm, heavy with the weight of her stones, her gabardine gown buttoned tightly to her neck and her wool petticoats scratching her legs, Saylah jumped from the wagon and watched the driver disappear in a welter of dust and a rumble of loose wheels. He had pointed in the direction of the Ivy house, and without a word, left her behind.

Saylah did not mind. She felt no regret at turning her back on the school, though she grieved for the girls she had left behind. She sang quietly as she went.

I hear the wind
that whispers of dawn light
upon the water.

The Salish sang those words when their mourning had ceased.

It was a warm summer day and the leaves of the maples were golden, the aspens pale green in the fine, filtered light. Saylah's hair was restrained in a tidy knot by hairpins that hurt her head and reminded her how much she disliked the heavy, complicated way the Whites chose to dress. When a breeze touched her bare neck, she sighed with pleasure and reached up to take the pins from her hair. It fell loose down her back and she liked the way the breeze lifted it into the fragrant air, let it drift down to rest on her flushed cheek.

She was not frightened of what lay ahead. She had learned to quell her fear long ago, when she stood face-to-face with a cougar about to leap. Nevertheless, she shivered with expectation as she turned down the well-worn path shaded by gnarled oaks that grew in uneven lines along the way.

Brow furrowed, she moved pensively through the shifting shade. Then she came to the end of the path and stepped from the shadows of overgrown trees into a clearing thick with grass. In the distance she could see the outline of a house, but that did not interest her now. Her gaze was drawn inexorably to a stump on the far side of the clearing. Once the tree had been a magnificent cedar, cut, no doubt, to clear land for the house. But the stump was taller than usual, and the bark had been carved, over many years, she thought, and perhaps by many hands, into a roughly textured deer.

Saylah was mesmerized by the power of that lifeless buck which, though caught forever in rigid wood, seemed to live and breathe, even to stir in order to look at her with the soft eyes some gentle hand had shaped. The animal rose on its back legs, front legs bent in a graceful arc. On its head was a set of bone antlers that spread like the branches of a tangled tree. Only once before had she seen such magnificent antlers; those she had left on an altar with her blessing and her prayers for the People who had held them sacred.

Moving in a trance, she crossed the clearing, unaware of the dew that clung to her gown, impatient with her buttontop boots which pinched uncomfortably, slowed her down and held her back. She bent and tried to work the shoes free, but without her buttonhook, which lay at the bottom of her bag, the task was not easy. She found a twig and pried the buttons loose, dropped the shoes and her stockings beside her bag.

With a sigh of pleasure, she looked up, caught again by the power of the carved animal. When she was near enough, she touched the roughly shaved wood, ran her fingers down the side of the deer to its strong yet graceful legs. The wood was many shades and many textures; some had been exposed to the seasons for several years, some for only a few, some for a mere month.

She stood for a long time, transfixed by the texture of the wood, the ridges where the knife had not struck true, the planes that edged one into the other. Trailing her palm across the cedar, she moved around to see the animal from another angle.

Saylah stood paralyzed, painfully aware of the rapid beat of her heart. This magnificent buck, so like the one she had killed years ago in the mists of legend that had become her childhood, was not a buck at all, but a doe. Whoever had taken knife in hand had not thought of the antlers that proclaimed this beautiful animal a male as the blade slipped through the rich red wood. Some unknown artist had given shape and substance to a memory, a precious piece of an old story, told and retold.

Saylah pressed her hand to her heart, which beat frantically against her palm. She knew she had come to the end of her journey.

Until this moment, she had clung to the past, and now it had come back to her, made new. She smiled as she had not smiled for three years, freely and without restraint.

Then it came to her that she was not alone. She gasped and turned to see a white man, not much older than she, staring at her thoughtfully.

"Forgive me," he said when he recognized her distress. "But you seemed lost in your thoughts, and I didn't want to interrupt. I've never seen anyone look at the deer in quite the way you did, like you'd found an old friend."

Saylah stared at him, speechless. How had he guessed her thoughts, well-hidden from the eyes of most Whites?

"Forgive me again," he murmured. "We haven't been introduced. I'm Julian Ivy. You must be the woman the missionaries sent."

She heard it then, the suppressed pain in his voice, the effort he made to sound at ease. "They call me Saylah." She noticed his muslin shirt, the sleeves rolled to the elbows, his earth-stained trousers and mud-caked shoes. He had been hard at work when she disturbed him.

She looked more closely at his face, at the lines between nose and mouth, carved deeply by sorrow, she guessed. She saw the film of sweat on his skin, his dark brown hair, blown into disorder by the wind.

He offered his hand in the greeting of his people. She was surprised he did not shrink from the touch of an Indian and a stranger. Saylah put her hand in his. Only then, as his fingers closed around hers, did she look directly into his hazel eyes. What she saw there made her ache with compassion and a fear she could not name. Those eyes were full of suffering, deeply rooted sorrow, a burden too heavy to bear, which he carried on his shoulders, and had for far too long.

Others might not have seen these things in Julian Ivy's eyes; he had become a master at disguising what he felt. But to Saylah, it was as if he held a mirror that reflected her past, her secrets, her pain. Her sorrow gleamed on the polished surface like afternoon light on a green rippled lake.

"Saylah," he said, breaking the stillness that had fallen between them, trying out the name on his tongue like a ripe red berry, "have you come to stay?"

She did not look at his smiling lips but at his eyes, which told his stories without words. Within those eyes was a plea he did not know existed, but she heard it just the same. She felt it as she had felt Kitkuni's fear on the night of her marriage. As she had felt Koleili's yearning when she named her Frenchman of smoke-dreamed memories. As she had felt the despair and confusion in Yeyi's eyes when she lay dying.

But this plea Saylah could answer, because it was also her own. The lilting song of a stray breeze stirred, then settled into stillness. "I will stay," she told Julian Ivy, "for as long as I am needed."

PART II

SAYLAH

Victoria, British Columbia
1879

Chapter

——— ⇌ 19 ⇌ ———

Nineteen-year-old Julian Ivy put his foot on the worn shovel and drove the blade deep into the earth. The damp soil gave and gave as he forced the shovel down, arms taut, back rigid with frustration. The blade hit a rock and the handle vibrated in his hands, making him curse under his breath.

"Damn!" he said. "And damn again!"

He wrestled with the shovel, trying to work his way around the rock, which resisted all his efforts to dislodge it. He grimaced, every muscle in his body strained. Intently, he maneuvered until he held the rock and not the other way around. With one powerful thrust, he lifted the pile of debris and tossed it over his shoulder with a grunt of satisfaction.

His cotton shirt was soaked in sweat, clinging tenaciously to his back, emphasizing his broad shoulders and well-defined muscles. Mud covered his worn boots and pant legs, dusted the front of his white shirt brown.

Julian shook the longish brown hair out of his eyes, and with it the sweat that dripped down his sun-browned forehead. Pausing, he rubbed his sleeve over his face and glanced back at the house. He frowned, thinking of his father lying, eyes closed, face shadowed, in the hollow worn in the bed. Julian's throat clenched in bitter sadness.

Tensely, he turned back to the land—the rich, fertile earth, firm and unchanging. The rains had been heavy this summer; the alders and spruce, fir, pine and dogwood were lush and green with the moisture that still hung in the air. It was a good time to plant the five new apple trees he had bought for next to nothing from his neighbor, Edward Ashton. Again Julian glowered. He would rather have gotten the trees elsewhere, but he had had little choice. Edward had offered a bargain, and there was not much money to spend.

Julian pushed the thought away. The late summer air was crisp, the scent of pine sharp, along with the musty odor of disturbed soil. His gaze wandered along the boundaries of the ranch, toward the woods, the clearing, the river that glistened silver in the morning sun.

It had not changed, would never change. That was why he loved the rugged vastness of the land, the salt sea air that he could taste and feel, the trees that rose, ancient and regal toward a wide, cloud-dusted sky. He felt at home sunk to his knees in damp soil, covered in sweat, the shovel worn smooth by the work of his hands.

He hurled another shovelful onto the growing ridge behind him, letting his frustration drain away in the rivers of sweat that streaked his body. Dropping the shovel, he unbuttoned his shirt, letting the suspenders fall around his hips. Removing the soaking fabric, he tossed it under a gnarled oak, then turned, ready to contend with the next challenge.

With an energy born of sorrow, he dug resolutely into the earth, the air cool on his naked back, long since tinted brown by the kiss of the sun. He had come to get away from the house, where regret filled the air like invisible smoke.

Out here the air was fresh, swept clean of human grief by the ceaseless wind. He lifted a heavy load of soil and tossed it aside. As he moved, the muscles across his shoulders rippled, ridged by sweat and the strain of his furious digging. The breeze ran over his skin like the gentle touch of cool fingers, and sunlight touched him in an intermittent caress. His body had begun to ache with the exertion, but he welcomed the pain; it was safe and familiar.

Impetuously, he bent to grasp a handful of earth. It felt damp and heavy in his palm. He sniffed the fragrance of loamy soil, of musty secrets long buried. The color was deep, the texture moist and luxuriant. Julian breathed in and smiled, crumbling the dirt that drifted downward, a few particles clinging to his callused skin. He stood, the hollowed-out earth up to his waist, surrounding him in the smell, taste and texture of the land, mingled with the odor of his own sweat. His slightly wavy brown hair brushed the tops of his sunburned shoulders, and he shook it so the sweat flew out in tiny droplets.

He realized he was grinning and climbed out of the hole, annoyed. With renewed vigor, he attacked the ground, shaping it to the depth and width he wanted. He worked laboriously, obstinately, until he was satisfied with the five fresh holes where the apple trees would soon take root.

In triumph, he rested his hands on the shovel as if it were a sword at his fallen enemy's throat. He smiled because tomorrow his enemy would rise again and he would be there, waiting, eager to begin the battle once more.

Julian shook his head at his own sense of melodrama. He had been thinking like his father—or the man his father used to be, smiling, full of optimism, with a sparkle in his eyes. But that man was gone. Wincing at a pain so sharp it was almost fury, Julian turned his back on the house once more.

"You don't have to do that, you know," Jamie Ivy murmured into his wife's ear. "I'm perfectly comfortable. Except I keep expecting something. . . ." He trailed off and tapped his fingers pensively on the arm of his chair.

"Ye've no need to fret," Flora assured him. "'Tis pleased I am to see ye up, and happy to give ye a little extra warmth." After arranging a soft wool blanket around Jamie's legs, Flora sat at his feet, resting her head on his knee. "What might ye be expectin'? There's been nothing new here for many a month. Except another Indian girl is comin' from the school," Flora breathed, intensely aware of the pressure of her husband's leg against her back, the weight of his hand on hers. It had become a ritual with them, sitting quietly every morning, enjoying the stillness after Julian left the house. She always waited eagerly for this one hour when they could be alone together.

Jamie stared at the heavy velvet drapes that covered the windows. For a fleeting instant, he thought he saw a glimmer of light, an image of the future undimmed by the filmy haze of the past. *Another Indian girl is comin'.* It couldn't have been that.

He caught his breath and rested his hand affectionately on Flora's curly blond hair, restrained in a bun which rarely lasted out the morning. Every now and then, she made him wonder if tomorrow might not be better after all. He glanced at her rosy face and bright blue eyes. Unexpectedly, he smiled. "I wish I could give you something pretty."

Flora grinned, delighted by his smile. "All I want is to warm your cold hands, *mo-charaid*. The heat from the wood-burnin' stove is no' enough for ye." She noticed he was pale, his skin almost translucent; his brown eyes seemed larger, deeper, more full of pain than ever.

"What is't that bothers ye?" she asked in the Scottish Highland accent that was still pronounced after years in British Columbia. Her parents had come from Scotland to work for the Hudson's Bay Company when Flora was ten. So many of the officers and settlers had been Scottish that the accent and the songs had flourished, even in this wild new place. She clung to the sound of her people, kept alive by her Highland lilt long after her childhood memories had faded.

Richard James Ivy tilted his head curiously, as if he listened to an unfamiliar voice. His curly light brown hair, which had grown too long, fell over his forehead, and Flora reached up to push it back. He caught her hand and held it. Even so slight a gesture made his wife shiver with pleasure.

"It's nothing new," Jamie replied at last. "Just memories that linger overlong." But that was not quite true. Something was stirring in the shadowed room. The stale air had been disturbed by a hint of unseen breeze. The feeling made him uneasy and a little afraid.

His wife frowned at the suppressed pain in Jamie's voice. She wanted to ease that pain but did not know how. She could not begin to understand the disillusionment that had brought him to this small, dark, chilly room. "I'll open the curtains, and let the sunlight rid ye of the shadows."

Jamie's smile was bittersweet. "I've told you, the light hurts my eyes." Flora deserved much more than the half-lie, but her husband could not give it. He felt again the urge to deny the past, that stirring of light in his self-made darkness.

Flora nodded, leaned into the reassuring warmth of his knee against her cheek. "I'm still wonderin' why ye married me at all," she whispered.

Jamie took her face in his hands, which had grown frail from lack of use. "Because you were what I longed for. Sensible and warm and pretty. A woman to make this cold house home again." He slid his fingers through her hair, so clean and fresh, scented of mingled soap and flour.

Caressing her rounded cheek, he smiled and gently ran his knuckles over her soft skin. Flora slipped her hands around his waist and he leaned down to press his cheek to hers, to bury his nose in her disheveled hair, to inhale her fragrance and the pleasure of her full, sensual body.

She was soft and giving in his hands. When she sang to him, when her skin touched his and she looked up, her honest eyes full of hunger, she became something more than just Flora, who was pretty but not beautiful, plump and not slender, practical and not graceful. She became his eyes and ears and hands; she made his body live again.

So little meant so much. Her fingers on his shoulders, circling, soothing, kindling his desire, which he had thought long dead, reminded him he was real, he was loved, he was not alone and without hope.

Flora kissed his cheek with moist lips, trailed them to his mouth and touched it lightly. Jamie groaned and pulled her close. She was of the earth, and she bound him to it with her warmth and strength. She sat in his lap, her head in the curve of his throat, her hand warm on his chest beneath his shirt. He could feel her breath on his cool skin, her arms, heavy and languorous about his neck.

Tears came to Flora's eyes, but she blinked them back. Her Scottish pride, as much as her concern for Jamie, would not let her weep. She was strong and capable and as Jamie had said, eminently sensible. But she had not made his cold house warm. Or at least, she had at first. She had thought they were happy together; he had been thrilled when she gave him another son. He loved Julian, his first son, but, at nineteen Julian had grown away from his father. He was too old to cuddle, too old to tickle and laugh with and frighten with ghost stories on cold winter nights.

Flora bit her lip, despite the urgent motion of Jamie's hands over her back. He had always been a man who found great pleasure in all things, despite the melancholy that sometimes came upon him when he thought of Simone. He never spoke his first wife's name, but Flora knew. She did not try to fight this alluring shadow. She knew she could not win.

"Why did you marry *me?*" Jamie asked abruptly, startling her. He braided his fingers in the small of her back and waited, his breath unsteady with desire.

"Because ye had stars in your eyes, no' money or ambition or the image of your own bonny face. Just stars and dreams." As she spoke she realized her mistake. The stars had faded from Jamie's eyes a year ago, and the dreams had gone with them.

"I'm sorry." He looked away, his gaze wistful, full of things he could not express and she could not understand.

"I'll no' be havin' any of that. 'Tis happy I am to be with ye, Jamie. And that's the God's truth." He needed her. That she *could* understand. He was her husband, her companion, the father of her child—a troublemaker, Theron, if ever there was one, but the boy was so lovable you forgave him almost anything—and that was miracle enough for Flora.

Jamie was still listening for a passing voice, watching for a flicker of light. He could not concentrate, now that the feeling had disappeared. He clenched his hands on the arms of his heavy mahogany chair, the only piece of furniture he had brought from his family home in England, the first he had installed in this house—the house of his dream. He had stood in the sun once, but it had been too hot and bright; the burns it had made were still deep and painful.

Flora felt her husband tense, try to relax. Her heart contracted in sympathy, but she said nothing. There was nothing she could say. She did not know what had changed Jamie from the man she had married. In the year since he had come back from Seattle, gray-faced and grim, he had not spoken a word of what had happened. If he had, she might be able to ease the pain a little. Flora was no fool. She knew she'd never give him joy—not the kind Simone Ivy had once given him. Flora wanted to give him something else, more lasting, more dependable and steadfast. "I'm here," she said softly, "if ye need me."

"I know," Jamie murmured. "Did you think I didn't?" As he kissed her, an unexpected breeze parted the curtains, revealing a trace of dappled sunlight before the heavy velvet settled, locking in the drifting shadows.

Theron Ivy was six years old and ever since his birthday a month before, he had been keeping a secret. It had been easy to do, because he did not know what the secret was. But today he meant to find out.

Early in the morning, when the sun still shone in streams through the large glass window in the main room of the house, he had heard his half-brother, Julian, leave, slamming the thick oak door behind him. Theron had rushed to the window, pressing his ruddy face to the glass, and watched Julian stride toward the orchard. His brother had looked around wildly, picked up the shovel, and begun to dig.

Theron clutched the fabric in tense fists. The curtains were usually kept closed, but he had risked opening them this once. He had been unable to resist when he saw the brightness against the fabric, felt warmth through the glass, and knew that the sun was shining bright. Such an event in the cool, cloudy island climate was too rare to miss.

Theron paused, the sun on his face, absorbing the heat and golden light. Then, his heart pounding with excitement, he closed the curtains, sneezing at the dust he had disturbed. He knew the look on Julian's face, the stiffness of his back as he began to work. He would be busy for some time, Theron was sure.

The small blond grinned, blue eyes sparkling, and crept toward the kitchen. He must be certain his mother was busy too. If anyone found him, he would be in trouble. Again. It seemed he was always in trouble—for asking too many questions or going off with his friend Paul or fighting shadows with branches in the woods. But this was different. This was important. If they found him—Julian or Flora—they would be very angry indeed. There would be no scolding followed by fond smiles quickly hidden. He was little, as his mother was always reminding him, and did not know much, but he did know that.

Walking on tiptoe in his high-topped shoes, he peeked into the kitchen.

The warmth engulfed him comfortingly, but the room was empty. The breakfast dishes had been washed and put away, the shelves neatened, the kettle left to gurgle on the battered cast-iron woodstove. A fire burned low in the huge stone fireplace, burnishing the copper pans hanging from the ceiling and the implements in rows along the walls. No one sat at the long pine table in the center of the room, surrounded by benchlike chairs with bright cushions Flora had made.

Theron sniffed appreciatively. Whether his mother was cooking or not, the kitchen always smelled of fresh baked bread and stew and cinnamon. He stuck his head farther around the door to get a better whiff, then remembered his errand.

With unnecessary care, he let the door swing to, then crossed the rug-strewn floor to his father's room. Theron bit his thumb as he pressed his ear to the door. It opened a crack, and he saw his mother seated next to Papa's chair. She was looking fondly at her husband and did not hear her little son, who nodded to himself and crept away.

Grinning openly now, he hooked his thumbs in his suspenders, which he'd talked his mother into letting him wear, and climbed to the second-story loft with the tightly closed sitting room at the top of the stairs.

He opened the door and paused, intrigued by the waiting hush that filled the room. He frowned, searching the corners as he usually did. But there was no one. Shrugging, he closed the door, holding the crystal knob so the latch would not click loudly. He took a deep breath and stepped into a different world.

The sitting room was lovely, the walls covered with paper patterned in climbing blush-colored roses and silver vines. There was an elegant velvet love seat, curved and divided so the lovers could face each other, small graceful tables with marble tops, shelves filled with tiny figurines and music boxes and prettily bound books. The mantel was carved oak, an ormolu clock in the center and graceful vases on either side. There were brocade-covered chairs and a beautiful painted fire screen before the stone fireplace. The lace inner curtains just showed beneath rose satin outer curtains interwoven with silver thread.

The cold, polished wood of the floor was covered by a thick Oriental carpet in shades of red and pink, lilac and blue. Theron stopped beside the table with the paraffin lamp, crystals dangling from the globe. He ran his fingers over them to make them tinkle as they swung together. He could never resist those crystals, though Julian had told him not to touch them. The sound was so pretty, like tiny angels singing.

He had heard the sound often when he played in the loft and had been drawn toward the soft tinkling. Julian's face had changed to thunder when he mentioned it and Theron had dropped the subject. But Julian's anger only made the boy more curious. He had decided the day before his birthday that since he would be six, and nearly grown, he should know more about the mysterious room. He had sworn in blood with his best friend, Paul, that he would find out that afternoon what Julian was hiding.

On that day, Theron had thought his brother was busy outside, as he usually was, and Flora was baking a cake for his sixth birthday, so he had crept up the stairs, paused with his hand on the knob, and waited for the sound of tinkling glass. But it had not come. Quietly, he had opened the door.

He froze, astonished, when he saw Julian standing in front of the open armoire, a small, beautiful chest in his hands. Julian stared at it longingly, then bitterly, then sadly; he could not make up his mind what to feel. He had opened it, only for a second, but the scent of roses had swept from under the lid so that even Theron, waiting at the door, had smelled it.

Julian had closed his eyes, his face contorted the way Theron's did when he tried to dig out a stubborn splinter. Julian had cursed violently, slammed the lid shut, and thrust the chest back onto the shelf. Theron, still holding his breath, bewildered, had crept down the stairs and hidden in his room until Julian passed.

He had not forgotten that chest, that scent, the confusing looks that had crossed his brother's face. These things had haunted his days and nights ever since. "It's all you talk about," Paul had complained. "Why don't you explore? Just go when no one's looking and see what you find." He'd lowered his voice and added nervously, "But don't get caught. People get real mad when you try to find out their secrets sometimes."

Paul was awfully wise, Theron decided. Today, at last, he was going to take his friend's advice. His heart thudding delightfully with fear and excitement, he moved toward the huge rosewood armoire, dragging the brocade ottoman with him.

By now his curiosity was so great he could barely breathe. He wished Paul were with him. Paul was two years older and wouldn't be afraid. He wouldn't keep looking over his shoulder to see if the shadows had turned to ghosts. Theron clambered up on the ottoman, forgetting all about being quiet, and reached one long, skinny arm toward the back of the shelf. He could just reach the chest. He moved it forward a little at a time until it sat on the very edge, one carved foot perched precariously, half on, half off the shelf.

Theron peered upward, biting his lip with apprehension. He listened for the sound of climbing footsteps, and wondered, for the first time, if he should leave the chest where he had found it. A tiny wind stirred the crystals on the lamp and he shivered, certain a hand would descend heavily on his shoulder at any moment.

His hands were shaking and he buried them in his pockets, where his fingers touched familiar rocks and bits of wood and colored glass. Paul had helped him collect the treasures. Paul, who rode a horse and did lots of grown-up things Theron wasn't allowed to do. "But I want to," he'd told his friend often. "I'm not afraid. I'm just as brave as you are."

Paul had stared, shaken his head. His brown eyes flecked with gold had darkened to the shade of the cedar he was leaning against. "I don't think I'm very brave." His face had looked gray in the dim forest light, like he was going to be sick.

Remembering the scene with unease, Theron renewed his vow to prove his own courage and see what was in the chest. Carefully, cradling the heavy wood in both hands, he went to sit behind the settee, where he could hide if someone came into the room.

Legs crossed, he rested the chest on the floor and stared at the top. It had been painted with angels a long time ago. He knew because the paint was cracked and smooth with age, the colors dim, blending together. But the angels were still visible, graceful wings spread, with gently smiling faces. Theron didn't see too many of those; he touched them reverently—the rosy cheeks, soft rounded arms, the yellowed wings.

The boy forgot his fear and smiled as he examined the sides of the box. They were carved with magical figures he did not recognize, except for the dragon his mother had shown him once in a book. He ran his fingers over the smooth wood, memorizing the dips and hollows and ridges. He was deliberately drawing out the moment of discovery.

Somehow he knew he would find treasure; he was as certain as a six-year-old can be. Finally, holding his breath, he twisted the tiny gilded key and lifted the lid.

The fragrance of roses rushed around him, like a breath held back for far too long. Theron smiled in triumph and sniffed again and again. He saw a daguerreotype in a delicate oval silver frame and picked it up, brow furrowed in concentration. He recognized the man; it had to be his papa, lots of years ago, but he'd never seen the woman before. Their cheeks were close together and she wore a white veil. She looked so small, so fine that she might break, like the reading glasses Theron's mother treated so gingerly. She was beautiful, this woman without a name.

Suddenly, Theron sat upright, slapping his leg. This must be Julian's mother. What was the name he'd heard whispered when they thought he couldn't hear? Simone, that was it! He rubbed his grubby finger over the picture. Where could she have gone? And why was her name spoken only in whispers? The mystery enthralled him.

He scratched his head, trying to figure out how she had kept her smell inside this box for so many years. He touched her face again, drawn by the fine bone structure, the pale cheeks and dark hair. She was prettier than anyone he'd ever seen. And she smelled so good, like flowers. Not like Theron's mother.

Flora Ivy smelled of fresh baked bread and woodsmoke, in a reassuring, familiar way. He was very fond of his mother's smell, of her ample lap was that always open to him. Nearly every night he climbed up to rest his head on her shoulder while she sang songs in the Gaelic. He didn't understand the words, but he loved the rhythm, the puzzling—and therefore fascinating—sound of the words. He usually fell asleep, protected by her dimpled arms and the cadence of her rich, deep voice.

But this mysterious lady was different, more elegant. She had secrets in her eyes, things he wanted very much to hear in words but knew he never would. Sort of like the Gaelic his mother sang so well. Was Simone dead like the squirrel he had tried to keep as a pet last summer? Julian had explained what death meant, but Theron had not really understood.

Reluctantly, he put the daguerreotype aside and picked up a thick red book that lay underneath. The cover was velvet and Theron rubbed it with pleasure. He'd never felt anything so soft. It was special, like the lady in the picture.

He opened the book to find delicate handwriting. He had not yet learned to read, and was wildly jealous of Paul, who had started school two years ago, but he knew the writing was elegant. He peered more closely; if he looked long enough and hard enough, maybe he could figure out what the words meant. He bet they held more secrets. He could tell by the velvet cover and the beautiful writing that the words would not be ordinary, but full of magic. Maybe they would explain where Simone had gone, why Julian never spoke of her, why Papa sat day after day in his room without moving.

Theron heard a sound and froze, suddenly chilled. They would take the chest if they found him with it; he knew they would. This time Julian would hide it where his brother would never find it. Well, he wouldn't let that happen. Theron held the book fiercely to his chest. They would not take his treasure away from him.

In the bottom of the chest was a brooch shaped like a bird with dangling earrings to match. There were so many brilliant colors in the stones that he reached out to touch them, but pulled his hand back. He was afraid of all that beauty. Beneath the jewelry lay fragrant dried rose petals.

Gently, he laid the book back in its hiding place with the picture of his father and the woman. He would find out what had happened to Simone.

Just the thought of her made him feel excited and fluttery. His curiosity burned.

Sticking his lip out obstinately, he closed the chest. He would take it to his room and hide it. They would never miss it. Julian had not liked it anyway; he had made that very clear. Theron held the chest so tightly that the shapes of dragons and griffins were etched onto his arms.

They all had their secrets, the adults who peopled his little world. There were many secrets here, but none for him. Until now. He decided he wouldn't even share this one with Paul. Now he would have a secret of his very own.

Chapter
◄═► 20 ═►

The hairs on the back of Julian's neck rose in warning and he dropped the shovel, instantly wary. Someone was nearby, someone who did not belong. He had become distrustful of strangers since Jamie's return from Seattle, and because of the priests. But he refused to think about that—the memory of his mother's tears that came at the sight of vestments or crucifix.

Pushing his hair back from his eyes, he peered about but saw no one. Then his gaze fell on the carved buck at the edge of the clearing. In spite of himself, he smiled. The sight of the deer always pleased him. It had changed over the years as different men worked the fine wood, but the antlers had not lost their regal spread nor the wood its reddish glow. This, at least, could not leave him. It was fixed, indestructible.

He saw a faint motion, waited and watched while a woman moved around the deer, running her hand reverently over the wood. Who was she and what—

"Damn!" he cursed for the third time that morning. He had forgotten the Indian girl was to arrive today to help Flora with her heavy load of chores. The girl had stopped, hand pressed to the wood, and Julian was struck by her graceful pose. He had known many Indians as they came and went, helping with the harvest, the housework, whatever must be done to keep the ranch alive. But he had never seen a native as graceful as this one. She was tall and thin, with a slender waist, not at all like the sturdy, stocky bodies of the other Indians.

He took a step forward, felt the wind on his chest, and realized he was not wearing a shirt. Quickly, he found the discarded garment and slipped it on, fastening the buttons haphazardly, snapping the suspenders into place. He was sweat-soaked and filthy, but that did not matter.

By the time he reached the carved deer, the girl had not moved. There was something disturbing about the way she stood motionless, absolutely still, as if she too had been fashioned from wood by skilled and patient hands. He shivered at the eerie sense that she was not of this world—not the world he knew.

She raised her head so sharply that Julian wondered if he had spoken aloud.

Saylah regarded him cautiously. She had heard his thought, if not his careless footsteps. Words flashed into her mind and vanished while she stood, speechless, caught up in the spell of the cedar deer.

"Forgive me," Julian heard himself say. Where had that come from? Why did he feel he had intruded where he had no right to be? This was his ranch. The Indian was the stranger. "But you seemed so lost in your thoughts and I didn't want to interrupt." He recognized his voice, but the words were alien things which increased his unease. "I've never seen anyone look at the deer in quite the way you did, like you'd found an old friend."

While the girl stood silent, Julian noticed her features were as unusual as her stature. Her nose was slender, her cheeks softly curved, her eyebrows finely arched above her eyes. Those eyes, fixed unwavering on his face, explained a great deal. She was a half-breed who wore her mixed blood in her body and her face, and most especially in her clear green eyes.

"Forgive me again," he said, and again the words surprised him. "We haven't been introduced. I'm Julian Ivy. You must be the woman the missionaries sent." He felt the need to identify her, tie her to a time, a place that he could understand.

"They call me Saylah."

He had begun to think she could not speak. The unexpected sound of her melodic voice took him aback. Without quite being aware of it, he extended his hand. He felt her surprise as her fingers closed around his. He tightened his grip, unnerved by the untarnished green of her gaze, so steady and direct.

"Saylah," he repeated resolutely. This time the reassuring timbre of his own voice broke the spell. Abruptly, almost rudely, he withdrew his hand.

"Saylah." He tested the sound on his tongue like a sweet whose flavor was unfamiliar. She had a name now. She was real. "Have you come to stay?"

He did not sound pleased at the prospect. Saylah smiled sadly. She too had felt a frightening jolt of recognition when he touched her hand. But her voice did not quaver. "I will stay for as long as I am needed."

Julian blinked at her, amazed, not only at the urgency of her promise, but at his own response. He was glad. "Saylah," he said for the third time, hoping to dispel his growing anxiety.

"That is what they call me."

Something in her tone made him look at her more closely. "What do you call yourself, then?"

"I am called by others. It is the way of the Salish."

"To let the whites give you a name?" he asked skeptically.

For a moment, Saylah hesitated. "The missionaries called me Sally when first I came among them. But I was only learning English and could not speak it well. The name came out as Saylah. This they have called me since."

The glint in her eye revealed her inward smile. "So you made it your own," he said.

She stared at the fluttering leaves of the cottonwoods. "I have tried." She did not like Julian Ivy's questions. They struck too close to well-buried memories.

Julian felt her retreat; she was as far away now as she had been in that moment of perfect stillness. Unsettled, he sought a remark that would ease the awkwardness. "I like your hair," he muttered, feeling foolish. Why hadn't he noticed before? The thick black strands fell loose down her back, completely unrestrained. He had never seen anything like it.

"Is it unusual?" Saylah asked, confused by his compliment.

He nodded. "Even in the wilderness the women wear their hair rolled or knotted or twisted up off their necks, tightly confined." He had always thought their dresses equally confining, made to hold them in, protect them—their hair, their bodies, their feelings. Only his mother had been different. Every thought had shown on her fair face; her gray eyes had revealed her pleasure, her sadness, her deep affection. Or so Julian had believed, foolishly, as children will.

Saylah watched him intently. "Do they? I did not know. I have lived only among my People and at the school. Does it make you uneasy that I am not like the others?" She had seen the admiration in his eyes, and her tone was teasing. When he did not answer, she added softly, "For three summers I have followed the rules of my white teachers. Now I must follow my own."

"You mean the Salish rules?"

"No." She spoke sharply, cutting off the single word—and any other questions—with grim determination.

Julian Ivy, who had learned through hard experience to charm, draw others out, making them reveal much while he revealed nothing, was at a loss. "You must meet my family," he said.

"It is why I have come." His formality reminded her, poignantly, of the pride Salish men felt so deeply, tried so valiantly to conceal. She had to struggle to catch her breath.

"Have you no bag?"

Blinking to get her bearings, Saylah tried to remember. It had been so long ago. "I left it in the clearing." She pointed.

"I'll get it." Abruptly, Julian put an end to the conversation. He passed the lines of oak, alder and cottonwood without noticing their fat green summer leaves, and though the meadow grass brushed his ankles, he was not aware of it. When the sun passed behind a cloud, he nearly tripped over the small carpetbag hidden in the grass.

He stared appraisingly at a pair of button-top boots with stockings tossed carelessly beside them. He had always wondered how women managed to wear the stiff boots, especially where there were no proper roads or sidewalks. At least not outside Victoria, which was several miles to the south. Not only did Saylah wear her hair down—he found a pile of pins under the shoes—she preferred bare feet to shoes and stockings. Suddenly, he liked her, observant green eyes or not.

When he returned, he found her staring at the deer. She closed her eyes, reached up to undo the top buttons on her high-necked gown. She let out her breath in relief, threw her head back, and inhaled, her face suffused with pleasure. The wind swept around her, lifted her blue-black hair over her cheeks, half covering her face.

Saylah did not seem to mind. She leaned into the wind, not bothering to brush the strands away. She moved her palm over the carved cedar, stroking it gently, intimately; almost, she made him believe it lived and breathed beneath her hand.

Julian looked down and saw that her feet were indeed bare, caked with dirt and mud. Her dust-grimed skin and windblown hair, her head, tilted toward the sky, even her dirty feet, reminded him of the freedom he had not felt since he was ten years old. He did not move, could not bring himself to interrupt, not while the envy still burned inside him.

Saylah looked up, sensing his presence, and smiled. Julian started toward the house in silence. There were no words for what he felt; he could not name it or dismiss it or understand it. He walked briskly, but she did not fall behind.

They circled the two-story house, and Saylah admired the porch that ran the width of side and front on both the upper and lower levels. There were many windows, though all were covered with curtains. The log house was carefully finished and much larger than she had expected.

Julian stopped before they reached the front door. He seemed reluctant to go forward, but stood staring at the ordinary house as if it were an enemy.

Saylah regarded him curiously. The mirror in his eyes had vanished. A flash of changing sunlight, perhaps, cut off by shifting clouds. Relief rose in her like a wave, but beneath the water swirled something dark, without shape or substance.

Turning away, she looked up at the house and noticed a single oval window high over the front door. The glass was translucent blue, like the palest sea on a day when it lay serene and unbroken by wind or wave. She stared fixedly at the unusual window, imagining the feel of the cool, calm water it reminded her of around her ankles.

Julian drew a deep breath. Though his expression did not change, Saylah felt his reluctance as if he had gripped her shoulders and left the mark of his fingers on her skin. He did not want to go in.

Suddenly, the front door burst open and a child in a red plaid shirt tumbled out. He stopped, bouncing on both feet in front of Saylah.

"Is this her?" the boy cried, barely able to contain his excitement. "It must be her. No one else is coming today. Are you sure you're an Indian? You look different. I'm Theron Ivy and I've just turned six."

The blond boy with the whirling arms took Saylah's hand and tugged. "Well? Aren't you coming in? I've been waiting for hours and hours with nothing to do—" He broke off, reddened, and looked sideways at Julian, who did not appear to notice.

Saylah felt Theron's warm, grubby fingers, and her own curled naturally around them. His blue eyes sparkled and his flyaway hair was rumpled. His shirt was half out of his pants, one shoe was unmercifully scuffed. She liked him at once. "I am sorry to have kept you waiting. I was listening to the wind and admiring your carved deer. I am afraid I thought only of myself."

Theron puckered his brow. "It's okay. I do that sometimes. Julian says *all* the time, but he doesn't know *everything*." Upon consideration, Theron was afraid Julian might very well know everything and that trouble was sure to follow. He decided to change the subject. "You have pretty eyes. Doesn't she, Julian?" He stamped his foot in annoyance. He didn't want his brother to notice him, but he kept asking silly questions. "Well, I mean . . ." He trailed off miserably.

Julian started and looked down at his half-brother. He should have known Theron would already have Saylah in hand. "This is Saylah, who's come to help your mother," he explained. "Say hello politely."

Theron opened his mouth to retort indignantly that he had already said hello, but thought better of it. "Good morning, Miss Saylah. Isn't it a lovely day?"

Obviously, he had heard someone speak those words before. Saylah laughed and nodded agreement. "Lovely," she said.

Julian shook his head. Theron was impossible, mostly because one could not stay angry at him long enough to teach him manners. Reluctantly, unable to delay any longer, he went into the house.

Saylah stopped inside the door, surrounded, all at once, by a profound silence. Julian and Theron might have disappeared, so complete was her sense of isolation. She swayed at the eerie sensation that somehow, in stepping over the threshold, she had stepped into her childhood.

She stood at the end of a large, dim room, and though a portion was cut off by a loft overhead, the rest rose toward the slanted ceiling, high into the shadows like the Longhouse of her ancestors. Three ridgepoles supported the loft. Though they were simple sturdy beams, she could easily imagine bears and cougars carved into the wood. There were low-burning fires in the twin stone fireplaces that faced each other at the far end of the room.

She could not make out many details in the spacious interior of the house; it was too dim. But the smell of must, old fires and cold ashes was strong. The disturbing feeling passed, but the gloomy interior, the heavy, dank air and the fragrance of old wood shook her deeply, made her yearn for what she had lost, though she had thought that yearning dead long since.

"So ye've come after all," Flora called. She came from the long, dark hallway to the left, brushing wisps of hair off her forehead. "'Tis sorry I am that I was no' there to greet ye."

"Flora!" Julian cried with obvious relief. "This is the woman from the Indian school. Saylah, my stepmother, Flora."

Flora was tall and softly rounded with Theron's blond hair and blue eyes. Stepmother. Saylah wondered if Julian's mother was dead. Had she been too frail to survive in the wilderness, as so many of the Strangers' women were?

Flora, she saw at once, would not let the wilderness defeat her. She was sturdy and healthy, pretty in her own way, with a round face and strong hands. She was wiping them now on her flour-splattered gingham apron, which covered a practical cotton twill dress of green and blue plaid. "I'm glad to see ye," she said, offering her hand. "I wanted to give ye a proper *failte*." She shook her head, flustered. "I mean greetin'. Sometimes I slip back into the Gaelic without thinkin'."

Saylah noticed that under the natural flush of her skin, Flora's face looked harried, pale. Despite her youth and strength, there was a fine line of worry between her brows.

"I also forget," Saylah said. "Sometimes the North Wind blows all but Salish words from my head and I cannot speak, except in the ancient language. Yours too I think is very old."

Flora smiled in gratitude and more than a little surprise. Like Julian, she was used to silent Indian girls who chose a name and left it behind at each new place they stayed. Not one of them would have thought to reassure her as Saylah had. She peered more closely at the girl, puzzled by her stature and delicate features until she noticed the clear green eyes. "No' old enough to be forgotten," Flora said, adjusting her apron and her expectations. "I was plannin' to be there when ye arrived. I know they leave ye standin' in the road, like ye'd no' a feelin' in your heart. But my husband's no' been well."

"They told me," Saylah said. "I would like to see him."

Flora opened her mouth and closed it, too startled to think of a reply. None of the other girls had bothered about Jamie. But Saylah sounded more than curious; she sounded determined.

"Not now," Julian said too quickly. He felt an unreasonable urge to block the way to his father's room. "He's resting." The lie sounded harsh and hollow, even to his own ears.

Saylah felt the tension that eddied around the little group like a chill winter wind. Julian Ivy was afraid and she wanted to know why. She wanted to know why the name Richard James Ivy had haunted her since the moment she first heard it.

Flora was shocked by Julian's rudeness. She looked at Saylah helplessly. "Jamie is ill and rarely leaves his room."

There was much she had not said, but the weight of those unspoken words vibrated in the somber air. Saylah nodded. She had learned patience early; that lesson had only grown deeper at the missionary school.

"Well," Flora said too heartily, "ye've just barely arrived, and with the dust of the road still upon ye. Ye must want to change and wash up, put your things in your room."

"Can I show her where it is?" Theron asked, tugging on his mother's apron.

Saylah noticed his voice was subdued. He was trying to keep quiet, and from the strained expression on his face, she guessed it was not an easy task.

"But who will carry her bag?" Julian asked. He still held it in his hand—he had slipped the shoes, stockings and hairpins inside before he picked it up.

"*I* can do it!" Theron declared proudly. "I'm six now." He began to bounce on the balls of his feet.

Saylah suspected he would not be quiet for long.

"All right," Julian said, winking at Flora and ruffling his half-brother's hair affectionately. He understood that this small thing was very important to Theron. "I need to get back to work anyway. I'd appreciate your help."

The little boy grinned triumphantly at Saylah. Theron's unfeigned pleasure made her smile in response.

"Your room is next to mine," he confided. "Have you ever had a room all to yourself before?"

Saylah thought of the Longhouse, the dormitory at the school, the summer hut she had shared with her mother. "No."

"Well, come on, then!" He headed to the right, nearly tripping over her carpetbag, tugging and pushing with intense concentration. He glared at Julian, daring his brother to embarrass him by trying to help.

Julian stayed where he was, pretended not to notice the boy's struggle.

Flora smiled at her son, then at Saylah. "I'll be in the kitchen when you're ready." She pointed to the hallway opposite the one Theron was aiming for. "'Tis on the right and easy to find. But mind, I'd no' be wantin' ye to hurry. Rest for a while and put your things away. I know 'tis a strange house and no' like home."

Saylah's eyes felt painfully dry. Not once had any white person understood that she might prefer the freedom of her childhood to the civilization of their world. "Thank you," she said. "I will come to you soon."

Flora shook her head. "When ye're ready," she repeated. "No' a second before."

Saylah nodded and turned to follow Theron as he grimaced, biting his lip, and dragged her bag over the wooden floor. Though she had had only a glimpse, she would not forget how Julian stood, legs spread, arms crossed, a sentinel bent on keeping away intruders. His father's room must be nearby. She felt Julian's fear like a choking dust that did not lift or clear when she left him behind.

She knew, even then, that the fear was not for himself, but for the man they called Jamie, whose face she did not know. She felt a flicker of doubt, a gnawing curiosity, a determination that frightened her. Nothing had touched her as deeply since she left the Salish behind. She focused on Theron's bent, curly head. She was not certain she wanted to re-awaken those long-slumbering feelings. Better to leave them in shadow and peace.

Chapter

21

At dinner, the Ivys sat around the large pine table in the kitchen. The whitewashed walls and huge, snapping fire made the room brighter and more cheerful than the rest of the house, but Saylah was not comfortable. She had been surprised to discover that Flora had set a place for her with the family. There was a place as well for Jamie, at the head of the table, where Saylah guessed he had not sat for some time.

"'Twill be a beautiful night for the moon," Flora observed as she passed a bowl of green beans to Theron. "Ye have some, mind," she scolded when the boy tried unobtrusively to push the bowl along to Julian. "I'll no' have ye wastin' away in my house. Jamie would be sore disappointed in ye." She glanced at the head of the table, expecting her husband to concur. She blinked at the empty chair, dismayed, even after so long, that he was not there to answer.

Saylah looked away from Flora's distress to Theron, who was healthy and in no danger of wasting away. He grinned and crunched down loudly on a bean.

"Are ye cozy in your room?" Flora asked, determined to remain cheerful. Determined not to let her husband's absence mar this first night's meal.

"It is pleasant, thank you."

Theron crossed his eyes at her; he thought her first private room deserved more praise than that. "I'll show you the rest of the house after supper," he insisted.

Saylah smiled back. She could not resist his enthusiasm. She had brushed her hair and braided it when she changed her gown, and knew she looked neat and correct. Yet despite Theron's obvious approval, she felt out of place. She had not expected the Ivys to accept her, to invite her to join them at their meal. She had thought she would have to fight for these things. Now there was no struggle and she was uncertain how to respond.

She was also distressingly aware that Julian's eyes strayed more than once to his father's empty place.

Saylah stared at the clean plate and folded napkin, the glass, sparked with rainbow light from the restless flames. She felt Jamie Ivy's presence in that moment. Not like a gust of cold air in the midst of the fire's heat, but rather like another warmth—abandoned, fading, but not yet gone.

"And what of ye?" Flora asked her stepson. "Were ye happy with your work today? Are the new trees ready? I've seen the apples growin' bonny on the others. Golden they are, and bright green and red." She would not be put off by stiff answers and distracted airs. Her family would talk to her no matter how difficult it was for them. She knew no other way to keep them together, near her, warm and alive.

"I've planted all five," Julian said.

"I thought a ranch—I have been told there are cattle and wheat and oats," Saylah said.

"We have a little of each here. Originally, we planned a cattle ranch. But somehow the apple orchards crept over more and more of the land. It's the fruit that keeps us alive now." Julian turned to Jamie, smiling, for confirmation or an answering smile of pride. But Jamie wasn't there.

"Paul and I can help pick this year," Theron announced. "We can even show Saylah how. Have you ever picked apples before?" His eager blue eyes were fixed on Saylah's face, his lip held between his teeth while he waited for her answer.

"No, I never have. My People sometimes eat crab apples, but those are not the same."

Julian did not hear her. He hated the cold emptiness of the chair at the head of the table, the void Jamie had once filled with stories and wit and laughter. The silence of his absence lingered, even through Flora's questions and Theron's chatter. Tonight, Julian was deafened by that silence. He looked away.

Saylah stared down at her rabbit stew, but she was listening, watching, sensing the unnatural hush where Richard James Ivy should have been.

How many times a day, she wondered, did Theron or Flora or Julian turn to speak to empty air?

"'Tis quiet here, especially in winter," Flora pressed on. "I hope ye'll no' mind."

"I am used to solitude. I value it and seek it."

"I've heard that about the Salish," Julian interjected. "I always wondered why."

Saylah did not meet his gaze. "Because it is their way."

Julian shook his head. She had mentioned her people several times now, but had told him nothing. Jamie would never have allowed that. He would have drawn her out long since, made her regale them with stories of her other life.

"I don't like being alone," Theron said, striking the table to emphasize his point. "I don't know how Papa can bear it."

Flora and Julian stiffened. "Perhaps he has no choice, or has come to believe he has none," Saylah suggested. She was only guessing, because she wanted so much to reassure Theron.

Julian glowered at the clean plate and glittering glass. "There's always a choice," he muttered. Then he fell silent. Once again, he had said too much.

Julian could not wait to get away when the meal was finished. "I'm going for a ride," he called to Flora. "As you said, the moon tonight is too fine to miss."

He did not wait to see his stepmother's reaction. Breathing deeply of the pine-scented night, he went to the stable, eager to leave the house behind. But when he entered the stall where he kept his horse, Phoenix, it was empty.

"Lizzie!" He slapped his hand on the wooden divider in exasperation. "Not tonight." He groaned and pressed his forehead against the cedar plank.

Lizzie Grant was young, healthy and pretty, but unfortunately, Julian thought in despair, she had an unorthodox sense of humor. Several months ago, when he'd been too restless to sleep, he'd decided to take a long night ride. But when he went to saddle his horse, Phoenix had disappeared. The stall door had been closed and latched, so he'd known the horse had not escaped. Since Lizzie was the only person besides Julian who Phoenix let near, he'd bet his life that she'd taken him.

In a rage, Julian had gone to her cabin and, finding the horse grazing contentedly nearby, he'd pounded with both fists on the closed door.

Blond hair brushed and brown eyes glowing, Lizzie had welcomed him with a smile.

"You stole my horse!" he'd shouted before she could distract him from his fury.

Eyes wide and innocent, she'd pointed at Phoenix. "But he's right here, safe and fed and happy."

Julian had placed his hands on either side of the door and leaned toward her menacingly. "How was I to know that?"

"You're here, aren't you?" She refused to back away, could not hide the sparkle in her eyes. "I know you ride at night a lot. I thought for once you might like to be with me instead."

Julian had taken several deep breaths in an effort to calm both his anger and the insidious desire that had begun to overtake him. Lizzie wore a low-cut green gown and leaned toward him enticingly. "Why," he said, enunciating each syllable with care, "didn't you just ask?"

She'd crossed her arms and pouted, forcing the curve of her breasts upward. "I did," she said haughtily, "but you didn't answer." She looked him up and down, noting his flushed face and the arousal he could not hide. "At least until now."

Giving up the struggle, Julian had laughed and followed her inside.

Since then she'd taken the horse many times. When Julian didn't come looking, she sent the animal home in the morning, usually with a small gift tied to his saddle. The first had been a handmade doll with blond hair, brown eyes and a painted face with turned-down lips and teardrops on her cheeks. The next had been a package beautifully wrapped which held a very old, very fragrant potato.

He had been amused by her tricks until now. Tonight Julian was not in the mood for the walk to Lizzie's cabin. Tonight he wanted to ride far and fast, to escape the apprehension he'd felt since he first saw Saylah gazing at the deer. Lizzie was fun, but Julian did not want fun. He wanted to be alone.

He had decided to forget his ride when he saw the note pinned to the stall door. Against his better judgment, he lifted the lantern from the hook and held it close to the tattered paper.

I know you worked hard today, digging all those horrible holes for your apple trees.

As usual, she had not bothered with a greeting. She was too impatient for such social niceties. It was one of the things Julian liked about her.

—— *159* ——

You're probably too tired to be any fun. Probably don't even have enough energy to chase after your horse, let alone me. Too bad. I feel like playing. Maybe another time.

Lizzie

Julian cursed under his breath, ripped the paper from the nail, and crumpled it in his fist. The thought of her laughing at his weariness made him angry and careless. This was Lizzie's little game, and he couldn't let her win.

Shaking his head in irritation, he set out, jaw rigid and fists clenched, over the path lit by the moon. He knew the way well to the narrow valley where Lizzie's brother had built a cabin before disappearing to follow the gold he was sure would make him rich. Just like Jamie.

Julian kicked a clump of tangled bracken; dew scattered in the cool night air. By the time he reached the hill above the cabin, he was tired and resentful. "Why do you go to all this trouble?" he'd demanded of her once. "Aren't you busy enough at that saloon in Victoria, singing and dancing for lonely miners?"

He'd meant to make her angry, but she'd only laughed. "You're the one who works too hard, Julian Ivy. You need to rest now and then, come to Victoria yourself." She leaned close to whisper against his lips, "I'd rather sing and dance for you."

When he continued to glower, Lizzie had shrugged. "At least the miners know how to have fun."

Considering himself exceedingly virtuous, Julian had replied, "I have no time for fun."

Undaunted, Lizzie had sidled up, hips swaying. "None at all?" She'd run her tongue invitingly over her lips. "Are you sure?" She'd given him a smile that was a smoldering promise.

Julian had discovered that, after all, he could spare half an hour. He'd stayed until nearly dawn.

But that had been different, he thought now, grimly. Though the sky was clear and the moon bright, he did not notice the lush landscape. He was concentrating on his anger, which had grown with each step. Tonight he was not in the mood to laugh. Why couldn't she take him seriously for once?

He was at the front door before he realized there was no sign of Phoenix. The cabin was dark and deserted. He pounded on the door in disbelief, long after it was clear no one was home. His feet ached, and his shoulders and lower back, from the digging he'd done earlier. The walk hadn't helped. And now there was no sign of Lizzie.

—— 160 ——

Then he saw the note tucked under the rusted latch. He squinted in the moonlight, trying to decipher her shaky scrawl.

Couldn't wait any longer. Had to get some air and Phoenix was restless. If you come lookin', you might find me. Then again, you might not know where to look. And I know how tired you are.

Lizzie

It's a good thing she isn't here, Julian thought, *or I might well strangle her*. The game, which hadn't been funny in the first place, had now become serious. Besides the fury that made his vision blur and his pulse pound, he was worried. The woods were dangerous at night, and neither Phoenix nor Lizzie knew how to protect themselves.

He was sorely tempted to leave Lizzie to her fate, but that last little jab—*I know how tired you are*—stuck in his throat.

Besides, if anything happened to her, even through her own foolishness, he would never forgive himself. And, he realized even through the red haze of his anger, he would miss her.

He sighed heavily. Where in heaven's name would she be? And how could he find her, even in bright moonlight?

"You know where I'd like to take you?" she'd whispered as he lay tangled in the sheets beside her. "Someplace where there's a pretty little spring, with rocks to sun myself and grass soft enough to sleep on." She'd winked meaningfully. "Someday I'll meet a man there at night, under the moon, and I'll fall desperately in love and throw you and Phoenix over."

Julian had kissed such thoughts out of her head. But now he remembered she'd pointed out a grotto as they rode through the woods together. She'd be there waiting; he was sure of it.

When he found her, he'd carry her away, all right, but not to shower her with kisses. He was breathing heavily by the time he reached the grotto and was relieved to hear Phoenix nicker in greeting. No note this time. Just let him find Lizzie and she'd see how tired he was. He stepped around an outcropping of rock and saw the horse standing quietly with Lizzie in the saddle. Her blond hair was tangled with Phoenix's mane, and her cloak fell in elegant folds down his sides.

She didn't move when Julian came near. She was waiting to see what he would do.

He suppressed the urge to shout out his frustration; the sound would echo off the stone walls and frighten Phoenix. "Lizzie," Julian said slowly, succinctly, in a voice that was dangerously low, "are you mad?"

She tossed her head so her blond curls tumbled back over her shoulder.

"Oh," she said, pouting, "you're going to be difficult. And it's such a beautiful night. I thought we might—"

She was grinning. That's what unleashed the fury he'd been trying to hold back. The knowing smile, the gleam in her eye that said she'd won. "Don't you know that there's a cougar running in these woods? It's killed several farm animals, even attacked a bull once."

Lizzie shrugged in unconcern. "I have Phoenix. He'd protect me."

Julian fought to keep his temper. "A cougar can outrun Phoenix, and if a bull didn't stop him, I don't think he'd be afraid of my horse." He paused. "Or even of you."

Lizzie pressed her hands to her cheeks. "Oh, my!"

Julian gaped. Her cloak had fallen open and she wore nothing underneath. Nothing but her button-top shoes to protect her feet. Her body glowed in the moonlight—full breasts, tiny waist, softly rounded hips. He felt a rush of desire, then remembered how she'd brought him here. "If you think—"

"I didn't know it was dangerous," Lizzie yelped in mock terror. "I'd better get back where I'll be safe." Swinging her cape wide to show him the full extent of her naked body, she turned Phoenix sharply. Without a backward glance, she swept the cloak closed and rode away, leaving Julian standing in marshy earth, his mouth open, his face red with fury, the memory of her soft white body all too vivid in his mind.

"I'll kill her," he shouted to the uncaring stones. "I swear I will!" He could hear her laughter carried back to him on the wind. This time his rage boiled over.

He began to run, following the tracks of horse and rider. His head was pounding and he could not think. He could feel the hot blood flowing through his veins and pulsing at his temples. His breathing was harsh and ragged, but he did not slow down. His fury pushed him on; he was not aware of the cold, rising wind or the clouds that drifted across the moon.

When he came to the cabin, Phoenix was not in sight and the door was barred against him. He pounded on the unyielding wood until his fists were raw. "Open the door, damn you, and tell me what you've done with my horse."

Lizzie waited a long time before she answered. "Since the woods are so unsafe, I sent him home. I know it'd break your heart if he got hurt."

Julian closed his eyes; even then the flaring colors behind the lids echoed the erratic pulse of his blood. "You'd better open this door, Lizzie. I'm not laughing. Do you hear me?"

"I hear you. And that's exactly why I *won't* open the door. Besides, the way you're leaning against it, I don't think you'd be worth much tonight anyway. You must have walked eight miles."

Julian thought of breaking a window so he could reach inside and fasten his hands around her neck, but he had not quite lost his mind entirely. He sat on an upended barrel and waited for his heart to cease pounding, his breathing to return to normal, the rage to subside so he wouldn't have to commit murder. "You'll open the door for me, Lizzie. You can tease all you like, but you'll open up in the end."

But she didn't.

Eventually, he found he could breathe without pain. The rage lingered much longer while he clenched his fists and thought about what he would do when he saw her—if he ever did again. She had dragged him over half the Saanich Peninsula, knowing he'd worked hard, knowing he was tired. She'd played her little game, oblivious of his discomfort and his feelings and even his health.

"It's not my fault if you can't resist a challenge," Lizzie called. "Any sane man would have stayed at home and soaked his feet in a tub by the kitchen fire. You didn't have to follow me, you know."

Julian raised his head and stared, eyes narrowed dangerously, at the tightly closed door. He started to reply, growled something indistinguishable, then sighed in defeat. The aggravating thing was, she was right. If he hadn't been so stubborn, if he hadn't been determined to prove she couldn't best him, he would have ignored her notes and sat out under the garry oak at the ranch, where it was quiet and he could rest.

Instead, he'd tramped over hills and through mud, up riverbeds and down rock faces just because of his damned pride. He was a fool, that's what he was. Without quite realizing it, he began to chuckle. Lizzie knew him too well. And whose fault was that? He had to admit it; she'd beaten him this time. He chuckled harder, then laughed aloud.

Only then did Lizzie open the door and reveal that, somewhere along the way, she'd discarded her cloak and high-button shoes.

Chapter

22

Gradually, lingeringly, Saylah fell into her dream. The water caressed her, sang to her softly, while light sifted through the leaves onto the still surface. She touched the changing patterns, and light danced on her brown, glowing skin.

Then she heard the voice, a stranger's voice calling a name she could not hear. The breeze carried the sound rippling through the treetops, but she could not catch it.

She awoke, wide-eyed and vaguely distressed, well before dawn. After three years, she still awakened before sunrise on those days when she craved solace. She looked out the tiny window and felt that she would suffocate in the darkness of the unfamiliar room. She had been there for two nights, but it still felt alien to her, with its simple frame bed, small bureau, washstand and white china pitcher.

She rose in darkness and found her wrapper. She would go to the river and bathe. Then this feeling of heaviness would leave her. As an afterthought, she took one of the sheets from her bed and tied the ends, making a kind of bag that she could toss over her shoulder.

She stepped into the hallway, tiptoed past Theron's room and into the main room. The twin fires smoldered, but did not dissipate the chill. Saylah had begun to wonder if it cam from Jamie's withdrawn breath.

She knew Julian and Flora saw him daily, but Saylah had not yet been allowed to meet him.

She looked at the log walls, hung with a cross-cut saw, an old rifle, a beaver trap, a mining pan and two Salish hunting bows that puzzled her. There was nothing new or pretty—no paintings or embroidered hangings or portraits like the ones that had hung in the missionary school.

The things on the walls belonged to Jamie, Theron had informed her. She had not been surprised. She felt his presence every moment; he hovered in dark corners as certainly as he slept behind his unyielding door. Whenever his family gathered, he was there—beside them, inside them, around them.

Because his name had called her here, Saylah could not find solid ground in this house of shifting shadows until she saw his face, spoke to him, began to understand his intangible power. She felt a growing sense of urgency that would not let her rest.

She shivered at the chilly darkness. "Why are all the curtains closed?" she had asked Theron the first afternoon.

"Because the light hurts Papa's eyes."

"Flora said your papa does not leave his room."

"But he will someday," Theron had said emphatically, trying to make himself believe it, "and we don't want him to go back because the light is too bright."

Saylah had not been convinced.

She sniffed, felt a drift of scented breeze. There was another presence in this house, more mysterious than Jamie, more ethereal, like the delicate scent of flowers in a hidden cave.

The name Simone floated toward her in Theron's eager remembered voice.

"You smell good," he had said one morning after she bathed in the river and dried herself with hemlock boughs. "Not like Mother, or even that other lady." He had blushed furiously and tried to change the subject, but Saylah would not let him.

"What other lady?"

"Julian's mother!" the boy had blurted out, glancing furtively over his shoulder to be certain no one else would hear.

"I do not see how you can know what she smells like, but I have felt her too, especially in the loft. Her spirit lingers here. I wonder why?"

Too excited to be wise, Theron had taken Saylah to the narrow stairway which led to the loft. Just beyond the top of the stairs, he showed her the tightly closed door with a crystal knob, too fragile and beautiful for this huge and practical house.

She would have known Flora had not created this room, even if Theron had not told her. The faint scent of roses greeted her, the sight of exquisite wallpaper, a thick carpet and elegant furniture. She was certain she could hear the echo of voices that had only just faded into stillness. Yet she could see the room had been abandoned for a long time; dust lay over tables and trinkets, rosewood and brocade, except where recent footprints had disturbed the fine film. Saylah was certain if she lingered long enough, listened hard enough, Simone would come and speak to her. It was a foolish notion, yet—

"Don't tell them I brought you," Theron had pleaded. "They don't like me to come here. Mama said Julian wanted to take all this away, but Papa wouldn't let him."

"I wonder why?" Saylah mused. Every other trace of the chimerical Simone had obviously been stripped from the house.

Theron gave the now-familiar glance over his shoulder, then tugged on her skirt so he could whisper in her ear. "Paul says that his mama says that Simone was very beautiful, and a woman like that keeps a hold on a man." He frowned. "What do you think she means?"

"I do not know," Saylah had replied. "But who is Paul?"

Theron had grinned. "Paul Ashton is my best friend. He's eight, and he doesn't care that I'm only six. His papa is my papa's best friend too." He bit his lip, considering whether to say more, but Saylah's kind eyes drew the words from him against his will. "He used to be, anyway. Paul's family came here all the time to visit. They don't anymore."

"That makes you unhappy?"

"I miss them," Theron said. "Sometimes I get lonely. *You* know."

"Yes. I think I do." But she had no time for her own unquiet memories. Already she had become entangled in the secrets eddying in the faint light that spilled through the partially open curtains. A man who did not leave his room, a family who would not say why, a woman who was gone, yet lingered still. An unguarded remark of Flora's had revealed that, so far as anyone knew, Simone Ivy was not dead.

Two ghosts, alive, unseen, unheard, ruled this house as surely as the tide ate away at the windswept shore.

Saylah shook away the memory of that morning with Theron, shook away her nagging questions and curiosity. She felt the need to leave behind secrets and ghosts, along with the image of Julian's hazel eyes, shuttered one moment, full of light and anguish the next.

She looked forward to her daily bath in the river, though Flora did not understand why she would not use the huge metal tub in the kitchen. It was difficult to heat the water and fill the tub with buckets, the woman had explained, so they usually shared the water—once a week when they took their baths beside the blazing kitchen fire. Saylah shuddered at the thought.

With intense relief, she stepped barefoot into the gray morning. The air was damp and cold; it made her skin tingle, made the gloom of the house rise from her shoulders and disappear into the darkness.

Hurrying over the rough ground, she avoided stones and roots and bracken. The crisp morning breeze whispered through bent oaks which marked her path toward the woods. Her long black hair flew out behind her, and the distant song of the river called.

She laughed aloud as the woods closed around her. Pausing, she touched a fir, following its rivulets and crevices with her fingertips. Her whole body was awake now—awake and alive. She yearned to watch the sunrise as she used to do.

Crouching on a hilltop, she heard the wind calling. Her wrapper flew open, but she did not notice, any more than she would have noticed the strips of supple cedarbark that rose and fell in the breezes of her childhood. She was happy to be free of the awkward clothes the Whites were so fond of, happy to be alone and waiting for the sun, surrounded by the fragrance of the forest, damp with sea air.

The first hint of color appeared in the sky, tinting the low clouds pink. Saylah looked out over the land that fell toward the sea, wild and so lush that the criss-crossing roads were well concealed. The shimmering lilac light of dawn wove its way upward, above the trees topped with clinging mist, above the billowing clouds to the sky that turned from deep gray to purple to rose.

Saylah breathed deeply of the late summer air. It was not silence she sought, for she loved the songs of birds, the whisper of the breeze, the murmur of the river among the green trees. Her stillness lay, not in the absence of sound, but in the absence of turmoil.

For a long while, she crouched, her hair more like a cloak than the pale wrapper, and let the stillness take her. She felt calm, serene, alone. For the first time in many moons, she was acting without thought. Even when she lived among her People, she had been restrained—by the faith of others, their belief in her wisdom, her purity, her strength. Now, suddenly, she was free.

Finally, she stood, a silhouette against the rising sun, her dark face lifted to the light.

Then she turned, running lightly, stopped to gather some mock orange leaves and followed the sound of rushing water until she reached the river. Along the way, she began to gather boughs of fir and cedar and put them in her folded sheet.

She stopped, head tilted, when she heard a hollow sound beneath her feet. She stamped her foot, and an echo rose from the ground. She bent down to examine a tangle of moss, ferns and kinnikinnick, pushing damp greenery aside until she uncovered an old warped cedar plank.

Impulsively, she stood on the cleared space and danced a few steps, hearing with pleasure the thumps that rose around her, like the beat of a huge hollow drum. Curiously, she dropped down to examine the plank. It was loose at the edges. When she lifted it, she stared down into a deep round hole. It must be a well like the one that had provided water for the missionaries. An abandoned well with the heart of a drum. She dropped the plank back into place, rearranged the moss and ferns, and turned at last toward the river.

Dropping her wrapper on the bank without a thought, she stepped into the water. The chill went through her body, making her shiver violently, but it felt good—clean, pure, exhilarating.

Slowly, the dust of the Ivys' grief was washed away as Saylah felt the touch of newly made soap, ducked beneath the water and rose, swinging her hair upward, flinging water into the sky. She glanced back once, warily, then laughed at herself. No one was watching. There were none from the school to scold and bind her.

When Saylah raised her arms to the sky, the sun touched the water on her dark skin with radiance. For too long her songs had been silent. Now the words came back to her slowly, carried on the wind, in the scent of the trees and the flowing of the waters.

Julian was repairing a broken stretch of fence, his booted foot on the lower rail, a hammer in his hand, when he heard movement at the edge of the woods and looked up, expecting a cougar or deer. Instead, he saw an apparition, tall and white, floating on the mist at her feet. The evanescent light made her wraith-like, ethereal. He shook his head to make the image go, but it remained, came closer.

Then he saw the long black hair clinging to arms and breasts, the thin white wrapper and bare feet. Saylah. She must have been bathing; the cambric clung to her damp skin and her hair was heavy with moisture. He felt a surge of disbelief. Her hair hanging loose and unrestrained had been one thing, her discarded stockings and shoes another. But this—

Her body was clearly outlined by the thin, wet fabric, and her hair did not hide the swell of her breasts. The wrapper was not fastened; he could see her dark skin in flashes as she crossed the clearing. Moving gracefully, sensually, and above all, heedlessly over his meadow.

An image of Lizzie, naked in the moonlight, flashed through his mind.

He could hear her laughter, see the sweep of her arm that had revealed, then hidden, her lush body as she turned away. So Saylah knew Lizzie's game, and played it better. Her unusual green eyes, turned inward, as if she were unaware of his presence, were more intriguing, more alluring than Lizzie's openly seductive gaze.

She paused beneath a dogwood to touch the dew-wet leaves, caress them, press them to her cheek. She moved unselfconsciously, smiled in genuine delight. She was—he could think of no word to describe her. He realized he was staring, transfixed, and cursed violently under his breath.

"Have you lost your mind?" he snapped when Saylah was close enough. "You'll make yourself ill wandering about half dressed."

She did not understand his bitterness. "It is you who looks ill," she said. "You are very pale." Instinctively, she tried to touch his cheek with a soothing hand.

He backed away, looking at the green and golden leaves, the dark earth, the bracken—anywhere but at her body.

Troubled by his odd behavior, she shifted the weight of her burden of boughs and tried to think. "I fear you have been working too hard. It is early. Should you not be sitting warmly in the kitchen with Flora and Theron?"

Julian's stomach tightened in inexplicable disappointment. Angry at her pretended innocence, he glanced up. It was not her body he was avoiding, he realized, but her probing eyes. He faced her squarely, jaw set in a stubborn line. "I think you should go in."

How had she known he would be watching, drawn irresistibly to the curves of her body in the dawn light? She used her natural grace of motion, the fall of her lustrous hair, the shape of her parted lips to create and enhance her power. She was desirable, sensual and deceitful. Just like Simone.

She had not moved, but stood regarding him curiously.

"Go, I said." He spoke more harshly than he had intended. With all his strength, he pounded a bent nail into the wood, splintering the post with a single stroke.

Saylah stiffened. "The dawn is not yours to give, so you cannot take it from me. What I value, what is mine because it belongs to no one, I will enjoy as I choose."

She stared at the half-raised hammer, the shattered post at his feet, his red cheeks. "I think it is you who should go in before you harm yourself—or someone else."

Julian laughed coldly, gazing openly at her body. "There are degrees of danger," he said.

Saylah followed his gaze, perplexed. She saw how the fabric clung, how the wrapper fell open, revealing her breasts. A memory stirred. Glancing at Julian's fierce expression, she heard again the vague and formless threats, the missionaries' warnings about the appetites of men. She remembered the word *immodesty* and the word *lust* and the word *danger*.

For the first time, she tried to recall those forgotten warnings. They had had no meaning for her in the days she had spent at the isolated school. She had gone there to learn about her mind, not her body. She raised her head to meet Julian's accusing eyes. "I grew up among the Salish. They do not think as you do. They do not lust after things they cannot have. To us clothes are for protection, nothing more. Our bodies are natural, not shameful, meant for work and pleasure, not false and meaningless restraints." She spoke slowly, clearly, so that even he might understand.

Folding the wrapper over itself, tossing her hair forward so it fell heavy and dark to her waist, concealing her breasts, she added, "I had no wish to make you uncomfortable. For that I am sorry. But I am not sorry for what I believe, what I was born to believe, though you call it crude. I see in your eyes that you think I am here to make you desire me. It is not true."

His expression was doubtful.

Saylah felt the last of the stillness leave her. Julian had wrenched her sharply away from the beauty of the dawn. *This* was reality, not the water, the trees, the songs of solitude and peace. She should have guessed those things had come too easily. Now, just as easily, they had gone.

"You do not believe, because for you it is easier, safer, to judge and thereby make your choice." She did not know why she continued when he could not hear or understand. So soon had her mirror become warped and distorted. It shook her that Julian Ivy should judge her so harshly when he knew her so little.

Julian saw that she regarded him steadily, no secrets hidden in the clear depths of her eyes. He could not doubt her sincerity. She had closed the wrapper and swung her hair forward. For him, he realized, not for herself. She had no sense of the power of her body, did not know how to use it as a weapon. "I didn't understand," he said in a choked voice.

So he believed her after all. But now it did not matter. Battered as it had been, her pride was still bright and strong within her. She squinted at Julian, who examined his hammer with exquisite care. "Sometimes I forget I am no longer Salish."

That made him look up. "But you're only part Indian."

Saylah winced and looked toward the blaze of sun on the carved cedar deer. "It is the best part." She felt his alarm and realized she had revealed more than she would have wished. "I understand your shock at seeing me appear from out of the mist, but I do not understand your anger." She met his eyes, briefly, one last time. "Do you?"

He did not answer her challenge, but bettered it. "You speak very formally, very precisely. Is it to set you apart from us? To make you seem better because you're different?"

Saylah held her wrapper in fingers gone white with tension. "It is because for most of my life I spoke only the language of my People. It is not always easy to turn my Salish thoughts to English words." She meant to stop, but something urged her on. "It is because, if I cannot speak as my People do, I wish to hold the rhythm and cadence of their language. It gives me comfort."

Julian was stunned by her confession, more stunned by his own rush of compassion. Her face was expressionless, her back erect, but her agitation showed in her whitened fingers which threatened to tear the thin cambric wrapper. "I didn't mean to be rude. It's just—"

"It is just that I surprised you and you do not like to be surprised. It is just that I told you the best part of me belongs with the Salish, and you, a Stranger, do not wish to believe it. It is just that you misunderstood the way of my thoughts and so the way of my body. Perhaps it is just that I am not ashamed, though you looked at me with such disdain. Perhaps you cannot bear to be mistaken. Or perhaps you do not wish to examine your heart and see where your anger smolders inside you. You do not wish to know."

Before he could answer, before he could see her distress, she whirled away. All at once the morning air was cold on her damp skin. Silently, she glided back to the house.

Julian stared after her, furious and speechless. There was nothing he could say. Because she was right.

Chapter

23

"I heard there's been some trouble." Sandy hair combed, morning coat open to reveal his brocade waistcoat, Edward Ashton leaned casually over the stall in Neil MacKinnon's barn.

A forkful of hay in his rough, callused hands, Neil paused to shake his head mournfully. His untidy red hair was scattered with pieces of straw, his gray eyes clouded with weariness. "When is there no' trouble, I'd like to know? Four strong sons and no' one with the brains of a sow, I'm thinkin'."

Edward shook his head in sympathy. "Have they gone off to sell your stock again?"

Tossing the hay into the stall he had just cleaned, Neil picked up another forkful. "'Tis that and more. Sold 'em to a man they'd never met for half their worth, and the pigs I was planning to slaughter for our own food this winter. They got enough to treat their gurrls to dancin' and carryin' on in Victoria, with a little left by for me."

Neil snorted in disgust. "Brought it to me proud as can be, like 'twas a great gift, and me without a grateful bone in my bent old body." He looked up, running a hand through his hair and adding to the disorder. "Be glad ye've only the one and him still a bairn. They'll break your heart and leave ye starvin' and shed nary a tear for their sins."

"I'm sorry to hear that." Edward crossed his arms on the top of the stall divider and regarded his neighbor with compassion, at the same time assessing the nature of his loss. "You know I'd be happy to help you out, old friend."

Neil raised an eyebrow, but inside he was grinning. He had been hoping Edward would drop by, hoping he would offer a solution without being asked. You could always count on Edward for that. He understood pride, even stubborn Scottish pride, though he was American, New York born and bred. But Neil didn't hold it against him.

The Scotsman eyed his friend, noticed the friendly smile, the slivers of gold in his brown eyes. Not, Neil thought shrewdly, that he'd risk having his Annie around Edward more than necessary. There was something about this tall, fine-boned man with his unusual eyes and handsome face—cleft chin and all—that drew women like hollyhock drew hummingbirds.

"I've been thinking about those twenty acres on the north side near my far pasture," Edward continued, resting his booted foot on an overturned bucket. "If you'd like to sell them, put a little money by that your sons don't need to hear about, I'd be willing to offer a good price." He smiled with genuine pleasure. He'd been wanting those acres for a long while now. He'd already bailed his neighbor out several times by buying up small pieces of his 450 acres when the wheat and oat crops weren't as good as expected or the cattle fell ill or the MacKinnon boys began to meddle in their father's business.

Neil MacKinnon was a man forever in need of cash, and Edward Ashton always seemed to have it. What's more, he seemed to know when MacKinnon was getting desperate enough to let some land go. Edward was never satisfied with the size of his own ranch. He had started with 324 acres, all he'd been allowed to file for back in 1864 when Jamie Ivy and he had taken parcels next to each other. Now he had almost five hundred acres, every one of them generating profit.

"Well, now, and wasn't that just what I was thinkin' last night when the moon would no' let me sleep for worryin'. 'Tis many a time ye've saved my hide, Edward Ashton, and I'll no' be forgettin' it. Don't think I will." Neil pulled a straw out of his hair and began to chew it absently.

Delighted at such an easy victory, Edward put out his hand for his neighbor to shake. Each challenge was a test to him, each victory a confirmation that became more necessary as the victories multiplied. He'd thought the need would fade in time, as he proved himself worthy again and again. But it hadn't.

"You're a fine man," Neil added, gripping the offered hand firmly. "A body can depend on ye."

Edward shook his head, although MacKinnon's praise was like balm to an open wound. "A man like you doesn't need to look for people to depend on. You're honest and you work hard. It's not your fault your sons don't share your many virtues."

"Tell my Annie that. She blames me." Neil sighed, but he was pleased. He'd been lucky to get Edward for a neighbor. Most of the men who had come to Vancouver Island to make their fortunes were rough and prickly and never bothered with pretty words. But Edward Ashton was charming and warm. What if he did manage to get what he wanted easier than the others? Was that so surprising? A kind word went a long way in this wilderness. "I tell her 'tis God's joke on a proud, unbendin' woman, but she only glares at me with those eyes of hers."

Edward laughed, though he knew MacKinnon really believed in the hand of God. Edward had given up that luxury long ago. He made his own luck, had done a good job of it too. "I'll drop by this evening to work out the details. And if I come upon those sons of yours, I'll tell them there's another gold rush on the mainland. That would get them out of your way for a while."

Neil came around the stall and slapped his friend on the back. "I'll be prayin' that ye meet 'em away down the road."

The two men smiled companionably before Neil went back to his work and Edward left, swinging his hat in his hand. He whistled, pleased with his morning's work. Sophia would be proud of him. He had worked hard, overcoming challenge after challenge, each greater than the last, to convince himself he could succeed. But with Sophia—

He shook his head. She told him it was enough for her. That she was more than satisfied with her life on Vancouver Island. She was extraordinary, this woman who had blocked the door of her father's three-story Victorian mansion in Boston and said, "I'm going with you. Just try to leave me behind."

"Isn't she afraid of the wilderness?" Jamie Ivy had asked once. He himself had left his wife Simone and their young son in the East until he had a house to settle them into.

"Sophia doesn't know what fear is. Besides, she said she'd had enough of Boston and Beacon Hill, of men with high starched collars, the social register in one hand and piles of gold in the other. She wanted to be free of all that." Edward had spoken with pride of his wife's strength of will. He, more than anyone, knew how lucky he'd been to catch her.

But did she know? Did she ever catch a glimpse of the demons that drove him? A shadow moved beneath the maples with their fine-spun yellow leaves, reminding him there was always darkness hidden somewhere in the too-bright light of day.

Edward took a deep breath of clear, crisp air. He had won today. He would not think of the specters that slithered through his dreams at night. The shadow fled through the shifting light, and he followed until the sound of water over stones told him where he was going.

The Indian girl was waiting, naked, a garland of wild roses in her hair, her skin damp with beaded water. Edward paused to admire her as she moved across moss-covered stones with the waterfall at her back. She moved her brown body in undulating curves that sparked desire within him, called out to his need, promised passion and then peace.

She made him aware of his own tall, broad-shouldered body, muscular and healthy in all ways. She swayed, and he responded instantly, fervently. The girl motioned with her hands—working hands, not soft and white like Sophia's, but brown with the warmth of sun and earth. Her black eyes were wide, her nose flat, her face more square than oval. Water glistened on her breasts, her hips, her long black hair. She parted her lips to wet them sensuously with her tongue.

Edward began to remove his well-made clothes. "I'm glad you're here. I've been thinking of you." He spoke huskily, a plea and a promise in his gold-flecked eyes.

"I have felt it in my dreams. That is why I have come."

He did not know the Indian girl's name, though she had met him here before. He did not want to know. All he wanted was to take her body, hold her against him, to feed the endless hunger that tormented him day and night. He wanted to forget the need to win, to blot out with the power and fury of his passion the tiny, prickling fear he did not understand. He tossed his coat and hat aside and entered her open, welcoming arms.

Sitting cross-legged on the parlor floor, eight-year-old Paul Ashton stared at the blurry newspaper photograph his mother was pointing to. Despite her expensive pearl velvet morning gown, which was in grave danger of becoming crushed and wrinkled, she had joined her son on the patterned Chinese carpet. Their auburn heads were bent over the newspaper from Victoria, their cheeks nearly touching as they examined a woman with a rigid smile. Sophia's hair hung in loose curls about her shoulders; it had not yet been tugged, pulled, pinned and twisted into a proper style for the day. Paul's hair, though much shorter, was equally disheveled. He had forgotten to brush it.

The housekeeper, Clara Ferguson, passed, clacking her tongue loudly in disapproval. "Shouldn't wonder if you start going about in your underclothes next," she muttered. But she was smiling, and Paul and Sophia knew it.

"What's the game today?" Paul asked eagerly, attempting, unsuccessfully, to keep his hair out of the brown eyes flecked with gold he had inherited from his father.

His mother covered the story beneath the photograph with her hand. "I saw this woman's enchanting face lying on the breakfast table and could not resist its charm," she said. "I wondered at once who she was, but I thought it would be more fun for us to guess than to simply read the story." She settled herself comfortably, leaning back against the settee. "You tell me your story about her, and I'll tell you mine, and then we'll see who's closest."

Paul examined the prim-lipped woman with hollow cheeks, her dark hair pulled severely back over her ears. She did not look as though she knew what laughter was, much less how to do it. He crossed his arms and pursed his lips, thinking. "I say her name is Ethel Lucille Davies." He had read the name once, though he couldn't remember where, and was proud of his inspiration. "She's awful old, probably almost thirty—an old maid." He grimaced at Sophia. "Who would marry her anyway? I couldn't look at her face every morning before I was properly awake."

Sophia ruffled her son's hair. "It's enough to make you stay in bed altogether, or sneak out the window by a dangerous tree limb just to avoid such an eventuality," she said.

Glancing at his mother from the corner of his eye, Paul raised one eyebrow in perfect imitation of his father's favorite expression when he was amused or skeptical. "You'd have to buy a special house with a tree outside the bedroom window, and test the branch to see if it was strong enough."

Sophia narrowed her lips in mock disapproval. "You've diverged from the story of Ethel Lucille."

Paul turned his attention back to the photograph. "Ethel Lucille came from England, where she lived with a maiden aunt." He paused, gnawing on his lower lip. Then he grinned. "Because the Victoria city council wants her to start a library. She's devoted to her books, you see!" he cried in triumph.

Sophia wondered how her eight-year-old son knew a word like *devoted*. What's more, he was far too good at imitating Edward. "Is she now?"

"Oh, yes," Paul said earnestly. "She had them with her on the ship. She'd kept them in tidy piles in her aunt's cottage for years. Only on the way to Victoria, the ship hit some rocks in the Sound and sank."

"Poor, distraught Miss Ethel. Whatever did she do?"

Paul sat up, backbone rigid. "She gathered her books, tore the door from the captain's cabin, and abandoned ship, swimming in the icy water but keeping the books afloat. So now she's a hero. Ethel Lucille doesn't look very happy, but she is. She just doesn't think it's proper to show it."

Sophia threw back her head and laughed. "I don't even want to try a story," she gasped. "It can't be as good as yours."

"But you must," Paul said sternly. "It's part of the game. Rules are the thing, you know. Can't break the rules."

Sophia frowned. She suspected Paul was quoting her father from one of his voluminous letters, but decided not to pursue the question. She was having too much fun. "All right. I'll call her Abigail Wilson Smythe. She looks so severe because her husband wants to obtain the post of Governor of British Columbia, and she knows it's a serious business. They've put in her picture instead of her husband's because he was too shy to stand in front of the camera. Abigail is feeling a bit peeved."

Sophia tapped her lips with her forefinger. "She's just had a long talk with Teddy, that's her husband, and explained that this time she will go in his stead, but that, really, if he's going to go making great plans, he must follow through himself. He shall have to overcome his shyness, and that's that. She explained to the photographer, who sympathized, but regretted that she felt the need to express her feelings at such length."

She crossed her arms to indicate she was finished, thereby uncovering the story underneath the photograph. "Now," she said, "what does it really say?"

Paul started to read, began to chortle until he was doubled up and rolling on the floor. Consumed by curiosity, his mother picked up the paper and read about Mary Ann Lawrence, who had married one man in England, one in New York and one in Victoria. She became bored rather easily.

Now, however, all three had converged on Vancouver Island and were promising disruption and general mayhem if Mary Ann did not abide by her several marriage vows. She had been heard to remark that the husbands took things far too seriously and ought to worry a little more about enjoying themselves and a little less about causing a scandal. She herself was quite capable of that without their help. "No wonder she looks so grim. She is trying desperately not to laugh at the photographer, who probably thinks she should be ashamed."

"Scandalous," Paul snorted. "Utterly scandalous."

Another word bigger than he was, Sophia thought. Her son was stretched out on the rug, arm flung above his head, chuckling in spurts. Sophia shook her head. "We're not very good judges of character, you and I. We shall have to try to do better."

Paul doubled up laughing, and his mother joined him, until both were breathless.

Clara found them in a most unbecoming tableau upon entering the parlor a few minutes later. She tapped a letter against her hand and did not speak a word. Her squinting eyes and prim lips told them everything. "Mr. Palmer dropped by to leave this, Mrs. Ashton," she said in her most formal voice. "He was in Victoria yesterday and picked up the post. I thought it was most kind of him, but he refused to share a cup of tea with you. Perhaps he guessed what he would find."

Sophia rose and took the letter, noting, as she did so, the glint of mischief in Clara's eyes. "You may bluster all you like, but we know you too well. If we behaved properly, you'd give notice in an instant, you'd be so bored," Sophia informed her with equal formality.

"No doubt," Clara said, turning sharply on her heel so they would not see her laughing.

From his awkward position on the floor, Paul saw his mother's skin turn gray. He leapt to his feet and peered at the letter. "It's from Grandfather, isn't it?"

With a sigh, Sophia nodded. Her father had not approved of her marriage to Edward Ashton, had refused to answer her letters for years after she left Boston. But she had continued to send him news, and lately, now that Paul was growing up, he had begun to write again. She fervently wished that he hadn't.

"Shall I read it to you?" Paul asked. "It doesn't upset me as much."

His mother smiled at him fondly and settled herself on the horsehair sofa. "I am not made of breakable china, Paul. That's exactly what I've been trying to explain to my father. Here, come sit beside me." She opened the envelope, breaking the formal wax seal.

Dear Sophia,

I have read your latest letter with horror. Have you lost your mind? How can even you be so foolish as to remain in such a lawless place? Do you not worry that you are in danger, not only from the savages who people those islands, but also from the influence of your less than wise husband? Do you not realize your helplessness, and my grandson's, with no one there to protect and direct you?

I am convinced absolutely that that godforsaken Island is no place for my grandson to be raised. How can he possibly be educated properly or even associate with the proper sorts of people? How, for that matter, can you, who were raised for better things?

You must not be unfair to young Paul just because you are selfish and think only of your own pleasure.

Sophia dropped the letter and began to pace before the low-burning fire. It was late August, and though the mornings were brisk, the days were usually warm. As she walked, grasping the folds of her skirt distractedly, she grew flushed and pale by turns. "I wish he'd never forgiven me," she said.

Paul picked up the letter and read the last line, which he was fairly certain his mother had not. It said, "Come home to me. Please."

He ran his fingertip over the words that made him hurt inside. He thought his grandfather might feel that way too. "Mama," he began, "do you know what he's saying?"

Sophia shook her head so her hair flew wildly about her shoulders. "I know it, unfortunately, all too well."

She had not meant to speak so harshly. She tried not to let her father upset her, but nearly always failed. She still wanted to please him, even after all those years of silence, when she thought he had forgotten her.

She realized her son was watching in concern. "I'm sorry, Paul. He always affects me this way. Leave me alone for a bit. I'll soon be myself again, I promise."

Paul shrugged helplessly, but knew there was no point in arguing. When his mother made up her mind, not the Governor or the Queen or all the foreign princes could change it. "I hope so," he said. "I wouldn't want to give the flowers I've gathered to Clara. They would only make her sneeze."

"I shall appreciate them," Sophia assured him. "What on earth would I ever do without you?"

"Wander helplessly in the wilderness, I should imagine," he replied in his father's words and his rich, laughing voice.

Chapter

24

Flora stood in the kitchen, cutting up leftover venison for the stew she was making for supper. She had opened the checked gingham curtains, pleased with the warmth of the sun despite the heat from the huge fireplace and the wood-burning stove that smoldered under the tin kettle. She reached up with one sticky hand to push the unruly hair from her cheek, wishing she had Saylah's thick, straight hair. Flora's own hair was neither short nor long, but halfway between and so curly that no matter how she restrained it, there were usually more tendrils around her neck and forehead and cheeks than in the knot at the back of her head.

She thought of Jamie, alone in his dark room, and a murmured prayer came to her lips, as it so often did these days.

Saylah stopped in the doorway. Restless after her confrontation with Julian, she had stayed in her room only long enough to dress and quickly braid her hair. Thinking longingly of warmth and light, she had headed for the kitchen.

mFlora was damp with sweat from the heat of the fire, and her tight collar was unbuttoned. She was not simply mouthing words like many of the whites who prayed in church; this prayer came from her heart.

A deeply rooted instinct sent Saylah across the plank floor to cover

Flora's hand with hers. She had been told too often it was for this she had been born. "Your voice is strong. I could not help but hear," she said.

Flora looked up, embarrassed. "Ye caught me prayin' to the Lord, though ye've nothin' but my word that 'twas no' the kelpies I was callin'. Sometimes I need to hear my own voice, when the quiet gets so loud it hurts to listen." She did not know why she spoke so freely, but she felt easy looking into Saylah's compassionate eyes. Those eyes—she had seen them before. Flora's mother had had such eyes. Eyes that saw more than you could touch with your fingers or hold in your hand.

"The school was that kind of quiet," Saylah replied. "I used to whisper the songs of my People under my breath while the missionaries talked of knowledge and wisdom yet did not try to know the hearts of we who listened. Their words were cold, like blasts of winter air."

Flora was shocked, but only for a moment. She had met several of the missionaries who ran the school, had heard a few cold and heartless remarks. "Can ye forgive them?"

Saylah started. "Who?"

"The missionaries, for what they tried to make of ye, what they tried to take *from* ye."

Saylah looked thoughtful. "There is no need to forgive them. I chose to be there, to learn what I could not learn on my own. They took from me only what I allowed them to take, and that was very little." She paused, hesitated, then continued. "They taught me what I felt the need to know. I do not think of them unkindly."

"'Tis a saint we've found," Flora said under her breath. "And no doubt a saint we're needin'." She raised her voice. "I've finished with the meat for stew and have a mind to get some vegetables. I've no' shown ye the garden yet. I've worked hard to make it grow, but 'twas no' all work, if ye ken what I mean."

"I know what pleasure it brings to work in the earth. It is not the same as the toil the missionaries speak of so fondly. And I am always happy to feel the air on my face."

Flora stifled a smile and nodded with approval. "Well, so ye shall." She wiped her hands on her apron once more and opened the plain pine door eagerly.

Both women stopped when the door closed behind them, Saylah to let the breeze caress her face and Flora to admire the carefully tended rows of her garden. "I've three areas, ye see," she said proudly. "One for vegetables, one for herbs, and one for flowers, though the flowers are near finished for the year."

Saylah heard the pride in Flora's voice, saw her bend over wispy green leaves to pull a weed, then lovingly pat the soil back into place.

"'Tis here I like to spend my mornin's, after I've been to see Jamie, of course." She looked up to find Saylah watching; there was an air of expectancy about the Indian, a deep and troubling curiosity, but she remained silent, her questions unasked. Flora was impressed by her restraint. She sat back on her heels and motioned the girl down beside her. "If ye don't mind gettin' your gown a bit dirty."

Saylah laughed in her silver voice and Flora paused. Such pure, lovely laughter. She had not heard the like for many a long month.

Saylah herself seemed surprised by the sound. "I am Salish," she explained. "I wore no shoes until I joined the missionary school, no long dresses or petticoats. I spent most of my life kneeling in wet sand or on mossy banks or burrowed in among forest vines and roots. If my gown gets dirty, it will wash clean." She leaned forward, pressed her hands into the tilled soil. "It is so good to smell the earth again."

Saylah's face was transformed as she looked beyond the garden to the forest, raised her hand, full of earth, inhaled deeply, let it fall, crumbling through her fingers.

"This is where ye belong, no' inside a stout, dark house," Flora declared.

Saylah looked her in the eye. "I belong where I am. Do not pity me because I wear white clothes and live in a white house. That does not change the earth and sky, the trees and wind and water. Such things cannot be taken from me, so I shall never be in need." She remembered Julian snarling, *I think you should go in*, but closed her ears against the sound.

Flora nodded and turned back to the garden. "In autumn we'll be bringin' in the vegetables and storin' them for winter," she explained, "and dryin' the herbs. We've no' enough meat smoked and put by, but there's time yet." She didn't sound at all certain.

Saylah was only half listening. She knelt, hands buried in the soil, wondering why anyone would take the time and effort to clear and till and plant such orderly rows of vegetables when just down the hill was a forest full to bursting with herbs and roots and tasty bulbs. Flora, or more likely Julian, had put up a fence, carefully, watchfully, to keep the forest out, yet the forest itself was a garden richer, more lush, more fertile than any man could plant.

"I suppose ye know all about growin' things," Flora said, "and here I am makin' a fool of myself."

"You could not do that, not when you speak of a place where you are happy." She would have to find a way to get Flora into the woods, to show her its treasures without hurting her pride.

Flora beamed, wiping her damp forehead and leaving a smear of dirt behind. "That I am, lass." The clouds drifted over the sun, casting a long shadow on the earth. "Even now."

In companionable silence, the two women walked through the garden to the edge of the apple orchard with its five new trees. "I have never seen such fruit," Saylah said. "It is beautiful."

"Aye, and precious too, as ye'll soon be learnin' for yourself."

They worked their way back to the vegetables, dug up some potatoes, carrots and onions, then went inside to prepare them for dinner.

No sooner had Saylah shut the door than she heard a thunderous cracking of wood and stared out the window, hand at her throat.

Flora joined her curiously. "What is't?"

She followed the girl's intent gaze to where Julian stood at the far end of the house, cutting logs into pieces small enough to be carried inside for the double-sided fireplaces of fine, unusual stone.

He raised the ax high and brought it crashing down, recklessly splitting a piece of oak in two. He knocked aside the fragments, thrust another log in place, and swung again, wildly. At first it looked like he would miss, but at the last instant, he aimed and broke the solid log in half. His face was set in rigid lines, his aristocratic features blurred by sweat and dust, his hair wet, dirty and tangled.

Saylah gasped when he swung the ax for the third time, waving it in a circle over his head. It slipped in his damp grip; he caught it just before it flew off into the sky. Nostrils flared, Julian used his sleeve to wipe the grime and sweat from his face, stained with more than the heat of the sun.

Gripping the windowsill, Saylah tried to still her racing pulse, to swallow the unpleasant taste in her mouth. She felt a flicker of recognition at Julian's violence, but forced the thought back into darkness. Her palms grew damp with the strain of trying to silence the clamoring voices in her head. "Why is he so angry?" she asked when she could speak calmly. She did not stop to wonder if the question was rude or intrusive or presumptuous; she only knew she must have the answer.

Flora glanced at her in astonishment, stunned as much by Saylah's pallor as by her question. "I don't think 'tis anger—" She broke off to stare at Julian battling the woodpile with fierce resolution, incautiously endangering himself and any other who might pass by. All at once, after so many years, she saw what Saylah had recognized in a few brief seconds. Julian was eaten up with rage.

She was disturbed by his frenzy, but more disturbed that she had never noticed it before. She had not wanted to. She knew there was nothing she could do for him, just as there was nothing she could do for Jamie. "Did ye never learn no' to say what ye're thinkin'?"

Saylah whirled, raised her hands in instinctive defense, but Flora's eyes held no accusation, only admiration. Perplexed, the girl considered. "With the missionaries I learned quickly never to reveal my real thoughts. They did not wish to hear my truth; they had their own, you see. But among my People—as long as what I said was not untrue or unkind, I always spoke my thoughts." She looked away. "But that was long ago."

The sharp splintering of wood drew Flora's attention back to Julian, bent over the stump, kicking away the damaged log so furiously that they heard the crack as it met his booted toe.

Saylah bit her lip, fighting back a wave of empathetic anger. She was so distressed that she did not notice Flora's hand holding hers.

"I didn't know 'til ye made me see it that he was angry. Grieving, aye, that he is, and has been since I first knew him."

"His father has been ill for so long?"

Shaking her head, Flora drew Saylah away from the window. "He lost his mother when he was but a bairn." She would not meet the girl's eyes, and her voice was strained.

Saylah contemplated Flora's pinched lips. Perhaps, after all, she had misunderstood about Simone. "How did she die?"

Flora shrugged with elaborate unconcern that fooled no one. "She's no' dead, so far as I know. I thought I'd told ye before." The sound of the ax biting into wood disturbed them for the third time, and Flora wrung her hands. "Poor lad."

"Surely he is no longer a boy."

Flora concentrated on the one thing that could calm her troubled thoughts—her work. She began to peel potatoes while Saylah sliced carrots and onions. "In some ways, he never was a boy," his stepmother said sadly.

Saylah felt the same unnerving sense of recognition. "Because of his father's illness?"

Flora straddled a chair and leaned her elbows on the clean pine table. "Sit, lass, for I'll no' be answerin' such questions twice. I don't know why I'm answerin' once, if I tell ye true. Except that ye remind me of my mother, God rest her soul, and she was a good woman, kind and caring and wise."

Saylah began to object, but Flora waved a hand to stop her. "Hear what I've got to say while I've still a mind to speak. Even before Jamie became ill, he was no'—well—a practical man, I suppose ye could say. My Jamie dreams the dreams and has the visions, and Julian makes them real."

Without being asked, Saylah found two cups, added tea and the water that had been kept hot on the stove. She still marveled at how easily and quickly she could cook on a wood-burning stove. She thought of the endless ash-covered rocks it had taken to boil a single cup of water, and was impressed by the ingenuity of the Stranger who had thought of a better way.

She offered a cup of tea to Flora, who took it gratefully, and cradled her own in her cold hands.

"How can I show ye what I mean?" Flora gazed upward for inspiration and it came, like a whisper from the smoke-stained ceiling. "There was the time long since when Jamie decided to make his fortune trappin'. He was so enthusiastic, he bought all the gear, and wantin' to catch beaver, naturally, my Jamie got only bear traps. Julian traded them back, makin' sure that this time they had the right kind. Then they went to set the traps. Julian was lookin' for sloughs and channels upstream. He'd talked to the old trappers, ye ken, and learned the best way to catch lynx and beaver and marten.

"But Jamie had his own ideas. He said they should go downriver if the others had gone up. To try new places, he said, that had no' yet been discovered. Jamie was always one for seekin' out new places. Julian followed, knowin' he'd have to come back later and move the traps his father set."

Flora shook her head affectionately. "And Jamie, ah, Jamie. He was enjoyin' the beauty of the woods and the sound of the runnin' river and the sigh of the wind so much that he put the traps down, one after another, and not one did he set so it was ready to spring."

Chin in her hand, she imagined the scene. "Julian sneaked back later and moved them all, set them, and waited to see what he would catch. While he was away, Jamie had discovered the wheat was growin' tall and golden, and he'd watch it wave and ripple by the hour. Cast a *sian*, a spell on him, had that wheat, and he forgot all about traps and furs and the money they could bring."

Saylah began to like Jamie, who seemed to hear the call of his heart and follow where it led him.

"So 'twas Julian who remembered, who went out daily 'til the traps were full. When he brought the animals home, 'twas he and I who skinned 'em and prepared the pelts. Julian had learned from the Indians, and well they taught him too." She smiled at Saylah, unafraid to admit that the Salish had known what the whites did not.

Saylah grinned back.

"'Twas then that father and son went into town to sell the pelts. Jamie, bein' the charmer he is, gathered the men, captivated them, while Julian bargained like the best of them, so they came home that night with money in their hands. Julian was that proud, he fairly burst with it." She paused, rubbing her chin thoughtfully.

"Jamie came back from Victoria with somethin' more. He brought new stories—magical stories of great men and evil and how the good men won the day. We all listened by the hour, bewitched, we were, and no denyin' it. But 'twas Julian's good sense that let us eat that winter and bought the seed for next year's grain and some new apple trees. That's how 'tis with the two of them. Jamie dreams and Julian works." She glared at her half-empty cup. "'Twas like that once, anyway."

Saylah remembered Julian's fury. "Is he angry because he must care for his father and do the hard work alone?"

Flora considered, swirling the tea leaves in the bottom of her cup. "The lad loves Jamie so much, he would do anythin' to make him happy or keep him safe. Besides, Julian likes to work hard, to see the fruits of what he's done. 'Tis why he loves this ranch. Jamie bought the land and started the clearin', but 'twas Julian who made it last." She glowered at the scrubbed tabletop. "Sometimes—" She hesitated, met Saylah's steady gaze, and went on. "Sometimes I wonder if he works just to be workin', no' because the work needs to be done."

"Does he work to forget the past and not to build the future?" Saylah knew the answer before she asked. Had she not looked in the mirror of Julian Ivy's eyes a few days past?

Flora was startled by Saylah's perception. "I've had such a thought now and then, especially since our Jamie's been so ill." She seemed to realize how much she had revealed and rose abruptly to empty her cup into the cast-iron sink with the high, worn pump handle waiting to be primed.

Saylah wanted to ask about Jamie's illness, but she sensed Flora's withdrawal. "Do not ever wish these things unsaid," she murmured. "They have helped me understand and I am grateful. I would never use them to hurt Julian or your husband."

Flora couldn't help but believe her. There was a sense of quiet determination about her, as if she were accustomed to acting with authority. She had not learned such a thing at the Indian school. It had to be bred in her from birth or the missionaries would certainly have rooted it out and destroyed it.

Flora put out her hand while the steam from the boiling potatoes rose around her in clouds.

Saylah took the hot, damp offering and squeezed it firmly. "I am glad I have come," she said.

For no reason at all, Flora felt a tiny lifting of her spirits. "Perhaps the Lord's blessin' has touched us at last."

She spoke out of hope and simple trust. It frightened Saylah, that trust. The Salish had trusted her too. A long time ago in another world. She had left them behind—her People, her Chosen, her sacred power. She started to shake and turned away so Flora would not see her weakness.

Chapter

25

In the afternoon, Julian found Saylah working in the garden.

"Come," he said brusquely, "my father's asked for you."

Saylah felt a surge of excitement. She would meet Richard James Ivy at last. "When did he ask?" She knew Julian had not been back inside the house since she'd seen him cutting wood. The memory made her shiver, but there were other things to think of now.

Julian stared at the orchard, avoiding her eyes. "This morning."

Saylah stood to face him. Their meeting at the edge of the woods hovered between them, a lingering taste of bitterness in the air. Gripping her long braid in her hand, she said stiffly, "Why did you not tell me sooner?"

"I was working."

Saylah considered his unyielding expression. "Then why have you told me now, when you wish so much to keep me away?"

Julian stiffened in surprise, but quickly recovered his composure. "Because my father wants to meet you. I can't deny him that, no matter what I think of his decision." He did not add that Jamie had talked about a wind that had blown through his darkened room on the morning of Saylah's arrival, speaking through the play of light on shadow. Jamie believed she had been sent to them for a reason.

Julian had been shocked by the fervor in his father's eyes as he stared at the curtains and waited for another breath of wind. For the first time, Julian had begun to fear for Jamie's sanity. That was why he had not gone to Saylah, why he had looked for hard, demanding work to make himself forget. But another memory, of a white-clad specter in the mist, had survived his violent exercise and was with him even now.

"I know you are afraid for your father's sake," Saylah said, splintering his thoughts. "But I do not wish to harm him."

Julian wondered if she could read his mind. He shivered, though the air was warm. "I never thought you did," he called over his shoulder as he started toward the house.

Saylah followed in silence, but she felt Julian's distress, absorbed it as the clouds absorbed the morning dew. She asked no more questions. She would know soon enough.

She was startled when Julian opened the forbidden door and drew her quietly into his father's room. She saw a huge walnut bed hung with brocade curtains, a fine Persian rug, a carved chair and low marble night table. The oil lamp that burned on the burnished surface did little to lighten the darkness.

Saylah glanced at the face on the pillow and forgot Julian hovering protectively beside her. Her heart ached for the man with tumbled light brown curls and cheeks so pale they were translucent. Though he was a stranger, his fragility touched her deeply and at once. He was not like a man, but the spirit of a man, drained of color and warmth; all that remained was a fleeting beauty.

Even when they were ill and dying, the faces of the Salish had been full and brown and the strong shape of their bones had not altered. Saylah had seen other white faces pinched with displeasure or discomfort, pale from lack of sun, but their expressions had been alive and vital.

She stared at the dark eyelashes that lay on Jamie's pallid cheeks, his curved and faded lips, the slight uplifted corners of his mouth. It drew her closer, that face—so beautiful, so inexpressibly frail, so infinitely vulnerable.

She felt a stirring of warmth that had not touched her since she left the Longhouse. She felt his pain go through her body as she used to feel the pain of her People. She had forgotten the midday sun beyond these shrouded windows, the family who dwelt outside this little room, even Julian, who stood beside her. She was suspended in a world where shadows consumed the light.

She moved closer to Jamie Ivy.

Suddenly, she was staring at Julian's broad shoulders. She blinked at him in confusion, struggling up from the depths of her vision. Julian blocked her way to the bed, her view of Jamie's face. "Don't touch him!"

He spoke fiercely, every muscle tensed. She knew he would not hesitate to strike her, even break her, if she tried to hurt his father. They stood in the pool of yellow lamplight—strangers, enemies, bound by a thread so fine that Julian could not see it. He did not believe anyone could understand this kind of pain. Once Saylah had believed the same.

She took a step back. Her eyes held a question but no fear. Julian realized she was not intimidated by his strength or his anger, only perplexed. It was that more than anything which made him add more quietly, "Please don't disturb him. He's resting. I haven't seen him look so peaceful for a very long time."

Saylah shook her head, disturbed. "Not even when he sleeps?" She spoke in a voice that was strangely like music, though it could not possibly have awakened Jamie.

"Not even then."

Saylah stared at the place where Jamie's head rested. Although Julian's body blocked her view, he had the feeling she could see right through him to the dented pillow, discolored satin quilt, the pale white of his father's cheeks.

"Then he is very troubled." She met Julian's wary gaze levelly. "I know of such things. Illness of the body and spirit. Among my People I studied healing, and at the school."

She had never expected to learn medicine from the Strangers. But then a white doctor named Helmcken had come from Victoria when a girl fell ill with scarlet fever—the Red Sweating Sickness. The doctor had cured her quickly and efficiently, kept her apart from the other girls to insure that no one else became ill. Saylah had been dumbfounded. She had sought him out and he had told her of the drugs he used. "More complex versions of your roots and leaves and herbs," he'd said.

When he saw how fascinated she was, he had explained about ailments of the body, not the spirit. He told her if a doctor understood the body, he could cure many more afflictions, save many more lives. Even then, Saylah had thought the white doctor wrong to dismiss the spirit so completely.

But she had learned a great deal, had gone away thoughtful, haunted by the knowledge that she might have saved more of her People if only she had known what Dr. Helmcken knew. The thought left her sick with regret and grief.

"I think I can help your father." When Julian remained stubbornly immobile, she added, "It was for him that I came. I know that now." It was not the whole truth, but the part of it which Julian, in his pride and pain, might be willing to accept.

He shook his head. "You came to help Flora, nothing more."

"If that were so, the school would have sent Sarah or Betty or Jane. But they did not. They sent me." She decided to take a chance. "When I heard the name Richard James Ivy, I knew I must come here. The name called to me."

"Jamie," Julian murmured.

Saylah tilted her head, bemused by his tone. The single word was full of affection, grief, despair, adoration. It was, quite simply, a caress.

"We call him Jamie."

"Jamie." She wanted to feel the name on her own lips.

Julian hovered, unwilling to move away. He was wary of this stranger who was not like other women. If she were, she would have struck him when he found her in the garden. Saylah had spoken no word of reproach for his behavior that morning. Her one concern, even then, had been for Jamie. With a sigh, Julian stepped out of her way.

Saylah knelt beside the bed, reached out gently to touch Jamie's forehead. It was cool and damp. She turned to Julian, who watched closely. His mask had slipped and grief showed in his hazel eyes. Saylah wanted to reassure him but did not know how. "What exactly is his illness? Have there been doctors to see him?"

Julian's protective wall rose between them, clear and weightless, but impenetrable. Yet Saylah knew he was struggling with every ounce of his will to keep the wall in place. His long-practiced control was wearing thin. Gently, she insisted, "I must know if—"

"Several doctors have come," Julian snapped. "Among them the most famous on the Island, Dr. Helmcken from Victoria."

Saylah's eyes widened but she did not interrupt.

"They all said the same thing. That there's no hope."

"He is that ill?"

Julian did not want to answer. "Not precisely."

Confused, Saylah formed another question, but a sound from the bed stopped her.

"Julian?" a slurred voice said. "Have you brought her?"

"Yes, Father. She's here."

Saylah focused on the pale, luminous face on the pillow. Jamie's eyes were glazed with sleep, and he did not seem aware of her presence.

"This is Saylah. She's come to help Flora."

"Has she?" Jamie's voice was little more than a whisper, but the mist had cleared from his eyes. For a long moment, he stared at Saylah in silence. His eyes were blank, then full of bleak despair.

Saylah had never seen that look before. Not in Koleili when Hawilquolas died or even in Kitkuni's mother when she lost her faith and her last child all in an instant. Not even in her own distorted face in a lake edged with ice.

With painful clarity she saw that Jamie had released his soul, leaving only the shell of his body. She touched his hand, which reached blindly for something to grasp. Saylah was struck mute by his pain. She held his elegant, long fingers, so pale that the blue veins showed beneath the skin, so delicate they looked as if they could hold nothing, not even empty air.

"Your eyes," Jamie whispered with difficulty. He peered at her, looking for something. "Come later. Now I must rest."

He squeezed her hand and a current flowed between them. She did not want to let him go, but felt Julian shift restlessly beside her. She felt his protective wall quivering at its foundations.

"We should go," he said.

Saylah released Jamie's hand and rose. "I am happy to meet you, Jamie. I was welcomed here by *Ah-tush,* the deer that stands at the edge of your land. It is beautiful."

Jamie smiled vaguely, but it was enough. "Yes," he muttered. "Very beautiful." He closed his eyes.

She felt Julian's impatience and reluctantly left the room. Outside the door, she paused. He blocked the way as he had that first afternoon.

Now that she could not see Jamie's beautiful face turned hollow and empty, she began to think again. "What happened to make him this way?" She sensed it was not an illness. Such despair came from the soul, the battered heart, the spirit.

Julian formed a lie in his head, but the truth came from his lips. "I don't know." His shoulders drooped with misery and frustration. "He never speaks of it."

Saylah touched his arm lightly. "I will try to help him." She wondered as she said it if she could. He had fallen far into the darkness. It would be a long way toward the light.

"You'll have to ask Flora if it's all right. She nurses him." He was grateful to shift the burden of deciding onto his stepmother's shoulders for once. She was sensible and would not be bullied into what she did not wish to do.

"I will ask her if I might make him some fir needle tea. It would give him strength."

Then she was gone. Julian stood watching the graceful motion of her body in the bulky gray wool gown. Something she had said drifted back to him. *I heard the name Richard James Ivy and knew that I must come. The name called to me.* What did she mean? And why did he believe her?

* * *

Before the sun sank into the sea, Saylah climbed the stairway beside her room as she did each day. She passed Simone's sitting room without a glance and stood in the center of the huge, empty loft. It was lined on two sides by windows and doors that opened onto the upper porch.

There was a diagonal wall topped by a slatted railing that went from the edge of the sitting room to the far side of the cabin. From there Saylah could look down on the main hall and see where the family gathered between the two stone fireplaces.

The roof began to slope up above the low windows, giving the room an unusual shape, but Saylah did not mind. She loved the loft better than anyplace in the house. Her favorite window was the oval of blue grass she had noticed that first day. When she gazed through it, she saw the world in shades of blue, as if floating underwater. She was fascinated. The whole spacious room called to her.

She knelt beside a window; she could feel light and heat radiate through the curtains of shimmering blue shot with silver thread—silver on blue, like the path of moonlight on the sea the night she had walked with Hawilquolas and learned of his ancestor, alone and buried in a White Man's grave.

Saylah leaned closer to the warmth and felt the whisper of Simone's breath on her cheek, urging her to follow her instincts and throw open the windows, but it was not her right.

Turning away, she went to the low railing. There was no one in the main hall; the only motion was the flicker of flames that cast an eerie glow. Outside, it was full daylight, yet in the hall it might as well have been black midnight.

She stood for a long time, waiting, though she could not say for what. Flora came from the kitchen and tiptoed toward her own room. Theron followed, finger to his lips, warning himself to silence. They moved unnaturally, like puppets, carved and painted by someone else's hand. Jamie's.

Saylah leaned toward the shadows, made deeper by the firelight. Shadows full of secrets, heard in a breath of wind as a sigh is heard, without words or meaning. There was a chill in the musty air like the chill of a tomb.

Saylah gasped and cried out soundlessly. The demons sleeping within her stirred and she fought back a wave of terror.

She had lived before in a house tainted by acrid air, full of the dead, the dying, those without hope. A white-hot flash shot through her, reminding her she was real, and only human.

She shuddered. She had been hovering in limbo for three winters, neither living nor dead; coming back to life was painful. She released the rail and turned to look once more at the broad expanse of the loft. Here the ghosts were friendly. She knelt and closed her eyes, head back, skirts in a tangle of white and gray around her. With her hands on the floor, she felt the polished wood, and the sense of gloom lifted gradually, taking with it her gnawing grief.

Chapter

—◄ 26 ►—

"Dear Papa," Sophia Ashton wrote in her most elegant hand, dipping her pen into the crystal ink holder on her ivory inlaid Chinese lacquered desk.

In your recent letters—composed, I have noted, almost entirely of questions—you have asked for more details about our life on Vancouver Island. So, dutifully, I sit down to relate them, since I have a free moment from working in the garden and the murky gloom of the root cellar, where I will be spending part of each day next month supervising the storage of our vegetables for winter. I stopped on the way through the kitchen long enough to use the rusty water pump to wash the clots of mud from my hands. Now only the rims of my fingernails bear witness to the morning's activities.

Sophia paused to glance at her father's small pile of letters, all of which had arrived within the past twelvemonth. For Paul's sake, Douglas Charles was willing to forget past wrongs and start again, by berating his daughter soundly and often for her many failures. Sophia sighed and dipped her pen once more.

But I digress. Or perhaps not. The root cellar is, after all, very much a part of my life on this isolated ranch. Aside from preparing the vegetables for storage, I will spend much time and effort this autumn overseeing the slaughter of our fat, healthy pigs and their butchering and placement in the smokehouse. I hope things go as well this year as last; I only ruined four aprons with the blood.

Delicately, Sophia pushed an auburn curl behind one ear and straightened the sleeves of her lilac cashmere gown, edged in velvet braid and tiny pearl buttons.

How I enjoy walking through the smokehouse, admiring the hanging slabs of pork. It is dark, of course, and close, and the smoke makes one choke and cough horrendously, and I must, naturally, take care to avoid the pools in the worn hollows beneath the meat.

She did not mention that she sat now in her parlor on a lacquered chair with a blue silk cushion. The room was most notable for its pale blue silk wallpaper, matching brocade chairs and velvet settee, royal blue velvet drapes with inner curtains of French lace, and the rare plush Brussels carpet.

She would like to see Douglas Charles' face when he read her missive. He would drop his pipe, no doubt, and ruin his fine quilted smoking jacket. He would never imagine that when she finished the letter, she would take up her sewing to make a needlework pillow for Annie MacKinnon.

She did not mean to be cruel. She just wanted to tease her father, to punish him for the chilly silence that had been the only thing that marred her happiness for the past fifteen years. And now that the silence was ended, each letter was filled with predictions of disaster, recriminations, demands that she return home, where his grandson could be raised in the proper moral and social atmosphere. With few words and no sound, he managed to shout with reverberating loudness his complete lack of faith in his daughter.

Sophia sighed. She was thirty-three, old enough to know better. She wondered if her father understood how much he hurt her every time he said she would not—could not—survive in such a place. She had his pure Boston blood, did she not? His obstinate will? And she had something better yet—her husband.

Chin in hand, she thought fondly of Edward, his eyes alight with yearning for adventure and excitement. His eyes were tawny brown flecked with gold, his fine sandy hair slightly waved; it felt soft and giving beneath her fingers. He was a man to depend upon—tall, muscular, with broad shoulders to carry the weight of their success. But she had not known that then. She had taken a great risk in marrying him, one risk in a life full of predictable hours and days, months and years.

> In the autumn, when the vegetables have been dug up, the meat quartered and hung, I enjoy the smokehouse almost as much as I do the field edged by wild forest, where we keep the cattle. I never tire of watching the bulls and their antics. They seem so natural a part of this wilderness in all its rough and untamed beauty.

She looked at the lovely room pensively. She was not quite certain how the huge log house a few miles outside Victoria had been transformed into this beautiful home. It had happened so slowly, a little at a time, as Edward became more and more successful.

Sophia laughed with delight at the thought. In the middle of the wilderness, he had built her a palace. Her father, a successful lawyer who had lived all his life on Beacon Hill, could not have done the same. Yet her father had no respect for Edward, had always despised him and all he represented; he did not try to disguise that hatred in his letters—another recrimination, another lapse of faith and trust.

> Do you remember, Papa, when you suggested ever so gently that I should not marry Edward?

"I will *not* have you wed that blackguard!" Douglas Charles had roared until the crystal chandelier tinkled madly and the maid slunk away to the safety of the kitchen. "Not if I have to send for the sheriff and the mayor and the judge himself and post them at your doors and windows. He is nothing but a wastrel, a charmer. He will use you up like a bottle of fine whiskey and toss you aside as easily. Mark my words! Edward Ashton will never set foot in this house again."

He had not done so; Sophia had met him in the garden one night and they had been married by the very judge with whom her father had threatened to imprison her.

> You will be happy to hear that we are quite happy, even after fifteen years. He understands me completely, you see, and I him.

Douglas Charles had never looked closely enough to recognize the streak of recklessness in his own daughter. He had not understood her boredom with Boston society, her horror of marrying into one of the fine old families and turning into a matron with pursed lips and haughtily crossed arms at twenty-two. Edward had understood at once. For the first time in her life, she had met someone who shared her desire for adventure, for laughter, for *fun*.

"Fun!" her father had snorted with disdain. "What a common word. A word to be ignored and forgotten, I should say. Now, responsibility, respectability, maturity—those are words to live by. I have not trained you in the law so you might go romping off to some godforsaken country in pursuit of *fun*. I fully intend for you to marry another lawyer and become part of his business—not just his hostess and the mother of his children."

At that precise moment, Sophia had discovered her corset was far too tight and had gone into a fit of coughing which Douglas Charles did not recognize as laughter because he never saw the overbright glitter in her gray eyes.

I know you thought Edward reckless and irresponsible, but that's not true at all. Why, at this very moment he is at the neighbors chatting charmingly while I plan and organize the preserving of vegetables and meat.

She smiled when she thought of the real reason for Edward's visit to the MacKinnons. He'd planned it carefully, as he did everything. He wanted excitement, yes, but he also wanted luxury and a home to come back to. Sophia wondered if her father could begin to conceive of the five hundred acres they owned, the river, the forest, the fields of wheat and oats. It was breathtakingly beautiful and nicely profitable as well. Sophia loved this place as much as Jamie Ivy did—or had. Edward shared that love for what they had built out of nothing.

I must say that we suit each other very well. Even you would have to agree.

"I should say not, and most emphatically, too!" Paul had bellowed, pacing up and down the drawing room in his father's velvet dressing gown that dragged behind him like a royal robe. He had sniffed hugely, nose in the air, disdain written all over his pliant eight-year-old face.

Unforgivably, Sophia thought, she and Edward had been convulsed with laughter. Their son had been imitating Douglas Charles, and Paul was a very good mimic.

"Deplorable state of affairs!" the boy had boomed to regain their attention. He tapped his father's empty pipe on the table for emphasis and glared balefully at his parents, lips pursed.

Edward and his wife had laughed until tears ran down their cheeks. Where had he learned a word like *deplorable*? Sophia wondered. It

—— 197 ——

reminded her that she and Edward had better take more care about what they said. Paul seemed to absorb a great deal he was never meant to hear.

The boy had begun to strut again. Between gasps of laughter, Sophia took her son's shoulders. "We are quite ill-behaved to encourage you this way. It's unkind to make your grandfather seem a fool."

Paul had peered at his mother earnestly. "I don't think he was a fool, or that he tried to be unkind." He paused, brow furrowed. "He just didn't want to let you go."

Sophia's smile had disappeared. Paul had his father's brown-gold eyes and his mother's auburn hair, but just now Douglas Charles looked up at her through Paul's young face. "It will break my heart if you go," her father had whispered brokenly. Why hadn't she believed him? Why hadn't she bothered to tell him it would break *her* heart if she did *not* go? Edward had made himself a part of her; she could not imagine life without him, except as bleak and endless winter.

Paul had noticed his mother's distress and began to strut again, this time more flamboyantly, swinging his trailing robe over his arm. He had picked up a small round mirror on which a porcelain figure usually sat and placed it over his eye like a monocle. He clasped his hands behind him and cleared his throat several times. "Can't be done, don't you know," he intoned, his accent heavily British, his face reminiscent of an overdried prune. "Fffmmmph, fffmmph, ffmmph, dignity, fffmmph, fffmmph, family honor, fffmmmph, tradition, ffmmph, ffmmph, proper behavior." He pretended to peer at Edward accusingly through his monocle.

Sophia laughed in spite of herself. "Where did you learn that?"

"Jamie did his father, the Earl, for me once."

Edward and his wife had exchanged uneasy glances. Jamie's name, once commonplace, was mentioned rarely now. Things had changed, though Sophia could not understand exactly why.

You have said you are worried that we do not have the proper kind of people with whom to keep company here. Calm your fears, Papa. We have many friends, though because of the nature of the land, most of the early officers of the Hudson's Bay Company, who started the fort at Victoria, married Indian women. They were the only ones hardy enough to withstand the uncivilized country. But now other women have begun to come. Our neighbors and close friends, the MacKinnons, are Scottish, Highlanders who said they used to sit down for dinner with the sheep back home. Neil MacKinnon makes us laugh so much that it is worth sloughing through the mud to get to his front door.

Also, since Victoria has grown so much, many enterprising English merchants have come with their families to build huge houses and begin new dynasties. They're our own brand of royalty, you might say. So you see, you needn't worry. We are all very jolly and intimate, and not at all lonely.

Sophia did not mention Simone Ivy, who had had more royal blood in her veins than all of Boston society put together. But then, Simone had stayed only five years. Not strong enough to last it out, Edward had said. But his wife thought he was wrong. Beneath that delicate beauty, beneath satin and lace, velvet and pearls, had lived a spirit stronger than any Sophia had ever known. Certainly stronger than her husband, Jamie, who had hidden himself behind closed curtains and refused ever to meet the sunlight.

You will be delighted to learn that our other closest neighbor is the second son of an English earl who divorced his first wife to marry the good solid daughter of a Highland coppersmith. We started our ranches together and Richard James Ivy is Edward's dearest friend.

Nibbling absently on the end of her pen, Sophia stared at the painting of a light-scattered glade Jamie had given the Ashtons on their fifth anniversary. There had been a strange distance between the two families since Edward and Jamie had gone to Seattle a year ago. Sophia had not asked her husband why. She did not think she wished to know. She only knew she missed Jamie a very great deal.

You have hinted rather frequently that I am not quite as responsible as I might be, but I assure you, I have settled down considerably since Paul was born. As you know, we waited a long time for a child. And now that he has come, even Edward has changed.

Sophia laid down her pen and tried to put her thoughts in order. It was true that Edward had changed, but she couldn't put her finger on how. Sometimes she actually felt a shiver of fear when she woke at night to find him awake, so distant that he did not hear her call his name.

She did not want to admit that she was afraid of what she didn't know. Purposefully, she picked up her pen.

Dear Paul is such a blessing to us. He is always off exploring in the woods and brings back the most amazing things. Once it was a muskrat that he thought we could raise along with the chickens. Once it was a wounded weasel, but Edward was really quite firm about that. He wouldn't have it in the house for longer than a week, and then he made Paul keep it outside.

You would be proud of his interest in science, and all the wild roots and bulbs he brings home and tries to make us eat. He has not yet run into a grizzly bear, though he has followed the tracks many times. Rory MacKinnon met one face-to-face and has the claw marks on his leg to prove it. You know how boys are; Paul feels that the MacKinnon boy has outdone him and he wants to catch up.

Sophia smiled at the memory. Paul had indeed wanted to catch up with Rory MacKinnon, who had fled shrieking from the grizzly. Paul had been as close behind the older boy as Rory's flying feet would allow. He had not gone into the woods for at least a week afterward.

As for my own safety, I can put your mind completely at rest on that score. You seem particularly concerned about the Indians, but really, you need not worry. The Salish no longer use bows and arrows; the Hudson's Bay Company gives them guns instead, and they don't take scalps like the Apaches. There *is* one village called the Haida. They are very bloodthirsty, but they live on an island a little to the north and do not come down this way very often.

Besides, Edward has bought me a huge watchdog to guard the house. I still make a wide circle around him when I pass, and I always toss him a piece of raw meat. It's just that I'm not certain he can tell the difference between me and the enemy. But Brutus should do very well if the wolves do not get him.

Sophia looked up when Clara came in, feather duster in hand.

"You're looking very pleased with yourself, I must say," the housekeeper observed.

Sophia's smile broadened. "I was just telling my father about our vicious watchdog."

Clara snorted. "*There's* your vicious watchdog for you." She pointed the feather duster at the velvet settee, where Brutus, who was seven weeks old, had curled himself around a needlework pillow, which he had pawed and nuzzled into shape, so his body was protected by the bulk of the pillow and his nose just rested on the edge. His full black tail hung over the arm of the settee. A trail of black hair showed how many spots he had tried before selecting this one.

Sophia rose to pet him; she could not resist. Brutus grunted, thumped his tail, and gazed up at his mistress through one half-opened eye. Sophia laughed and Clara joined in. It was difficult not to; Sophia's voice was so clear, like crystal goblets touching rims, so full of pleasure and delight. It was infectious, that laughter.

Still grinning, Sophia returned to her letter, reading aloud as she wrote.

Oh, dear. Brutus seems to have fallen asleep. But I'm sure he'll awaken the instant someone tries to disturb me.

Clara burst into loud and tuneless song right above Brutus' head. The puppy raised his ears slightly but made no other sign that he had heard. "Lift your ears at me, will you!" Clara cried with mock terror. "Ooooh, he'll be a monster when he's grown, that one. I shouldn't like to get in his way, I can tell you."

Both women chuckled and Brutus thumped his tail twice.

So you see, Papa, my life is very full. I am quite busy, delightfully happy, quite satisfactorily sociable and imminently safe. You needn't worry about me or Edward or your grandson for a minute.

Your Loving Daughter,
Sophia Ashton

Chapter

27

Saylah returned to her room at sunset. She noticed that in her hurry this morning, she had left open the drawer of the small bureau which held her long flannel nightgown, two shirtwaists and a skirt, an extra gown and a pair of drawers, which she rarely wore except in the worst chill of winter. Beneath these Stranger's clothes she had hidden the shredded cedarbark skirt and pounded bark top she had made in secret at the school. Her cambric wrapper, draped over the bedstead, had not quite dried, because she had not lit the fire in the wood-burning stove.

On the bureau she had laid out her sacred stones. She ran her hand over the fern trapped in still green water, the earth-colored stone with an indentation that fit her thumb, the white feather in shiny black.

Her hair fell forward onto the bureau, blocking the little oval mirror as she reached down to open the drawer. She took out a stack of bundled pages—her collection of Salish stories. She had begun with the stories of Tanu and her magic in an attempt to try to understand what had happened among the Salish. She had become enthralled with recording these little pieces of her past, and had added other stories of her People and then the stories of the other girls. She touched the ink-filled pages with reverence, as she had once touched the sacred antlers. This was her magic now—her People preserved forever in the legends they most loved. She held the pages to her chest, then slipped them back under the clothes. They were her one luxury, the only real link between this life and the one she had left behind.

She felt a wrenching nostalgia that frightened her with its intensity. She had become used to the school, but this room was small and narrow, with a single iron bedstead covered in white linen sheets, a thick blanket and a chenille spread. To her it seemed tiny and confined; her breath came in short gasps, as if there were not space enough or air enough.

She did not light the lamp, but sat on the bed near the single square window. Saylah stared out longingly, her hand pressed hard against the glass. She had never grown used to gazing through glass that held her away from and distorted the world beyond. She did not understand the need for such a barrier; she wanted to shatter it and let the outside in.

"You want to smell the air, don't you?" Theron asked. He thought Saylah looked very sad, like his father when he stared at nothing, or Flora when she looked at Jamie and he did not look back.

Saylah turned, surprised but not frightened by the boy's sudden appearance. "Yes," she admitted candidly. "Yes, and to watch the sunrise. I love to feel the air on my face, and the light and the wind. They remind me of home." Her throat grew tight and dry.

"I thought so." Theron swaggered a little because he had been right, then crawled up on the bed and sat next to her, whispering confidentially, "I know because I want to too. One time I threw a toy at the window to try and break it. Julian made me stay in my room for *three whole nights!*"

"Julian?" Saylah asked mildly. "What did your father say?"

Theron grimaced and bounced on the mattress. "They didn't tell him. They said they didn't want to upset him. But sometimes I don't think that's it at all. I think it would only make him laugh."

Saylah gazed at him seriously. "Have you told them that?"

Biting his lip, the boy shook his head. "They don't listen to me. But I'll tell you a secret if you promise not to tell."

He grasped her hand tightly, his eyes full of hope. Saylah nodded.

"Sometimes I go into his room when they're busy and make him laugh anyway. He's always glad to see me. He says so, and I can tell by his face. The Look goes away when I'm there."

"What look?"

"The Look he gets when he's sad. Sometimes he sees things"—he groped for words as he tugged at the worn chenille spread—"things from before. They remind him of something. I don't know. When we're alone, he never gets the Look." Theron paused, sniffing tentatively, then inhaling huge gulps of air. "That's not you," he said accusingly. "But it smells like the woods."

Saylah smiled. "I told you I wanted to bring the outside in. So that is what I have done." They crouched down and she lifted the spread to show him the fir, cedar and hemlock boughs under the bed. "Now I can pretend I am sleeping in the forest among the friends of my childhood. I lie here at night and the scent of pine drifts over me like a blanket. You see that I have also put them on the bureau. Now the room does not seem so small or close, because it reminds me of the woods and the breeze through the trees."

Theron was impressed. He inhaled again, puffing up his chest and his sun-red cheeks. He let out his breath in a huge sigh. "I think you should bring the woods into the rest of the house. It's not as good as sunlight, but it's awful nice." His tone was light but his blue eyes were pleading.

"That is what I have been thinking. But I do not wish to offend your mother."

Saylah heard footsteps approach and Theron saw her glance up. He scrambled off the bed, on which he was not allowed to climb. "Mama won't mind." He smiled mysteriously. "You'll see."

She was sorry when the door closed behind him and she was alone. Turning back to the window, she pressed both hands against the cold, unfriendly glass and rested her forehead on the window.

Long after dinner, after Flora had kept the others talking while they ate, cleaned up the mess, and sat between the fireplaces of stone, after the fires had roared and died down in the main room, Saylah heard Julian slip into the room across the hall from hers. She had been waiting and was ready. Earlier, she had heated a small bowl of water and brought it from the kitchen. Now she bruised some cottonwood leaves and steeped them in the water. She pounded woodfern roots to a pulp, added a little water to make a salve, and carried the bowls across the hall.

The door was ajar. Julian sat on the plain bed, elbows on knees, hands spread, palms upward, his head falling forward, too heavy to hold upright.

She balanced both bowls in one hand and tapped on the door.

Julian snapped to attention, his face full of suspicion. "What is it?" He had not intended to sound quite so cold, but she had startled him, and he did not like that. He was so tired.

Saylah stood inside the door, staring, not at his face, but at his lacerated palms. "I have come to treat your hands."

Julian glowered in the light of his paraffin lamp, glanced down at his hands. They were cut, the blisters open and raw, the calluses split and caked with blood. It must have been all the wood-cutting. But that had been this morning. Odd that he had not noticed the pain. He glanced at Saylah suspiciously. "How did you know?"

"I watched you for a little while. Swinging the ax with so much violence must have injured your hands. So I have come."

She made it sound like a duty, he thought. A responsibility she could not ignore. He did not protest when she knelt on the bare floor, her bowls beside her, and took one of his hands in hers. She used a soft, supple cloth of some material he did not recognize and gently rubbed liquid into the broken skin. Julian winced once, then made no move and no sound.

Saylah did not look at him, but kept her attention on her task, disinfecting both hands with cottonwood, then smoothing on woodfern salve. Her fingers stroked gently, smoothing the rough skin, soothing the pain that flared and faded and flared again.

He watched in fascination the circling motion of her long fingers, graceful fingers, gentle fingers that touched his lacerated skin like magic. His hands grew warm in hers; she cupped each with one palm while she eased in salve with the other. Where her palm touched the back of his hand, he felt a strange heat, a friction he could not explain, because her hand and his were still. Only her fingers moved on his palm, massaging in the fragrant salve. She ran her fingertips up his scratched fingers, down again to the dry cracked skin between.

Deftly, she alleviated his discomfort, at the same time warming his body with her practiced touch. He was caught by the shimmer of lamplight on her hair that cloaked her body and brushed the floor. In the half-light it sparked blue, then black, glistening like a high, dark mountain pond ruffled by the night wind. He could smell the scent of fir in her hair as her fingers did their magic dance on his open, vulnerable palm.

"Does it help?" she murmured into the hush that had fallen upon them.

"The pain is gone," Julian said reluctantly. He did not want her to stop. She didn't.

Instead, fingers still massaging, circling, hypnotizing, she raised her head. "I meant, when you hurt your body like this, does it help to ease your anger?"

Julian stiffened. "Anger? At what?"

Saylah looked into his rigid face, hazel eyes hidden by half-closed lids. "At your father, I think."

Julian was horrified. "Because he's ill? That would be wrong. It would be selfish."

"Selfish," Saylah muttered. "Yes." Again she felt a jolt of recognition. How many times would she see herself reflected in this house of little light? This house of strangers holding close their secrets and their sorrows.

"Well then, this work that costs your body so much, does it ease your spirit?"

She released Julian's hand and wiped her own on soft cedarbark.

Julian saw her retreat, felt the cold night air now that her warmth had been withdrawn. "My spirit is none of your concern." He did not like the cold, but he liked even less how easily she had caused it by moving away.

"No," Saylah replied, rising with dignity from her place on the floor. "I suppose it is not. I must learn to accept that. But I was taught differently." She backed away, the bowls held tight against her chest.

As she reached the door, Julian relented. He could not let her go in anger. She had made his hands better, after all. "It does help for a while. It makes me forget. Isn't that how you calm *your* spirit?" he asked.

Saylah blinked at him, opened her mouth, closed it. Then she said softly, "I have always gone to the woods and the water to find my peace."

"And does it always help?"

She shivered when she thought back to days of fever and death and isolation. "No," she said, before she closed the door. "For some kinds of sorrow there is no relief. You know that, Julian Ivy, as well and as deeply as I do."

He did not move or speak or try to stop her. He sat, ashen, unmoving, staring at his hands, bandaged in soft, supple cedarbark, and remembered the mesmerizing motion of her fingers, the silver soft sound of her voice, sliding like a fine-honed blade between his ribs to where his pain lay hidden.

Chapter
—◄ 28 ►—

Julian raised his head from a fragrant cloud of tousled blond hair. Though the air outside was brisk, his naked body was covered in a fine sheen of sweat that accentuated the muscles in his arms and chest and back.

Lizzie traced those muscles with her fingertips, running her tongue over moist lips, undulating her soft white body in invitation. She wrapped one leg around Julian's, pulling him closer, smiling at the jolt of excitement that went through him.

She smiled a dazzling, intoxicating smile, ran her hands over his back, damp with sweat and smelling of the rich dark earth. She shivered as she dug her fingers into his buttocks; her brown eyes glowed at the tremors that ran up and down her spine. She raised her head, showing off her graceful neck, and stretched luxuriously, opening her body to him. His weight pressed down into the mattress and he tangled his hands in her hair and kissed her hard.

"Lizzie," he whispered, "you are a witch." He was not thinking now of the wild chase she had led him on a few nights past. Then he had wanted to strangle her. Now he wanted only to feel the pain of her fingernails digging into his back, the pain that flared to pleasure, arousing him further, kindling in him a hot bright coal that sent sparks shooting through his blood. Feverishly, barely keeping his body under control, he took her mouth, inhaled the heat of her, the smell of her body, liquid with passion and sliding up and down beneath him.

She put her hands around his neck, flicking her tongue over his lips, teasing, until he tired of the game and thrust his tongue into her mouth. She closed her lips around it, sucked greedily, while they lay together, panting, their bodies crying out for release.

Lizzie gasped when Julian raised his head and took her nipple in his mouth, circling it with his tongue, nipping, smiling at her little moans of pleasure. He felt his own need raging, his nerves tingling, the blood pounding in his head.

He entered her roughly, and she purred and moved her hips around and around, drawing him deeper. The smell of his sweat was in her nostrils, and she licked the damp edge of his shoulder, bit into the sun-browned skin, leaving a tiny circle of marks. He rocked with her, pressing, pressing down and down, making her body quiver and tremble at the desire that shook her. She gripped his back, demanding her own pleasure, and he began to move more slowly, circling his own hips, feeding the need inside her, teasing it from ember into flame.

She arched her body and threw her head back in delight at the splintering torment, the ripples of heat that made her cry out. "Julian!"

He covered her mouth with his, swallowed her screams, her pleasure, the heat of her flushed face. He began to quiver from head to toe, to feel the pressure rising, rising inside him, choking him with its power. The sparks flared, blazed, and he groaned aloud, tangled his hands in her hair and pulled, shaking violently in one last, furious surge of exhilaration. The sparks fell, burning, into coals again, smoldering deep in his chest.

Lizzie kissed him, biting his lip gently, running her nails up and down his back until she shuddered and lay still. She held him for a moment, but no longer. She did not want him to get too contented. Slowly, she rolled and climbed over him, sitting astride his thighs, wiggling her hips suggestively. When he reached for her, she slipped away.

The game was on again, Julian thought with a satisfied grin.

Lizzie threw a wrapper around her shoulders and started for the small wood-burning stove. "Want some tea?" she asked coyly, knowing he wanted more than that.

Julian propped himself on his elbow to watch her move. The wrapper hung open; every time she turned, he caught glimpses of naked, damp skin. Languidly, he stretched while she poured from the pot into a fragile china cup. An odd thing for her to have in this one-room cabin.

She was lucky to have that. If her brother had not stayed long enough to build it, she would have had to follow him or live upstairs at the saloon in

Victoria, like some of the other girls did. He was glad that hadn't happened.

His eyes narrowed as he watched Lizzie speculatively. He wondered sometimes about her secrets. All women had them; he had learned that when he was very young, long before he knew how much he needed the warmth of their bodies for his release. His stepmother, Flora, was the only woman he'd ever trusted completely. She had no deception in her, only warmth and sympathy and the desire for a man to need her.

Lizzie was swaying over the teapot, tossing her tangled hair down her back. Julian took a deep, harsh breath as his body responded.

"What's the matter?" she asked, grinning. "Can't get comfortable?"

Julian decided to tell the truth. "I was just thinking how awful it is to want you so much and trust you so little."

She stopped grinning, mouth open to object, but she couldn't think of what to say.

"It doesn't matter," he said. "It's part of the game. And you know how much I like the game."

Lizzie was not mollified. "You didn't like it much the other night. At least, not at first." She couldn't help smiling, remembering what had followed. Which made her stop to think how odd it was that he'd come back so soon. Usually she was lucky to see him once a week. Sometimes he stayed away for a month at a time.

Julian shrugged, got up slowly, slipped on his shirt and looked around for his boots. "I changed my mind. Couldn't you tell?" Now he was grinning and though she fought it, Lizzie had to respond. That's how it was with Julian. Not surprising, really. Everyone said that's how it'd been with his father too.

As Julian dressed, he saw the edge of a hat under the bed—pale leather with a red and green plaid band around it. He smiled bitterly. The hat didn't belong to him. But then, he had known about Lizzie before. "You don't come around often enough," she'd told him more than once. "I just like the company of men too much."

"Your tea," she said, bowing in front of him so her breasts brushed his chest and her hair clung to his hot, wet skin.

Julian said nothing, merely took the cup and drank. Then he caught her with one arm, holding her in a tight grip. "That's malt whiskey," he said, "poured straight from the teapot. I saw you."

Lizzie giggled with delight. "Thought I'd give you a little surprise. You know how I like surprises."

He thought of the hat under the bed. "Yes," he agreed, "I suppose I do."

When he sat down at the rough pine table, he noticed the present he had brought her at least a month before. "It doesn't look like you've opened that book once. It's covered with dust." He wondered why he had brought a volume of poetry at all. Perhaps he still harbored a tiny hope, or maybe he'd just wanted to prove something to himself.

"What do I need with books?" she asked, rubbing up against his side. "I got what I got. That's plenty for me." She put her elbows on the table and sighed. "Besides, books don't talk. I *like* to talk, to hear other people's stories—real people, who live and breathe and smell like work or flowers or cheap perfume. These book people—they're flat and stiff. Ink and paper people who don't know how to laugh."

She paused, winded by such a long speech. "And you know that most of all, I like to laugh." Her smile was sweet and inviting. Julian could make her laugh when he wanted to. His rare smile changed his sun-browned face, made it younger, softer, more touchable. But his body was every inch a man's.

Julian looked into her sparkling eyes and thought that she was happiest when two bodies were intertwined in tangled sheets. She had no grace, no beauty inside.

He groaned at a vivid image of Saylah kneeling beside his bed. He could still hear the sound, the anguish of her voice: *For some kinds of sorrow there is no relief.* He did not want to think about that. To remember how she had touched his scarred hands gently, how the lamplight had shimmered over her hair.

Fiercely, Julian shook the thought away, leaned across the table, and kissed Lizzie hard on her parted lips. "I have to go. There's work to do."

Lizzie pouted; he always had work to do, and she did not like to be alone.

She ran her fingers through his wavy brown hair, which still fell boyishly over his forehead, brushing the top of his straight, chiseled nose. His angular, aristocratic chin and cheekbones were free of beard, mustache or curling sideburns, though all were popular among the other men on the Island. Somehow that only made him look younger. Except for the cast on his hazel eyes which hid his thoughts but told her without words that he had grown too old too fast.

That was why she'd started the game with Phoenix, why she'd made him chase her through the moonlight, waited until he laughed aloud to let him in. His pain hurt her, and she couldn't heal it. She couldn't stand that. She'd always been able to make men forget everything but the pleasures of their bodies and hers.

She didn't like feeling this way, like she couldn't win no matter how many times she defeated him. "When will you be back?"

"I don't know." Julian rose, driven by a force he could not explain, and hurried into the yard, where his horse was tied. He mounted, then sat, puzzled, on the worn leather saddle. His hunger had not been appeased today. He ached with the power of it, lessened not one bit by the struggle with Lizzie, the release of their passion. He was not satisfied and he didn't know why.

Phoenix nickered in protest and Julian felt a weight behind him on the horse. Then Lizzie's arms were around his waist. "It wasn't enough for you today. You want to come back in and try again?"

Julian stiffened. How did she know? Was he really so transparent? He gave her an irresistible smile. "Not today," he said softly, dangerously. "Maybe after you return Geordie MacKinnon's hat."

Lizzie felt the rigid line of his back, the sudden chill in his eyes, and thought she was looking at a stranger. His anger rose between them like shards of splintered glass—cold, controlled, unforgiving. She had never seen anything like the sudden transformation in Julian Ivy. She wanted to run, but was perched precariously behind the saddle, caught between Julian's sharp-edged anger and the restive horse. "Geordie didn't—he just dropped by. I'd been alone so long. I thought it didn't matter."

"It doesn't." Carefully, Julian dismounted, lifted Lizzie down, his hands gentle at her waist. He didn't want to hurt her, just leave her behind. He himself was astounded by his anger. It had come upon him so suddenly, so long after he had seen the hat. Perhaps Simone had come and touched his cheek with her cold hand. What had been heat and hunger and confusion had changed in an instant to cold, hard rage.

Lizzie could not find her voice. He was acting like a gentleman, but she smelled danger in the air. She watched in appalled silence as he turned his horse and rode away. Her last glimpse of him was lying flat against Phoenix's back, the horse galloping at breathtaking speed over the sloping ground, the wind blowing Julian's hair straight back. She had the feeling he would ride like that for hours, fast and furious, with ice like dirty snow caught forever in his eyes.

Chapter
29

Saylah carried a small tray to Jamie's room. She had prepared fir needle tea, boiled hemlock bark and pounded licorice root for his various ailments, though she wondered if they would be enough. He frightened her, this man who looked like the ghost of an angel. He who had made this house and this family into a pale, reflected image of himself.

She pushed the door open and stopped, overwhelmed by the elaborate room lit only by a low-burning lamp. She had not noticed the opulence yesterday; she had seen only Jamie cradled in white linen.

There was silver silk fringe on the burgundy bed hangings which echoed the silver roses on pearl-gray wallpaper. The wine velvet curtains were heavy and rich, as was everything in that still, dark room.

"So you've come back."

Jamie's voice was clear, unblurred by sleep, and it startled her. Saylah managed to hold the tray steady, smelling the steam that rose from pottery mugs—the scent of home.

"Yes," she said, turning to the frail man propped on embroidered pillows against the ornate headboard. "I have come back, as you knew I would. I had no choice, it seems. The things which guide me sent me here."

Jamie Ivy looked at her with new interest, and she realized there was a flicker of life in his brown eyes. Even his translucent skin had a touch of color this morning.

"What things guide you?" he demanded. "Your sense of charity? Compassion? Or is it pride? Do you want to be the one to cure a man who can't be cured?"

Saylah put her tray on the bedside table. Marble-topped, she noticed, and uncluttered with the tiny details of daily life. She drew up a chair and sat down. "I do not think you can understand the forces which compel me. I myself do not understand. I know only what must be done. Nor can I say it is not pride." She leaned forward suddenly, her eyes locked with his. "How do you know you cannot be cured?"

Jamie felt a ripple of fear, the pull of her eyes, which asked for the truth and would recognize a lie. He did not know how he knew these things, but he *knew*. "You might as well take your medicines and go," he said, waving the tray away. "I don't wish to be one more doctor's experiment."

He had not answered her question, except through the tremor in his voice. "I am not a doctor, and I do not believe in your pretense at bitterness and anger, though you would have me go away hurt and frustrated and so leave you in peace."

Saylah touched his cool hand. "I see the gentleness in your eyes. It goes deep, deeper than even you wish to admit." She released him and sat back. "It will not hurt you to drink the teas. They are made of herbs, picked by my hands, dried beneath the sun, put back into the water which the sun took from them."

"You misunderstand. I'm not afraid. It's just that I don't want—" Jamie broke off, gripping the bedclothes too tightly.

Saylah stared at his claw-like hands and pellucid face, his dark eyes shining unnaturally in the dim light. She tilted her head, listened to his labored breathing, the rasp of a cough beginning in his chest. He retreated from her without moving, shrank into himself so that he seemed small and shriveled and old. But Flora had said he was only forty-seven.

It struck her then like an icy hand on the back of her neck. He did not want her infusions because he did not wish to recover. The thought made her desperate. "You choose to die," she said, disguising her turmoil with the tranquil music of her voice.

"I wouldn't say I choose to live." It was a simple statement of fact, toneless, and therefore frighteningly real.

He wanted to die; the truth lay in his eyes. The spark was gone because he had willed it away. Her head pounded dully and she fought back the weakness she could not afford. "If you will not let me make you well, will you let me make you more comfortable?"

Jamie Ivy felt the strength in Saylah's body, bent toward him, her face

— 213 —

half in shadow. He felt the warmth in her skillful hands. She did not tell him pretty lies or try to persuade him to change his mind. She did not lecture or weep or plead, not even with her eyes. He covered her hands with his and pressed them palm to palm. "If it would please you."

Saylah did not look away, did not allow Jamie to do so. "It would ease my pain a little."

"Pain?" he repeated. "Over me? Someone you don't even know?"

Smiling sadly, Saylah murmured, "I cannot bear to see hopelessness. I do not have the strength of will to face it. Especially not in you. I have seen how your family loves you, waits for you, praying every day that you will recover. For myself and for them, I cannot bear it. But I did not come here to heal my pain."

Jamie felt a lump in his throat and found he could not swallow. "Why *did* you come?"

"Because I am needed."

His curly light brown hair was rumpled from sleep, but his eyes were clear and wide awake. "Perhaps you are. My head aches. Have you a cure for so small a malady?"

Hesitating, Saylah rose. "If you will permit me to be too familiar. I must sit on the bed, hold your head in my lap."

Jamie shifted obligingly. He trusted this woman instinctively, irrationally, though long ago he had learned to trust no one.

She began to massage his temples with her fingertips. He closed his eyes, lulled by the motion, by the sound of her voice. She was singing.

> Rest and put your burdens down
> The sand will give beneath their weight.
> Rest and seek the stillness—
> Cool, alluring, soundless—
> In the ebb and flow of the sea.

Jamie drifted, aware of Saylah's hands as they moved over his shoulders, down his back, up again to his temples and the vein that showed through the fine-drawn skin across his forehead. Her voice came to him from far away, whispering, chanting, singing him toward the light.

"What happened to make you give up hope?"

He sat up sharply, turned and saw her fine-boned face surrounded by black hair, unbound around her shoulders. Her green eyes were luminous, kind, forgiving. He had not seen such eyes for a very long time. Once Simone had looked at him that way, and he had fallen—far and forever.

The silence lay between them, infinitely fragile, full of things unspoken, of threads so fine-spun that they were invisible. Jamie found that he

—— 214 ——

wanted to give her an answer. "I was walking around in a dream for most of my life. Then one day I woke up."

Walking in a dream. Saylah felt a shock of more than empathy, more than compassion. She felt an affinity that made her shiver. She had walked many dreams in her lifetime. Koleili's had been one, Hawilquolas and Tseikami's another. Then there had been the dream of her People, and Kitkuni's dream, and Colchoté's. The dream of Tanu, She Who Is Blessed.

For three years, she had been floating in a different dream. Not her own, but someone else's. Someone she did not know. But that dream too was over. It might have ended long ago. She was no longer certain. But now she was awake.

The rush of realization brought with it the tingling pain of a limb too long immobile, forced abruptly into motion. Her hands went hot, then cold. She began to tremble.

She closed her eyes and prayed for the stillness she so desperately needed. It came slowly, drifting down in the yellow lamplight, falling through the shadows, resting on her bent shoulders until she straightened and the stillness seeped into her blood. "Tell me."

For a moment, Jamie had been frightened by her pallor. He was so relieved to hear her voice that he answered without thinking. "I was a fool for a very long time, until I finally opened my eyes and saw the world as it really is." He shuddered.

"Was it so awful?" But she knew the answer. She too had seen the truth, and its cruelty had nearly destroyed her.

Jamie did not want to lie, because her hands felt pleasant on his shoulders, and because he knew with a bewildering certainty that she would never lie to him. Not like the others who had forged their word like precious gold, and with a flick of their fingers, turned it to dust. But there were things he could not speak of. Not yet. Perhaps not ever.

Saylah was afraid. She felt that she could reach through Jamie like a wisp of smoke. His substance, his spirit, was lost and wandering. "I have been thoughtless," she told him. "You owe me no answers. I am only a stranger after all."

Fragments of sound filtered in from the main room beyond. Flora's voice, Theron's, Julian's.

Jamie stiffened, winced as the spirit returned to his body and, with it, the pain.

"Do you hear them?" Saylah said.

"You said they were waiting for me." Jamie listened, eyes half closed; to him each word was a drop of water in a dry, hot desert, a touch of color on a burned-out hillside.

Saylah was amazed that he had heard and understood. She thought carefully before she answered. "They wait."

"But they know I never come out."

"That does not stop them from waiting. They have not forgotten how to hope, only how to make the hope real." Saylah's melodic voice filled the lamplight and the shadows. "I do not say this to hurt you, but only to reassure you."

"I thought—" Again Jamie broke off. Again he clutched the bedclothes with his hands. "I thought they had let me go."

"No," Saylah said softly. "They do not know how."

Chapter
30

After dinner that night, Saylah joined the family between the fires in the main room. She needed the warmth of the crackling flames, their red-gold radiance against her cold skin.

She had not accomplished much with Jamie, did not know how to help him. The knowledge left her frustrated and despondent. And now, though Flora and Theron chattered as if she had always been among them, Julian would not meet her eyes. She had been a fool to show him that she recognized his pain, but she had not been able to keep silent.

He stood at the fireplace, using a poker to jab at the snapping wood. Theron sat at Flora's feet, quiet for once, watching the flames. Flora herself held some sewing in her hand, and her lute lay beside her chair, untouched. Julian did not turn when Saylah sat down, but Theron gave her a wisp of a smile.

"How is Jamie?" his wife asked, trying to hide her anxiety. She had kept the question inside all day, but she couldn't wait any longer.

"I do not think he has changed, though his head no longer aches and he did not cough while I was with him this evening."

Flora sighed with relief. It was not nearly enough, but it was all she had.

"Is that good?" Theron asked. He could not keep his questions inside;

they burst out whenever he opened his mouth. "I mean, is he really better?"

Saylah could not lie to him. "I do not know."

Julian snorted in disgust but did not turn from the leaping flames. Theron glowered fiercely at his brother's back, but Julian was oblivious.

Silence fell and Theron pressed himself as close as he could to his mother's legs. Flora sewed industriously, to keep her hands busy, her mind from wandering toward the room where her husband lay. Julian stared into the fire, waiting for the flames to shift, to alter their shape, their heat, their color. But they did not change. Nothing did.

The past lay like a fine film of dust over everything in the room. It rested on the shoulders of the Ivys, drifted through their hair, tasted dry and bitter on their tongues. Saylah felt their unhappiness, absorbed it until her hair too was filmed with the dust of a past she did not understand, her mouth bitter with a taste she did not know.

Then a door opened and Jamie stood on the threshold of his room, lit from behind by pale lamplight, a silhouette with a white-painted face. Saylah was surprised at how tall he was—thin, elegant and aristocratic, even in his illness.

Julian looked up, astonished, then frightened.

"I thought it would be pleasant to join you tonight. It's been a long time since I spent an hour with my family."

Saylah stared in disbelief. Jamie met her eyes and nodded imperceptibly, but she saw and understood. He had listened. He had heard.

Flora went to help her husband and he leaned against her, smiling at her with affection.

"You can't sit here." Julian waved toward the carefully crafted but rigid chairs gathered near the fire. "I'll get your chair. You'll be more comfortable." He spoke quickly, trying to cover his delight and concern as he carried in the huge mahogany chair with its carved lion's claw feet, its regal back and well-worn leather seat. Julian placed it close to the flames.

When Jamie was seated, his son knelt before him. "Are you sure you're up to this?"

Jamie put his hand on Julian's shoulder and squeezed. "I'm sure. Do you think I'm so feeble that I can't sit by my own fire for an hour or two? I grow weary of the company of shadows. Not very good companions. They never respond to your questions, but they grow and flutter and eventually make the whole room their own. Out here they won't know where to find me."

Julian looked sharply at Saylah. What had she said to bring about this extraordinary change in Jamie's behavior? Because she was not certain, because she had caught the flare of Julian's excitement and pleasure, she smiled and shook her head.

Theron, who had been sitting open-mouthed, chose that moment to erupt into motion. He grinned, bouncing on the balls of his feet, started toward his father, stopped, then stumbled forward until Jamie's knees stopped him. Jamie held his youngest son by the shoulders and looked at him intently.

"Have I got dirt on my face?" the boy asked, rubbing vigorously at his cheek just in case.

"No," Jamie said softly. "It just seems to me that you have grown since your birthday. Maybe you've learned something important that's made you older."

Theron reddened in agitation. Could his father know about the chest? But no, he was not angry. His hands on the boy's shoulders were gentle, his expression full of affection.

Impulsively, Theron threw his arms around Jamie's neck. "I'm glad you've come out. Now you can talk to Saylah." He assumed a grave expression and whispered, "She's good to talk to, you know. She listens with her whole body."

Jamie smiled at the twinge of pain his son's rough embrace caused him. It had taken so little to make Theron smile. He had not been fair to the boy. "I've already spoken to Saylah," Jamie declared, half smiling. He held Theron away from him and admired his healthy round face, unruly curls and clear blue eyes. "One can hardly ignore what she says."

Flora was completely at ease, behaving as though her husband joined them every night. She put aside her sewing and leaned forward, dimpled elbows on her knees, hair curling about her face. The line between her eyes was less pronounced, and there was color in her cheeks, but then, the night was cold and the flames from the fire were warm.

"Come," Jamie whispered.

"I'd rather stay right here and look at ye," Flora declared. And that was that.

"Julian," Jamie said, "sit beside me."

Julian drew his chair close to his father's, Theron sat at Jamie's feet, and the two women together across from them. To his surprise, Jamie felt his pain recede. "Will you play for me?" he asked Flora.

Saylah had expected sullen silence, but realized she had misjudged Jamie Ivy. He really did not wish to hurt his family. Tonight his eyes were warm and his voice gentle.

Saylah forgot all that when she heard the first few lilting notes of Flora's lute. A moment ago the room had been full of dust and the smell of burning fir. Now, quite suddenly, it was full of magic. Saylah turned to gaze in wonder at the stringed instrument which Flora stroked tenderly, as she would a lover. The music that rose from beneath her fingers was so pure, so clear and sweet that it brought back to Saylah the birdsongs of her youth. The music curled through the air, drifted on the smoke, wove an impalpable gossamer spell.

Even Julian forgot himself. He leaned forward, hands clasped loosely between his knees. Saylah noticed for the first time that he wore a clean shirt and wool pants. His hair had been combed back from his face, emphasizing his broad forehead and sculptured cheekbones. Even his lips, relaxed, parted in soundless empathy with the flowing music, looked less rigid, soft and pliable and warm.

Before she could wonder at her own thoughts, Flora began to sing in a strong, clear voice.

> Then, when the gloamin' cooms,
> Low in the heather blooms
> Sweet will thy welcoom and bed of love be!
> Emblem of happiness,
> Blest is thy dwelling place—
> O! to abide in the desert wi' thee!

Even Theron had stopped fidgeting and sat with his back against his father's legs, eyes half closed, chin resting on his knees. Saylah smiled while the music made its way around and inside her, in the smoke that swirled and eddied, the sparks that flared and died, the cadence of silvery notes that danced and dipped and rested in her open palms.

Never had she imagined there could be music such as this. At the school, music had been forbidden, except for the hymns which they'd sung every Sunday in the bare little chapel. Those hymns and the organ that echoed up and down the valley had been the only part of the Strangers' religion that touched her. That and the candlelight. Drums and fire, booming rhythm and flickering light, these things she could understand and worship, but the words had been meaningless, empty.

But this song was airy, ephemeral, like the brush of a butterfly wing on her cheek. The music of the Salish—the all-powerful, all-encompassing beat of the drums—made her want to dance, to celebrate, to dream a spirit dream, to feel the rhythm of the earth move within her. She had been hypnotized by the sound of the drums that echoed and amplified her own heartbeat.

Flora's music made her want to drift, to close her eyes, to weep. Instead of her heartbeat, the lute echoed her thoughts, her hidden pain. It was so soft, so tender that it frightened her. And yet she did not want it to end.

When the last note faded, she found she did not wish to move. But for the others, the stillness had become a threat, a reminder of all they faced and all they feared.

Saylah forced herself back to the present. She leaned forward and met Jamie's eyes. "I wish that you would tell the story of the carved deer at the edge of your land. It is so beautiful, so full of power."

Jamie blinked at her. He seemed confused and ran his hands through his hair, further disturbing the uncombed strands. Then the intensity of her gaze brought him fully awake and her eyes drew him in, as they had done before. "You want to know about the deer."

Saylah nodded, watching Julian out of the corner of her eye. He had grown tense and was shaking his head in warning. His father did not speak about the past.

"Yes," Jamie said unexpectedly, "it's been a long time since we told stories together. I miss that."

Julian and Flora exchanged startled glances but did not object. Instead, they moved closer, eagerly.

Jamie leaned back in his chair, hands curled on the carved arms. "I came to Victoria from England, you see, where my father, the Earl, was still running the family estate. I was a second son; there was nothing for me there. But here—here I had heard that gold tumbled through waterfalls so bright and glittering with wealth that they blinded all who looked upon them.

"Julian was only a baby then, so I left him"—Jamie hesitated, added quickly—"on the far coast of Canada, where we'd been trying to start a farm." His smile was wistful. "I wanted the gold because it was rare and beautiful. Because few had ever touched it, held it in their hands, shaped it to remake their lives. And once I saw Vancouver Island, I knew it could happen. Here was a wilderness where dignity and stodginess and tradition did not mold lives into hollow, meaningless things."

He groped back through his memories, found one, and grasped it. "My father didn't want me to come. He'd never wanted me to do as I chose, since I chose to call myself Jamie. 'You should be called Richard,' he told me. 'A good, solid name with tradition behind it. Jamie has no dignity.' I didn't want that sort of dignity, not if it meant moldering away forever in the English fog. 'I'm for adventure,' I said.

"So I came, and in Victoria I met Edward Ashton, who had come with his wife for the same reasons." Jamie's eyes clouded. "At least, I thought they were the same. A song called me here, as clear as Flora's and just as lovely. I could not help but answer; the lure was too strong." He frowned.

"I don't think Edward remembered songs, not that kind anyway, the kind that live inside you and drive you on to make just one dream real."

He paused, unused to talking for so long, and the crackle of the flames grew loud. Saylah felt herself slipping into a time when the fire had been the center of her world.

"So we found a river that the sunlight made into gems and mined there until Edward decided there was no gold. We tried trapping for a time, but we were both dissatisfied. We realized at last that what we wanted was a home.

"So we went searching. I found this valley full of flowing waters and unexpected springs, smelling of pine and cedar, with meadows to be planted and huge old oaks to guard it. I knew it was home the moment I set foot here. It called me too, just like the gold. 'This,' I told Edward, 'is where I shall build paradise. This place asks for such a thing. Can't you hear it in the wind?'" Jamie rubbed his chin thoughtfully. "But I don't suppose he could."

The room had fallen silent; even the snapping flames were muted and their light kind. It softened Jamie Ivy's face, transforming him into a man who glowed with inner fire, with enthusiasm that radiated outward to his family, who listened raptly, their faces touched with adoration. Saylah saw how they loved him, and understood why. His charm was not studied or practiced or false; it was the irresistible charm of a man who believed in miracles and tried to make them real. His eyes were incandescent in the wavering light; Saylah could not look away.

"When we were ready to clear the land, we found the tallest, oldest cedar. An Indian said it had sickness in the upper branches which would spread if we did not cut it. That tree was beautiful, and I couldn't bear to see it rot, so I decided to take it down. We worked on it for a whole day with that saw." He pointed to the two-handled cross-cut saw Saylah had noticed earlier. "The misery harp, Edward called it, though I never understood why. Not then, anyway."

Theron had turned to face his father and sat with his elbows on Jamie's knees. He had not moved since Jamie began to speak.

"While we worked, the smell of cedar was sharp in the air and the breeze was rising. We coughed and sweat rolled down our backs and into our eyes and our muscles screamed, but we didn't care. Our hands were covered with blisters that rose and broke and rose again, dyed by the bark and blood and our own sweat.

"Eventually our arms gave out and our stomachs began to rumble and we found that while we worked, a wolf had been at our bag of provisions. I sat down for a minute to think. I remembered my father back in England with his very proper house and garden, while above me the wind wailed

— 222 —

and snarled through the trees. I wondered what he would say if he could have seen me then. There was no dignity in the sweat and dirt that ran down my face, no dignity in the grime, the smell of bodies heavy with work, palms red with blood and rough with broken skin. No dignity in sharing one grimy whiskey flask with my friend as if it were the finest claret in England. No dignity at all, or, at least, none that my father would understand. But I looked around me and was gloriously happy, and that was all that mattered." His eyes were glazed with memory and satisfaction.

"Edward built a fire—I'd never gotten the hang of it, you see—I thought we'd have to make do with water and berries when I saw a huge buck cross the ridge on the far side of the clearing. He paused with the sun behind him, silhouetted in the afternoon light."

Tears burned in Saylah's eyes, but she fought them back.

"We took our rifles and started around the edge of the clearing, downwind so he wouldn't smell us, stepping on pine needles so we wouldn't make a sound. When we got to the far side, I saw the buck on a hillock. He was even more magnificent than I'd thought; just the sight of him made me ache. His antlers rose against the sun like bent, grasping fingers, rigid with years of reaching toward a light too high to touch."

Saylah ducked her head, hands crossed, grasping her upper arms. She closed her eyes and let the words take her back and back to a night on a moonlit river when she had sung a buck to its death.

"Edward raised his gun, but the buck must have caught our scent. Just as he fired, the deer began to run, but my bullet caught him and he fell. It broke my heart to watch that proud buck stumble, but we were hungry and didn't have a choice. We carried the carcass back to the fire and left it while we finished the tree. I didn't tell Edward, but I hadn't the heart to cut that animal to pieces. He'd been so beautiful. I felt like I'd betrayed him."

His eyes were misted with sorrow for the dying buck, pride in his skill, affection for his friend. He leaned forward to point at the rifle on the wall. "That's the gun I shot it with. I bought another and put this one up for good. It was important somehow."

He paused, unable to speak. "Anyway, we worked and worked and when we were done, the tree fell so there was nothing but the stump, one man high, looking lonely and abandoned in the dusk. We returned to the fire and found the deer gutted and skinned and venison roasting over the flames."

"How?" Theron asked, so wide-eyed that the question came out a gasp. "Was it magic?"

Jamie smiled down at him. "I thought so for a moment. But then I saw a movement in the trees and remembered the Indian girl who sometimes followed Edward, doing chores for him, cleaning his clothes and cooking while we were out looking for land. When we'd eaten, she came from the woods with the antlers cradled in her hands like something sacred.

"She knelt on the other side of the fire and reached out with those antlers so near the flames that I gasped and half rose to stop her. But she only smiled, a mysterious smile I couldn't understand, and then she spoke."

"What did she say?" Theron prompted. "Was it in Indian so you couldn't understand?"

Jamie shook his head. "She spoke in English, telling us the antlers would bring us luck, that many had tried to bring the buck down, but we alone had done it. She said we should take the horns, which held the power and magic of the deer, and make that power ours. 'It is right that this should be,' she said. 'This only have I come to tell you.' I saw then that her hands were still red from the blood of the animal.

"She disappeared, leaving the antlers behind. I picked them up and, with my knife, carved out a hollow on top of the stump. I put the antlers there, and Edward and I rigged them to stay. 'It's our first marker,' I told him, 'to show where paradise began.' He just shook his head, as he often did, and stepped back to admire our work."

Jamie's voice had grown stronger, and the droop of defeat had left his body. "I looked at the outline of those graceful curved bones in the moonlight, touched the bark of the cedar, the soft fuzz on the antlers and knew this land was really mine. It was not a dream. This place, this wind and water and rich green earth, this moment, above all others in my life, was mine and mine alone. I knew even then there would never be another like it."

Chapter
31

Jamie was silent, his eyes cloaked in the half-dark of a moonlit night long past. He smiled and his face was transformed into an image unbearably beautiful, unutterably fleeting.

"The next morning," he continued, the lingering hint of an angelic smile on his lips, "I looked at the stump—beautiful and furrowed, like it had already been carved by rain and wind. That's what gave me the idea of carving a deer underneath those antlers, as fine as the buck himself. In a way it would be a tribute to him. I started carving, though we had little time for it once we began to build our ranches. Edward's is just down the way," he said, pointing for Saylah's benefit.

"But whenever I got the chance, I worked at it a little, and the priests and missionaries who come through began to work at it too. Some even came asking, looking for our deer, wanting to be part of it." He paused, obviously moved that something which meant so much to him also had meaning for others.

"When I sent for my family, Julian carved on it bit by bit. Over the years, it grew into the buck it is today."

"Doe," Saylah whispered. "A beautiful doe."

"What?" Julian asked. Her voice was hoarse with emotion, and reminded him that she had stood looking at the deer, touching it reverently, as if she had known and loved it for a lifetime.

Saylah shook her head, but Jamie had heard her. He guessed what she meant, realized with a start that of course no one would have made the animal a buck, despite the huge curved antlers. No one had ever noticed that before. But it was the tone in her voice, the quiver of her hands that made him take notice.

She raised her head to find everyone watching expectantly. She looked only at Jamie. "I wonder if you know that what you created is a miracle. Because it was made by many hands and many knives over many years, it is more than a sign of your victory. It is a sacred carving touched by many hearts. I did not know man could make something so precious, especially not a white man. I was wrong."

Saylah leaned toward Jamie. This man of mist and silver and golden firelight would slip into his room tonight to become a sad ghost of the man who sat here now, she mused. Already the glow was fading as the present replaced the magic of the past. She wanted to take his hand, to hold him here, in this moment, before he turned his back on his dreams. But she did not have that power.

As the stillness lingered and became strained, Theron jumped up and ran to Saylah. "Mama has sung a Scottish song, and Papa's told an English story. Will you sing us a song of the Indians? I heard one once, but I couldn't understand the words." He gripped her skirt in chubby fingers; young as he was, he seemed to sense that once the circle around the fire was broken, it would never be complete again.

Saylah started to shake her head, then changed her mind. Perhaps, after all, she could hold Jamie here.

Her own memories vibrant within her, she began to sing a song of her childhood.

> The moon lights the path of the water,
> Glides down the path of the water,
> Follows the path of the water,
> To the place where *Ah-tush* waits.
> Tonight I will not touch you,
> Tonight I will not harm you,
> Tonight, rimmed by moonlight,
> I am not hungry or cold or alone.
> For *Ah-tush*, the deer, is beside me.
> A reflection in the water,
> A silent watching brother,
> A friend in the moonlight that guided me here.

After the words died out, she looked at Julian, changed by the firelight and the presence of his father. Once again he held the mirror, not the thick, distorted glass of the window or the missionaries' tiny oval frames, but the mirror of the sunlight on the water, the mirror of the sorrow and the burden that they shared.

They walked together to her room and he stood outside, hands in pockets, hair falling forward. "I must tell you—"

Saylah felt an irrational fear. She could see the gratitude in his eyes, his dazed and wondering smile, and guessed he was going to thank her for bringing Jamie back to them. His brittle wall—the barrier between his living and his pain—could not withstand such an admission. It would crumble at his feet; he was not yet ready to face what lay on the other side. He started to speak and she put her palm against his lips to stop him.

Julian paused, reached up to press her hand closer, so she felt his warm breath on her skin. He kissed her palm gently, cupped her hand in his.

They stood, not moving, bound within a moment that spun itself out endlessly—fragile, full of possibilities. Yet they stood apart, strangers. Her hand on his lips was a caress, but also, somehow, an impediment. Neither moved. Neither could. They were caught, carved, still—waiting for something nameless that did not, would not, come. They were suspended, though they stood firmly against the floor, leaned hard against the wall. Only the meeting of palm and lips was light, barely perceptible—evanescent.

A door slammed behind them and Julian started, released her hand, and tried to speak. But no words came. He turned slowly and crossed to his room. He closed his door, leaving the hallway long and dark and empty.

Saylah trembled at the stirring that curled from her hand up her arm into her chest. She could still feel Julian's palm against her skin, his breath and the moist pressure of his mouth. She had never felt anything so acutely—the cold and the heat, the poignant pleasure and the fear.

But tonight she would be alone, so close to the memories of her People and the life she'd left behind that it made her ache inside. The kindling warmth, the re-awakening of yearnings born in an instant and long ago forgotten, Julian's breath and his parted lips, could not change that.

Chapter

32

Flora sang an old Gaelic marching song. Her voice rose through the steam of boiling dumplings, and she tapped her foot on the polished wood floor. Her cheeks were red from the heat, her hair disheveled, though it was still early and the sun had not yet topped the trees. She was enjoying herself.

She blew a stray hair off her forehead and plunged her hands with vigor into a ball of fresh dough.

"You are singing!" a voice cried from the open back door.

Flora froze, hands covered with flour, and turned to see an Indian girl with flowers in her hair. She smiled and held up her empty basket.

Flora motioned for her to come in. The girl had been working for a neighbor, Mr. Palmer, for some time, but Flora did not know her well. She came often to buy vegetables and apples, but, like the other Salish, did not speak much and kept her thoughts and secrets to herself. She had been startled by the sound of Flora's soaring voice into letting her mask of indifference slip, revealing her pleasure. "'Tis a lovely mornin' is it no', Ah-mah?" Flora asked.

The girl nodded, though Ah-mah was not her true name. The name her People called her was too precious to be shared with Strangers who would not understand, so she told each what they wished to hear. Some, like Edward Ashton, who knew her body as he could not begin to know her soul, did not use even the false name she offered, but Flora was different. The reflection of her face in Flora's eyes told the girl the Scotswoman saw not "an Indian," but the girl herself, or as much as she wished to reveal. So she asked Flora to call her *Ah-mah*, the word for the sad-voiced loon, a bird which the Salish girl honored.

"Sit and have ye a cup of coffee," Flora insisted, pouring out the dark brew and leaving white flour prints on the handle of the dented pot. She went back to kneading her bread. "Aye, 'tis singin' I feel like today," she said, responding to Ah-mah's original exclamation. "Mayhap 'tis because my work is lighter than before." She glanced back at the girl. "We've a new girl, Saylah, from the missionary school. She's taken a load off my shoulders, I can tell ye."

"You mean you have less work, more time to rest now that she has come, this stranger?"

Flora chewed her lip thoughtfully. "'Tis more than that, I'm bound, and she's no' a stranger either. More like a companion, a healer of old wounds, I'd call her."

"So." The single word, uttered in Ah-mah's soft voice, spoke many thoughts.

"She's taken me through the woods each mornin' to show me some new herb growin' under a tree, or a bulb I'd no' have guessed would taste as sweet as new onions. I've gone the past few days on my own, gatherin' this and that for our supper. 'Tis cooler in the woods than in the garden, more welcomin', mayhap." She would not soon forget that first day in the forest, when Saylah had shown her tiny hidden twinflowers, moss-covered trees that hung out over the river, making images in the water, red-breasted nuthatches, warblers, a graceful hawk.

Flora had enjoyed herself thoroughly, had forgotten the tasks that awaited her at home in the excitement of that day of glorious freedom. She had brought back an apron full of herbs and roots and used them that very night to cook the grouse Julian had brought. By showing her all the things she could gather in the woods, Saylah had given Flora a reason none could dispute to escape the house from time to time. Not Jamie, darling Jamie. But the house itself, which weighed on her shoulders, bending them forward.

Ah-mah nodded. She knew these things very well.

"Saylah has a way with Theron as well. She keeps him laughin' or workin' 'til he's too tired to be makin' trouble, and has him thinkin' the work is play. And my Jamie, well, 'tis no' enough to say she has magic in her hands. If his forehead burns, she makes the fever go just by layin' her palm on his skin. She makes miracles, does our Saylah, and no doubt about it."

Ah-mah stared, her fingers restless on the weave of the empty basket. She had heard of another who made miracles, who had left the People and disappeared. But that could not be. She was dreaming again when she should be working. "It seems," she said slowly, "that the one you call Saylah has given you hope."

Flora stopped what she was doing, contemplated Ah-mah in wonder. Why did it always take a stranger to see what was so clear, so simple, so extraordinary? "Aye, that she has."

"I caught it! Throw me another and let me see how many I can hold at once!" Theron shouted up to Saylah, who was clinging to a tall fir, her skirt gathered around her waist, her bare feet balanced on spreading branches, her hands and face stained with fragrant pitch.

She had worn her cotton bloomers, remembering Julian's cold appraisal. She knew that to the Whites a woman's body was something to be wrapped, disguised, altered by steel and bone. She had known she would be climbing trees today, which did not disturb her, but she did not wish to upset Theron.

Especially not when he had surprised her so pleasantly. The morning after she had shown him the boughs under her bed, he had brought Flora to Saylah's room so she could see for herself how fresh and clean it smelled. He had clung to his mother's hand, gazing at her with pleading eyes. "Couldn't we put branches in the rest of the house too? Then everywhere would smell this good."

"So few of the flowers are in bloom and they are difficult to find," Saylah had interjected. "But the fir boughs would do as well. They would cover the smell of the smoke." She did not say that they would add color to the toneless gray of the house.

Flora had been delighted.

Several days later, Saylah had found the time to get away for a few hours. Once the early mist burned off the ground and out of the treetops, where it had floated all morning, she and Theron had set out to collect fir, cedar, hemlock and any fallen leaves Saylah could fit in the voluminous pockets of the gingham apron she had borrowed from Flora.

With a dramatic whisk of the knife, more for Theron's pleasure than for her own, Saylah cut another branch and sent it floating downward. Theron stood, face tilted up, watching with concentration. As the limb got closer, he began to shift position, back and forth, side to side, bouncing on his feet in an effort to be at the precise point where the bough would fall. He had missed more often than not, but this time, the limb landed safely in his outstretched arms.

"Ha!" he cried in delight. "I caught it!"

"I am making it too easy for you. I will have to practice throwing them in a spiral to confuse you."

Theron laughed, dropped the branch on the growing pile, and turned to wait for the next one. Saylah tossed it to the side, and before Theron could get to it, another little boy leapt in and caught it neatly. "Now we've both confused you!" the newcomer called, laughing.

"Paul!" Theron was delighted to see the auburn-haired boy with gold and brown eyes, whose fine bone structure promised that one day he would have a very handsome face.

"Saylah," Theron shouted, "this is my best friend, Paul Ashton. His father and mine built their houses here together. I think they've known each other forever." He scratched his head, trying to conceive of such a great length of time. "Paul," he added, pointing upward, "that's Saylah. She came to help Mama."

Paul stared at the bare feet, gathered gray skirt and white bloomers and shook his head. "By climbing trees?"

"She's very good at it," Theron said, defending his new friend staunchly. "Much better than you or me."

"That's because we don't climb trees at all," Paul pointed out sensibly.

"Do you not?" Saylah called. "Then you must learn."

"Could we?" Theron asked, jumping up and down in his excitement.

Paul, who was eight and thought he ought to be more restrained, tried hard to disguise his pleasure. "I wouldn't mind all that much."

Saylah smiled. "Well then, I will teach you." She slid down the tree trunk, bracing her feet lightly on swaying branches as she went, surprisingly graceful, even in her awkward garments.

"But there're lots more up there!" Theron protested.

"We must take only a few from each tree, especially when there are so many."

"Let me pick the next tree!" Theron cried. His voice echoed upward through the cool green darkness, making the needles tremble.

Indulgently, Saylah ruffled his hair. "You enjoy speaking loudly in the woods, do you not?"

Theron nodded. "At home Mama's always telling me to talk in whispers, and it makes me tired. Sometimes I think we *live* in whispers."

Saylah peered at his round, glowing face and wondered if he understood how right he was, how sadly right. "Now," she said, "Theron, you seek out the best tree and we'll wait here. Then you call to us until we find you."

The boy raced off, kicking up needles and earth as he went. Paul was too busy staring at Saylah's brown skin, delicate features, and green, green

—— 231 ——

eyes to notice. He thought she was beautiful. More beautiful than any woman he'd ever seen, except his mother, he thought loyally.

"Are there other boys of your age here?" Saylah asked.

Paul shook his head, unable to find his voice. It always happened when he was faced with extraordinary beauty. It moved him so deeply that he could not speak. Finally, he muttered, "Theron and I are the only ones I know. My father's ranch is over there"—he pointed in the distance—"and our families used to visit all the time."

"But not anymore?" Saylah thought it odd that she had not heard more about the Ashtons, since their ranch was so close and Jamie had known this boy's father for so long.

Paul frowned. "Not so much. I don't know why. But I come to see Theron anyway. Isn't that him?"

Saylah too heard the distant call, and the two set off through the shifting patterns of colored leaves. Saylah could have found Theron at once; she could see the impressions he'd left in earth and fallen needles and leaves, but she pretended to be confused while Paul searched. Finally, they found the younger boy because he was chuckling at their confusion. He could not stifle his laughter and gave himself away.

They glanced up to see him hidden among the low branches of a fir tree. He laughed so hard he fell from his perch, and Saylah and Paul hurried to catch him. Then they all began to laugh.

Saylah shimmied up the tree and began cutting branches, making the boys guess where she would drop them. They circled the trunk, eyeing each other, both determined to catch the most, but neither able to figure out what Saylah would do next. Sometimes she dropped them end down, so they would be more difficult to catch, and Paul and Theron wrestled over who would add those to their pile. Because he was older, Paul always won, so Saylah would drop two extra in Theron's direction.

When she was satisfied with the piles of boughs, she climbed down and showed the boys how to grasp the tree with their arms, using their feet to find branches on which to brace themselves. She showed them how to shimmy upward a little at a time, and when they finally made it halfway up two small firs, they looked around from their new height, crowing in triumph.

"I can see the whole world!" Theron declared. "All the way to the ocean."

Paul was less vocal. "Oh!" he cried, and, "Look!" Though scratched and somewhat bruised, with bark and needles in his hair and sap all over his skin, he was enchanted. If he practiced, he thought, he could climb all the way to the top of the biggest tree and see everything from a height no one had reached before.

Saylah smiled up at the boys, shading her eyes with her hand while she sought the path of the sun through the breaks in the leaves and branches. "We should get back to the house. It is time for the afternoon chores, and Flora will be worried."

Theron shook his head. "She won't be worried. She knows we're with you."

Bending to hide her pleasure at his confidence, she began to gather up the branches.

Theron and Paul shimmied down the trees without Saylah's grace and experience, but full of pride at their accomplishment.

"I hope we have to gather branches every day," Theron said as they started back. "I don't even mind helping."

Saylah laughed. He had done much more playing than helping, and it made her feel good to know that the color in his cheeks was healthy and would linger for most of the day. She had brought him a breath of fresh air, she thought, smiling.

But even Theron knew she had given him more than that. Much more.

Chapter

33

When Saylah left the boys, they were in the kitchen comparing scratches for Flora's benefit and talking all over each other in an attempt to describe their morning. Flora had sent Saylah a look of glowing gratitude over their bent heads. "Ye go and arrange the boughs now. 'Twill give ye a little peace."

Saylah had moved through the house, making intricate arrangements of branches, until none but the sitting room was unchanged by her touch. She was just crouching before the fire in the main room, replenishing the smoldering wood, when Julian came in.

He stopped inside the door, sniffing, as Theron had done, trying to decide where the scent was coming from. Then he saw the low chest, covered with fir, cedar and spruce boughs twined together with a pattern of gold and shaded green leaves in the center. When he glanced around and discovered the other arrangements on every available surface, he also discovered Saylah, watching him curiously.

"You did this," he said.

It was not a question, but she could not tell if it was an accusation. "I have missed the smell of the forest. In my childhood it was always there, along with the sound and smell of the sea."

Julian sniffed again. It was amazing how some branches spread artfully

—— 234 ——

around a room could give it a new feeling of life. But he should have known that if anyone could accomplish such a thing, Saylah could.

Although he had not planned it, he found himself kneeling beside her. She still had streaks of sap on her face and hands. Wonderful hands, he thought, staring as she held a piece of alder toward the flames. Her fingers were long and thin, graceful, her hands fine-boned. Yet there was nothing weak about them. He had seen her carry a load of firewood that Flora, who was robust and did not hesitate to work hard, would not have attempted to lift.

"I like it," he said. He felt a surge of gratitude—again—and wondered how much he would owe her in the end. Already she had done so much. It troubled him—the power she had to change their lives.

"I hoped that you would."

Julian was unnerved by her admission. "What were you smiling about when I came in?"

Saylah glanced up. He knelt very close to her, so he could see the dirt stains on her skirt, the twigs and leaves in her hair. She could hear his breathing, rhythmic and strong. He was watching her intently, searchingly. She thought he was looking for something.

He must have risen early. Already there was the shadow of a beard on his cheeks and upper lip, and his hair, wetted back, had fallen forward, waving across his forehead. His question eddied between them, but she did not hurry to answer. She had to take care with Julian, the sometime mirror of her childhood and her pain.

Saylah shifted her weight, backing out of his curious gaze. "I was smiling because I like to watch the flames climb high and explode as I feed them. I do not *feel* the warmth so much as I *know* it will chase away the chill. It is satisfying to build a fire which is so beautiful, so full of power."

Julian heard what she said. At least he thought he did. Not simply the words but the meaning underneath. "You like your work."

She smiled again, a smile so wistful that it caught in his throat. "The Salish always enjoy their work. Everything we do, most of the day, is work, except at night, when we gather and tell stories. But it is pleasant work, satisfying work. We are always happy as we gather fruit or hunt for elk or prepare food."

Julian frowned. He too used to find pleasure in the everyday tasks on the ranch. Now they had become a kind of purging, a release from pain. "You are never unhappy? And why do you speak of 'we' as if you're still one of them?" It bothered him more than he wished to admit. He did not want her yearning for the life she had left behind. Glowering into the fire, he turned from the sight of her face.

"I have told you before that the best part of me is Salish, told you also

—— 235 ——

that you did not wish to know this. Yet I cannot wish it otherwise. The Salish songs and prayers run in my head and the beat of their drums fills my ears at night. To forget those things, to hear them no more, would be to die." She paused. "I am not yet ready to die. I have chosen to survive."

Julian regarded her in the firelight. Her brown skin, hooded eyes darkened by heavy lids, her thick black hair, even her tall, willowy body seemed more Indian than white. Nothing had changed, yet she was not the same. Without moving a muscle she made him see in her the blood of her Salish ancestors. "What do you mean, you have chosen?"

She was silent for a very long time. Already she had felt shards of the past slicing through her woven veil. She had thought those sharp and dangerous fragments buried deep in the earth long ago. But for Julian's sake she said quietly, "There was a time when it would have been easier to let the water take me, to drown in my grief and thereby end it. But I have never chosen the easy way. My People would not allow me that luxury."

Julian shifted, desperately uncomfortable. Saylah's eyes were too wise, the words she spoke too familiar. He rose.

"You think my spirit is too strong, but you are wrong. I am a fool, and weak, but this I have not chosen to let you see."

Julian was not appeased. "I only came to get some bread and cheese and check on my father. There's much to be done still." He spoke rapidly, betraying his unease.

"Yes," Saylah agreed in a whisper. "There is much still to be done."

Chapter

34

Julian went down the narrow hallway to his father's room. He paused with his hand on the door, closing his eyes in silent supplication, the smooth oak cold yet familiar against his palm. He never knew what he would find inside, and yet he never ceased to hope. Perhaps, after all, he was a fool. Resolutely, he pushed the door open.

He blinked, trying to discern shapes in the darkness, and saw his father seated in his chair, face to the double glass doors that opened onto the porch, though the heavy wine-velvet curtains did not let in a streak of light. Jamie did not turn his head as his son crossed the worn Brussels carpet, though Julian made no effort to be quiet.

He paused, uncomfortable here, as he always was.

"You don't like this room, do you?" his father demanded.

Julian whirled to find Jamie watching him, wide-awake, keenly observant. "No, I don't." He had never liked the huge, canopied bed or the chandelier, made of hundreds of tiny crystals. These things seemed ridiculously out of place in the wilderness of British Columbia, as did the watered silk wallpaper, the heavily carved French armoire, the Pembroke tables and brocaded maple chair with a curved, arched back. "All this opulence is unnecessary."

"You're lying to yourself and to me. That's not why you dislike it so much."

Rigidly, Julian muttered, "Why, then?"

Jamie cupped his hands in his lap, hidden by the folds of his velvet dressing gown. "Because Simone created this room, and you don't like to be reminded of her."

Julian flinched. He wanted to look away, but could not give his father such a victory. Instead, he sat, abruptly, on the brocaded maple chair. He had told himself that what he hated were the heavy velvet curtains that kept out the light, the shadows clustered around his father in the darkness, the gloom of stale, musty air.

He swallowed dryly. Jamie was right; he had been lying to himself. Everywhere he looked, Julian saw Simone. She had made the bedroom irrevocably hers so that even after she had gone, it belonged to her. And Jamie had refused to change it. That's what Julian hated most of all.

He wanted to take an ax to the shimmering crystal chandelier, to tear the curtains from the bed, the paper from the walls, and take back the house from the ghost of his beautiful, sensual, tender and heartless mother. "How did you know?" He managed to force the words past the blockage in his throat.

Jamie looked sadly at his oldest son, who thought he hid his pain so well. Jamie himself was safe, seated in his huge chair, its back carved like a lion's royal head, its arms and feet curled claws, with its well-worn seat of wine-colored leather. Or so he had thought. "I lived with her too. I know what it's like to love her."

Julian leaned forward, hands on knees. His father had never spoken of Simone before. Not once since she had left them nine years before. Julian noticed with unease that Jamie's light brown hair was indistinguishable from the shadows at his back, his brown eyes nearly black. Only his pale oval face showed in the gloomy light.

Wearily, Jamie sighed and stared down at his hands. "But you didn't come to talk about your mother."

Glad of a reprieve, unable to calm the turbulence that forced the color into his cheeks and drained it away, Julian took a deep breath. "I just wanted to see how you're feeling, to spend a little time with you."

"You're wondering if Saylah's medicines are helping, I suppose." A light—fleeting but undeniable—flared in his onyx eyes.

"I suppose I am." Julian waited anxiously for another sign that there was life and energy in Jamie's shell of a body. He would not let his father go as easily as he had lost Simone. This time he intended to fight. And Saylah had given him hope.

Jamie leaned back, resting his head on polished wood. "I don't know. Something changes when she touches me, but the change doesn't last. Only when I feel her hand on my forehead . . ." he trailed off.

Julian stifled a gasp of alarm. He did not want to hear this. Yet it was why he had come. He made himself speak normally, distinctly, ignoring the strange longing in his father's eyes. "She healed my hands," he said, and wondered why. "She's not like the others who've come and gone."

Jamie's eyes were glazed. "She loves the deer. She knows how much it means."

"She knows a great deal." Julian fought to keep his voice steady. He could see Saylah now, this moment, leaning toward the deer, her hand pressed lovingly to the wood, her eyes half closed, as if in prayer. The image haunted him. "She's here, but she's somewhere else at the same time. And she doesn't look *at* things, she looks *into* them." He heard the note of mistrust in his voice. Was he warning Jamie or himself?

"If you don't like her, why don't you send her away?"

Julian was astonished. "I didn't say I don't like her."

"Didn't you?" There was a glimmer of a smile in Jamie's eyes.

Julian frowned thoughtfully. "When I first saw her, her hair was down; she'd taken out the pins and left them with her bag in the field, along with her shoes and stockings. She was barefoot, and not in the least concerned that I knew it."

Jamie tilted his head, intrigued. Today he was not a ghost; today he had made himself into breath and flesh and warmth, just as he had the night when he'd joined them between the fires.

"She opened her collar when she thought I wasn't there. She tore at the buttons like they were suffocating her. Then she threw back her head and breathed more deeply than I've ever seen anyone breathe, all the way down to her toes." He smiled at the image, so vivid that he could feel the drifting hair across her cheek. "It looked like she was tasting the air."

"As if it were rare wine," Jamie mused softly.

"Yes," his son whispered. Now that he had started, he could not seem to stop. This was how it used to be when he talked to Jamie about his problems, his small victories, his plans. But they had not sat together like this for a long time. He had missed it.

"One morning I saw her coming back from a bath in the river, wearing only a wrapper." He paused, disturbed by the memory. "I thought she was teasing me, but she wasn't. She doesn't think like we do."

"And for that I thank God," Jamie interjected.

To hide his irritation, Julian said, "Theron says she's not happy in her room. He says it holds her too tight."

"Why doesn't she ask for another?"

"Because it's not her way." Julian touched Jamie's locked hands gently. "Theron says she likes the loft. She smiles when she's there, he says."

Jamie sat upright. "The loft? And you want to give it to her?" He peered curiously at his son.

"I thought it would be kind to let her use it."

Jamie smiled hollowly. "If you let her use it, she'll make it hers. Are you willing to allow that to happen?"

Julian did not know what to say, did not understand what his father was afraid of.

At his son's silence, Jamie went limp, gave in to the images that had been tugging at him all morning, calling him back.

Julian saw at once that his father was gazing inward, toward a memory, an old, half-healed pain. He was sinking into the shadows. They were thin and shifting, those shadows, wisps of smoke-like mesh, but Julian could not reach through them. He watched, helpless, as Jamie sank from pain into blankness.

"Papa?" Julian cried desperately. He squeezed his father's cold fingers, but there was no response.

Face rigid, Julian rose abruptly. *Perhaps you are angry at your father,* Saylah had said. *Angry at his illness? But that would be selfish,* he had declared self-righteously. He was chilled, suddenly, and afraid. But he would not show it. The pretense of his strength was all that he had left.

He turned to leave the room, as well as the stranger enfolded in the safety of sweet, beguiling memories. He closed Jamie's door carefully, then opened the front door and slammed it shut behind him. So loud was the crash when it hit the frame that the crystals on the chandelier in Jamie's room danced, playing a soft, tinkling tune. But no one heard it.

Saylah knelt in the loft, arranging the pile of cedar boughs Julian had brought up the steep stairs for her. She was making a bed in the room which was now her own. Theron must have noticed how much she liked the loft and told his brother.

"You can't bear being closed into that tiny room, can you?"

She'd been touched by Julian's question. "It is only that I am used to sleeping in the open, in the woods or the Longhouse. Even at the school, it was a huge, long room. It is hard for me to change."

He'd promptly brought her there and offered to move her bed and other furniture up the stairs. "We've never really used this room. I don't see why you can't have it, if you don't mind that the privacy isn't complete."

She wondered if he knew she would sleep with a ghost and the scent of roses. "It is that which I love—the windows, the low wall, the roof that slants upward forever."

"I wish we'd thought of it sooner." Julian's tone had been kind, but his voice unsteady. He had, she knew, been thinking of other things. He had left her to bring a thin mattress, which she placed over fir boughs on the floor, the little table for the lamp, and a low chest for her clothes. There was already a long-unused wood-burning stove.

Now night had fallen, he had gone, and she was alone. She smiled and unbraided her hair. Carefully, she arranged her stones next to the low bed, touched them gently, whispered her sacred prayers.

> Let sleep come easy, moon of brightness,
> Let it bring rest.
> Let it bring rest.

Saylah picked up the lamp and went to the window, kneeling on the low bench beneath. She drew aside the curtain, which shimmered, even in the lamplight, and set the lamp on the bench. She was startled to see, not the starred blackness of night, but her face reflected in the glass. She started, looked away. She had not seen her own face in a long time.

She had avoided the few small mirrors at the school, believing they would not reflect the truth but the white man's image. They had been poor quality anyway; the missionaries did not wish to encourage vanity in the Indians. Saylah had preferred the wavering image in a pool of clear water, but she had not sought one out for some time.

All she would find was the face of a stranger, a specter, a reflection of what used to be. She did not know the woman Tanu had become; she felt that she was half formed, waiting, and the sight of her face would be vague and undefined.

Unnerved by the reflection in the window, Saylah paused to stare at her burnished skin, the black hair that fell about her shoulders, obscuring her body so only her face seemed to float in the glass. She leaned closer, examining her softly curved cheekbones, parted lips and arched brows above green eyes.

She did not feel the usual aching emptiness, but a tiny tremor of recognition. Perhaps she was beginning to learn who Saylah was. Perhaps, after all, she was walking through her own dream now.

Chapter

35

As he wandered along the well-worn path beside the river, Paul Ashton dragged a bent stick through the soil, making a wavy pattern that pleased him. He liked the noise of the river, the plopping sound when he tossed a stone into its center, the faint trickle where the ferns grew so close that they met over the water. The green lace fronds made a low secret place among the cattails where he could hide.

Paul's arms and legs no longer ached from the day when he and Theron had climbed trees while the Indian, the woman with amazing green eyes, had watched. He had wanted to go back every day since, but his mother had needed him. There was a great deal to do to get ready for autumn, when the crops and vegetables were harvested, the animals slaughtered to be smoked and cured for winter. Paul hated that part and had been glad, finally, to get away.

Dragging his stick, he stopped to examine a fallen log covered with gray, green and pale yellow moss. He crouched, tracing the swirls and indentations with his finger. So many patterns, so many years of decay that had changed to beauty. Paul breathed in the damp air, which he loved, though it made his auburn hair curl in the most frustrating manner.

When he rose, he heard splashing and low voices. He froze, eyes squeezed closed, praying he had been mistaken. But then it came again, the rasping groans, the deep sighs. He was only eight years old, but Paul Ashton knew what those sounds meant. At five, he had gone to the barn one day and climbed halfway to the loft before he realized his father was already there. With a woman. Paul had not seen her face. He had not wanted to. He had heard her voice and knew it was not his mother's.

He had crept away, shuddering at the glimpse of bare white skin and tumbled hair and the sounds coming from the bodies strewn with hay. He had been violently sick when he got to the river, had sat with his back against a boulder, shivering. Eventually, the sun had come to warm his chilled body and the horror had become anger—hot and fierce. He had not really understood, but one thing he knew instinctively. Edward Ashton had betrayed Sophia. What Paul had seen was secret and sordid and wrong.

He had stayed away from home for a long time, walking aimlessly, kicking up tufts of grass and tossing them into the river, throwing stones so hard against a tree that his arm had ached for a week.

That had been the first time. There had been others. But Paul had not grown used to it. Even now he felt ill and wanted to run, to put the voices far behind him, but he could not move. The air was cool, just touched with mist, and he thought he would choke on it. His father laughed deep in his throat.

"You won't ever forget me, will you?" Edward Ashton said huskily.

Paul bit his lip, confused, as always, by that question. His father did not speak it with warmth and love. Often Paul had tried to work out what he heard in Edward's voice. It wasn't arrogance either, but a sort of desperation.

The boy wanted very badly to understand. He was certain if he could know this one thing, he might be able to forgive his father's betrayal. If he could not understand, he would have to hate Edward, because Paul Ashton loved his mother.

He shook with anger that turned to hurt rage when he thought of Sophia's gray eyes, her face, so familiar and so tender. Paul knew his mother was strong, but not strong enough for this. He would have to protect her, as he had for three years. He wanted more than anything to go to her now, but she would know he was upset. He could never hide that from her. And he didn't want her to guess why.

Edward groaned and suddenly Paul was running, stumbling blindly, trying to outrace what he didn't wish to know. He hurt inside, everywhere, and the hurt got tangled with the anger until he could not tell one from the other. His breath began to come in sharp gasps, and a pain shot through his side. He ran toward the barn, toward the pony his father had bought him.

He had to get away, and if his feet would not go fast enough, then his horse would. He did not guide the animal; he was too upset, doubled over, choking for breath, his face, wet with tears, buried in the pony's mane. The horse followed the most familiar path. Sensing Paul's distress, he ran faster and ever faster toward the haven of Jamie Ivy's house.

He would not think of his mother, Paul vowed. He would not. He would make himself forget, one way or another.

Every morning Saylah brought Jamie herbs to build his strength, to ease his cough, and boiled hemlock bark for his sensitive eyes. Sometimes he spoke to her like an old friend, sometimes like an unwelcome stranger, sometimes not at all. It was in those quiet moments that Saylah began to reveal to him fragments of her own past—small glimpses of her joy and pain and sorrow. Jamie listened and understood, but did not respond. He sensed that she did not want his sympathy.

He did not leave his room after the night when he told the story of the deer. The effort had drained his strength. One morning Saylah found him standing with the heavy drapes clutched in his fists. She could not tell if he was drawing the curtains closed or trying to wrench them open. She stood for a long time, the tray of steaming cups in her hands. "You should go outside," she murmured. "I can feel your yearning."

He spoke sharply, with alarming clarity. "All I yearn for is peace." He did not turn or incline his head; he spoke into the heavy folds of the wine-colored drapes. "That's why I came to this island. It was in my blood—the wild beauty, the untouched land full of possibilities, the ocean, which all the powers of England could not transform into something other than what it was. The mountains were magnificent, isolated, and perfect in their isolation. So peaceful."

He half turned, the velvet still clutched in his hands. "You understand, because you understand the earth. You're part of it."

"How did you know?"

Jamie smiled a smile that wrenched her heart. "Julian told me how you looked at the deer with the wind in your hair, your bare feet covered with dust, breathing in the air like it was precious and sweet and would give you strength. I understood, because I used to feel the same." He did not give her a chance to respond.

"But one day the ground was no longer firm beneath my feet; it shifted and changed and betrayed me." His voice was muffled by old, dusty fabric. "The music of the wind, which had been soft and alluring, became melancholy, infinitely sad, and finally harsh and icy cold."

He faced her fully, and the pallor of his skin emphasized the burning darkness of his eyes. "I can't bear that discordant sound. I can't bear the sound of my exile."

With great care, Saylah set down the tray, in order to hide the shaking of her hands. But she could not hide the color that stained her cheeks. She swallowed dryly.

Jamie shrugged and the weight on his shoulders was faintly visible in the dim, transforming light. "If I stepped outside for a single moment, the island might be too beautiful, as beautiful as I remember, and that would break my heart. Or it would be too cruel, too real, too ugly. And that too would break my heart."

Saylah hurt for him, where the layers of pain had formed deep inside her, scar upon scar, covering the wound but never touching or healing it. She wanted to weep for Jamie—and for herself. "I have always sought a means to silence the discordant sounds you speak of. It is not easy to find. For anyone."

Jamie tilted his head and looked at her with compassion. "In death I think one finds such peace. In life—" He paused. "I don't know." Still he did not release the velvet, creased and damp beneath his grasping fingers.

"Why have you told me these things?" she asked at last.

"Because you'll listen. You will hear me. You seek understanding. You need it, I think, as much as Julian needs to avoid it."

"You do not realize—"

"Please," Jamie said, "go. I need to be alone."

Saylah could not ignore the melancholy, the misery in his tone; it echoed her own unspoken anguish. She must reach him soon, before it was too late, before he curled into the safety of the darkness, and embraced it so tightly that she could not pull him free.

"Please."

This time she went, closing the door behind her. She paused, her skin damp with sweat, her head spinning. She realized that Jamie had meant to awaken her demons so she would go away quietly and tend her own wounds, leaving him the false peace which was all he had been able to attain. But her wounds would wait. She had survived once; she would do so again. And so would Jamie Ivy. Thus she had sworn and so it would be.

Chapter
━━━►◄ 36 ►◄━━━

Theron and Saylah stood at the edge of the apple orchard, holding the two Salish bows she had found on the wall in the main room. "Where have they come from?" she had asked Julian once. "Some Indians left them for Jamie after he fed them and let them stay here for a night," Julian had explained. "He always treasured those bows. I'm not sure why."

Saylah was grateful, whatever the reason. She had needed to get away from the house after her talk with Jamie, and Theron too had been restless. She had suggested using the morning to teach him how to shoot the bow.

"Go," Flora had said. "My Jamie would no' be mindin' a little calm and quiet today." She had smiled at Theron but whispered so only Saylah could hear, "I'd be needin' a little of that myself."

With great relief, Saylah had taken the boy outside, where they spent the morning collecting cedar sticks to make arrows. She knew the forest well, and located feathers that had drifted down from bird nests overhead. "I'll get them," Theron insisted. "I promise to be careful so they don't get broken." He dug among the needles and bark, finding black, gray and speckled feathers which he cradled in his hands like spun glass.

He perched beside Saylah, watching in fascination while she carved and notched an arrow, then attached the feathers to the end.

When she had finished, she showed Theron how to set up a small target on a fence post.

"I got it in the middle," he shouted, "so we can't miss."

Saylah smiled to herself and took the bow in her hands. It had been a long time since she held the fine curve of polished wood. She cradled it, felt its light weight, its elasticity.

"When are you going to shoot one?" Theron demanded. He was quivering with excitement, gaze fixed on the taut string. Like the arrow she placed against the bow, he was ready to burst free, to fly through the cool summer air. Overcome, all at once, with the boy's impatience, Saylah let the arrow go. It hit the target near the center.

"You did it! I can't believe it. Let me try!"

She was as surprised as he that she had not lost her knowledge of the bow, which once she had held easily, indifferently. Now the chance to use it again was a blessing and a joy.

"Look!" Theron shouted. "There's a squirrel. Can you hit it?" He jumped up and down, too excited to stay still.

Shaking her head, Saylah made him sit on a boulder. She knelt beside him. "If you harm an animal without reason, the spirits will be angry. If you are genuinely hungry or the animal threatens your life, then is it allowed. The animals are glad to give up their lives to feed us, the Changer teaches."

Theron looked confused. "Who is the Changer and why would any animal be happy to die?"

Saylah locked her hands around her knees, enjoying the fragrance of the freshly turned earth in the nearby orchard, the heat of the sun-warmed rock. "The Changer is another name for the one who you call God. And the animals are pleased to give up their lives to help man live and prosper because they know they will be blessed. They know they are giving a precious gift."

Theron rubbed his forehead to brush away an annoying thought. "When I went hunting with Julian and he tried to shoot a deer, it ran. It didn't seem happy to me. Not even a little."

"I did not say the animals will stand and offer up their lives without a struggle. They do not wish to make it easy for us." She stared into the distant woods, narrowing her eyes to see the hidden creatures that lived in its protection. "Julian enjoys hunting sometimes, does he not?"

The boy nodded emphatically.

"He likes the challenge, the skill and excitement of the chase."

Brow furrowed, Theron considered. "I guess so."

"So," Saylah continued, suppressing a smile, "perhaps the animals enjoy the chase as much. Just because they must give up their lives does not mean they must do it easily." Julian's image came to her, strangely vivid, but she concentrated on Theron. "After all, there is no challenge, no excitement in standing and waiting. But when people kill for no reason, for sport or anger or pleasure, the animals grieve. The Changer grieves. They are less willing to offer their gift another time." She took Theron's face in her hand and looked into his clear blue eyes. "You must learn always to take a gift that is offered, for it is unkind to refuse, but never to take what is not offered freely, for that is selfish."

Theron thought of the sweet-smelling chest hidden in his bedroom cupboard and stiffened with guilt. He opened his mouth to confess, closed it with a snap. He could not give it up. He had to see it, touch it, smell it.

His thoughts were interrupted by a shout which he recognized with joy. "Paul!" He jumped up to greet his friend.

Paul was leaning forward on his brown pony, whose sides were heaving and wet with sweat. Paul slipped off the animal's back and took its bridle in his hand. "Do you want to come exploring?" he asked without preamble.

"I do not know if that would be wise," Saylah said, peering at Paul's red face and glittering eyes.

"We won't go far," he promised earnestly, a little desperately.

Saylah felt sorry for him, yet she was apprehensive. She was relieved when Flora came out to join them.

"I saw ye through the kitchen window," she told Paul. "'Tis glad I am that ye're here. Theron's been missin' ye."

"I want to take him exploring," Paul said. "I'll leave the pony in the stable to rest. And we'll be very careful. You know Mama trusts me in the woods."

"That she does," Flora said. "Well then, if ye give me your word that ye'll no' be gettin' into trouble."

"We never get in trouble, Mama," Theron objected, grinning.

Flora shook her head, laughing. "Keep one eye on Theron and one on your back," she told Paul.

"I will." The boys went off toward the barn, chattering. At least Theron chattered. Paul was strangely silent.

Saylah watched them go, brow furrowed.

"Don't be worryin' your head about those two. Paul is older than his age, if ye see what I mean. We can trust him. And Theron has so little chance to play, so little freedom. I'd have him know there's a world outside this house that 'tis worth fightin' for. But now I'd best be back at the pots and pans."

"I will help," Saylah offered.

"Ye'll do no such thing. Stay outside today. Ye'll find enough to keep ye busy." She nodded over her shoulder, where Julian had just emerged from the woods with three rabbits he had killed for their dinner. Flora grinned. "I've a feelin' *he* could use a little target practice. See if ye can teach him that there're other things to learn," she said cryptically, and hurried away, apron strings flapping.

Saylah went to meet Julian and took the animals from him. She examined them critically, noting the damage the bullets had done to meat and skin.

"I'll take them to Flora," Julian said.

"I will prepare them. I need only an apron and one of your sharp knives. The steel cuts more precisely than the shell or bone my People use."

She disappeared into the kitchen and returned at once, her hair pinned loosely at the back of her head. The borrowed apron covered most of her plain gray worsted dress. She pushed back her sleeves and sat on the ground, lifting the rabbits without flinching.

Julian stood open-mouthed as she slit them, cut away the skins, and laid them out for tanning, removed the entrails, and finally sliced the meat, leaving most of it in one piece. He had never seen anyone, man or woman, do the job so neatly or so quickly.

When she was finished, she was covered with blood—her arms, the sleeves of her dress, her legs, where she had drawn up her skirt to keep it free of stain. Her face was dusty and smeared with red, yet she seemed unaware of her appearance. The task was all that mattered.

"Shall we make a stone fire pit and cook them outdoors with a little alderwood in the fire to add flavor?" she asked, looking up, a smear of blood on her cheek.

Julian was so stunned he did not object. "How do we go about it?"

She showed him, gathering wood from the kindling pile and stones from the corner of the garden, where she had been saving them for such an occasion. She set a fire and watched it burn low, placed the stones on top, lined the pit with salal and skunk cabbage leaves, and added some wild onions and camas bulbs. Then she added more stones and covered it all with dirt.

"It should be ready by dinnertime," she told him cheerfully. It had made her happy to perform the tasks that had once been so familiar, even though her hair had come loose and brushed the dirt as she knelt. Her hem was as filthy as her hands. She sat on the back step in front of the kitchen door. "If you'd killed those rabbits with an arrow, we could have saved the hides and sold them. And there would have been more meat besides."

Julian shrugged. "A gun is faster, more efficient."

"There is no weapon more efficient than an arrow truly aimed. Besides, it is more of a challenge to hunt with a bow. The rifle makes it too easy. You lose the pleasure of stalking your prey."

Julian threw back his head and laughed. "What do you know about stalking prey?"

Saylah was disturbed by his laughter; it was too harsh, too brittle. "I used to hunt with the men. I would hunt with you if you used a bow. Would you not enjoy the change?"

Julian considered. She did not look wise or serious or fearsome now. She looked tired and dirty and quite pleased with herself. He liked her that way, smiling, with her hair coming loose around her shoulders. "I might at that," he said softly. "I might very well enjoy it."

Saylah took the larger bow, a fine weapon made from a flat strip of yellow cedar tapered at the ends. The string was made of twisted cords of animal sinew and was taut and undecayed. She took the few arrows the Indians had left behind, along with the one she had made, then demonstrated for Julian as she had for Theron.

He watched with interest, leaning on his rifle while she took her stance, balanced herself by bouncing a few times on the balls of her feet, and raised the bow.

"It is a matter of concentration," Saylah said. She was aware that Julian was probably needed elsewhere, as he always was, aware that he too knew this and chose, for once, to ignore it. She took a carved arrow with a bone point from the waistband of her gown.

"You must listen and watch and wait, once you have tracked your prey and know it's near." She crouched and aimed for the same fence post which bore the mark of her earlier practice. She stared at the post until it filled her vision, drew back the string, sighted. At the last instant, she whirled to fire at the fence post far to her right. The arrow impaled itself neatly in the wood.

Julian had stopped leaning casually on his rifle. She had changed direction swiftly, yet her aim had been true. As if she had been aware of more than the target in front of her, of all the possible targets. Dropping his rifle, he came closer, touched the bow with admiration ill-concealed. "Show me."

Saylah gave him the weapon and stood behind him, guiding his hands until he held it correctly. She moved closer so her body was pressed to his and they could move as one while he loaded the arrow and drew the string taut. Breasts against his back, hips against his hips, hands over his hands, she stood unmoving.

The bow had suddenly lost its importance. Julian was very still, very tense. He felt the slight quiver of Saylah's chin on his shoulder and knew she felt the tension too. The air seemed to sing inaudibly, with promise, with expectation and doubt. Julian understood these things; the heat that flared between a man and a woman when they stood close, even if it were merely to test a bowstring. But he did not think Saylah understood. "I wish I could see your eyes," he murmured.

Taut as a fine thin birch that quivers in high wind, Saylah forced herself to speak. "Why?"

"To see what you're thinking."

She did not answer. She did not know how. Silence enveloped them, and they stood with the string pulled back and the arrow in place. Julian's wavy brown hair tickled Saylah's nose, along with a scent she did not recognize. A soap that was clean and fresh but had not the natural scent of thimbleberry or mock orange. Yet it was pleasing. Her own hair blew around his shoulder and down his shirtfront. She saw the stubble of his beard, felt the smoothness of his cheek above it. The scent of fir was strong and the leaves of the aspen, the alder and dogwood flitted in the intermittent breeze. Her body trembled as his heat penetrated her thin wool gown, and her own skin grew warm and sensitive.

They stood unmoving, as they had outside her room, hand to mouth and breath to skin. Something seemed to hold them in place, to keep them from going forward or retreating into the safety of the past. They could only exist in this moment of intense connection, unwilling to recognize the invisible bond that wove itself between them, that spun out from the tension in the air, the heat of their bodies, the erratic rise and fall of their breath.

Saylah's heartbeat slowed, then raced, and she felt the echo of that irregular beat in Julian's broad back, in the pulse at the base of his throat which betrayed his own agitation. She leaned forward and he leaned back. The breeze whipped around them, lifting her long black hair up and across his face. All at once he released the arrow, shocking them both with the jolting motion. They stumbled backward as it landed in the ground well beyond the fence post.

The thread was broken. Saylah sighed at the tension that ebbed from her body a little at a time. She went to get the arrows, collecting them slowly, catching her breath, aware all the time of Julian's eyes upon her, curious, intent.

Without a word he took the arrows she handed him and fired them one by one until all four were gone. "We need more arrows," he said, breaking the silence between them at last.

"Yes," Saylah agreed.

"Aside from that," he continued, "I can't master the bow here. Let's go into the woods and practice. You can show me how it's really done among trees and vines and hanging moss. Not at all like this nice little fence post in a clearing. I need the real challenge."

Saylah was strangely hesitant. "Now?"

"Why not?"

There were many reasons why not, but prominent in Saylah's mind was the image of Flora's distress this morning, her plea that Saylah take Theron away. *My Jamie would no' be mindin' a little calm and quiet.*

It was a good day to take Julian into the woods. "I do not object," she said at last.

He grinned, taking the bow in one hand and Saylah's arm in the other. "Good." The single word carried no hint of anger, no resentment, frustration, pain. Just expectation and pleasure.

Saylah smiled. He sounded like a child anticipating a rare treat. *I never had a childhood,* she had told her mother once. *They took it from me long ago. But Kitkuni gave it back to you,* Koleili had answered. *At least for a little while.* Perhaps she could do the same for Julian.

Chapter

37

It did not take long to reach the woods. The shadows of trees moved toward them and Julian stopped, peering into the cool darkness. "Will you show me what you know? The forest was once your home, wasn't it? I want to see it through your eyes."

Saylah heard his low, alluring voice all through her body. No one had ever asked her to go back, to become what she had once been—a Salish whose soul burned brightest in the woods and wind and waters. Especially not Julian, who could not hide his resentment at her heritage.

His hand tightened on her arm, and she nodded. She could not resist his smile, or the force that drew her back into the freedom of her childhood and the magic which had been as real as her breath or her agile young body.

She moved forward until she was enfolded by tall fir and cedar and spruce, by tinted light filtered through fluttering leaves. Nearly unaware that Julian was beside her, she stopped, then closed her eyes and tilted back her head so she could feel the speckled light on her lids. She tried to empty her mind of all she had learned since she left the Longhouse.

She straightened, amazed at how easily it fled, how quickly the silence came. She was intensely aware of her surroundings, sensitive to the changing light, the smells of earth and trees and air, the movement of animals not seen but felt, the sound of branches shifting above her, the rush of the river which called her with its song. She heard it all, tasted it, felt it in her body. She did not realize until that moment how completely she had closed herself off from this bittersweet communion.

Every nerve was alert, almost painfully so, every instinct prominent, every emotion stripped of pretense, every sensation, every remnant of her childhood was with her now. She was vulnerable and totally without protection.

Julian watched, mute with awe. Saylah's body, the angle of her head, the placement of her hands changed slightly as she leaned into the colored light. But her face became that of a stranger, as if a veil had been removed. Her features were the same, yet not the same. For the first time, he saw the purity that had been diluted and defiled by the knowledge of the Whites. Here, with the changing light upon her face and her soul lost in another, older world, she was so beautiful that he caught his breath—and held it.

He felt the jolt that shook her as the last of her defenses fell away. *But you're only part Indian,* he had said. *It is the best part.* Only now did Julian believe it.

He saw how she opened her eyes, luminous with her new awareness. She looked about, alert, absorbing everything around her. She was at home, at peace from within. He knew, as she reached out unselfconsciously to take his hand, that he could trust her completely. She had revealed herself to him; her soul was naked and unprotected. That vulnerability touched him, reassured him in a way nothing else could have.

"You will need a beaver skin to hold your arrows." Saylah spoke in the hushed and reverent tone of one who worships the place in which she stands. "Come, I will find one."

"The beavers have been pretty much killed off by the trappers," Julian replied in the same hushed tone.

Saylah shook her head. It was the way of the Whites to kill unthinkingly, unwisely. "Then we must sing a hunting song."

He waited.

> O *stiqayu*, quicksilver wolf,
> Living spirit of our ancestors,
> Who knows the secret places of the forest—
> Come hide within my shadow,
> Guide me
> To the prey I seek.
> Lend me
> Your far-seeing hunter's eyes
> And your fearless hunter's heart.

Julian heard the bushes rustle, sensed movement in the half-darkness. He felt a warm rush of breath from an animal that has been running. But when he whirled to look behind him, there was nothing but the swaying branches of a hawthorn tree.

Saylah laughed and tugged on his hand. "We have our answer. We must go." She ducked beneath low branches, stepped easily over moss-covered logs, around the kinnikinnick and twinflower vines that covered the forest floor. She did not hesitate, despite her bare feet. This was her home. She was safe here.

"I will find a beaver," she said. "I know where they hide."

Julian followed, mesmerized by her confidence, the light touch of her hand. She had become the leader, he the follower, and he was not used to that. Yet he submitted to Saylah's authority without question. It was why he had come with her.

As they moved toward the river, she froze, raised her hand, and Julian stopped where he was. She crept forward, kneeling over scattered twigs and grasses and mud beside a small offshoot of the river. She examined the ground closely, then motioned Julian forward.

"It is all right. A beaver has been here recently, but he is gone." She peered up and down the river, one hand dipped casually into the chilly water. "We shall look for him upriver, where I hear fast-running water. He will have heard it too and answered its call."

"Saylah." Julian pointed to the edge of her skirt, dampened by the vegetation, covered with clinging leaves and twigs that had caught in the fabric. Now it had fallen into the river and was weighted down with mud as well.

She smiled and shook her head. "How foolish to think I can track while wearing such a garment. If we did find the beaver, he would run away, laughing at my awkwardness." She undid the buttons deftly, pulled the dress over her head, and draped it across a juniper bush. The petticoat followed, until she wore only chemise and drawers. "This is not what I would wish to wear, but it will not hinder me so much."

To his surprise, Julian was no longer shocked by her behavior. He saw that she acted automatically, concerned, not with propriety and modesty, which belonged to his world, but with efficiency and practicality, which belonged to hers. He had felt the change in her; she was Salish now, and a Salish would not endanger the hunt with foolish and unnecessary hindrances. He noticed with interest the otterskin pouch she wore on a cedar twine rope around her waist.

Saylah followed his gaze. "It is for my medicines. I keep it with me always." She began to move again. "I would wish that these clothes were not so white. They do not blend with the trees and foliage like my cedarbark skirt." Kneeling, she brushed her body with damp earth and twigs and leaves that clung, dulling the bright white of her clothes. She threw a handful of leaves and soil at Julian. It hit him on the shoulder and he fell back, smiling.

"Oh," she said, "I suppose you do not need to dull yourself. Your shirt is already green and your pants bark brown. Perhaps I should have looked more carefully before I decided to help you." She grinned playfully.

To his astonishment, Julian grinned back. He had never seen this Saylah before. He could feel her pleasure in her new freedom and he wanted to share it. "Ah, but my face," he said solemnly. "It is much too white to fool a clever beaver."

Saylah pivoted, on her knees in the leaves and vines snarled around her legs. "We could crush some dogwood leaves and dye it green."

Julian laughed. "I think a little grime will suffice." He took some soil and dusted it over his face. "Well?"

"The beaver is more clever than you suppose, but it will do." Then she was off again. Occasionally she bent to examine a plant at the base of an oak, a bit of moss suspended from drooping branches, the ferns that carpeted the floor of the woods in such profusion. She tore off bits and pieces, pulled a small plant up by its roots, and added these to her pouch.

One moment the sun came out from behind the clouds piled one upon the other to linger at the edge of the water. "Now we can walk in the sun, as friends," Saylah said.

Julian fell easily into step beside her. "I never had a woman for a friend before."

She lifted a branch of hemlock and pressed it to her face, inhaling its sharp scent. "Flora is your friend."

Pausing to stare into the rushing water, Julian sighed. "I suppose she is."

"Lush and fertile as it is, this island seems for some to be a friendless place."

Julian glanced at her sharply. "I used to think Edward Ashton was my friend. Then one day he wasn't there anymore. His eyes were different, like a stranger's eyes." He picked up a pebble and tossed it into the river, whose song was to him no more than the meeting of water and stone.

"And then there was Jamie. Always Jamie. Even when I was a child I felt he was more my friend than my father."

"And now?" Saylah prompted.

Julian scowled. "Now, well, he isn't Jamie anymore, is he?"

"I think," she said carefully, "that somewhere inside he is still the man he used to be. But he does not wish to know it."

Julian swung around, grasped her shoulders in his hands. "Why? In God's name, *why?*"

His fingers were digging into her skin, but she did not wince. "Because for him it is too painful."

"For him," Julian repeated, trying out the sound of the words, finding them bitter. "For him. But what about for us?"

The fevered look in his eyes made her want to take his head in her lap, to lay her hands upon his closed lids until the fever was cooled and gone. "Come," she said, "we are nearly there."

Julian released her, eyes hidden by half-closed lids. He had thought for a moment that she had an answer. Swallowing his disappointment, he followed her to a low waterfall, where the land fell away from above and the boulders had gathered at the edges.

Saylah examined the area carefully, climbing up slippery rocks without hesitation. She leapt back to the ground with a shout of triumph. "He has been here. He will return. Let us find a place to rest and wait. I saw a clearing at the top of the waterfall."

Julian hesitated. He knew that clearing and did not want to go there. But Saylah was already climbing, motioning for him to follow on the gentle slope of the hill. She was wet, her hair long and gleaming on her back, her already brown cheeks darkened with pleasure. She stopped, clinging by one hand from a precarious hanging rock.

"Do you come with me? Or are you afraid of the spirits of the woods?"

"I'd call them ghosts," he muttered under his breath. "Ghosts better buried and forgotten." Yet he found himself climbing the hill, his heart thudding dully with apprehension.

He stood at the edge of the copse bordered by oak and aspen, to watch Saylah. She had found an old stump and leaned against it, her face to the sun, smiling slightly. She raised her head and looked at him. She had felt his presence, though he hadn't made a sound.

"You do not wish to be here?" she asked quietly. His face was stiff with the effort to disguise his feelings, but she knew him well enough to understand. She felt his pain more intensely now that her defenses had been left behind. "There is no threat in this copse where the sun reaches through the trees. It is warm here and pleasant."

Julian moved forward, drawn by her voice, her musical silver voice, her silky voice that burrowed easily inside him, where knives of flint or steel could never make their way. "I know what it's like. I've been here before. Many times." He sat beside her, leaned against the stump and closed his eyes. But he did not turn his head to the sun. Instead, he fell back into memory—a past long forgotten, a pleasure long suppressed.

Saylah watched and waited. She did not touch him; he knew she was there. She knew he was not ready for that. Drawing her knees to her chin, she contemplated the drifting clouds.

"My mother used to bring me here." Julian spoke hoarsely, as if the words had been dragged from him. His hazel eyes were gray, drained of color by the memories that assaulted him.

Saylah stared at the river that meandered by, widening into a pond before it fell, rushing and roaring, over the tangle of boulders. When she sensed that Julian had recovered his composure, heard his breathing return to normal, felt him lean against the stump, she risked another question. "What did you do here, your mother and you?"

He shifted uncomfortably and she leaned close, until her shoulder touched his. "Come," she said, "I am enjoying my afternoon by the river, my return to the spirit of my people. Do not leave me alone with my happiness. Tell me a story."

Julian hesitated.

"Did you come to escape the shadows in the house?"

He glowered. How did she come to know so much? "Not really the house," he said reluctantly. He had lived a long time in the black solitude of his pain, and Saylah's smile was kind. "It was different then, with the windows open and the light streaming in. She told me she brought me because she needed to walk, she said she feared she would turn old and ugly with her skin sagging around her collar." Unconsciously, he smiled. "Even then I didn't believe her. She wanted to take me away from the endless work. She would bring a picnic in a basket and never tell me what was inside until she laid it out on a linen cloth just here by the stump."

He stared up at layers of gray clouds and white that moved and shifted in the sky. "She liked it here because it was shady yet open to the light, and because the ferns trailed in the water and the bees hummed overhead. She refused to let me think of all that needed to be done and fed me 'til I was swollen with tiny sugared biscuits and delicate sandwiches and rich jam and chocolate. She always brought a decanter of sherry and poured herself a glass and gave me a sip. She said I must not tell Papa, that it was our secret, but we both knew Papa wouldn't mind. And we played games with her French songs."

"Will you sing one for me?" Saylah asked. She thought fleetingly of a French song that had haunted her own childhood, but pushed the thought aside.

Julian put his hands behind his head. "Funny," he said, "but I remember exactly the one she sang most often."

> *Sur le pont d'Avignon,*
> *Tout le monde y danse, danse.*
> *Sur le pont d'Avignon,*
> *Tout le monde y danse en ronde.*

> *Les beaux monsieurs font comme çi,*
> *Les belles dames font comme ça.*

The words were strange yet somehow familiar to Saylah. "So she brought you here to rest."

"I suppose so. I never wondered why at the time. Only later—" He broke off and the words caught in his throat. "I knew even then that she would go. I was eight years old, and I knew."

This time Saylah didn't press him. Instead, she rose, took his hand, and headed back into the woods. "We will wait farther upstream, where the beaver will not expect company."

"Saylah," Julian called in alarm. "Watch . . . out!"

The last word echoed as they tumbled head over heels down a sharp incline that she had not seen coming. She had been looking back at him. She rolled, her feet tucked under her, and stopped at the bottom, more muddy than ever, her hair a wild tangle of sticks and dirt and leaves. Saylah looked at Julian, sprawled beside her in a clump of bracken.

At the same moment, they began to laugh, choking and gasping as they tried to catch their breath.

"Hush!" All at once Saylah fell to the ground and lay flat. "There is someone coming."

Julian held his breath, turning deep red with the effort—for he knew he would laugh if he breathed even once—until he heard the sound of breaking twigs and snapping branches. He looked at Saylah's clothing, or lack of clothing, her general dishevelment, and knew no one must see her like this, especially not with him. "We have to get away."

Saylah had been looking frantically around. Now she motioned toward some bushes and began to crawl there on her hands and knees. Julian followed, urging her to hurry. When both were hidden behind copper bushes heavy with whorls of leaves, they looked at each other and began to laugh again, helplessly.

"Shhh," Julian whispered. "You'll give us away."

She nodded but kept chuckling. She felt a hard, unyielding wall crumble inside her, and its falling made her laugh. She couldn't stop.

Julian was enchanted. He had never heard anything quite as captivating as Saylah's laughter. He had to find a word for the high, pure sound, to name it in order to understand why it affected him so deeply.

The crunch of footsteps came closer, waking Julian from his trance. Hazel eyes wild, he grabbed Saylah in desperation and pressed his lips to hers to silence her. That only made her laugh harder. She put her hands on his chest and gripped the dirty fabric and laughed into his half-open mouth. Julian felt her breath and her laughter and the pressure of her hands, and he too lost control and laughed back against her warm lips. They held each other, gasping, while the laughter built inside them, bubbled up into their united mouths.

Finally a crashing among the trees broke through their hysteria. Holding their stomachs, they peered out at a farmer with a pail in his hand. The rusted handle had dyed his palm red, but he did not seem to notice.

"Mr. Palmer," Julian whispered so softly that Saylah had to press her ear to his lips. "We let him share the water because his stream isn't always enough."

The man, who at first glance appeared old and gray, was really about thirty-five with sandy hair and a pair of round, wire-rimmed spectacles that barely clung to the end of his nose. His hair stood up in clumps; Saylah understood why when he scratched his head this way and that while he crouched beside the river where it broadened into a pond. He rocked back and forth on his heels, squinting into the water for a long time.

Saylah covered her mouth with her hand. She felt the laughter coming again and dared not make a sound. She pinched Julian warningly when he couldn't stifle a single gasp.

Mr. Palmer didn't notice. He had begun slowly, carefully, to pick stones out of the water, rinse each one and place it in the bucket. He was not happy with just any stone; he picked up several each time before he found one that suited him. Finally he lifted the bucket, testing its weight. "Ah," he muttered, "just one more."

As he leaned forward to pick up the stone, his spectacles slipped off the end of his nose and into the water. Oblivious of the splash, tiny compared to the noise as he dropped one stone and chose another, Mr. Palmer took his bucket, rose, and sauntered back into the trees.

"He'll need his spectacles," Julian gasped. "He'll walk straight into a tree without them. I've seen him walk into trees *with* them. Though how he'll even find them is beyond me. But we don't dare—"

He broke off when Saylah darted out from behind the bushes, stood at the edge of the pond, and dived into the water. He saw her feet disappear, saw a flash of white fabric, then her head burst out of the water. She stood, dripping and laughing, the spectacles on her own nose, one hand closed in a tight fist. She had found something besides the glasses. She squinted at the blurry world around her and shook her head. Carefully, she removed the spectacles, glanced about for a moment, saw a large boulder, and placed them precisely over a rise in the rock.

"He's coming back!" Julian hissed. "Hurry!"

In an instant, she was back, soaking him with her sodden clothes, tossing her long wet hair over his back so that he gasped. She rolled away, shaking with laughter, unable to face him for fear she would reveal herself to the poor, befuddled farmer who had come collecting stones. Julian too was laughing. What was it she had told Kitkuni once? *I have not yet learned to teach with laughter.* But perhaps she had, after all.

They stifled their mirth when Mr. Palmer appeared, feeling his way along from fir branch to oak, from oak to spruce, until he reached the edge of the pond. He frowned darkly into the water. "Never find them in there. Can't be done." He sighed in despair, then looked up and saw the gray blur of the boulder, the light glinting off something round and smooth.

Mr. Palmer reached out, knocked his spectacles sideways, but somehow managed to catch them before they slid all the way down the rock. They shone with beads of water, and he gazed at them in disbelief, scratching his head and muttering under his breath. Finally he shrugged and turned to go.

Saylah and Julian watched in silence as he struggled with each branch that blocked his way as if it were an enemy who had come upon him while he was not looking. When he had disappeared a second time, they noticed he had left his bucket of carefully selected stones.

This time it was Julian who leapt over the bushes, picked up the bucket, and glanced around wildly. He saw a fir whose branches were thin arms that protruded like steps on a ladder built by a madman. He climbed halfway up the tree, well out of Mr. Palmer's reach, and hung the bucket there. He started down, aware that at any moment the man might reappear, but paused to look back at the swinging bucket. It wasn't fair to make a man like Mr. Palmer attempt such a climb. Quickly, he retrieved the bucket and jumped to the ground, hanging the rusted pail on a low branch he was certain the farmer could reach. Then he heard the bumping and banging through the trees and made a running leap toward the bushes.

—— *261* ——

He cleared them, but caught his pants on a branch and tore a large hole in one knee. Saylah pulled him down beside her and held him while Mr. Palmer, totally flummoxed by now, looked about for his bucket where he had left it. He had given up in disgust when he saw it hanging, swaying slightly.

He scratched his head so furiously that his glasses began to slip off his nose, but he caught them with one bony finger. With a deep sigh, hair standing on end, he retrieved the pail. He stomped away, muttering more loudly than usual about mothers who couldn't manage to keep their children at home where they couldn't go about bothering harmless men.

Saylah and Julian clutched each other, rolling with laughter. When he came up for a gulp of air, Julian gasped. "How can we behave this way?"

"How can we not? We must learn to take the moments that are offered as they come. They are few enough already. Besides," she added with a smile, "we did no harm. He would have had to return for both things anyway. I have simply saved him some groping in cold water." She grinned at the memory of his perplexed expression.

Julian was holding her, shaking with mirth. Without thinking, he leaned forward to kiss her again, but this time their laughter stilled unexpectedly. Saylah felt the touch of his lips all over her cold, wet skin, like a warm skimming breath. Their bodies were pressed together, legs and arms entwined, her hair wet and clinging between them.

Julian was stunned by the prickling of his skin, the heat that came and went in his face, the soft pliancy of Saylah's lips. He had kissed more than one woman in his life, but never like this, never a kiss born of laughter that changed so quickly, so fiercely, to desire. She shivered in his arms and he forced himself to let her go, though his breath came in gasps and his heart beat furiously.

A cool breeze ran over their wet bodies, reminding him of where and who they were. Saylah was flushed, her teeth chattering with cold, and he himself was shaking. "It's too cold here. Let's go back to the waterfall, the broad flat stones that catch the sun when it comes out. We can dry off and get warm."

Saylah nodded mutely. She didn't trust herself to speak. She thought of Colchoté's kiss, full of longing and sadness and desperation. She followed Julian, feeling again the tingling warmth along her arm, her hip, her naked throat. With relief, she saw that he also did not wish to speak. He indicated the warm rocks and stretched out. Silently, she stretched out beside him.

Julian noticed that her hand was still closed tight, and he brushed her locked fingers. "What is it?"

"I found a stone of my own." One finger at a time, she opened her fist to reveal a clear pink stone streaked with gray. "It called to me and I could not resist."

Tentatively, he reached out to touch it. It was warm from the heat of her palm.

"I have many sacred stones," she said, "but none found in the midst of laughter." She closed her fingers around it in a protective caress.

Unaccountably, Julian's eyes began to burn and he bent his arm across them as if to shade them from the sun.

Saylah lay back, the stone clutched in her hand, and let the heat soak into her. She began to feel drowsy, strangely contented. She was enjoying herself, she realized. For the first time since she had left the Longhouse, she felt no need to hurry, no need to find a useful task, no need to keep her mind and fingers occupied.

Then, in an instant, she was up, crouching, alert. She put the stone down and reached slowly for the bow that lay between them.

"What is it?" Julian raised himself on his elbow.

She pointed to the base of the waterfall. The beaver had returned. It waddled along, following the bank, in search of the perfect twig.

Without a sound, Saylah reached back, found an arrow and fitted it to the string. She seemed barely to disturb the air around her as she shifted her weight and took aim. "I must strike near the head," she whispered, "or the skin will be useless. And I must kill him with one arrow, not merely wound him, for that would be too cruel."

Even though Julian heard, she did not seem to have moved her lips. He crouched beside her, watching in fascination. She was so still that even her hair did not move in the breeze. Her concentration on the animal was complete, unbreakable. It frightened him, that stillness, though he could not say why. He only knew that for her, in that moment, there was nothing but the beaver and the bow and the arrow that must reach its mark. He did not think she could hit the animal from this distance, certainly she could not judge well enough to hit a particular part of its body.

He held his breath and watched her pull back the string with a steady hand, crouch on the balls of her feet and yet keep perfect balance, stare directly at the beaver so her gaze seemed to connect, to form an invisible line between them. This was Saylah as she had once been—magnificent, confident, fearless and free. Once they went back to the world, his world, this Saylah would disappear; nothing but a round pink stone would remain. He could not bear the thought and looked away.

That's why he did not see her release the arrow. He heard a hiss, like a night whisper, and turned to see the animal lying motionless on the bank below. "I don't believe it," he blurted out.

—— 263 ——

Saylah did not hear. Her eyes were closed and she whispered Salish words he could not understand. He suspected she was praying. Quietly, he leapt down the side of the boulders and picked up the dead beaver. The arrow had pierced its neck from side to side, killing it instantly and preserving the skin. He looked up at Saylah who was smiling broadly. *There is no weapon more efficient than an arrow truly aimed.*

When he rejoined her, she said quietly, "Now that you have seen, do you believe?"

So she *had* heard him. "How can I do otherwise? It's incredible."

Julian's praise was rare but sincere. Saylah smiled and touched his hand. This time it was he who tensed and reached for the bow, he who crouched, staring, his heart pounding dully.

She glanced up to see what had caught his attention. A huge golden cougar walked at the edge of the trees, alert, searching. "He must have smelled the beaver's blood and come to see what he could find."

Julian was not listening. He inserted an arrow in the bow and pulled the string taut. He aimed along the shaft, his face cold and stiff with the intention to kill.

"No!" Saylah cried.

Julian paused, but his eyes never left the dangerous cougar. Saylah's hand was on his arm. She made no explanation, only the plea of her fingers through his sodden shirt. He drew back the string a second time.

"No!" Saylah gasped again, but this time he ignored her. His concentration was on the sleek animal that had so deftly avoided capture until now. Carefully, he released the arrow.

He felt a jarring that made him lose his balance and the bow went flying from his hand to land on the boulder below. Saylah had knocked it away. He glared at her in disbelief and anger.

"I could not let you do it."

"Why?" It was the only word he could manage through the unpleasant taste in his mouth.

"The cougar is sacred."

Julian took a deep breath that did not begin to fill his empty lungs. "Maybe to you. But to us it is a menace. It kills our chickens, harasses our cattle. I once saw a man mauled by that cat. It was ugly and brutal, Saylah."

She shook her head vehemently. "A cougar would never—" She broke off, horrified. The cougar was sacred among the Salish. It would protect her People, always. But these were not her People. These were the Strangers, the destroyers, the unknown.

She had no protection against them now. Her defenses were down, every nerve exposed, susceptible, raw. She could not guard against the power of her memories. She folded in upon herself. "No!" The word was torn from her by a brutal and unfriendly hand. Pain rushed over her like the storm-tossed waves of the sea, heavy with wind and salt and swirling foam. She lost her balance, fell against the force of her pain, the tide racing inward to her unprotected soul. She shivered, chilled through, unable to think or see beyond the anguish that engulfed her.

Slowly, so slowly that she was not sure when it began, she realized someone was holding her. Someone's arms were tight around her, protecting, not confining. The heat of someone's body was making the cold retreat, a little at a time. Julian held her close, her head on his shoulder. She was not, after all, alone with the savagery of her pain. If he had not caught her, she was certain it would have swept her away.

She gasped for breath, struggling to hold on, to bring life and warmth into her empty body. She had left the magic of her childhood behind. She was back in the world of the Strangers. There was nowhere else to go.

When the trembling had subsided, Julian whispered, "You're cold." He took off his shirt, dried by the sun, and wrapped it around her shoulders, circling her with his arms.

Tentatively, Saylah looked up, appalled that she had revealed her weakness. But when she saw Julian's face, she knew his own protective wall was quaking. It stood on water which could not hold its weight, though it had been reduced to spun-glass threads, like a fragile crystal curtain. It was just a matter of time until it shattered. But he was not ready. She looked quickly away.

They sat for a long time on that ageless boulder formed of wind and rain and the rushing of waters. They sat, shoulder to shoulder, back to rigid back, held captive by the fear of their own feelings, of the pain that could destroy as easily as it might heal. Some force unnamed, unspoken, held them intertwined; they could not escape the woven web, but neither could they bear to hold it in their hands and feel its texture, know its weight, its promise.

Julian did not speak for a long time, then the words tumbled out, unwise and dangerous. "I didn't realize you hurt so much. You're always so contained."

"I thought the pain had left me," Saylah whispered.

He shifted gingerly, avoiding her gaze. Her storm had raged and lost its power. His had not yet really begun. She picked up the new smooth stone, placed it in his palm, and wound her fingers with his. They sat unmoving, hand on hand, with the gray-streaked stone between them, bound by silence more tightly than by words.

"We should go back," Julian said.

"Soon," Saylah replied. "Too soon."

—— 265 ——

Chapter

——⊰ 38 ⊱——

Sophia Ashton was in a temper, even though she was wearing her favorite brocaded alpaca dress of teal blue, which set off her gray eyes and auburn hair nicely. At her throat were the matched pearls her husband had brought back from a trading trip the year before; she wore matching earrings and a small pearl brooch. She paced the floor in the drawing room, her fine kid boots making no mark on the thick Persian rug.

"My dear!" Edward exclaimed, coming up behind her. "You are a vision."

Sophia whirled, hands on hips. "A vision of what? A leprechaun? Or perhaps a frog transformed into a prince." She spoke sharply, but Edward merely smiled.

"Neither, I shouldn't think. More like a duchess." Whisking his hand from behind his back, he presented her with a spray of purple asters, the last of the summer flowers.

Sophia fought the impulse to give up her temper and smile, even when Edward retrieved the flowers from her limp hand and arranged them with care in the lace-edged neckline of her gown.

"You've gone to a great deal of trouble for an afternoon beside the fire," he observed with a twinkle in his brown eyes sparked with gold. His sandy hair was tousled, and he tried to smooth it with his hand. With the other, he caressed Sophia's throat above the flowers.

"I meant to go into Victoria with Paul. He's outgrown his boots again and Clara is too busy to trim his hair. Since I need to see the dressmaker, I thought we could have a pleasant afternoon together."

Edward listened gravely, rubbing his chin between thumb and forefinger. "And what, might I ask, has so cruelly spoiled your well-laid plan?"

Sophia punched him playfully in the arm, but refused to smile. "He's not home yet. He went to walk in the woods this morning, but he promised to be back by noon." She frowned and began to pace again. "He's seldom late."

Edward heard the concern in her voice and caught her by the shoulders. He wanted her to hear him, and besides, he liked looking into her softly rounded face, her gray eyes tinted pale blue by the teal of her dress. "He's a smart lad, is our Paul. He'll have discovered a pioneer trail and followed it to Cowichan or some such nonsense, forgetting entirely that you'd be wearing your most flattering gown and pacing before the fire. You know how young boys get distracted."

Sophia sighed and leaned against her husband. "But Brutus has been barking for the longest time, and I feel uneasy. I can't explain—"

At the sound of his name, Brutus raced about and began a high-pitched moan that made Edward cover his ears. "*That* is a bark?"

Sophia's lips actually twitched, but she hid her smile by bending to pat the dog. "That's just it. It's not normal. And Paul wouldn't forget. I don't feel right, that's all."

"Superstitious?" Edward asked, drawing her close again. "Worrying about ghosts?"

Sophia straightened her spine and raised her chin. "Certainly not." She rested her hand on the mantel, forgetting the packet she'd hidden there. The paper crackled and Edward peered closer.

"Ah!" he breathed. "So that's it. Letter from your father, I imagine. Has you upset again. Can't say I'm surprised."

Clenching her fists, Sophia cried, "He has no sense of humor. He's nothing but an old stick!" She blushed at her childish outburst, but Edward was delighted.

"Well then, I'd say it's a good thing you're here with me and not back in Boston with him." He hugged her, then backed away and slowly began to run his fingers up the tailored sides of her gown. "Don't you agree?" he asked wickedly, arching an eyebrow.

Sophia grasped his hands. "Don't do that. You know it makes me laugh, and I'm trying very hard to worry and be angry."

Edward threw back his head and laughed. "You're too beautiful to worry," he said when he'd caught his breath. He tucked in his rumpled shirt and smoothed his trousers, watching Sophia with admiration. He could always make her laugh; she was willing to put unpleasantness behind her when he made the effort to bring her around. She had the strength of will to do that, yet never forget her duty or her power. She was a rare woman, and he was lucky to have her.

"Ah-ha!" his wife exclaimed. "I have you there. You made a mistake and bought me a mirror on your last trip to Victoria."

Edward was determined not to let her win. "I thought that was the pearl brooch."

Shaking her head in a manner which denied argument, she said, "That was the time before, and you aren't going to distract me with inconsequentials." She did not admit that when she had first seen the delicate silver filigree on the mirror, hairbrush and comb, she had been enchanted. "I looked long and hard into that mirror, Edward Ashton, and I know—"

He started to interrupt, but she touched her finger to his lips. "I shall admit I'm not as ugly as Pierre, the prize bull, but the mirror told me quite frankly that I'm not beautiful either." She had known that even as a girl. She was attractive enough. Her eyes were dark-lashed and piercing—the mirror had told her that as well—her auburn hair thick and wavy, her dimples charming. She would not crack a looking glass, but neither would she ever make men stare open-mouthed, as they had at Simone Ivy.

Edward threw up his hands and stomped about in mock rage. "Then the glass is defective, a bald-faced liar. I shall return it tomorrow and demand another to replace it."

Sophia gave up the fight. She laughed until her side ached. "Just suppose, my dear, that the new mirror says the same," she managed to gasp.

Her husband paused, pretending extreme consternation, pulling wildly on his muttonchops. Then he pounded his fist on the mantel, crumpling his father-in-law's letter quite by accident in the process. "Then I shall return it as well until I find one that is not so damnably flawed."

Tears ran down Sophia's cheeks as she laughed. "My father would be deeply shocked by your language in front of a delicate female."

Edward looked around wildly, gripping his throat in fear. "Where? Where is she? Can't have delicate females living in the wilderness. Far too dangerous. Just you remember that."

Sophia kissed him on the lips and he stopped his ranting to pull her close. He kissed her ear, the line of her throat, the tiny hollow where her wild pulse beat. Then he tangled one hand in her hair and dropped more kisses from her throat to the cleft between her breasts. He removed the asters and placed them on the mantel, drawing them past her nose so the scent hung for a moment in the air.

Edward breathed deeply as Sophia leaned into him and he covered her parted lips with his. When she wound her arms around him, her breath warm and demanding on his cheek, he raised his head. "Wouldn't you rather worry? You said—"

Sophia slid her hand inside his shirt, tangling her fingers in the fine gold hair that covered his chest. "I'm far too busy to worry just now."

Edward smiled benignly and began to search out the fastenings on his wife's teal blue gown.

Chapter
━━◄ 39 ►━━

Once Flora had set them free, Paul and Theron headed straight for the forest.

"We don't usually go this way," Theron said.

"I'm bored," Paul announced petulantly. "I want to do something new."

Theron considered his friend closely. Something was wrong; he could tell. Paul was pale and restless and he kept twining his hands together before and behind him. But every time Theron started to ask a question, Paul glared so fiercely that the younger boy subsided.

Paul began to move faster and faster until Theron had to run. "Hey!" he shouted. "Wait for me!" He was puffing, trying to keep up on his short, chubby legs. "Can't you slow down, even a little bit?"

Paul glanced back, saw his friend's red cheeks and ragged breathing and felt immediate remorse. He had been so intent on losing himself in the woods that he had not thought of Theron at all. "I'm sorry. We'll go more slowly from now on."

"Where *are* we going?" Theron demanded when he could speak without gasping.

Paul shrugged. "I'm just wandering. I had to get away. Far away."

"From what?" The older boy was moving quickly again, and Theron struggled to keep up. He was worried about his friend. Paul looked sick and sounded desperate, and his brown-gold eyes flicked back and forth, resting nowhere.

Paul stopped so abruptly that Theron crashed into him and they both fell backward into a clump of bracken. Bugs and a snail or two scattered, and Theron grimaced with distaste. He knew boys were supposed to like that stuff; Julian had told him. But he preferred soft brown squirrels and rabbits. If that wasn't good enough for Julian, well then, too bad. Just now it was more important that he push Paul off him so he could breathe.

Brushing the bits of fern from his back and the drops of moisture from his hair, Paul regarded his friend seriously. "Don't you ever want to run away for a little while? So you can't hear them telling you what's good and bad?"

Theron stood somewhat awkwardly and nodded with vigor. "Especially when the bad things are always the most fun."

"Well, that's how I feel today. I want to find a place they don't know about where we can be left alone." He put his hand on Theron's shoulder. "You'll understand better when you're older, like me."

"I guess," the younger boy said, trudging after his friend, who had started off in yet another direction, purposely avoiding the path. "But if I'm going to be lost forever in the woods, I want to know why."

"You won't be lost forever, silly. I'll find the way out. I'm smart about those things. My parents always say so."

Theron looked doubtful, but was not in the mood to argue. This looked very much like becoming a secret—this place Paul would find where no one else could discover them. Theron was thoroughly addicted to secrets. He crossed his arms over his chest. He'd just wait awhile and see what happened.

"Quiet!" Paul hissed.

Theron stopped where he was, petrified by the tone in his friend's voice. Paul was standing behind a great cedar, peeking out into a clearing. His face was so white it might have been a piece of parchment in the book Theron had found, and his body was rigid with fear.

Theron squinted, trying to see, but the foliage was too thick. He was just about to turn back the way they had come when Paul whispered, "You'd better come here. I don't know which way she'll break."

Theron's heart began to pound. He didn't like the sound of that at all. Who would break? He heard a low growl and a snarl and found he could not swallow. He picked his way through the ferns toward Paul, his pulse racing. By the time he reached the tree, his palms were damp with sweat.

"Look," Paul whispered. "Isn't she beautiful?"

Theron, who had closed his eyes in silent but fervent prayer, looked up.

He knew Paul was afraid; he could feel him shaking, feel the clammy skin of his arm. Yet his eyes glowed and he seemed unable to move or look away. Suspiciously, inching around the tree until he could look out and still be protected, the younger boy glanced into the clearing.

There, in full view, lay a cougar, stretched out in a moving patch of sunlight. Her fur was sleek and golden, her eyes golden-brown, like Paul's, and her teeth, when she opened her mouth to yawn, were huge and glittering white.

Theron thought he might very well be sick. He leapt back, using Paul as a shield, and closed his eyes again. "I heard it growl," he managed to stutter.

"A flicker was teasing her," Paul explained. "Good thing it could fly fast. That cougar's paws move like lightning."

Now Theron knew he was going to be sick. "What if it smells us? Julian said they can smell people and stalk them 'til they can't get away."

Paul shook his head. "The wind isn't right."

"I don't care if it is or not. I don't want to stay here."

"If you run, she'll hear you. You have to stay still," Paul warned, deadly serious.

So that's why he was shaking, Theron thought. Then he heard Paul gasp, and in spite of himself, looked back around the tree. A rabbit had entered the clearing on the far side. The cougar watched it lazily, tail twitching. Then it became motionless, inaudible, part of the waving grass, its golden eyes on the small brown rabbit.

Paul felt sick and wanted to turn away, but knew they dared not make a sound. Theron was clinging to his legs, digging his nails into the fabric of his trousers until Paul winced in pain. Yet he did not move. Theron's eyes were shut tight, but Paul could not look away. He saw the rabbit twitch its nose, munch on a leaf, and hop nearer the waiting cougar.

The air was so hushed that the boys could hear their own breath and tried to hold it, praying for a breeze to rattle the leaves overhead.

The cougar was poised, waiting. Nothing moved but its eyes. Suddenly, the entire forest seemed to erupt into motion. The cougar was in the air, paws spread before and behind, tail raised. In another instant, the rabbit was clamped in deadly jaws and its blood dripped onto the trampled grass. Paul retched silently and the cougar raised its head, then turned back to its prey. Proudly, the cat carried the rabbit into the woods.

Paul gripped the tree so hard it cut his arms, but he didn't care. His stomach lurched and rolled and his body was covered with sweat.

Theron squeezed his eyes together so he wouldn't cry. All he could do was hold on to Paul, who was older and wiser and would get him away from there before his heart burst with the blood rushing through it. They stood together, trembling, pale, but unable, somehow, to leave the clearing. Or was it the tall cedar that kept them from falling face down into the bracken?

They waited, hardly daring to breathe, until long after the sounds of crackling brush told them the cat had disappeared in the other direction. They were frozen where they stood.

Finally Paul released the tree to look at his scratched arms. He was still shaking, but his heart had stopped pounding and Theron had let go of his legs. They looked at each other and wondered what to do. Neither seemed able to think. Paul took a deep breath. He had brought his friend here, after all. He had to get him safely away.

He took Theron's hand and they started off in the opposite direction from the one the cat had taken.

"I used to say I wanted to see a cougar close up," Theron whispered.

"I know," Paul agreed, shuddering. "I always tease Mama about running into grizzlies."

They fell silent, considering the wisdom of making further wishes. When they found a huge oak with protruding roots that made a small hollow underneath, they sat down, wrapping their arms tightly around the twisted roots for support. "I'm hungry," Theron said. Slowly, his optimism began to return.

Paul dug in his pocket and brought out some nuts and two grimy candy balls. He gave half to Theron and they munched contentedly, happy to be alive. Theron thought about telling Flora and Saylah about the cougar but decided against it. They'd never let him play with Paul in the woods again. So there it was, the secret he'd been hoping for. He was altogether delighted.

"Come on," Paul said finally. He didn't really want to move, but they had to get up if they were going to find their way home. Somehow the adventure in the woods had lost its allure.

Only when they stood up and looked around did Paul realize he had no idea where they were. He had never seen this part of the forest. He tried to look at the sun, but it was hidden behind the clouds. Besides, he couldn't remember how to tell the direction from the sun, though his father had taught him once. He gnawed on his lower lip. He thought they had come through a narrow opening of trees, so if they went the other way, they should be heading home. "This way," he said with more confidence than he felt.

"How do you know?" Theron demanded, hands on hips, ready to dig his heels into the ground if he had to.

"I don't, but it's better than sitting here for the rest of our lives."

Theron's blue eyes grew wide and round. "You mean we might miss dinner?"

Paul didn't want to think about what they'd miss. "You can stay here if you like, but I'm going to try to find my way home."

Theron stuck his jaw out stubbornly, but when Paul ducked under a low branch, he gave up sulking and started to run. "I'm coming!" he cried. "Wait for me!"

They trudged for hours through thick trees and snarled underbrush until they were hopelessly lost.

"Saylah told me if you get to the river you can always follow it and be safe," Theron offered tentatively when Paul seemed to run out of ideas.

The clouds had looked like they would clear earlier, but now they were thick and gray overhead. The boys were shivering and cold and desperate. The normally murky woods had grown positively dark, though the sun had not yet set. They could barely find their way without walking into trees and fallen logs and jutting boulders.

"They'll notice we're gone and come after us," Paul said.

Theron perked up. "Sure they will."

Paul sat under a tree, looking dejected. "I hope so."

Theron sat next to him, elbowing him in the side in a gesture meant to reassure. "Saylah will find us," he said firmly. "I know she will. She'll find us."

"If you believe it so much, why do you keep saying it?" Paul demanded querulously. He did not want Theron to know how frightened he was.

Theron crossed his arms and glared up at his friend. "Because it sounds nice. And that makes me feel better."

Paul shook his head. "I'm sorry. We shouldn't fight. That won't help."

"It would help me," the younger boy declared with a dangerously jutting lip.

Paul laughed out loud, but Theron didn't see what was so funny. He concentrated on thinking about Saylah. She would know what to do. They just had to wait.

Then they heard it; the crackling of twigs nearby. They had listened to that sound too closely earlier not to recognize it now. They looked at each other in terror. "The cougar," Paul whispered. Then he clapped his hand over his mouth.

"Maybe the wind's wrong now too," Theron offered. It came out like a croak.

"Shhh!" Paul put his finger to his lips, stared at the heavy underbrush where they'd heard the sound. He pointed the other way and Theron nodded stiffly.

He was afraid to move a muscle. Maybe it's not hungry, he thought desperately. Maybe the rabbit had been enough. It took every ounce of courage he had to stand up and follow his friend, who was creeping forward, step by step, watching for twigs, placing his feet carefully on full green ferns that would muffle any sound. Theron did the best he could; at least he had practiced being silent more than once. He hoped they'd just leave the cougar behind and concentrated on watching Paul's feet and following his trail exactly.

They went along for several minutes in silence, with only the rustle of the breeze overhead. Then the crackling of twigs began again and they knew the cougar was behind them. Perhaps even following their trail.

Theron felt the nuts and candy rise into his throat, but he fought back the nausea. The fear would not go. Every moment it became more clear that the cougar was not out for an idle stroll. It was following them.

Paul looked back once, desperately. The expression on his face turned Theron's blood to ice. He knew then that they were going to die, be torn to pieces by a golden cat with glittering white teeth.

The boys began to run. They did not know what else to do. The cougar was running too. And it was much faster, much more agile, more familiar with the woods. Finally Paul called back over his shoulder, "We can't outrun it. We have to hide."

Theron looked around wildly at the same firs and cedars, spruces and alders, birches and oaks they had seen all day. None would be good for more than a moment's shelter. He was gasping for breath, certain his heart had stopped beating long ago, and he hurt all over. Paul was about to collapse too. He could hear his rasping breath. Theron wanted to sit down and cry, to shout for Flora or Saylah or even Julian. He wanted to fall where he was and let the cougar come and have it be over.

But he kept running. Until he saw the log. Paul saw it at exactly the same moment. It was long and hollow, with a knothole halfway down. The moss had grown over it long since and hung over the end like a curtain of beads. The far end was tight against a stump, perhaps its own.

"If we hide in there, the cougar can't follow," Paul said.

Theron chewed furiously on his already raw lip, eyeing the narrow log with distaste. He grimaced, but when he heard a sound behind him, he glanced at his friend's set jaw, then raced for the log and crawled inside.

The boys had to wiggle along, scraping arms and legs against the sides. The log was not much bigger around than they were.

"The end!" Paul gasped when they were wedged in place. "The cougar's small enough to work its way in. I saw a boulder nearby. I'll use it to block the hole."

Theron didn't want his friend to move, but he didn't want to die either.

He lay immobile, hearing his own breath, and his pulse, which sounded like thunder in his ears.

Paul wriggled halfway out and saw that he could reach the boulder. He struggled to dislodge it, then shifted it, an inch at a time, toward the end of the log. As he pulled it closer, he wriggled back inside, until he wedged it securely into the end. "Now," he said with satisfaction.

"Now what?" Theron whispered. It was cold and dark, and the sides were damp and smelled strongly of moss. If it hadn't been for the knothole just above his arm, there would have been no light at all. Theron was afraid he couldn't breathe. And he could hear the cougar approaching. He felt Paul stiffen and try to move, but he had no room.

There was a loud slap at one end of the log, followed by a low, deep growl. Paul closed his eyes and prayed, more fervently than he ever had before. He was cold with fear, yet covered with sweat, and he could hardly breathe in the damp, murky interior. But that was nothing compared to the huge, sleek animal who was sniffing around the log from end to end.

Theron started to cry. He knew he was being a baby, but he couldn't help it. He could hear the cat as it brushed past the spot where he lay huddled.

"Shh!" Paul demanded. "You'll just make her angrier."

Theron choked back his sobs, bit his lip until it bled. His heart pounded so fiercely that it hurt.

Then, all at once, there was no more light. He looked up in terror to see the cougar's paw over the knothole. The paw disappeared and her nose filled the hole, sniffing. She growled in triumph and pushed her paw through the hole, swiping at Theron's exposed arm. He tried to draw away, but there wasn't any room. He opened his mouth in a silent scream. Terror blocked his throat. He could feel the air whoosh as the paw moved back and forth. Then he felt a searing, a tearing on his arm, and the cougar withdrew a bloody paw.

Theron gasped, sobbing at the horrible pain.

"What happened?" Paul hissed.

"My arm" was all his friend could manage. The pain was throbbing up his arm and shoulder until it mingled with the hot, pulsing fear. The boys could smell it, even over the moss and rotting wood.

Paul rasped back, "Take off my shoe and jam it into the hole. I can't reach my foot."

Theron lay shivering, unable to move as the paw came close, retreated, came closer.

"Do it!" Paul cried. "Please!"

It was the *please* that jolted Theron into action. It was so shaky, so full of terror. With his unhurt arm he reached above his head. Paul's foot was practically resting on his hair. Tugging and pulling, Theron got the shoe off, though he thought he'd broken the buttons. He didn't care. He struggled for a minute, then wedged the boot into the hole.

The cougar growled, hissed, snarled. It battered the log with its paws, nudged it with its head, pushed and pulled, driven now by the smell of Theron's blood. The log began to rock, back and forth, slowly at first, then more and more quickly. Suddenly, it came loose and began to roll.

Theron let out his breath in a rush of pure terror. The boys lay helpless while the log bumped and scraped over rough ground. Paul was afraid he would vomit and fought the urge desperately. The smell in the log was already overpowering. Theron clutched his friend's feet, but could not hold him steady. Over and over the log went until the boys' heads were spinning, their stomachs lurching, their elbows and knees striking the rough sides again and again.

Finally the rolling slowed, then stopped. The boys lay in pools of sweat, teeth clenched, waiting. There was no sound. Perhaps the cougar had dislodged the log but could not follow its path. Neither spoke the thought aloud. They could not have found the words even if they wanted to.

For a long time they lay cramped and aching, but each moment brought more hope. Then Paul tensed and Theron groaned. They could hear the cougar's roar and it was close.

The cat approached; they could hear her moving back and forth. She pawed at the surface of the log, but it did not give. Miraculously, the rock had not come loose. Theron did not know what lay at the other end. He did not want to know. Ever.

For what seemed like hours the cat paced, then suddenly, there was silence. Theron risked opening his eyes and saw through the now empty knothole a tiny bit of light. He waited, holding his breath until it exploded. He covered his bloody, throbbing arm with his hand, trying to ease the shooting pains. He was cold. So cold and hurting and tired.

"Maybe we can get out now," Paul said when the sounds of the cat did not return. He could barely speak, he was so choked by the tight confines of the log, the fetid air, and the sense of panic that welled inside him.

"What if she comes back?" Theron croaked. "What if she's out there waiting?"

Paul gulped but nothing happened. Theron was right. They would have to stay here until—until when?

"We'd better not move until they find us," Theron said, his face covered with tears. He was glad Paul could not see them.

"No!" Paul's panic, too long held in check, burst free. "I can't bear it! Really I can't! I can't breathe. Oh, God, I can't breathe."

Theron fought back his own terror. "We got away from that cat, didn't we? I'll bet we can escape from a log a whole lot easier. We just have to wait, is all. We just have to wait."

"What if they don't come?" Paul was sobbing now, in shock and terror and panic.

Theron refused to think about that. They had to come. Please God, they had to.

Chapter

—◄ 40 ►—

Julian led Saylah around the back of the house, to the door at the far end of the hallway, where their rooms were located. Both wanted to wash up before anyone saw them; they were covered with dirt, twigs were caught in their hair, and their feet were crusted with mud. Saylah's dress was wrinkled and stained from the bush she had hung it on, and Julian's clothes were torn in several places. They did not want to worry Flora, so they slipped inside and went directly to their rooms.

That is why they did not see the smart carriage pulled by beautiful but restive horses sitting in front of the house, nor hear the muffled voices in the hall. It was not until Saylah left her room and entered the main hall that she saw the two visitors huddled around the fire with Flora.

As soon as she saw the three rigid backs, the heads—one blond, one auburn and one sandy brown—held stiffly, Saylah knew something was very wrong. And it had nothing to do with Jamie. Her hands went cold and her vision blurred, faded, came back into focus.

"Where's Theron?" she asked, forgetting, in her distress, that no one knew she was there.

All three jumped, all three turned, alarmed, to regard her in dismay.

"Saylah!" Flora cried. "Thank the Lord ye've come at last."

"Theron?" Saylah repeated through a dry, parched throat. She was

— *279* —

aware of the two strangers watching her intently, but kept her attention on Flora.

"That's just it, ye see," Flora said, twisting and untwisting her hands in her apron. "We've none of us seen him since mornin'. Nor their Paul either. We hoped he was with ye."

Saylah was drinking in Flora's fear. Her cold hands began to shake and she had to clasp them tightly. After several steadying breaths, she addressed the visitors. "You are Paul's parents?"

"By the Black Stone of Iona!" Flora cried. "Where are my manners? Saylah, 'tis Edward and Sophia Ashton, sure enough, come to ask after Paul."

"I wasn't worried at first," Sophia burst out. "Not until the sun began to set. He's never stayed out so long before, you see. He's always careful not to worry us." Her gray eyes were clouded with apprehension. "When Flora told us about you, we really had hoped . . ." She trailed off miserably. "But you haven't seen them, have you?"

"Not for some time. But I will find them." Saylah spoke in her most soothing voice, the voice that had lulled her People, calmed them, made them hear her words inside, where they knew how to believe. She felt sure the Ashtons had been here for a while, yet Sophia had not removed her fur-lined cape, nor Edward his greatcoat. That, more than anything, revealed their agitation.

Now the man came forward, slipped his arm around his wife's shoulders. "How can you find them in the dark? The forest is much too large, the undergrowth too thick. And we've no idea which way they've gone."

Saylah straightened her shoulders, annoyed by Edward's lack of faith, though why he should have faith in a stranger she did not know. But he looked at her with his brown-gold eyes in a way that made her more apprehensive than she already was. "I am of Salish blood. I spent many years living in the woods, coming to know them well. I have followed the tracks of a deer in the darkness, slept and dreamed by the river whose path flows through my blood. I will find Theron and your son."

"What if it's too late?" Sophia asked shakily. "What if something has happened? I can't think why else Paul would worry us so." She looked at Edward pleadingly, but he did not know how to reassure her.

Julian had joined them by now, and Flora was telling him what had happened. He glanced miserably at Saylah. If they had not lingered, behaving like children, if they had come back as they should have to their chores and their responsibilities, they would have known long ago that the boys had not returned. They could have searched while it was light, while there was still a chance of finding them.

Saylah swallowed dryly. It had been she who insisted they stay, she who urged Julian to forget the ranch and lose himself in the river. She had caused this catastrophe. It must be she who made it right.

"It's all my fault!" Sophia cried, looking from one to the other. She had expected them to bring relief, but they brought more questions, more uncertainty.

"Of course it's not!" Edward declared just as Flora snapped, "Nonsense!"

Sophia shook her head wildly, releasing some of her curls from their confinement. They fell about her shoulders, glinting red in the firelight. "I wrote to my father, you see, teasing him about the danger of living on the ranch. I told him Paul was looking for a grizzly. It was a mean and stupid thing to do. And this is my punishment from God."

Saylah regarded the woman intently. "Is your God so cruel that he would punish a child for some words you wrote while laughing? That does not seem just to me. I do not think the gods are unkind. You did not lead Paul into the forest. Only if you had could you take the blame." The words of reassurance came easily, but Saylah did not hear them in her heart, where her own guilt flourished.

Sophia stopped shaking to stare in astonishment.

"What, exactly, *has* happened?" Edward demanded. "What good does it do to stand about discussing it? We should go, now, and find them."

If they can be found, Saylah added silently. She knew Paul and Theron were in danger, had known it the instant she entered this room full of fear. "Let Julian and me go alone," she said. "Too many people would cause confusion and create more danger."

"That's right," Flora said as cheerfully as she could. "Let the young people go. Saylah's tellin' ye the truth when she says she knows these woods. Many's the day she's taken me out to gather herbs and roots."

"But can you trust her?" Edward whispered low, but not low enough to be inaudible. "You barely know her."

"I'd trust her with my own life, that I would, and my son's as well," Flora said, puffing up her chest while a flush of anger climbed up her cheeks.

It was then that Saylah remembered Jamie's few references to Edward Ashton, the ambivalence of his tone. They had once been close friends. But that did not matter now. She looked at Julian. "Do you have something I could wear? I will not be able to crawl in this dress, or move silently."

Julian took her arm, grateful for something positive to do. "I think you'd fit into some of my old clothes."

Saylah did not hear Sophia's gasp of surprise. She was listening to her inner voices, which bid her hurry, hurry. "Bring your gun," she said as she grabbed the clothes and went to change. She closed the door behind her and began to undo the tiny buttons she had fastened a few minutes before. All the time the wind was rushing in her head, crying, "Hurry, hurry!"

Saylah and Julian set out with two oil lanterns, though Saylah claimed she would not need them. She wore a pair of Julian's trousers, hooked around her waist by an oversized belt, an old cotton shirt and a hand-woven sweater. He had offered her a greatcoat, but she said it would be too bulky, though the night had turned cold. She had braided her hair tightly and pinned it up, out of the way.

Julian followed her, crouching low, his lantern casting weird shadows over her huddled form. He did not know how they would find two small boys in this huge forest, he only knew he trusted Saylah as he'd never trusted anyone. He had seen her blend into the woods with the ease of the animals who made it their home. If anyone could find a trail, she could. He hoped to God she did. He could never face Flora again unless he carried her son in his arms.

They ducked in and out of thickets, under low branches, zigzagging from trees to clumps of brush to tiny clearings. Julian had no sense of their direction, but Saylah did not hesitate. When branches struck her face, she brushed them carelessly aside. When the sounds of animals came near, she held her lantern high, threateningly, and the sounds disappeared.

She had seen where the boys entered the woods that morning, so she went straight there and searched the ground until she found what she was seeking. Footprints in the soft, damp earth. "If it were sand, we would be lost," she whispered. "The spirits are kind."

Julian didn't think so, but he didn't argue.

Saylah was so intent on following the footprints that she almost missed the broken ferns where the boys had fallen. She examined them carefully in the false, fitful light, and from there, found her way to the tree where they had stood for so long. She was confused by the markings; the boys had not been moving, yet the prints were very deep. She touched the soil, rubbed it between her fingers.

After that they lost the trail. She did not know why. The tracks had been clear enough until now. Saylah tried to keep her pulse steady, her breathing even, but she was afraid. Hurry, hurry, rang in her head, but she could find nothing to hold on to, no sign that Paul and Theron had been here.

Julian was the one who found it. He shouted in triumph. "A gumball wrapper!"

Saylah was beside him in an instant, studying the impressions on the ground between two gnarled oak roots. "They rested here," she said. "They were safe then."

"What—" Julian began. But she was gone, following the signs that were now visible once more. Broken branches low on a tree, snapped ferns, occasional footprints, disturbed plants. She realized soon enough that they were crossing and recrossing the same ground. It seemed they had been traipsing through this grim, unfriendly forest for hours, yet they could not find a pattern to the footprints.

She began to feel dizzy. Hurry, hurry, hurry. But there were too many signs, as if the boys had run in circles. "They must have been lost," she called back to Julian. *Lost.* The word echoed dully in her ears.

Julian sensed her rising apprehension and tried to calm his own rapid pulse. He thought of Paul and Theron lost in the woods in the dark, without a weapon, without wisdom, probably without hope. Then he heard Saylah gasp, saw her fall to her knees.

He was there, his hand on her shoulder, trying to hold her upright. She swayed, moaning out words he could not understand. "What is it? For God's sake, tell me."

She looked up and he saw that her cheeks were colorless, her eyes dull. She opened her mouth, but no words came. She began to sway again, keening out her anguish.

"Please," Julian cried, "tell me. I can't bear not knowing."

With an effort, she forced the words through parched lips. "The cougar," she said. "It crosses their path many times."

Julian nearly dropped the lantern. He felt something settle in the pit of his stomach, cold and hard as lead. He did not speak. The only words he could say would have torn her apart.

"I did not know," she said. "I would give my life to protect them. I did not know." She had heard those words before, lived through this hell, this helplessness caused by her own blindness. Many lives had been lost the last time. How many would pay now for her mistake?

Julian forced his voice up into his throat, which was raw and painful. "How could you know? Just because you see the track, we don't know what happened. Let's find them before we grieve."

She looked up into his face, his gleaming eyes. He was not going to blame her or remind her of what she already knew.

"Come," he said again.

Saylah rose slowly, painfully. He took her hand and felt how clammy it was. She was shaking, struggling to regain her composure. Julian said nothing, just held her tighter. Eventually, the trembling stopped and her skin grew warm in his.

"This way, I think," she said. "The trail seems to veer off sharply."

She did not say that the footprints were those of two boys running and that the cougar's deep paw prints were close behind. She looked ahead, sang and prayed, her lantern high. She felt a sense of unreality, as if she were running in a dream—or a nightmare. Never before had she followed a cougar in fear, stalked him as a threat and an enemy.

She noticed that Julian held his rifle cocked and ready. His eyes moved restlessly from side to side. He was watching, waiting for the animal to strike.

"There is no need for that," she said in a voice that was not her own. "The cougar is gone."

He peered at her through narrowed lids. "How do you know?"

She stopped in the middle of the rough path through broken vines and tangled greenery, made eerie black by the night. "If he were nearby, I would feel it." Her eyes blazed in the quavering light of the lanterns, in what seemed to him a challenge.

"There are other animals," he began.

"I would know if there was danger. I was taught to know such things. *We* are safe."

Julian believed her, and tried to ignore the slight emphasis on the word *we*. They moved forward again, slashing at low-hanging branches and creeping vines. They carried the lanterns carefully, trying to avoid the thick branches that could so easily catch fire. At least here, deep in the forest, the sun had not penetrated to dry the dampness from fir and oak and pine.

Saylah pressed ahead without speaking until she stopped at a stump with a low, dark depression beside it. The earth was packed down, saturated with moisture and crushed leaves. "Something heavy lay here recently," she said. "And here the footprints stop." She bent to examine the ground at the far end of the depression and found the dirt scuffed, then marked again and again by a cougar's paws. She frowned, concentrating. She could not stop the flare of hope because there was no blood, no fragments of clothes, no signs of struggle.

Then, when Julian held up his lantern, she saw the path where the log had rolled. She looked around the stump once more, at the place where the footprints stopped. "They were clever," she said breathlessly. "They must have crawled inside a log where the cougar could not go. The cat must have jarred the log loose."

Even Julian could see its erratic path downward; even he could see the cougar's paw prints following. Together, not speaking, afraid to make a sound, they started down. It took them a long time to get to the place where the log had come to rest. Saylah held her lantern high just as Julian came up beside her. He saw the log, battered now, covered with tattered remnants of moss, and started toward it.

"No!" Saylah gasped. She reached out, her arm rigid across his chest to stop him, for she sensed he had not heard. His attention was on the log and what might be hidden inside it.

When he felt the pressure of her arm holding him back, he tried to push it away. He had to get to the boys if they were alive. Suddenly the air was so cold it hurt to breathe, and his heartbeat slowed, threatened to cease.

"Hold up your lantern!" Saylah cried. The urgency in her voice finally got through to him. He looked at her blindly for a moment, then raised his lantern and glanced from end to end of the fallen log. For the second time, he nearly lost his grip on the rusty lantern. "God in heaven!" he panted as the chill moved slowly through his body.

The log had come to rest against a slight rise. One end was planted firmly on disturbed but solid ground. The other lay at the edge, where the hill dropped off sharply into darkness, emptiness.

Saylah saw the look of horror on Julian's face, just before she began, slowly, to move forward. She was as cold as Julian, as frightened and stiff, q(5)but something more than fear drove her forward. She sang silent prayers, calling the spirits back to her. They had left her when she saw the cougar's tracks, but she needed them now, their protection and their guidance. Why would they not come? *Is your god so cruel that he would punish a child. . . .*

"No," she whispered. Nor would her spirits punish Paul and Theron for her mistake. She must believe that or there was nothing. She had to believe.

In the unnatural light of her lantern, she found the circling prints of the cougar, which veered off and disappeared into the woods. There was no sign that she had been dragging any heavy object, nor was there a trail of blood. No doubt the ledge had made her wary, or she had scented better game and given up the chase.

"The cougar?" Julian managed to choke out.

"Gone," Saylah replied. She knelt beside the log, glanced once more into the empty branches above her, and touched it gently. Her body shook with a tremor of heat, and her breath escaped in a rush. She knew the boys were inside. But were they hurt? Never before had she felt such fear, such cold, gnawing fear. There was a flutter of movement inside her, she saw Julian through a strange blue mist, kneeling nearby, and the fear grew dim. The spirits were with her. They had come back.

"Hello," she said softly in her musical voice. "Are you there, little ones?" She did not want to frighten them if they slept, to jar them back into panic. She heard a tiny movement inside the log and nodded at Julian, who brought the lantern closer. "It is over," she whispered, "we are here to take you home."

Chapter

— 41 —

Theron was dreaming. He was cold, very cold. He wanted the heavy quilt his mother had made for him, but she was not paying attention. He trembled and shivered, rolling from side to side to get away from the flames. Why did they keep putting him so close to the fire? Heat followed cold, and he could not stop shaking.

He opened his mouth to cry out because he was afraid, but no sound came. He couldn't move. He couldn't breathe. A searing pain slashed through him and in its wake he saw a sharp and terrible silver claw flashing through the darkness. He tried to shrink back, to curl into himself, to look away when the moonlight touched it with brilliance.

He rolled again, shuddering, cold and then hot, and watched a rabbit hop by. Why was there a rabbit in his bed? Why was it so dark and cold? Why couldn't he move his arms and legs?

He heard breathing and knew someone was near, struggling for each harsh, ragged breath. Theron wanted to ease the sound of the rasping breath, but the pain flooded through him, leaving him helpless.

Then he heard a voice, a magical singing voice. He struggled to open his eyes, but they were heavy and streaked with flares of color. The harsh breathing stopped and the cold grew sharper for a moment. The voice came toward him, enticing, beguiling, as the world began to spin. Then there were hands, warm hands, gentle hands, pulling him away from the spinning and the darkness, holding him close, wrapping him in soft, warm fur. A face floated above him, and he reached up to touch it, but his arm was heavy and the pain ran through it like fire.

Theron lay inert as the nightmare retreated, then the cold, the darkness, and finally, the fear.

Sophia and Edward sat close to the fire, their parchment-white faces reddened by the heat. Flora paced behind them, trying to hide her panic. For the first time in many months they were three friends together, without barriers or doubts or secrets between them. They were bound together by their fear.

Flora stopped every few minutes to put a reassuring hand on Sophia's shoulder. She had already made them cider with a little soothing Scotch whisky. She had swallowed a cup herself, but it had not warmed the cold place inside her. A door opened and everyone swung to look at the thick oak that shut out the chilly night, but that was tightly closed.

"What is it? What's happened?"

Three faces turned to Jamie, who stood in his velvet robe, staring blankly at the Ashtons, huddled near the fire, and Flora, pale and wandering over the vast hardwood floor.

For a moment Flora could not think what to say. No doubt Jamie could feel the fear in the air, it lay so thick and cumbersome around them.

She went to take her husband's arm. "Theron and Paul seem to be lost. But Julian and Saylah have gone to look for them."

Jamie glanced from the Ashtons, who gaped at him open-mouthed, to Flora and back again. They must have been very much afraid indeed to come here uninvited. "I'll sit with you and wait," Jamie said.

"No, *mo-charaid*, 'twill tire ye too much. We don't even know how long—"

Jamie took his wife's shoulders in his hands. "You're thinking they may never come back, but you're wrong. Saylah will find them. She won't give up until she has them in her arms."

"How can you be so sure?" Edward asked.

Jamie faced his friend with the lion-gold eyes and said tonelessly, "Because I know Saylah. Even when a cause is lost, she will fight. She'll bring our sons back to us."

Sophia's eyes filled with tears that Jamie should comfort *them*. Jamie, who had lost all hope. "God grant that you're right."

Jamie smiled crookedly and slipped his arm around his wife. "I don't think God has anything to do with it. Saylah does not believe in our God.

She says he's too full of flame and threats and resounding warnings. She prefers her gentle spirits."

Flora stared at him. "How do ye know so much about her?"

"Sometimes we talk." He moved purposefully toward the fire and sat on one of the handmade chairs. Flora sat beside him, shaking her head.

Edward and Sophia exchanged self-conscious glances. Edward could not take his gaze from Jamie. He stared at his old friend's pale, translucent face and gripped the arm of the rigid bench. He had heard Jamie was ill, but had never imagined this. This was not Jamie, but a ghost, an apparition with Jamie's unruly hair and huge brown eyes. Even the eyes were different. There was no spark, no light, no curiosity. Not even a flare of anger or long-suppressed rage at the sight of Edward Ashton's face. It was as if Jamie's soul had left his body—his soul and his spirit and his memory. Edward struggled to hide his horror.

"You're not comfortable," he said unsteadily. "Let me bring your chair." He did not wait for a response. He had to get away, at least for a moment.

Inside Jamie's room, Edward leaned heavily on the ornate back of the chair. First Paul had not come home, and now there was Jamie. Always Edward had dealt with problems easily, quickly, finding the practical solution, pushing aside the unpleasant memory. But now he could not think; there was no simple answer, nothing he could do to change what was and what had been.

He clenched his fists until the blood drained from his fingers. Paul was missing, maybe badly hurt, even dead. He closed his eyes in denial. And Jamie, his dearest friend, had gone away and left him alone.

Edward stiffened his shoulders and stood upright. He must not let this happen. He must be strong, resilient, as Jamie never had been. He must overcome this empty, aching fear and sorrow. It would weaken him and drag him down.

Resolutely, he carried the chair into the hall where the twin fires blazed. He placed it next to Jamie and offered his hand. Jamie hesitated, then took the extended healthy hand. Gently, Edward guided his friend into the lion chair.

"Edward," Sophia said gently, "come sit beside me. I'm cold."

He slid his arm around her, drew her willing body close. It felt good, Sophia's head on his shoulder, her weight against his. He touched her hair tenderly, and she smiled for the first time in hours.

Silence fell over them once more, heavy and oppressive on their bent shoulders.

Then the door opened, the wind rushed in, igniting the flames, before Julian and Saylah stepped inside, each carrying a tightly wrapped bundle in their arms.

Sophia rose, hand to her throat. "Paul?"

"He's alive," Julian said. "Chilled and frightened, but alive."

Jamie stared at Saylah, waiting.

She met his gaze. "Theron too is chilled and frightened. He has a wound. I could not see it closely in the torchlight, but I think it is from the claw of a cougar. He has a fever. I must put him to bed and prepare my herbs."

The weight of the child in her arms grew heavier by the moment as her fear for him rose in her chest. She had to force herself to think of Paul. Holding Theron closer, as if her warmth could protect him from the fever and infection that had already taken hold of his small body, she said firmly, "Paul would do best on the bench between the fires, I think."

She turned to Sophia. "If you could wrap him in your cloak and give him something warm to drink. A little at a time. He is in shock. He must be kept warm until he comes back to us. I will send Flora with disinfectant for his scrapes and bruises. I do not think they are serious."

She paused, started to turn away, and added, "If you could be there when he begins to see clearly, it would ease the shock."

Sophia, who had stood in the same room with Saylah for a few minutes, who knew her not at all, listened closely and followed her instructions carefully. There was a quiet authority about this half-breed, a confidence that soothed and subdued.

When Saylah started away, Julian touched her arm. "You will need things from the kitchen? I've seen you boiling water and herbs for Jamie. Tell me what to bring."

His voice was matter-of-fact and reassuring. "Hot water in a large pot, an empty basin and many small cups," Saylah told him. "The disinfectant Flora keeps in the far cupboard, and the gauze." Silently, she thanked the spirits for leading her to the school where she had met the white doctors. Their disinfectant would do more, quickly, than a difficult preparation of pounded roots. "Also a basin of cool water and cloths for the fever. I have my herbs with me, but there are more stored in a cedar box beside my bed. I will need them all. Though how I will keep them warm—"

"I started a fire in the stove in Theron's room," Flora interrupted. "I knew he would be cold."

Saylah smiled at her gratefully, but the smile was thin and tense.

"Let me help!" Edward cried. "Surely, Julian, you can't carry all that by yourself."

Julian surveyed Jamie's friend suspiciously. He was certainly eager to be of assistance. Was he trying to prove something to Jamie? Or perhaps himself? But that did not matter. They needed Edward Ashton tonight whatever had happened in the past. "You start collecting things in the kitchen while I go get the herbs," Julian directed.

Jamie watched helplessly as everyone dispersed to do what they could. While they were planning, he had tried, surreptitiously, to rise more than once. But he was too weak. He could stand, but he could not bend and lift. He saw his son's blond head disappear down the hallway, and his eyes were damp with fear and frustration.

"Jamie." Sophia knelt beside him. She had seen that Paul's torn clothes were dry, and had wrapped him in her fur-lined cloak, before drawing the bench where he lay closer to the fire.

Jamie looked up at her, bewildered. He had forgotten she was here.

"I must make Paul something to drink and find some cloths to clean away some of the dirt. But I don't like to leave him alone. Do you think you could sit beside him, talk to him a little? I don't want him to think he is alone."

"Of course." Jamie wished he could do the same for his own son; he had heard the tremor in Saylah's voice and knew Theron was still in danger. But at least Jamie would not be alone and useless. Though Sophia offered her arm, he rose by himself. First he sat in the nearest chair and pulled it close, but Paul seemed restless and Sophia hesitated, afraid to leave him. Jamie slid onto the bench and cradled Paul's head in his lap. A verse came to him from his distant childhood. Quietly, he began to sing.

> Oh, the cuckoo she's a pretty bird,
>   she singeth as she flies.
> She bringeth good tidings,
>   she telleth no lies.
> She sucketh white flowers,
>   for to keep her voice clear;
> And the more she singeth cuckoo,
>   the summer draweth near.

Paul's eyelids fluttered, then stopped, and Sophia crept away. She could not explain the tears on her cheeks.

Flora asked no questions on the way to Theron's room, where she drew down the covers and turned up the lamp. Saylah felt the warmth embrace her and was doubly grateful for Flora's foresight.

"Ye'll need more blankets. I'll see to it. And I'll be makin' certain the men don't burn away their fingertips tryin' to boil a little water."

Saylah nodded, her face strained in the yellow light of the paraffin lamp. She was aware that Flora stood unmoving while she removed Theron's torn jacket and shirt, as well as his filthy trousers. His mother gasped when she saw the nasty blood-clotted wound. Saylah bent to examine the four long scratches on the outside of his lower arm.

"The cold must have slowed the bleeding, and the wounds are not so deep that they have damaged the inside," she said as steadily as she could. She paused to draw several deep breaths. The scratches were swollen and red, full of pus and poison. "The danger is from the infection. I will need the disinfectant at once."

When she touched Theron's skin, it burned, and his face was deeply flushed. "Already there is fever. It must be broken. I did not ask for a pitcher of water, but I must try to make him drink, at least a little." She heard the hollow sound of her voice, weary and without emotion. She could not seem to make herself smile at Flora or ease her worry.

"Ye'll have it."

Saylah glanced up, but Flora was already gone.

Theron kicked out, muttering words that had no meaning. He beat helplessly against the mattress with his uninjured arm. Saylah felt a jolt and realized he was trying to free himself from the log. He did not yet understand that he could move as he wished. He tossed and thrashed while she tried to hold him steady. Tenderly, she smoothed the hair back from his forehead, rested her cool palm against his hot skin.

Saylah knew before she raised her head that Julian was behind her. He offered the disinfectant without a word, laid out the bowls he had brought, and the cedar box. Edward placed the hot water on the potbellied stove and gave her the cloths draped over his arm. He hovered for a moment, glanced at Theron's face, then left the room.

Saylah began to work quickly, applying the antiseptic, dipping the cloths in cool water, sorting the herbs for the red cedar seeds that would break the fever. Julian helped as much as he could, leaving everything within her reach, testing the heat of the water, wringing out the cool cloths and placing them on Theron's forehead. Saylah did not thank him; she was afraid if she spoke aloud her gratitude, she would also release her tears. And she had no time for weeping.

Julian saw how exhausted she was; her brown skin had grown dull and pale, her hands trembled as she drew up the covers. But he did not suggest that she stop. She could not rest until Theron was safe.

Through her eyes he saw the image that haunted her now. He saw her reach out to knock the bow aside and let the cougar run free. Again and again she pushed away the bow. Again and again the great golden cat disappeared into the trees, where it stalked new prey.

Saylah bowed her head, but the vision did not go. It would follow her through light and darkness, sun and shadows, dream and nightmare for a very long time to come.

Chapter

42

Theron was delirious. He thrashed and moaned while Saylah cleansed his wound, medicated and bound it, not with the supple cedarbark of her childhood, but with clean gauze which Flora provided. Obstinately, Saylah teased at the boy's parched lips with a few drops of water on a spoon until he had swallowed enough to satisfy her. Then she prepared the warm infusion made from the seeds of red cedar. Patiently, gently, she held spoonful after spoonful to his lips. He would need it to break the fever that racked his small body.

She put a poultice of skunk cabbage leaves on his forehead to draw out the heat. As she bathed him with cool cloths, she treated the scratches, bruises and abrasions that covered his arms and legs, face and hands. As she smoothed soothing woodfern over his cuts, he groaned.

"If someone must die," she murmured, "let it be me. It was *my* mistake, not Theron's."

Saylah had replaced the poultice on his forehead for the third time when Flora came in. "Ye must stop or ye'll make yourself ill as well," she said firmly. "There's naught to do now but keep him cool, and I can do it as well as ye. Besides, I'd like to sit and watch him. I've missed my little bairn."

Saylah could not argue. Flora wanted to care for Theron herself. Wanted him to need her as a son needs his mother. The girl nodded and rose. Flora took her hands as she started for the door. "Thank ye for all ye've done. Julian says we'd no' have found them 'til mornin' or mayhap longer without ye."

"It was my responsibility."

Flora grinned. "But that'll no' be makin' us any less grateful now, will it?"

Suddenly, Saylah was chilled through and she headed for the blazing fireplaces in the main hall. Julian was there, rubbing his hands near the flames, glancing now and then at Jamie, who had not gone back to bed.

Paul lay wrapped in his mother's cloak, looking around him tentatively, trying to remember what had brought him here. Sophia and Edward sat at either end of the bench, where their son could see them. Edward had finally discarded his greatcoat. Beneath he wore a linen shirt. Saylah had expected a waistcoat, a morning coat, even a cravat. Sophia's teal alpaca gown trimmed with lace was elegant and out of place in this simple room. But the expression on her face when she looked at Paul made everything else unimportant.

The boy shivered constantly, but the color had begun to return to his cheeks. Flora had seen to his scrapes and bruises and discovered he had no other injuries.

When he saw Saylah, his eyelids flickered. The color that had begun to creep back into his cheeks left him. Without hesitation, she went to kneel beside him, took his hands in hers, and held on tightly.

He opened cloudy brown-gold eyes and stared at her. "Theron, how—is he?"

"He has a wound on his arm, and a fever, but he will be well cared for by those who love him."

"I promised to protect him. I promised to take care—"

Saylah pressed his cold fingers, forcing him to meet her eyes. "And you did. You kept him alive by outwitting the cougar. You were so clever to think of the log. If you had climbed a tree, she might have followed. But she could not get to you inside the log. You had wedged the rock in so tight."

Paul regarded her doubtfully. The memory of that damp, cramped log, of the sniffing and snarling cat, the darkness and cold that had stopped his breath, was hard to bear. "How do you know I thought of it?"

"Because you are older, and I have seen how you think and consider when Theron wishes to plunge ahead heedlessly."

Paul had to fight back sudden tears. He couldn't cry. Not right there in front of everybody. Saylah's fingers tightened on his and he swallowed

noisily. "I promised we wouldn't get in trouble. If I hadn't run away—"
He broke off abruptly when he realized what he'd said.

"It could have happened at any time to anyone," Saylah interjected
before anyone noticed the boy's careless remark. "I knew many hunters,
men who lived in the woods, who knew them as well as you know your
own house. Hunters trained to track and kill, who were set upon by
grizzlies or cougars or wolves. It was their way of life to *know* when danger
was near, to kill before they could be harmed. Yet they came to the
Healers, bleeding and ill, while the animals went free, unmarked by the
hunters' arrows."

Paul listened intently, mesmerized by Saylah's voice and her reassuring
warmth. He held on a little longer, pulling himself out of the dark hole of
his guilt with the pressure of her strong brown hands.

"You saved his life, Paul. You should be proud. Now you have known
the worst, have you not? Now there is nothing to fear. And think of the
stories you will have to tell."

Lips curved in a hint of a smile that spoke of his gratitude, though he
could not, Paul nodded.

Saylah released him and rose to find Sophia looking at her in wonder.
"That was very kind."

Frowning, Saylah replied, "It was necessary." She felt the prickling of
the skin on her neck and turned to find Jamie watching, eyeing the
Ashtons warily, surreptitiously. She felt there was a question on the tip of
his tongue, but he did not want to ask it. He wanted to find the answer in
their faces, lit by two sets of roaring flames.

She tried to understand, but her thoughts were weary, confused and
troubled. Wordlessly, she sank to the floor near the fire. She was not aware
that her own face and hands were scratched. The pins had been torn from
her hair, and long black tendrils drifted across her cheeks. She glanced at
Julian, whose face brought back images too vivid and too painful.

Numb with horror, she looked to Jamie for some sense of what was real.
Surely this room full of strangers, the brown-haired boy who had laughed
with her, held her and kissed her a few hours past, were not real. But
Jamie, in his velvet robe, his hair, as always, falling over his forehead, was
somehow very real. "You are not weary from sitting up so long," she said.

It was not a question, but a statement. "No. There is much to distract
me." He glanced at Edward with the same perplexed expression, the same
unspoken question in his eyes.

Saylah noticed that Edward avoided meeting those eyes. He pretended
to be watching Paul, rubbing his hands to make him warm, concerned that
he might still be in shock. But his shoulders were unnaturally stiff, and the

color in his cheeks was not born of the firelight. Inexplicably, she pitied him.

"You know," Edward Ashton said loudly, surprising everyone, including himself, "this reminds me of something that happened not long after this house was finished."

Jamie sat up straighter, leaned forward, suddenly intent.

Edward opened his mouth and closed it once or twice; Sophia wondered where his practiced charm had fled to. She glanced at Jamie and felt the same anxiety that had troubled her for a year. These two men used to be the best of friends. She drew her son closer, trying to disguise her disquiet.

"What happened?" Julian prompted when Edward did not continue. He had seen Jamie's reaction and sensed that his father wanted to hear what the other man had to say.

"Yes," Saylah agreed. "Tell us a story."

"Do, Papa. I want to hear." Paul shuddered, though not from the cold. It had come to him in a flash why he'd gone off into the woods to begin with. But he knew if his father would talk a little, relax, begin to tell stories, he could make his son forget. Edward had that power to charm away unpleasant memories.

Even Sophia was curious. "Go on," she said, touching her husband's shoulder.

"You remember, Sophia. I'd come over here to join Jamie and Julian"— he broke off, paused, and continued—"for dinner. We had roast venison, if I remember, then brandy by the fire. We used to spend hours sitting here, between these two walls of flame. It reminded us, Jamie and me, that we were in the wilderness, but we were safe. I'd left Sophia at home, you see, in case it should snow again. I didn't want her in danger."

Sophia smiled. She had not heard Edward reminisce, especially about Jamie Ivy, for a very long time. Raising one eyebrow, she smiled crookedly. "You didn't want me too tired to rant at the workmen the next day, you mean. The house was not yet finished," she told Paul, "and your father was busy making great plans and eating vast meals. That's why he couldn't follow the carpenters from room to room as I could, seeing that things were done properly." She laughed; there was no resentment in her tone, only affection.

Jamie had relaxed as Sophia spoke, resting his head on the back of his chair. His hands were folded together on his lap, easily, as though he were quite comfortable. This was what he wanted. Edward and Sophia talking about the past.

"There was snow on the ground when I left home, but no wind and the clouds looked frail and white, not gray and threatening. So I didn't worry about riding over to visit." He realized what he was saying and smiled at Sophia in chagrin.

"But I'm so much smaller, you see," she chuckled. "I'd have frozen through, no doubt, just getting from there to here. But being broad of shoulder and tall of build, Edward always loved the cold. It invigorated him, excited him."

"It was like a challenge, I guess, the way this Island was a challenge when we first came here and chose our land." Edward's eyes glowed. He did not look at Jamie, but was speaking directly to him.

"The trees, the twisted branches and green firs looked different in the snow. Just touched with white that glittered like crystals, thousands of crystals, catching the sunlight."

Paul relaxed as the brandy began to have an effect. His body hurt everywhere, but the sound of his father's voice was soothing. That was funny. That Papa could drown out the sound of that cougar snarling and spitting and pawing the log. He couldn't remember exactly what it looked like anymore.

"Remember, Jamie? You came out to meet me before the sun went down and we saw the crystals turn blue and purple and pink? Remember how the splintered sunlight glittered on the snow?"

"Was it whiskey in a tall glass that made it shine, do you suppose?" Sophia asked, finger to her chin, brow furrowed as if she were figuring a difficult problem.

Julian was grateful to her. He'd seen Jamie flinch, and he wanted to change the subject. "It seems to me—"

"No," Jamie interrupted. "I remember." He had not moved, but was no longer relaxed. His eyes were luminous, fixed on the familiar face of his friend. "I remember everything."

"Anyway," Edward continued, stretching out his legs, settling into a familiar hearth, a familiar warmth, "it was beautiful." He grinned at his wife. "Whiskey and all. We stood outside, watching so long that the soup burned away in the pot. But we didn't care." His eyes had grown hazy, his speech slightly slurred.

No wonder Sophia had mentioned whiskey, Saylah thought. Edward must have drunk several glasses while he waited for his son. Though smiling, Sophia was watching her husband, puzzled by his behavior.

"We sat here drinking and eating and singing those old songs that sound so grand when you're warm and dry between two blazing fires, and outside the wind has begun to howl. Eventually, we roused ourselves and I started home. It was blowing like the devil out there, but I knew Sophia would worry if I stayed. Besides, I'm a stubborn man. Like to lie in my own bed on a night so cold it'd freeze your heart."

Sophia did not interrupt with a humorous remark. Edward paused, lost in memory, oblivious of Jamie's watchful eyes or Julian's curiosity or Sophia's dismay. "It started to snow pretty hard on the way. My horse lost his footing more than once. I remember looking up and seeing the snow hissing down around me, spinning like pinwheels with the cold wind behind it. It's usually so pleasant on the Island. I'd never seen a blizzard like this one. I was too surprised to think clearly."

"That's where you came into it, Sophie, while I was out wandering in frozen white whirlwinds. Maybe you should tell it from here." He glanced at Jamie. "Or you. I don't remember much, after all."

"No," Jamie said softly. "You know what happened now, even if you didn't then. I want to hear you finish it."

Saylah had never heard that particular tone in Jamie's voice before. She couldn't decide what it was. Not calculating; Jamie could never be that, but he knew exactly what he was saying, and why. But she could not concentrate. She was listening for Theron's cry, feeling again his raging fever.

"Sure," Edward said jovially. "Sure. I'll do that." He smiled at his old friend warmly. "Well, anyway, seems Jamie and Julian were awakened next morning by Sophia, who'd ridden over alone. She'd searched through the snowbanks for hours, combed both sides of the trail for some sign of me. The snow had stopped early in the morning, you see. She came to ask if I was here. She hadn't seen me since the past evening.

"Jamie told her when I'd left, and she sat down between these fires and cried. 'There was a blizzard last night, the worst in years. He can't have survived it. I've lost him, I know I have.'" He squeezed his wife's arm. "That's what she told me she said, anyway. An extraordinary woman, my Sophia. She wasn't frightened by the snow or cold."

"No," Sophia agreed, all laughter gone from her voice. "I was afraid of losing you. And when Julian agreed, and the Indian girl who was cooking for them then, I broke down. Everyone was certain Edward couldn't have survived."

"But Jamie wouldn't have it," Edward cried. "Said I knew my way around. I'd probably found a cave to wait out the storm and was snowed in. Said he and Julian would go looking and promised Sophia they'd find me too. She'd lost hope, but he gave it back to her."

Saylah felt Julian take her hand. Without thinking, she turned her palm up to link her fingers with his, but did not look at him. She didn't dare.

"So the two of them, Jamie and Julian, bundled up and went out. And they found me, by God. My friend Jamie found me. I owe him my life."

Saylah suspected Edward owed his life to Jamie's optimism and Julian's keen sense of direction. Jamie alone might have frozen to death himself.

He was sitting forward in his chair, scrutinizing Edward with an expression so intent, so probing, so full of pain that even Sophia noticed.

"He saved my life," Edward repeated. "No other way to say it." He paused, apparently unaware of Jamie's expectant silence. "The funny thing was"—he rubbed his chin; the memory perplexed him—"I was standing next to my horse when I saw them coming. And I thought I'd left their house just an hour past. Couldn't figure why it was light already or what they were doing out in that cold. I didn't remember a thing about that night, except looking up into those whirlwinds. Lost about six hours and didn't know how. Never did find them either. Those hours—I still wonder what they were like. Sometimes I dream about it."

"Weren't you half frozen when they found you?" Saylah asked, since everyone else was silent, waiting for something which she sensed would never happen.

"Now, that's the oddest thing of all. I was cold, of course I was. They brought me back here and it took a good three hours with both fires blazing to warm me up. But I didn't have frostbite, no missing fingers or toes." He wiggled his fingers to prove his point.

"It's true," Sophia said. "I couldn't understand it. It was a miracle, just like finding our Paul."

"That wasn't a miracle," Julian said with an edge in his voice. "That was Saylah."

Saylah did not hear him. She was thinking back to a story she had heard when she was very young. A Salish from another village had told it. He was Sooke, she thought. She tried to remember what he had said. Something about finding a white man clinging to his horse, unconscious. The hunter had taken him back to the Longhouse, wrapped him in blankets, and forced warm infusions down his throat. He had slept without waking and slowly grown warm from the circle of fires. The infusions had made certain he would not wake, just as they had warmed him and fought away the chill.

A little after dawn, the Sooke hunter, with the help of his friends, had taken the man back to where they'd found him. The storm was over; they knew he wouldn't freeze, not with all the heat they'd poured down his throat. They'd hidden in the trees and watched him wake up, look around, bemused. They'd even seen his friends come to rescue him. They had roared with laughter over his confusion, knowing he would never remember what he had never seen.

Saylah regarded Edward Ashton with a slight smile. They had not hurt him, had, in fact, saved his life. But they'd saved their pride—foolish, the other Salish would have said, to save a Stranger—by playing that little joke on him, leaving him befuddled for years afterward. The strange thing was, no one had believed the Sooke. But it made a good story, so they had listened and smiled and pounded their drums.

She heard the pounding in her memory, inside her head, in the beating of her heart. Then it was real, it was Jamie, eyes closed, beating a sharp rhythm on the arms of his chair. He was looking at her, watching her slip away, calling her back with the tap of his fragile hands.

She rose in a dream, in a dream took those hands and led him to his room. She had forgotten Edward Ashton and his story; now there was only Jamie, looking at her with pleading brown eyes.

He was pale, his skin tinged blue in the uncertain light. She pressed her palm to his chest and listened, took his wrist and felt its erratic pulse. For the first time it struck her that perhaps, after all, the sickness was not solely in his spirit, but also in his body.

> O that our dreamings all, of sleep or wake,
> Would all their colors from the sunset take . . .

She raised her head, startled by the sound of his voice.

> From something of material sublime,
> Rather than shadow our own soul's day-time
> In the dark voice of night.

Saylah wondered if he was speaking to Edward, friend and stranger, who had held them all in thrall.

Jamie took her hand. "John Keats wrote those words, or sang them with his pen, as you sing your healing songs and prayers. Listen for just a little while to the silence he left behind."

All she could do was draw the covers up around him, sing softly, soothingly, and rest her head on his shoulder so he'd know that she was there, she would not leave him, he was safe and warm and not alone.

Chapter

43

Julian stood at the door just after dawn the next morning. He held his rifle tightly in his hand—so tightly that his fingers ached, but that was good. He wanted to remember what it was to hurt, though he couldn't ever know the fear and pain Paul and Theron had felt. He wanted to feed his slow-burning rage against the cougar who had cost them all so much.

He was waiting for Edward. Today they would go into the woods and hunt the cougar down. Even if Julian's anger were not so fierce, it was too dangerous to let the cat live.

He stared out the crack of the door, watching for a man on horseback— not the half workhorse, half mount that Julian rode, but a beautiful gelding who skimmed the ground and made a man think he was flying. Julian stiffened and spun, gun in hand, when he felt a feather-light touch.

Saylah backed away from him, away from the dangerous light in his eyes, away from the gun, pointed a little too far outward. She tried to tell herself that he was suffering, just as she was, over what had happened to the boys. But she suspected it was something more. She was shaken by the glazed expression in his eyes, which looked through her, beyond her, to a place where nothing could defuse his building anger. Slowly, he rested his rifle on the floor, his hands on the stock, and stared down at his splayed fingers.

"You go to hunt the cougar," Saylah said when he did not speak. Had his rage burned away the memory of what they had been through yesterday? Did his anger, like her pain and guilt, weave a barrier of silence over what had happened between them? "I will go with you."

Julian raised his head sharply. "No!"

"I can track him more easily—" she began.

"Perhaps. But in daylight it shouldn't be difficult for us. Unlike Paul and Theron, we're armed and know the danger. I don't think it would be kind if you went along."

Saylah shook her head. "Yesterday I acted from instinct when I knocked the bow from your hands. My instincts were wrong. I know this." It was not easy for her to say, even now, while Theron lay unconscious in the other room. "The cougar cannot be allowed to live and attack others."

For an instant, Julian woke from the red haze of his helpless anger. "I meant it would be unkind to you." He would never forget the look on her face when she saw the cat's tracks crossing the boys'. Or earlier, on the boulder, when the mention of the cougar had struck her like a muscled fist. He had seen her anguish, felt it in his own body. He did not understand what had caused it; he only knew he would never willingly cause her that kind of pain again. Or himself. "You stay with Theron," he said firmly. "No one else can help *him*. Only you have that skill. Anyone can stalk the cougar."

Saylah knew he was right but did not want to let him go. She felt the tension in his body, the building pressure that would lead, inevitably, to an explosion. She felt it coming, rising upward like the wind burrows beneath the waves before it brings them crashing onto the calm shore. Julian's cold glare was a challenge. She raised her hand, then let it fall. She did not have the power to stop him. Not anymore.

Edward arrived just then, and Julian touched her shoulder—the light and hurried touch of a stranger—before he slipped out the door.

By the time Julian reached him, Edward was waiting at the edge of the woods. Julian brought Phoenix from the barn, where he had already saddled and bridled him, and joined his father's friend. Edward's face was dark and thunderous. Like Julian, he needed this task to vent his helpless rage at what had happened to his son.

The two men did not speak as they entered the woods. Not because silence was necessary, but because they had nothing to say to each other. Julian led the way to the last place the cougar had been sighted: the bluff where the log had come to rest. When Edward saw how it lay over the edge, he gasped and went white, grasping the pommel.

"Do the boys know how close . . ." He trailed off, unable to speak the words aloud.

"No." Julian was as shaken as Edward. It was one thing to see this in darkness, by the light of a lantern, another altogether with the sun overhead, unshielded by clouds. "They couldn't see from inside the log, and when we took them out, they were barely conscious." He swung down from the saddle and kicked at the log until it rolled free, down the slope to a hollow surrounded by huge gnarled roots. Then he remounted.

"What was that for?" Edward asked. He was shaking and chilled, despite his heavy overcoat lined with fur. Unconsciously, he had grasped his rifle, as if it could protect him from the knowledge of how close his son had come to death.

"In case the boys come this way again. I think they will someday, if they ever find the path. Boys have a morbid fascination with danger, or don't you remember? I'm just making sure they never see how near death was, long after the cougar had left them alone."

Edward stared at Julian with admiration. He himself would never have thought of such a thing, and Jamie—well, Jamie was not a man to whom practical thoughts came easily. Julian was obviously quite different from his father. Then again, he was little more than a boy himself. It would be easy for him to remember what Edward and Jamie had long ago forgotten.

Edward closed his eyes, saddened and unable to say why. An image of his Indian girl, naked among the cattails with flowers in her hair, flashed across his lids, and he felt physically ill. "Why did you run?" he had asked Paul this morning. His son had refused to answer and looked away.

"Are you coming?" Julian called. He had ridden ahead, expecting Edward to follow.

But Edward found it difficult to tear himself away from the sight of the moss-covered, battered log that had saved his son's life. He was struggling to keep the thought from forming in his mind. He was good at that— pushing an unpleasant thought down until it did not reappear. But this time he could not do it. Was it possible Paul had lost himself in the woods because he had seen something that had upset him deeply?

Edward straightened and set his jaw in a rigid line. There was work to do. He must not waste his time with pointless questions. Feeling slightly queasy, he followed Julian, who leaned down from Phoenix's back, following the cougar tracks from the night before.

Julian held his rifle across the pommel, primed and ready, praying for danger with every step of his horse's feet. He did not want this to be easy. He wanted a struggle, a chase, a meeting of two enemies with equal skill and an equal desire to kill. He wanted the game to begin, so he would not have to think, but to act from instinct and the black heart of his rage.

There was no more conversation. Edward lagged behind, but Julian did not care. He wanted to take the cat alone. He wanted this kill to be his.

He was disappointed time and again in the course of that endless day. Just when the tracks seemed to grow fresh and he smelled the animal on the wind, it disappeared and they had to start again. He was off and onto the horse's back so often that his thighs ached with the effort. The hand that gripped the rifle had ridged blisters, and the palm was chafed and red. He thought, fleetingly, of Saylah kneeling beside him, rubbing her salve into his torn hands, and the ache in his body curved inward on itself.

His kicked Phoenix forward again, and yet again. Sometimes he felt so weary he fell back and let Edward lead. He began to hurt everywhere, from muscles held taut for too long, but he welcomed the pain. Unlike the demons in his head, it would leave him in time; it could be soothed by ointments and gentle hands.

Twice he caught sight of new spoor and the rage came back, pulsing in his head like the frantic wings of wild trapped birds. His nostrils flared, his body stiffened, and he listened with his eyes, his ears, with every sense he had.

But always, in the end, the cougar slipped away. At last he realized the cat was leading the hunters, easily, carelessly; like an animal who smells no danger in the air. Julian's vision came and went in a blur while the blood pounded and raced, throbbed against his suddenly fragile skull. When the forest became so thick with undergrowth, the trees so close together that he could not ride anymore, he tied Phoenix to an arbutus and continued on foot. He no longer cared if Edward followed. He was blind to everything but the tracks of that cougar, deaf to all but the sound of the animal's breath, its padded footfalls on the tangled greenery.

The darkness was cool and green, but Julian felt uncomfortably warm. He crouched and crept forward, crouched and crept, until, at long last, he saw the golden cougar that had stood in his path yesterday, had paused, unknowing, in the path of Julian's bow.

This time it would not go free. His fingers slid down the barrel of the gun and he realized he was sweating. He dried his hands on his flannel shirt, keeping his gaze fixed on the cat that crouched warily on a wide, graceful branch of fir. The cougar raised its head, made radiant by the sunlight, which touched the pale blue fir and turned it silver. A golden cat on a feathered silver bed, swaying slightly in the breeze, so beautiful that he knew he must destroy it.

Edward had crept around the other side of the tiny clearing to block the cat's escape. He braced his rifle against his shoulder and peered through the trees. Even from where he sat, motionless, Edward saw the blazing light in Julian's eyes, the hatred and the need to kill. Edward waited. Let the boy have his moment. The older man had seen more than enough blood in his life. He did not need one more trophy to prove his courage—not this kind of trophy. Besides, the cat had not harmed his son. Julian had stalked the cougar for the blood of his family. He had the right to fire the shot that brought the animal down.

Slowly, so slowly that the motion was nearly imperceptible, Julian raised his rifle and pointed it at the swaying cougar on his natural silver throne. He held his breath and prayed the wind would not shift, as it had so many times today when they were close, so close they could smell the kill. The blood pounded in his ears and he prayed about that too. That the cougar could not hear it, couldn't smell his rage as easily as the golden cat smelled fear.

Julian's finger traced the trigger, found its place, began, with infinite patience, to draw the mechanism back. Suddenly, the cat stiffened, ears up, back rigid. It knew he was there. Its golden eyes met his—glittering, wild, unafraid. Julian did not hesitate. He drew a deep breath and fired, saw the cougar leap and snarl, then stumble from its regal perch. For an instant, it was frozen, head up, tail raised, red oozing down its side. Even then it was beautiful. It made no sound as its sides heaved with the struggle to draw breath. No sound, Julian thought. How strange. Its power took his breath away, gave new life to his fury.

He fired again, though he knew the animal was dying. He must do more than kill it; he must break it like a brittle twig. The cougar, rigid and royal a moment before, seemed to melt, to lose control and slide to the ground. It fell, sprawled awkwardly, covered with its own blood, a stain of red on a stain of gold against the thick green grass.

It was dead. Its power was gone, and its beauty and grace. Its yellow eyes stared blankly at the cloudless sky; they might never for a moment have been filled with hate and cunning and the lust for death.

"Damned good shooting!" Edward cried, emerging from the shelter of two moss-covered spruce. He looked down at the cougar. "I'd begun to think we'd never get her. Can't tell you how relieved I am."

Julian did not hear a word, did not even realize Edward was near. He knelt beside the corpse and his rage seemed to spill out with the last pulse of the animal's blood. The rushing in his ears faded, his painful grip on the rifle loosened. He had destroyed it. It was beautiful no more, just useless, broken, weak.

But the cougar is sacred! a voice in his memory cried. He flinched, the rush of triumph gone. He wanted, inexplicably, to weep. He knew then that the anger had not left him; it lay inside, where it had grown and festered long before this cat had tried to take his brother's life.

He did not know that his hand was dark with blood, that as Edward stared in astonishment, Julian stroked the red-stained fur again and again and again.

At her post beside Theron's bed, in the straight-backed chair she had chosen over the cushioned rocker, Saylah had drifted off to sleep. Her dream was full of shadows and she stumbled to escape them. Far ahead, lost somewhere in the thick, thriving forest, she heard a cry of pain, of outrage, of defeat. A high and piercing death cry that turned her blood cold, like an ice-bound stream in winter.

She sat up sharply, wide awake. Not Theron, she cried silently, praying to every spirit who had ever touched her with its power. But she knew it must be the child, because her heart beat slowly, raggedly, with grief and guilt and sorrow.

She leaned over the bed and touched Theron's forehead. It was hot, not cold, and his chest rose and fell with his labored breath. He was sleeping. The delirium had passed.

Saylah sighed with a relief so profound it left her limp and frail. She wrung out the warm cloth in cool water and replaced it, then sat once more in her straight-backed chair.

She shivered as the memory of her dream moved through the darkness. She had heard a death-cry, felt it ripping through her body. Whose?

Only then did she notice that she was shaking violently and her hands, her body were cold with sweat.

Chapter

44

Theron awoke with a keen aversion to secrets of any kind. He was confused to find himself in his own bed, more confused by his scrapes and bruises, the tight bandage on his arm. It throbbed with pain and he stared at it blankly.

"So, you have decided to wake up at last."

The boy moved his head gingerly, afraid it would burst. "I'm hungry," he declared when Saylah bent over him, and he smelled the scent of fir in her hair.

He blinked several times as images flickered through his mind. He remembered that smell, and her face above him, white and blurry. He remembered rolling down a hill, and silver streaks that must have been stars. He remembered a fear so deep that at the first thought of it, he screwed his eyes closed tight. Behind his lids, a graceful golden cat flickered among the vibrant colors.

"It is all right," Saylah murmured. "You are safe and I am with you." She did not tell him that the cougar was dead. That would come later, when he was ready to hear, when her voice would not tremble at the memory of Julian's distorted face. He had come back from the hunt a stranger—distant, silent, racked with pain. Somehow, Saylah would have to make it up to him.

Flora appeared in the doorway, a bit of mending in her hand. "I was thinkin' I heard voices. . . ." She trailed off when she saw Theron's tight-closed eyes and rigid mouth. "He's awake?" She looked at Saylah with hope and dread, pleasure and relief.

"He is. I have just been telling him that there is no danger here, just those who love him."

Theron opened one eye warily. "You sure it's all right?"

"I am sure."

He looked to his mother, who smiled and seemed to shrug a heavy burden away. "Never have I been more certain of anythin'," she whispered. Flora leaned down to kiss her son's cheek, touch his hand. She did not say more for fear the tears of relief that brimmed in her eyes would fall and frighten him. "I will get you some broth." She dropped one more kiss on his forehead and slipped away.

Reluctantly, Theron opened the other eye, squinted at the room around him, then relaxed and smiled. He thought of asking about the bandage, winced when he moved his arm and a shaft of pain ripped through it. Maybe he'd just leave that 'til later. He concentrated on Saylah. The sight of her reassured him.

Saylah guessed that he did not remember what had happened. The delirium had burned that night away. It would come back eventually, a little at a time. She had seen it before in hunters who had fallen into delirium from their wounds. The details would return, but not the feeling. There was a shadow on their memory where the pain and fear would have been. She hoped it would be the same for Theron.

Theron had opened both eyes wide and was staring at Saylah. She was sitting with her hair in a thick braid over her shoulder, wearing a white thing he couldn't name that made her brown skin look warm and rich. On her lap was a pile of papers, in her hand a pen. On the table beside her was an inkstand.

"What's that?" he asked with the tiniest bit of belligerence. He didn't want her to notice that he wasn't asking about his arm.

Saylah put her hand on the top page gently, like a caress. "This is my secret," she said.

Theron grimaced and remained silent.

"I thought you liked secrets. You told me you had many of them. You seemed very proud."

He remembered, all at once, the painted chest. That was a secret and it made him happy. But there were other secrets that were bad. He was sure of it. He didn't want any part of those. He rubbed his head, alarmed by the dull ache there.

Saylah leaned above him, rubbing his temples with cool fingertips, offering him a warm cup to drink from. Theron sniffed, wrinkled his nose, and shook his head.

She took the cup away and sat down, unconcerned. "Your mother was saying last night that because of your injuries, you might have to stay in bed for weeks. I told her you would recover soon if you drank my medicines. But she did not think you would want to. I suppose she was right."

Theron reached for the cup which she had left on the bedside table and drank it down. He grimaced horribly for her benefit, but she seemed unmoved.

"How long *will* I have to stay here?" His voice was plaintive.

"A few days, I think."

Theron sighed with all the resignation of a very old man. "What will I do for all those hours?"

Saylah considered, hands folded on the papers in her lap. "I suppose you could tell me a secret or two."

Theron thought longingly of the chest. But he didn't dare tell her. Or did he? "What if you can't *keep* a secret?"

"Well, if I told you *my* secret—"

"We could trade!" he cried, then winced at the pain in his head. "Then you couldn't tell on me and I couldn't tell on you."

"That is almost what I was thinking."

"You start," Theron suggested warily. He wasn't sure about this. What if she got angry and took the chest away? But she wouldn't do that. Not if she gave her word.

Saylah told him about the stories she had been collecting since she left her People. Indian stories of their traditions, their legends, their history.

"But what're you writing now? Has an Indian come to tell a new story?"

Saylah smiled. "Not exactly. But Edward Ashton told a story that reminded me of another, a Salish story I had heard long ago and forgotten. I wanted to save them both."

Theron's blue eyes widened. "Would you read them to me?"

"Not all at once. You would sleep through most of them. But one at a time, yes. Would you really like to hear the stories of my People?"

Even in his discomfort and confusion, Theron noticed how her voice softened when she spoke of her People. It made him want to cry. "They must be better than Paul's stories, and I listen to those." He frowned at a flicker of memory which quickly vanished. "I have a secret too," he said to distract himself. "It's in that little cupboard next to the bureau. But you have to promise—"

"I promise," Saylah said solemnly. She laid her stack of papers aside and knelt beside the bureau. It took her a minute to find the tiny handle that blended into the wall. When she pulled it, the wall opened to reveal a small cupboard. Saylah reached inside and pulled out the most beautiful chest she had ever seen.

She ran her fingertips over the painted lid, admiring the angels as Theron had once admired them. "This is a great treasure. It is very beautiful. Where did you get it?"

He bit his lip. This was the tricky part. "I found it."

Saylah turned the key, opened the lid, and the scent of roses drifted upward. She knew then where he had found it, knew too that it had belonged to Simone. Her face did not reveal her thoughts. "Tell me about it."

Theron did, with increasing enthusiasm, letting her examine each piece inside and telling her the stories he had created about them. "And no one wanted it. No one wants it now." He paused, holding his breath. "Do I have to give it back?"

He did not know that, at that moment, Saylah was incapable of saying no to him. She took out the daguerreotype and caught her breath at the fragile beauty of the young woman at Jamie's side. Saylah touched the beautifully bound book and glanced at the pages, filled with elegant writing. She squinted to try to make it out, but realized it was not English. Finally, she lifted the book and saw the pearls, a kingfisher made of jewels. She had never seen anything like it. Even the most complicated beading did not compare to this. Why had Simone left it behind?

Saylah felt suddenly that she knew the woman, understood her heart. She wished she could understand the words Simone had written. As she ran her fingers over the parchment pages, she felt a fine-spun thread that bound the two women together somehow. A thread of shared pain and a blurred but vital memory.

She did not wish to close the chest, to shut away the pull of that invisible thread. She was pensive as she replaced each item where she had found it. "This chest is very precious, Theron. It must have meant a great deal to Julian's mother." She paused. "It is true no one wants it now. Perhaps someday they will. And then I think you must give it back, because it is so valuable, and because it is not truly yours." She noticed the boy's quivering lip and added quickly, "But that will not be for a long time, I think. And if you are careful, if you treat this very gently, then I think it will be all right. But you must not ever touch it with dirty hands, or tear these pages, or loosen the stones in the jewelry."

Theron sighed with relief and remembered he was hungry.

"It will be better now," Saylah whispered, "because someone else will know it is safe, someone who values it as you do. Simone would like that, I think. To know that someone still smells her scent with pleasure, wonders about her, touches her things with reverence."

"Would she?" Theron made the mistake of sitting up. Saylah caught him before he fell heavily back onto the mattress. Gently, she lowered him into place.

"She would. Very much. *I* would like to know, if I had left my home and my family behind, that they took out my treasures sometimes and touched them and remembered me. It would make me happy, even if I were very far away." Her eyes were damp, and she busied herself with her herbs. She did not see Theron reach out awkwardly to try to touch her cheek; his arm was not quite long enough and she turned away too soon.

Sophia Ashton was determined not to ask where her husband had gone after he returned from the hunt, victorious, but silent and withdrawn. He had sat beside his son for a long time while the boy slept, watching the flicker of his eyelids, the tangle of his auburn hair on the pillow, the whiteness of his hand on the down quilt.

Sophia had joined him more than once, but he hardly seemed to notice. He was watching Paul too closely, waiting for—what? A sign that the damage had not gone deep? Reassurance, now that the cougar was dead, that that night would be forgotten? In the end, Sophia had been more concerned for Edward than for Paul, who slept peacefully, without nightmares to make him toss and turn and sweat on his fine linen sheets.

"What is it, Edward? What are you looking for?" Sophia asked, hand on her husband's arm. When he did not answer or turn his head, she added softly, "Don't worry, he'll be all right. He has suffered, but he's strong, our son."

Edward looked up, pale and haggard, dark circles around his eyes; it had been two days since he had slept. "Like you, Sophia? Is Paul strong like you? Or like me?"

Sophia was appalled at the despair, the defeat, the fear in his voice. She remembered how he had laughed that night with Paul's head on his lap and Jamie listening intently. How her husband had taken them back so easily to a time when there had been no bitterness and no fear. It had been like magic; Edward the conjurer had drawn them all into his glittering woven web. "Paul carries a little of each of us inside him. He is doubly strong, doubly able," she said.

Edward listened, repeating her words like a litany or a prayer. "Doubly strong, doubly able," he murmured again and again. But the chant could not drown out the sound of his own voice, shouting in silence, "Doubly cursed!" He bent over his son, caressing his tousled hair. "I'd never want to hurt him," Edward declared. "Never!"

"Of course you wouldn't." Sophia was shocked and confused. "It was the cougar that hurt him. Why on God's earth would you blame yourself?" Perhaps she spoke a little too forcefully, because of her own sense of guilt over the letter to her father. She had joked about Paul's danger, and it had been real.

Sighing at the memory, at the way, without a word, Edward had risen and left her, Sophia patted Brutus' sleek black head. She hated Edward's secrets and his unspoken nightmares. She tried to pretend they were not real, but the image of her husband kneeling by her small son's bed wouldn't leave her in peace. How could she pretend with the sight of his furrowed brow so close she was certain she could reach out and touch it, smooth the lines away with her fingertips, kiss a smile onto his rigid lips?

"Are you thinking of your father?" Paul asked.

Sophia jumped, her heart racing, her hands less than steady. She had thought her son asleep. She touched his shoulder where the covers had fallen away. He leaned up on an elbow, watching her with his father's gold-flecked eyes. "Why would you think that?" she asked to give her time to still the rush of joy that came with the sound of his voice, his face, softened with sleep, no longer unnaturally pale.

Paul shrugged, which was not easy, since his muscles ached horribly and his head pounded with a fear he had to push away with all his strength. He smelled clean linen, and his mother's lilac perfume, and it almost concealed the smell of a damp, rotting log. The rustle of her petticoats as she moved almost disguised the sound of harsh breathing, inside and outside the suffocating darkness. Paul fought his way back to the scent and sound of his mother in a pale velvet gown, her hair tied back with a satin ribbon. He reached out and she took his hand.

"When you think of your father," he explained carefully, to keep his memories at bay, "you always screw up your face that way, and your eyes get dark, because you hurt."

Sophia was not prepared for Paul's unerring perception. She forced a smile to her lips. "It's true, my father hurts me," she said, because that was easier, because Paul need never know that sometimes Edward hurt her too, by closing himself away from her, by leaving her when his eyes grew haunted, instead of giving her his pain and asking her to heal it. She frowned and tried to remember what she had just said. "But I've written him a very long letter and answered all his questions, so perhaps he will stop now."

Paul braced his shoulders and tilted his head so he could stare down his nose. "A letter indeed!" he snorted. "How one found ink and pen in the wilderness is beyond me." He shook his head with mock dismay. "Madness! Trying to put two words together in such a place. Don't tell me you can think with the wind always howling in your ears."

Sophia laughed and Paul dropped his pose. "You know what Papa always says. If you frown, you'll make wrinkles in your forehead."

"Yes," Sophia agreed fondly, "I know what your father says. I shall try to do better."

"You couldn't do better," her son said matter-of-factly. "Except, perhaps if you and Grandfather could be friends?"

"I don't know. I'm afraid he'd ask too much of me. He'd want me to be different, and I can't be."

Glancing around the room, Paul noticed his father's absence. "Where's Papa?" he asked warily.

Sophia gave up the struggle. "I don't know." She buried her head in the covers and repeated, "I don't know."

Paul stroked the back of her head gently, so gently that she would never have guessed that a hard golden light gleamed in his eyes. He parted her hair and rubbed her neck, brushed it lightly, like a whisper of cool breath. "He'll be back soon," he said. No hostility betrayed him, not a hint of the hurt anger that had grown so large it filled his elongated shadow across the sunlit bed. "He always comes back, doesn't he?"

Chapter

45

Julian rode Phoenix hard, bending his head into the wind, trying to outrun the sight of the dead cougar—a nightmare that followed him into the daylight. He had done what he could to make things right by destroying the cat, but the feeling of helplessness had not left him. He was possessed by an angry energy that would not let him rest.

By now the autumn wind had swept away the last lingering wisp of summer, and the cool air of the changing season rushed over him. Branches slapped at his face, but he did not notice. Nor did he hear the tranquil music of the river, which was buried beneath the thunder of Phoenix's flying hooves. In the fragmented glimpses of green, blue and gold that flashed by, he saw the vivid red of uncontrolled fury that had driven him to hunt the cougar, the white-hot rage that had not faded to gray.

Julian was not surprised when he found himself approaching Lizzie's cabin, though he had not planned to go there—not after the last time, when his resentment had unnerved him almost as much as it frightened her. He remembered how pale she had grown, how still. She had not deserved his cold anger then, just as she did not deserve his desperation now. But the need to escape his demons was so great that it hurt.

For a long time he sat on his horse and looked at the tiny cabin at the edge of the woods. There were quaint blue-checked curtains in the windows. He had always thought them out of place in Lizzie's haphazard, boisterous life—an attempt to make her tiny cabin seem more like a home and Lizzie herself more like a wife. Julian flinched at the thought. He had never given her much more than pleasure, and he realized now it wasn't enough. Pleasure could not fill the chinks in the walls where mud and moss had been dislodged, or straighten the uneven door, or reinforce the crumbling logs which had never been strong, and now were old and weather-worn.

Julian tightened his grip on the reins and Phoenix raised his head curiously. "It's all right, boy. All right," he murmured automatically. But it wasn't.

He tried to ease his conscience by remembering that he'd seen Geordie MacKinnon riding this way more than once in the past few weeks, an expression of bemused pleasure on his face. Julian realized then that he had told Lizzie the truth. It didn't matter. And yet—

He sat for a long time, waiting, though he could not say what he waited for. Not until Lizzie came to the door and saw him, stood regarding him warily. Her usually tousled blond hair was carefully combed and she wore a ribbon in it—green, to match her simple gown with lace around the low neckline.

That ribbon, that tiny bit of color tied so neatly in a bow, made Julian ache, but not with longing. Lizzie met his gaze unblinking, curious, a little afraid, and he thought how pretty she was, with her heart-shaped face and lushly curved body. The hunger flared within him, the urgent need to feel her naked skin beneath his searching hands, but he clenched his jaw and did not move. It was Lizzie's choice this time, not his.

She bit her lip, full, pink and moist, surveyed him a moment longer, then slowly raised her hand in greeting and invitation.

Julian dismounted and walked Phoenix the rest of the way, struggling to contain his impatience; he was starved for the sensations she stirred inside him, the overwhelming release of their bodies joined in a frenzied embrace. But he must not lose control. He must not let her see the depth of his need, which even he could not understand.

She stood waiting in the doorway, her full green skirt swirling around her ankles. As he approached, her eyes betrayed her uncertainty. Julian tied Phoenix to the branch of a garry oak, breathed slowly, drawing the air in, feeling it escape in a rush. When he knew it was safe, he turned to her and smiled.

Lizzie grinned in response. She knew that rare and radiant smile, trusted it because he did not give it freely, recklessly, falsely. Julian Ivy did not smile like that unless he meant it. There was no hint of ice in his eyes,

—— *315* ——

no anger. Lizzie sighed with relief and put out her hands in welcome. She did not realize until Julian took them how much she had missed him. The fear of those icy shards of anger had made her forget.

"You look lovely," he said awkwardly. Compliments and pretty words did not come easily to him. His mother had spoken beautiful, lyrical phrases in her accent sprinkled with singing French words. Even Jamie found it easy to recognize beauty and name it. But Julian was not like them. They had lived in a mist-woven world he could not understand. His feet were firmly on the earth. But he owed Lizzie something—something more than just his smile. He had hurt her, been cruel and careless, but did not know how to tell her so.

"So you're back," she said, drinking in the sight of his face, his windblown hair and hazel eyes. "I thought you'd gone for good." Her voice quivered a little, but Lizzie was good with her voice. She knew how to smile with a touch of sadness, to draw a man toward her with just a hint of hurt in her wide brown eyes. But with Julian, sometimes, she didn't have to pretend.

Her hands felt soft in his, clinging, though *he* held *her*. She drew him inside, kicking the door shut with her foot. He glanced around at the tidy table, the potbellied stove free of dirty pots, the bed, made neatly with her homespun quilt.

"You were expecting company."

She shrugged. "Three hours since, I was," she said with unconcern. "I'd just about given up. Then you came. Want something to satisfy your thirst?"

She offered her most appealing smile. Julian noticed she had unhooked her dress so it fell from her shoulders, revealing the curve of her breasts above her chemise.

"Don't bother with the teapot this time," he said, running his hand down her neck to her bare shoulder. "Just give me whiskey . . . for now." His eyes glistened and his hand trembled above her breast, telling her he wanted more than whiskey, but not yet. Not just yet.

"Whatever you say." She went to fetch the bottle, reaching up to the high shelf for a glass, turning so her dress fell farther down her body, uncovering her waist. It took her a long time to find the glass; she chewed on her full lip and swayed as she groped in the cupboard.

At first Julian watched with appreciation the white curve of her breasts, the nipple that showed now and then above the thin fabric of her chemise. But when she came back to him, whiskey in hand, flaunting the tantalizing curves of her body, he was dismayed to feel his rising hunger swirl back into fury. He finished the liquor in a single swallow. It burned down his throat, fueling the desperation he thought he had left outside.

"You've gone away," Lizzie breathed huskily. "Where are you?" She leaned forward to give him a better view.

"Somewhere you don't want to go."

Lizzie didn't hear; she was busy with the buttons of his shirt. Her hands shook with eagerness. She was hungry too, starved for the torment and the pleasure he could give her. She drew him to his feet, stood so close that her breasts touched his chest and he felt her breath at the base of his throat. She slipped her arms around him, pulling up his shirt and sliding her splayed fingers over his back.

He knew with a certainty that left him shaking, as she flicked her tongue along his neck, that this time her body could not give him what he needed. Fiercely, he buried his hands in her hair, tilted her head up and kissed her, hard and long and deeply.

When he released her, Lizzie gasped, fighting for air. She thought her knees might buckle, but he caught her, held her tight with one hand while with the other, he ripped the ribbon from her hair.

Quivering with delight and expectation, she said, "I heard about how you stalked the cougar. Hunting must be good for the blood. Killing that cat sure made yours run hot."

Julian went rigid and struggled not to let her see his turmoil—or the chill that had killed the heat in his blood. She pressed against him, her breasts moving with her rapid breathing, her lips hot on his skin. Her fingertips traced alluring paths over his back, down to his hips, inside the waist of his trousers. He barely felt Lizzie's practiced touch. All he could see was the terrifyingly real image of the dying cat, of blood on golden fur, of the blinding rage that had made Julian a stranger, even to himself.

Lizzie moaned and deep within the sound, he saw the image of Saylah's ravaged face, once in cloudy sun, once by glaring lantern light. Her devastating pain burned against his eyelids in bursts of vivid color. A kind of pain he could not know or understand. It was too much for him to carry, that anguish born of memories she would not share.

Lizzie paused, saw that he was slipping away, and desperately pressed her lips to his. She would not let him go so easily. She knew how to reach him. She untied her chemise, freeing her breasts, and opened his shirt to brush her nipples over the dark hair on his chest.

"Julian, honey, you're not paying attention." She unfastened his pants, ran her hand down over his hip and between his legs.

His body responded, but he could not banish Saylah from his thoughts. Even now he felt a strange desire that had nothing of passion in it. His hunger would not be eased by hands and mouths and skin to naked skin. This hunger was deeper and more dangerous.

"Julian!" Lizzie was frightened by what she saw in his eyes—not the reflection of her face, but a strange creeping mist. She stopped moving her body enticingly, threw her arms around his waist and held him, head resting on his shoulder.

Julian looked down at her, felt the desperation of her grasp and closed his eyes in pain. Gently, he tilted her chin up; tenderly, he bent to kiss her, slowly, so warmly that she melted against him.

He lifted her in his arms and carried her to the bed, where he undressed her, opening her chemise gradually, touching her soft white skin with tongue and searching fingertips. He dropped the wispy garment on the floor and reached for her drawers, covered in pale embroidery and edged with lace. These too he removed slowly, lingering over her waist, the swell of her hips and legs as he pulled the fabric away from her naked skin. She lay quivering while he cupped her breasts, teased the nipples, ran his tongue down the cleft between.

He made love to her not wildly, graspingly, as he had before, but leisurely, luxuriously. He drew out her pleasure, leaving the heat of his hands on her skin not through the raw power of his touch, but through its feather-light brush against her tender, aching body.

He made love to her for the first time without greed or feverish need or rough demands. He trailed his moist tongue from her breasts to her stomach and down between her legs while she curled her fingers in his hair, cried out, quivering, and spread her thighs. Julian kissed away her voice and, with his lips, made her cry out again.

She glowed, she flamed beneath his body, finding a pleasure sweeter than she had ever felt before. The tears on her flushed cheeks told him she knew she would not feel it soon again.

It was all he could give her, this tenderness, this slow and sensuous arousal of her need before he satisfied it tenderly, his own hunger forgotten. He gave her the gift of momentary wonder because he knew no other way.

Julian Ivy had never learned to apologize, just as he had never learned to say good-bye.

Chapter

46

Edward Ashton was very drunk. He was in Victoria, leaning heavily against the bar in a saloon whose name he couldn't recall. John Thomas Howard and his wife Nellie, who owned the place, had tried unsuccessfully to talk to him. They were always glad to see Edward, who was not afraid to spend money on the best scotch whisky in stock.

Edward Ashton had taste, Nellie thought, and a lot of charm to go with it. Unconsciously, she smoothed back her wild red hair and straightened the bodice over her ample breasts. Edward wasn't a snob like so many of the wealthy in Victoria, who held their noses in the air like anyone but their relatives gave off a bad smell. Edward knew how to laugh, and he wasn't choosy about his companions. So long as they were entertaining, he was always happy to see them.

But Edward wasn't himself tonight. Nellie smiled at him compassionately. Poor man, he probably needed a sympathetic ear, and didn't even know it.

Several people had tried to engage him in conversation; Edward could always be counted upon to tell a good story which either kept them laughing, doubled up with pain, or held them spellbound until the last word. He didn't brag about his success or hold himself apart. And he was a generous man, always willing to buy a friend a drink. He was one of the most popular of all the Howards' customers.

But tonight he didn't want to talk. He'd said no more than four words the whole night. He just kept admiring the saddle and book on the bar beside him and staring dismally into his drink.

Two or three women had approached him, thinking he looked lonely and in need of a friend, but he had sent them away. He was concentrating on scotch at the moment—pouring it out neatly, drinking it down quickly, waiting for it to warm the cold spot in the middle of his chest—and did not wish to be distracted. It was exceedingly important that he do all this correctly, though he could not remember why. It had been perfectly clear at the beginning of the evening, but his memory had grown foggier as the night progressed.

What he was *not* doing, he assured himself, was thinking about the hurt and accusation in Paul's eyes. He was *not* thinking about Julian Ivy stroking the dead cougar or the look of horror on his face. But most of all, Edward was *certainly* not thinking about Jamie Ivy, the expression in his unwavering brown eyes. A thing like that—why would he bother his head with it? What was there to think about, after all? An old friend, a little disagreement, a man with an unforgiving heart. Was that Edward's problem?

"Certainly not!" he exclaimed rather loudly, slurring the words together.

"Excuse me?" the Englishman beside him said primly.

Edward glared at him, considered knocking his bowler hat across the room, but decided against it. He didn't want to fight. He wanted to drink. That's why he'd come here, and if this thin, dark-haired fellow—who reminded him a little too much of how Jamie had looked when he first stepped off the boat from England—couldn't understand such a simple thing, then Edward would just have to explain it again. "I was saying—"

The Englishman heard *Iwassshsshaying*, and decided not to pursue the discussion. "Oh yes, indeed yes. Most interesting." Casually, he left the bar and went to sit at a table.

Edward rubbed his chin in confusion. Odd sort of man, he thought. Starting up a conversation, then walking away. But what could you expect, anyway? Now, Jamie would never have done that. Edward pounded his fist on the bar. He wasn't *thinking* about Jamie, and that was that. Otherwise, what was the point of drinking a whole bottle of scotch all by himself?

His elbow struck something, and he blinked in confusion at a small, beautifully tooled saddle. Then he smiled and the confusion retreated. He had forgotten about the saddle, and on top of it, the book. That was what had brought him to Victoria. He touched the saddle gently, caressed the fine seat, breathed in the smell of fresh leather. It was perfect, the workmanship superb. Just what he'd been looking for to fit the pony he'd bought from the MacKinnons that morning. He'd refused to leave it by the door when he entered the saloon. He wanted it near him, where he could feel it, touch it, smell it. He rested his hand on the ornate cover of the book. Beautiful. Who could resist such a treasure? He had done well.

That's precisely what he'd come here to do. Why had he forgotten? He never forgot his business, never lost his clear head. That was too dangerous. If he didn't stay clear-headed, he wouldn't succeed. He frowned. This wasn't a success at all. This was his one failure.

He felt someone beside him, someone who would not go away if he ignored them. He looked up to find the Indian girl with the flowers in her hair. He wondered sometimes if she followed him. She wasn't the first woman who had done so. Nor did he ever disappoint them.

She looked at him, his bleary red eyes and shaking hands, and knew he was more than drunk. He was in pain. It was true that she followed him, but not out of desire—though his touch was gentle and he knew a woman's body well, how to worship breasts, hips, thighs with hands and breath and warm moist lips.

She followed him because she was afraid for him. Something burned in him; she had seen it the first time he held her, felt it move inside where he thought it was well hidden. That glowing heat was too bright, too fierce. Now it was just a white-hot coal spitting sparks into his blood that gave him the madness, the need for release. But one day he would become flame. And then he would burn himself up.

Edward squinted at her high, square cheekbones, her wide black eyes, so deep that he fell into them like falling into a cool, dark pond. Her hair was braided neatly, but when loose, it fell around him, enfolded him, protected him. Her nose flared like the nostrils of a wild animal when he touched her, and her brown and sun-worn hands were rough against his skin—rough and painful and tantalizing. "I want you now," he whispered. He'd let her hold him and make him forget, then he'd make her forget that any other man had ever touched her. To hell with the scotch!

She smiled. He never called her by name, but that didn't matter. She had not told him the truth anyway. To Flora Ivy she said her name was Ah-mah; she told Edward she was called Skayu. He didn't know that Skayu meant ghost. He didn't know that the first time she had seen herself reflected in his eyes, she had known that to him she would never be more than a spirit without substance. A body to hold, a woman to ease his hunger and whose hunger he would inflame.

She ceased to exist for him the moment he looked away. Sometimes she thought he actually believed that he alone gave her life and warmth and pleasure. That he had the power to create and destroy. She let him think it, because this golden-eyed man needed her so much, because inside he burned.

"Come with me," she said. "There are things better than whiskey to dream about tonight. Come with me. I am waiting."

Edward took the girl's hand and her fingers locked with his.

"What are you making now?" Theron demanded testily.

Saylah looked up, startled by the question, which had come unexpectedly from a restful hush, punctuated by the boy's regular breathing. She had thought he was sound asleep.

He had slept heavily, off and on through the past several days, slowly regaining his strength, if not his optimism. Flora came often, bringing food and sheets and bandages and the smell of soap and baking. Sometimes she sent Saylah away to rest, but the girl preferred to stay at Theron's side, where she could watch him, though the danger was long past.

"Your hands are never still," the boy muttered accusingly.

That much was true. To keep herself busy while Theron slept, she had begun by carving arrows for Julian's bow. But soon the beaver pouch was full and he took it with him. "To practice," he'd snapped before she asked.

He had refused to meet her eyes, and Saylah was glad. There were things she did not wish to see just now. But she could not forget the thunderous expression on Julian's face, or the sound of the ax as he cut more wood than the family would use in three winters. Just as often, he practiced with the bow, as if his whole existence depended on his skill.

"There's nothing more efficient than an arrow truly aimed." He'd thrown the words back in her face, like a challenge or a threat. Yet she had heard the despair beneath the taunt. She had ached for him then, and the hurt had not eased.

That's why she had begun to make other things, more difficult, more exacting, demanding more of her attention.

"Saylah," Theron groaned, "you're not *listening*. I asked what you're making."

She noticed the dark circles around his eyes and his normally red cheeks which had not yet regained their natural color. "Of course I am listening. Do I not always listen to you?" She reached out to clasp his hand briefly, in reassurance. "I am making rattles and drums and wooden beads."

"What for?" Even through the haze of half-sleep, the boy was curious.

Saylah smiled mysteriously, thinking of the abandoned well by the river, and the smooth, echoing wood. "For celebrations."

Theron liked the sound of that. "What kind of celebrations?"

"The kind I knew before I came here, when I lived among my People."

"Oh." The boy fell back against the pillow, too sleepy to ask more questions. Soon his eyes closed and his breathing grew calm and regular once more.

Saylah went back to the pieces of hide and cedar and bone, the long sinews she had fashioned. It gave her pleasure to work with these remnants of her past, but not simply for herself or the memory of her People. She hoped the drums and rattles would bring Julian pleasure too.

It was late, nearly time to take Jamie his evening tea. Saylah sighed and noticed the sun was sinking low, burning its way through the curtains on the window. "They should be open. You need light and air to make you well," she had told Theron. "But what if Papa comes to see me?" the boy had asked wistfully. The curtains remained closed, though Saylah knew that Jamie would not come.

Since the attack, Jamie had become even more taciturn, more silent and withdrawn. Now he had shut Flora out. "Och, he talks to me, right enough," Flora had said mournfully, "but he's no' really seein' me, if ye know what I mean." Jamie lived in the darkness of his room, and Saylah sensed the shadows were closing in around him. She had tried to reach him, but he did not seem to hear. She had come to dread her evening visits, the sight of his parchment-white face and dark, empty eyes.

She rose precipitously and, careful not to wake the boy, unwound the gauze from Theron's arm to replace it with a fresh bandage. She froze when she felt insistent eyes upon her.

Slowly, very slowly, she turned to the doorway, where Julian stood watching. His gaze was full of turbulence, a turmoil that compelled and threatened her all at once.

"I came to see how Theron is," he said.

Saylah motioned toward the bed. "He is better every day. I am certain the sleep heals him more than anything."

Julian leaned over his brother, noticed Theron's peaceful smile. "I think he's having a pleasant dream. He's lucky."

Before Saylah could respond to his caustic tone, he moved closer, staring at the uncovered wound. He examined the swollen red skin, the deep parallel gouges in fascination. Julian reached out with a claw-like hand and traced the marks without touching them. Softly, he murmured under his breath, "The cougar is sacred."

Saylah straightened, shaken by the timbre of his voice, the words he chanted like a prayer, the strange burning look in his eyes. In the air above his brother's arm, he traced and retraced the mark of the cougar. The brown in his eyes had been shadowed by the green. Now they were the color of the sea, of an island lake before a storm.

He caught Saylah's gaze and held it. This time he would not look away or let her turn from him in fear. This time they would face each other without flinching.

Saylah's hair was tightly braided, her face unnaturally pale from the days she had spent inside the house. But her eyes, fixed on his face, were translucent green—unveiled for the first time since the day when they lay on the riverbank, their bodies pressed together, quivering with laughter. He had kissed her to stifle the sound, but the kiss had become more. Almost, he had forgotten. She had willed him to forget.

But now he knew the truth; Lizzie had made him see it. What stood between Julian and Saylah was the mirror that reflected one upon the other. He could feel its cold surface, feel it undulate with the warm touch of his hand.

Saylah knew what he was thinking; he reached out through stale air and held her so she could not run. "You did not come to see your brother."

"No." He would give her no more than that.

She had to ask the question, though the answer was suspended in a shaft of bright sunlight between them. "Then why have you come?"

Julian did not move closer, did not move at all. "We've been somewhere together, you and I, where no one else can ever go."

His voice brought back the clatter of a falling bow, the fleeing cat, the rush of her pain. It brought back the moment when she'd seen the tracks of the cougar crossing the tracks of two little boys. It brought back the log, moss-covered, battered, barely clinging to the hillside. Saylah closed her eyes. "That place is dark and dangerous. We must not go back, or even remember that we have been there."

Julian stared at her, incredulous. "What *should* we do?"

Saylah chose her words carefully. "We must turn our faces forward and put that place behind us."

"You mean, pretend it never happened?"

She did not answer, merely gazed at him with cool green eyes.

Julian shook his head wildly. "It's impossible."

"Yet I have done it before." She spoke calmly, but her hands began to tremble.

Then you're stronger than I am. The words rose to his tongue but he did not speak them. His pride would not let him. Besides, he wondered now if they were true. "What about the laughter? Should we forget that too?"

Saylah flinched, unconsciously running her fingers over the rattles, the taut deerskin, the cedarbark on the bedside table. She thought of what they meant, and her heart—which once, in a moment of anguish, she had thought would cease to beat—took up the rhythm of remembered drums. "Do you not see," she said, "that that is the most dangerous of all?"

—— 324 ——

Chapter
47

Saylah dreamed of standing in cool, clear water, of starlight swirling beneath her hands, of the voice, distant and indistinguishable, calling a name she could not hear. When she awoke, the light was shining through the lustrous blue curtains, filling the room with the warmth of the sun, keeping out the chilly autumn air. She lay unmoving, breathing in the scent of fir, uneasy at the memory of her dream. This time the voice had been Jamie's, calling to her, pleading. But for what?

Now that she had helped Theron heal, now that he was safe and free of nightmares, she had but one thing to give.

Tapping gently, Saylah opened Jamie's door and peered inside. He was not in bed, but stood facing the double glass doors hidden by drapes. He held the curtains in his hands, which were pellucid in the dim light. His face was tense, his eyes open wide, staring at nothing. Saylah knew Jamie Ivy was not looking at worn velvet or thinking of the view the drapes concealed. He was gazing within, to the past that had betrayed him, bewildered him, abandoned him to this present filled with sorrow.

"Jamie," Saylah whispered. Her eyes were damp, her voice hoarse with compassion. The man at the blind window did not speak or nod or move one muscle of his tightly clenched hands. He was dwarfed, made insignificant by the huge, canopied bed, the thick curtains, the carpet, soft and rich beneath his feet. Even his dressing gown—quilted velvet trimmed in gold silk braid—was too heavy, seemed to weigh him down and hold him apart.

Saylah forced herself to breathe. Never, in all the years of her life, had she seen anyone more isolated, more terrified of his loneliness, which he had chosen but could not bear. "Jamie," she repeated, "I am here. Come back to me."

He wanted to fight, to stay where he had been hiding in his memories, but he could not resist the lure of her voice. She alone understood the depth of his pain, the quality of the shadows clustered at his back. Flora loved him, gave him all of herself, but she could never understand. Her soul was free of darkness. Only Saylah had felt her own darkness, carried her own shadows heavy on her back. Only Saylah knew what was deep inside him where even he did not wish to go.

He had to let her bring him back. He revolved slowly, gazing at her through the uncertain light of the low-burning lamp. She held the familiar tray of three cups. The steam rose around her, blurring her face, so that, almost, he could believe she was a dream. Her eyes were dim, obscured by smoke and shadows, and her hair hung long and free to her waist.

He had asked her to leave it that way, flowing inky black and rippling as she moved, giving luster to the plain gray gown she wore. Black on gray on smooth warm brown; she melted into the darkness of his room, into his daydreams, which had become his life. Jamie stared at her across the room and knew that one day she would set him free.

"Come," she repeated, "drink your morning tea."

Jamie released his grip on the curtains and came toward her. "I was very far away," he said.

"I know." She spoke quietly, reaching out to steady his hand when his fingers trembled on the hot cup. She touched him briefly, felt his cool skin, the ridges of veins beneath her palm.

The steam wavered, a vaporous screen between them. "Why did you bring me back? I was happy there."

Saylah shook her head. "You were not happy. You were horribly alone. I could not bear to watch it."

He winced at her honesty, took the cup, and moved away. "Perhaps that loneliness was easier—"

"No," she interrupted, "not for you or for your family."

He whirled, spilling hot tea down the front of his rich velvet. "What has my family to do with it?"

"Everything." Saylah set down the tray, forced back the wave of

—— 326 ——

empathy that made her want to leave him alone and in peace. She gathered her strength around her and said firmly, "You are taking them with you when you slip into the past. You have chosen to die. They have chosen to follow."

Jamie stared in disbelief. "I meant to set them free." They had spoken of this before—too often. Saylah took his arm and guided him to the chair with the carved lion's claws. Another magnificent beast, wooden and powerless, another remnant of what had been. She knelt, her hands on Jamie's knees. "Did you think to set them free by hiding in your room, by cutting yourself off from them, refusing their help or their kindness or their comfort?"

He listened, mesmerized, frightened by the phantoms that hovered around him, the specters he had not recognized until Saylah made them real.

"They love you, Jamie. You cannot hide from that." She saw the cast on his eyes which dulled the brown to gray, felt his unwillingness to believe.

"But I never gave them anything I promised." He smiled bitterly. "And I promised so much." He gripped the claw-like arms of the chair with bloodless fingers. "I failed them. I'm a fool and I hate myself for that. I can't even bear the sight of my own face."

Saylah put her hands gently on his. Her palms were warm. "And yet they love you. Enough to die for you or with you."

Jamie pulled away. "You're talking nonsense."

Saylah was perplexed. Why did he deny the affection his family felt for him when it could soothe him, heal him, ease his pain? But he did not want that. He wanted to suffer. "If you do not believe, then come with me. Let me show you."

Jamie's skin turned sickly gray.

All at once, Saylah understood. "You do not keep the curtains closed because the light hurts your eyes. It is because you do not wish to see." She spoke sharply, in anger.

He opened his mouth to object, but could not lie. "Perhaps."

"That is your choice, to remain in darkness. But must you take your family's sight as well?"

"What do you mean?" He feared this new and furious Saylah whose green eyes blazed with accusations.

"How long has it been since you have seen the rest of this house?" she demanded.

Jamie blinked at her in surprise. "Not long ago I sat by the fire when the boys were lost and Sophia and—Edward came."

"At night there is firelight. It is not the same."

"What am I to do?" he asked helplessly.

"Come see it with me. That is all I ask."

"Why?" He was struggling to deny his impulse to do as her golden voice bid him, to follow her, safe in the protection of her shadow. "Why are you doing this?"

Because I think that I will lose you, because I have become part of your sorrow and Julian's and Flora's. Because, above all, I am afraid of something I cannot name. But she did not say these things.

Her mouth was dry with compassion, her throat raw with fear at what she might be risking. Jamie's sanity, his health, perhaps even his life? But the Ivys could not go on this way much longer, or the house would fall in upon itself. "Because I care about Flora and Theron and Julian enough to fight for them."

Jamie glared, his cheeks bright with color. "They can fight for themselves. They're strong."

"Yes," Saylah conceded. "In some things and in some ways they are very strong. But they have no protection against their love for you. They are struggling with all they have to make this a home where you will wish to live."

Jamie's cheeks were pasty, his eyes overbright with apprehension. "Show me," he said at last.

Saylah knew how much the words had cost him. He rose awkwardly from his chair, but she did not offer help. That would have been cruel just now. Instead, she followed as he moved slowly across the room. When he reached the door, he put one hand flat against it, willing it open. He could not make himself turn the knob.

Saylah slipped in front of him, peered through a crack, and saw that no one was about. She opened the door wide and Jamie stepped behind her into the main hall.

She had removed the fir and cedar boughs the previous evening, intending to replace them today. The fresh scent of the woods had gone. There was only the tamped-down ashes of the fire and the damp mustiness of the huge room through which fresh air did not blow. The room was murky, kept in darkness by thick curtains.

Jamie stopped, appalled. He was used to this heavy, dank air in his own elaborate room. There it was soothing and safe. Here in the huge, barren hall it was suffocating. He looked around, bewildered. This room used to be full of light and welcome, even in winter. He had put in many windows, many more than the other ranchers, for Simone's sake, because she loved the light and feared the darkness. Now the hall was grim and cold and empty. Saylah hovered close, her hand protectively beneath his elbow.

Jamie swayed, but steadied himself without leaning on her hand. "Are all these shadows mine?"

For an instant, Saylah hesitated. "Yours—and Simone's. And now Julian has inherited them from you."

Jamie moved away unsteadily, went to touch the saw, the mining pan, the rifle. "I put these here many years ago. There's nothing new."

Saylah said nothing. She ached for him, but knew no other way to make him see.

Jamie wandered like a stranger in the house he had built. He did not know this room, this cold and unforgiving place. When Saylah took his arm to guide him down the hall past Flora's room and Theron's and Julian's, he did not resist.

Step by step, they climbed to the loft and the half-wall that looked down on the world he had created. Jamie stopped, gripping the railing, grateful for something to lean on.

Just then the front door flew open and Theron burst into the hall, calling, "Mama! You'll never guess what I found!" His arm was bandaged, but that did not slow him down. His cheeks were red with cold and his eyes sparkled with excitement.

Saylah touched Jamie's arm.

He leaned forward, gazing with affection at his smiling son.

Flora came out of the kitchen, flapping her apron wildly. "Hush!" she cried in a whisper. "Your father had a restless night. I'd no' want to disturb him."

Before she had finished, Theron grew still, as if his spirit, bright and vital an instant before, had drained away.

Flora saw the light go out of her son's eyes and put her hand on his head in an offer of comfort, an apology. Her own cheeks were pale and drawn with worry. Above Theron's head, she looked at the door of her husband's room. Thinking herself unobserved, she gazed at it with all the love she could not express, the longing she could not reveal.

Jamie sucked his breath in sharply. He felt he could look right through his wife and son; they had no substance, no spark of life. In silence they disappeared into the kitchen.

Jamie sagged against the wall. For him Flora and Theron had not moved; they were frozen in that moment when the light had left their eyes. He would never forget Theron's glowing face turned ashen, Flora's hand on her son's head. That simple caress had been a gesture of defeat.

Jamie began to sway, but Saylah was beside him. "I did not intend for you to see that," she whispered. The expression on his face was tearing her apart. She put her arms around him from behind and he leaned against her, listened to the beat of her heart, which was steady and reassuring.

"No," Jamie said shakily, "how could you know that Theron—" His voice cracked and she held him tighter.

"I will take you back to your room. You have seen enough."

He was silent for a long time, struggling against himself. Then he straightened and moved forward. Saylah let her arms fall away. "I want to see the rest."

"I do not think it wise— You have been ill—"

Jamie was not listening. He had moved past her and was examining the bed of pine boughs she had made on the floor, the stones in their small semicircle on the red cedar box she had fashioned, then carved with the head of Thunderbird, Owl, Wolf and Raven. She had placed the box, a kind of altar to her childhood, beside the bed.

Jamie knelt. "This must be your sacred place," he said. He seemed glad to turn his attention to her, to give himself time in which to build his strength again. "You brought these with you from your village?"

Saylah looked at the clear pink streaked with gray. "All but one," she said.

"May I touch them?"

She nodded, watching as he ran his fingertips reverently over the round stones. He lingered on the black with the white feather and the captured fern beneath clear water. He smiled thinly. "You, at least, have made this house yours. I'm glad."

Saylah's eyes were painfully dry. She clasped her hands firmly behind her back.

Jamie replaced the stones, then stood in the middle of the large open room. "I built this for Simone. She wanted a room surrounded by windows. She loved the light here. She said it was not like this anywhere else on earth, that it was magic."

Saylah was captivated by the wisp of tender memory that transformed his face. Her fear for his family burrowed deeper inside her. Did the man who stood with his eyes on a shimmering past remember Flora, who trusted him and gave him all she had?

Jamie turned slowly. He sensed Saylah's dismay and rubbed his eyes, as if to dislodge the last vestiges of sleep. "If you're worrying about Flora," he said, "you needn't. She knows that I love her. She knows more than you think. But Simone—" He tried to keep his gaze on the present, on the slender woman with wise green eyes, but he began to slip back again, to the sound of a lovely French voice, an elegant but gentle hand, a face so beautiful that even now the memory made him ache. "Simone was different. No one will ever be like her. No one can take her place. Flora knows that too.

"She's wonderful, my Flora." His tone was full of gratitude. "Simone is gone." He spoke with grim finality and started toward the sitting room.

Saylah was there before him, blocking the door. "No."

Jamie glowered. "They're *my* memories and it's my pain. I have to learn to accept it. You can't do that for me." He paused. "Though I believe you would if I let you."

Saylah's eyes were damp. "I would. I am strong. I can bear it."

"And I can't?" He was not hostile, only confused. "You have memories and pain of your own. Why do you try to carry the pain of others besides?"

Saylah wanted to say she had put the grief behind her, but the words would not come. *It is not that the light hurts your eyes,* she had said to Jamie, *but that you are afraid to see.* She shook with the rising misery that had engulfed her when she sat with Julian on the rock. "It is how I was trained. It is all I know."

"It seems all I know is how to make others suffer with me, especially those I love." His laughter was harsh, brittle.

Saylah put her hand on his mouth to stop him. "Please."

Jamie smiled sadly, reached for the crystal doorknob and turned it. He stepped inside, stopping when he saw the rose and silver wallpaper, the velvet settee, the satin and lace curtains. "It's exactly the same." He sniffed, and his face softened with memory. "I can almost *feel* her."

Saylah shivered at the same cool whisper of air that had touched her the last time she entered this room.

Jamie tilted his head. He felt it too. Compelled by that invisible breath, he went to the settee and picked up a needlepoint pillow. "Simone used to lie with this under her head. She would tie her hair back with pearls and they would come undone and fall over her shoulders, twined into her hair." He buried his face in the pillow and took deep, gasping breaths that sounded like uncontrolled sobs.

Saylah touched his shoulder and he looked up, dry-eyed but despairing. He dropped the pillow, looked around once more, and left the room without a word. He had said them all. Saylah closed the door gently behind him.

He paused at the head of the stairs. "I'm tired of ghosts. I want to see who lives here now."

Saylah nodded, too shaken to respond. She helped Jamie down the stairs and guided him first to Flora's room. He opened the door and glanced inside. The room was large, very tidy and sensible, like Flora herself. There was an old rocking chair with faded flowered cushions that looked inviting. Jamie wondered how often his wife had sat there with Theron on her lap.

On the bed was a frilly, hand-embroidered pillow. Jamie picked it up curiously. "This doesn't look like Flora."

"It was a gift from her mother, she said. She treasures it for that reason. I think she loved her mother very much. I think she misses her, even now."

Jamie dropped the pillow. "I didn't know. She never said."

Next Saylah pushed open the door to Theron's room. Toys and clothes were scattered, as if a wild wind had blown inside these walls, frustrated and unable to get free. It belonged to a boy full of energy and life, not the solemn-faced young man they'd seen in the hall. Saylah closed the door quickly and took Jamie's arm. "Let me take you back. You are weary."

"I haven't seen Julian's room."

"But you must rest." All at once, Saylah was afraid. "It would be foolish to tire yourself more."

Jamie faced her, waited until she met his gaze. "If you are afraid to show me the truth, how am I supposed to have the courage to face it?"

She had no answer. Was this the same man who had hidden himself away for so long, refusing to look into the light? She felt deep respect for Jamie, but it did not ease her fear.

She straightened, drawing on *his* strength. She had brought him this far. They must go on. "Here," she said, indicating the door across the hall. She turned the knob and they went in.

The room was in semidarkness, like the rest of the house. Jamie stopped at huge twin bookcases that rose along each wall. They were dusty and bore no marks of fingertips or reaching hands. "He hasn't touched his books for a long time," Jamie murmured. He had always been proud of these overburdened shelves, of the things Julian had learned, his insatiable need for knowledge. Where had that hunger gone?

"I think he no longer finds what he needs here," Saylah whispered.

The bed was neatly made without a wrinkle to show that Julian might have sat there while he put on his boots that morning. In fact, the whole room—the desk with its chair pushed in, the nightstand, the bare wood floor—looked untouched, unlived-in.

Saylah clenched her hands and swallowed dryly. She could see that for Julian, this was nothing more than a place to sleep when he was too exhausted to do anything else. It was not a place to live, to feel, to breathe and grow.

There was a sound outside the window.

"What's that?" Jamie asked, eager for a distraction.

"It is Julian, I think. Using the Salish bow that used to hang in the hall."

"I didn't realize he knew how to use a bow."

Saylah smiled. "I taught him."

"And he *let* you?"

She regarded Jamie intently. "Why should he not?"

Jamie rubbed his temples to ease the ache there. "Julian likes to learn things on his own. He doesn't like to admit that anyone else knows more than he does." Intrigued, he turned to the window.

He stood for a long time, eyes closed, hands on the windowsill. When he reached out to draw back the curtains, she wanted to stop him, but did not move. As he had said, it was his choice, his memories and pain.

Jamie opened the curtains and stood blinking, blinded by the sunlight that had not touched him for nearly a year. He swung away, took several breaths, then looked again into painful whiteness. He put out his hand and Saylah took it, massaging it gently while he struggled with the light. At first he saw nothing. Then, slowly, a figure took shape.

Even soft and out of focus, the sight was disturbing. The sounds, though muted by the glass, were equally so. Jamie's eldest son was indeed practicing firing arrows into a distant target. He had attached his beaverskin quiver to a post behind him at shoulder height, so he could reach back and grab an arrow as soon as he let one fly.

He stood, legs spread, bracing his upper body, every movement full of impatience and frustration. He shot arrow after arrow without pausing. The tree that was his target was riddled with holes. Some of the arrows had been so well aimed, they had split others down the middle, but Julian did not stop to notice or admire his expertise.

Saylah felt a constriction in her chest. She had seen Julian often since that day when he had faced her in Theron's room and asked her to remember. They had gone forward, as she'd said, pretending that no danger lay behind them. They had spoken to each other pleasantly, sat together by the fires at night, worked side by side. Not once had he mentioned the things she had told him to forget. Now his body spoke them more eloquently, more poignantly than his lips could have.

From where he stood, Jamie could see his son's profile. Julian's expression was taut, unyielding. He was moving like a powerful machine, with occasional bursts of violence that revealed his hurt and anger. Jamie leaned heavily on the windowsill, making smears on the wood that had been so long untouched. He had forgotten Saylah; he was alone in the room with his son.

Julian ran out of arrows. He cursed at the empty quiver, swung away from it toward the tree. He pulled out arrows recklessly, breaking off the points of some. Then he turned and Jamie saw his face straight on for the first time. There was a moment when Julian let his mask slip to reveal his naked pain.

Saylah gasped and fought to breathe.

Jamie put his hand on the window, fingers spread, pushing with all his strength, willing that single gesture to heal all Julian's grief and loss. "I'm leaving him alone," Jamie groaned, understanding for the first time exactly what those words meant to his son. He rocked back and forth, staggered by what he'd done. "I didn't know," he whispered brokenly.

—— *333* ——

When there was no response, he looked up. Saylah had pressed both hands to the glass and her body was tense, like Julian's. She echoed his stance, legs spread in a challenge, back rigid, arms straight before her. Even the tilt of her head was the same. Except that in Julian's eyes there burned a cold, implacable flame, while Saylah's eyes were damp with tears and an empathy so profound that something inside Jamie twisted. Twisted and shattered.

"You're right," he said. "I'm very tired."

Saylah started, fought her way back to the small, barren room. Gradually, her body grew slack, she relaxed her arms, and took her hands from the window. She saw Jamie's haggard face and began to close the curtains.

He put his hand on her arm. "Leave them."

Astonished by the command, Saylah did as he'd bid her. His strength and courage had seeped away, leaving him weak and vulnerable. Saylah was afraid for him. Deeply afraid. More than anything, she wanted to wrap him in the thick satin quilt on his bed and make him warm again, safe again, blind again. She put her arm around his waist and he leaned against her as she helped him to his room.

She settled him in bed, and he did not protest. He did not speak at all, merely reacted to her touch like a limp doll with a bemused look on its painted face. Saylah hurried to the kitchen, relieved that Flora was in the garden, and made him an infusion of restorative tea, with a bit of herb to make him sleep.

Jamie held the cup with both hands, but he couldn't keep them steady. Saylah sat on the edge of the bed and cupped her hands around his. She did not like the bluish tinge to his skin or the rhythm of his pulse, which thundered, then barely moved through his veins. He winced and she knew he was in pain.

"You're very gentle," Jamie said, "very tender. Your hands seem wise."

"I have had much practice."

Jamie glanced up, no longer bemused, his gaze unnerving and intent. "And you'll have much more, I think. But Saylah, little one, that will never heal *your* pain. Sometimes I see it—a flicker, a moment's darkness, 'e'en like the passage of an angel's tear that falls through the clear ether silently.' Keats, you know. Sometimes he haunts me."

Before she could reply, Jamie began to cough. She gave him a steaming cup to drink from. Slowly, the coughing eased and he lay back, eyes closed. The tiny blue veins on his lids touched Saylah and made her want to weep. She turned to go.

When she was at the door, he stopped her.

"Saylah?"

She glanced back.

"Open all the curtains in the house, except here. I prefer the darkness. As I said, that's my choice."

"Of course." Her heart pounded erratically; in spite of his pain, he wanted to make things right. She turned again.

"Saylah?"

"Yes?"

"Julian won't be entirely alone, will he?"

She struggled to find her voice. "No, he will not."

Jamie smiled then, with such sadness and tenderness that Saylah could not bear to watch. Yet she took a step toward him.

"Go," Jamie whispered. "Tell Flora what I've said. It will please her, I think."

"Yes," Saylah agreed. This time he did not stop her, and she left the room and closed the door, leaning against the solid oak. Without it she would have fallen. Her legs were shaking and she could not see through the sheen of her tears. She had learned a great deal about Jamie this morning. Somehow he had seen beyond her protective veil to the things she had thought hidden or long dead. He saw so much, despite his desire to see nothing at all. He was a rare man, a man met once in a lifetime.

She felt cold and vaguely desperate. It was too much to lose. "Jamie," she said into the stillness of the gloomy hall, "I was wrong. Forgive me." But she knew it was too late for that.

Chapter

48

"I can no' believe it!" Flora cried with delight. "'Tis the work of the kelpies, that's what it is."

"It is not!" Theron cried indignantly. "Saylah did it. She can do anything." He stood beside her, shoulders straight, head high, proclaiming his loyalty.

"Aye, well, she can do a great deal, anyway," Flora agreed. Her face glowed with pleasure.

Saylah could not resist Flora's enthusiasm. She smiled back, but the hope in Flora's eyes disturbed her.

Theron was jumping up and down, undeterred by the damage he might do to his healing arm. "What are we waiting for?" he demanded. "The sun'll be down before we even start."

Flora grinned at her son. "'Tis barely ten in the mornin', lad. I think we've time enough."

"Yes, but—"

Throwing up her hands in mock surrender, Flora said, "All right, then. Let's be at it." She looked around the main hall appraisingly. Her gaze settled on the far wall with its floor-to-ceiling draperies. "Come," she said to Saylah. "The sun's hidin' behind all that cloth, and I've a mind to bask in it, just for a little."

Theron could no longer contain his impatience. *"I'm* going to help. I'll do the bedrooms." He was gone before his mother could protest.

Flora looked after him fondly. "He's no' very good at hidin' his feelin's, I'm afraid."

"No," Saylah said, smiling. "It is one of the reasons I like him so much."

The women moved toward the far end of the hall. In silent consensus, they went to the center of the heavy, dark curtains. Each grasped the worn fabric in one hand. They paused; then, with a flourish, they dragged the curtains open, rattling the rings as they moved away from each other to uncover the row of high, broad windows.

Saylah stared, the velvet swinging in her hand. The morning sun streamed in patches from among the clouds, penetrating the coating of dust on the thick glass and illuminating the long, dark room. It was as if a wall had been knocked down and the daylight allowed, at last, to enter. The windows looked down over the hill to stands of oak and arbutus and dogwood. The apple orchard was off to one side, the lush woods stretching beyond.

The cedar logs, dulled to gray by the darkness, glowed a warm, red-streaked brown, and the sun glinted off the saw blade, the dented mining pan, the barrel of the rifle. The stones in the two fireplaces, each hand-picked, each distinctive in shape, color and size, made a random pattern that was fascinating and beautiful. The well-kept wooden floors gleamed in shades from butter-gold to beaver-pelt brown.

Shaking her head in disbelief, she found Flora staring, transfixed, at the motes of dust that drifted and tumbled in the streams of light. Suddenly, both women sneezed, overcome by the dust sifting down from the curtains and the windows, undisturbed for so long.

Flora blinked and rubbed her nose, leaving a smudge of dirt on her cheek. "'Tis amazin' how bonny dust can be when 'tis touched with sunlight," she said. Though she was a tidy person, she showed no inclination, just yet, to remove the layers of dust from the glass or wave them out of the sun-bright air.

Looking at Flora, her apron coated with dust on top of flour and gravy and other mysterious stains, her blond hair tipped with beige, her cheek streaked with dirt, Saylah felt a tightening in her chest, a fierce surge of affection. "Yes, it is beautiful." She smiled and Flora smiled back and they stood, watching dust particles dance in the light.

"What have you been *doing?*" Theron squealed when he saw them holding the curtains. "I've got all the bedrooms, and I've even *cleaned* them."

Flora and Saylah turned to see the boy waving one of his best shirts before him. It was black with dirt and dust flew from its crumpled folds, making Theron cough and sneeze.

Flora gazed heavenward and sighed dramatically. "Did ye have to use your Sunday shirt? And look at ye! Ye're head to toe in dust. I'll have to stand ye under the pump to wash it all away."

Theron was not impressed. He grinned, white teeth gleaming in his dust-coated face. "Come and see," he said, waving his flag of triumph and starting another burst of sneezes.

"I'll come if ye drop the shirt where ye stand. Ye'll be paintin' the whole house with dirt and 'tis me who'll be washin' down the walls."

The boy let go of the filthy garment and gave one more ferocious sneeze. Laughing, Saylah and Flora followed him down the hall.

Proudly, he stood in the doorway to his room, pointing at the window. Saylah had to choke to stifle a new wave of laughter. Indeed, the window was clean—except for an occasional curved streak of gray—up to a point. Above Theron's height, where he could not reach, the glass was thick with dust and grime. The clear glass below only emphasized the dirty area above.

" 'Tis a fine job ye've done," Flora managed to gasp. "Mayhap later we'll bring in a ladder and finish it up." She smiled tearfully and glanced about, reacquainting herself with the house that had been hidden in darkness.

Theron glowed and insisted on showing them every room. When they came to Julian's, he frowned. "The curtains were already open in here. I wonder if Julian—" He broke off, grasping Saylah's sleeve in horror. "We didn't wait for Julian. We should've *waited!*"

Saylah barely heard him. Through the window, she could see that Julian had gone. But that was not what held her attention.

Flora stared at the glass, glanced quickly at Saylah, and turned back again to the window. The lower portion had been wiped clean, but higher up, where the dust was thickest, were the distinct impressions of handprints on the glass.

Saylah stood on the upstairs porch, the French doors open behind her. Leaning on the railing, she gazed beyond the woods to the sea. Not until she opened the luminous blue curtains had she discovered that from here, at last, she could look at the sea. She had missed it with an ache she had not acknowledged until that first view of blue water drifted with mist.

Flora and Theron were busy washing the rest of the windows. Afterward, at Saylah's suggestion, Flora would look in on Jamie, sit with him, sing to him if he wished.

"He will want you there when he wakes. I do not think he should be alone," Saylah had murmured, too low for Theron to hear.

The boy had been so excited, between sneezes, that he'd been determined to open every set of curtains in the house. But when they reached the sitting room, Flora had stopped him. "I'm thinkin' some ghosts should be left to rest in shadow."

When she noticed Saylah's pallor, she'd asked, "Why do ye look so frightened?"

"It is only—" Saylah stammered, not wanting to hurt Flora, not knowing what to say. "I have noticed her presence sometimes, and I wonder . . ." She trailed off, dismayed by the words that would not come.

Flora squinted at the girl curiously until a thought struck her. "Mayhap my Jamie told ye how he feels about"—she hesitated, then forced herself to go on—"about Simone. But I'd no' have ye grievin' for me." She pursed her lips thoughtfully. "I can no' change what happened to him before I came, though 'tis often enough I wish that I could." Blue gaze steady, she added, "I'd no' want him to forget her, ye ken, only to forgive her, so he can be at peace."

At a distant shout from Theron, she had cocked her head and disappeared before Saylah could respond.

Now the girl listened, but Flora's voice had faded. Saylah smiled triumphantly, feeling that she had fought a long battle that the opening of these doors had ended. She knew it was not true, but just now, for this moment, she would enjoy the victory. She shook her hair free of dust, breathed deeply, smelled the salty fragrance of the sea and leaned closer, while a painful ecstasy welled within her.

She longed to sit and watch the waves lap gently on the beach, to dig for clams and scallops and mussels, to feel the damp, grainy sand on her bare feet. Her memories were bright, vibrant and painful, but she could not turn away any more than she could have turned from the handprints pressed into the dirty glass.

Julian had finished his target practice and chopped up two fallen logs for firewood. It had not been a pleasant morning. The work had neither appeased nor exhausted him; his frustration and sorrow lay close beneath his skin. He dropped the last logs onto the pile carelessly, so they rolled back down, spewing dust, bark and soil as they went. With a muffled curse, he left them and went around the side of the house.

He stopped when he sensed a movement above and looked up at the porch overhead. Saylah leaned there, her hair blowing over her shoulders, across her face. But the strands could not hide the light in her eyes, the tint of red in her brown cheeks, the slight smile on her lips. He stared, taken aback. She looked lovely, healthy, almost happy.

It was a long time before he realized the doors stood open behind her and all the upper windows were uncovered. He examined the rest of the house and saw it was the same downstairs. There was no hint of velvet or satin or even lace undercurtains. Just glass, endless, clear and radiant with morning light, despite its film of dust.

For a full minute he could not breathe. Then he called up to Saylah. She smiled at him and motioned to the open doors.

Impatient, full of questions, Julian grasped the squared-off pole at the far edge of the porch, stepped on the railing and shimmied upward. He moved quickly, with agility, catching the slats of the upstairs porch and pulling himself up until he could swing one leg over the railing.

Saylah regarded him calmly. "It is a good morning," she said, with a hint of a smile.

Julian could not help smiling back. "Why?" he asked when he caught his breath. "What happened?"

"You are too impatient, I think. You might have fallen." But she was grinning, pleased that his earlier mask was gone.

Julian shook his head and tried to look grave. "But I didn't. I'm too clever."

"So clever that you split and break the arrows I have made for you so carefully. If you do not take more care, I will not be able to keep up."

Julian actually looked sheepish. He had ruined many arrows in his frustration, and he knew how hard she worked to make them. He had been touched when she presented him with the first set, though he had not found the words to tell her so. Instead, he told her how he enjoyed shooting with the bow. It was a new challenge, a focus for his restless energy. "I wish you wouldn't spend your free time working, especially when I'm so careless with the arrows. You need time of your own."

Saylah wondered why he was so concerned. He himself got few hours of sleep and spent most of every day, from dawn until dusk, working on the ranch. At night he went over books full of figures. She had watched him covertly and knew that those figures turned to nightmares the moment he fell asleep.

"I do not mind. I enjoy such tasks. They remind me of home. Of sitting cross-legged near glowing coals, knee to knee with the other women, the salt air all around us. We could look out at the sea while the smell of steaming clams drifted past. We worked hard summer and winter, but our work was also our pleasure."

She bit her lip. She had said too much. Besides, Julian had not climbed up there just to hear her talk of things that were lost. He had come because of the light through the windows. "I opened the curtains as your father asked."

Julian gaped at her, uncomprehending. "*Jamie* asked you?"

Saylah nodded.

He stood immobile, too stunned to take it in. Then it hit him with the force of a roll of thunder in a raging sky. He grasped Saylah's shoulders exuberantly, let her go, took her hand. He did not know what he was doing. His heart beat with excitement and the first hope he had known in a long time. He caught her other hand. "Will he get better now?"

"I believe he will try," Saylah said carefully.

Julian shook his head in disbelief, ran his fingers through his hair and laughed aloud.

Saylah had never heard that note of triumph in his voice before; the burden had slipped from his shoulders for the moment. She laughed with him, in spite of what she knew. His joy was irresistible, as powerful as his anger and pain.

Julian had been careful and afraid and angry for so long, he had forgotten what it was like to feel like this. Impetuously, he picked Saylah up and swung her around. "*You* did this. You!"

She tried to push him away, though the morning air caressed her and Julian's strong hands held her gently. "No!" she cried.

He was smiling, exultant, but it would not last. "It was Jamie's decision."

He was not listening. She could not bear to ruin his pleasure, but she would not give him false hope. He still held her waist and his face was flushed, his eyes bright with flecks of green and brown. "Julian!" she said.

Her tone broke through his elation at last. He looked at her questioningly.

"I do not know if it will be enough." She waved vaguely at the windows.

The laughter faded from Julian's eyes, and he loosened his grip but did not let her go. "At least it's more than we had before. I'm grateful for that."

He was thanking her, Saylah realized. They stood looking at each other, unmoving, her hands on his chest, his hands at her waist. They were held apart by the length of their arms, by all that lay unspoken between them.

Julian broke the silence. "When I saw you from down there, your expression was beautiful. What were you looking at?"

"The sea," she answered, grateful that, for the moment at least, he had abandoned the subject of Jamie's recovery. "I always lived at the edge of the sea, with the sound in my ears, the damp air in my mouth, the water swirling around me. I found it comforting—the lap and swell of waves, the foamy white lace on the sand, the changing tides."

Julian released her and leaned on the rail as she had done. "The sea looks like it's breathing and the mist is its breath." Before she could answer him, before he turned to see her face, he looked toward the clearing, where the deer rose from the roots of an ancient cedar. "Look!" he said. "It's very different from up here."

Saylah nodded. The antlers were more impressive when she looked into their heart; the prongs spread like the graceful branches of a tree and the colors of the carved wood glowed with morning light.

"Let's go do some carving," Julian whispered. "Jamie would like that."

Saylah smiled up at him. "Yes."

He caught her hands and held them together palm to palm. "I know it was Jamie's decision. I also know he would never have made it without you to guide him. That doesn't make him your burden, Saylah. Only your friend."

Chapter
49

That afternoon, Paul and Theron met in the stable for the first time since the night of the attack. Paul curried his pony with exaggerated care, and Theron helped. They fed the animal, petted it, talked to it, long after the pony was content. Yet they did not leave, because outside the barn was the woods. Both boys were thinking it, but neither wanted to say the words. Finally, Paul took the plunge.

"We can't stay here forever."

Theron hesitated, rubbing his bandaged arm.

Paul touched the bandage lightly. "Can I see it? I didn't get a scar. I can't even prove it happened."

"Why would you want to?"

Shrugging too casually, Paul said, "Well, to impress a girl someday, or tell a story like our fathers do. You know."

Theron had not thought of that. But now he remembered how Saylah had caressed the wound. "Saylah said her people called it the Mark of the Cougar. She said it was like a badge of honor." She had told him the hunters would have been proud of such a scar, which proved their bravery. All at once Theron felt sorry for Paul. Moving toward the light that came through the open doors, he unwrapped the gauze to reveal the four parallel claw marks, covered now with dark scabs. The redness and swelling had gone away, and it only hurt sometimes, when he forgot and swung his arm too fast.

Paul examined the wound in awed silence, running his finger gently around the ragged red, trying to imagine what it would look like when it was healed. He bit his lip, blinked rapidly several times, finally looked up at his friend. "I'm sorry," he said. His face was very pale, very strained.

"What for?" Theron was confused. First Paul had been envious, now he was sorry. It didn't make any sense.

Paul swallowed dryly. "For taking you—there—that day. It wouldn't have happened if—"

Theron kicked at a clod of dirt. "Saylah said the same thing, and Julian. That it was all their fault. I think it's silly. It's the—" He paused, unable to say the word, but knowing he had to, or Paul would keep looking at him with huge, sad eyes forever. And that would be awful. "It's the cougar's fault," he said obstinately. "So stop being stupid."

Paul's eyes were suspiciously damp, but instead of crying, he laughed. He leaned close to whisper, "Mama said it was *her* fault, and Papa—well, he didn't *say* anything, but I know he thinks it's his. That's why he gave me this present." He held up a leather-wrapped package, and his eyes clouded over, but he forced his ugly memories down.

"Maybe if everyone feels so bad, we can get them to make us taffy twice a week," Theron suggested. He grinned. "It would make them feel better."

Paul giggled, though he had grown out of the habit at least two years earlier. "Maybe it would. Come on. I want to show you something."

Theron stood where he was, arms crossed. "You have to help me tie this back. Saylah'll be mad if she sees I took it off. And I'm not going anywhere till you show me what's in the package."

Paul was astonished. Theron did not seem any different from the boy he'd been before that night in the woods. Yet Sophia had said he'd almost died. Paul tried to tell himself he was no different either, but he wasn't very certain. Carefully, he replaced the bandage on Theron's arm. "Come on."

"The package," the younger boy repeated.

"It's just a book."

"But it's a *present*, you said." Theron bounced with anticipation.

Paul gave in and unwrapped the leather to reveal a large book with a beautiful hand-painted cover and pages whose edges made a swirled design when the book was closed. Theron took it reverently. It reminded him, somehow, of Simone's chest. Inside were large ornate letters and hand-painted pictures of animals.

"The stories are about the animals' secret lives. You know, the ones we don't know about." Paul's voice trembled, excited but wary. Because Edward had given him the gift, he had not touched it for several days; his anger and fear had been too raw. But the book lay on his bureau in full view, inviting, mysterious. Eventually, his curiosity overcame his distaste and he opened the cover, caressing the painting with sensitive, searching fingers.

He thought of telling Theron why he had run that day, why he had not wanted to touch this book that was supposed to be so beautiful it would make him forget, like his father's warm voice and compelling stories. But Theron was too little. He wouldn't understand.

"I wanted to keep it someplace special. Like the secret place I found in the woods. That's where we're going now." He paused, drew a circle in the dirt with his toe. "It's what I was looking for—that other time."

Theron pursed his lips. He still wasn't too sure about secrets, despite the nice ones he shared with Saylah. But Paul looked so eager he couldn't refuse. Besides, he didn't want to go back into the house. Even though it was brighter now, being inside wasn't the same as feeling the wind on his face and in his hair. He shrugged. "Okay."

Paul nodded and started toward the woods. The look in Theron's eyes told him perhaps his friend was not as unconcerned as he seemed. When the two boys reached the edge of the clearing, they stopped, hesitated, shifting from foot to foot.

Images sliced through Theron's mind—a flashing paw turned silver by the light, the cramped murkiness of a mossy log, the breathlessness of running, knowing you can't run fast enough. The fear came back to him, and his body went cold. He rubbed his hand across his forehead and found it was covered with sweat.

Paul was not faring much better. He felt like he couldn't breathe, like the trees would close around him and he'd never be able to get free. He thought he could hear the animals breathing, hidden in the bracken and snarled vines, waiting—

Tentatively, Theron reached out to take his friend's hand. They glanced at each other, ready to turn and flee. Then their eyes met, and their clammy palms. They seemed to find courage in those two tenuous bonds and knew they had to go on. The forest loomed before them, a huge, breathing darkness full of danger, until they took one step at a time and moved into the cool shadows, smelled the scent of fir and cedar, felt the ground give beneath their feet.

They stopped, and Theron shouted, "I'm not afraid of you!" Both knew the cougar was dead; Theron was not talking to the cat, but to the woods themselves, to all the lurking dangers that were hidden in their depths.

Nothing moved but the wind in the trees, and far away, the fading echo of Theron's voice. He smiled and the boys unlinked their hands. The fear retreated.

Paul listened for a moment longer, heard the silence, free of threat. With a sigh of relief that shook the kinnikinnick trailing over a dead tree stump, he moved in front to lead the way.

This time he was not lost in bewildered memories, and he easily found the narrow path. In a short time, the boys ducked under a spreading fir. Paul pointed in triumph to an Indian plum that sprawled up the edges of a huge flat boulder. "Here it is!"

"What?" Theron looked around, but saw nothing out of the ordinary.

Paul knelt next to the Indian plum and pushed it aside, motioned for Theron to follow. Then he disappeared behind the bush. Theron was perplexed until he caught the tangle of leaves in his hand. Behind the drooping branches was a hollow, cave-like area. The boulder jutted out above, but sloped back sharply below. It was just high enough for the two boys to sit.

"This cave'll be just for us. Our secret. No one else can come in, ever!" Paul declared. Then he added quietly, "We'll be safe here."

Theron wriggled in, scuffing his boots and his corduroy trousers, to settle cross-legged beside Paul. The Indian plum hid them from view, yet let in enough light to see by, making patterns of lace on the soft dirt floor. Theron was awed.

Secrets, he decided with a firm nod of his head, weren't that bad after all.

Julian twisted and turned, disturbed by his dream. He was sitting in a boat on a gently lapping sea. He knew he could not drift off because a woven rope went back through mist and foam and hills of sand to a stout cedar. He could not see the land or the tree that kept him safe, but he knew they were there.

Then a storm blew the sea into a roiling cauldron. The wind screamed, dipped beneath the water, carrying the waves higher and higher. He knew he could have ridden them out; the boat was light enough to rise with the swell of the furious sea. Except that the rope held him back, tied down when he needed to rise, to let his boat ride free in the midst of the storm.

Julian gasped when the rain poured down, mingling with the wild salt sea to soak his clothing until it hung heavy and cumbersome around him. He could not remember how to free the rope; his thoughts, like the boat and the sea, were spinning out of control. He shivered, chilled through, and struggled to keep his head above water. Then he saw the enormous wave rise above him, higher and higher. It was leaden gray, except when a shaft of sunlight broke through the clouds, turning it glorious turquoise and azure and emerald. He stared, enchanted, while the deadly wave rose higher, until he knew it would come crashing down upon him. He could not get away; he could not move, could only cling desperately to the sides of his fragile boat.

He awakened, gasping for air, fighting the surging water all around him. It was a long moment before he realized he was safe and dry, twisted hopelessly in the quilt on his bed. He lay waiting for his breath to calm, remembering, not the terror as the water crashed over him, but the colors, brilliant as jewels, more beautiful than any he had seen before. He could not understand his fascination with those colors that would have brought his death.

He rose, though it was not quite dawn, and dressed in the dark, picking up yesterday's shirt, stepping into his trousers. The sky was beginning to lighten, slashed with pink and lilac and violet, muted near the ground by fine morning mist.

Julian left his room, turning to the stairway that led to Saylah's loft. He did not want to go there, where the memory of her face—twisted by pain, lightened by laughter, transformed by the breath of the forest—would torment him. Yet he was drawn up the stairs by a compulsion he could not resist. Julian wanted to tell her his dream.

He reached the head of the stairs, thinking she would be asleep, or already gone to the river to bathe.

But she was not asleep. She was poised on the window seat, her white nightgown falling to the floor, her hair hanging loose down her back. She did not see him because her face was turned outward, toward the rising sun. She was waiting, he guessed, for the last light of dawn.

There was about her that quality of stillness which he had seen before. She was at ease in her own room, curled up with her flannel gown to protect her from the chilly glass. She sat in perfect solitude, absolutely and intensely alone; yet there was no sadness in her loneliness. Her face was in profile, a clear silhouette.

Julian wanted desperately to hold that stillness in his hands, to breathe it in along with the pure morning air. Even the sight of her anguish had not moved him this deeply.

He wanted to feel for himself what he saw in Saylah's profile—serenity, unruffled calm, a clear pool of water whose surface is smooth, like satin. Even when the wind comes, ruffling the satin into tiny swells, the heart of the water is unmoved, immutable.

Saylah had left him. She had drifted into another world, far beyond his reach.

He wondered, in that frozen instant, how the sun had ever risen without her. How much time had been wasted before she began to sit like this, motionless, taking the beauty into herself? How much of that beauty had dissipated—forgotten, lost in the too-bright light of day—before Saylah was born to gather it, remember it, make it live in her magnificent green eyes?

Chapter
━━━►► 50 ►►━━━

"Ye've gone daft, that's what!" Flora exclaimed to her husband, who stood facing her, fully dressed. She had not seen him in flannel trousers, a fine linen shirt, a cravat for so long that she had not yet recovered from the shock. And now he was making wild suggestions that made her heart beat with hope.

"Not a huge party. Just a small one. Perhaps twenty people or so, if they remember how to find their way here." Jamie pushed a lock of hair from his forehead with a flourish. He thought it was a grand idea. "Just to show everyone that I'm not a recluse or a madman after all. I'd enjoy shattering all the myths they've woven in the past year about my mysterious illness."

Flora stood with her hands on her hips. For an instant she saw a cast on Jamie's eyes, but then it was gone. Her husband had changed in the past week. Somehow, in a way she could not understand, her Jamie had come back to her. "Everyone we know'll be rememberin' the path to Jamie Ivy's house," she said fiercely, forcing herself to concentrate on what her husband was saying and not his sparkling eyes and the color in his cheeks.

Flora's slow, wistful smile made Jamie's chest tighten and his breath catch in his throat. He sat in the claw-footed chair and motioned her toward him. "Come," he said softly. "There's room enough for two, remember?"

Flora hesitated, trembled at the rush of tingling warmth that filled her veins. Yet she was afraid for Jamie—and for herself—as she sat and he drew her head against his chest. She reached up to clasp his hand when he slid his arm around her shoulder. She was afraid if she didn't, he would slip away, forget her.

Flora's heart slowed when she felt the heat of her husband's body mingle with her own. She smiled. It felt so good, so natural to sit as they used to, absorbing each other's breath and pulse and heartbeat. "I've missed ye," she sighed.

Jamie rested his chin on the top of her head. Her curly blond hair was freshly washed; the familiar fragrance moved him, and his body responded quickly, forcefully. In that moment, he wanted to weep, because he was alive after all. "You can't have missed me as much as I've missed you." His voice shook and he fought to keep it steady. He had forgotten what it was to be strong, to desire, to ache for Flora's touch, her scent, her gently searching fingertips. "But I did not forget how beautiful you are."

Flora knew she was not beautiful, knew too that Jamie believed what he said, because he saw her through his eyes; open at last, they made magic of what was plain and ordinary. She shifted uncomfortably, remembering that Saylah had made him see again. Saylah, whose gift radiated outward like invisible light, whose grace was contained but undeniable. "What about Saylah?" she said before she could stop herself. She was ashamed of her jealousy, which flared suddenly but brightly. "She's very lovely."

Jamie tipped up Flora's chin. "It's not how she looks, but how she sees right through me, no matter how I try to hide."

Flora's common sense had left her. She knew Saylah's power, had seen it as she healed Theron. The girl had not simply touched his wound or laid a cool cloth on his forehead; she had given him her hand, and through it flowed her will, her warmth. She had become Theron, made him part of her. Flora had never seen anything like it.

And now, here was Jamie, full of energy and enthusiasm, dressed and talking of a party. Saylah had done that too. Flora wanted to weep in gratitude and envy, in fear at the strange, invisible web that bound the girl to those she sought to heal. "Ye're sayin' that she knows ye in a way I never can."

Jamie held her with his eyes, no longer clouded with mysteries. "I would never wish upon anyone the things Saylah has suffered. I don't even know what they are. I only know she recognizes my pain because she's felt it. To understand it, you would have to feel it too. You don't want that, Flora. *I* don't want it. I don't want you to share my misery, but to make me forget it." Tenderly, he caressed her cheek, her parted lips with his fingertip.

"It's true that we're bound together, Saylah and I. Bound in the past and afraid to let go. But don't ever envy her. The cost for her wisdom was too high."

"Forgive me." Flora's eyes were damp, her fingers locked tightly with her husband's. "'Tis just that ye've been away so long, and I thought—" She broke off and kissed his forehead, brushed her lips over his. "Never mind. It makes no matter."

Jamie wrapped his arms around her plump, warm body and breathed her in like fragrant wine. He kissed her and she sighed against his mouth, sinking into the pleasure that had long been denied her. Jamie made her feel desirable, a woman whose body came alive after a deep slumber.

"I know how 'tis with Saylah. I know."

"But you see," Jamie murmured, brushing her curls with the tip of his nose, kissing her temple, inhaling the scent of skin warm from the heat of the stove, "she does not know how it is with us. That's why you should pity her, my Flora."

Flora agreed without words, with her hands and her lips and the motion of her body.

They settled closer, resting against each other, smiling. "It's too quiet here, too isolated," Jamie said. "I miss the people who used to fill the house with noise." He rubbed his chin thoughtfully. "Besides, Julian is too much alone. Theron has Paul, but there are no other children, no young women and men. My boys should have many friends. And you need the company of other women. Don't think I haven't noticed. A party would remind people that a rutted road through the woods doesn't have to be a wall between us and the rest of the world."

Flora did not think he was telling her everything, but she did not say so. "I have Saylah to keep me company. She's worth a great many of the others I've met." This time she spoke without envy.

"We were lucky to get her."

"I'd no' be sayin' 'twas luck that brought her. She was sent, and no' just because we need her. I've a feelin' she needs us too." She bit her lip. "I'm worried about her. She works too hard and gets no rest."

Jamie nuzzled his wife's neck. "That's why I want a party." He kissed her again, amazed at the hunger that he had thought forever dead. He pulled her closer and she curved into his body. "There'd be songs, dancing, new people, talking. It would bring the house back to life, and all the people in it."

Flora smiled with tears in her eyes and returned his kiss eagerly. She had just locked her arms around his neck when the door burst open and Theron erupted into the room.

"Papa, Mama, come see! Come see!" He bounced from foot to foot, unable to stand still. He grasped Flora's hand and tugged. "You have to come see!"

Reluctantly, his parents rose and parted, made curious by Theron's excitement.

The front door had been thrown wide open to the cloudy morning. Despite his improvement over the past week, Jamie was not yet ready to face the sunlight. He hovered in the shadows while Theron dragged Flora outside.

She gasped when she saw a beautiful white pony, saddled and bridled, standing in the clearing. Paul Ashton held the reins, but that did not stop him from dancing around, enjoying everyone's astonishment. Saylah and Julian stood nearby, staring.

"What—? Where?" Flora stammered.

"My father bought the pony for Theron," Paul cried. "He missed his birthday, and wanted to give him a late present."

"He had the saddle made special," Theron chimed in. "Isn't it the most beautiful pony you've seen ever?"

Flora exchanged a long look with Saylah, who seemed bewildered, and Julian, who seemed suspicious. She herself could not help but wonder what motive Edward Ashton had for presenting a boy of six with this magnificent gift. Especially since, until the night when the boys had disappeared, Edward had not seen Theron for nearly a year.

"Mama! You didn't say it's wonderful." Theron tugged at her skirt, demanding that she share his delight.

Flora put her hands gently on her son's shoulders. He was healing, but not yet as strong as he thought. The gentle pressure of her palms held him down, forced him to stop and remember to breathe.

Saylah knew she could have calmed Theron in an instant, but her job was done. She had made him well, now Flora must take up the task of making him take care. The boy smiled up at his mother, and Saylah felt a pang, not of envy, but of longing.

When Theron was quiet, Flora moved toward the sleek white animal. "'Tis certainly excitin'." She turned to Paul while she patted the pony's arched neck. "But would ye no' be thinkin' 'tis a mite too much of a gift for so tiny a boy?"

Paul's hooded eyes hid his thoughts. "That's how Papa is. He likes to give presents, and they're always good ones."

He sounded belligerent and more than a little defensive.

"But why now?" Saylah asked.

Her question was drowned out by Theron's shout when he remembered his father in the shadows. "Papa!" he cried. "I can't believe it. Can you?"

Jamie regarded the pony thoughtfully, while Theron propelled himself toward his father, hugging him until both nearly toppled over. "Paul says I can't ride 'til I practice and learn how." He grinned expectantly up at Jamie.

"Then we'll have to find someone to teach you, won't we?" Jamie liked the feel of Theron's small weight against his legs, the sight of his sparkling eyes and rosy cheeks.

The boy fiddled with a button on his father's waistcoat. "Couldn't *you* do it?"

"Well, I—"

"Paul's father taught *him*," Theron interrupted breathlessly. "He said they were together for hours and *hours*, practicing. You have to practice a lot, Paul says."

Jamie felt a stab of pain at Theron's unconcealed longing. He knew he could lie and make his son happy for a little while, but what good would that do? Through dry lips, he said, "I'm sure Julian will have time to teach you. He's a better horseman than I am anyway."

Theron set his jaw in a stubborn line. "But Julian's not my father. *You* are."

Jamie felt helpless and foolish. How could he explain that he did not have the strength of will to undertake such a simple task? How could he explain that he was a coward, hiding in the safety of his room?

Theron gripped his father's brocade waistcoat tightly, and would not let go. Jamie coughed, cleared his throat, rested his hand on his son's head. "I wish I could do this for you, Theron, but I can't. I'm sure Julian would be happy . . ." He trailed off miserably.

The boy blinked back the moisture in his eyes. "Who taught you to ride?" he demanded. "Your father or your brother?"

Jamie gasped as if he had been struck.

Theron was horrified by the look on his father's face. "I didn't mean it, Papa. Really, I didn't. I just want to be with you sometimes."

With difficulty, Jamie recovered his composure. "And so you shall be," he said carefully. "Things will be different from now on. I won't be hiding anymore. You can come to me anytime." But he wondered, as Theron's smile returned, if after all, he was not making a promise he could not keep.

Julian saw Jamie's pallor and touched Theron on the shoulder. "Papa and I need to talk."

The little boy grinned and wiggled his eyebrows in a ridiculous imitation of Flora when she was attempting to look severe. "Do ye now? Weel, it sounds important, that it does." He dropped the accent when Paul called to him. "Have to go." He tumbled outside without looking back.

Julian and Jamie watched with affection as he disappeared. Then Julian turned back to his father. He had seen Jamie's look of dismay at the sight of the pony, but he'd also seen that his father was not surprised, only curious. That was odd, Julian thought. Then he realized Jamie was fully dressed. That was odder still.

"Well," Jamie said as the two men gravitated naturally toward his darkened room, "Edward has certainly made an impression on Theron."

"On everyone," Julian replied, pulling the door to behind him. For the first time he was not aware of the ornate atmosphere of the room. He was aware only of his father, who, despite his pale skin and too-thin body, was not behaving at all like an invalid. "But I don't think it's a good idea. Theron's too young for a responsibility like that."

Jamie looked away. That Julian, who had carried the world on his shoulders since he was four years old, should say such a thing, and without resentment, made him want to weep. But, like his son, he was ignoring the obvious, the unspoken questions that hovered between them. "Did you see the look on Theron's face? There's not been much in his life to bring that look."

Julian paced restlessly. "But don't you wonder why all of a sudden Edward gives such a gift? It must be worth a small fortune. The pony is exceptional."

"Yes," Jamie mused, "and beautiful." He faced the French doors, hidden by dark velvet. "I doubt Theron has ever seen anything like it." He paused and added, "Or like Edward."

Julian was watching his father closely. "Do you think Edward acted out of guilt?"

Jamie stood with his back to his son. "I wouldn't presume to guess why Edward Ashton does what he does." The words he did not say, but which lingered in the air like a hot, unpleasant rush of breath, were *or what he has done.*

Julian listened for bitterness but heard none. He felt a sense of urgency, a need to understand what had passed between the two men on the night of the cougar attack. There had been ghosts in the room that night; Julian was sure of it. "Maybe he wants to start over."

Jamie turned, head tilted, eyes blank.

"To start your friendship over," Julian explained.

There was a long moment when the ghosts began to eddy in the small drafts of air in the enclosed room. Then Jamie murmured,

> . . . I saw
> Too far into the sea, where every maw
> The greater on the lesser feeds ever more—

But I saw too distinct into the core
Of an eternal fierce destruction . . .

He paused, listening to the ghosts, then met his son's curious gaze. "You don't start over with a friendship. You just go on."

"What if that *is* what he wants?" Julian persisted.

"I am a fool, I admit, but I'm not altogether blind. Besides, Flora is always talking of forgiveness. Edward is my closest friend." He turned again toward the blind window. "You just go on," he muttered under his breath. "I suppose that's what Saylah taught me. That it's possible to go on. It won't be like it was before; nothing ever will be. But you can move forward." He paused, sensing Julian's confusion, his distress, but Jamie could not help him now. "If Simone came back tomorrow, somehow we'd all go on, even then." He did not know what had made him say it, though he had felt her presence more strongly in the days of his recovery.

"Simone is dead," Julian said coldly, implacably.

"No," Jamie said just above a whisper. "I'd know if she were. She's alive, somewhere. And she won't be back; she's chosen never to return. But still I can go on." He met his son's chilly hazel eyes. "And so can you." When he saw Julian would not respond, he forced himself to smile. "That's why I want to have a party here."

It took an instant for Julian to let go of Edward Ashton and Simone, another to understand what his father was saying. "A party?" The words seemed foreign to him, incomprehensible.

"Indeed. I've already told Flora. The ranch is too isolated for her. She's used to a large family. She had ten brothers and sisters, you know, and her father worked for the Hudson's Bay Company. There were always others about. She misses the noise and confusion, I think. This house has grown far too quiet." When Julian did not respond, he continued. "We could invite the MacKinnons, the Brodies, the Buchanans, Mr. Palmer, of course, and some people from town. I think it would be quite festive."

Julian felt a tiny leap of hope, a moment of happiness that overshadowed what had gone before. "A party," he repeated.

"That's what I said. I thought you might go into Victoria to get some things we'll need. Ale and punch and plenty of flour and sugar for bannocks and cookies and cakes." He moved toward his son and touched his arm. "You haven't been to town in far too long, you know. It's not healthy at your age. You should be wandering from saloon to saloon raising hell."

Finally, brilliantly, Julian smiled. "I doubt if you ever wandered and raised hell in your life, so how would you know?"

Jamie shrugged. "Edward told me. He was quite the hell-raiser at one time, I understand. And besides, I do know you're too much alone. There's a world out there, Julian, full of so many things worth seeing and touching and feeling and enjoying. So many things you refuse to go in search of."

Julian went pale. How had his father learned so much about him? It was true that he had not gone to Victoria, except when it was absolutely necessary, for a long time. He'd been afraid to leave, afraid of what he'd find when he got home. But now, for the first time, with Jamie standing dressed and full of plans in front of him, he felt a twinge of excitement.

Victoria was a beautiful city, a welcoming city. He used to love to go there for no reason at all, to drive down to the sea or visit the shops or slip into one of the saloons. He had lost his enjoyment in such things without even realizing it.

"Papa," he said, "you're wiser than you know."

Jamie grinned back at him. "Wiser at least than I was. For now that will have to be enough."

Paul and Theron huddled over the makeshift desk they had constructed of boulders and planks inside the light-speckled cave. Paul had brought his inkwell and pen, which Edward had bought for him when he started attending school, and several pieces of parchment taken from Sophia's desk drawer.

"But I don't understand," Theron said, chewing on his lip while he watched Paul form careful letters on the blank parchment. "If your mother already wrote to your grandfather, why do *you* have to?"

Paul sighed with exaggerated patience. "I don't *have* to. I just think I should."

"But *why?*" Theron persisted.

Paul snorted in exasperation. "Because I think Mama might make him mad, and then he'll make her mad, and they'll just shout at each other forever and never say a thing."

The younger boy regarded his friend skeptically. "But if she makes him mad, won't you make him madder?"

Paul frowned. He hadn't thought of that. He pushed the auburn hair off his forehead in annoyance. "Not if I'm careful. That's why I asked you to help."

"Oh." Theron was taken aback. His reluctance disappeared in a burst of enthusiasm. He rubbed his chin thoughtfully, as he had seen his father do.

Paul was chewing on the end of his pen, which dripped ink onto the parchment in an ever-widening pattern. "I don't even know what to call him."

"What's his name?"

Paul glared at his friend severely. "You don't call your grandfather by his name."

Theron leaned over the paper, looking for inspiration in the ink-splotched parchment. "I guess not." He stared blankly for a while, then said, "My grandfather's name is Theron. Papa named me after him." There was another long pause during which both boys gazed at the ink spot and Paul held the pen poised in case of a revelation.

"Who're you named after?" Theron asked when his mind remained stubbornly empty.

Paul waved his hand in dismissal. "A friend of my father's."

"Really?" Theron's eyes lit up with interest. "Who was he? Did you know him? Did he do something wonderful?"

The older boy began to nibble on the end of the pen again while he narrowed his eyes and tried to think. "I don't know. Papa knew him a long time ago. But he must have done *something* important. Mama said she wanted to name me after Papa, but he insisted on Paul." He shrugged, dismissing the subject. "That doesn't help me now. We need to think about the letter. I have to say something important, or Grandfather won't pay any attention."

Theron grinned. "He might if you make him laugh."

For a moment Paul sat, pen in the air, letting the words sink in. Then he bent over the rough plank and began to scribble furiously.

Chapter

51

"So they're going to have a party," Sophia observed, spreading her full white skirts around her on the delicate stool of her vanity and tapping her index finger on her chin. "Paul said Jamie was better, but I never thought—"

"In my humble opinion, you think far too much anyway." Her husband, who stood behind her, leaned over to undo the top two buttons on her cambric wrapper. Her silver mirror reflected his handsome face; even in the glass, the lure of his eyes was nearly irresistible.

Sophia laughed and leaned against Edward, her auburn curls crushed against his linen shirt, which he had not yet buttoned. He caught his fingers in her hair and held her head pressed to the cool skin of his chest. He felt safe with her weight against him, safer than he had felt in many weeks. He saw his face reflected in the mirror and shifted slightly so she would not see his expression. He was afraid.

The feeling had been building since the night when he had sat between the blaze of Jamie's fires. Edward shuddered at an urgency building so slowly, so stubbornly, so intensely that he could not fight it. He gripped Sophia tighter and she cried out when he pulled her hair.

Freeing herself with difficulty, she turned to look up at him. "Does the

358

thought of attending the Ivys' party upset you so much? You didn't seem ill at ease the last time."

Edward began to pace. "No, it's not that." Lately, he found he must be always in motion, going somewhere, doing something to keep the thing growing inside him from erupting. "You are burning inside," the Indian girl with the flowers in her hair had said. He had laughed and made love to her so violently that both had lain trembling for a long time afterward.

Sophia contemplated her husband, elbows on her knee, chin in her hands. She felt an agitation within him that perplexed her. Always before she had been able to recognize his distress, to talk him through it, sitting with his head in her lap, brushing back his sandy hair with her strong and tender fingertips, the sound of her voice flowing over and around him, bringing him back to the reality of solid ground. Ground that would not shift or change or open up and suck him into darkness.

His need for her made her feel whole and invulnerable. Her father was wrong; she had not failed. She had done what few others could—created a life, a home, a haven for her family in this wilderness.

Even Paul was stronger than she'd realized. Sometimes he had night-mares where he could not breathe through the musty darkness that threatened to suffocate him. But in the daylight he had left the night of the cougar behind him.

Sophia's only regret was that he was so often gone now, exploring with Theron, teaching him about his pony, doing all the things that young boys did together, without their mothers to watch or worry over them. Sophia and Paul still played enthusiastically their morning games with books and newspaper. They laughed together and sometimes Edward joined in. Sometimes, but not often enough.

This demon that plagued her husband was something she could not fight, the disquiet which made him restless, like an animal wild with the craving for freedom but caught behind iron bars.

"If it's not the party, then what is it?" she asked.

Edward stopped. The sound of her voice, steady, calm, curious but firm, was a gift whose price he could not name. It held him up when he might have fallen. He turned so she would not see how deep it went—the gnawing need for the reassurance of her voice. "Who can say?" He tried for his usual glib response, but could not quite make it real. "It's Jamie, I suppose, and his changes in mood. Don't people who are dying simply die? Not Jamie. He decides he's not going to leave us after all, then commands our presence at his coming-out party."

He was shocked at the venom in his tone. Sophia was staring at him open-mouthed.

"You don't mean that, Edward."

—— *359* ——

He collapsed like a skin in the shape of a man from whom all the bones had been removed. His hands dangled loosely between his knees and his head fell forward. "No," he said in a strangled voice. "I thought I had lost him, that he'd turned his back on us and would never turn around again. But he has, hasn't he?" He looked up at his wife pleadingly. "Do you think he's forgiven me?"

Sophia's mouth was very dry, and words were difficult to form. She had wondered, worried, imagined what had ended the long-standing friendship, but Edward never offered an explanation. "Forgiven you for what?" she said carefully.

Edward's head snapped back and he sat rigid, the gold of his eyes lost in the brown. "You know how business is," he replied stiffly. "Things don't always work out. You have to accept that, don't you? It's part of life."

He rose regally, his former need encased in a chilly cloak of indifference, and left the room without another word.

Sophia stared after him, shocked, silent, more than a little afraid.

Chapter

52

Saylah stood by the carved deer, waiting for Julian to bring the wagon around. For the first time, she had asked a favor of the Ivys. Tomorrow was the party Jamie had planned so carefully for the past few weeks. Flora had already prepared apple and berry pies, cakes and bannocks, biscuits and cider. Saylah wanted to add something of her own.

Besides, she had been longing to go down to the ocean ever since that first glimpse from the upstairs porch. She had offered to make a seafood stew if Julian would take her to the beach when the tide was low. Flora had agreed at once.

"Been workin' too hard and too long, lass," she'd said. "Ye'll make yourself ill if ye're no' careful. Take the whole day if ye've a mind. And if ye bring back no' one single clam, who's to know but ye and me?"

So today Saylah was free. She felt light-hearted, expectant, like a child awake through the long hours of darkness, who springs from her bed at the coming of the light.

She leaned close to the carved doe, pressed her palms against the cedar and felt the warmth, the weight of the many hands that had shaped it. She wanted to be one of those hands, to make her own mark.

Taking a pocket knife from her otterskin pouch, she considered the graceful line of the hind legs, still joined and solid, unfinished.

Singing to herself, she began to work. Each cut made the fragrance of cedar stronger, each flick of her knife brought back the memory of hollow bowls and spoons and curls of bark. Each piece of raw wood revealed beneath the worn outer bark brought her childhood closer, until she could smell it, feel it, touch it.

"You look so happy, I hate to disturb you," Julian called, waking her from her trance. "But we'd better be on our way."

The horse pranced in place, echoing his master's impatience. Julian was smiling, looking forward to their outing. For the last two weeks, he had seen Saylah often but spoken to her rarely, and never alone. The preparations for the party had added to his regular workload, and he had been with Jamie a great deal, talking as they used to, becoming reacquainted.

Julian leapt down to help Saylah up to the high-sprung seat of the wagon. He noticed her dark gray plaid dress was brightened by a long wool scarf Flora had knitted in green, to match Saylah's eyes.

"It is a good morning," she said with conviction, drifting in the warm, safe memory of her past.

"Better than I've seen in a while," Julian replied, admiring the cloud-scattered sky, the trees, swept free of mist, the dew on their thick branches sparkling like gems in the sunlight. The days had turned slowly, inevitably, deeper into autumn, and the leaves had changed to gold and yellow and red and royal purple. But today the air was warm, promising one last reminder of summer before the cold came to stay.

Julian rode for a while in silence, enjoying the feel of the wind in his hair. He was intensely aware of Saylah beside him, her hip pressed to his. "What is it we're looking for anyway?" he asked finally.

"I will gather clams and scallops and mussels for a stew. It is a special dish which my People make for feasts and ceremonies." Saylah closed her eyes, imagined the smell curling toward her in the rising breeze.

Julian's hands grew damp around the worn leather reins. "Do you know your voice changes when you speak of your past, like you're singing a lullaby. I've always wondered why you came here." He hesitated. "Why did you leave them if they mean so much to you?" He did not want to hear the answer, yet he had to know. Especially since that moment when he had seen her face against the window, a silhouette rimmed with the light of dawn.

He shivered. The longing in her voice had sought out his fear and breathed it back to vibrant life. She had said they would move forward, but that was a lie. They hung suspended, motionless, in her pretense that nothing had changed.

Too distracted to notice Julian's distress, Saylah thought of her last days with the People. She could still see vividly the unspoken accusations, the look of horror on Shaula's face, the strangers who had stood waiting for something she could not give. She remembered Hawilquolas' voice. *I think you have grown so used to being right that you do not remember what it is to be wrong. No Head Man lives forever, no shaman, not even a Queen.* Her heartbeat paused, grew ragged with remembered pain. "I had grown into someone they did not know. I had no choice."

Julian sighed. How good she was at speaking, yet telling him nothing. "But you want to belong to them, isn't that true? You want to return."

Saylah stifled a gasp at the wild sorrow, the yearning that engulfed her. She turned away, arms crossed to keep the memories in—to keep Julian out.

But this time he did not intend to let her go. He breathed deeply, considered one last time, and said, "Tell me a story about your child-hood."

Saylah heard her own words whispered back to her, and shut them out in an instant. She half rose on the worn wooden seat. "Look!" she cried. "It is the sea."

Julian shook his head in defeat. He had lost her—again. Reluctantly, he stopped the wagon under the trees at the edge of the sandy beach. She leapt down before he could help her, running toward the sea, arms outspread. For a moment he thought she would not stop until the water rose around her ankles, her waist, her neck, enfolded her like a familiar cloak discarded long ago. She tossed aside her boots and gathered up her skirt; by the time she reached the water, she was once again the girl he had first seen, hands pressing into cedar, head back in the wind, inhaling air much purer and more rare than what he breathed.

Saylah felt the water whisper around her toes. Though it was icy cold, she laughed aloud. She sensed that Julian had not followed, had left her alone to enjoy what he could not understand. She was grateful. Grateful for the scent of salt in the air, the water lapping gently on the sloped beach, the wet sand against her bare feet.

She tasted the sea on her tongue, felt it mist over her face. She filled her sight with the blue and gray swells that shifted to green and turquoise and azure. She had come at last to the sea. The pain receded once more into darkness.

When she saw an airhole, she looked about frantically. She found some driftwood tangled with seaweed, tore away the translucent green vines, and found two pointed sticks.

She began to dig, turning up wet sand in clumps, uncovering clams and scallops, leaving a trail of tumbled earth behind her. The smell of shellfish mingled with the salty air and the sea mist to make her remember, and, remembering, to forget.

When Julian could bear it no more, he left the wagon and went down to the water. Saylah was walking slowly now. She had tied her skirt up around her waist and filled the hollow with clam and scallop shells. The fabric was dripping wet, as was her petticoat. Sand clung to her hands, her feet, her dress, and her hair had fallen free of its loose braid.

She stood with her back to him, feet spread, relaxed, carefree, at ease. He knew she was smiling with delight. All at once he wanted to feel it too.

Saylah turned, holding a clam shell, and Julian was there. She opened her arms in invitation, though perhaps she did not know it. Julian knew then he had been waiting for this moment for a very long time. He took her hands, feeling the damp, clinging sand, the chill of the water, the shell pressed hard against his open palm. A rush of heat blinded him, then her face grew clear—a face he had never seen before. She was not beautiful in the way Simone had been, but she shone with joy, with the mist of the sea upon her, at one with the earth, with he whose fingers were locked with hers.

Saylah felt the pressure of his grasp and a distant memory flickered in the back of her mind. She was intensely aware of the touch of his hands, but it was more than that. She felt palm pressed to callused palm, with the striated clam shell between. It made her skin tingle, the pressure of the shell against her skin and his.

She shivered with delight, with confusion, with desire. She wanted more than just this touch, more than her hands bound to his, but she did not know how to ask, how to tell him of her need. She parted her lips in a silent cry that shaped itself into words of longing. "They never taught me to be a woman."

With his body, with his voice, Julian answered, "I will teach you."

Yet she could feel the barrier of his protective wall between them. His hands shook with the power of his hunger, and Saylah wept, without words, in mourning. When the wall fell, he would have to stand in the unkind light of day and *see*. To face the truth about himself, his father, the dreams that could not be. He was not ready. That truth was too bitter, too ugly, too painful to bear.

Saylah gasped and swayed forward.

"You're shaking," Julian murmured. Her hands were damp, but not with the sea. She was filmed in a cold sweat.

Saylah gripped him tighter, drew him closer. The warmth that began in their clasped hands spread upward, found its way into her blood, where it smoldered and took her body from her control. She could not release herself from Julian's hold.

"I'll teach you," he whispered.

She wanted to learn. She leaned toward him willingly. She closed her eyes but saw his familiar face in every detail—the shadow of a beard that had begun to grow, his square chin, high forehead and wavy brown hair. And his eyes of hazel that turned to green and reflected her own.

Julian brushed her lips with his and the moist, gentle touch made her quiver, seeking the pressure of his tender mouth. Her desire was so bright, it took her sight away and gave it back, made clearer and more beautiful. Julian's hands, his lips, his face, she wanted to etch inside her exactly as they were in that moment so they could never change.

It was too soon. A cry rose through her body, alive with sensitivity to the air, the moisture and Julian's sweet breath. It was too soon. They were not ready. The wall would crumble, and without its support, they would fall.

They would fall and fall into darkness and the memory of blood.

Julian could not escape her; her fingers were linked too tightly with his. He remembered, with a jolt of pain that took his breath, the cougar's matted fur in his hand.

He closed his eyes to force away the image of the blood, but the vision grew brighter, the pain more intense. *The cougar is sacred!* she had cried. Sacred and beautiful and more dangerous than the hungry wolf, *because* of its beauty which compelled, commanded, exuded power and strength and immortality.

Julian shuddered. The cougar was not dead. It lived in his eyes, in his hands taut and ready on the trigger, in his fingers making paths in the wet, matted fur. Saylah had brought it to him, as she brought all beauty and all pain. He could hear her breathing harshly, as if she had run a very long way, as if she were afraid of what ran behind her.

"We are living in our dreams, in our nightmares, you and I," she whispered. "When Jamie turned from the darkness, we turned toward it. It is time to turn away again. It is time."

Julian heard the rhythm of her voice, but the words flowed around him and away. He looked at Saylah, at her luminous eyes—full of compassion, desire, and something more. Something without a name, like the lust for blood that had pushed him to kill, which lived within him, though its voice had grown quiet, subdued. Almost, he could believe it had left him. Until he looked into the mirror of Saylah's eyes.

He kissed her again, more urgently, his lips warm and persuasive. He would force the sound of the cougar from inside her head. He would hold her until they were both free.

Saylah shuddered, moaned as he released one hand and drew it up her shoulder to her naked throat, up her throat to her ear, into her damp, windblown hair.

Her heart was pounding against his as he pulled her closer, the clam shell pressing its pattern into their palms. "It's all right," he said. "I won't hurt you. I want to make you remember the touch of our bodies and nothing else."

She wanted to believe him. She wanted to learn, finally, what other women knew about the bright white heat pulsing beneath her skin. She wanted to appease the yearning that was hunger and need and pleasure— aching, endless pleasure. She wanted to.

But she couldn't. She couldn't let the wall collapse or she would fall. Slowly, agonizingly, she unwound her fingers from his. Slowly, she drew back her head until the sea air whispered between their lips. Slowly, she took the clam shell—beautiful, ringed with gray and blue and cloudy white—and put it in his hand, closing his fingers around it, as if that tiny gift, picked off the sand and held between them for so short a time, could fill the void she had opened inside him. And deep within herself.

Chapter

53

Some say that kissin's a sin,
But I say that willna stand:
It is a most innocent thing,
And allowed by the laws of the land.

Flora sang lustily, her voice carrying through the house, bringing with it the enticing fragrance of simmering seafood stew, spiced cider and baking apples.

Sniffing appreciatively, Theron grinned at Paul. "I *like* having parties. Even smelling is more fun."

Paul nodded enthusiastically, but did not look up from the last grouping of branches mingled with bright autumn leaves that he and Saylah were arranging on a low table.

When they were finished, Saylah stood back. "Have we done our job well?" she asked Theron.

"I think it's beautiful!" He stood in the middle of the main room, admiring the intertwined boughs of fir and cedar that the three of them had just finished draping along the walls.

Saylah smiled at the pride in his voice and the healthy color in his face. His wound had healed cleanly, leaving four long scars of which Theron was more proud than he was the draped bows. He could not wait until the party, where he could show everyone the Mark of the Cougar and tell them his story.

"Of course you think it's beautiful," Paul said in his matter-of-fact tone. "You helped make it." He smiled indulgently at his friend.

"Can we go out now and talk to the pony?" Theron pleaded. "We haven't named him yet, and I'm sure he's awful lonely."

"Would he be less lonely if he had a name?" Saylah asked solemnly.

Theron looked at Paul, shaking his head at her ignorance. "Of *course* he would. Then he'd know who he *was*. He's standing out there all alone, not *knowing*. Don't you think he *wonders*?"

Saylah did not answer. Though she stared at Theron, she did not see him, but a wavering image from long ago. Kitkuni sitting on a boulder, shivering, saying sadly, *They will give me a new name.* Why was the memory so full of pain?

But she knew why. It was because of the morning she had spent with Julian on the beach. He had awakened her body, a voice deep inside her that cried out in need, and with it, long-slumbering feelings she had struggled for many years to forget.

When Theron tugged impatiently at her skirt, she made herself focus on his face. "I think your pony must wonder often who he is," she said. "I would not leave him alone and nameless for a single day more."

Satisfied, the boy motioned to his friend, who balked. Paul had discovered the wonderful fragrances coming from the kitchen. "Maybe we should visit your mother," he suggested. "She might be sad because we've spent all morning with Saylah."

> 'Tis lang since it came in fashion,
> I'm sure 'twill never be done . . .

Flora's song soared, her throaty voice sweeping over them.

> As lang as there's in the nation
> A lad, a lass, wife or a lown.

Theron grimaced comically. "She doesn't sound sad to *me*. Besides, she isn't alone. Ah-mah is helping. The cakes she makes are almost as good as Mama's." He smiled and whispered conspiratorially, "There's so many pies and bannocks and baked apples, I don't think they'd notice if half of them were gone."

Paul saw Saylah's amused glance but decided to ignore it. "Maybe we should get a snack for the pony. It might make him less lonely, just in case we don't think of a name."

"Just in case," Theron agreed exuberantly. He headed for the kitchen, abandoning the bits of branches and needles strewn about the room.

Paul followed, glad that here, at least, he wasn't in the way. His mother was busy choosing clothes and jewelry, having a bath, making Clara do her hair for the party. And his father—Paul did not want to think about Edward. There was something strange about him lately, something frightening. And it had gotten worse as the party drew nearer.

He liked it better at the Ivys', where everyone shouted directions from one end of the house to the other, smiling, burying their arms in flour up to the elbows or bringing the sweet scent of fir into the house. "I'll see you tonight," he called as he disappeared into the steamy kitchen.

With a mixture of pleasure and regret, Saylah watched the boys go. They had kept her mind occupied, her thoughts far from a curve of beach and the imprint of a shell in her empty palm. Just then the Indian girl who called herself Ah-mah appeared.

She smiled at Saylah, a secret smile, shared with few, which held the knowledge of their People. Only to Saylah had she spoken her true name, Alida. She had known from the moment of their meeting, from the first time she had looked into Saylah's green eyes that she was also Tanu, She Who Is Blessed, who had disappeared one night after the Red Sweating Sickness had taken many of her village. Alida spoke in Salish, enjoying the sound and rhythm of the words she heard so rarely now. "Flora has sent me to discover if the house is ready for its many visitors."

Saylah listened to the words, and the old longing possessed her, to hear again the Salish drums, their speech and prayers and songs. "It is ready," she replied in Salish.

Alida of the watching eyes nodded and walked away. The girl had the short, square body of the Salish, the black eyes and jutting cheekbones. Saylah wondered if this mysterious girl was not a ghost from the past—a reminder of all she had left behind.

Purposefully, Saylah turned from her thoughts to her work. Since yesterday on the beach, she had concentrated on cleaning, washing and cooking. She had also skinned the animals Julian brought and prepared the huge pits in which they now cooked slowly.

"Saylah, *mo-run*," Flora called, "ye've done more than your share. Come and I'll show ye somethin' I've been savin' for a surprise." She had washed away the flour and butter, cream and nutmeg, and left her apron in the kitchen. "'Tis time to be gettin' dressed, I'm thinkin', and ye with only those gray gowns that the missionaries gave ye from the goodness of their hearts." There was a trace of irony in her voice. "But I've a mind to do somethin' about that." She led the way to her bedroom, where two gowns lay on the bed.

"This one's mine. The single elegant gown I own. I've no' worn it for over a year." Lovingly, she draped the beautiful red and green tartan over her arm and stroked the fabric, then laid it aside.

"This one, now," she said, tapping her finger on her chin, "this once belonged to my mother. 'Tis no' in the latest style, no bows or ruffles or bustles, but 'tis lovely all the same. I want ye to wear it."

Saylah stared at the blue-green muslin gown with a wide blue sash and sweeping skirt. The bodice was simple and scalloped, the sleeves full and gathered at the wrists. As Flora held it out to her, she thought of Yeyi's borrowed wedding finery, made her own by Kitkuni's loving hands. There were no beads or shells to make this gown precious, but Flora's expression was enough. "I will find a way to thank you," Saylah said. "It is lovely."

"And just the color for your eyes, I'm thinkin'. As for thankin' me, what ye've already done is worth more than that dress over your arm. 'Tis priceless, your gift. I'm happy now." She bit her lip, hesitated, then added quietly, "I'm no' feelin' so angry anymore."

Saylah was startled. "I thought you must feel resentment over all you and Theron did not have, all that Jamie kept from you by hiding in his room. Especially when what you longed for was so close within your grasp. But you convinced me that you had conquered that anger."

Flora sighed. "I'd almost convinced myself. 'Tis my mother and father who taught me that ye do the best ye can without complainin', unless there's a way to make it better. I tried, but I could no' find a way this time." She shrugged. "So I prayed my prayers softly and sang and talked loudly, to convince myself and Theron and Julian that we'd survive, that the world was no' fallin' in around us."

As she spoke, her shoulders slumped and her busy hands grew slack. The words seemed to drain from her the strength that had kept her going, kept her smiling, kept her from despair. Now that it was safe, she could let go. Flora leaned back, closing her eyes wearily. "There were times when I hated Jamie. I wanted to shake him and make those misty eyes *see* me. But I loved him so much I could no' feel that way for long. He was no' even aware how much he was hurtin' us until ye showed him. I thank ye for that, lass."

She smiled faintly. "I'm no' a saint, don't be thinkin' I am. For I hate Simone too, and no' just for leavin' her family behind. Why couldn't she have taken her ghost as well, and left me a life to go on with?"

Shaking her head, Flora sat up straight. "I should no' tell ye these things."

"I do not mind. I would like to hear what you are thinking."

Flora peered at her with narrowed eyes. "Well, I'm thinkin' that ye're no' a saint either and 'tis time ye realize it. Ye'd rather I talk about me so ye don't have to admit what's in your heart. But that doesn't stop ye from hurtin' and it doesn't make the confusion go away, now, does it?"

Saylah stiffened. "I do not know what you mean."

"I'll wager ye do. I'm talkin' of Julian and ye. I've seen how he watches ye and listens for your step."

Saylah collapsed on the bed, pale and shaken. "Does he?"

"Are ye blind that ye don't see it yourself?" Flora was concerned at Saylah's pallor. "Or do ye no' wish to be seein'?"

Clutching the beautiful gown, Saylah fought against the voices rising within her. They spoke through rhythm, the familiar beat of ancient drums, but louder, more insistent, so she could not ignore them. She could not put into words and sentences the turmoil inside her. There was no way to express the primitive impulses that had begun to rule her body.

She had tried to drown them out by dancing on the drum that used to be a well. Beside the river she could pretend she was alone; there the spirits gathered, offering comfort. Though she danced out the cadence that possessed her from within, the voices would not leave her.

"What is it, lass? Ye can talk to me. I've a brain in my head and a fair quiet tongue in my mouth when need be."

Saylah had to struggle to find her own voice above the others. "It is not that I do not trust you. It is just—" She broke off, uncertain. How could she explain something like this to a woman like Flora? A woman who was not haunted, like Saylah, with a thousand long-dead ghosts, a whisper of wind whose message was lost in the treetops, trailed through the white-streaked blue of the skies. "It is just that there are no words for what is inside me."

Flora considered for a moment, absently stroking the gown in Saylah's lap. Finally, she murmured, "There are words, all right. 'Tis just that ye've no' found the right ones yet. 'Twill come to ye in time."

Saylah started to shake her head, but Flora cupped her chin and held it. "I know there are other voices for those who can hear them. I've the blood of many a fey Highlander in my veins, and ye don't forget such things, even if ye know them dimly, from deep in your memory, where the souls of your ancestors lie."

Her blue eyes darkened to slate. "Ye see a great deal more than others, *mo-ghraid*, and yet ye see nothin' at all. Close your eyes for a little and then ye'll begin to feel, without the patterned sunlight to distract ye. Ye may laugh at an old woman lost in the woods and the wild, but ye can no' laugh at the wisdom of every Highlander who's gone before me, blind, with the Sight like a shadow on their eyes."

"So," Edward Ashton said quietly, "here you are."

Sophia rotated on her stool and her wrapper fell open, revealing her small breasts and smooth white skin. "I'd begun to wonder if you'd be back in time—" She broke off to grimace at his coat as he tossed it on a chair. "Have you been working with the cattlemen again? You're covered in mud. How will you ever be ready in time?"

Edward laughed, too loudly. "I see your bath is still full of water. Perhaps I'll recline among the scent of lilacs and make myself ready for the fête." He started for the tub and raised one leg as if to step in.

"You wouldn't dare!" Sophia knew as soon as the words were out that she should not have said them. Edward had never been able to resist a challenge. Still fully clothed, he stepped into the tub and slid down into the scented water.

"Care to join me?" Edward held out his arms, smiling expectantly. He knew she could not resist him.

Sophia shook her head in dismay. "There's not enough room for you, let alone both of us. Come out of there at once."

To her astonishment, Edward rose, dripping streams of water on the Persian carpet. "Just as you wish, my dear." He came toward her, an unmistakable glimmer in his gold-flecked eyes. "Come here. I want to hold you."

Sophia backed away, laughing. "You're mad, Edward. Completely mad."

He stood in a growing puddle on the rug and tried to look hurt. "I don't think it's mad to want to hold your wife and smell her lovely body next to yours. I thought it was rather endearing, actually." He flung off his wet clothes and dropped them in a sodden heap.

"But Paul will be waiting." She made one last attempt to divert him.

"You mean he actually came home today? I should have thought he'd feel obligated to stay and help test every pastry in the house."

Sophia laughed. "I think he did that too. But he had to change his clothes."

Her husband shook his head gravely. "Shouldn't wonder if his own are too small with all that rich food in his belly. I shall have to lend him some of mine."

"Edward!" Sophia grinned. "He's only eight years old."

He took a step back, eyes wide in astonishment. "Only eight, you say? Then he can't wear my clothes. How silly of you to suggest it. He'd look like a clown, no question about it." He began to move forward. "But about *my* question—" He raised his eyebrows suggestively and ran his fingertips over the breast exposed by his wife's open wrapper.

Sophia noticed his sandy hair was damp and had begun to curl around his neck. She tried to look away, to maintain a moment of sanity, but Edward opened his arms and she went to him. It had been so long since he'd teased her this way. She did not really mind that the moisture was soaking into her wrapper, or even that the rug squished beneath her feet.

But she gasped when Edward hugged her so tightly that she could not breathe. "I suppose if you can't give me pneumonia, you'll strangle me to death."

He raised his head and the laughter had gone. His eyes devoured her, greedily, almost desperately. "I want you," he groaned. He caressed her, sliding his hands underneath the wrapper, finding the sensitive places on her neck, her back, her buttocks. He was burning and he needed to feel her cool hands upon him, soothing away the gnawing, licking flames.

When he covered her mouth with his, nipping at her lower lip and tossing the wrapper onto the floor, Sophia backed away. She had never seen Edward quite like this. "We'll be late for the party." She did not want to admit the real reason she was hesitating. She was afraid of him. Afraid of the golden glow of his eyes, the restless pawing of his hands, the tight arch of his body, like an animal ready to pounce.

"The party be damned!" Edward bellowed.

His wife struggled to remain calm. "If you don't want to go, you needn't."

Edward snorted in disgust. "They'd think me a coward if I hid myself at home."

Sophia was bewildered. "They'd think you were ill, if that's what I told them. Why on earth would you say—"

"Please, Sophia," he whispered.

His voice, so suddenly hushed, frightened her as much as his anger. "I don't know what you want," she said.

"You," he said. "Just you. I need you."

Sophia's eyes filled with tears. Her husband had never had to plead before. She should not have doubted him. Who else had ever looked at her that way, as though he might cease to breathe if she refused him?

She smiled, touched his chest tentatively. Both were naked now, and though his skin was damp and cold, the moisture had dripped away into the rug. "Why didn't you just say so?" She kissed the hollow in his throat.

Edward pulled her close and guided her toward the bed, kissing her nose, her cheeks, her parted lips as they moved. His arms were tense around her, his body no longer cold, but burning hot. With a sigh that shook Sophia with its sorrow, he fell onto the bed, and she fell with him. She crouched above him, ran her hands over his face, rested her cheek on his forehead, covered his body with her soft white cool one.

"Edward," she whispered, "everything is all right. I love you. Remember, I love you."

He gripped her shoulders, peering into her gray eyes, searching for reassurance. "God help me if you don't!" he gasped. "God help me!"

He silenced her response with a kiss that sent heat from his mouth into hers. Unaccountably, she shivered.

Edward rolled over until he loomed above her and tangled his fingers in her scented hair. He kissed her again, breathlessly, shuddering at the desire that surged through him, the need that gathered in his chest, his throat, his mouth, pressed tightly against hers. She lay beneath him, her breasts barely rising above the supple line of her girlish body. He leaned down to suck one nipple, then the other, cupping her breasts in his hands, leaving on her skin a wide circle of his sweat.

Edward's touch broke at last through her apprehension and ignited her own desire. He writhed, so their bodies rubbed, chest to chest, legs wrapped around legs, hip to hip. Everywhere he touched her she felt his heat penetrate, until she writhed with equal pleasure, squirming to grasp his buttocks in her hands, to tantalize him with the light insistent pressure of her nails along his spine.

Edward moaned and sucked at her breasts while he reached between her legs and made her squirm with the dexterous motion of his fingers. When he sucked and teased her nipple with his tongue, she shuddered and pulled him closer.

Pressing his face into the softness of her breast, he felt her quiver and whisper his name. Edward smiled and raised his head, lowered it again between her parted thighs and flicked his tongue in and out, up and down. Sophia gripped his hair until the pain made him wince, but he did not stop. He covered her with his hot, moist mouth, sucking, licking, stroking, massaging her buttocks while she cried out again and again.

When she began to buck, unsatisfied by the spasms that shook her from head to toe, he moved slowly up her body, using his tongue, until he reached her mouth. He covered her parted lips just as he entered her and began to rock furiously.

Sophia felt the world begin to spin. She could not bear the powerful sensations that shook her as Edward thrust inside her again and again, while the room spun in and out of focus.

He undulated, thrust, entwined his tongue with hers, seeking the cool release that would stop the heat before it consumed him. Suddenly he froze as the ecstasy shook his body, then he thrust again, more fiercely, calling out, sobbing, groaning, pleading. He shuddered as the poison left him, shooting outward and away, where it could not hurt him anymore.

Exhausted, relieved, dizzy and weak, he buried his face in his wife's white, pulsing throat.

Sophia trembled for a long time, damp with sweat, agonizingly aware of Edward's weight across her body. He had awakened in her feelings she had never thought to feel, and once the need raged, he had slaked it. Yet she felt strangely light, as though she had lost some part of herself. As if Edward had sucked the strength from inside her to replenish his own, leaving her vulnerable and shaking. For the first time in over fifteen years, her husband had left her empty.

Chapter

54

Carriages, wagons and horses crowded the clearing in front of the Ivy house. Not a single invitation had been declined. Everyone remembered the parties Jamie Ivy used to give, and it was nearly winter, when the already isolated families became more cut off from the rest of the world. This was their last chance to enjoy themselves among a crowd, and no one wanted to miss it.

Inside, the house looked festive, with hanging boughs everywhere. On each table were arrangements of vegetables and brightly colored autumn leaves. The tablecloths of bright red and green tartan, along with the brilliantly colored gowns and huge fires, gave the room depth and radiance and warmth.

Besides the firelight, there were candelabra on every table. The light seemed to shimmer off ruddy faces; the sound of rustling skirts, hearty voices and muffled laughter was enhanced by the crackle of the flames.

Jamie stood at the door, eyes alight with excitement. His hollow cheeks had filled in and the natural color had returned to his face in the past several weeks. His dark curly hair fell over his forehead, but he did not bother to brush it back.

He wore gray wool trousers, a silver, blue and lilac waistcoat, white silk cravat, and a gray morning coat with tails. "Jock Buchanan!" Jamie called as Flora's brother and his wife approached. "And Jeannie, looking prettier than the last time I saw you." He offered his hands which the Buchanans took firmly.

"'Tis too long since last we saw ye," Jock exclaimed, his arm about Jeannie's waist. "We've missed Flora"—he leaned over to kiss his sister affectionately—"and your stories and the music that used to spill from your windows."

"No doubt you've also missed my whiskey," Jamie whispered so only Jock would hear. "I remember many nights by the fire when we drank and talked until dawn."

The Scotsman smiled. "Aye, that as well. Ye've been cruel to keep yourself hidden this way."

Jeannie hugged Flora, who stood beside Jamie in her bright gown, her hair piled on her head, a pearl comb showing through her blond curls. "Your husband's a charmer, Flora Ivy. There's none like him. We've missed ye both."

Like the other guests, the Buchanans were quickly drawn into the center of the crowded room.

Saylah stood in the darkness of the loft looking down. She could hear Jamie greet each guest by name, see how they returned his smile, how it warmed them before the flames ever came near.

This house, once dreary and full of shadows, was full now of life and noise and color. The ladies wore gowns of wine and red and green, rust and teal blue—ruched, ruffled and trimmed with lace. Some, like Flora, wore simple tartan dresses with round necklines and full skirts, the plaid of their clan draped about their shoulders and fastened with a brooch. The men, though less brightly colored, looked magnificent in frock coats and waistcoats and snowy white cravats.

"I see you've brought your fiddle, Neil," Jamie called to the MacKinnons. "I suspect there'll be many damp eyes in the house before you've gone your way again. I've heard you make that fiddle weep."

"Weepin' or laughin', I'll make it sing, as Conall will his flute and Archie his hand harp. Ye give the party, we'll bring ye the music!" Neil MacKinnon shouted in a rumbling Scottish accent. "Even Annie can no' be complainin' about the awful racket here."

His wife grinned. "Ye'd be surprised what I can do when I've a mind to, Neil MacKinnon."

"I hope you've a mind to enjoy yourself," Julian interjected. "Otherwise, I'm afraid you'll be disappointed."

He stood behind his father, dressed in a rich brown coat and trousers and a waistcoat of gold watered silk. His wavy brown hair had been

—— 377 ——

brushed back from his forehead, and his eyes gleamed from the candle-light.

Saylah clutched the rail of the half-wall, feeling cut off from the motion and color and sound. This was not her world; she could not understand or be a part of it. The family had taken her in, but she had no place among the strangers who laughed and drank and ate together like old and intimate friends.

Yet the music, the rustle of starched petticoats, the cheerful voices called her, brought memories of other rhythms, other pulses, other colors. The firelight danced over the faces below, transforming them from moment to moment, from brilliant light to shadow to radiance again. It was painfully familiar and yet so strange. She had not been near so much laughter and goodwill since Kitkuni's wedding. So many years without a celebration. Saylah almost turned away, but she felt someone watching.

Julian had looked up to see her at the railing. His hazel eyes glimmered with admiration. She touched her hair self-consciously. She had forgotten the elaborate hairdo Flora had insisted on, the lovely gown she wore.

Julian's eyes told her she was not alone, then Jamie looked up, and Flora, to follow the young man's gaze. All three smiled broadly and Jamie mouthed the word *beautiful* as he waved her down to join them. Drawn by rhythms she could not resist, bewitched by the flickering firelight, compelled by the look in Julian's eyes, she went to the stairway.

When she reached the bottom, Julian was waiting. He watched her glide toward him, her feet barely touching the ground. The blue-green of the gown, the flattering upsweep of her hair, softened her somehow, as the damp sea air had softened her. He stood unmoving, mesmerized.

Saylah felt the warmth of his appraisal and paused a little apart from him. Their eyes met and held until each smiled, slowly, irresistibly. Saylah felt a shock of pleasure and distant memory. *There is an intimacy that has nothing to do with the joining of bodies.*

She knew then that Julian was right; it was impossible to forget where they had been together, no matter how dark or dangerous that place had been. Impossible to go forward without looking back.

He offered his arm and she took it, resting her fingers lightly on his sleeve. He covered her hand with his just as lightly, wary of a touch that would awaken feelings best left slumbering. He released her quickly.

They reached the door as the Ashtons arrived. Saylah felt Jamie tense, become more aware, as if listening to a voice so faint he had to strain to hear it.

Edward made a courtly bow, then slid his arm around Sophia. "It's good of you to do this," he said to Jamie. "It's been too long since we've all been together."

"It's nothing compared to the gift you sent Theron," his friend replied. "It was quite a gesture."

Sophia, dressed in a royal blue gown with a French-lace collar and violet silk underskirt, smiled thinly. "I told him it was too much, but Edward's very stubborn."

"Theron is daft for the pony, that's the important thing," Flora said. "Come in! Come in and join the party!"

"Where's Theron?" Paul demanded just as the younger boy called from across the room, "There you are, Paul."

Theron came running, but Edward stopped him, crouched down to examine his scars intently. "Quite impressive," he said. "You're a very lucky boy."

"Is that why you sent me the pony?"

Edward glanced up at Jamie, who was watching with that same expectant expression he had seen the night of the attack. "Partly," he said. "And partly because you were so brave. I wouldn't have liked to be in your place. Yet here you are, fully recovered and chipper as anything. Amazing."

Theron blushed, but before he could reply, Paul led him away.

"Come in and enjoy yourselves," Jamie said. He took his wife's arm and led her away from the door, into a group of boisterous guests.

"I did not know there would be so many people," Saylah whispered, though Julian could barely hear her over the noise.

"Some are neighbors from the ranches in the area and some are from Victoria. Papa used to do business in town and we entertained often. Everybody knew Jamie. That's how it seemed then, anyway."

"That is how it seems now." Saylah could not accustom herself to the crush of people. She was distracted when another couple arrived—a small blonde hanging tightly to the arm of a red-headed man.

Julian stiffened. "Geordie MacKinnon and Lizzie Grant, this is Saylah."

"'Tis good to meet ye this lovely evenin'," Geordie exclaimed. He was looking forward to this night. Lizzie was on his arm, pretty as any Highland spring day, and he knew Jamie Ivy never stinted on food and drink. He squeezed Lizzie's hand.

She smiled, but her attention was on Saylah. There was something about the woman—perhaps her dark coloring, or her fine features and extraordinary eyes, or the way she held herself with such dignity. Lizzie could not look away. Julian did not touch the half-breed, but was very much aware of her. Lizzie knew the signs.

"Lead us to the punch before we dry up and are carried away by the wind!" Geordie cried. He did not intend to linger and give Julian time to stare at Lizzie. Unerringly, he headed toward the laden tables.

Julian released a taut, indrawn breath. "I believe I'll have a drink. I'll bring you some punch." In an instant, he had disappeared.

Saylah noticed that nearly everyone had a glass. The men were drinking whiskey, gin and cider, the women sherry, brandy and wine. The smell of alcohol was strong, yet she felt no threat in the air, no suppressed violence. These people were merely enjoying themselves; no demons had come into their eyes. It was early and their eyes were still clear.

When Julian returned and handed her a cup of apple cider, she saw that the tension had left his body. Whatever had disturbed him had lost its importance. Grinning, full of goodwill, he took her arm and introduced her to everyone.

Several men had seated themselves and begun to play their instruments, tapping their feet and singing along, though the noise was so loud that words filtered through a phrase at a time.

O Mary, mild-eyed Mary,
By land or on the sea . . .

The floor vibrated with the rhythm of their music, and Saylah paused, absorbing the unfamiliar meter. She had forgotten what it was like to let the music inside, let it lift her beyond the green earth to the world of the spirits. An idea came to her slowly, a little at a time, like the moon revealing itself from behind a silver screen of clouds.

They drifted toward the entrance, where Julian closed the door, shutting out the wind and the cold night. "Lizzie is drawn to you," Saylah said quietly.

He tightened his grip on her arm but did not consider lying. Somehow, with Saylah it did not seem right or even possible. "We were drawn to each other once."

She looked at him closely. "And not long ago."

"No, not long ago, but long enough." He wanted to add, *Before I saw you on the beach in your sea-soaked dress. Before we stood with water, salt and sand between us, yet nothing between us at all. Except for the blood of the cougar.* Julian knew Saylah was not ready to hear those things, so he drew her toward the cleared area between the two blazing fires.

And when with blossoms laden
Bright summer comes again,
I'll fetch my nut-brown maiden
Down from the bonny glen.

"We're going to *dance*," Theron cried, hopping from foot to foot in his excitement. "Papa *said* so. Will you dance, Saylah? I want to *see* you!"

Saylah wondered when he had begun to emphasize every other word, but she knew. After a night in the woods that had taught him life was more of an adventure than he cared to know. Yet there was no flicker of fear in his face as he told one guest after another about the cougar attack and proudly showed off his scar. Paul, she noticed, was a little envious.

She went to join the older boy. "Theron says we will dance. Does he even know how?"

Paul shook his head emphatically. "He'll probably run around stepping on everyone's toes, but they won't mind."

"Do you know how to dance?"

Paul smiled. "A little. My mother taught me. But I might forget the steps."

"Among so many people, I do not think anyone will notice."

Nodding agreement, Paul observed in a whisper, "If they don't stay away from the whiskey and cider, *they'll* be the ones to forget the steps."

It was true that the drink table was the most popular spot in the room, though it was remote from the warmth of the fires. The men stopped often, refilling their glasses again and again. They were laughing, slapping each other affectionately on the back, singing along with the musicians. They did not seem to be causing any harm.

Suddenly Julian was beside her. "Come dance with me. It will make Papa happy. He wants everyone to be happy tonight."

"But I do not know how!" Saylah objected as he took her hand and guided her toward a small cleared area.

"I'll teach you!" Julian shouted above the music and laughter. "Look, even Papa is dancing."

Jamie twirled Flora, who beamed at him, breathless, but singing along just the same. Jamie too was grinning, but something in his manner unnerved Saylah. She could see the strain it was for him to turn and whirl, stop and start. Beneath his high color, his skin was gray. Yet she knew he would not sit, even if she told him he did not look well.

Jamie Ivy was tense, expectant; he was waiting for something, and until that happened, nervous energy kept him going. Saylah could feel the tautness of his muscles, the rasp of his breath, even from where she danced. He had not had this party simply for his family, to re-introduce them to the world beyond the borders of his ranch. He wanted something, wanted it so badly he would risk his health to get it. And he meant to get it tonight.

Chapter

55

It was not long before Flora also noticed her husband's ragged breath, the strain it took to smile and follow the intricate steps and not reveal his weariness.

"If ye don't let me sit, I'll collapse on the floor," she said loudly. She was breathing heavily from the exertion, so Jamie believed her.

"Here, Neil, ye've had that comfortable chair for long enough. Don't be so greedy," she called, propelling Neil onto the floor, where his wife caught his arm and made him dance. Jamie sank gratefully into the abandoned chair while Flora sat on the arm beside him.

"They came back," Jamie whispered. "They all came back."

"Of course they did, *mo-charaid*. They'd no' be forgettin' ye so quickly. They'll always come back to a man like ye."

Jamie stroked her arm, covered her hand with his.

Flora rested her head on his shoulder.

Saylah sighed, let Julian pull her forward. She could hear the music more clearly now and was surprised at how pleasant it sounded. It was not like the beat of drums and rattles, nor even like Flora's lute, but it flowed around her, making her want to move and sway. She smiled at Julian. "Teach me."

Julian caught his breath at the sight of her face upturned and smiling. He had never seen her in anything but gray or black; this blue-green gown made her eyes more luminous than ever. The scoop neck and full sleeves were flattering, and she moved gracefully in the wide skirts, though they were unfamiliar. Flora had braided her hair and piled most of it on her head, leaving one long braid twined with ribbon over her shoulder.

She looked soft, approachable, and her smile was so sweet, so alluring that he had to remind himself they stood in the middle of his father's house with people all around them. He took her hands, showing her the steps one at a time while she tried to copy his movements. Saylah took her rhythm from the quivering of the floor, the strings of the fiddles, the stamping of feet.

Once Julian began to swing her around, she found it was not easy to move in the heavy skirts and many-layered petticoats Flora had given her to wear. She stumbled, laughed, and stumbled again. Only the circle of Julian's arm kept her from falling. "I thought I was very clever to learn so quickly," she confided. "The spirits are punishing me for my pride."

Julian was surprised she would joke about such a thing. "I don't think the spirits have much to do with the weight of those petticoats."

She saw the question in his eyes and smiled. "My People try always to laugh at such human weakness. I think they are wise."

"I think your people sound fascinating. I want to know more about them—about you."

Saylah started to speak, but the dance drew her away. By the time she faced Julian again, the words had left her. But she knew they would come back, later, when there were no other watching eyes.

Julian lifted her, swung her around and around. She heard the rise and fall of his breath, more rapid with each turn, felt the weight of his hands at her waist, gentle but firm, saw the warmth in his hazel eyes, which shifted in the changing light.

Saylah felt someone watching and turned to find Lizzie regarding her intently. The blonde's gaze was curious, and she was frowning, yet Saylah felt no hostility. Then Julian's arm tightened around her and she forgot Lizzie's bewildered brown eyes.

She felt light-headed, unafraid, and did not know why. Julian touched her cheek fleetingly as a song came to an end.

"You are very gentle," she murmured.

"You are very beautiful."

No man had ever told her that before. She felt warm, suddenly, and safe, a part of the crowd, no longer a stranger. "There is something I wish to show you," she said. "But you must meet me later, when the people have gone."

Julian's eyes widened. "Meet you where?"

"Beside the carved deer." At the astonishment on his face, she shook her head. "I will teach you to dance as my People do."

"I want to dance with Saylah." Theron tugged on her skirt, oblivious of the rent he had just made in the fragile woven light between Julian and the girl.

Julian ruffled his brother's hair. "Be careful of her. She's young, you know, and easily broken."

He said it with a smile, but Saylah was shaken just the same. She turned with relief to Theron, who stepped on her toes repeatedly, not even in time to the music, but she did not mind. He was smiling, happy, alive, and she had nearly lost him. The thought chilled her, and she realized that he and his family had become too dear to her. She had not meant to care for them so much, only a little, so their loss would not hurt deeply. She was not certain she could survive such pain a second time.

But it was too late; Theron wriggling, his hands clasped in hers, told her so. She lifted him in her arms and spun him until she stumbled on her skirts.

Theron jumped down, grinning. "Julian should have told *you* to be careful." He cupped his hand and she leaned down so he could whisper, "Don't worry, I won't tell him."

She could not help laughing as they wheeled around the floor, knocking into other couples and bowing in apology.

Julian watched them, smiling, until he felt someone beside him. He knew the smell of lilacs, the warmth of the body that reached him even through his suit. "Lizzie—" he began.

"Indian women are very mysterious, aren't they?" she interrupted. "I guess that's what makes them so fascinating. I guess men can't resist all those things they don't understand. And she looks more mysterious than the others. Maybe she's got more secrets. Maybe that's why you can't tear yourself away."

"You know nothing about Saylah," Julian replied.

His voice was soft, without censure. It was not his tone which made Lizzie turn pale, but the way in which he said *Saylah*. She had never heard anyone say a name that way, as if it were sacred. The sound hit her like a blow, told her she had said too much. How she wished she had not had the third glass of sherry. She was making a fool of herself.

She didn't even know why. It was just that she was certain no one would ever touch her the way he had. Now that she had felt tender and gentle hands, she could not bear the thought of living without them. "Sorry," she muttered, brushing Julian's arm. "It's nothing to do with me."

She was gone before he could reply, but Edward Ashton took her place. He smiled conspiratorially, as if the two men shared a secret. "Couldn't help overhearing. The little girl's right, alas. If we could just find out their secrets, understand them, if you know what I mean, we could resist them," he slurred a little drunkenly. Then he too was gone.

Julian stared after him in astonishment. What on earth had the man been talking about?

Edward headed directly for Saylah, who had swung Theron in so wide a circle she was in danger of falling. She would have if Edward had not caught her and held her upright. Gasping to try to catch her breath, she put Theron down and he ran off to disappear with Paul.

"Now that I've rescued you, you must return the favor and give me this dance. I've been waiting all evening for such an opportunity."

Saylah knew he was pretending; she had seen how he looked at Sophia all night.

They danced awkwardly, and Saylah wondered how you could give someone a dance when their mind was not with you, though their hands touched yours and their feet followed the patterned steps.

She did not have long to wonder. Soon Mr. Palmer, whose spectacles she had rescued from the pond, tapped Edward on the shoulder. The newcomer was as inexperienced as Saylah, so she felt at ease, though each time she saw the light on his thick glasses, she was overcome with a desire to laugh.

When Mr. Palmer went away, Saylah sank, exhausted, onto a stool near the fire. Slowly, the pace of the dances grew slower, the music softer, and the dancers fell away, one by one. People gathered along the walls, between the two fires, on chairs and benches and even the floor.

Jamie smiled benevolently at his guests and watched Edward take a seat nearby. He held Sophia's hand tightly, but she was not smiling. Edward sensed Jamie's appraisal and stiffened, leaned against his wife, who gave him her shoulder and held him upright.

Flora felt the tension in the air and decided it was time for a distraction. "Give us 'Dumbarton's Drums'!" she cried, loud enough to be heard above the din.

Everyone cheered, and Neil MacKinnon held his fiddle to his chin, drawing the bow deftly over the strings.

> Dumbarton's drums, they sound so bonnie,
> And they remind thee o' thy Johnnie;
> What fond delight doth steal upon thee,
> When Johnnie kneels and kisses thee.

Saylah was enthralled by fiddles, flutes and hand harps, mingled with rising voices in the lilting cadence of the song.

Thy love he is a handsome laddie,
And though he is Dumbarton's caddie
Someday ye'll be a captain's lady,
When Johnnie tends his vow to thee.

Jamie listened, eyes closed, not in sleep, but so he might let the words and rhythm enfold him, the way it used to. How often had they sung this song by firelight or torchlight or under the distant shimmer of stars? He slipped into the feeling those nights had brought, that the men were bound together, invulnerable, that they would stay this way forever—young and full of songs and energy and hope.

Even Julian was singing, and for the first time, Saylah realized the Ivy family was not alone, that their world was wide and full of people. People who sang and danced together, creating a rhythm that drew them closer as the beat of Salish drums had drawn her People closer.

"What're you thinking?" Julian asked.

"I am thinking of the drums," she said.

"Dumbarton's drums?"

"There are others," she told him. "I will show you—the power of the drums."

"Let's have a story!" Jock Buchanan cried when the last note had faded and the floor had ceased to vibrate with the memory of tapping feet.

"Who will tell it?" Neil MacKinnon demanded. "There're too many voices all clamorin' to be heard."

"Why, Jamie should tell it," Jeannie Buchanan said. "'Tis his party after all."

Jamie, who sat in the mahogany chair with Flora beside him, shook his head to bring himself back to the present. He had been smiling sweetly, and the smile lingered as he said, "Let Edward do the telling tonight. He knows the stories as well as I do."

Saylah leaned forward, suddenly tense. She knew intuitively, without doubt, that this was what Jamie had been waiting for.

"Take us back, Edward, to the beginning, when we came searching for wealth, when we believed every story we were told. Take me back and tell us about the gold."

There were shouts of approval. "Aye! Take us back!"

Edward shifted uneasily, hands on his knees. Jamie was waiting, not in anger or derision, but in expectation. Edward swallowed dryly. "If you must hear it—"

"Aye, so we must!" several shouted together.

Men and women moved in closer to hear Edward's story. His eyes glowed golden in the firelight, like the eyes of a lion, and his handsome face grew pensive.

Julian leaned heavily on the mantel, listening and watching. *You just go on*, Jamie had told him. *That's what Saylah taught me.* Julian was not sure it was possible.

"We had heard there was a gold rush in British Columbia, though from different voices in different lands." Edward felt Sophia press close, and he was grateful.

"We met on the ship that brought us to everything we ever hoped for. It brought us to Victoria."

The men cheered mightily, repeating, "Victoria!" with as much gusto as they had sung a few minutes past.

"We followed the other miners, Jamie and I, out of the city and into the hills, until we came to a green valley with a fast-rushing river and the song of the birds to accompany us day and night. Jamie took one look at the luminous water and said, 'Edward, my friend, we've discovered Paradise!'"

Another cheer rose toward the ceiling, echoing off the beams, floating down into the flickering firelight. Jamie had closed his eyes again, remembering.

Edward grinned at the faces gathered around him. "Now, Jamie and I, we're not alike in every way. I liked the valley well enough, but I liked it a lot better when I discovered tiny chunks of gold that glittered among the pebbles. To me, *that* was beauty, those little pieces of shining gold."

The men laughed, slapping their thighs and spilling their drinks down their white starched shirtfronts.

"My friend Jamie worked hard. He told me he meant to make this dream the one that turned all others pale. But he got caught in the beauty of the place and not the beauty of the gold. He was mesmerized, transfixed by the rush of shimmering water, the falling of pebbles and stones caught now and then in flashes of sunlight.

"He watched the water plunging over tumbled boulders, sending up showers of drops that might as well have been jewels or embers or flecks of brilliant gold. How, he asked me time and again, could such a place *not* be rich with wealth enough for one man, two, a hundred? How could the rush and glimmer and swirl be any less than a miracle sent to answer the prayers of men, even soulless men like me, who did not believe in God?"

Edward spoke with such reverence, such awe, that he made his friend sound like a saint untouched by harsh reality.

Julian glowered, confused by his tone. Earlier he had been drunk and unwise. Now he seemed clear-headed, except that all the sharp corners were softened by invisible gauze. Why? Why silence for so long and now this dream-like version of an old, well-worn story?

"Back then I just listened, shaking my head. I'd begun to doubt a long time back that the gold was in that valley. I left Jamie to his worship; I wanted him to have that feeling as long as he could before we moved on.

"I began to talk to other miners and the men who wandered through, trapping or seeking land or other riches. There were other gold fields they said, but they were running dry."

He gazed down at his hands, clasped between his knees.

"Then I heard land was going cheap, that the Company wanted to encourage settlers, and I'd seen a great deal of Saanich while Jamie watched the river. So I sat next to my friend one day and shook him awake from his dream, in order to bring him here. He was the one who guessed that it wasn't gold or coal that would make us rich, but the land itself. He saw that wealth when all I saw was how many chunks of gold we'd gathered in a day.

"He saw what the miners and trappers never stopped long enough to recognize—that the miracle was right here in the earth and the forests and rushing rivers. I used to think I was wiser, but it wasn't true. There are men who learn the truth and know it when they see it with their eyes and touch it with their hands, and there are men like Jamie, who feel it inside. I never did feel it the way he did, though I came to know it later, when I saw the ranches grow and prosper.

"But I always wondered what it would have been like, just for a moment, to see that river like he did, like a miracle, like Paradise. I don't suppose I ever will now."

Edward reached for his wife's hand, and it was there, warm and familiar, closing around his. He squeezed her fingers, and though his touch was gentle, she felt he was holding on to keep from falling. Sophia remembered vividly the violence of his lovemaking earlier that evening. She was even more frightened, somehow, by this quiet anguish that had no words, and, for her, no explanation.

Silence fell and Jamie touched his cheek to Flora's, eyes closed, remembering the sight and sound of that river—the icy water on his palms, the rocks smooth as satin, the green of the valley reflected in the water.

Julian took Saylah's hand as she looked from Edward to Jamie and back again. Both stared blindly at the present while the past glittered in their eyes. They were slipping, sliding backward to a place no one could follow. Saylah wanted to touch Jamie's arm, to lure him back to this moment, but she did not move. The look on his face was so full of peace and wonder that she wanted to weep at his beauty.

Chapter

56

The boys had slipped away during the singing. Theron had decided it was time to show Paul his secret chest at last. They had closed the door with care, and Paul sat with his back against it, so no one could surprise them.

"But I don't think they will," the older boy observed, thinking of the glow the whiskey had put in his father's eyes. And Edward Ashton was not alone. Who would come in search of two small boys in the midst of all that joviality?

"Maybe," Theron muttered unintelligibly from the floor where he was trying to work the hidden latch free. "But if *I* saw anybody sneak away, *I'd* think they had a secret, and *I'd* want to know what it was."

"Not everyone's like you," Paul said. He wondered why he was whispering, when the stamping of feet, the laughter and the voices were so loud.

Theron grinned in triumph when he slid the cupboard open and brought out the chest. He sat down with the treasure in his lap, running his fingers over the painted lid. "Well?"

His friend was dumbfounded. When Theron had told him about Simone's chest, Paul had not expected this. "It's beautiful!" The painting looked so old and fine, the angels so graceful, their faces round and glowing. "I think it must be worth a lot of money." He was whispering again, afraid to be discovered and have the chest taken away before he'd had a chance to look at it closely. No wonder Theron had hidden it.

Theron lifted the lid and the scent of roses drifted on the air. "Sometimes I just sniff and sniff," he said. "No other woman smells like that." He lifted the old photograph reverently and passed it to his friend.

Once again, Paul could not find his voice. Not only was Simone Ivy the most delicate, lovely woman he had ever seen, but the young Jamie was also handsome—a different man from the one who presided over the noisy party. "I can't believe you found this," he finally managed.

Theron glanced nervously at his friend, but Paul would not betray him now that he wore the Mark of the Cougar on his arm, and they shared the secret of the cave. "You know what I wonder?"

Paul was gaping at the photograph. "What?"

"I wonder if she'll ever come back."

Dropping the picture, the older boy glowered at his friend. "I hope not!"

"Why?" Theron demanded. "I want to see her. And I know Julian does, even though he won't talk about her. And Papa—"

"It would be awful!" Paul gasped. "Don't you understand? What about your mother? Don't you think she'd mind?"

Theron hadn't considered that. "Why would she? If it made everyone happy?"

Shaking his head in despair, Paul took the chest and settled it on his own lap. "It wouldn't make everyone happy at all. Believe me, I know."

Lower lip jutting obstinately, arms crossed, Theron said, "But *I* want to see her."

His friend patted his shoulder. "I know you do," he sighed. "But what if she's evil? She left your father and brother, didn't she?"

Theron snorted in disgust. "How could anyone who smells like roses be evil?"

Paul could not explain it, could not even try, so he merely said, "You can't have everything you want."

Theron was not convinced. "Why not? She's awful rich. Look." He held the jeweled kingfisher up to the light of the paraffin lamp.

Paul shrugged. "You can't be rich *enough*, that's all. You just can't, ever."

After Edward's story, there was more playing, more dancing, more drinking. Though Saylah moved about the room, she kept an eye on Jamie. The smile had not yet faded from his face, and it troubled her.

"What is it?" Julian asked. "I know something's wrong."

"I am not certain," she told him. "I wish I could be."

"Let's have a last song," Flora said when the fires had begun to burn low, "for my Jamie's weary."

"Aye," Neil MacKinnon said, slurring the word slightly. "'Tis a wee bittie weary I am myself. So what shall it be? 'Ye Banks and Braes'?"

"Aye, 'tis the very one," Jock agreed, and Edward Ashton, who had said little for the past hour, added, "The perfect one."

Saylah leaned against the hearth, grateful for the warmth of the fire, wondering at the premonition that turned her cold. One by one, the men picked up their instruments and began to sing.

> Ye banks and braes o' bonnie doon,
> How can ye bloom so fresh and fair?
> How can ye chant ye little birds,
> And I sae weary, fu' o' care?

Saylah shivered and wondered why the song was so perfect. She noticed Julian was also perplexed, but Jamie kept smiling and stroking Flora's hand.

> Ye'll break my heart, ye warblin' birds,
> That wanton thro' the flow'ry throng,
> Ye mind me o' departed joys,
> Departed, never to return.

After that, people began to drift away, stopping by Jamie's chair to say good-bye. Julian went to the door to wish them a careful trip home, leaving Edward and Sophia, Flora and Saylah in the huge room that still smelled of sweat and good food and laughter.

Flora and Sophia moved toward the door, and Saylah backed away when she saw Jamie rise. Unexpectedly, he reached out to grasp Edward's hand. "Old friend," he whispered brokenly. His grip was too tight; there was a plea in his grasp, his voice, his brown eyes fixed on Edward Ashton's face.

Edward could not breathe. He did not know how to answer the silent question his friend was asking, how to ease Jamie's fevered melancholy. He could not bear it—the heat of that familiar gaze—so he turned away. He coughed loudly, attracting his wife's attention, and Jamie let him go.

Only Saylah saw the strength of those clasped hands, the plea in Jamie's eyes. He had asked Edward for something he could not give, not because he did not want to—Edward's sorrow was so real that she could feel it in the air—but because he did not know how. Only Saylah saw the inexpressible sadness with which Jamie released his friend. She felt that sadness heavy in her chest, throbbing with a pain so sudden and sharp that she gasped.

She knew the truth then; it glowed in the firelit shadows, raced like fingers of flame up the walls, screamed to her through the gray of Jamie's skin, the unnatural red in his cheeks. She could not bear the knowledge. Not alone, not this time, not like before. Not ever again.

Flora leaned over Theron, smiling as she drew up the quilt, ran her fingers lightly over the scar on his arm before she slid the arm under the covers. His face was rosy from excitement, but he slept peacefully. He had not even opened his eyes when she lifted him from the floor where he'd been sitting with Paul when both fell asleep.

"Good night, wee one," she whispered. She kissed his forehead and turned down the lamp. "Dream ye of burns and the braes and the bracken."

When she rose, she was unnerved to find Jamie waiting in the doorway. She had kissed him good night after the Ashtons left. He had held her close for a long time, then turned toward his room. Now he had discarded his fine clothes and wore his velvet dressing gown. His face was full of tenderness as he tiptoed in, bent to touch his son's cheek, then took Flora's arm. Her heart fluttered with apprehension. "What is it?"

He motioned her into the hall, and she followed, closing Theron's door behind her. "What—"

He stopped the question with his lips on hers. "I want you with me, that's all. Say you'll come with me."

She gazed up at him in astonishment and delight. Though he often held her during the day, sat with her on his lap, kissed her and caressed her in his great lion's chair, he had not taken her to his bed for nearly a year.

She started to answer, but her throat was choked with tears. She nodded, Jamie slid his arm around her, and they made their way through the destruction in the main room.

Saylah and Alida were clearing away the mess from the tables, collecting empty cups and plates and bottles. Flora paused to call out, "Leave it for tomorrow. Ye've done enough, ye two. Get ye some rest."

"It is nearly done," Saylah replied, noting how tightly Jamie held his wife.

As was her custom, Alida watched in silence and did not speak. She continued piling plates and stacking cups, but she listened, storing away the words in a secret place where she could always reach them.

"It is you who must rest," Saylah insisted when she saw Flora hesitate, "you who deserve peace tonight. If we can give it to you, it is yours."

Flora smiled and followed Jamie into his room, lit by the welcoming light of the chandelier.

Her husband tossed his dressing gown aside and Flora saw he was naked beneath. She smiled and slowly undid the brooch that held her plaid. She unwound it leisurely, aware that he was watching.

Jamie sighed when Flora unhooked her gown and let it slide to the floor. It was good to see the rounded curves of her body, the gleam of her hair in the candlelight. She removed the pins, let the blond curls tumble about her shoulders; he thought they looked like burnished gold. Her skin was white and silky, and she moved unconsciously, not trying to seduce him, not shifting her body so the shadows fell in the hollow between her breasts, not swaying with the candlelight.

She did not hurry as she unhooked her corset, laid it over the chair, along with her chemise, then slowly stepped out of her drawers. She stood for a moment, naked. He ached for her, wept silently for her, wanted her so much that he was afraid if he spoke a single word she would disappear. He tossed back the covers and slid between them, making room for her beside him.

Flora sensed the need for silence; for some reason she could not guess, Jamie did not wish to speak. But that was all right. She preferred it this way, with the muted light, golden and warm around them, and the touch of their bodies, skin to skin. She sighed and settled next to him.

Jamie pulled her close, so her breasts touched his chest, and she wound her legs with his. He could smell the scent of her, warm and reassuring. He had been so cold before, but Flora would make him warm. Flora would always keep him warm.

She raised her head and he kissed her lightly, barely brushing his lips over hers. She shivered and slid her hand across his chest, up to his shoulder, where she caressed the line of his throat, the curve of his ear. She seemed to know without being told that he did not wish to make love, but only to hold her, breathe in her nearness and her love for him.

"I'll never leave ye, Jamie," she said softly. "Never."

"I know." His eyes were damp and he buried his face in her tumbled hair. Tenderly, he began to rock her. Clinging to each other, they rocked—warm and safe and tightly bound together.

Eventually, exhausted from the preparations and the party, Flora fell asleep with her head on Jamie's shoulder. He listened to her deep, even breathing and it soothed him, calmed the pain in his chest that took away his breath.

Long afterward, he lay awake, with her weight against his body and her breath on his cool cheek. For a long time he lay—watching and waiting and wishing she had the power to heal him.

Chapter

57

Julian was more than a little drunk. Because he was uncomfortably warm after all the dancing, he went to his room to take off his coat and waistcoat, finding the buttons awkwardly shaped and too large for the holes they had fit through easily earlier in the evening. The cravat had settled permanently into an intricate knot at his neck, and it refused to respond to his dexterous attempts to loosen it. Finally, he pried it open with a buttonhook and tossed it triumphantly across the bed.

He felt a sense of urgency as he ran his fingers back and forth through his hair, trying to remember what it was he had to do. He stood sharply upright and nearly fell backward when he heard Saylah speaking inside his head.

Meet me beside the carved deer. I will teach you to dance as my People do.
mJulian smiled, delighted by the idea, by the memory of whirling with her, the scent of fir that clung about her, her hand clasped in his. Picking up his coat with exaggerated care, he slipped out the side door and stumbled toward the deer. At least he thought he was moving toward it, but the slope of the ground seemed to have changed, rising up when he least expected it to block his path, dropping off sharply where before it had been smooth and level.

"Which of those drunkards did this?" he demanded aloud of the trees that used to circle the clearing but now marched toward him in orderly lines. "Who dug up the hills and put them where they don't belong?" Glowering, he waited for an answer, but the only sound was the autumn breeze.

Annoyed, but possessed by the same sense of urgency, he stumbled on until, quite by accident, he found himself standing with his arms wrapped tightly around the deer's middle. "Where'd you come from?" he asked severely, making it clear that this time he would have an answer.

The deer, however, did not respond. Nevertheless, Julian hung on to make certain it didn't move again. After some time had passed, although he was not certain if it had been minutes or hours, he began to feel the chill of the night breeze. He had dropped his coat and could not remember where, though it lay over his scuffed leather boots and wrapped around one leg.

He held on and shivered, determined to persevere. Julian looked up when he heard a strange noise and saw a white figure in the distance. The figure drew closer, tinkling and rattling, its belly strangely distended, hair flowing wild around its shoulders. He decided there was no point in fleeing; everyone knew that ghosts could outrun you.

"Julian?"

He frowned and peered closer at the figure in white. "Saylah?" He felt dizzy with panic. "Are you a ghost now?"

She lowered her head to hide a smile, surprised that she could smile at all. "You are drunk, I think."

"Certainly not! I'm resting, that's all." She came closer and he was not so drunk that he didn't notice the glow of her skin in the moonlight, the spontaneity of her smile. She was wearing her wrapper and there were many bulges beneath it. In one hand she held a clam shell as if it were fine crystal.

"What's that?" he asked.

"The ember for our fire." With her free hand, she unwrapped his arms from around the deer, took a bottle of whiskey from under her wrapper and gave it to him to carry. "It would help if you would bring this, and your coat," she added when he tried to move and couldn't. "Though you will not need it, if I am right."

"You're always right, aren't you?" Julian demanded. "And why do we need an ember? Can't we use a match?"

She took his arm. "No," she said as they moved toward the trees, "I am not always right. You just want to believe I am."

"Not always," Julian muttered, remembering that her perceptions were often too acute and painful. Besides, she had changed the subject. "What about the match?"

"We do not need a match. We will make a fire as my People do, with a smoldering ember from the home fire. Tonight we will do things in the old way, as I was taught when only a child."

Julian frowned. He was not certain he liked the sound of that, though her voice was so sweet, so soothing that he decided to withhold judgment until later. "Where are we going? Can't we dance here?" This was more a practical suggestion than a romantic one, since he was having trouble keeping the ground at its proper level and wasn't sure how far he could walk and yet remain upright.

Saylah put her arm around his waist and encouraged him to lean against her. "There is a better place. It is hidden and apart, where we will not disturb the others. Do not worry, I will lead you."

When he reached the edge of the forest, Julian balked. "It's not safe in there. All kinds of danger. Teach me to dance here." He wondered, for the first time, how he would manage to dance at all. His feet did not seem inclined to move as he instructed them.

Saylah withdrew her arm. "I know of the dangers in the woods. We will be safe. The fire will keep the animals away and the drums will keep them quiet."

"Drums?" Julian looked around wildly.

Saylah touched his face and he froze. "You must trust me or I cannot teach you." With both hands, she drew his head down to hers. "Do you trust me, Julian?"

Even in the uncertain light, even in his drunkenness, her eyes were green and clear and wise. *I will stay as long as I am needed.* "I trust you."

He felt her sigh of relief throughout his body. She had been holding her breath. His head spun and he would have taken her in his arms, but her unwavering gaze stopped him. "Come," he managed without slurring the words, "show me."

Saylah's eyes misted with tears, but she blinked them back. Taking his hand, she ducked under fir branches and alder, oak and pine, finding the path easily, by instinct.

Julian was silent, concentrating on following her lead. He became aware of the night sounds around him, the sighing wind, the hidden animals, the insects hovering in air and trees. His head began to spin again.

"Wait here," Saylah said, "and please hold this for me." She gave him the shell she had cradled so carefully.

Julian held it out before him. "But I can't see."

She knelt to put a number of things on the ground. "Wait," she said, "soon your eyes will take in the moonlight and things will become clear again."

She began to gather leaves that seemed bound together somehow.

When she flung them aside, he saw that she had woven a kind of tarp with skunk cabbage leaves and nettle twine. It had covered a circle of stones which he realized was a fire pit, and a large flat platform he would not have noticed if it had not been for the four large stones at the corners.

"That's the old well. We covered it long ago."

"Tonight it is a drum. Usually, you see, there are the drummers and the dancers. I had to think of a way to do both, alone. I was lucky to find the well."

Rubbing his chin, where a thick stubble had begun to grow, Julian tried to understand, but the words swam in his head, disconnected, their meaning lost in the swirling darkness.

The tarp had been damp, already covered with dew, but the fire was dry. Saylah took the shell and inserted a curled piece of bark, then blew gently, coaxing the ember until the wood caught. She placed it carefully in the fire, already laid with dry tender. Then she took another piece of bark and lit it from the ember.

Soon the fire was roaring and Julian felt its warmth creeping into his chilled body. Saylah raised her head.

"Come," she said, "sit here."

He sat beside the platform, where she'd placed a cedarbark mat. "You've planned this for a long time, haven't you?"

She was untying her wrapper, but paused to smile at him. "Yes, a long time. First I made the drums and rattles, though I was not certain why. Long before that I had discovered this well. I danced upon it, heard the sound it made, and knew I would bring you here someday. I did not know when until tonight."

"All this for me?" he asked incredulously.

Saylah pulled her wrapper closed and crouched before him. "And also for me. You said you wanted to learn about my People. This is the most sacred thing that I can teach you."

"To dance?"

She shook her head. "It is much more than that. Not merely to move to the beat of drums, to the cadence of rattles and the sounds of the night, to change with the firelight, altered every moment by the breeze. To dance, yes, but also to celebrate. That is what I wish to teach you."

Julian scratched his head in confusion. "Isn't that what I've been doing all night?"

"In your own way. But I want to show you my way."

He held up the bottle of whiskey. "What's this for?"

She rocked back on her heels. "I see that the liquor makes you relax. It is important to let go of everything—all the thoughts in your mind, the worries, the responsibilities. I know it is difficult for you to release these things which are so much a part of you, so I have brought the whiskey."

Julian set the bottle aside. "I won't need this."

"I am glad," she replied, "but remember it is there." Slowly, she slipped the wrapper down her arms, tossed it aside, away from the fire, which had begun to leap and crackle. Saylah turned and the glowing light revealed her, barefoot, her hair unbound and falling down her back. She wore a necklace of bear and cougar teeth, a supple top made of pounded bark and a shredded cedarbark skirt that lifted lazily in the breeze. There was a small drum fixed by a leather thong around her waist. She wore anklets of scallop shells and deer hooves.

When she moved, Julian saw that she wore nothing else on her slender, bronzed body. He groped for the whiskey and took a long drink after all. He put the bottle aside as she began to sway with the movement of the firelight, to tap her feet on the wooden platform, to swing her hair out and back.

She raised her arms to him. "Come, let us dance as my People dance and you will see that there is nothing else." Her voice rose like a silvery thread of song, held taut and glimmering by the breeze, released and falling as she moved.

"I don't understand." But he thought he did. How could you misunderstand the sinuous movement of her body, her reaching arms, her alluring voice—calling him, enticing him.

"You will see," she chanted, "you will feel it. When the drums beat and your body answers, and the pulse of your blood and the rhythm of your heart, there is nothing else in all the world." She stamped lightly, making her anklets jingle, and began to tap the drum at her waist. "But you will feel it only if you are not afraid."

Julian took another swig from the cold bottle. "Afraid of what?"

Fluidly, Saylah began to turn and sway. "Of all that is sacred, all that is in the drums, all that is in you—hidden, but still brilliant and beautiful. If you are not afraid, you will see."

Julian was paralyzed with drunkenness and desire. Every motion of her body seemed to lure him nearer the brink of foolishness. Her voice flowed over him like mist in the wind, fueling his hunger. He wanted her. He had wanted to hold her and become her for a very long time. And now she was singing his hunger back to him, weaving a spell with her body and her hands and her irresistible golden voice. He struggled to hear what she was saying, but the words meant nothing. Only the sound. "I'll look like a fool."

Saylah laughed, breaking the rhythm for the first time. "As I did when I tripped over my skirts and all were watching? At least here there are none but you and me. None to see or hear or judge you. We are alone, Julian, with the magic of a Salish campfire and the beat of Salish drums."

He could not move. He was fascinated by the sensuous motion of her body, the cadence she created with feet and hands, shells and hide, wood and bone. Julian took another drink and another, but the needs of his body grew more acute, not less.

"Watch," she murmured. "Your body will know when it is time to join me." She raised her hands and her face toward the sky, lit by the moon that penetrated the lacery of leaves overhead. "Watch, and listen to the snapping of the fire, feel the warmth of its flames, which reach out to draw you into its heart. Listen to my feet on the smooth, cool wood, to the hollow, stirring rhythm, to the tapping of my fingers on the skin of the drum. See the movement of the flames"—she swayed toward the firelight, imitating the undulating motion—"feel the heat in the dampness on your skin." She ran her finger up her arm and left a trail through a film of sweat that made her body luminous.

Your body will know. . . . He half rose, hands outstretched, ready to pull her into his arms, to feel her skin pressed close to his. But she had spun away and he sank back onto the cedarbark mat.

She danced, stamping her feet against the wood, hearing the tinkle of her anklets, feeling the power of the fire, of the past, of the voices from inside her, too long contained in silence. Raising her arms, she turned and turned again, caught up in light and heat and rhythm, in the intricate steps that her feet remembered, though her mind had long forgotten. She swayed toward Julian, inviting him with open arms, inviting the spirits who hovered in the trees, who called to her, embodied in the beating of the drums.

Slowly, lyrically, she began to sing.

> Blazing golden fingers,
> Luminous dancing flickers,
>   Come.

> Touch my cold hand—shaking, shivering.
> Reach my still heart—waiting, fluttering.

> Smoldering orange fingers,
> Shimmering fiery flickers,
>   Come.
>   Surround me.

"What's that?" Julian asked, breathless and enthralled by the hypnotic motion of her body.

"That was Tanu's song," Saylah said sadly.

"And who is Tanu?"

"She was Queen of my People. She died long ago." She whirled away, stamping, tinkling, beating, beating softly on the hide of her waist-high drum. Her hair spun out around her, catching the firelight, blue-black and radiant, falling into shadow, drawing her toward darkness. Her body undulated with the songs that filled her, lifted her beyond this cold autumn night to the memories of her ancestors.

Julian saw her turning, turning, spinning into a world where her eyes were blind to the thick-growing trees and the fire and the heat of his body. Quickly, in terror, with a need so great it stopped his breath, he stepped onto the platform to catch her before she whirled away forever.

She felt him there, caught his bent, reaching arms, and grasped them with hers. They stood with half the length of their arms between them, hands on each other's elbows, bound together. He tried to break the hold of their locked fingers, to draw her closer, to taste her parted lips. Then Saylah looked directly into his eyes and he felt a chill down his spine that jolted him finally, fully awake.

He remembered her voice, distant but distinct: *To us our bodies are natural and not shameful, meant for work and pleasure, not false and meaningless restraints.* Her eyes were not veiled with promises or desire. Her hands on his skin were not seductive, but firm. *This is the most sacred thing that I can teach you. To dance, yes, but also to celebrate.*

Julian was sober in an instant. He had been struggling for weeks to get her to talk to him, to break through the reserve that held her apart. Now, without his asking, she'd ripped away the veil and spoken from the heart—not just with words, but with her hands and her body—and he hadn't even heard.

Saylah gazed into Julian's eyes until he saw that she had not left him behind. Her eyes were open wide and pleading for him to follow, to lose himself in this ritual, this world he could not understand.

She wanted to give him something she would give no other—a glimpse of her true spirit. She was whispering intimate secrets, deeply hidden, and all he'd heard was his own desire. He felt small and insignificant, secretly angry that he should always feel that way. She was so good and he so base.

Saylah saw these things in Julian's eyes. For a moment, she hesitated. She had been so careful, so quiet, so safe. Yet she could not turn away. "You were listening to another voice," she said, "just as I was when you spoke of the cougar. I did not wish to hear you, but only my own voice and my own truth."

She paused, then whispered, "I was not wrong to bring you here. You were not wrong to come. If you will listen now, if you will try to hear me, we will dance."

Julian felt tears burn his eyes. She had made herself vulnerable to him, uncovered her secret shrouded soul. He saw it, lucid and incandescent in her eyes. He understood what it had cost her to take this risk.

"I wanted you to know what it is to lose yourself in celebration," she said. "There was no other way to do it. Was I wrong? Are you unwilling?" Her voice quivered, revealing her uncertainty.

Julian's throat grew dry and tight. "I'm willing," he said. "Show me."

She smiled as he had never seen her smile before, openly, with excitement and expectation, even happiness. She looked very young, like a girl who denied the years that had come between her and her childhood. She had stepped back in time and trusted him enough to take him with her. His hands tightened on her arms and Saylah winced.

Julian's naked need, his desire awakened the hunger inside her. For a moment, she wanted to end the dance and let him touch her, hold her, teach her all she had never learned.

She knew one refuge from the weakness of her body. Slowly, imperceptibly, she began to lift one foot and then the other, to push against the platform, to make her anklets jingle. Clutching Julian's arms, she swayed in time with the rise and fall of her feet. Without knowing, without caring, without fear, he began to sway with her, slowly at first, feeling the moistness of her palms against his skin.

He lifted his feet as she did, but his boots were loud and harsh on the platform. He removed them and tossed them aside, surprised by the feel of the wood beneath his feet. "It's smooth. There are no splinters."

"I rubbed it many times with dogfish scales to make it so," she said, stamping her feet one at a time, releasing his elbow to strike the drum around her waist. She did not ask more of him, or guide him, or force the steps upon him.

They moved together, feeling the firelight, the flickering firelight, as, slowly, they began to circle, arms locked together. Her shells jingled in a music strange and of a different beat, yet he listened, captivated by the sound, the moving light, the drum under his feet which played as he danced.

They moved faster and faster, lifting their feet, tapping the skin drum, moving toward the fire and away and back again, answering the voices of her People and the night.

When Julian's body glistened with sweat, he removed his shirt and threw it into the darkness. They twirled, released each other, spun apart, still beating out a song, singing out a rhythm. He made his, she made hers, and the two songs blended and rose on the wind. Firelight gleamed on Julian's muscled body, the fine curly hairs of his chest, the sweat that ran in rivulets down his heated skin.

Saylah paused, lifted the bear- and cougar-tooth necklace, put it over his head so it came to rest on his damp chest. "Now the cougar is no longer between us, but binds us in his beauty and his rage."

Julian leaned toward her and she leaned away. She leaned toward him and he leaned away. They circled, stamped and beat the drum while the old voices cried in their blood. She gave him the gift of her memory and her rituals and her history. She spoke it with the lithe motion of her hands, whispered it in the curve of her hips, shouted it in the leaping of her long legs over the golden fire.

Julian told his own stories with his work-worn hands and his sun-browned muscles and his strong legs. The fire blazed up, too near, and he stood back, uncertain.

Saylah laid her palm on his heaving chest. "A friend told me once, and I tell you now, 'There will never be another moment like this one. Not for you or for me. Do not destroy it with your fears. There is no fear. There is only you and me and our friendship and this glorious night. We are alone in all the world and everything you see is ours.'"

Julian believed her. How could he not? She was not made of human flesh, but of songs and silver voices and the cadence of the drums. She was quavering firelight, red and golden, and a fall of blue-black water made lucent and rippling by the flames.

Yet when their eyes met, she was still Saylah. He was caught in her magic, lost in her past, lifted beyond what was hard and real anguish. He danced with her among the trees, and the woods became their shelter and their haven and their cradle. It became, for that one night, their home, where they were safe and free and full of an exaltation they had never known before and would never know again.

Chapter

58

Saylah awoke under the blanket of skunk cabbage leaves with Julian's body curled around her own. She could feel his warm breath in her hair, the curls on his chest brushing her back, his hips pressed to hers, his hand around her shoulder, holding her against him. She felt safe and warm, though the chill on her cheeks told her the morning was brisk and cold.

It was not yet dawn, and she lay unmoving, smiling at the memory of how they had danced until both collapsed, exhausted, in the damp bracken nearby. They had curled together naturally, and she had drawn the makeshift blanket over them. They had fallen asleep, comfortable in the world she had created—the world of her childhood, and now, her womanhood.

Yet he had not touched her out of hunger, not even when they lay nearly naked, side by side. Her weariness had dulled her desire, her exaltation burned away all memory of the strange new yearnings of her body. Now she twined her fingers with his and lay still, content.

She knew when Julian awakened, because he squeezed her hand and buried his face in her hair. Then he slept again, his even breathing like a soothing whisper of song.

Saylah watched the dawn come through the trees; the light called her, and she slipped reluctantly out of Julian's arms, away from his warmth and his reassuring pulse. She stood in a small clearing, gazing up at the fragmented light. The rain-streaked leaves quivered with any breath of wind, and the air was heavy with moisture, the trees laden with green and silver moss.

She was alone, the world was encompassed by this quiet place of distant rushing water and shimmering leaves, and life was clear and simple and free from pain. In that moment of dim green stillness, she felt at peace.

Julian awoke a second time to see that Saylah had wandered away. He followed quietly, not wishing to disturb her. He stopped when he saw her standing naked, enfolded by the deep, wet darkness of the forest.

The clouds moved and the sun pierced the layered leaves, touching Saylah's face, her outstretched hands with radiance—brilliant amidst the play of moving shadow on her palms. Motionless, head back in silent communion, she absorbed the light that filtered through leaves, through rain and moss and clouds, to touch her face with a pattern of ever-shifting lace.

Saylah smiled, felt Julian watching, and turned.

He held out his hand and she took it. It felt warm and reassuring in hers. They walked back, fingers laced, to the glowing embers of the fire and sat on the platform, side by side.

"What are you thinking of?" Saylah asked. "You are not really here beside me."

He smiled and she wanted to trace that smile, to carve it into her memory.

"I'm here," he said, lifting their clasped hands toward the fire. "But I was remembering something . . ." He trailed off, unwilling to continue. Unwilling to bring the past into this moment which was completely theirs.

Saylah put her free hand on his shoulder. "Tell me, and then you will no longer carry it inside you."

"Maybe you're right." He stared down at the ashes of their fire and said, "When I saw you among the trees, I remembered a day when I came upon my mother in the woods." He paused, fighting back the anger that always came when he spoke her name, the bitterness that was poison in his blood.

"She wore a rose silk gown with silver braided trim and French lace at the throat. I remember she'd pulled her hair back with a single strand of pearls. The hem of her gown had caught up nettles and pine needles and broken bits of fern which clung to her, tenaciously, as if to weigh her down and hold her back."

He took a deep breath. Now that he had begun, the words came rushing out, too long damned up inside him. "I noticed her fingers spread against the bark of a fir. They looked so fragile, so pale compared to the aged, weather-beaten tree. Her face, her skin, were soft and white, unmarred by age or pain or grief. At least I thought so then.

"All I knew was that her gown, her face, her pearls, seemed precious and out of place in this confusion of trees and ferns and shadows and piercing wind. There were silver threads in her gown that glittered like liquid gems. She was so delicate, so elegant, so foreign to this rough place that took your energy and your passion and dried them up like the furrows on the battered old trees."

Saylah squeezed his hand but did not interrupt; his gray-green eyes were drained of color by the disturbing memory.

"I felt a pain in my chest and could not breathe. I thought that she did not belong here. I *knew* it. She belonged in palaces and long corridors with gilded walls and thick red carpet. She called to me then, shifted the folds of her cashmere pelisse, and swept up her belled skirt in her hand. It broke my heart, that gesture. It belonged to a stranger who had fallen by mistake into a world she could not understand and in which she did not belong. I never forgot that moment. I never will."

Saylah was silent, considering what she knew of this strange woman from Theron's secret chest. Finally, she said, "What brought the memory close again?"

He gazed into the smoldering coals of the fire. "When I saw you with the light on your face, I thought how you belonged here, that you seemed to find your strength among these trees. Then I remembered Simone, and how lost she was among them."

Saylah wanted to say that she ached for him, for the sound and feeling of his sorrow. But he knew that, or he would not be where he was, unclothed, unprotected yet invulnerable.

"We should go back," he whispered. "If Flora and Jamie can't find us—"

Saylah started at the sound of Jamie's name, the memory of his ashen face last night. "Yes," she said softly. "We must go back." But she did not want to leave this place, the bond that had been created by drums and fire and the cadence of their feet upon the wood. She did not want to leave the warmth of Julian's body or the clasp of his hand.

But she must go, because Jamie needed her, and she could not fail him.

In silence, they dressed, doused the fire and re-covered the platform, then moved off through the trees toward the closed and darkened house.

By the time they had slipped in the side door, returned to their rooms, and dressed, the sun had begun to blaze through the windows and light the house, which felt strangely empty after the party the night before.

—— 406 ——

In her plain black gown, hair neatly braided, Saylah went directly to Jamie. Flora was just leaving the room, her plaid over her arm, her blond curls tumbled and uncombed. There was a thin line of worry between her eyes, but she smiled with relief when she saw Saylah. "I'm sore afraid we overtired him last night. He's no' himself this mornin'."

"I will do what I can for him."

Flora heard what she did not say and reached for the girl's hand. "He's been much better these past weeks, happier."

On a drift of stale air, Saylah heard a faint, remembered voice. *When those who love you want you to be happy, it is easy to make them believe it is so.* All at once she missed Koleili so much that she had to fight to keep her thoughts on Flora. "Jamie has tried very hard. He wanted to see you smile again. And so he has."

"He held me gently, as he used to, and I felt his heart beatin' against my ear." Flora's eyes were misty, her smile sweet and wrenching.

They wish so much to see contentment instead of sorrow, happiness instead of pain. It is not difficult to let them see only what they wish to see.

Saylah forced her own grief inward and reached for Flora's hand. "If you will make him a broth and heat the water for his tea, I will take care of Jamie."

Flora nodded and headed for the kitchen, grateful for something to do. Slowly, Saylah turned the knob and opened the door.

Jamie was sitting in his lion's chair, but this morning he was not dressed. He wore his velvet dressing gown, and had not combed his hair. His face was haggard from lack of sleep, his skin tinged slightly blue.

"You have had much pain," she said.

Jamie nodded wearily. "Too much, and for too long."

"It is your heart, is it not?" She wanted to touch his forehead, his ashen cheek, but something held her back.

Jamie nodded. "My heart, it seems, has lost its strength. The struggle to go on beating is too painful."

"Let me ease it. I can find the roots and leaves you need. I know of hearts that sicken with weakness. I know that they *do* go on beating." She hurried on before he could stop her. "Dr. Helmcken told me that with rest and care, a man can live for many years with such a heart."

Jamie looked up. "What kind of life would that be for me? More shadows, more darkness, more lying still and careful in my bed. If I choose to live, it must be to live completely, exuberantly, as I used to. And that isn't possible. The damage goes too deep."

Saylah did not argue because she knew that he was right. To live each day as if he were a piece of crystal that might shatter at the slightest touch would be no life at all for Jamie Ivy. He had been born, as he had said, to live unafraid and unfettered. Anything else would be unbearable—for him as well as for those who loved him. She sat on the brocade maple chair and faced him, waiting.

"John Keats wrote many things that moved me. But there's one line I can't get out of my mind. 'Beauty is Truth, Truth Beauty. That is all ye know on earth and all ye need to know.'" He smiled again, drifting in his thoughts away from the pain in his chest. Drifting, as he had last night, to a time before the pain, when his smile had not been touched with sadness.

Leaning forward, Jamie tapped Saylah's knee. "When I believed the poet was right, anything was possible. But now I know it's a lie. Now I know that truth is ugly and harsh and it hurts, here." He touched his chest lightly, then his head. "And here as well." His eyes locked with hers. "You know I'm right. You've seen it too."

It hit Saylah like a blast of icy rain that he had made his choice, and that she could not bear to lose him. "We have all seen such truth." She took his hands urgently and held them tight. "But we are lucky, you and I, because for a very long time, we saw and understood and lived the *beauty*. As long as we believed it, it was true. Most people never even glimpse it."

Jamie was stunned. "Not even for a moment?"

"Perhaps for a moment now and then," she conceded, "but never for years, like you and me." She had been blessed in spite of all the sorrow; she had been happy walking in her People's dream, in their faith and their affection. All of that had brought her joy. She felt tears sting her eyes, but she forced them back.

Shaking his head, Jamie turned his hands so they gripped hers. "It never occurred to me that others didn't see it."

The floor seemed to shift under Saylah's feet. "It makes it easier, I think, for them to survive."

Jamie thought of what he had suffered and knew that she was right. "And yet I pity them."

"As do I. That part of my life which it hurts most to remember, that alone I would never give up, even to stop the pain." And yet she had done so. For four years she had done so. She had been a fool to give up so much and gain so little—not happiness or peace, but emptiness and freedom from her gnawing sorrow. She fought back the waves of anguish that overwhelmed her. Jamie. She must cling to Jamie.

He was resting his forehead on their linked hands. "Last night I went back to the days when I believed in the beauty. I slipped into my memories and I knew again what it was like, that wonder. I *felt* it. But I can only find that feeling in the past. I'll never find it in the future." His eyes grew dim and she knew he was thinking of Edward, of the moment when he had turned away.

She shook herself free of her own dangerous memories and met Jamie's clouded gaze. "What did Edward Ashton do to you to make you give up?"

Jamie stiffened, then shook his head. "It doesn't matter. Can't you see that?"

"You are making an excuse to avoid speaking aloud what you do not wish to relive."

Abruptly, he rose, pulling her with him, their hands clasped together. "Come." He moved toward the window.

When they stood in front of the heavy velvet drapes, he released her hands and pushed the curtains aside, letting the morning light spill over them.

Saylah gasped. He had never stood in the light of day since the first moment she met him, except to watch Julian slipping away. Now he blinked and did not turn from the sun.

"Look at me," he demanded. "Look in my eyes and see that I'm telling the truth. What Edward did doesn't matter. If it hadn't been him, it would have been someone else, something else." Leaving the drapes open, he began to pace, hands clasped behind his back. "Don't you see, it's simply the way the world is. If Simone or even Julian had been the one to wake me up, it would have been the same."

Because he had faced her with the sun on his face and in his eyes, Saylah believed him. He spoke with no ill will, and there was no deception in his gaze. He could have hidden his anger in the shadows, but not in the light. Perhaps he had known that all along.

Yet she could not help but believe that if Edward had met his friend's eyes, if he had apologized or wept or shown regret, it *might* have made a difference. It *might* have given Jamie a reason to believe again.

Jamie seemed to read her thoughts. "I think you don't understand Edward. He seems to have everything, but I suspect he's never really been happy—not deep inside. He doesn't know how. He has suffered more than I have, and long before he knew me. My friend Edward is driven to succeed, possessed by that need. I sometimes wonder if it won't destroy him before . . ." He trailed off and stared beyond Saylah to the dust dancing in the sunlight.

She gasped, but held the breath in tightly. As Jamie spoke of his lost friend, she saw how fragile he had become despite his apparent improvement, how frail his hands, how like old parchment his skin. She saw the lines of pain etched into his face, deep and irrevocable. He stood with his empty hands open before him.

"I want to go back, back to my memories, when I was happy. Please let me go."

She felt a tearing inside of something precious and irreplaceable, but did not let her anguish show. *You must learn to let go,* Koleili had whispered. "I knew I would have to set you free a long time past." Her voice was steady, because he needed her strength now, not her sorrow. "It is the others who will not wish to let go."

"Can't you tell them, explain?" Jamie pleaded.

"I will try, but they will not wish to hear me."

He leaned against the bedpost, drifting, drifting back. "It's selfish of me to pray for escape."

Saylah swallowed dryly. *Do not hold me here when I wish to fly free.* "It is selfish of us to pray for your continued imprisonment. We are all selfish. We know no other way to be. I will speak to the others—" she began.

Jamie caught her wrist and held it. "Tell them I am falling back into my dreams. That I have nothing more to give them. 'Now, in sleep, he is at rest.'"

He made it sound like the end, but it was not. "Look at me," she said as he had earlier, "and remember what I say. Because you have dreamed, you understand the dreams of others. There are few who can do that, fewer still who can bring to our lips the things we would hide away in darkness. You see inside our dreams and nightmares and so we share them with you.

"I think you have heard more secrets, more confidences than others hear through many lifetimes. You have given more comfort than most men know how to give. People want to dream with you. They want to be worthy of the world you imagine."

His eyes were wet, but he blinked the tears away. He saw a flicker of color out of the corner of his eye and moved toward the window, grateful for the distraction.

Julian was holding the reins of the pony while Theron sat on its back. They made a slow circle around the flat ground, then another. Theron called out, laughing, and Julian smiled back at him encouragingly. He kept a close watch, and when the boy bounced a little too high and started to slip out of the saddle, Julian was there to catch him.

He did not chastise Theron, but stood patiently, explaining, bending the boy's leg to show him how to grip the horse, demonstrating how to hold the reins.

"Julian'll make a good father someday," Jamie murmured. "He's had a great deal of practice, after all."

Somehow, Saylah knew he was not referring to Theron.

Just then Julian turned toward the house and paused when he saw the break in heavy velvet at his father's windows. He saw Saylah and Jamie watching and smiled, calling something out to Theron, who also turned, wide-eyed, to stare at the open drapes.

The young boy waved frantically and Julian stood smiling, thinking that now, once and for always, his father had come back to him. Saylah saw his gratitude, felt it, even through the heavy glass and the distance between them. She rested her forehead on the cool window and choked back the despair that blocked her throat.

Jamie cried out, reaching for her blindly. "He doesn't understand."

She did not raise her head, though she felt Julian's questioning eyes upon her, Theron's laughing gaze and Jamie's claw-like hand. In the back of her head, she heard a warning voice. *The People have freed you. Be grateful that you need no longer carry the burden of their faith.* And yet three sets of eyes told her it was not so, that once again, she had taken the burden on her shoulders.

"Please," Jamie whispered.

They asked so much of you. You are only human, Tanu, but they did not tell you that.

"I will tell them," she replied. As she turned away, she knew she would never forget the look of gratitude and joy on Julian's face. The joy had been for Jamie, the gratitude for her. Now she must shatter his hope, his happiness, his faith.

She turned to leave the room before she betrayed herself and her duty and her love for Jamie, which threatened to change, in that moment, to bitterness.

Chapter

—=◄ 59 ►=—

Julian was waiting on the upper porch, leaning on his elbows and watching the distant sea. Saylah did not need to see his face to know what he was feeling. "Julian," she said.

He turned, smiling with the memory of the past night, easy in her presence as he had not been before. He took her hand casually, intimately. "I never thought to see my father through that window again. You make miracles, did you know that?"

The People believe in you because you give them cause. If you gave them cause to turn from you, they would do so.

Not Julian, Saylah cried inwardly, he who has seen the darkness and the beat of drums with me. He would not turn away. But what if he did? And Flora and Theron, who believed in her too. What if they closed her out and made her a stranger?

mHer body went rigid, her chest tight with pain. She could not bear to lose another family. She had lost so much already. But so had Julian.

"What's wrong?" he asked, drawing her into the circle of his arm. "You're cold and shaking."

Saylah looked up, startled. She wanted to lean against him, to enjoy the warmth of his hand on her shoulder. But she had made a promise.

"What is it?" he repeated in concern. "Tell me." When she did not answer, he tilted her chin up and stared into her clouded eyes. "Are you sorry about last night?" He winced at the thought, but he was tired of games and shadows and threats he could not understand. "Do you want to become strangers again so the danger goes away?"

"It does not ever go away." She sighed and rested her palms on his chest. "Listen to me, Julian. Hear me. I do not regret what passed between us in the darkness or the dawn. It is not that which troubles me now."

"Then what?"

She curled her fingers into the soft flannel of his shirt. "It is Jamie."

"But I saw him at the window. He opened the drapes and looked out. And he's been much better lately. You know that."

He sounded like an eager young boy, ready, for the first time in his life, to believe the best. His smile broke Saylah's heart. "Your father appears to be better, but he is not well."

"Then you can cure him." His eyes were wary, but his voice was certain, unwavering, like his faith.

Saylah's breath escaped in a rush, as if he had struck her. "I thought once that perhaps I could cure his body."

The wind came up beside them, lifting the hem of her skirt, ruffling Julian's hair. He brushed it back impatiently. "But not his mind? Are you saying he's mad?"

"I am saying his heart is not strong, that it may fail him. But it is more than that. Jamie is a man in love with beauty, with gentleness and miracles and simple human kindness. These things exist, they are real, but he cannot see them. I am saying that he cannot live outside the dream; it will destroy him."

Julian released her and turned to stare at the trees, bent and swaying in the wind. "What am I supposed to do, give up?" He spoke harshly, echoing the bite of the ax into splintered wood.

Saylah went cold. "Jamie cannot bear the sight of your pain. If you call him back to you, he will come."

"But you don't think that would be wise." It was more an accusation than a question.

"It would not be kind. Death means the end of pain and sorrow. Give your father that solace. Find the strength to let him go." Julian would not look at her, but he was listening. His body was rigid with waiting. "I know it is not easy."

He revolved slowly. "You don't know. You can't begin to imagine how I feel."

Saylah stared at him, shaken beyond reason. *You have seen your fear and come to know it well. You are in turmoil.* "I have come to love Jamie too. To lose him will tear me apart."

"I don't believe anything would tear you apart." Julian wanted to be cruel, to hurt her, to release the seething storm raging inside him.

No one lives forever. Not a Head Man or a shaman. Not even a Queen. Saylah choked back a cry of anguish, tried to think clearly through the tumult in her head. "It is not your grief that churns inside you and makes you speak this way, but your anger."

Julian smiled bitterly. "Why, because you told me the truth?"

She took a deep breath and fought to break the grip of something violent and raw that rose in her body. "Your anger is not for me."

"For whom, then?" He spoke coldly, derisively.

"I have told you before, for Jamie. You are angry because he has given up."

"Then I should pity him." He crossed his arms and leaned against the railing, shutting her out.

Nothing has changed except that you have understood the truth at last. Now you must learn to accept it. Her head was whirling, but Saylah grasped the railing and held herself upright. "Do you not understand that by choosing to die, he has chosen the easy path? Why should you not be angry? Jamie will find peace and rest, but your sorrow will go on and on."

Saylah wanted to leave him, to turn from the sight of his mocking disillusion, but she was held motionless by thoughts of Hawilquolas and Koleili, who had welcomed death, had begged her to set them free. Their faces rose before her, the sound of their voices, their cold, dead bodies and the smell of the death root, sweet and ineffably bitter.

Julian heard her gasp, and the sound penetrated the haze of his despair. Her eyes were bleak, her face ravaged with grief. Why had he never thought she might have lost someone too? Why had he not listened when she told him the place they had been together was dark and ugly, that it had left their fears exposed and raw, their weaknesses written in the tracks of a cougar in the dark, wet earth?

Julian took Saylah's shoulders and felt her tremble. She was cold as polished stone. "Forgive me," he said, but she did not hear. "It's not your fault. Forgive me, Saylah. Please."

The last word rang in her ears as she struggled to escape the whirling images, the frantic feeling of loss and grief that threatened to overwhelm her. *You must go to the woods to seek your peace, to restore the stillness that is necessary to healing your tortured heart.*

"Saylah, don't leave me. I'm sorry."

She blinked up at him, at his eyes, which came slowly into focus, at his face, sunburned and dearly familiar, at his hair, tossed by the wind. He was still with her. She forced her feelings into silence, into calm, into darkness.

"Help me," Julian said. "I need you."

She reached up to touch his cheek. *I would give you that stillness in my hand if I could, but you must find it for yourself.* "Yes," she said. "I will help you. I will try."

Her voice shook, and she seemed small and fragile beneath his work-roughened hands. He remembered then the young girl he had seen last night, the girl who had danced with joy, shouted that all the world was theirs. He wanted her back. He wanted for all she had said to be true.

"Julian says Jamie is going to die," Paul announced somberly one evening after dinner.

Sophia looked up sharply from her snifter of brandy. "But he looked so well at the party. He was almost his old self again." She stared down the table, across the heavy damask cloth, the gleaming china and crystal, in which the light from the candelabra sparked and touched off tiny flames of color. Edward did not raise his head, but his hands were white and fisted on the table.

"I overheard Julian say it's his heart and there's nothing they can do." Paul spoke the words but did not really understand what they meant. All he knew was that he felt hollow and desperate inside. "He said Jamie's had some attacks and they didn't even know it. But he can't hide it anymore."

Edward sat with his shoulders slumped forward. One hand opened and closed around the handle of his enameled silver knife.

"Poor Flora," Sophia said, her eyes fixed on her husband's bent head. "She loves him so much. Does Theron know?"

Paul scowled. "No one's told him. I guess they think he's too little. But he knows anyway. He doesn't talk about it, just mopes around a lot. Julian's trying to teach him to ride the pony. I think he hopes it'll make Theron forget. But it won't. They think he's just a baby. They don't even remember he was attacked by a cougar and lived. How can you be a baby after that?" he demanded furiously.

Sophia curved her fingers around Paul's. "Don't worry, my dear. Theron will speak up when he needs to. And he won't be left alone and neglected. If I'm not mistaken, Saylah will take very good care of him."

Paul sighed and nodded. "Saylah listens to him. She's the only one."

Frowning, Sophia ran her finger around the rim of her glass, making the crystal sing. Only now did she really hear what her son had said, begin to absorb its meaning. She felt unbearably cold, unutterably sad. Somehow, she had always believed that Jamie would come back to them one day. She did not want to stop believing. "What will Julian do? He worships Jamie."

"He'll survive," Edward snapped. "It's what we all do, isn't it?" When he saw the hurt in Sophia's eyes, he lowered his voice. "I don't mean that's all there is to life." But perhaps, after all, he did. "It's just that everyone has made so much over Jamie Ivy and his illness, as if people didn't get ill and die every day. As if, somehow, he's special."

Sophia set her glass down hard, and brandy splashed up the sides, glowing amber in the candlelight. "You're the one who described a man like no other in your story at the party. Or don't you remember?" Edward had not spoken much since that night. His broad shoulders seemed bowed under a heavy weight and he no longer held his head quite as high. The violence she had felt in him when they made love had not returned, yet he was further away from her than ever. She could not begin to guess what he was thinking. "Won't you miss Jamie? I thought he was your best friend."

Edward's eyes met hers across the table. "He was. And I've been missing him for a long time now." Beneath the bitterness was sorrow, shrouded and concealed by a film as dark as smoke. The wavering light settled in the hollows of his cheeks, on his forehead, in the cleft in his chin. His skin was burned from working in the sun, but underneath it had no color or warmth.

The demons that drove him had begun to sap his strength, to make him more of a stranger every day.

Biting his lower lip, Paul watched his parents, and listened, and tried to understand. But nothing made sense. He wished he were older, and smarter, that he could hear the things underneath the words that eddied around him. Something wasn't right in this house, and for once, he didn't think it had to do with Edward's other women. There had always been other women, but never before had there been this sense of waiting, of currents of danger that ate away at the laughter like the sea eats away at the shimmering sand.

Paul knew Sophia was hurt and confused; her face said what her lips did not. He wanted to be angry at his father, but Edward's face too was distorted by pain. There was a silent battle going on between them, and Paul couldn't think whose side he should take, because he didn't understand what they were fighting for—or against. All he knew was that his home was full of the shadows that had haunted Jamie's before the curtains came open and the sun poured in.

And now, even in the light, the shadows waited, as did everyone, for Jamie to die.

Chapter
60

Douglas Charles sat at the rolltop desk in his library in Boston, tapping his fingers impatiently on the glossy oak. For once, the sight of his gleaming shelves lined with fine leather-bound books did nothing to soothe him. He was puzzled, angry and uncertain.

Douglas Charles was not the kind of man who enjoyed being uncertain. He liked things to fall neatly into place, in their proper order, according to consequence. He liked things to be right or unquestionably wrong; he disliked intensely any murky in-between.

For the third time, he picked up the letter he had begun that morning to his impertinent and ungrateful daughter in British Columbia.

Sophia,
    Do you take me for a fool? Trying to frighten me with images of rifle-bearing marauding Indians and unsavory neighbors with disgustingly middle-class wives, and worst of all, the nauseating details of your daily life. Have I ever given you reason to think me feebleminded? Did you think I would quake with fear for your safety? Indeed, it is more your mortal soul that concerns me now. Because it seems that, far from being threatened by these dire developments, you have been corrupted by them. The bulls and their antics, indeed! How unutterably vulgar!

For the third time, he dropped the unfinished letter and rested his double chin on his hand. He scratched absently at his muttonchops and considered the other thick missive, received as he was dipping his pen once more into the inkwell to continue his diatribe.

He had not recognized the handwriting, though the postmark was Victoria, Vancouver Island. Curious in spite of his low-boiling anger, he had put Sophia's letter aside and broken the somewhat lopsided seal. He had been utterly astonished by the contents. Just to be certain he hadn't been working too hard and begun to imagine things, he picked up several pages of smudged and blotted parchment, perched his spectacles on his nose and began to read.

Dear Mr. Charles,

My name is Paul Edward Ashton and I'm your only grandson (at least that's what Mama says when she wonders out loud why you've never even asked for a photograph of me, and since Mama doesn't lie, I guess it must be true). I am writing to introduce myself, though Mama says you don't really want to know me. I think she says that because she thinks you don't care about her, but I don't see why you would bother to write so many letters (I counted, and there are sixteen, just in the past six months) to someone you don't care about at all.

I know Mama just wrote, but I thought I'd better write too, because she was smiling and looking pretty pleased when she posted that letter, and she usually scowls a lot and tears up lots of paper when she writes to you. I think she might have said something to make you mad (not because my mama is bad—she's the most wonderful mother in the whole world, but sometimes she doesn't know how to answer all your questions and that makes *her* mad, so I thought she might've tried to make you mad back).

I know Mama cares about you a lot, because she stomps around and mutters to herself and sometimes even cries every time she gets a letter. I guess if she really didn't care, she'd throw your letters in the fire the way Papa does with the people who want to be his friend because he's rich and not because he's Papa. He says they don't care about him and that's why he burns the letters. But Mama doesn't burn yours. She keeps them on her desk in neat little piles and stares at them for a long time and even forgets I'm there. Of course, *I* don't like it very much, but it might make you feel better.

Douglas Charles swallowed dryly and reached up to loosen his cravat, but he'd already untied it. He scowled at the crumpled letter in his hand. He was not usually forgetful, and he didn't like it one bit.

The thing is, Mama doesn't understand why you're still so angry that she married Papa, since it was a long time ago, and he makes her laugh and tells her she's beautiful and trusts her with all kinds of important things. Mama likes to laugh a lot (every morning she spends at least an hour making *me* laugh. She says it's a good way to start a day, and I think she's right. I don't guess you go in much for laughing in the morning, do you? Maybe you should practice. I found out you can learn just about anything if you practice hard enough. But if you don't want to, that's all right. I'm sure there are lots of other nice things about you). And next to laughing, she likes being trusted.

But Mama doesn't believe you trust her, because of all your questions, even though I told her I thought maybe you were just really curious, since you've never traveled or seen all the things she sees every day. But that's not the worst part. She doesn't think you might have hurt feelings just like she does. But I think you do. I think you must miss her a lot (because she's so wonderful and so pretty and so much fun). If she wasn't here when I woke up in the morning, I might get mad and write mean letters to whoever took her away too.

I think she *would* believe it if you didn't ask quite so many questions, and if you just said things a little different than you do. See, my mama doesn't really hear *what* you say. She just hears how you say it. I asked her once why she married Papa when you didn't want her to. She said it was because Papa gave her a choice. He asked her to marry him and go away with him, and then he let her decide. I guess I can say that my mama doesn't like being told what to do. She's got real strong thoughts of her own. She's just a strong person, I guess. I heard Papa tell her she's just like you, so I thought maybe you'd understand if I explained it carefully.

I don't like my mama stomping around and getting mad at your letters. It makes me sad. I tried to tell her once that I thought you might be sad too, but she didn't believe me. Maybe you could tell her yourself. Maybe you could even make her laugh if you tried real hard. Then she'd be much happier, and maybe you wouldn't have to spend so much time thinking up hard questions. Maybe you could just tell her things about what you do all day and what funny things happened and how much you miss her.

I'd appreciate it if you didn't tell Mama about this letter. I don't think she'd like it at all. But I had to write. I just had to, or else how would you know all these important things?

Yours Most Sincerely,
Paul Edward Ashton

With a snort of anger, Douglas Charles dropped the letter among the scattered papers on his desk. His spectacles fell off the end of his nose and bounced, on their thin satin ribbon, against the front of his brocade silk waistcoat.

"Impertinent young pup!" he said to no one in particular. "How dare he tell me how to handle my relationship with my daughter!"

His face was growing redder by the moment, and he puffed air in and out in blasts, scattering the papers further. Then he sat back, arms folded. Of course, the boy was only a child. No doubt he'd thought he was helping out.

And it was true that Douglas didn't laugh much anymore. Now, when had that happened? He used to laugh all the time. He remembered when Sophia was little, they'd actually rolled on the floor, convulsed, over something her pretty mother had said.

Douglas frowned and sighed. There was his answer. Ever since young Natalie Charles had died of tuberculosis, her husband had found fewer and fewer things amusing. Until now, so many years later, so long after he stopped grieving whenever he woke up beside her empty pillow, almost nothing seemed funny.

But for a child to pry into his personal life like that. It was unthinkable, unpardonable, inexcusable. That Sophia had raised her child to behave in such an outrageous manner was more proof, he thought grimly, that she had lost all sense of pride and what was right and proper when she ran off with that gigolo. Except, it seemed, the gigolo had made her rich and Douglas himself had never given her a penny or a kind word for the last fifteen years.

Papa makes her happy. Douglas shivered at a nonexistent draft. Damn this Boston weather anyway. There'd be snow before nightfall, if he wasn't mistaken. And he never was.

Or was he?

Chapter

61

Julian stood outside his father's room, watching Flora hold Jamie's hand, offer food which her husband refused, and tea, which he sipped lethargically. He was not even trying to pretend anymore. His hair was matted and dirty, his skin so pale it was translucent. He wore a stained nightshirt, open at the neck. His hands lay immobile at his sides. His eyes were glazed; he did not see Flora's misty eyes or the tears she could not keep from falling now and then.

Julian clenched his fists and fought the urge to beat them against the wall. He knew sometimes his father was in pain, but Jamie was not in pain now. He was drifting, smiling slightly at something no one else could hear. His eyes were focused on another time and place, another dream that was prettier than this one, easier to live inside than his own home, where his family loved him. Jamie was happy, in his ow. way, happier than he'd been in a very long time. Julian wanted to shake him hard, to make him see his wife's tear-streaked face, understand her grief, feel her tender, heartbreaking touch—just once.

Julian felt himself losing control. His clenched fists were shaking and he could not contain the frenzied feeling of helplessness that overpowered him. *It is not your grief that churns inside you and makes you feel this way, but your anger.*

When Flora rose, he slipped out of sight. He did not want her to see his fierce compassion, which he knew would break the last of her waning strength and bring her to her knees. Nor did he want her to guess at his rage. Every muscle in his arms was taut and ready to snap. He watched his stepmother disappear into the kitchen, took several deep breaths that did not begin to steady him, and entered his father's cave of webs and shadows.

Saylah was picking apples and dropping them into her apron, held up by the corners, when she felt a tremor go through her. Her skin grew clammy and her vision blurred. She had to get back to the house, craved the safety of the walls around her. She was choking on a fury she could not explain, driven by a need she did not understand. She ran recklessly, letting the apples fall to the ground, where they lay in the dappled sunlight, bruised and red and forgotten.

By the time she closed the front door behind her, the need had become a compulsion and she had to fight for breath. Then she heard voices in Jamie's room. She leaned against the wall, uncertain and afraid. But those voices had called her. She had to go, though every instinct cried out that she should run.

She stopped beyond the door, just out of sight, and saw Julian with his back turned. She could not see his face, but the rigid line of his body, the tendons in his neck, the unnatural angle of his head told her enough. "I need to talk to you," Julian said stiffly.

Jamie looked toward his son, but did not see him.

"I said—" Julian began.

Jamie reached out a frail hand and his son could not ignore it. He fell to his knees so suddenly that Saylah gasped and covered her mouth to disguise the sound.

Julian knelt, one hand holding his father's, one lost in the tangled covers, his head bent in supplication. "Papa!" he said in a strangled voice. It was the voice of a child, abandoned, frightened, desperate.

Saylah had forgotten how young Julian was, barely nineteen. He had fooled her with his competence, his will, his dedication, into thinking he was a man in control. But underneath, he was still a boy who had lost so much—his mother, his faith, all the years of carefree pleasure he should have had.

Jamie looked at him with affection, his feelings drawn in the fine blue veins beneath his skin. "Jules, my Jules." Jamie's eyes were full of tears. His boy had come back to him. His little boy, who sat on his bed, enraptured by his father's stories, while Simone sat nearby, holding Jamie's hand and humming.

Julian's head came up sharply. Only his mother had ever called him Jules. Then he saw the name his father's lips were forming. "Listen to me, Papa. You must listen. I'm Julian and I'm a man. Simone has been gone for a very long time. She left us alone, remember? She ran away."

In panic, Jamie gripped his son's fingers until his nails dug into Julian's skin. "But I can go back to her. If I close my eyes and concentrate, I can go back. And she's there, Julian. She's there, just as she used to be."

He smiled at the thought, at the gift that awaited him if he wished for it hard enough. The gift of remembering the happiness, of passing over the pain and anguish and betrayal and neither seeing its stark outline, hearing its harsh discord, nor feeling its sharp sting.

Julian prayed that Flora could not hear. *Why should you not be angry? Jamie will find peace and rest, but your sorrow will go on and on.* He was horrified by his father's vulnerability, the pitiful plea in his eyes. "Why must you go back? Why can't you stay with us?" When Jamie flinched and looked away, Julian took his shoulders. "Why?" he repeated. "Why?"

Jamie shook his head.

"You're not even trying," Julian cried. *You are angry because he has given up.* The slow-boiling rage rushed through him, and this time he could not fight it. "Damn you, you're not *trying*."

"You don't need me."

Julian stared. His father had spoken clearly and his eyes were focused on his son's flushed face. The memories had gone.

"You built this ranch and made it succeed. By yourself, Julian, without my help. Even before I hid from the sunlight, you didn't need me." Jamie had not spoken so lucidly for weeks.

Julian was alarmed by the abruptness of the change, the ease with which, at last, his father had come back to him. The anger tasted like bile in his throat. "You don't seem to understand." The effort of will it cost him to keep his voice steady took the last of his restraint. "I made the ranch succeed, barely. But I did it for you. Now you won't even look at it. You haven't seen this year's crop of apples. How healthy they are, and how plentiful. You don't even *know* what I've done for you here. You don't even bother to ask."

Jamie was stunned by his son's fury. The fog of confusion threatened to settle, but he shook his head until it left him. "I always thought you loved the land. More than I did, more than Edward. I just admired it. You seemed to understand it."

Julian released his father's hand. The huge, canopied bed with its curtains and silk fringe was closing around him, shutting out the air, cutting off his breath.

He rose and began to pace. Words roiled within him, but he did not want to speak them. He could never take them back again.

"Julian," Jamie whispered, "tell me. I need to know."

Julian whirled. "Then I'll tell you," he said, more harshly than he'd intended. "Yes, I love the land. It doesn't change. I can depend on it. It won't abandon me, ever. Not like my family does. First *Maman*, and now you. You've chosen to leave me, just like she did. All you could think about was your pain, not mine or Flora's or Theron's. Do you think it's any easier for us? Do you think I can ever forgive you for this—for choosing the past over your family, over me, your own son?"

By now Jamie was sitting up, his face a pallid mask in which his eyes were mist-filled wells of darkness. "I never meant to hurt you," he said carefully. "I meant to free you from my foolishness, my weakness."

Julian revolved on one heel, jaw clenched. "I never wanted freedom, not from you. And your dreams—what you call foolishness—are what kept me going all these years." He sighed and his rigid muscles went flaccid. "Don't you see, I have no magic in me, no vision. Just a strong back and willing hands. You were the one with the passion. All I had was obstinance and physical strength."

His voice broke and he turned away, staring blindly at the heavy drapes. "*You* gave me something to hope for, to reach for."

Jamie shook his head. "But there were so many dreams, so many visions unfulfilled."

For the second time, Julian spun to face his father. "But that's just it. You were never satisfied with what was. There was always another dream to work toward, another goal to seek. And now you've turned your back on everything. I worshipped you, didn't you know that? I never thought you were a coward, to give up so easily."

Through the haze of his own making, Jamie looked at his son, really looked. He saw hazel eyes burning with passion, pain and rage, a handsome face, racked now with sorrow. He saw the rigid line of his muscled body, the strength that flowed from him, even in anger. The hard work he had done, the struggle to survive had toughened him. He didn't even know how strong he was inside, how capable, how talented, how passionate. And he was just nineteen. When he was older, he would be a man that others gravitated to naturally, as they had once leaned toward Jamie. But Jamie had had nothing to give them but inspiration. Julian had the strength to give them more.

"I believed in you," Julian said passionately. *"Believe* in you. Just as I believed in my mother."

Now, at last, Jamie looked away.

> My spirit is too weak—mortality
> Weighs heavily on me like unwilling sleep,
> And each imagin'd pinnacle and steep
> Of godlike hardship, tells me I must die.

"Don't quote Keats to me, Papa. *Talk* to me. I need to understand."

Jamie stared at him, speechless, and Julian knelt again beside the bed. What more could he say? There was nothing here for Jamie anymore—except his family's love. And that was not enough. Julian buried his face in the sheets.

Jamie ran his fingers through the dark waves of his son's hair. "It's hard to learn to think of others when you've thought only of yourself all your life, as I have."

His hand on Julian's head was more than a caress; it was a benediction. "Just because I've suffered is not enough reason to make you, all of you, suffer too. Nothing gave me the right to do that. Forgive me if you can."

His face was gray around the edges from the searing pain in his chest. His son did not look up and so did not see. "I'm sorry, but I can't bear the pain anymore. I'm not strong like you. I'm weak, and the world is too cruel."

"Not *our* world," Julian muttered. "This ranch is ours. We can make it whatever we want it to be."

"But don't you see, we'd have to fight, and I'm tired of fighting. I can't do it anymore. Forgive me, but I can't. Not even for you."

Julian felt his father's hand in his hair, heard the misery in his voice, and the tension slowly left his body. The pain was blinding, unbearable. But the rage that had flared inside him for so long, bright, hot and destructive, slipped out with his tears—the only tears he had wept since he was ten years old and his mother had kissed him and left him behind.

Chapter

62

Saylah did not see Jamie wince in pain or Julian bury his head in the sheets. She had not heard a word since Julian had cried, *I believed in you. Believe in you.* The words rumbled through her like the harsh beat of a discordant drum, calling up things she did not wish to remember. Things she had buried so deep in her memory that she thought they would never touch her again.

But that cry for help, that unforgiving indictment, tore away layer after layer of protective gauze, leaving her exposed. Her skin grew damp with sweat and she realized she was shaking. Bewildered, she stared down at her outspread hands. They trembled like the feathers of a bird who has the desire to fly but not the strength to lift his wings. She drew her breath in and held it, fighting for control, but the shaking went on as the gauze was quickly, finally, ripped away.

She looked around wildly. She had to get away, to be alone.

She began to run, blinded by anger, despair, and deep gnawing pain. She had to escape it before it destroyed her. By instinct, she found the door, the clearing, the path to the woods. By instinct, gasping for breath, pleading for comfort, for peace, for the violence inside her to stop, she headed for the river—her refuge, her solace, the home of her heart.

She stumbled repeatedly, catching her feet on vines and clumps of bracken, keeping herself upright by clutching branches that pierced her skin with their needles and sharp twigs. The boughs of fir and cedar slapped her face, leaving long scratches in her soft brown skin.

Saylah didn't notice. All she knew, all she dared to think of, was the water, the healing water, the song of the rushing water. It kept her going, even when she tripped over a root and fell, sprawling, feet caught in kinnikinnick and twinflower.

Trying desperately to catch her breath, she scraped her way out of the dirt, hung for a moment, pressed to a silver birch, her chest heaving, her side shot through with pain. Then she ran again, through mist and chilling cold, reaching ahead to clear a path, choking on the scented air she had always loved.

The pain swept over her in waves. *I believed in you.* The words rang in her head, made her bend forward to stop the searing pain. But she could not stay still or the tumult began again, roaring through her like the sea in a dark and threatening storm.

Just when she thought she could not go on, she came upon the river and collapsed, gasping, her hands in the frigid water. The cold crawled up her arms but did not slow the chaos of fear and grief and desperation inside her.

"Damn you!" she shouted, stunned by the rasping sound of her own voice, the acrid taste of the words. "Damn you all!"

She was shaking so violently that she fell, curled in on herself, shuddering at the ugly rage that filled her body and spilled from her lips. It was so raw, so deep that she knew she could not survive it. Her body would fly apart, and her soul, torn to pieces by this fury that she could not name.

Was it the Ivys who had set this seething anger loose? But no. They had trusted her, shown her nothing but kindness. Then it struck her like a sharp wet slap across the face, in a moment of rage frozen in ice, which bore the shape and size and image of the Salish, her People, her family and her past.

"Damn you!" she shouted into the treetops until her voice echoed all through the forest. Her People, who had turned their backs on her, had stared with disbelief and horror in their eyes. Her People, who had called her Queen, then spit on her name, her title and her power as if it had never been—and could never be again. Her People, who had betrayed her because she could not make a miracle, just one more miracle in her blessed and magic life.

By now Saylah's lips were blue with cold and bitterness, her skin deep red. She had taken her hands from the water and it puddled on her skirt. She clutched her arms with chilled fingers and rocked, shuddering, unable to stop the storm. She remembered Shaula's eyes, the eyes of a stranger. She remembered Yeyi's rasping, fevered whisper.

It is easier to say you are weak than to believe the Changer is so cruel that he would let this happen. If I believe in you, I must doubt him. Tell me what to do. And Tanu, still alive, still full of power and magic and faith, had told her, *Believe what will give you peace,* Ladaila.

Saylah was weeping, fighting for breath as the tears ran down her reddened cheeks. She leaned toward the river, rocking with the pain, rocking and weeping, and cried, "Believe in *me!* Why couldn't you believe in me?"

She could see her face in the water, the face of someone she did not know and did not wish to know. "I believed in you, my People," she whispered. Not just Yeyi and her small black stone, but all of them. "I believed everything," she gasped. "Everything you said, every story told by firelight, every blessing you promised or placed in my hands. Everything!" But it hadn't been enough.

She sobbed uncontrollably, racked by a rage that had hidden in silence for three long years, denied, refused, unrecognized. Now that it had broken free, she could not stop it. She did not even try.

Her People had given her power, her strength and her purpose, along with their faith and affection. Then they had taken it away as easily as they snuffed the torches above their pallets before they went to sleep. They had taken everything and turned away; their fear had mattered more than her pain.

"I hate you!" she shouted. "I hate you all!" She had always hated them, since that moment when they stood and looked at her with empty eyes, and yet she had not known it. "I hate you!" she screamed like a child who knows no other words to say. "Please," she wept. "I'll never forgive you."

I'd no' want him to forget her, ye ken, only to forgive her, so he can be at peace. The memory of Flora's voice, calming, sane, gentle, startled Saylah out of her rage. She raised her head, her face streaked with tears, and listened.

On the wind, in the trees, in the fast-rippling water, she heard the songs of her People, remembered their faces and the illness that had taken everything they had—even the One they most believed in. *Can ye forgive them, do ye think?* Flora had asked her once.

She drew her knees to her chest, teeth chattering, shaking from the inside, where the black venom ran. Can you forgive them? Can you? She closed her eyes, rocking, trying to ease the agony, but it would not go. Yet she heard their voices all around her, knew each one, and welcomed it, even in the small, dark cocoon of her fury and pain.

She began to pray to the spirits of the woods; she could feel them nearby, watching and waiting. A twinge of sharp pain flared in her chest, and she knew then that she must forgive her People. If she didn't, she would not survive.

She was trembling, but the blindness had left her, and the terrifying force of her rage. Her breathing had begun to steady, though her skin was cold, so very cold. The weight of her anger held her down, pressing her into the soggy earth, where she would never breathe again.

She had to choose. She thought of Colchoté, who had always believed, even when she did not want his belief, but only his affection. She thought of Hawilquolas, who had sent her off to seek her own peace. She thought of Koleili, who had pretended all her life to be strong for her daughter's sake. Then, slowly, she was able to remember Yeyi with her head in Tanu's lap, spilling out her worries. Enis, kneeling with a small round stone, thanking her for making Kwahtie well. Eventually, she conjured the image of Tseikami's face—he who had deserted her before the others, knowing what he left behind.

She uncurled her body, slowly, laboriously, knelt on the riverbank, her hands spread over the water. "I do not know what my blessing is worth, but I give it to you, all of you, freely." The faces came to her, crowding her sight—Alteo and Kitkuni and Shaula and the others.

Saylah breathed deeply, then doubled over with a pain so sharp it took her breath and the beat of her heart. She had seen those faces so clearly that it hurt. In the air, in the wind, in the sighing of trees and the murmur of water came a voice. "Now that you have forgiven them, it is time to let them go."

She shook her head wildly. She could not bear that too, not now. To give up her family, her childhood, all she held sacred, all she had loved. She thought she had left them behind long ago, but it was not so. She carried the ghosts of her People on her shoulders. Not just the memory of their faces or their friendship or their deaths, but the crippling weight of their memory. Living or dead, in anger or love, she carried every Salish she had ever known. Quietly, without complaint, without knowledge, she had always done so.

It was time to take that last burden from her back. She rose, moving by instinct. One by one she picked up autumn leaves—some red, some pink, some yellow or gold or brown or deep rich rust—small ones, long ones, fat ones, curved and graceful, frail and dry, some curled at the edges, already close to death.

When she had enough, she returned to the singing river, with the remembered beat of the drums at its heart. She knelt on a dry patch of bracken and held the leaves up, then dropped them on the water one by one. "This one I call Wahan," she murmured, "and this one Enis, and this Kwahtie. This I call Yeyi, this Shaula, this Alteo, and this"—she brushed the leaf across her cheek—"this I call Kitkuni. This I call Tseikami, who betrayed me most of all, and this Twana, and Old Grandmother and Old Uncle."

The largest and brightest she kept for last. "This golden one, so thin I can see my fingers through the veins, I shall call Koleili, my mother. This red one, large and strong, not easily broken, I name Hawilquolas. And this leaf of rust, tough, resilient, yet beautiful to my eyes and the tips of my fingers on its surface, I shall call Colchoté."

She dropped the last one into the river and watched it join the others, turning, swirling, meeting and parting, skimming the clear, cool surface of the water, gliding like silent dancers until the river carried them out of sight.

Saylah sat on the bank, aching, frightened, alone and free, and at last she wept, hands buried in her heavy wool skirt, for the loss of all the people she had loved.

Paul and Theron were riding together on Paul's pony, practicing for the day when Theron could ride his own alone. They had been strangely silent for two healthy young boys. Paul was thinking about his father and Theron about his, and neither could express his own confused thoughts.

Finally, they put the pony in a stall with some water and oats and went into the woods on foot, looking for diversion. Suddenly, Paul gripped Theron's shoulder. "Shh! Someone's crying."

Theron frowned, peering through trees and underbrush and falling leaves toward the harsh, rasping sound. "Is it Mama?"

He looked so upset that Paul put his arm around the younger boy's shoulders. "I don't think so. I just saw her in the kitchen window when we put *Mo-run* away."

"Well, who, then?" Theron demanded impatiently. He was over-wrought with forebodings and fears and dull aching pain and hardly knew what he said anymore.

Paul didn't mind his friend's sharp tone. He had become used to brittle, frayed tempers in the past few weeks. "Let's go see," he suggested. He knew Theron wouldn't be satisfied until he'd solved the mystery, and besides, it gave Paul something to do besides cower at home in the shadows, waiting for the world to come crashing down around him.

Theron followed his friend through the trees, hands pushed deep into his trouser pockets. It made him feel a little safer, pushing his hands as far as they'd go into the warm lining. As they went, the sobbing grew louder, then began to fade.

Paul motioned for him to stop behind a giant garry oak, and Theron clutched the rough bark, sticking his head around the trunk. He gasped and stuck his fist in his mouth when he saw Saylah crouched beside the river, her hands covered with mud, her gown wet with water and tears, her brown face streaked and swollen. Though Paul grabbed his arm, he pulled away.

"Saylah!" He cried in alarm and more than a little fear. "You've been crying."

Paul followed Theron reluctantly. "I'm sorry," he said awkwardly, shifting from one foot to the other. "We didn't mean to jump out at you. It's just that we heard someone crying, and we thought—"

"You thought what?" Saylah asked, burying her hands in her lap. Her voice shook and she concentrated on keeping her body still, her turmoil hidden. Theron's thunderous expression frightened her.

"But you never cry!" he exclaimed vehemently. "Never!"

Paul shook his head in warning, but Theron wasn't looking.

"Because you do not see me does not mean I do not weep." But Theron was right. She had not wept since the day when she had sat beside Colchoté and grieved for her mother and the father of her heart and her friend. That day she had learned that although Tanu was dead, she could not disappear or be forgotten. All she could do was leave behind the place in which she had been born, the People who had made her Queen.

Three years of sorrow and anger had come spilling out as she knelt on the marshy bank. Saylah had lost track of the movement of the sun. She did not know how long she had crouched there, but the moisture had crept through her heavy wool gown to the skin underneath. She was chilled and exhausted, too tired to explain what this child would not understand. Yet Theron stood there, watching her belligerently.

"Is it because of Papa?" he demanded. "Is that why you're crying? Did something happen to Papa?" His face was very white.

Saylah sighed. "No, Theron. Your father is the same. It was an old grief, that is all. An old grief that had collected too many tears. I could not hold them back anymore." She was cold inside as well as out, and empty. The rage, the grief, even the hatred had filled her until today, made her believe she was whole and strong and real.

Now she knew what it was to be truly alone—without her People, her past, the stories and spirits and the beat of ancient drums. Now there was nothing. She was hollow. Her soul had floated down the river with the swirling autumn leaves.

Theron's lower lip began to tremble. "But you never cry," he repeated stubbornly. "You're Saylah."

—— 431 ——

He spoke as if Saylah were someone, not an empty shell so light and without substance that a sudden wind would carry her away. There was no longer anything to hold her down. Except for Theron and Flora and Jamie.

She began to shake and bent toward the river to rinse her face in the icy water. She couldn't let Theron see how barren she was. *You must carry no doubts in your heart. They will weaken you, and we need you strong and wise and whole.*

"Don't leave me!" Theron shouted. He watched the water stream over Saylah's dark skin, saw her shiver and stare sightlessly before her. "Don't!" he shrieked.

Paul stared at his friend, perplexed. Theron was behaving very badly. "I think we should go," the older boy said firmly.

Theron stood his ground, arms crossed, legs wide apart, issuing a challenge. "I won't go without Saylah."

She motioned him toward her. He came, reluctantly, and she put her hand on his shoulder. "I cannot go back with these eyes to betray me. The others would not understand."

Her touch seemed to calm him, change him. Theron hugged her, clasped his dirty hands around her neck. "So what? They can't make you tell them what's wrong. Just say it's private."

He whimpered as she closed her arms around him, holding him close. Poor Theron, who was told nothing. He must want to talk about Jamie very much, about the illness and his mother's frozen smile and Julian's fury. But no one ever thought to explain. That's why he had become so demanding. He did not know how else to get what he so desperately needed.

"I'm scared," he whispered. "More scared than I was of the cougar." He raised his head enough to see her face clearly. "Is my papa going to die?"

She could not lie to him, despite the hope that burned in his blue eyes. "Yes, Theron, he is."

"But *why?*" He beat his small fists helplessly against her shoulder. "Why?"

"Because his heart is not strong enough to keep him alive."

The hope flickered once, then disappeared, and Theron buried his head in her long black hair. Paul felt tears burning his own eyes and decided it was time to go. He slipped away silently.

"I'm scared," Theron repeated in a whisper.

"Do not be," she said. "When Jamie is dead, he will be happier, and free of pain. You want that for him, do you not?"

The boy looked up through bleary eyes. "I guess so." He tightened his hands around her neck. "But what'll we do, Saylah?"

"You will go on. You do not believe me now, but it is true. You will go on and the pain will slowly begin to ease, and someday you will smile when you think of Jamie. That is when you will know that the grief has left you, though sorrow lingers."

Theron blinked back tears. She was talking to him just like she talked to Julian, not like he was a baby who couldn't understand. "Do you promise?" he asked, lower lip quivering.

"That I will promise."

She held him for a long time, because she liked the weight of his small body, reminding her of her promise and her duty. His warmth was a gift that began to dissipate the chill in her hollow body.

Finally, Theron raised his head, frowning. "If someday it will be all right, why were you crying?"

Saylah smiled sadly. He could not really understand. Not yet. "I will tell you, but I do not wish for the others to know. I was grieving for my People." Even now the word came out garbled and she fought back tears.

Theron's eyes lit up. "You mean it's a secret?"

Saylah gave him a crooked half-smile. "It is secret and to me it is sacred. Will you promise not to speak of this?"

"I promise!"

She smoothed his dusty hair back from his forehead. "I thank you," she said. "And I make you a promise. If you have a question or you do not understand, come to me. I will tell you what I can. I know you are no longer a child in here." She tapped his chest. "You should know what the others know."

Theron snuggled up to her, not caring that her dress was sodden, her face swollen and red. He held on as if to let go would be to tumble backward into gloom and sorrow and confusion. As if, once he fell, he would never stop falling until the darkness swallowed him and he could not see the light.

Chapter
63

That night the Ivys sat around the table in the kitchen with the huge fire crackling behind them. There was duck for dinner, with potatoes, carrots, bannock cakes, gingerbread and dried berries for dessert.

"I know you were with Jamie all morning," Saylah said, grateful for the food, though it could not begin to fill the emptiness inside her. "You should not have taken so much time over dinner."

Flora looked up wanly, pretending she did not see the redness in Saylah's eyes, her puffy lids, the unnatural color of her cheeks. "I was happy to do it. It gave me somethin' to keep my mind busy."

She had shined the silverware and piled wood by the huge stone fireplace that was the most cheerful spot in the room. Julian looked toward it longingly. He wanted to curl up on one of Flora's flowered cushions and let the heat and light invade him until the sweat broke out on his skin. He would let it run down his neck into his collar, down his chest and his back without wiping it away. He would feel cleaner then, lighter.

He glanced at Saylah, who would not meet his gaze. "I spoke to Papa today," he said.

"I know." She did not know how she managed the simple words. She only knew she could not look into his eyes and see that poignant look of something shared but unspoken.

"I'm glad ye spent some time with him," Flora interrupted, sensing Saylah's unease. "He was tired after ye'd gone, but he seemed more at peace." She reached over to pat her stepson's hand. "If only I could stop his pain as well." She sighed. "But even Saylah can no' be doin' that."

Theron's fork clattered on the table. "Saylah can do anything," he said solemnly. "But when can I talk to Papa? I've waited and waited, but he's always too tired or asleep or something." Yesterday he would have whined or shouted; now he just looked pleadingly at his mother.

Flora opened her mouth to object, but saw Saylah nod slowly. "Well, tonight then, if ye promise no' to upset him."

Julian choked on his cider, but no one seemed to notice.

"I'm practically grown-up," Theron declared. "I'll be very careful. Won't I, Saylah?"

"I believe you will," she said.

"I might even make him laugh." The boy picked up his abandoned fork and attacked his dinner with renewed energy.

Julian stared miserably into his plate. *He* had not made his father laugh, but had caused him more pain. He turned to Saylah, but she would not look at him.

After dinner, when the dishes had been washed, dried and placed back on the shelves, Theron ran off to comb his hair before making his visit to Jamie.

"I'll go warm myself before the fire out there, where I can put my feet up and yet be hearin' Jamie if he calls." Flora smiled at Saylah and Julian and left them alone.

They pulled up chairs in front of the fire with coffee mugs in their cold hands. Saylah did not want to be there, but could not bring herself to flee. She felt Julian waiting and searched for some comfort to give him. But the well of words inside her had run dry and she began several times before an answer came. "Sometimes there are hard, unpleasant things that you cannot hold inside, even if it means hurting another."

Julian leaned forward, his palms cupped around the warm mug, the firelight caressing the chiseled features of his face. "I went to speak to him today—I knew I'd waited too long, that there was too much boiling inside me. I didn't believe you when you said I was angry, but you were right, as always."

Saylah's eyes ached with dry tears. "I am not always right. I have told you that before. But I know that no one can heal Jamie's spirit, no matter how much they love him."

"No." It was not easy for him to admit, even to Saylah, even now. Julian thought with an ache of despair of the long afternoon spent at his father's side, talking of the past—of Simone and the deer and building the house, of Flora, of Theron's birth, of all the good memories—until he saw Jamie begin to slip away. He had left his father smiling, staring at the blank wall where, for him, the world was painted in vibrant color. Julian would not forget the sweetness of the smile as long as he lived. It had broken his heart.

"I've failed too," he said bitterly. "I'm giving up just like he is." He held out his hands and stared at them, looking for the answer in the scars that criss-crossed his palms. His helplessness hurt far more than his anger.

Saylah reached out to cover his hand. "Kindness is not failure, Julian, unless you allow it to be so."

He felt the touch of her hand all through his body and did not move for fear she would withdraw it. Though he was acutely aware of the woman beside him, he continued to talk of his father. Just now, it was safer.

"If the dream is so necessary, why can't he find it again?"

Saylah shook her head. Julian was stubborn. He would cling to hope until the thread broke away in his hand. In the deep hollow well that was her soul tonight, she admired him for that, though it would bring him pain. She began to move forward and back in the rocking chair, her bare feet touching the polished wood floor. "Have you ever awakened from a pleasant dream and tried to sleep again, to bring it back? But you cannot get it back. It is gone the moment your eyelids flutter open and the light of morning filters in."

Julian followed the slow, creaking motion of the chair. "I tried to make it real for him. I thought that I *could* bring it back."

Saylah winced at the remorse in his voice. When would he stop blaming himself? When would he learn to go forward? She stopped, her feet flat on the floor. Did she want him to go forward as she had, from a world rich in culture and feeling and song to a world without meaning or rhythm or depth? "Jamie would have to do that for himself, and he cannot. He is safe in the cocoon of his memories. It is the only way he can survive."

Glowering into the flames, Julian snapped, "By dying?"

Saylah began to rock again. She needed the motion, the constant soothing creak of the old, well-worn chair. "Sometimes I think your life would be easier if you were Salish." The words fell easily from her lips, though she did not know what made her speak them. Julian had raised his head, ceased staring blankly into the fire. She had to go on now.

"The Salish do not fear death, but the pain and disease that comes before it. They believe a person's soul floats away from the body, into the air. Only the empty shell is buried high in a tree. The spirit wanders free until the Changer makes it live again, as a rabbit or deer or a gurgling stream. Each vine, each fern, each aged and furrowed tree has a spirit that was once man or woman or child. The Salish's dead ancestors do not leave them; they hover nearby in their new forms, protecting the People from harm.

"Death is not even sleep to them; it is birth and life and all that grows and prospers."

Julian peered at her through narrowed eyes. "I've heard the Indians wail and moan over a body. I've even seen them weep."

"It is part of the ritual to release their human pain. Even if they do not fear the world the soul will enter, they will miss the person they cared for—their friend, wife, child. They grieve deeply, Julian, and weep many tears."

For the first time since he'd known her, she had spoken of the Salish as "they" not "we." He wanted to ask why, but some instinct kept him silent. He watched her rocking, her toes pushing against the floor, her hair coming loose from its braid, as usual. He stiffened, forgot his own distress, and noticed the signs of her tears. He felt an icy fear that stopped his heart.

How could he have been so blind, so absorbed in himself that he did not see her pain? Once more she had become a stranger; something fundamental and necessary had changed in her. Her green eyes were perfectly clear, perfectly still, perfectly vacant. Yet her voice had been so warm, so convincing.

Julian found it difficult to breathe. He set his mug on the floor and clasped the arms of his chair, trying to dispel the sense of foreboding that clutched at him. "Saylah!" he cried.

She looked up, intent, wary, alert. Julian's cry had gone through her like a shard of ice from a winter pond. She began to shiver, clasped her hands tightly in her lap. When he rose and took those hands, drew her up from the chair, she did not resist. She could not. Her strength had left her along with her music.

Julian stared into her eyes and shuddered. Impulsively, he pulled her against him. He closed his arms around her and she leaned into him, craving his warmth, the touch of his breath on her clammy skin. That breath, scented with hot coffee and blueberries, would tell her she was real and alive.

She raised her head, Julian lowered his, and their lips met, not gently, but desperately, clinging, warm and moist, as they sought reassurance one from the other.

The kiss shook Saylah deeply; something dark and frightening moved within her. Her skin was so sensitive that his lightest touch made her want to cry out, to push away the dark thing, the thing moving upward from her hips to her chest and her throat.

Julian twined his fingers in her hair and despite her fear, she sighed as he brushed the nape of her neck. With his other hand, he caressed her back, willing the life back into her eyes, willing her to feel his need and share it.

He teased her mouth, nibbling at her lower lip, flicking his tongue along the sensuous fullness. The fire was hot on his back, and he turned so it would reach her and the chill would leave her body, which trembled in his arms.

Against her will, Saylah touched his chest through the flannel of his shirt, felt his heartbeat, strong and even on her palm. She felt his lips on hers, asking things of her which she had never given, did not know how to give. Especially now that she was empty.

With her hair wound around his hand, he nuzzled her neck, kissed the hollow at the base of her throat, moaned her name into her cool brown skin.

Saylah began to shiver as the dark thing moved more wildly inside her and Julian raised his head. Struggling against the lure of his arms, her own need, and the memory of his seeking lips on hers, she broke away, gasping, shuddering—chilled and frozen by the whirling darkness.

Julian stood, chest heaving, and demanded, "What, in God's name, are you so afraid of?"

Saylah looked him in the eye, sought the careful lies, the lies of protection, the veil of gentle, soothing lies, but they were gone. "I am afraid that it is not true," she said.

"What isn't true?" Confused, frustrated, angry, he swallowed huge gulps of air that did not reach his lungs.

She could not stop herself. "Everything I believe in, all that is sacred. I am afraid that none of it is true."

He gasped and stumbled, because, suddenly, there was nothing to hold him upright. "Then it's not Jamie who's leaving us," he choked at last. "It's *you*. You're the one who made us laugh and taught us and gave us hope. If everything you believe is a lie, then so is everything you've done. And so are you."

He could not bear to look at her; it hurt too much. He left the room without a word and did not see her kneel on the smudged floor. She crawled, shivering and blind, toward the one thing she believed in and worshipped still—the light and heat of the golden-red fire.

Chapter

⟹⊲ 64 ⊳⟸

In Edward's dream, he and Jamie wandered among the trees that circled a deep blue lake near Seattle. They were singing, thinking of their wives, left behind.

It was July, the sky was dappled with clouds, the water lapped gently on the shore; they surveyed with pleasure the landscape, the undulating lake, the tiny caps of white.

Jamie's voice floated out over the water, where white streaks of cloud were reflected, as in a shifting mirror. He leaned closer to try to touch one, but the bank gave way beneath him. He fell into the water, which snaked around him, pressing down his arms as he reached for the shore. He struggled, gasping, while the streaks of white shattered and whirled in a circling funnel with Jamie at its center.

Edward stood, horrified, on the bank. He started to reach out to help, but was frozen with revulsion. Jamie was his dearest friend, fighting desperately for his life, but Edward could not bear to touch him.

For a long time, he stood with his hand half outstretched, then let it fall to his side. He shuddered at the image of his friend's frantic face, clenched his fists until raw pain shot up his arms.

But he could not make himself reach over that clear blue water.

Jamie choked as he flailed in the vortex that was sucking him under. He tried to shout, but no sound came. He saw Edward take a step back, drop his arm. Jamie's eyes widened in disbelief and a terrible, gnawing hurt. Then he slid beneath the blue, roiling surface of the lake and did not rise again.

Suddenly the water was everywhere, filling Edward's mouth, his nose, pressing against his temples. The pain was fierce, unbearable. The water rose above his head and he could not breathe, he could not fight free, he could not stop the endless, awful pain.

He awoke, thrashing in the sheets, covered in sweat, gasping for breath. A dark foreboding clutched at his chest until he thought his lungs would burst. He had to get away. He had to try to outrun it.

Sophia reached for him, but he did not see her. He rose, threw on the clothes he had worn the day before, left his wife with her hand outstretched and no one there to take it.

Edward ran down the stairs two at a time. Let her be there, he pleaded silently. He could not be alone now; he would fall apart, shatter into thousands of dangerous glittering shards.

He threw open the front door and stepped into the thick morning mist. Around the corner of the house, he heard a movement, and then she was beside him, the Indian girl with the flowers in her hair. He took her hand and pressed it to his chest to slow the thunderous beating of his heart.

She had known he would need her and was there, as always, waiting.

They stood without speaking, hands pressed against his heart, until he knew that he was safe. He could breathe again. He was not going to die.

From the sofa in the parlor, Paul watched his father disappear into the mist with the Indian girl. When they had gone, he let the satin curtain slip from his fingers. Arms wrapped around his knees, he pulled his legs close to his body, trying to hold in the pain, the anger, the disgust that overwhelmed him. But he could not do it.

Saylah dreamed of still water, of starlight through the branches, the voice of the wind. She wanted desperately to hear that voice, to understand the words, but the sound rose too high above the trees, beyond her grasp.

She awakened shivering. The emptiness had not left her, had not been filled in her restless sleep. It was a constant reminder of all she had been and could no longer be, an echo of Julian's hurt, bewildered voice. *If everything you believe is a lie, then so is everything you've done. And so are you.*

It was true. Right now, this moment, it was true.

She rose, naked, to sit beside her carved cedar chest. Reverently, she picked up each stone, smoothed it with her fingertips, held it to her cheek, seeking the magic that did not come. These were merely stones, lifeless, cold, unyielding. Even the black stone with a white feather that had carried Yeyi's soul was empty now.

Saylah blinked, though there were no tears. This bleakness, this bewildered, hollow feeling was beyond tears, beyond the anguish she felt as she ran her hand over the rattles and shells, the small buckskin drum. Today the pieces of her past were lifeless; they had no meaning.

"Saylah?" Flora called up the stairs. "Do ye think ye might be comin' down soon? Julian's already gone out, we've a visitor, and I'm no' wantin' to leave Jamie alone."

"I will come," Saylah replied, astounded that her voice was no different. There was nothing in Flora's tone to alarm her, yet all at once she was full of dread.

She dressed quickly, her fingers clumsy with familiar buttons, her pulse beating out a persistent warning. She braided her hair and hurried downstairs to the kitchen. She would take Jamie his morning tea and sit with him for a while, pray that he did not notice how little of her there was beside him. Pray that this feeling was not a premonition, that it would leave her as the ghosts of her People had left her—alone and in silence.

She stopped when she saw a strange man seated at the table.

"Och, there ye are. Saylah, 'tis Father Bouchard, come to look in on Jamie. Is he no' kind?"

"Very kind." Her tone was flat, without inflection. Saylah looked at the man with thick gray hair and a long, uncut beard which did not quite cover his religious collar. Nor did his bushy eyebrows disguise his piercing silver eyes. She had met many priests at the missionary school, but had not seen this man's face before, had never even heard his name.

Yet she hated him on sight. Hated him, feared him, and wanted him gone. But the feelings were not her own. "Julian," she whispered in agitation. She opened her mouth to speak and remembered she had no power, no instinct she could trust, no way to explain to Flora how strongly Julian felt, how strongly Saylah felt the need to do this thing for him. She could not believe her own feelings, let alone Julian's. What if he were right and they were nothing more than lies?

Julian was up before dawn, saddling Phoenix as light and color crept into the sky. Bent low above the horse's neck, he rode through half-light touched with lilac, trying to outrun his thoughts. He headed for Elk Lake, hoping to find quiet in the broad expanse of blue-gray water, the clear waves lapping gently on the sandy shore.

But the motion of the heaving horse, the damp morning air heavy with the scent of pine, could not help him escape the memory of Saylah's stricken face when she told him of her fear. He remembered with sick dread the icy panic that had gripped him, closed his eyes against the sound of his cruelty, born of his own fear. *Everything you've done is a lie. And so are you.* The worst part, the part that made his stomach twist and churn, was the knowledge that she had believed him, that she had not fought back, denied his accusation or slapped his face in fury.

Something had snapped in Saylah the day before—something fragile and infinitely rare. Julian twisted the reins until they cut into his palms. She had lost her faith, her magic. He kicked Phoenix's sides and the animal plunged through slashing fir branches and oak and aspen, over trailing vines and rotting, moss-covered logs and the mud that lingered after the past night's rain.

Julian thought he might be ill. Saylah had been pale, frightened and broken, and he had offered her, not kindness, but the brutal cut of a sharp-edged knife. He realized he was shaking. He had forgotten his greatcoat and the air was bitingly cold. He could not bear the thought of how much he had hurt her.

He had nearly reached the lake when he sat upright, pulled sharply on the reins. He had to go back. "Julian." He heard his name in the thick morning mist, a plea, a warning, a question all at once.

Julian glanced around, but nothing stirred except the languid branches of the trees. When he lifted the reins, he felt a surge of inexplicable anger, then hatred, deep and bitter. A sense of foreboding engulfed him, a shadow on the winter-cold ground. In an instant, he had wheeled Phoenix and started toward home, driven by an urgency he could not understand.

When he reached the last hill before the clearing, dimly through the trees, he saw a burro tied to the rail in front of the house. Julian paused, though there was no sound, no movement, no threat. Yet the urgency had become panic—uncontrollable and all-consuming.

Julian peered more closely at the animal, confused by his feelings. Then it hit him; he knew who owned the burro.

"No!" Julian shouted into the wind and shifting fog. "No!" In desperation, he kicked the horse forward, oblivious of the uneven ground or the muddy tracks of wagons or thrusting roots. He had to get back, to get that man out of the house, to wipe the priest's face from his memory so he need never think of it again.

He had to hurry or he would be too late. He could not let that happen. Not again.

After a little, when Edward lay beside the Indian girl, his hunger eased but not his tension, he reached for her again. She was not there. He sat up abruptly, heart pounding, to find her sitting on a flat boulder, watching him pensively.

"Come back," he said. "I want—"

The girl shook her head. "It is not that you want, Edward Ashton, but that you need. And what you need I cannot give."

Startled, he fought to conceal his distress. He knew what she was going to say; he had said it many times himself. He grew bored easily once he knew a woman's body, once she no longer had the power to make him forget. It struck him for the first time that he should have left this girl long since. But something drew him back to her again and again. Perhaps, as he had told Julian, it was the secrets in her eyes. He felt frightened suddenly, bereft. He wanted to protest, but his pride would not let him.

She sensed his pain, felt it in her own chest, tight with pity. "It is time," she said, each word distinct and separate from the other, "that you learn my name."

Edward blinked at her, confused and close to panic.

"I am not a ghost or a spirit, I am not called Skayu or the Girl with the Flowers in Her Hair. The People call me Alida. Because I will not see you again, I wanted you to know."

Reaching out to grasp her hand, he murmured, "I'll learn your name if you like."

Alida wanted to weep with compassion. Her desire for him had dwindled, though his hands and his urgent hunger could always make her respond. She was surprised by that, surprised that, as he had told her many times, she would not forget how he had touched her, the passion he had made her feel. But now the pity was greater than the pleasure. She carried it on her shoulders like a flat, heavy stone. "If you began to use my name, you would become a different man, and I do not think you are ready for that." She spoke gently, trying to soothe the turmoil that smoldered and flared, flared and smoldered in his eyes.

Holding his hand lightly in hers, she whispered, "I can give you my body, but that is no longer enough."

"How do you know what I need?" He just managed to keep the panic from his voice.

"Perhaps I know what you do *not* need." She stared at the lines in his

—— 443 ——

palm, traced them with a fingertip. She did not look up because she could not bear to see his pain. She was moved by anyone who suffered, touched by their sorrow. But Edward moved her most deeply, because she could not heal his pain. She had to stop trying, or in the end, his sorrow would become her own. "I must go from you, Edward Ashton," she said, "because inside you burn, and I can no longer quench the flames."

She rose and he stared at her in disbelief. She was going to walk away and he knew, even in the grip of his frenzy, that she would never once look back. There were other women, he reminded himself. There was always Sophia. "Don't go! I'll tell you what I did to Jamie," he cried. Perhaps if he told her the truth, she would stay. Women always wanted to comfort a man who confessed a weakness—any weakness.

Alida paused, not because she wanted to know what had happened between the two men, but because she heard the desperation in Edward's plea. He needed very badly to tell someone about the guilt that was eating away at him, that had made him into a distorted image of himself in the past few weeks. To listen just once more; this single thing she could do for him. She seated herself cross-legged beside him. "Speak then," she said. "But speak the truth."

Now that she sat watching him with her wide black eyes, he hesitated. Then she smiled, touched his hand, and he knew she was the only person he *could* tell—the only one not involved and who would not blame him. He stared at the thick green bracken, glimmering with drops of dew.

"Over a year ago," he began, "we went to Seattle, Jamie and I, to see about buying some land. I'd heard we could make quite a profit, and I'd made many such investments before, and many since. But this time Jamie wanted to go with me. He wanted to take the risk too."

He paused, tugging up bits of broken fern, rubbing them between his fingers. He could feel the girl's gaze upon him, but did not look at her. His eyes were glazed and his voice slurred. "The deal was more complicated than I'd imagined, and we were working with an unscrupulous man. I'd always known that, but Jamie trusted everyone. He didn't want to believe in evil or cruelty or corruption. So the man decided to cut him out, to take his money and give him nothing back. He called my friend a fool, right to my face, and I didn't—" He broke off, staring blindly at the trees and boulders crowding the edges of the glade.

"You did not what? Defend him?"

Somehow, coming from her lips, the words were not so harsh or ugly. Edward gripped Alida's hand, and the poison buried inside him for so long came spilling out into the daylight. "I didn't strike the man with my fist for maligning my closest friend, I didn't tell him what I thought of him.

I just stood there and did not protest when I realized what he meant to do."

Alida nodded gravely. "Did you tell Jamie the truth?"

Edward scowled. "I did. I don't know why, even now. I'd lied to him before, but that time—I couldn't. I felt so powerless, so dirty. And the way Jamie looked at me . . ." He trailed off miserably.

"How did he look at you?" The girl felt tears in her eyes that never wept and was amazed by her empathy for Jamie, her compassion for Edward.

He flinched, remembering vividly the expression in Jamie's eyes that night. "He'd always refused to see the ugliness all around him, but when I told him his money was gone but mine was not, when I told him he'd been cheated, he opened his eyes wide, and the first thing he saw, *really* saw, was my face. He looked at me as if all the brutality he had refused to recognize was suddenly in me, a part of *me*. The dreams fell from his eyes that night and the truth—the tragic, cruel truth—was me, his friend who had betrayed him.

"I remember he called out for Simone in anguish, staring into *my* eyes. I realized then that though she'd been gone for years, he'd never recognized her betrayal. He knew it would destroy him. But that night, he looked at me and saw her face, lost to him forever, so that even *her* sin became mine. He saw reflected in my eyes the woman who had left him."

"Did you tell him you had been wrong, ask for his forgiveness and try to make him see things as they really were?"

Edward bowed his head. "I couldn't. Not while he stared at me in such horror. And later—well, it was too late. That's why he gave up, because of that moment when I forced open his eyes, and because I never made it right. That's why he's dying now."

Alida stiffened. "No," she said. "You are wrong."

"What do you know about it?"

She squared her shoulders. "I know it is a little thing, what you did to your friend. It was Jamie who made it more, and you who let him. I know that Jamie Ivy is an extraordinary man. He is special, blessed. No one on earth is powerful enough to take his will to live. Not even you."

Edward wanted to believe her, but he couldn't. "You didn't see the look in his eyes. You don't know what it's been like—"

"I have seen your suffering," she murmured, "as I have seen his. The two are not the same. You have told me the thing which has made you unhappy, restless, hostile over the past moon, but that is not the thing which makes you burn. That burrowed within you long before you met Jamie Ivy, I think."

Edward did not really hear her. He felt a strange lightness in his head, like a cumbersome weight had been lifted away. He had wanted to tell someone—Sophia, Flora—but he had been a coward. He could not have borne it if they looked at him as Jamie had. He would never forget those brown eyes full of pain and horror and fear. Then Alida's warning penetrated his turbulent thoughts. "But I've told you the truth. Surely now you'll stay with me. I've told no one else, ever. Just you."

Alida bowed her head. "I am honored, but I say again, it is only part of the truth—the part you understand. There is more, and it is that which I cannot face." She rose for the second time, for the second time started away.

"Don't go!" he repeated. *Don't leave me alone with my demons*, he added silently. But she heard.

Alida's smile was bittersweet. "Forgive me," she said. "I wanted to be more for you, but I could never be enough." Without a sound, with less than a whisper of motion, she was gone, consumed by the forest from which she had once come.

Chapter
65

Flora stood at the foot of her husband's bed, watching with despair his shallow breathing, the gray cast of his skin, the glazed look in his eyes. He must have had another attack during the night. Thank God the priest was there.

She glanced at Saylah, who stood at Jamie's bedside as she had all morning. She had not eaten, had not paused to make his tea. When Father Bouchard moved toward Jamie's room, Saylah had followed, silent and obdurate. Flora did not protest, but she was curious. The girl was behaving oddly, not speaking, just waiting. Her wary expression told Flora that Saylah herself was not certain what she waited for.

Jamie had looked at the priest just once. He had glanced up, squinted in the dim light, and frowned. When he tried to speak, Saylah leaned down, her ear near his dry, parted lips. All she heard was "Simone. No. Wrong."

It wasn't much, but enough to tell her that perhaps, after all, her instincts had been correct.

"I must be alone with him," Father Bouchard said firmly. He had draped his embroidered vestments over his robe, drawing out the heavy jeweled crucifix he wore around his neck. His hands were folded over a Bible, a rosary and a cross.

"Why must you be alone?" Saylah demanded.

"To give him extreme unction. To perform the last rites." He turned imploringly to Flora.

Flora had seen her husband's distorted face as he tried to speak, and as a Scot, she had never learned to like Catholics overmuch. "Saylah cares for Jamie. It is her choice."

"It is *not* her choice!" Father Bouchard cried, forgetting his meek demeanor. "It's the law of the holy Catholic Church. Richard James Ivy must be given the last rites."

"But he may no' die for a long time yet," Flora said as firmly as she could.

The Father sighed heavily. "I will be here for a single day. There are others who need me. If this man is to have the last rites performed, it must be now."

"What are last rites?" Saylah asked stiffly.

Father Bouchard cleared his throat. "I must cleanse him of his sins before he dies so he has a chance to enter heaven." His tone implied it would probably do no good; his eyes blazed the message clear and coldly—Jamie Ivy was going to hell. "As a man of God, I must do what I can."

Saylah nearly choked on her rage, so hot and quick that it stunned her. "This man has committed no sin. There is nothing for which he must be forgiven. All he has is pain and regret. Can you not see that?" She pointed to the beautiful face on the pillow, a face already of another world.

Father Bouchard did not bother to look at Jamie. "You don't know his history. It's not a pleasant one. He has been touched and corrupted by evil, I fear."

Drawing a deep breath, Saylah confronted the priest. "That is not true. I see what I must know in Jamie's eyes, which are full of kindness and a sadness greater than you can understand. I know he has never willingly hurt anyone, though others have often hurt him. He has never sought revenge, never found relief in anger. He loves his family, would do anything for them." She spoke softly, out of deference for Jamie.

"He has not lived according to the laws of God, keeping himself pure, avoiding sin, obeying the sacraments so he will be worthy to enter the afterlife, which all good Catholics seek."

For a moment, Saylah was speechless. "Your religion is very strange," she said in a dangerously low voice.

Just then Julian burst into the room, face red with fury, but when he saw Saylah blocking the priest's path, he paused. Her jaw was rigid with determination, her eyes bright with anger. Gripping the doorknob tightly, Julian waited.

Saylah was aware of his presence, but did not look up. "In the world of the Salish, the only sin we can commit is to lose respect for living things, for the spirits inside them, for the Changer who made earth and sky and waters, and for those things themselves. This we believe.

"Our only obligation is to absorb the wonders with which we have been blessed, to open our eyes, our hearts and senses to the beauty in the world, to feel every moment of our living on the earth."

The priest tried to interrupt, but Saylah ignored him. "We do not expect our People to be perfect. Mistakes are made, recompense is given. We are taught to laugh at our own weakness, but there are no priests to do it for us. Our spirit must be pure; no one else can cleanse it if it is not so. Who made you believe you had such power?"

"The Pope of Rome and the Catholic Church, which see you savages for what you are. We are civilized. *We* are blessed."

"It does not sound that way to me." Before he could contradict her, she plunged on. "The Salish do not concern themselves with death until it comes. We do not live our lives so that someday we die properly. That would be to stare down a dark tunnel and see nothing but the blackness, while all around the tunnel there is light and life and growth.

"We do not live to die, nor do we cast another's soul into darkness. It is difficult enough to shape our own."

Shrugging, Father Bouchard muttered, "What has that to do with me?"

"Nothing," Saylah replied. "That is what I mean. I do not think you are wanted here. I know you are not needed. Jamie Ivy's spirit will fly, no matter how hard you try to weight it to the ground."

She looked at Flora, who nodded emphatically, then to Julian, who stared, open-mouthed. He could not hide his admiration and relief. "Saylah speaks for all of us," he said. Theron had heard the commotion and rushed in wearing pajamas, hair standing on end, to see what had happened. Julian took his little brother's hand.

"My father needs his family and his memories. He doesn't need you. I think you should go." He spoke calmly, but his voice quavered and he squeezed Theron's hand to distract himself.

"Ouch!" his brother cried. "Who's that man? He dresses funny."

"His name is Father Bouchard," Flora told her son, "and 'tis nothin' to us how he dresses, since he's leavin' now. Are ye no' on your way, Father?"

The priest sputtered, clutched his Bible, turned red in the face, but he could not argue against all of them. At the door he stopped. "Say what you like," he snapped, "Jamie Ivy is going straight to Hell." Then he was gone.

Theron started to cry and Flora lifted him in her arms. "'Tis all right, *mo-run,* he doesn't know your father. He's just an unpleasant man, though I'd no' be knowin' why he had to come and hurt our Jamie." She bent to kiss her husband's cheek and left the room.

Saylah went with her, followed by the unexpected sound of Jamie's laughter. Julian pushed the door closed and gaped at his father in astonishment.

"You've found yourself an extraordinary woman," Jamie said.

Julian was so taken aback that he responded. "I think it was she who found me."

"They told her to come and she chose to obey. It's not the same thing."

Julian was not certain he understood. "Once she told me it was for you that she'd been sent here."

"That's because she knew you'd believe it. And it's partly true. But there's more to it than that. The truth is never simple." He drew a deep breath, then said vehemently, "Don't let her go, Julian. Don't be a fool."

In his agitation, Julian began to pace.

"Forget about my dreams," Jamie insisted, "and think about your own for a change." He noticed the deep lines in Julian's forehead, the pallor beneath his sun-browned skin. "She won't turn into smoke and drift away. Not unless you let her"—he paused—"or force her to."

Julian whirled. "How can I be certain of that?" He didn't understand Saylah; she had too many secrets, too many mercurial shifts of mood. He remembered her face in the light of the fire last night, the exclamation of fear that had confounded him and hurt him.

With a sigh, Jamie settled back against the pillows. "You can't ever be certain. You just have to take the chance."

"Like you did?" Julian sneered.

His father grimaced in pain. "I had eleven years with Simone. I wouldn't give those up for anything, certainly not to avoid the pain of her leaving. Eleven years of happiness. Don't you remember that? Or do you choose not to?"

His voice was hushed. "Besides, I always knew somehow that I wouldn't have her forever. There were parts of her that I could never understand."

Julian gasped at how closely Jamie echoed his own thoughts. Fortunately, he did not have to speak. Jamie was smiling oddly to himself.

"Then Flora came along and gave me so much. I wish I could have given her more."

"You gave her what she wanted—a family, Theron, your affection. And most important, your magic. She's never regretted marrying you, and she never will."

Jamie peered searchingly at Julian. "You believe that."

"I do." Julian paused to gather his thoughts. Jamie had made him forget why he had lingered, made him forget his fear and anger. "Papa," he said firmly, leaning on the bed with both hands, "what about Father Bouchard? I didn't want him near you. He cursed you."

Jamie shook his head. "No man can send another to hell, Julian, no matter how much he wishes he could. Whatever I believe or do not believe, I know that. A man makes his own hell as well as his own heaven." He took his son's hand. "You have to remember that Father Bouchard is one man and not the whole of the Catholic Church. No doubt he is overzealous, but he believes he's doing what's right. Not all priests are like him. Your mother found great solace in the Church when she was young. She spoke often of the kindness of the priests, the sense of peace and beauty her religion gave her. And whatever else she may have been, Simone was not a fool.

"Forget Father Bouchard. I'm not afraid of where I'm going. I know it will be restful there, that the songs will be gentle. Talk to Saylah. She understands."

Julian felt an irrational jealousy. Saylah knew Jamie as his own son could not.

Jamie's weak fingers fluttered. "You have no idea how much she cares, do you? Go to her. She's waiting."

"I'd rather stay."

"I doubt it. I think," Jamie said carefully, "that you're as stubborn as I am. Go. I want to be alone."

They both knew it wasn't true, but Julian was weary of fighting. "If that's what you want."

Jamie glowered at his son. "You haven't heard a word I said. Or is it just that you can't believe? What I want doesn't matter."

Shrugging in defeat, Julian turned to go. He realized he was reluctant to face Saylah because of his cruelty the night before. He didn't understand his own motives any more than he did hers. "You'll be all right?" he said.

"I'll be all right."

There was nothing further to keep him there. He squeezed his father's hand and went into the hall.

Saylah leaned heavily against the wall, not yet certain the danger was past, though her churning emotions had begun to subside.

Julian took her shoulders in his hands. "I don't think you could talk with that much passion if you were talking lies. The only lie is the one that made you doubt yourself at all."

Saylah blinked at him in confusion, until her own harsh voice came back to her. *I am afraid that everything I believe in is a lie.* She looked at Julian's face, at the faith in his hazel eyes, which had been cold and hard last night. Gradually, it came to her that he was right. She was no longer empty. The spirits were around and inside her. She could feel their presence like a soothing balm, and her pulse was the pulse of her ancestors' songs.

Julian swallowed convulsively. "What I said last night was unforgivable. But I'm asking you to forgive me."

Saylah bit her lip, remembering how he had left her alone, bleeding from the wound he'd opened. "I will do what I can," she said. But she did not pull away from the weight of his hands on her shoulders. "Tell me about Father Bouchard. I sensed your hatred so strongly that I felt it too, snarled up with and shadowed by fear. What has he done to you?"

As he stared at her, it came to Julian that they had gone too far. There was nothing he could hide from her. Nothing he did not wish her to know. "It's a difficult story to tell. Tonight I'll explain."

"It is Simone's story, is it not?"

"It is," he said briskly, but would say nothing more.

By the time Edward left the glade, long after the girl had disappeared, the clammy wetness had gone and the terror had begun to ease. Her name ran through his head like a litany—Alida, Alida. Odd that he had heard it just once and now he could not forget it. His anger at her desertion had left him weak and shaking. He knew he would forget her, like the others, but none of them had seen his demons; none had ever tried to heal him, except Sophia. It frightened him that this Indian girl had come to know him so easily. He had lost the knack of hiding his distress beneath a facade of unfailing charm. He must get it back. That power was necessary to him, vital.

Alida had given him her body, that was all. In her supple brown skin he had found release from the nightmare that lived in bright flashes of color behind his eyelids. That was what he must remember. As soon as the shaking stopped.

Finally, he rose to straighten his clothes, though not his uncombed hair. He hardly noticed the thick stubble that covered his chin. Because he was restless, he returned to the barn to get his stallion. He had not tried to guide the horse, but let it roam; his thoughts were frantic, his heartbeat erratic. He could not think clearly enough to plan even so small a thing as the path he wanted to take.

He was not surprised when the animal stopped at the crest of a low hill above Jamie's house. He saw the door open and a man come out, moving quickly, as if propelled by rage. Edward stiffened when he recognized Father Bouchard. He could guess why the priest had come. The man was known as the Harbinger. Wherever he went, grief followed.

When the priest had mounted his burro and ridden away, Edward looked down at Jamie's windows—blank and unrevealing. He watched those windows for many hours, but no one left the house, flicked back a curtain to peer out the glass, opened the casements to let in the air. No movement, no bustle, no sound or sign of life. All at once, he knew.

He knew too much, and always had. The years bound him to Jamie in a thick cord woven of memories—incomparable, beautiful, ugly, frightening—jumbled together like the ill-matched pieces of a puzzle.

Edward wanted to forget all that, to sit with his head in Sophia's lap while she massaged his temples, imbued him, through some magic he could not understand, with her strength and her faith. But he could not leave. Not yet. Jamie held him on that hilltop, aching and shivering, as surely as if he held the reins of Edward's horse in his frail hands. Only when the sun began to sink behind the rust-tinted trees, when the loneliness became too much to bear, did the reins slip free of his frozen fingers.

Edward sighed and turned at last toward home.

Chapter

— 66 —

Late that night, while the others slept, Saylah waited for Julian by the fire in the kitchen. Flora had stayed with Jamie most of the day, and meant to spend the night in her husband's room. "I want to be near him, that's all."

Father Bouchard had gone away, leaving behind a sense of impending disaster. Disturbed, Julian had also been with his father as much as possible, though he had left Jamie's room at least two hours since. Saylah waited, but he did not come. Perhaps, after all, he was not yet ready to tell Simone's story.

When she climbed the stairs to the loft, she saw a light beneath the sitting room door. Saylah paused with her hand on the knob. That Julian had gone there to wait for her, that he had chosen to tell his story surrounded by painful memories, made her shiver with apprehension. Quietly, she opened the door.

Julian sat on the velvet settee, looking oddly at ease in the kind glow of the paraffin lamp with its opaque globe and hanging crystals. The many-faceted drops of glass tinkled as Saylah entered, and she felt Simone's ghost in the rose-scented air. Julian looked bemused.

"I wondered how long it would take you to find me," he said. "You seem surprised. Where else but here can I tell how my mother left us? Where else remember that I thought I knew her so well? I knew the rustle of her skirts and tried to guess which one she wore by the sound and motion across the floor. Some were heavy with seeded pearls and velvet trim, some light—of silk and satin, so they made a different sound.

"And I knew her scent. It drifted around her like a fine, invisible mist. In darkness or light, eyes opened or closed in sleep, I always knew when she was near."

Saylah wanted to weep at the affection he could not disguise, the hurt he could not deny. His words were slightly slurred and she guessed he had been drinking. She drew up a chair and sat so close that her knees touched his.

"Isn't this room pretty?" he asked bitingly. "Pretty as a picture and just as flat." He rested his head on the back of the settee, his legs sprawled over the Oriental rug. Saylah noticed that despite his bitterness, he had removed his boots—covered in mud, worn and dingy, they did not belong in this lovely room. Her throat tightened in compassion. In the crook of his arm, Julian held a pillow done in petit point. Now and then he punched it, but did not seem to notice. His eyes were fixed on the crystals, swaying gently, making their delicate music.

"I've always disliked priests," he said, his voice overly loud in the hushed room. "They made my mother unhappy, you see. And she wasn't a woman prone to sadness. She wanted to enjoy every moment of her life, to feel the beauty and the pleasure, to breathe it in until it became part of her." He paused, leaned forward. "And she knew how to breathe it back out again so Jamie and I could feel it too."

With difficulty, Saylah remained silent. This was Julian's journey and he must follow where it led.

He fell back against the dusty velvet as the glow left his eyes and the color his cheeks. "She didn't approve of moping and grieving; she touched those feelings and they disappeared, like she had magic in her fingertips.

"Except when there was a priest around. She was Catholic, you see, and Jamie was too, back then, anyway. Simone could be smiling and open, singing a little song or telling a story, when she'd hear an itinerant priest was coming. She'd turn away, close in upon herself, become quiet and ill-at-ease. A completely different woman.

"I often wondered why she let them come. She told me once that the priests and ministers who traveled the Island deserved our respect. But while they were here, she never smiled, and sometimes I thought she was afraid."

He lapsed into silence. His eyes clouded over and he gripped the pillow so tightly that a seam began to give way.

"What was she afraid of?" It was time to bring him back, away from the morass of his remembered pain to the story he needed so badly to tell.

—— *455* ——

Julian blinked and stared at the tiny sparkling crystals. "I never knew. But I did find her once, by accident, kneeling under a huge old elm, her rosary in her hands. Father Bouchard sat beside her, listening intently. Her head was bowed and she was weeping. It's the only time I ever saw her cry—except the night she left. She was making her confession, I think, and it was tearing her apart."

Noticing Saylah's confusion, he explained. "She was telling him her sins and asking for forgiveness. Anyway, her tears made me want to take Father Bouchard, rip off his vestments and hit him in the face. He looked so smug, so unbending, and my mother so utterly miserable. That's the first time I understood what hatred was, how vile it tasted. I can still see her kneeling with the light on her hair and the glowing glass beads, her rich velvet skirt stained and crumpled on the ground."

Sweat had broken out on his forehead, and he leaned forward with the pillow between his knees. He kneaded it, pummeled it, crushed it with his fists, while the lamplight played over his restless hands.

"But what did you think he would do to Jamie?"

Julian shrugged. "I'm not sure. I just didn't want him near my father. He brings trouble and unhappiness; everyone knows it. But they're afraid to turn him away."

"I do not think he has the heart of a priest. He seemed almost—happy —when he said those horrible things. I felt he wanted them to happen."

"Self-righteous," Julian muttered. "All I know is, whenever he came, he or one of the other priests, he took my mother away and put a stranger in her place. I hated him for that. But I hated her too, because she wouldn't tell me why." Julian gasped, horrified by his unforgiving tone.

"She hurt and you wanted to help her, but she would not share her pain. Perhaps it was not that you hated her, but that you loved her too much."

"And then she left." The words were harsh, cruelly simple.

"Tell me."

Julian went back to crumpling the pillow. "I was ten years old. Father Bouchard was here that night, and I remember neither he nor *Maman* talked much." At the sound of the childhood endearment, he paused to glance around the room expectantly, but whatever he sought was not there. "Papa tried to fill the silence with a story, but no one was listening.

"After I'd gone to bed, *Maman* came to my room. She didn't say anything for a long time, just sat on the edge of the bed, smoothing the hair from my face. I knew she was upset; her hand was shaking. So I asked her what was wrong."

He rested his forehead on his clenched fists. "She never answered. She just said, 'Forgive me, *mon petit*.' I got scared then, like I'd never been before. My hands were clammy I remember and I was very cold.

"She said she had to go away, because of things that had happened a long time before. Things too dangerous to tell me. She said the only way to keep us safe was to go. I didn't understand." He looked up. "I still don't."

" 'Why are you leaving me?' I asked. 'I'm not leaving *you*, Jules,' she said, 'but I must go back. Back to where I started but did not end.' It didn't make any sense. She told me she was leaving a chest for me. When I was old enough, I could have it to remember her by. As if I'd ever forget. As if I could." He stopped when he felt Saylah's hand on his knee. With difficulty, he found his voice again.

"I remember she leaned down so her hair brushed my face. The curls were damp. She had been weeping. She asked me to kiss her good-bye, but I turned my head away. She pleaded, said she didn't want to remember me like this, but I couldn't move. I guess I thought if I refused, she wouldn't really go. I was such a damned fool."

His voice broke and Saylah held her breath, holding back the pain of the memories Julian was painting in her head.

"She said, 'Please, Jules, let me remember you loving me. I shall have to live on memories from now on. Will you not give me one little kiss to hold on to?' I didn't answer. 'Will you say good-bye at least?' I wanted to, but I couldn't turn from the wall. I couldn't bear to look at her.

"Finally, she kissed the back of my neck and left me. I remember how awful that silence was, without the whisper of her skirts, the beat of her heart, the sound of her voice. But her scent did not go with her. It hovered, choking me.

"I heard the front door close and suddenly I was free. I stood on the bed and threw open the curtain. There was a bright moon, so I knew I'd see her. She came around the side of the house, a single bag in her hand, wearing her hooded cape. When she reached the edge of the woods, she looked back.

"The moonlight fell around her, illuminating her face, pale and clear against the dark cloak. Not until that moment, when I saw the anguish that transformed her from a vibrant young woman to an image in marble, did I really believe she was going. But I knew it then. I started to cry and call out to her, but she couldn't hear. She disappeared into the woods. I let the curtain fall, covering the stark, vivid image that would never leave me. It never has.

"I don't know why she went, but I know Father Bouchard made her do it. Somehow he made her go."

Saylah let the silence settle. "Listen," she whispered, taking his hands. "It is important. It seems to me that your mother did not have a choice, or was made to believe she did not. She did not want to be cruel, but she knew no other way." Julian let the pillow slide to the floor. "Try to forgive her. Only then can you free yourself from her ghost, which haunts you even now."

"Jamie says she's alive," he muttered without looking up.

"That does not mean you cannot carry her spirit with you. It lives in this room. She left part of herself behind, Julian. This is where she wanted to be. Forgive her. I think she suffered much more than you. She had to make the choice, you see, and to make such a choice is an agony you cannot conceive."

Something in her voice caught his attention. He looked up to see the compassion in her eyes—empathy for Simone, and understanding, and something more.

"You've made that choice too, once." It was not a question and Saylah did not deny it.

"Let her go, Julian. It is time."

"I did that long ago."

"Then why does the bitterness linger and eat at you, even after so many years?"

Julian stared into Saylah's clear green eyes and knew she was right. Yet he was reluctant to let go of his anger, the deep hurt which, nurtured and hidden, had made him strong. He had clung to his resentment; it made him less vulnerable. Or so he had believed. "Why?" he asked despondently. "I don't know why."

Saylah was slipping back to the muddy riverbank where she had set her autumn leaves afloat. Slipping back into bewildered rage, the grief she had denied for so long. She focused on Julian's face, shutting out the sound of rushing water. "Open the windows. They hold her in—her scent and her memory and her sorrow. Open them wide and the wind will bring fresh air, clean air that is not tainted with your painful memories."

Julian rose, holding in the tumult of grief and fury, remorse and sadness that whirled inside him. He had fought so long and hard to keep it hidden, safe, sacred. But now he had spoken it aloud. Simone was gone. He knew then that he had clung to the belief that she was there, in the room, waiting. That someday he would open the door and she would float toward him, skirts whispering her secrets.

His chest grew tight with pain, his throat raw with unshed tears. Slowly, he turned toward the windows. He stood for a moment with the aged satin fabric in his hands, then buried his face in the silken folds. Even here amidst the heavy dust, Simone's scent lingered. He wrenched the curtains open, pulling back the lace so sharply that he tore it.

"You do not need to throw away her memory with violence. You do not need to destroy."

Saylah's musical voice rose, filled the elegant room from the faded carpet to the pale painted ceiling. He stopped to listen, captivated by the sound. There was more of beauty in the world than just Simone. Much more.

"Let her go easily, gently," Saylah said.

Julian worked at the latch for a long time before it came free. Then he pushed the casements wide and the cold night air rushed in. He thought he felt the brush of a hand on his cheek as the fragrance of old roses drifted past to the open window.

When he turned back, Saylah stood in the radiant light, her black hair loose around her shoulders, green eyes luminous as she listened to the song of crystals that met and parted in the breeze. Somehow, without trying, without even being aware of it, she had exorcised a soft, lingering presence and made this room completely and inevitably her own.

Chapter

67

Jamie lay dreaming, though it was barely nightfall. He was walking through mist, alone and aware of every sound, every flick of a branch, every cry of the wind, every hint of bird's song. Now and then the mist cleared and he saw the beckoning water—blue when the sun found its way from behind the clouds, silver when the golden light was hidden by wisps of white. The lap of the water charmed him, and he moved toward it eagerly.

He heard a noise and whirled to find a cougar in the middle of the path. It was beautiful and regal, poised and deadly; its golden eyes never left him for a moment. He knew those eyes, had known them for a long time. He trusted them. Even now they called him back, away from the silver-blue water, away from the gentle swell of the waves, back toward the golden cat with its sharp white teeth and pointed claws.

He heard it breathe, heard each rise and fall of its chest while it waited, head high, for him to come.

"Jamie!" a voice called. The cougar faded, and with it, the mist and the distant singing waters.

"Take this. It will ease the pain."

His lids were heavy and his arm numb. There was a weight in his chest that was tearing him apart, a pain so piercing that it forced his eyes open at last.

"I am here. I am with you."

Saylah and her dulcet voice. Saylah and her wise, gentle hands. Saylah, chasing away the cougar, the unbearable weight, the pain, with the warm liquid she poured down his throat.

Exhausted, Jamie leaned into her arm, which supported his shoulders, and looked up at her delicately boned, dark-skinned face. "It's better now," he murmured. "And you are very beautiful."

She froze, unable to respond. She had seen how close Jamie was to death. Her throat closed at the thought, and she had to fight for air. Then he spoke those simple words. *You are very beautiful.* Because she could not find her voice, she clasped his hands and rocked him gently, showing her gratitude in silence.

Jamie understood. He sensed an unusual stillness and realized that for the first time in many hours, he and Saylah were alone. "My heart is weak. I think it will be soon."

"I know," she crooned. "But you are not alone." Flora had spent the day at Jamie's side, talking low, holding him in her strong arms, smiling sometimes, sometimes weeping. Saylah had looked in more than once, but had not disturbed them. She had sensed that, in their own way, they were saying good-bye.

In the afternoon, Flora had pretended to go cook, in order to leave Julian alone with his father. They too had talked and laughed and clung to each other. Even Theron had had an hour alone with Jamie. Saylah did not know what they had said to each other, but Theron seemed a little less bewildered, a little less frightened. Now all three had fallen asleep.

Saylah had been in the loft when she felt a piercing pain in her chest and knew the time had come. She had tripped when she tried to rise, found that her breath would not come easy. She had paused over her stones, cupping each in her palm, rubbing the smooth surfaces until her pulse steadied and her breathing became normal. Then she had come to Jamie and found him lost in a nightmare, his face distorted with pain.

With her fingertips and her herbs and the strength of her hands, she smoothed the pain away, knowing it was the last time. "It is a lovely night," she said, "warm, though so near to winter, and the moon has risen, pale and ghost-like among the stars." Her chest ached and her eyes were dry and raw. It was too much to lose. Too much.

"You have turned away from the religion of your birth?" she whispered. "You no longer believe in its laws and rituals?"

"I no longer believe in anything but you."

Saylah gasped, tried to object, but he interrupted.

"I believe in your strength, your power—to heal, to 'see,' to understand. But most of all, I believe in your heart. You're afraid to trust your own feelings, though like your visions, they are true. You're afraid to listen to your heart as you listen to the wind and the spirits and the voices of your dreams."

Somehow, Saylah found the strength to speak. "I am not afraid of what I feel for you." His curly hair was damp beneath her fingers.

"What you feel for me is safe. You've known from the moment you came that I would leave you."

"Do you think, because of that, I will not grieve?" She spoke sharply. More sharply than she had intended.

Jamie considered her face, floating above him in yellow light. "I think you'll lock your grief away, as you have before, and nurture the grief of my family. That your own sorrow will become a barrier.

"I told Julian it's hard to learn to think of others, when all your life you've thought only of yourself, as I have." Jamie did not give her a chance to respond. "It's harder still to learn to think of yourself when all your life you've thought only of others. But it's time for you to learn. Promise me, Saylah. It's all I ask."

"I will try." She did not meet his eyes. "How do you know so much about me?"

"I've had time for contemplation."

"And you are certain," she whispered, "of what and how I feel for you?"

"Certain?" He shook his head, but it made the pain shoot through his chest and he lay back, head on her curled legs. "No, I'm not certain of anything. But I've been wondering if you aren't confused by your feelings for me." He paused, searching for words. "Tell me about your father."

"He was a Stranger. I never knew him."

"But if you could know him," Jamie persisted, "what would you wish him to be?"

Biting her lip, she tried to think. She opened her mouth, saw Jamie's brown eyes watching her, watching— She did not speak and did not have to. Her eyes were wet with tears that would not come.

Jamie reached up to take her hand. "It's easier to love a ghost—a man you never really knew, except in the shadowed world of his own creation—than to take a chance on someone real. A ghost never changes, never hurts you, never makes mistakes, and because he has already left, you do not fear his going. It's easy to be a hero in the darkness, where no one can see the truth, much harder to be a man who stands in sunlight and is unafraid of the flaws it might reveal."

"Is that what you thought?" Saylah interrupted.

"Don't you understand yet? It doesn't matter what I thought. It's you

—— 462 ——

who must think now, you who must decide. You and Julian." He closed his eyes, shut out the sight of her face, made luminous by the lamplight.

"You and Julian," he repeated. "Tomorrow."

Saylah cupped his head in her hands and waited. One by one, the others reappeared. They slipped quietly into the room, the shadows, the wavering light. Flora in her dressing gown, Theron in his long white nightshirt, Julian in his shirt and trousers. Saylah had called to them in silence. In silence they came.

She rose to face them. "It is time to think of Jamie's spirit, which will soon leave us."

They had been expecting this, but it did not stop Flora's gasp of denial, Theron's fearful stare or Julian's reaching hand. Saylah did not flinch, though inside she trembled. "I would like to follow the rituals of my People. It would give me comfort, and perhaps you also."

Flora and Julian exchanged glances. "Do what you like," Jamie's wife said quietly. "It can no' harm him if it comes from your hand."

"I have made mistakes," Saylah said.

"Do ye think we're no' aware of that? But what ye do, ye do out of love. 'Tis all we care about."

Saylah nodded numbly and rose. Flora, Theron and Julian clustered around Jamie while Saylah placed shallow dishes of burning oil at the four corners of the bed, opened the windows to let in the night air. On the breeze that lifted the gauze bed curtains, Jamie's soul would fly. She brought out the death root and placed it near the bed. She did not name it; they were not ready to hear a word so bald and harsh and real.

Finally, she sat, while Jamie gazed up at his family. He would like looking at their faces in the flickering light. He would carry that image with him, not the shadows that surrounded and invaded them. Everyone spoke in whispers. A loud word would have been a violation in this room of soft light and unspoken grief.

Quietly, Saylah began to sing.

> The wind comes, dancing, singing
> Through the trees.
> The moon comes, glowing, shining
> Through the clouds.
> The hawk comes, proud and silent
> From above,
> And spreads his feathered wings
> In blessing.

When he goes, he carries with him—
Dancing, singing, glowing, shining—
One man's memory
And the rhythm
Of his slow-beating heart.

The words rose and faded, but the tap of her hands on her knees did not cease.

Theron was huddled at the foot of the bed, fighting back tears.

Jamie peered at his youngest son, brow furrowed in concern.

"Don't worry," Theron whispered. "Saylah says you'll have peace and no more pain. I'd like that, I think." He pursed his lips thoughtfully. "For a little while anyway."

Jamie smiled and touched the boy's hand. "Thank you," he said. "I'll remember."

Only sometimes he didn't remember. Sometimes when he looked at these people, they were strangers and he did not know their names. Sometimes all he could see was Edward and Simone and Sophia, all he could hear was their laughter as they tried to make a home out of a wilderness. Sometimes he was back in the huge down bed where he'd been born, with his mother warm and safe beside him. Sometimes he wandered among the memories, smiling, for they were kind memories, with the harsh edges smoothed away.

Julian saw his father's distant smile and felt a wrenching in his stomach. He knew Jamie had left them again, not forever, not yet, but for a moment, while he lingered in the past, which made him happy.

Julian wanted to make him happy. He had tried hard and fought so long. But he did not have what Jamie needed—a world untouched by harsh reality. Resentment rose like bile in his throat, but he forced it down again. He would not let Jamie go in silence and anger as he had Simone. Taking his father's hand, he conjured up a fragment of the past, when they'd been happy.

> *Sur le pont d'Avignon,*
> *Tout le monde y danse, danse.*
> *Sur le pont d'Avignon,*
> *Tout le monde y danse en ronde.*

He sang from the deepest part of his memory, where the words had lingered since early childhood, when the world had passed in a blur—as it did now. He remembered before the sight of trees or his father's face or his mother's rustling gowns, Simone's voice, the melodic French song, the tune, serene yet somehow tantalizing. He had never asked what the words meant, had never wanted to know. The mystery was part of the magic that had lifted him away from scented pines, the swing of the ax, the rush of the river over empty beaver traps.

The same magic that had taken Julian away now brought Jamie back to him. He opened his eyes and smiled at his son. "We used to play the dancing game to that song. We used to whirl and spin until we collapsed into the bracken. You might have been a child then, but it was long ago. Too long."

With difficulty, his voice cracked and dry, Julian went on.

> *Les beaux monsieurs font comme çi,*
> *Les belles dames font comme ça.*
> *Sur le pont d'Avignon,*
> *Tout le monde y danse en ronde.*

"I'll remember that too." Jamie's voice quavered as he fought to draw a breath from among the points of probing needles in his chest.

Flora rubbed his temples, undone by her own helplessness. Always before, she had known how to soothe him, distract him, make him stronger. But now there was nothing left.

"Just sit beside me," Jamie whispered. "Don't leave me." For the first time there was fear in his voice.

Saylah heard it and knew it was time to let him fade into his dreams. "Please," she said. The Ivys saw she held a small cup in her hands and let her through. She lifted Jamie's head, and, fighting for breath, he drank. She sat for a while, stroking his forehead, his hair, his pallid cheeks, until she felt his muscles relax and knew the herbs had taken effect. "Now," she said, "sit with him. He does not see you, but he knows that you are there."

She backed away, pausing to look at the tender smile on Jamie's face. "Now he can seek the spirits of the sky and not the rocks and thorns of earth." She looked up into Julian's questioning gaze. "He has left his pain behind, if not yet his body. This is not the time for wondering. It is time for the coming of spirits, the sighing of wind in the tops of the trees. It is time for your father to ride on the back of the wind. You have said you will not hold him here."

She put her hands on his chest. "You want to see him happy again, but you have not the power to make such a miracle. Look at him, how he smiles when forgetfulness comes over him, how he fights and grows hollow with suffering when knowledge returns. Do you not see, my Julian, that the greatest gift you can give him is the gift of peace?"

Aware of the waiting silence, Julian looked. Jamie was no longer taut with pain, his skin was not gray, but pale white, fragile like a gossamer butterfly wing. His face was relaxed, his smile sweet. "I see," Julian said. But how he wished, in that moment, that he was blind.

My Julian, Saylah had called him, with her hands against his linen shirt. She had not removed them yet. Julian covered her hands with his, but a movement from the bed made him turn. Saylah slipped away to get the death root.

She held the root to a flickering candle and its bittersweet scent drifted upward, curling around the shoulders of the three who stood beside the bed.

Julian smelled the strange fragrance and knew. He knelt, head bent so the lamplight would touch his face, to bid his father good-bye.

"Don't close the curtains in your grief," Jamie whispered, eyes closed, lashes dark against his sunken cheek. "Open them wide, even these that have been closed for so long. Don't follow me into darkness. The sunlight is a blessing." His voice faded, grew weak. "Don't turn away from it. Don't make my house a tomb again. Sing for me. I want to hear singing."

His eyes were still shut, he could not see his family, yet he knew they were there and they would hear him. He lapsed into silence. There was no sound in the room but his breathing and theirs, muffled by their wish not to disturb him. Gradually, his face relaxed and he smiled. The smoke from the root, fine-woven and unbearably sweet, circled Jamie Ivy's smiling face, his pale, blue-veined hands, his body, small and fragile beneath the quilt. Not until he was sleeping and would not wake did he open his eyes again.

Chapter
68

Dawn had begun to creep across the sky when the first knock came at the kitchen door. Saylah opened it to find Alida, veiled in wisps of morning mist, with cedar boughs in her outstretched arms.

"I have come to help." Her black eyes were touched with sadness, and she spoke in whispers.

"How did you know?"

"I did not think you would ask such a question. *Sowkwad,* the Loon, floated through my dream, singing her lovely mournful song. I awoke with tears on my cheeks, and I knew."

Saylah motioned her inside near the fire. She watched the Salish girl lay the cedar boughs on the table, reverently, regretfully.

"You will miss Jamie Ivy?" Saylah said in wonder. She could speak, though the others had fallen silent and numb. Her own grief lay coiled in layers of fine gauze and she did not probe or think of it. She did not dare. "I did not think you knew him."

"Everyone knew him," Alida said. "Before he hid himself away, he was always busy, always planning, always visiting—always there for those who needed him."

Saylah wanted to hear more about the Jamie she had never known. "You needed him?"

"Once. I broke my leg while working for another. Jamie Ivy was there. He saw that the other man considered me a burden. He did not even know me, but he splinted my leg as best he could and carried me home on his horse. Then he found a doctor and let me recover here, where I was safe and warm and fed."

"He was kind to care for you." Despite her resolve, Saylah choked on the words.

"He could do nothing else," Alida said matter-of-factly. "It was in his nature. He might have turned away from his own misery, but never from the pain of others. That is why I have come. I could not repay the debt before; he did not need me. But there will be much to do now." She looked about the cluttered kitchen, saw the eggs, ham and biscuits Saylah had begun to prepare. "You are trying to make them eat. I will cook. You speak to them. They will listen to you."

Saylah gripped the back of a chair until her knuckles were white. Alida was right. Julian, Theron and Flora sat around Jamie's bed, unmoving, frozen in that moment when he had asked them to sing for him. Only she had forced herself to turn away, to go on, to think of what must be done. But the silence inside her, the silence in that room, grown chill and stagnant, oppressed her. She wanted to go to the river, to unwrap her grief and hold it in her hands, to feel it burn its way up from her fingers to her arms, to her chest, to the dark secret place where her tears lay unshed.

Yet she was grateful for the work that lay ahead. She did not really want to see the shape and texture of her grief. She was afraid it might destroy her.

Sophia, Paul and Edward sat in the parlor, playing at word games when Mr. Palmer arrived, flushed and breathless in the doorway. Sophia rose, her heart pounding in agitation. The man's hair was uncombed, his eyes strangely unfocused, his breathing ragged.

"What is it?" she said. "What's happened?"

Mr. Palmer took three gasping breaths before he could speak. "Jamie Ivy died last night. I thought you should know."

Sophia stared at him, refusing to believe. "You must be mistaken. How do you know?" It could not be true. She would not allow it to be true. Quite suddenly, without warning, Sophia Ashton realized what it would be like to live in a world without Jamie. Barren. Empty. Without magic.

"The Salish girl who helps me around the farm. She had a dream, so I went over to the Ivys' first thing. It's true. Saylah told me."

Paul went to stand beside his mother. He was afraid she would fall if he left her alone. "When—" he swallowed the lump in his throat—"when will they—"

Mr. Palmer looked at the boy in compassion. "Funeral's tomorrow afternoon."

Sophia felt Paul's cold hand slip into hers and closed her fingers tight around it. The earth had shifted beneath her feet; she could no longer stand upright. But for Paul's sake, she must try to be calm. "They'll need help. I'll have Clara prepare some food. And Paul, do you think you could stay with Theron? I know he has his family, but what he needs is a friend."

Paul nodded, unable to speak.

"I'll be going, then. They'll need men to help with—everything," Mr. Palmer stammered. "I thought you should know."

He disappeared, but Sophia and Paul did not move. They clung to each other, trying to believe. No blessed numbness seeped through Sophia, softening the blow; it struck her full in the chest—a deluge of pain that took her breath, her strength, her reason. "I didn't know how much it would hurt," she said at last. "I didn't know."

She did not look at Edward, who had sat brooding since yesterday morning. She could not face him now, with his mysteries and his strange, distant silence which she could not penetrate. Sometimes he came to her like a child, asking for her sympathy, her serenity and her strength. But he would not take what she offered, would not give what she needed—for him to make her understand.

Suddenly her husband erupted from his huddled position and shouted, "It's a goddamned lie!"

Both Sophia and her son jumped. "But Papa," Paul said, terrified by the wild look in his father's eyes, "you knew he was ill. I told you. And you said—"

Edward had known. He'd seen the priest, the Harbinger, hadn't he? He'd known, but he hadn't believed it. He couldn't. "But he wasn't supposed to die, don't you see that? It's not right. It's not fair." He looked at his wife in a desperate appeal, but she had no answer, no consolation to offer. She watched him mutely, tears coursing down her cheeks.

"He's gone," Sophia said. "He's just gone." Saying the words, hearing them ring in her ears, brought waves of pain that shook the strongest part of her, the part that would not bend or break. If Edward touched her now, she would snap like a dried-out twig beneath his foot.

Edward was pale, his hands shaking, his eyes, for once, more brown than gold. "No," he shouted to the air, to the gods, to the weight that he carried like a boulder on his back. "Can't you understand? Jamie Ivy was not supposed to die. Not ever!"

By mid-morning, Neil MacKinnon, his wife, Annie, and his four sons had arrived. Annie brought fresh-baked bread and venison stew, Geordie his carpentry tools. "We'll be buildin' the coffin, Geordie and I," Neil explained. "Ye'd no' want Julian to take on such a task just now. Conall and Archie and Rory will dig the grave." He glowered, tried surreptitiously to wipe away a tear. "I suppose ye'll be buryin' him tomorrow. Have ye decided where?"

Saylah could see he was eager to be busy. His grief was a palpable thing, but he was too much a Highlander to break down and weep. Instead, he would work until his hands were raw and his pain real and visible on his bloody palms.

"We thought he might like to lie beside the deer, the first tree he ever cut here." Saylah had to look away.

"Aye, he'd like that, our Jamie. He was so proud of that stump of cedar." Neil began, brusquely, to instruct his sons in what must be done.

It was not long before Sophia and Paul came through the open door, arms piled high with food. Paul went at once to find Theron while Sophia stayed in the kitchen to help make order out of chaos.

"Edward could not come," Sophia whispered when Alida went out to pick some herbs. "He—he's not taking it well. I hope you can forgive him."

"It is not for me to forgive him," Saylah replied. "He must forgive himself."

A chill ran down Sophia's back. *He must forgive himself.* A simple statement, a truth so clear, so obvious that she herself had never guessed it. She was glad she had no chance to respond, because, at that moment, Jock and Jeannie Buchanan burst through the door. Flora's brother and his wife had brought more food, and went at once to join the MacKinnon boys, who would dig hard and long before a place was made for Jamie's coffin in the cold winter earth.

By nightfall, the house was full of human voices, full of tear-streaked faces and helpful hands. Just a few weeks past, they had come in celebration. Now they came in grief.

Eventually, lured by the sound of life beyond Jamie's door, Flora, Julian and Theron had come out. Saylah had even convinced them to eat a little.

When the neighbors came in from their labors to rest, Neil took Flora's hands. "Now, there was a man, was Jamie Ivy, and no' another like him in all the world. 'Twas the way he had of lookin' at things as if none were impossible. When ye were with him, he made ye believe ye could do anything."

Stiff and aching from her two-day vigil, grateful for the physical pain which distracted her from the leaden emptiness inside, Flora smiled sadly at Neil. For the first time, tears came to her eyes. "I'm glad ye're here."

Neil nodded stiffly. He had said his piece. It was enough.

The following morning, the day on which Jamie Ivy would be buried, John Thomas Howard and his wife, Nellie, arrived with a thin, bespectacled man in tow. "We heard about Jamie and thought you might need a minister. Brought one along, just in case. I know Jamie was Catholic, but we thought, because of Father Bouchard—damn the bastard to hell— well, we thought a Methodist would do just fine."

"I am grateful," Saylah said. "I did not think—"

"Don't worry your head about it," John Thomas declared. "Looks to me like your friends will make sure everything is done."

"You were Jamie's friend?"

"Everybody was his friend. Used to spend many an evenin' at the Royal Oak Inn with us. Always glad to see him, we were. He could tell a story that would make the sailors weep, and he'd give you his last shilling if it'd help, never mind that he had no money to get home. Why, he made friends of people who had no friends. Most people don't know how to listen, but Jamie had a way with him. People would find themselves telling their life stories. That's the kind of man he was."

Saylah did not know what to say. She felt lost and confused.

John Howard smiled and shook his head. "You didn't know much about him, did you?"

She drew herself up with dignity. "I knew enough to love him." She blinked, shocked that she had spoken so, especially to a stranger.

John nodded in understanding. "Never met man, woman, or child who knew Jamie Ivy and didn't love him."

Saylah believed him. The house was so full that people had to find places outside on both porches. Everyone brought food, willing hands, and quiet praise for Jamie.

Saylah was astonished. He had seemed to her such a private man, lost in the wanderings of his own spirit. But as Alida had pointed out, she'd come to know him too late.

She slipped deeper and deeper inside herself as the guests talked about Jamie and how they'd cared for him. The Salish respected the grief of others, left them to suffer in silence and dignity. The wailing and moaning that accompanied the preparation of the body and the placement of the coffins was part of a ritual, a dance whose steps had been mapped out many generations past.

There was no need for thought; one did what had always been done. In that her People had found consolation. But these friends of Jamie's, who felt the need to express their grief, shook Saylah's resolve, weakened her resistance.

She had seen Flora weep often. Theron trailed behind her, tears running unchecked down his face. She envied them those tears, yet did not wish to weep her own. Julian was stiff and silent. His eyes were dry, his face drawn and gray. Like Saylah, he could not yet let himself grieve.

It was gray and misty on the day Jamie Ivy was buried. His friends could find no flowers, so they gathered the last of the autumn leaves and tossed them onto the plain pine coffin the MacKinnon boys had lowered into the earth.

The mourners clustered around the grave, except for Edward, who stood alone at the far edge of the clearing. He was not listening to the service, but to Jamie's voice in his head, Jamie's heavy breathing as they cut and cut and cut that cedar down. He was seeing Jamie's face on the night of the party, when he had gripped Edward's hand so tightly, in supplication. For the last time.

"Ashes to ashes, dust to dust . . ."

The last time, Julian thought, as the minister spoke kindly of Jamie's life and death. This is the last time I will stand at my father's side.

". . . a man beloved by all he met."

Julian was blessedly numb, blessedly deaf to the kind words of Jamie's friends, blessedly immune to the tears that flowed around him like rain into an endless sea.

". . . came here to make a new life, a better life . . ."

No life at all. Julian felt a brief stab of anguish, but he forced it brutally down.

"He was a kind husband, a giving man, a man who loved his family above all else . . ."

Except his dreams, Julian thought bitterly. He had known for a long time that his father would die, but never guessed how he would feel when he looked into Jamie's sightless eyes for the last time. No spark, no life, no dreams, just emptiness.

". . . commend him to God's hands . . ."

From far away, Julian heard the others singing a hymn. Mechanically, he joined in without hearing his own voice. A low murmur, like the distant drone of insects, swelled and faded, swelled and faded.

Then, in the breeze that rippled from among the treetops, curling like a ribbon through the first chill of winter, came the words of an unfamiliar song.

> I have walked the earth;
> The paths that I have come to know
> Were made long ago by the feet of my ancestors.
> My life has been more than the echo
> Of a voice in a stone canyon,
> And less than the coming
> Of the blue ocean tide.

Saylah was singing. Her silver voice slipped among the mourners, curved about their turned-up collars, coiled itself around Julian's heart. He stared at his father's coffin, at the bright-colored leaves, and felt his empty stomach contract again and again.

> My life is a flame—warm and golden,
> My life is the mist—cool and white,
> My life is a river—rushing silver.
> My life is a cloud—
> That forms one day a wisp of white
> Fine woven and fleeting,
> And another day a gray dark weight
> Full of thunder.
> I flee before the sea wind
> Like a shadow eclipsed by light.
> And that is as it should be.

It was done. There was nothing more to say.

The MacKinnon boys lifted the shovels, but before they could toss dirt onto the coffin, Theron got on his knees and leaned precariously forward until he grasped a handful of the autumn leaves. His face was covered with tears, but he made no sound as he clutched the gold and purple pattern to his chest.

When the first clod of soil hit the wood with a dull thud, Julian shuddered and turned away. The others followed, stopping when he paused at the carved deer, whose hind legs were bound by cedar still. Impulsively, he took the knife from his pocket and chipped at the weathered wood, dropping strips of bark on the ground at his feet. "For Jamie," he murmured.

Flora stopped him when he started away. She took the knife and carved once, twice, three times, shaping one fine long graceful leg. She lifted

Theron and he too carved a tiny piece out of the ancient tree. Then Saylah took the open blade and stroked the wood, cutting away what was not part of the leaping deer. Carefully, she passed the knife to Sophia, who stood behind her.

One by one, the mourners accepted Julian's pocket knife and carved a mark on the animal whose antlers rose regally into the sky, touched now with sun, now with shadow. No one spoke; there was no need. The motions of their hands spoke for them.

It was a long time before the last mourner had left his mark, hollowed out the last unfinished piece of the carved cedar deer that had been Jamie's symbol—his promise and his hope and, eventually, his heartbreak.

The house blazed with light and life, laughter and tears, story and song when Saylah slipped out alone to the newly covered grave. She stood in silence, then knelt and took from her pocket a small round stone, rust-colored, with an indentation the size of a thumb. She held the stone, the sacred stone, placed it on the freshly turned earth at the head of the grave. Leaning forward, she pressed her hands into the soil, feeling its cool grittiness against her palms, forcing her weight onto her hands, eyes closed, lips parted in a soundless cry.

She crouched, unmoving, connected to the spirit of the man who lay in the narrow pine box by the touch of her hands on the earth above him. The wind lifted her hair across her cheek, sang songs of her childhood, songs of the Longhouse, songs of mourning and death and the life left behind. She listened, head tilted, hands buried in the earth while the darkness sang with the force of the wind. It was winter, chill and biting, and it was time to go inside.

"Sleep," she said tenderly. "Your peace has come to you at last."

Soundlessly, she moved away, back toward the warmth and light of Jamie Ivy's house.

Edward Ashton watched her go. He had stood long after the other mourners had gone, long after the MacKinnon boys filled in the grave and disappeared into the house. He had stood while the sun set beyond the trees, rimmed in russet light, while darkness fell around and inside him.

Now that Saylah had come and gone, he moved forward clumsily and knelt beside the grave. "Dead." He said the word slowly, intently, listening to the sound, trying to understand. "You left me." His voice was rough with pain and disbelief.

For a long time, he was silent, rigid, his hands clasped while he waited for an answer. When the silence swelled around him, when nothing moved, when even the wind whirled away into the treetops, he said, "I suppose you wanted me to explain."

Brow furrowed, he rubbed his forehead, back and forth, back and forth until the skin was red and painful. He sighed. "I'm sorry, Jamie. I'm sorry."

Alone in the unrelieved darkness of a night without a moon, Edward Ashton crouched beside his best friend's grave and wept.

Chapter
69

On the fifth sun after Jamie's death, Saylah rose and went down to the kitchen. Flora and Theron were already there, Flora preparing breakfast, Theron sitting in the rocking chair before the fire, watching his mother's every action, afraid if he stopped for an instant, she might disappear.

"'Tis glad to see ye I am," Flora called above the sizzle of browning sausage. "Julian's already up and away. He can no' seem to keep still, nor do I blame him."

Everyone had slept uneasily and risen early since Jamie died. Saylah was not certain what they feared most—the darkness or their troubled dreams.

"Saylah! You're here!" Theron threw himself at her, clasping his chubby arms around her legs so tightly that she nearly fell.

Every morning he greeted her as if he had never thought to see her again. She ran her fingers through his blond curls and wiped a stray tear from his cheek, which was rosy from the heat of the fire.

Flora gazed sadly at her son's burnished head buried in Saylah's dark skirt.

Saylah hesitated, disengaged Theron from around her legs. With her hand on his shoulder, she went to the pile of cedar boughs Alida had brought her. "There is something I must do," she announced. "If you will allow me." She picked up the branches in her arms.

Flora cocked a curious eyebrow. "And what might that be?"

With a deep breath, Saylah explained, "My People believe it is wise and healing to rid a house of the taint of recent death." In deference to their grief, she had waited several days before bringing up the subject. But she could no longer ignore the strong impulse that compelled her; it must be done now. "They singe cedar boughs and use them to clear the air in the room where—it happened, to chase away the ghosts, so the living may begin again."

"Ye'd no be needin' to do that for us," Flora said cautiously.

"It is as much for me as for you." Saylah spoke softly, but beneath the gentle tone was a fierceness that startled her. "It is difficult for me to break the traditions of my People." Her voice cracked. "I will not feel easy until it is done."

Flora gaped at the girl. She did not ask much for herself, and until now, had not let her grief for Jamie show. Tears stung Flora's eyes. "I'm thinkin' I'd just as soon keep Jamie about me."

"Yeah!" Theron declared. "We want his ghost to stay."

Saylah's compulsion grew stronger, pulsing against her temples, making her head ache. "This house has groaned for so long under the weight of many ghosts. Is it not time to clear away the past?" She understood Flora's reluctance too well. *It is easier to love a ghost. . . .* Like Saylah, she was clinging to shadows, praying they would ease her pain.

"It is not Jamie's ghost that you long for. It is Jamie himself. He has not left this house and will not, so long as you hold him in your hearts. But remember that he asked us not to follow him into darkness, not to shut out the sunlight. He wants you to go on."

Flora ducked her head to hide her tears. "How can we go on? There's nothin' to hold on to."

Saylah backed slowly from the room; Flora and Theron followed without being aware of it. She stopped outside Jamie's door. "He left you a great deal to hold on to—this house, his dream of success, Theron's future." She pushed the door open. "But not this room. It has become a haven for shadows and secrets and memories. Those things will hold you down and keep you back." As they hold me, she added silently. She stood in the middle of the dark room. "He said to open the windows. Among my People what a man asks at his death is sacred."

Flora peered through the gloom, already filmed in dust. "Mayhap ye're right." Theron pressed against his mother's side, chewing on his lip.

It was enough for Saylah. She went to the windows to draw the drapes and the lace curtains beneath. One by one, she pushed back the panels of dark velvet until the room was flooded with light that set fire to the crystals on the hanging chandelier. She threw open a window to let in the morning air. The colors, once dim and dull, sprang to life—rich wine, rose silk, burgundy carpet and watered silk wallpaper.

Flora gasped and Theron stared, wide-eyed. "Why, 'tis a beautiful room."

"You must have seen it before Jamie shut out the light."

Flora rubbed her chin thoughtfully. "Aye, but 'twas so long ago. I had forgotten." She stared around her, bemused, and felt a tiny lift, a minute lessening of the burden of her sorrow.

"Theron, will you help me?" Saylah held out a bough of cedar which the boy took gingerly. She singed the ends of the two branches and they waved them through the air. The smell of charred cedar permeated the room, drifted out the open windows. Theron began to wave his bough more energetically.

Quietly, Saylah sang Salish prayers, standing beside the bed and waving her branch to and fro. She knew that this ritual, however necessary, however healing, would not rid the house of ghosts. Nothing could do that until the inhabitants themselves let go. And they were not ready to do so—she least of all.

Flora waited respectfully for her to finish, tears running unchecked down her cheeks. She did not know what the girl had said, but the air no longer smelt musty. It breathed with the curtains that billowed and fell, billowed and swayed, dancing in the cool, clean wind.

"Sophia!" Edward called through the house. "Where are you? Not hiding under the bed again, surely? I did so hope we'd broken you of that habit."

"Edward Ashton!" his wife said, standing up from behind the settee, where she'd dropped her needlepoint. "I've never crawled under a bed in my life, and well you know it." She stopped when she realized her voice sounded normal, not hoarse from weeping and talking too much of what used to be and was no more.

"I don't see why not," Edward declared, unabashedly reversing his earlier opinion. "It's really quite cozy and private under there, providing Clara has captured all the dust balls and cast them to their wretched fates."

Sophia blinked at her husband in astonishment. He had just returned from Victoria, and she realized that in the weeks since Jamie's death, he had, at some point, ceased to brood and snap and turn within himself. There had not been a tirade in days. If she hadn't been so wrapped up in her own grief, she might have noticed sooner.

Edward's sandy hair was neatly combed, his sideburns trimmed, and the color had begun to come back to his handsome face. The cleft in his chin looked strangely alluring, complemented, as it was, by the sparkle in his eyes and the smile on his full lips.

"Why are you staring at me in that forward way?" her husband demanded. "I think your father must be right. You've forgotten all your manners. It's quite dreadful, really, but what can one expect in this savage wilderness?" He sighed dramatically and Sophia laughed.

She covered her mouth, startled by the sound. There had been no laughter in this house for a long time. Dropping her needlepoint again, she went toward Edward. Perhaps Saylah had been right, and he'd needed only to forgive himself for whatever he'd done to estrange himself from Jamie. She fervently hoped so, but would not ask. She was too glad to see him smile. Someday he would tell her, but not yet.

She swung her hips suggestively and Edward covered his eyes in mock dismay. "You see, what did I tell you? You've lost all sense of modesty. Now, I don't know if I can, in all good conscience, give you the very expensive, very elegant gift I've brought all the way from Victoria. You might spoil it."

Sophia paused. Was the gleam in his eye a little too bright, his laughter a little too easy? She considered her husband warily. But then, it was to be expected. You didn't forget a dead friend in a few weeks. She certainly hadn't forgotten. "What gift?" she asked, masking her thoughts with a light tone and seductive smile.

Edward gazed deeply into her eyes. "I seem to have forgotten what we were talking about." He circled her waist with his hands and drew her toward him, then kissed her on the nose.

"I should very much like it if you could remember," Sophia breathed. Whatever disquiet lingered in her husband's eyes, he was trying hard to remind her of how easily he could make her laugh, how charming he could be, how winning.

Edward disappeared and reappeared promptly, carrying a large parcel wrapped in silver paper. Sophia untied the string to find a thick green velvet riding cloak lined with beaver. She held it out, speechless. When she looked up, she was no longer laughing. "It's beautiful, Edward. I don't know what to say."

He was delighted with her reaction. "Say you'll run away and marry me, that you'll have my children and run my house and see to my laundry and comb out my hair and bathe me every Thursday with hot water you've carried from the kitchen with your own two fragile hands, put up with all my despicable moods, forgive me all my shortcomings, and adore me without restraint or condition, and I shall be satisfied."

Even as she laughed, Sophia's eyes were moist with tears. He was asking her, in his own amusing, inimitable way, if they couldn't start over again. "It's a big decision," she said, burying her face in the thick, soft velvet. "I shall have to think about it carefully, for at least a quarter of an hour."

The corner of Edward's mouth quirked up in a lopsided smile, and he bent to kiss the top of his wife's head. "I'm in a generous mood. I shall give you all of an hour." He lifted the cloak and put it around her shoulders. "But I'm not fool enough to let you out of my sight. Not while you look like that."

Sophia loosened her auburn hair and spread it over the hood of the cape. She felt her husband's arms close around her and she leaned against him with velvet and fur a warm blanket between them. "We'll see," she murmured, slipping her arms around his neck. "We shall see."

They were groping their way back toward each other through the fog of their grief, and someday—surely soon—they would meet again as they used to, in laughter and desire, without secrets or resentment.

Saylah was out collecting kindling for the winter fires, staring up at the dull gray sky, seeking relief in the shapes of clouds but finding none. She had left Flora cleaning the walls; Jamie's widow had already washed and polished the pans and dishes and silver, then scrubbed the floors. The work seemed to soothe her a little. Saylah herself had found no such peace.

She stopped short when she saw Julian sitting on a stump, staring at the apple orchard, bare now of fruit and leaves. He leaned forward listlessly, hands clasped between his legs. His dark head was bent, his expression distant, his gaze blank.

For the first time in many days, Saylah really saw him, and what she saw appalled her. Julian sat on the stump where he had split logs resolutely, furiously, frantically. Now there was no outburst of violence, no ax swinging wildly, no arrows striking one upon the other, sent hurtling into the bark by the power of Julian's inflexible will.

Grief, unspoken, unexpressed, had broken that will—forged from a lifetime of work and struggle and pain—like a dry, brittle twig. Saylah covered her mouth with her hands to hold back a cry of horrified denial. Her own protective numbness had made her blind.

She swayed, her knees weak, her heart pounding. Tears threatened, and the sorrow she had pushed down and away. Julian seemed made of rags, not bone, indifferent, inert. He did not care—he who had always cared passionately, desperately. She had been frightened by the force of his anger; she was devastated by the knowledge of his apathy.

She stood, chilled, uncertain, fighting for breath. He did not see her, did not sense she was near. She took a step forward.

Julian heard her approach and raised his head slightly. When she sat on a boulder beside him, he turned his empty gaze upon her.

"I thought you were working," she said shakily.

"At what?" Julian asked. His eyes were dust dry. "There's nothing more to do."

The chill moved through her body and settled in her chest. "How will you survive if you don't work? Action, motion, creation are necessary to you, like air and water and food."

His expression did not change. "What if I don't want to survive? Have you ever thought of that?"

Saylah bent double, arms crossed over her stomach. "I have thought it."

The breathless misery in her voice made a bright splinter of pain slice upward through Julian's body. "It should have been me who died. Jamie had the magic, it was him the people loved. All this"—he gestured to encompass the ranch—"is here because of him. And now it's all for nothing."

Saylah felt herself falling, but she had to hold on. "Do not tell me you spent all these years and all this effort just to give Jamie a dream. Do not tell me you were not excited when you turned over the first clod of dirt to dig a place for the first apple tree. Do not tell me you were not filled with wonder when you saw the first blossoms on the trees you had planted with your own hands. And when you sold the first box of apples, do not say you were not exultant over what you had accomplished. For you, not for Jamie." If he denied it, if he turned away, she knew she could not bear it.

She gripped his arm so tightly that Julian winced. "Do not say, even once, even in your madness, that you do not love this land for its beauty and its richness and the challenge that it offers. That love was not for Jamie. You chose to succeed. Perhaps at first it was to help your father. But not anymore. You did it because you had to prove you could, and now because you cannot imagine life without it."

Julian stared at his hands, the nails grimy, the palms blistered and callused. Her urgency broke through the fog of insensibility in which he had moved since his father's death. He felt a churning in his belly, but gritted his teeth and pushed it down.

Drawing her knees up close to her body, Saylah pulled herself inward, where the last of her strength lay. "Do you not yet see that Jamie was a light too bright to blaze forever, so bright that he must burn himself out? Once he did, the beauty was gone and the inspiration. He did not want to be empty, ordinary. He could have borne anything but that. You cannot die for others, Julian. It is not your responsibility."

She choked on the words, because once, she too had wanted to die. For her People, who were ill and helpless, whose suffering she could not ease. Why had the spirits let her live?

The question struck her hard, like a closed fist. She shook with guilt because she had survived. All these years, she had known it, wished it, fought against the knowledge she could no longer escape. "I should have died," she muttered.

"What?" Julian asked, uncomprehending.

She looked up, afraid to meet his eyes and see her own reflection. "I said we are alike, you and I. It is strange that I should be here, that I should have come to know you."

Julian felt a surge of bitter grief mingled with unutterable tenderness. He looked at Saylah's delicate face, at her clear green eyes, and pulled her roughly toward him. He kissed her hard, locking his arms around her.

She groaned, just once, before she wrenched herself away. Julian made her feel things again. Things she had forced into darkness, far from memory or the too-bright light of day. She wanted to go back to a time when she felt safe, protected, happy. She wanted to lose herself in the concealing shadows of Jamie's dark room. She could hide there. She and Julian.

She rose without a word, and Julian followed, frightened by the frenzy in her eyes. When she began to run, he kept pace, wondering what she was running from and why he followed. What had she said to jolt him from the drugged paralysis of his dream? He wanted it back, that soothing oblivion in which he did not feel or remember, but the sound of his rasping breath, and hers, was too loud, too harsh. He could not shut it out.

Saylah flung open the front door with Julian close behind her, and stumbled forward until she paused, gasping, outside his father's room.

"No," Julian said when she reached for the knob. "I hate this place."

Through a fog of doubt and terror Saylah heard his voice. Somehow it steadied her, brought her back from the shadows to the dim light of this cold, bleak winter day. The beating of her heart subsided, and the spinning in her head. Finally, guardedly, she spoke. "I wonder if you have ever really seen this room. I think you are afraid to. Do not let your fear guide you, do not pretend there is no pain. You were not afraid to believe in your father; do not be afraid to grieve for him."

She did not know where she found the words. Closing her eyes to her own fear, she opened the door and drew him inside. Sunlight streamed in the windows, painting rainbows over the walls. The room did not smell of death, only emptiness. Saylah threw open the French doors so the breeze rushed in. She needed air in order to remember how to breathe.

The afternoon light brought into sharp relief the beautiful old bed, the lion's chair, the burgundy carpet and drapes, the living colored brilliance of the crystal chandelier. Julian gaped, unable to absorb the change.

Slowly, Saylah turned. "Jamie has a grave, Julian, beside the deer he loved. It is dark enough there. Let him lie alone."

Julian was transfixed by the reflected rainbows that danced on the silver wallpaper. He had begun to shake. The churning spread from his stomach to his throat. A book lay open on the bedside table. Jamie's book, left there, no doubt, as he lay dying, too weak to reach out and close it one last time.

Julian picked it up, turned it over, and, in the unfamiliar light of this lost room, read the marked passage haltingly.

> When through the old oak Forest I am gone,
> Let me not wander in a barren dream,
> But, when I am consumed in the fire,
> Give me new Phoenix wings to fly at my desire.

He faltered over the last words and Saylah saw his face was wet with tears. Despite her agitation, she could not turn away. She was drawn into his pain, into his arms, where she held him while he wept.

Julian shuddered. Jamie was gone, so far and so completely that even this room, which had been his haven, did not belong to him anymore. The light had taken it over, made it new. He held Saylah tighter, sensing that she shared his ravaged grief.

Their nerves lay close beneath their skin, and they held each other, screaming in silence. *I think you'll lock your grief away and nurture the grief of my family, that your own sorrow will become a barrier.* Lost in the sound of Jamie's voice, Saylah clung, but did not weep.

Julian could not stop shaking; he could not stop the agony that washed over him in waves. Saylah's arms around him, her cheek against his, drew the pain out, destroyed the last of his defenses.

She felt his tears soak through her gown. His pain had become her pain, his wilderness her sorrow. It came to her, as he held her and cried for his lost childhood, his lost happiness, his lost father, that he had become necessary to her. She had suffered his grief and anger, she had shared his childish laughter, she had danced with him in the darkness to the rhythm of remembered drums.

For all the things that he had lost, she had found one she had never thought to feel again.

When his weeping had ceased, when his eyes grew clear and focused once more, he lifted her braid and ran his fingertips along its thick, shining length. Her hair felt heavy and smooth, the design simple, yet intricately beautiful.

—— *483* ——

The pain had not left him, but the ugliness was gone. The festering edges of his wound could begin, gradually, to heal now. "Don't ever leave me," he murmured.

She started, moved by the anguish in his voice. "I have said that I will stay as long as I am needed."

"That's not what I mean."

Saylah did not wish to look at him. She was afraid of what she would see. *We have been somewhere together where no one else can ever go.* She turned toward the sunlight coming through the open windows, reached for that light, held out her hands, and let it settle on her palms. "I know what you mean," she said softly, but would not say any more.

Chapter
70

Theron sat alone in his room long after Paul had gone away. His friend came every day to see him, and Theron was glad, because he was lonely and afraid a lot. His mother tried to comfort him, but she was grieving too, and he didn't want to make her hurt any more than she already did.

Paul was a good friend, because he chattered when Theron wanted to listen, and listened when Theron needed to talk—about Jamie, or Saylah and Julian, or what would happen to them now.

Theron did not talk much about the secret chest. When he tried, his throat closed up and his eyes filled with tears. He thought probably he would just dry up and the wind would carry him away one day if he didn't stop crying.

Now that the room was quiet, Theron went to the place where he kept the chest and brought it out where he could sit with it between his legs. He opened the lid and the scent of roses drifted upward faintly, more faintly than before. "I didn't know it would go away," he muttered, ducking at the harsh sound of his voice against the walls.

He must have opened it too often to hold the daguerreotype and touch the diary, running his fingertips over the mysterious words. And now he had other reasons. On the day he died, Jamie had given his son a miniature painting of the Earl, the original Theron Ivy, in the same kind of embossed silver frame that held the daguerreotype of Jamie and his bride.

"But it's your father," the boy had cried. "You can't give your father away."

Jamie had stroked his son's hand gently. "I won't be here to look at it anymore. But I want someone to have it. Someone who'll take good care of it. And since you carry my father's name, I thought it should be you."

Theron had been speechless. He'd held the miniature carefully, staring in wonder at the image of the man in his hand. He was younger than Jamie, who looked so much like the Earl that Theron had gasped in amazement. For the hundredth time, he held the miniature and the daguerreotype side by side and stared at the two men, both beautiful, both gone.

He felt the ache that he had come to dread and looked into the chest at the leaves he had taken from his father's grave. They had dried out and crumbled into bright pieces of gold and orange that mingled with Simone's red rose petals. Theron wished the leaves had a scent, like the flowers. He picked up some fragments and sniffed them hopefully.

He bit his lip, but it didn't stop the tears. "Boys aren't supposed to cry," he'd told Paul that morning.

His friend had chewed his lip thoughtfully. "I've seen Papa cry, and if he can, *you* can."

The younger boy had nodded, unable to speak.

Theron let the crumbled leaves slip through his fingers and come to rest on top of the diary. Someday, when he could read, when his eyes had stopped watering every time he thought of his father, he would read that book. Then maybe he'd understand why Jamie had left them. Maybe.

Saylah had not been sleeping much. At night, when the house grew quiet, the dreams came, and the voices. They touched her grief, which was too tender to look upon, too raw and ugly. It was too soon after the moment by the river when she had huddled and wept and watched the last leaf disappear. She could not bear such pain again so soon.

At night, as she lay on her bed of fir needles, the voices came to haunt her. *I want you to have someone. Not to be so much alone,* Koleili had told her. Yet Saylah felt more isolated every day. The Ivys were beginning to heal, growing strong again, wiser from the teaching of their grief. She could have been one of them; she knew that. But her fear would not let her take the chance. *Most of all I believe in the power of your heart.* What if Jamie had been wrong? What if her heart was not strong enough to bear even one more sorrow?

Don't ever leave me. She felt Julian's fingers on her braid, caressing the woven pattern, drawing her close without the movement of her body.

She listened to the windless night, twisted and turned, bedeviled by images of dark, shrouded rooms and faces with hollow eyes and endless streams of salty tears. She covered her ears to shut out the voices, closed her eyes tight to stop the visions, but they would not let her rest. She could find no solace, no calm, no peace. *Do you not see that we create our own peace and our own sorrow? You, who are strong, must make your own choices.*

At last, with profound relief, for she found some solace in the work of her hands, which kept her demons quiet in the daylight, she sensed that dawn was near. Saylah rose, put on her wrapper, and crept down the stairs. She would bathe in the river and drown out the voices.

The air was cold, the scent of pines sharp in her nostrils. She shivered and hurried through the trees toward the river. Standing on the bank, she watched the water rush by, icy and clear in its carved, twisted path. She was mad to think of stepping into that surging water, but she felt unclean. She wanted to wash away the ashes of burned cedar from Jamie's empty room.

Dropping her wrapper on the bank, she ducked into the water, gasping as its icy fingers closed around her. For a moment she could not catch her breath. When the current lifted her, she caught a low branch from a sprawling oak and hung there, suspended, cold, uncertain.

She did not like the feeling. Saylah dropped back into the water, balancing herself between two boulders. She reached for the soap she had made and scrubbed her skin until it was red with cold and the abrasive rubbing of her fingers. She should not be here, alone and naked in the winter river. But there was no one to stop her, no warm body to curve against, no gentle hand to reach out and bid her stay.

Why should you not be like other women? You have a right to the same happiness. To lie beside a man, to know there is someone to keep you safe, to hold his child in your arms and feel its warmth and breath and life. She remembered Theron sitting in Flora's lap, his head on her shoulder, her arms wrapped protectively around him. They had grown closer in their grief. But Saylah was alone.

She gritted her teeth to stop her shivering. She wanted so much to be warm, yet she sat alone in the freezing river. She wanted to weep, to shout, to curl in upon herself. She wanted Julian to hold her. She wanted rest, a moment, time enough for the roaring voices to grow silent.

She was so tired—tired of fighting the emptiness, of trying to deny the pain of Jamie's loss. She had taught the others to mourn, but she could not. It took all her strength just to walk and speak and pretend that the awful, gaping void did not exist.

She could pretend no more. It was draining her dry. She rocked, mouth open in a soundless cry, weeping without tears, too weak to leave the water, too weary to care. As the light crept up from the sea, she grasped the oak branch to hold herself steady, stepped from the water onto the marshy bank.

She found a hemlock bough and tried to dry herself, but her muscles would not work properly. Finally, she wrapped her thin garment around her wet body and sat with a twig in her hand. She could not think what it was for. She stared at her tangled hair, dripping steadily into the bracken. Awkwardly, she reached up to try to work the knots free, but it was too difficult. She let her hand drop and her head fell forward.

Julian stood nearby, watching. Saylah looked exhausted, too tired to lift her own hand. He had been riding in the darkness, as he often did of late, thinking about her, worrying as the sun began to light the sky. Then he had heard noises in the water.

Shocked and disbelieving, he'd come to find her sitting in a wet wrapper, trying to comb her hair, giving up the effort with a weary sigh. Something was very wrong.

He slapped Phoenix on the side and sent him home while Julian approached Saylah warily. "Saylah?"

She tilted her head but did not answer. Julian's heart pounded furiously as he knelt beside her. "Saylah!"

She felt his breath in the chilling air, but could not lift her head to see his face. "Julian," she said, but no sound came. She was too cold to speak, too tired. Too late she realized that her wrapper clung but did not hide, covered but did not warm. Her strength had seeped away with the soap that had floated in rainbow bubbles down the river.

Then she felt his hand on her arm.

"You're frozen through," he whispered. She shivered violently and he cursed under his breath.

"Let me warm you." He did not wait for an answer, but took off his greatcoat and wrapped it around her. He was frightened by her silence, the way she leaned against him without protest. She trembled and he pulled her closer so the warmth of his body would reach her. "Don't you know it's winter? You'll make yourself ill."

He talked to fill the silence, to quiet his growing apprehension. He rubbed her back and felt the heavy mass of her wet hair. His fingers were caught in the dark strands and the chill moved from her body into his.

He looked around wildly and noticed the woven mat she had used to cover the old well and the fire ring. Perhaps the wood was still dry. "Come," he said, "I want to get you warm."

When he rose, she did not protest, but leaned against him gratefully. Julian felt dry tears sting his eyes. He guided her the last few steps to the place where she had taught him to celebrate. Leaving her wrapped securely in his coat, he uncovered the ring of stones and found dry wood beneath. With a prayer of gratitude, he piled it quickly and lit it with the flint and steel he always carried.

When the fire was blazing, he drew Saylah back into his arms, close to the heat of the crackling flames. She wanted to pull away, but she was so tired and the fire felt so good. Almost as good as her head on Julian's shoulder and the strength of his arm around her waist. She did not want to see his face, but something drew her head up, inexorably, until she looked into his eyes. She stared, dumbfounded by the concern, the compassion that softened his rough-carved features. But she must not think of that. It was too dangerous.

"Saylah, Saylah."

Julian repeated her name again and again and she fell into the reassuring cadence of his voice. She buried her cheek, bit by stinging cold, in his shirt. Just for a moment, she would let the tension flow from her aching bones. His warmth was so inviting, so solid, so necessary. For a moment, she would listen to his thudding heartbeat and rest, with the fire hot on her face, her hands on his flannel shirt. Just for a moment—

Julian felt her go limp and realized she was asleep. He liked the weight of her body against his, her head on his shoulder, though her skin was cold through and through. He opened the greatcoat enough to dry her wrapper, yet protect her from the morning air. It was a long time before the heat reached Saylah's body, crept beneath her chilled skin. She slid down until she lay with her head in Julian's lap.

He brushed the wet hair from her face, smiling. She had fallen asleep in his arms, soaking wet and nearly naked. She had trusted him that much.

Julian swallowed the lump in his throat, listened with relief to the sound of her even breathing. Her head was heavy and wet on his leg, her tangled hair still dripping. He touched it gently, glanced at her face, relaxed in deep sleep, and pulled a comb from his pocket. "I'll comb and dry your hair for you," he said, knowing she would not hear and so could not object.

He spread the thick strands in a fan across the woven mat on which she lay, then took a long, knotted portion and draped it over his leg. Gently, hardly daring to tug the comb along, he began to work at the snarls, one strand at a time. The heat of the fire turned his cheeks bright red and made his arm too warm, but he did not move. His fingers were involved in an intricate dance, a slow, painstaking parting of one interlocked strand at a time. The damp hair fell over his palm while he worked, looking up now and then to see if Saylah slept.

He sat with her hair over his hand, moving his fingers gently through the strands. He was intent on untangling each tendril without pulling or causing Saylah pain. He liked the feel of drying hair against his skin, gleaming in the wavering light of the fire.

Little by little, as Saylah's hair spread in a blue-black wave over the mat, as strand by strand he made it shine, the tenderness he felt for her grew.

Her face, relaxed in sleep, was beautiful, her lips curved in a slight smile. He absorbed the rhythm of her soft breathing, the soothing sound of his own tranquil breath. All worries left him, all memory of sorrow as he felt the weight of her hair in his hands. The feeling was so natural, as if he had known it for a very long time.

He felt that he belonged there, and he knew that even in her sleep Saylah could send him away if she chose. But he was no longer afraid of that, no longer afraid of the stillness he had envied. Now it did not shut him out, but called to him and took him in, told him more clearly than words that he loved her.

He had thought once that within such absolute stillness, deep emotion could not survive. He had been wrong. He had seen her celebrate, seen her throw aside restraint for a rhythm that vibrated from her body to his. He had seen her passion as she gazed into the midnight sky and gave herself up to the music in her blood. She had moved with the grace of a deer, with the power and abandon of a cougar, with the soaring freedom of an eagle. But more than that, she had taken him with her; he too had flown and leapt and danced and known what it was to let his passion rule his body.

Don't be a fool, Julian. Don't let her go. "No," he said fiercely. "No." Without the sight of her burnished face, delicate cheekbones and softly curved lips, without the sound of her lilting voice, without the feel of her hair in his hands, life would be cold and empty and barren.

Gently, breathing in the fresh smell of pine and clear island water, he buried his face in the long, shining strands.

Chapter
71

Saylah was dreaming, and in her dream she heard voices, far away and dim, but soothing and gentle. She was back among her People, lying on a cattail mat on a cedar shelf, while loving hands warmed her chilled body. She saw dark heads bent, felt the heat of fires built to chase away the cold, welcomed the many tender hands that cared for her.

A warm lassitude crept through her and her body grew heavy, too comfortable to move. Then she felt fingers in her hair. Someone was combing it, gently, carefully, separating the strands with a caressing touch. She liked how it felt, those fingers skimming through her hair, holding it toward the heat of the fire so she felt the warmth run up the strands to her forehead.

Only Koleili had ever combed her hair like that. But Koleili was gone. They were all gone. Even in her sleep, Saylah would not open her eyes. She did not want the dream to end.

Julian watched the changes in her face, the smile of contentment, the sigh of pleasure, the gradual easing of the lines of weariness and cold. In her sleep, she had let him console her. He clung to the thought tenaciously when her hair lay dry and full across his lap. He sat, stiff and uncomfortable, not caring about his discomfort, so long as Saylah slept with her cheek against his leg.

Saylah sank deeper into the darkness of the Longhouse, the fading voices, the lingering caress of hands. She sank beyond these things into a restful tranquillity where no dark things whirled in the shadows, no worries rose in the curling smoke, no pain followed, pulsing through her blood.

She was warm and safe, protected from the winter that raged beyond the windows. For a long time, she floated in hushed darkness, then she felt someone draw near. She saw a man who called to her, but would not step out of the shadows. A man whose voice was very dear. The sound made her ache inside.

The light began to flicker and she grew restless. He was there, talking quietly, but she could not understand. He called her, wavering in and out of sight—a wisp of smoke, a fleeting flame, a ghost.

The man was Jamie. Pain pierced her through and she reached for the shadow to pull it close. His voice grew louder but she could not touch his hand. "Death is peace, Saylah. You are a fool to try to call me back. I am happy in the shadows."

No! she cried, but again she made no sound.

"I am happy. Let me go." He swayed toward her and she saw in a sudden burst of light that his face was made of bone and his eyes were hollow and empty and dark.

When she woke up, she was sobbing, Julian was holding her, and Jamie was gone.

Paul Ashton heard laughter in the parlor and went to investigate. His father and mother sat side by side on the settee, giggling, while Edward wound a strand of his wife's hair around his finger. This was the third time in a week that Paul had seen them together, laughing. He simply did not understand.

"Paul!" Edward called when he caught sight of his son. "Come see. I've brought a new book from Victoria. It's from an English magazine called *Punch*, and it has funny pictures and stories." When he held out his arm, Paul moved forward warily.

There was no shadow in his father's gold-flecked eyes, no dark secret to turn his face gray, make him speak too loudly or not at all. His skin had been reddened by the intermittent winter sun, and he smiled as he used to do—almost.

"Paul, what is it? Don't you feel well?" Sophia asked. "It's all right, you know. It's an adult book, but you'll like it too. There's nothing 'questionable' in it." She screwed up her lips, prune-like, and uttered the word *questionable* in a thick British accent.

"Papa might find something. He's very good at that."

Edward threw back his head and laughed, but Sophia was not certain what her son meant. He did not lean easily against Edward's knee as once he would have. Perhaps Paul did not realize how much Edward had recovered in the last two weeks.

"Mrs. Ashton," Clara said from the doorway, "I need your advice about the menu. Mr. Ashton brought home fresh venison, no doubt the last of the year. I shouldn't like to waste it."

Sophia nodded, regarding Paul speculatively. She decided it might be best to leave father and son alone. "I'm coming right away," she told Clara. "You two enjoy the book for a while. There's work to be done in the kitchen."

"And my Sophia will roll up her sleeves and do it," Edward said with admiration.

She smiled, kissed his cheek, then Paul's forehead, before following Clara from the room. "Take care of each other," she murmured.

Paul stood stiffly, wondering at the affection in his father's voice. It seemed real enough. Taking a deep breath, he faced Edward directly. "There's something I want to know."

Edward felt Paul's intense gaze and closed the book with a thud. He was uneasy under that baleful stare, but refused to let his son see his distress. "Yes? What is it?" He leaned back on the settee, stretching his arm out casually, crossing one leg over the other.

Paul glowered, trying to think of the proper words, then blurted out, "Do you love Mama or not?"

Edward gaped at the challenge, the accusation in the boy's tone. His unease became wariness. He remembered these same eyes, this face, rigid with disgust on the morning after the cougar attack. Paul was too old for his age, that was the problem. He knew too much. Edward forced a smile to his lips. "I love your mother very much, just as I love you."

Paul peered at him skeptically, lips twisted in an unnatural curve. The question had been nagging him for a very long time. He needed to know the answer, to know if his father was going to hurt his mother again. Because he could not bear it if that happened. He had no idea how to stop it, but he knew he had to try. Still, he had been surprised when the words came out of his mouth just now. "Then why—why do you go off—" He blushed deep red and dug the toe of his kid boot into the Persian carpet. He could not say it after all.

Edward leaned forward, painfully alert. He had suspected Paul knew something, but it had not occurred to him that the boy would have the courage to confront him. Despite himself, he was impressed. Paul had suffered in silence, had not gone to Sophia, had not hurt her with what he knew. He had kept it inside, festering, no doubt, with his anger, until today it had erupted into this unanswerable question.

Edward knew all about festering wounds. He knew about cowardice— too well. Paul deserved better than that. And so did Sophia. "You've seen me with a woman—"

"Not just one," Paul interrupted, then stared furiously down at his shoe again.

Edward closed his eyes and stifled a sigh. How could the boy stand to look at him? He felt a wave of self-disgust that made his hand shake as he reached out to draw his son closer.

Paul stood between Edward's knees, staring into his father's eyes. "Whatever you've seen has nothing to do with your mother." He wanted to look away, to gather his thoughts, but knew Paul would take it as a sign of guilt. Since when did an eight-year-old boy have such an unwavering gaze?

Edward swallowed convulsively. "I've loved three people that way, the way I love Sophia, in all my life. The other two are gone now and forgotten."

Paul bit his lip. He wanted to believe, but was afraid.

Edward hurried on. "I can't tell you exactly how I feel about your mother. You're too young to understand all of it." He felt his son tremble, fight to keep his gaze steady. "But I will tell you this much. I couldn't live without her, not even for a day. I can't imagine trying. I've never known a woman like Sophia and I never will again. There *is* no woman like her." His voice shook, just a little.

Even Paul could not doubt his father's sincerity. He was not using his easy charm, his irresistible smile, his coaxing voice. Brow furrowed, the boy considered. He was not quite satisfied. "Then why do you have to—do those things?"

For the second time, Edward swallowed dryly. "I don't really know," he said. "There's just something in me that won't let me rest. I can't seem to find any peace—"

"Mama would give you that."

Edward shook his head. "She can't."

"Then who can?" Paul demanded.

For a long time, his father was silent. He released Paul's shoulder and ran his hands repeatedly through his sandy hair. "I don't know. No one, it seems. That's just the way it is."

Paul felt a rush of pity that could not quite stop the question that came unbidden to his lips. "Did Jamie die because of you?"

Edward flinched, stared helplessly at his fingers, clenched and white in his lap. In the back of his mind, a familiar voice spoke. *No man has the power to take from Jamie Ivy the wish to live. Not even you.* "No," he said, surprising himself. The words echoed inside his head, across the room, up to the ceiling, and Edward knew, all at once, that they were true. He sighed shakily at the flood of relief that swept through him. But Paul was watching, waiting, concerned and more than a little afraid.

"Jamie died because he was Jamie, because living had become a burden he no longer wished to bear. He made his choice, and I made mine, but that was a long time ago. He wanted peace and knew one way to find it. But he left us with too many memories to find our own peace. He left us to do the work."

"I wish I could help." Paul could not bear his father's pain any more than he could his mother's.

Edward's eyes burned. He had never realized what a remarkable son he had. But somehow, even that was not enough to fill the black hole inside him. "I know you do," he managed to choke out. He was learning to ignore the blackness, suppress it, to go on. He was a survivor, after all. He was going to survive, as always. No matter how deep the poison went.

Chapter

—— 72 ——

For the first time since she had arrived at the Ivys' several months ago, Saylah awakened with the sun in her eyes. She squinted, blocking the light with her hand, and gazed up at the sky through the wide windows. The clouds were thick and heavy, broken by patches of pale blue sky, and the sun was high. She had slept for too long.

Saylah sat up sharply, frowning as the wisp of a dream came back— hands on her cold skin, pushing away the chill, hands in her damp hair, soothing her into deeper sleep. Julian's hands.

She thought back to the day before, the dawn, the icy river, the lassitude that had drained her of strength. Then Julian had come and wrapped his coat around her and she had leaned against him, just for a moment. She remembered a blazing fire, the warmth that had crept through her, the strength of Julian's arm. She must have fallen asleep after that.

Then the other dream came back to her in a rush. The voice in the shadows, the plea for release. She had let go of the image in the shadows and wept for Jamie at last. All the while, Julian had held her, keeping away the cold. The rest of the day was a blur in her mind. She had moved through her tasks without thought or memory and sought her bed early. She remembered nothing more until the sunlight woke her. She knelt, surprised that her body felt so light. Somehow, the exhaustion had lifted from her shoulders.

Why, then, was she so afraid?

With shaking fingers, she dressed and went downstairs, Julian's face always before her—the compassion in his eyes, the kindness. She could still feel the weight of his arms tight around her, and it made her stomach clench in terror as she reached the foot of the stairs.

"So ye're awake. I thought I heard ye movin' about."

Saylah started at the sound of Flora's cheerful voice which woke her from the threat and the solace of her dream. She struggled for a moment to focus on Flora's familiar face. Gripping the rail, she tried to think of what she ought to say, but nothing came to her. She stared at the woman's curly blond hair and piercing blue eyes.

"How are ye feelin' this mornin'? Your thoughts seemed to wander far from your hands yesterday."

"I am better." The world was becoming sharp again and clear. "But I should have risen earlier. I have many things to do." She thought the words were right, but could not be certain; the sound of her disquiet was loud in her ears.

"Och, don't be daft." Flora waved her hand in dismissal. "Have ye no' done enough for us already?"

Saylah paled, concentrating on the smooth wood of the banister. "If I have done enough, then it is time to go." She realized with a shock that she had never thought about leaving this place, not since the day she arrived. She had never wondered when she would go, or if. Suddenly, she felt ill.

"Time—" Flora spluttered, then recovered herself. "Ye're talkin' madness. There's as much work to be done today as yesterday. We need ye as much as ever." She put her red, work-roughened hand over Saylah's. "But 'tis much more than that, and I think ye know it."

Saylah met those clear blue eyes, full of affection, and began to feel dizzy with fear. "I know," she managed to reply, but her voice sounded hollow.

Flora backed up, arms akimbo, regarding Saylah in dismay. "Ye'd best be eatin' something. Mayhap that'll help. Ye near starved yourself yesterday. And I've an idea ye'll no' be gettin' a chance later," she added mysteriously. She spun on her heel and started toward the kitchen.

Saylah would have stayed where she was, except she was so hungry that she felt weak. "I will eat," she told herself firmly, "and then the confusion will leave me." But she knew, as she crossed the main room, lit by two huge winter fires, that she was lying to herself.

* * *

"She's up, Julian. I saw her coming down the stairs," Theron shouted when he found his half-brother in the apple orchard. He had been running so hard that he could not stop in time and propelled himself into Julian with a force that knocked them both to the ground.

Theron was winded by his run from the house, so Julian lifted him and held him upright until he caught his breath.

"I didn't mean for you to kill yourself bringing me the message. Now your new shirt is covered with mud. It's even in your hair." Julian brushed away what he could, smiling affectionately at his brother.

"But you said it was *important*," Theron reminded him.

Julian grinned. He felt good today, strangely optimistic. "Not important enough to bring Flora after me for ruining your clothes. She's liable to beat me senseless with the broom."

The idea was so unlikely that Theron roared with laughter. Julian pushed him back toward the house. "You make sure she's eaten. I'll get the horse ready. And don't let her get away."

Theron's eyes grew round with incredulity. "Are you going to *kidnap* her?"

Julian smiled to himself. "Maybe. If she doesn't want to come. I have a feeling she might have other plans."

"Gosh!" Theron looked at his half-brother with new respect. "Aren't you afraid of her anymore?"

Julian froze in mid-stride. "Afraid of her? That's ridiculous."

Theron rubbed his scar absently through his thick wool coat. "I am, I mean, sort of. I mean, I'd *never* kidnap her. She's just so—so Saylah. She doesn't ever seem to wonder or be scared or ask questions. She just *knows* things." But there had been that time when he and Paul had found her crying. Theron bit his lip. He could not tell Julian that; he had promised to keep the secret. Besides, the memory frightened him.

"Maybe not everything," Julian mused, more to himself than to Theron. "She knows a lot of things, but maybe she doesn't know herself."

Theron puzzled over this all the way back to the kitchen, where he found Saylah finishing a plate of suspicious-looking greens and bulbs. Sometimes she ate things he'd be more inclined to step on. "Did you sleep good?" he asked.

Saylah smiled at him, but it wasn't real. "Yes," she said. "I feel better now."

"You don't look better. Does she, Mama?"

Flora scowled, but Theron didn't see it. He was right anyway, she thought. Saylah sat stiffly, her eyes clouded over, distant, the way Jamie's used to be. Flora winced at the pain that shot through her, even now, at the sound of her husband's name. Jaw set, she turned back to Saylah. She didn't like the girl's expression. Especially not today.

When Julian burst through the door, Flora wanted to warn him away, but she didn't know how.

"We're going for a ride," he told Saylah firmly.

"Do ye think 'tis wise?" his stepmother asked.

Julian glanced at her, brow furrowed, but she saw that he hadn't really heard. He was looking—and listening—only to Saylah.

"I do not wish to leave my work," she said. "I have wasted too much time today."

Julian shook his head. "It's winter. All we have is time. I want to take you for a ride before it gets too cold."

Saylah looked at his brown wavy hair, his sparkling hazel eyes, at his smile and his hands, which he leaned on the table beside her. The hands that had wound themselves in her hair. She stifled the urge to touch those deft, gentle hands, though she could not force herself to look away.

"I thought a little fresh air might do you good."

Saylah could not help but smile, though tiny sharp warnings pricked her skin. "I am outside in the air more often than you. I know its taste and smell and healing power."

Julian smiled back, noticing with regret that her hair was neatly bound in a braid. Then he remembered the smile on her sleeping face and the breath caught in his throat. "Come with me," he said. "I want you there."

Gradually, Saylah became aware of undercurrents in the air around her. Flora and Theron were listening avidly, waiting to see what she would say. She realized with both relief and dread that she could not refuse and shame Julian before his family. Not while the memory of her dream lay soft around her. "I will go," she said, "if Flora does not need me."

"We can do without ye," Flora assured her, "but just for the day," she added, remembering their earlier conversation.

Theron, who often woke up three times a night to check his mother's room and make sure she was there, heard something strange in Flora's voice. "You're not going to leave us, are you?" he demanded, grasping Saylah's hand.

His blue eyes were full of pleading, his grip on her hand desperate. "No, I am not. I have promised to stay for as long as you need me."

Theron released her with a huge sigh of relief. "Well, that'll be forever."

Saylah felt a wrenching sadness and turned so the others would not sense it. Julian was heading for the door and did not see her face.

Phoenix was waiting outside, saddled and bridled, stamping his feet with impatience.

"I told you we were going for a ride." Julian grinned.

He helped her up, then swung into the saddle in front of her. "Hold on," he said, grasping the reins. "I plan to make this a ride you won't forget."

She knew already that she would not forget. Julian dug his heels into Phoenix's sides and the horse galloped across the clearing and into the trees. Saylah felt the cold winter breeze in her face, saw the black branches of trees whose leaves had gone, the stands of evergreen that shut out much of the fleeting sunlight.

The wind whipped past, stinging her cheeks, lifting her braid and letting it fall against her back. Her skirts rose and fell with the motion, but she did not care. She liked the feeling that she rode on the air, that her feet never touched the ground. She liked the feeling of the horse's rippling muscles beneath her legs, the heat of Julian's body, encircled by her arms.

The clouds had covered the sun again, transforming the forest into a green cathedral. Saylah breathed in the cool darkness, the familiar scents she loved, the unfamiliar smell of a horse's sweat, and the smell of Julian's skin.

She knew he was smiling, though she couldn't see his face, knew he felt the same sense of freedom and release. They raced together among trees and low-hanging branches, through darkness and sunlight, stretches of chill wind and flashes of warmth.

Saylah held on, forgot everything but the pressure of her arms around Julian's waist, the beat of his heart through the fabric of his coat. She closed her eyes and imagined they were flying, skimming over the trees into the sky, dipping low above the river 'til the sound of the water echoed in her ears.

When the wind ceased, and the fluid motion of the horse, she sat, eyes closed, unwilling to come back to earth. Julian sighed with pleasure, acutely aware of her arms locked around him, her cheek pressed to his back. To Julian, the steel-gray lake streaked with blue, the fine-grained earth of the shore looked different, changed in some way he could not define. He was seeing it, for the first time, through Saylah's eyes, which now were tightly closed.

Finally, he shifted and Saylah sat up, gazing around vaguely, as if she had awakened from yet another dream. Julian slid off the horse and helped her down. They leaned, breathless, against the animal's heaving side, hands casually intertwined.

Saylah looked up to find Julian watching, a crease of worry between his brows. But his eyes were clear and full of an affection even she could not mistake. He reached out to brush a loose hair from her cheek. Instinctively, she flinched and turned away.

Julian stared after her, stunned. He had thought the barriers between them had fallen, that today she would talk to him, really talk. They would say what had been said in every way but words. He needed to hear the words. He breathed deeply, trying to draw strength from the air, but the thought of the cast on her eyes, the way she had winced at his touch, cut him like a twisted blade.

She walked down the shore, staring blindly at the billowing water. Her back was rigid, her arms stiff at her sides. She was once again a stranger.

Julian kicked a stone so hard it bounced into the lake, then, setting his jaw in a rigid line, he slapped Phoenix's flank. "Go wander, boy, but come back when I whistle. I think I'm going to need a friend."

Julian started toward Saylah and each step he took, each time his leather boots sank into the fine soil of the beach, he felt his anger grow. He had had enough of playing games, enough of the cold stillness in Saylah's eyes.

He came up to her and she recoiled when he reached out to touch her. His smoldering anger flared. Forcing himself to move slowly, he grasped her shoulders and swung her to face him.

"I want to swim," she said unexpectedly.

"It's too cold," Julian snapped, though those were not the words he wanted to speak.

"I do not fear the cold." Yet she feared something. It was wild and powerful and could easily destroy her—this nameless, faceless terror.

Julian glared at her. "Yesterday morning wasn't enough? Do you always have to prove again how strong you are?" When she didn't answer, he added, "I *know* you're strong. How could I not? What I want to know is—" He broke off at the grim penetrating chill in her green eyes.

"What is it that you wish to know?" She regretted the question when she saw the spark that leapt into his hazel eyes.

Julian drew a deep breath. "I brought you here so we could be alone, away from the house, the memories and the work, away from everything but ourselves." She stared blankly and he cursed under his breath. "I guess you don't understand what's happened between us. Or else you don't want to."

His heart was pounding in his ears, louder every moment that she gazed at him, unblinking. "I broke down and wept in front of you. I let you hold me while I cried for my father. Do you have any idea what that means to me?" he asked.

There was a flicker of feeling in her cool green eyes. Compassion, regret. It was not enough.

Julian shook her slightly. "A man doesn't let a woman see his tears. Hell, a man isn't even supposed to cry. But I stood there and wept and never for a moment thought of sending you away or pretending I wasn't being torn up inside. I let you inside, Saylah, *you* and no one else. I let you see the blackest, ugliest part of my pain, and then I let you ease it."

It's easy to be a hero in the darkness, where no one can see the truth, much harder to be a man who stands in sunlight and is unafraid of the flaws it might reveal. His fingers tightened on her shoulders until she grimaced and he let her go abruptly. "I thought you knew what it meant to share something like that, but I guess not. I guess you'd take any man to the river in the moonlight and play your drum and dance over the well."

This is the most sacred thing I can teach you. To dance, yes, but also to celebrate.

Saylah felt he had struck her, and this blow hurt more than his fingers digging brutally into her skin. "You know I would not. I told you, it was only you." She had given him her most precious gift, and he mocked it. Her own anger flared, shocking her with its depth and fury.

"And I'm telling *you*. It was, is, and will be only you. There's no other woman on earth I would have let that close to me." Julian began to pace in a small circle, turning his back, spinning to face her. "But I can't do it anymore unless I know—unless you tell me how you feel. I brought you here to hold you and stroke your hair and kiss you. I meant to tell you how much I love you. But you won't let me! You won't even look at me with your own eyes. I don't want to see those stranger's eyes. I want to see you!"

Saylah's world began to spin and in the center was a terror so deep it drowned her hurt anger. "You have seen much of me already. Perhaps too much."

Julian clenched and unclenched his fists. "I just told you I love you. I told you things I didn't ever want to say. But I did it because I know you're wary, I know you're not like other women, that you don't play their games. God in heaven, I wish you did. At least those games I understood." He raised his hand, cupped it, and held it close to her cheek. She did not move away, but her face was carved in stone.

"I thought you felt something for me. I thought I wasn't alone after all. But I can't go on thinking. I need to *know*!"

She opened her mouth in a silent cry, and the veil slipped for a moment, revealing her despair. It was enough for Julian. He pulled her close and kissed her until he was gasping for breath, until he felt her tremble, felt her relax against him, felt her hands come up around his neck and hold on—tight.

Julian groaned and closed his eyes, struggling against the angry urge that made him want to touch her everywhere, to make her admit she wanted him as much as he wanted her. But she shivered in his arms, her lips parted on a sigh, and he knew he could not do it.

Gradually, agonizingly, he raised his head. "Do you love me, Saylah?"

His lips were so close that she could feel his breath against her mouth. Her voice had left her, and cold dread lay coiled inside, choking out all other feeling.

"Tell me if you love me."

She saw what it cost him to ask her again and again, but she did not answer. She could not. There was no sound but the distant beating of drums inside her head. Drums and the echo of a man who was dead. *It is easier to love a ghost than to take a chance on someone real.* Saylah unclasped her hands and took a step backward.

"Tell me!" he snarled. "Just tell me, one way or the other."

Saylah struggled to find her voice, was horrified when she croaked, "Jamie—"

Julian went very pale. "I'm not Jamie," he said, "I'm Julian. If it's my father you want, go after him." He flung his arm toward the wind snaking over the lake, leaving in its wake gray tortured waves ridged in white.

What you feel for me is safe. You've known from the moment you came that I would leave you.

Julian swung away, then back again. He was a fool who could not give up, even when she flung Jamie in his face. "But if you want me, if you love *me,* then tell me so." His eyes gleamed with his need, his anger and his love, which was strong enough to keep him here, facing her in the chilling wind.

"I cannot," she whispered.

He froze at the soft murmured sound of her voice. "Why not?"

"Because if I say it, it will be true." Saylah gasped, fighting for breath.

Julian gaped at her, bewildered. "It will be true, or untrue, whether or not you speak the words," he said as calmly as he could.

Her eyes were no longer veiled but full of misery and hopelessness. "Did you really think your silence was a magic charm to keep you safe?" He would not let her go until she felt his urgency and it became her own. "Is that what you thought?" he persisted.

It doesn't matter what I thought. It's you who must think now, you who must decide. "I will never be safe again!" Saylah cried.

What, in God's name, are you so afraid of?

Julian fought to keep his head, which was beginning to whirl with doubts and questions and desolation. "Did you really think you were ever safe?"

It was a long time before she answered. "I believed it once. I thought I was protected, cherished, that no one could ever touch me."

Julian took a deep breath. "I'm touching you now, just as you've touched me. Do you feel it?" She leaned forward, just a little, but it was enough. "You can't deny it; I feel it in your hands, see it on your face and in your eyes."

Saylah felt a tearing inside, the pounding of distant drums, the erratic beat of her own pulse. *A ghost never changes, never hurts you, never makes mistakes, and because he has already left you, you don't fear his going.* She swallowed painfully. "If I love you, you will hurt me."

Julian's eyes burned at her look of desperation. "And you'll hurt me. It's the way people are."

I do not seek that kind of pain again. Twice I have borne it. Twice I have been strong. It is enough.

He saw her distress, and finally, he understood. "But there's more to life than just pain and sorrow. There's laughter and peace and celebration. You know that. You're the one who showed me. You *know* it."

Saylah struggled to speak over the rising sound of the drums in her head. "I know it exists, but not for me."

"Why not?"

She turned from him again. He followed, stepped in front of her, blocking the way. "Why not?"

"Because I do not deserve happiness."

Julian shook his head. He could not have heard correctly.

Saylah's throat was tight, her eyes burning. "It is because I am not enough. I have never been enough."

With an effort of will, he found his voice. "You're enough for me and more than enough." He saw her disbelief and spoke more quietly, but so distinctly that she would hear the truth in what he said. "When I was a boy and I imagined the woman I would love someday—the perfect woman, bred of all my dreams—I would never have dared imagine you."

She closed her eyes and he saw that his reassurance had not brought her comfort, but a pain that was tearing her apart. He forced himself to go on. "For whom, then, weren't you enough?"

"For my People—for Yeyi and Koleili, Kitkuni and Hawilquolas and Colchoté. For all of you—and Jamie. I failed them, and you, every one."

"But you said Jamie wanted to go. You showed us how to set him free."

Saylah shook her head frantically. "It was not enough. I should have stopped—" She broke off, crossed her arms over her chest protectively.

At last Julian began to understand. "Should have stopped what? The pain? Did you think you were a god with the power to ease all suffering?"

Do you not think it false pride to believe you alone could cure a sickness that our bodies have not learned to fight? Even you do not have such power.

She stared at him, eyes damp with tears of self-disgust.

Julian had to fight back anger, but this time, it was not for her. "Saylah," he whispered, "you're only human."

You are only human, Tanu, but they did not tell you that.

"But I should have been more. From the moment of my birth, they told me I was more. But I was never a true shaman."

Julian stopped short at the roar of thunder that reverberated in his head. Like everyone else on Vancouver Island, he had heard fantastic stories of the magical birth and life of a green-eyed Salish shaman, the Indian queen. She had disappeared one night and never returned.

That is Tanu's song, Saylah had cried as she danced in triumph. *Who is Tanu?* he had asked. *She was Queen of my People.* He looked deep into her luminous eyes and his heartbeat ceased. *"You* are Tanu, She Who Is Blessed."

Saylah shuddered and the blood left her face. "I told you, Tanu died long since." She spoke in a small, weak voice unlike her own.

Eyes narrowed, he scrutinized her face, half Salish, half white. Then he knew. "You were their queen."

As she looked at him helplessly, silently, unable to deny the truth, a wrenching fear stopped his breath. Only now did he understand fully what he was struggling against. "Listen to me," he said shakily. He did not touch her, sensed that to do so would make her flee without looking back. "Your people told you you were more because they needed to believe it. They needed you to hold them when they might have fallen, to give them something to have faith in when everything else was gone."

The spirits have chosen you, Colchoté had told her. And she had answered, *Once, perhaps, they chose me, but they have left me now. Whatever purpose they had for me has come to pass.*

"How do you know that?" she demanded.

Julian ran his hand through his hair, damp from the mist off the lake. "Because I needed to believe it too. I saw you once as your people must have seen you—a gift from God with the strength of will to lift me above my private grief."

Did you think I do not feel the pain of loss? I am not a spirit; I am a woman. Saylah shivered uncontrollably and the sound of drums grew louder.

With one finger, Julian forced up her chin so she would have to look him in the eyes. "But things are different now. Now what I see is a woman who is dearer to me than anything in my life before. Not because of your magic or your power or your wisdom, but because your heart is strong and kind."

Most of all, I believe in your heart.

"Because you saw through my anger and never once looked away.

—— *505* ——

Because you were not afraid to speak the truth, even when you knew we did not wish to hear it. Because you made me laugh and showed me the one thing you most treasured."

It is your heart, your self, your soul, that matters. Saylah stood motionless while the drums pounded and her pulse beat and her heart dragged in her chest.

"I do not need a shaman who makes miracles," Julian told her. "All I need—no, all I *want* is that you be Saylah and that you love me."

She whirled and covered her ears. The drums were pounding, pounding in her head, echoing through her body, taking up the rhythm of her tattered emotions, playing them back in the cadence of her fear, of an ancient, haunting song. But the song was too loud. Her head would burst with the sound, the pressure of those endless, throbbing drums.

You're afraid to trust your own feelings, though like your visions, they are true. She turned and saw Julian waiting, hand outstretched, despite his pride, his eyes full of hope and a promise no words could express or make true.

You're afraid to listen to your heart as you listen to the wind and the spirits and the voices of your dreams.

The ancient song ended, the drumbeat faded, and she moved toward him slowly.

I no longer believe in anything but you.

She was shaking as she opened her mouth, licked her dry lips, and whispered, "I am Saylah." She put her hand in his. "And I love you."

Chapter
73

Leaning on the railing of the upstairs porch, the French doors open behind her and the ranch spread below, sloping gently to the distant sea, Saylah listened. She heard the trees sighing, the river running past, the rise and fall of her own breath. These sounds brought to her a pleasant warmth, despite the chilly night air. She had been floating all afternoon on a soundless wind that carried her through Theron's constant questions, Flora's fond smiles and secret looks full of satisfaction, and the dull tasks of every day.

Julian had not been beside her, but she had been aware of him, always, wherever he was. She did not think back, nor did she dare to think ahead. She did not wish to shatter the fragile peace that had settled inside her. Now the others slept and she stood in the winter air, breathing with her body and her slow-beating heart.

She heard nothing, felt nothing, yet knew when Julian stood beside her. Her pulse raced and her skin tingled as she moved closer until their elbows rested side by side on the railing.

"I've been waiting a long time for this," he said. He did not reach for her or touch her, except where their arms met. He wanted to savor the unfamiliar stirring of a sense of freedom, of expectation, of elation that had filled him all day.

"You have stood here with me many times," Saylah replied.

"But not like this."

"No," she agreed. "It was different before." She felt a prickle of fear and moved closer yet, so they stood shoulder to shoulder.

"What is it?" Julian asked. He had learned to know her by the actions of her body, though he could not read her face; tonight there was no moon.

"It is strange to feel—so at ease with you. I have been so long alone, inside myself, where no one else can touch me." She looked at the dark outline of his face against a moonless sky. "I have not always wanted to be alone, yet I have treasured my solitude."

She paused pensively. "But it is more than that. Today we are both free, truly free, perhaps for the first time in our lives."

Julian stared at her, brow furrowed. "What do you mean?"

"Those we love bind us to them, though they may not mean to do so. And we do not fight these bonds. They are part of our caring. But now they—Jamie has released us. We should take our freedom, learn to know it."

"If you're afraid I'll try to take away your freedom, don't be. I've felt the tug of those bonds and felt them break, I've been alone and glad to be alone," Julian said.

They turned back to the dark landscape—shades of black on gray on pewter. "But you see," he continued, slipping his arm around her, sighing when she leaned into him without hesitation, "being together doesn't mean giving up our solitude, just our loneliness."

Saylah smiled. "Why is it that I believe you?"

"Because, somewhere inside, you know I don't want to intrude on the secret stillness of your spirit. I value it too much. I'll fight to keep it untouched and unbroken. Always."

Saylah smiled. He would protect her. Why did the thought make her shiver with apprehension, and, at the same time, fill her with hope?

"Tell me what you're thinking," he said, more to hear the sound of her voice than the answer to his question.

"That I am happy."

Julian took a step back and held her at arm's length, trying to read her face in the darkness. "You sound surprised. Weren't you ever happy before?"

"I was, or thought I was, for many years. But I did not really know what it meant. It came too easily. This happiness I have fought for, so I know it is a miracle." She lifted her face as he slid his arms around her and touched his lips to hers.

They clung for a moment, cool lips warming as they gave each other heat and strength and pleasure. For the first time, Saylah buried her fingers in Julian's wavy brown hair, felt its silky texture, smelled the fragrance of soap and pine. When he touched her lips with his tongue, she shivered and her skin grew hot, sensitive to the slightest movement of his body.

When he pulled her closer, she swayed back, drawing him with her, afraid to let go and afraid to hold on. Afraid of the whirlpool of desire and fear, need and exultation she felt. Never in her life had she stood so close to another human being, never had she risked so much for the call of her hungry body.

Julian raised his head, his cheeks flushed. "I want to stay with you tonight." He felt her stiffen and added, "I only want to hold you. I know you're not ready yet. But I can't bear to leave you. Not when I've just discovered you."

She could see his eyes in the dim light that filtered through the windows of the loft. She could see his sincerity and his need, naked on his face. It reflected her own.

She quivered with desire, with a yearning for the sound of his voice and the look in his eyes as much as the touch of his gentle hands—a yearning for his face in firelight, surrounded by the faces of their children, the exuberant noise of their laughter to reassure her.

When she was a child, Tseikami had taught her that the word *shaman* meant "to take flight." Since that moment, she had looked to the sky as her true home, the promise of all that was sacred. It came to her as Julian caressed her back with tantalizing fingertips, that he alone had the power to bind her forever to the earth. She had loved Jamie deeply, but his spirit had walked the skies long before she came to this house. He would never have held her back, woven her into the cloth of his life as Julian wished to do. She rested her head on his shoulder to hide her agitation. "Come," she said softly.

They stepped inside and Julian closed the French doors, shutting out the sound of the winter wind. He held the handles in an unyielding grip, trying to gain control of his desire. He must go slowly, carefully. He wanted her, all of her, not just in his arms, but in his breath and in his blood. He had waited a long time; he would not give in to his impatience now.

When he turned, Saylah was seated naked on the bed of fir, her hair falling around her. For an instant, he was too delighted to move, entranced by the curves of her body beneath her gleaming hair. She watched him curiously, but he sensed no fear. Yet he hesitated.

Saylah felt his distress and motioned him toward her. "Already you have looked inside and known the secrets of my heart. You have seen more of me than you see before you now. This is merely the shell that keeps my spirit safe. I have taken away what was not necessary, so I come to you with the weight of neither world upon my body—neither Salish nor white. It is right that it should be so."

Julian's ragged breathing grew calm with the sound of her silvery voice. She held out her hand and he bent to take it. He turned it over and kissed her palm, lingeringly. In another moment, he had removed his own clothes and sat beside her. Saylah turned down the lamp and reached for him.

He was certain she had never known a man, yet she was at ease and unafraid. He, who had lain with many women, could only think of her as delicate glass that might shatter at a touch. He smiled. Saylah, who was so strong. But he sensed that tonight he had that power. It was part of what she chose to give him.

Gently, she pulled him down beside her and slipped her arms around him. Julian kissed her forehead, her nose, her cheeks, twisted his finger in a lock of hair and kissed it too. His skin tingled with the touch of her body, her rounded breasts, smooth stomach and strong, slender legs.

It was she who touched her lips to his first, she who pulled him nearer, she who moaned, then buried her face in the thick brown hair on his chest. She felt she was playing a forbidden game which was all the more exciting because she did not know the rules.

Julian drew away, swallowing his own desire. "Lie against me and go to sleep," he murmured. He was amazed his voice was not a harsh croak, amazed that his hands did not shake when he touched her and she nestled close to him.

Saylah sank into contentment, into the solace of Julian's arms around her, his naked body at her back. "It is odd," she said, smiling without guile or sadness or regret, "that we have seen the worst of each other. We have walked together the darkest paths where the shadows pressed around us."

"That's true," he breathed into the fir-scented blackness of her hair.

"We have known the struggle and the grief. We have seen the sunset all around us. Let us turn now to the light. We must hold tight to the sound of our laughter, sing it louder than our songs of sorrow."

Saylah wondered if it was not dangerous to join cold reflection to cold reflection. Or would that melding of rigid glass into molten liquid give those reflections warmth and breath and life? When Julian kissed her, she knew it did not matter. She wanted to walk inside the man who was her mirror.

Julian wrapped his arm protectively around her, thinking they would not sleep, would not waste one moment of this intimacy, the texture of her hair across his skin, her weight and warmth against his body.

He would breathe with her breathing—listening, watching, savoring every moment. Except that, long before Saylah closed her eyes, he had drifted into sleep.

In her dream she stood high on a beach where a man and child sat talking above the pulse of the waves. Dark-haired, muscular and bronzed, the man spoke in a surprisingly gentle voice. "The end is not yet. There are too many answers not given, too many questions unasked."

"But what are they?" the child asked, and the moon shone on her black hair like a rim of silver light.

"That is for you to discover," the man said.

"But who will ask these questions and who will find the answers?"

The man took a stick and drew meaningless designs in the crumbling sand. "Some you have asked already, some belong to others. The answers will come from those who have answers to give."

When the child shook her head, the rim of light splintered and fell into the sea. "I have no answers."

"Are you certain of that? Are you certain the past is behind you, truly past?" The man did not look up; he spoke clearly, echoing the constant rhythm of the ocean.

"I know what I must do, what I have *chosen* to do," the child answered sharply.

The man smiled. "Just because you know your heart does not mean others know it. You must show them so your ghost no longer haunts their dreams."

The child shook her head wildly. "I left them long ago."

"*You* left them, but your ghost did not. You carried their ghosts for many years. Do you think they did not also carry yours? You have set your spirits free, but they do not know how. This one last thing you must show them."

"But how—?"

There was no answer. The man had risen and walked into the sea, where he disappeared beneath the shimmering water.

Saylah awoke with an unfamiliar presence beside her. When she saw Julian's arm draped over her body, she smiled. How easily she had slept beside him, when she'd thought she would not sleep at all. But now something called her to rise, and she slipped soundlessly from under his arm.

She knelt beside him in the darkness, drinking in the shadowed sight of his face, relaxed and vulnerable in sleep. She wanted to touch him, but not to wake him, so she barely brushed his extended fingers before she moved away.

She went to the low railing and looked down into the house in the glow of fading firelight. Jamie's house. Except Jamie had left it behind. It came to her then, as she gazed at the huge, empty room, that she was not simply giving herself and her solitude into Julian's hands. She was also giving up the world of her childhood.

Have you never thought that the two worlds of my grandfather are also in your blood? That someday you will face them both and have to choose as he did? Odd, how strong and sure the memory of Hawilquolas' voice, even after all this time, how clear and devastating his remembered warning.

She had answered with her whole heart, certain she knew all of the world that she need ever know. *I have chosen, long ago and for always.* Yet today she had chosen again, fulfilling that long-ago fear. Even then, the choice had not been hers to make. *There is a future I do not seek, but which will come to be, just the same.*

And so it had. This house, these thick walls, these fireplaces of sparkling stone would be her future, not the Longhouse or the summer huts of her memory.

She glanced at Julian, sound asleep, his hand on the indentation of her body in the bed. Saylah smiled sadly. If she chose him, she must also choose his world—the white world, the world of the Strangers.

Until that moment, she had always known, somewhere inside, that her heart was Salish, and her spirit which had brought her to this house. Until that moment, when the love she felt for another moved her more deeply, even, than the loss of her People, she had not understood that her spirit might reach one way and her heart another.

Her resolution did not waver, but ancient voices came back to her, and she leaned forward, listening. Even in the house, closed tight for the night to shut out cold and wind and snow, she could hear the movement of the water. That was a voice she understood, a sound which echoed the pulse of her blood, a sound which did not change from the one she had always known and loved. The voice said simply, "Dream."

Then she knew what she must do.

Chapter
74

Saylah knelt above Julian, staring at his body in the light of the low-burning lamp. His shoulders were broad from carrying the load of his father's dreams, from his own battle with the earth. There were many scars on his arms, his chest, from the heavy work he had done, the shovels that had slipped, the wire that had not bent the way he shaped it, the splinters of wood that had pierced his skin.

Gently, with her healing hands, she touched those scars, running her fingertips over the puckered ridges, the white curved half-moons buried among thick dark hair. In his sleep, he smiled, and she leaned down to kiss the path her fingers had followed.

Julian awoke, his body tingling, to find Saylah kneeling above him, an invitation in her clear green eyes. He took her face in his hands. "Are you certain you're ready?"

She smiled, for the first time in his memory, without pain or sadness. "I am certain."

He opened his mouth to object, but she tossed her hair back over her shoulder and revealed her golden body. Her breasts were small and round, tipped in dark brown, her skin made golden by the lamplight. Julian lay watching her, teaching himself to know the lines and curves of her body.

She moved gracefully, resting her hands on his shoulders, letting her hair drift over his skin. He shivered with anticipation.

"You are cold."

Saylah lay with one leg curved around his. Slowly, languorously, she spread her hair over him, to give him her serenity, her scent, the silken whisper of her song in the tendrils lifted by his breath, then left to settle on his naked skin. She touched his cheeks, trailed her finger down his throat to his shoulder and then across his chest, through her own thick, gleaming hair. She drew his head down to her chest so he might feel the pulse of her strange and powerful heartbeat.

To give him, to hold him, to warm him . . .

The words came through the windows with the harsh sounds of winter, echoing along the walls until he heard them and understood at last. To give *him* . . .

He sat up precipitously. "No."

She bit her lip, dismayed and confused.

"No," he whispered, so she would hear the tenderness in his voice. He watched her sway with the sigh of wind outside the brittle glass, and with his hands and lips and breath, he forbade her to touch him.

She had given him all she had—her wisdom, her healing, her strength and understanding, even her vision. Through her eyes, he saw not simply what was, but what was possible. She had given him her love. Now he wanted to give it back.

"Let me show you," he said, lifting her hair off his shoulders one strand at a time and watching it settle, featherlike on her waiting body. He followed each strand with his tongue, barely touching her skin, though she shivered and cried out and reached for him.

"You taught me how to celebrate in the way of your people. Now let me teach you mine," he said, caught by her glowing green eyes in the dim light. The scent of fir and cedar rose around them, and night pressed against the windows, seeking to enter with stray wisps of wind.

Saylah's pulse grew rapid and her skin feverish. "Teach me." She had thought she was doing this for him, to give him something to remember—a vow, unspoken, which told him she had chosen him above all others. Then he began, lightly, to touch her bare skin with his lips and seeking fingertips, burning away her inhibitions with his practiced touch.

She moaned and trembled at the desire that ran like fire in her veins. Julian had touched some primitive need, a rhythm so deeply buried that she had felt it only when the music of drums enfolded her, became her. When she danced, she had felt this pulsing, primal beat. But the voices that sang to her now cried out promises for the future, not legends of an ancient past.

Julian bent over her, cupping her face in his palms, kissing the side of her nose and the edge of her lips, the corners of her eyes, the tip of her chin. So easily, without knowing it was there, he tore away the veil of her past, and the touch of his magic hands drowned out the singing of spirits, the call of the world where her soul hovered among the clouds.

As he moved his lips over her face, he caressed her shoulders, tracing the curve of bone and muscle, the glistening skin that flowed into her arm. At the inside of her elbow, he kissed the brown skin, though his mouth was more demanding, less gentle.

He felt a stirring inside that threatened to take his breath, and his pulse beat out an erratic rhythm. To quiet his fierce need, he rested his head on her chest and listened to her heartbeat. He wanted to go easily, gently, so he wouldn't threaten the stillness he had promised to protect.

When Saylah tangled her fingers in his hair and called his name, he remembered the passion with which she had danced and beat her drum on the night of the party. He remembered, with a clarity that shook him, the look of rapture on her face. She had given herself completely to the passion, the cadence, the swaying and dipping of her body, until it consumed her.

He trailed his tongue down to her hand and pressed her palm to his open mouth, leaving the imprint of his moist lips, tracing with his finger the path his lips had taken.

Saylah closed her eyes and tilted her head back when he circled the curves of her breasts, stroked the nipples, teased them with his tongue. Deftly, tenderly, he stirred in her the passion she had so long denied, enticing her body upward until she arched to meet him, calling out his name.

He was enthralled by the look on her face, as expressive with her eyes closed as it was when they were open. Her throat was long, extended as she arched her back. Julian kissed the graceful line, and with his hands, caressed her stomach, her hips, her inner thighs.

He could feel her erratic pulse when he kissed her wrist. Her heartbeat was wild and ragged, her head spinning with color and sensation, with needles like fire and bursts of shivering ice. There was a single suspended moment when she hovered between earth and sky, and then her passion overwhelmed her. She began to move, not to her own measured beat, but to the rhythm of Julian's hands and lips, the call of his hungry, aching body.

Saylah was air and earth, water and fire all in one fluid motion that flowed from itself into itself, from the night into the dawn. She was lost, transported to a place where flame and song and heart were one compelling pulse that she could not ignore. It flared in her blood, brought her a joy so exquisite it made her weightless, freed her. Julian held her heartbeat gently while he sent her body spinning.

She was stunned by the feelings that surged through her body. She had felt nothing like it since the night of Kitkuni's wedding, when she had surrendered herself to the power and rhythm of the spirits, which had made her luminous, immortal. She had never thought to feel this way about something real and solid, something she could touch, see, know with her senses. She had never thought the touch of a human hand, the caress of human lips, could lift her outside herself and into the world where the spirits hovered.

She reached for Julian so he could hold her down, keep her from spinning off into the sky. She clasped her hands around his neck and pulled his head to hers. She wanted to feel his breath on her face, to stop the spinning and the heat that burned through all her veins. But his kiss was no longer reassuring; it was hot and fierce with hunger, beguiling and irresistible, as he tantalized her body with his sensitive wandering hands.

She breathed in the scent of his sweat and her heart pounded, the colors whirled, the night spun from darkness to light to moonlit night. Her face felt hot, as if she had lain too close to the fire. Her breasts, nipples erect in his hands, were washed by wave after wave of bright, fierce heat. Her fingers tingled as she ran them over his back; the inside of her elbow burned where he had kissed it. Her legs, wound with his, quivered, and she could not make them stop.

The tender power of his caress lured her closer and closer to a brink she did not wish to cross.

She could see the incandescent light beyond and feared it because it was so pure, so beautiful, so untouched. Surely if she fell she would despoil it. Yet Julian caressed her body with wise hands, gentle hands, hungry hands, drawing his pleasure from her sighs, her reaching fingers which sought to bind him to her. He could feel her tremble, feel the dampness of her skin, the moment when she opened her mouth and cried out as she fell over the edge.

But the radiance went on, brighter and more luminous. She floated, whirling, drifting in a sky with no land beneath, but clouds far and high above. Julian brought her back when he gently spread her legs and she smiled and took his shoulders and would not let go. There was a flash of pain, a stinging fire that spread, with the rhythmic motion of his body, over her skin, giving her a rosy glow.

She felt him move within her and knew that this was a miracle she could not have dreamed or imagined or hoped for. She had lost control and yet she was not lost; she was here, with Julian, rocking with his body, absorbing his heat, letting the pleasure explode in her as he called her name and kissed her hard and furiously.

Then he raised his head, rocking, thrusting with the motion of her body. Their skin met, cool and damp, and underneath they burned and exulted, cried out again and again.

Julian gathered her to him, buried his face in her hair, and shuddered, calling her name.

She held him tightly, afraid to let go, yearning to fall over the edge once more. And Julian, with his pounding heart and sweat-filmed body and a desire deeper and stronger than he had imagined, seemed to understand.

He rose, slid his hand between her legs, and circled with his fingers, drawing her closer, deeper, closer, filling her head with colors, the whirling of soundless voices, the splendor of that all-consuming, incandescent light.

When she began to sink through the weightless brightness, he shifted, whispering words that were not words, promises that had no shape or sound—only meaning.

Saylah's eyes grew damp and her throat ached. She brushed away the hair that clung to Julian's forehead. "I did not know," she said. Even when she took his hand and spoke the words "I love you," she had not imagined this. *They did not tell me how to be a woman,* she had cried. *I will teach you,* he had answered. Now that he had, nothing would ever be the same again.

The next time she opened her eyes, it was nearly dawn. Saylah woke Julian by brushing her hair over his cheek.

He gazed at her, eyes clouded with sleep, and smiled. Then he noticed how tensely she sat, leaning forward, hands on her bent knees. "What is it?"

"I must leave you for a little. I must go today."

Something inside Julian twisted with pain. "Why?"

Saylah stared down at her hands, wondering if he could understand. She raised her head and met his gaze. "I must ask for one more dream—a dream of my People and of my future. If I do not do this thing, the spirits will not let me rest."

He recognized her fear that he would not believe her, recognized too the sincerity in her voice. But he had fears of his own—deep and raw. "I don't understand."

"I must find the dream before I find my peace. It is how I have lived my life, what has made me the woman I am. You were right. Once the People called me Tanu, their Queen. I cannot turn my back on them now, nor on the spirits who shaped me. Julian," she cried fervently, "I cannot."

"But I love you."

"If you love me," she whispered, "you will let me go."

"How do I know you'll ever come back?"

"I have given you my word. This night, this touching of all between us that has not met before, was my solemn promise, given to no other man. I do not break my word." Saylah saw that he wanted to believe, was trying to believe, but the fear was stronger. This she understood. Had she not lived it too?

She kissed the hollow of his throat. "We must not doubt each other if we are to last. I have said I will return. When I do, I will come unburdened by the pieces of my past. I will come to you as myself and not a phantom made of memories."

She watched the shadows move over his face, the evanescent images of his trepidation. "Listen," she said, "while I make you one last vow, the vow of a Salish bride to her lover.

> "Until he spoke my name,
> I did not hear the small birds' songs.
> Now, unafraid, I turn to him only
> Who offers his open palm to the weary flicker."

Julian sighed; he reached up to close her eyes and rested his fingertips on the lids. "I can't look in these eyes and say good-bye, even for a little while. But I swear that I trust you. I give you my promise, the only gift I have."

Saylah's throat grew dry and tight. "It is more than enough. It is everything."

Chapter
75

Julian had promised not to hold Saylah back, not even to watch her go, but he stood in the loft, already barren of her scent and her magic and her graceful brown body, and watched her disappear into the woods. He was appalled by the sense of emptiness she'd left behind.

He had never meant to love her. He had thought of her first as an enigma, then, little by little, as a friend; he had not been able to keep her out. And now it was too late.

Too late because, having loved Saylah, every other woman would be a pale and lifeless shadow. He stiffened, realized with a sick feeling of dread that he did not believe she would return. How could he, when he had seen her in the woods, touched by dawn, dancing in moonlight? He knew how strongly the voices of her past called to her. To the Salish she had been a queen. He could not fight that enemy; he had no power against it. He stood, hands pressed to the cold glass, imagining her slender body, her long black gleaming hair, her voice, full of music, that he would never hear again.

He felt a small, warm body press up against his side. "She's *gone,*" Theron said. It was not an observation but an accusation.

Julian forced himself to look, not toward the woods that had taken Saylah, but at his half-brother, shivering and miserable with his nose pushed up against the glass. "She explained to you why she had to go. She said good-bye."

Theron's dirty hands left smudged prints on the glass. He glowered at Julian, screwing up his face. "That doesn't make me not miss her."

"No," Julian murmured. "I don't suppose it does."

Leaning his forearms on the window, Theron bit his lip to keep it from trembling. "She won't come back, will she?" His belligerence had evaporated in the haze of his pain. He had lost his papa, had dreamed about him night after night, expected every morning to see him sitting in his chair with a book lying open on his lap. He had wept and shivered and lain awake—cold and horribly alone.

But Saylah had always been there, she had understood, she had given him comfort. Now she had left him too. He pressed his forehead into the glass, as if he might get closer to her by pushing himself through to the other side, the magic side, where Saylah had been born.

He realized, finally, that Julian had not answered his question. A dark foreboding filled the hollow place inside him. "Will she?" he repeated shakily.

Julian's gaze was fixed on the woods, though Saylah had long since disappeared into them. "Will she what?"

"Come *back*."

"She gave me her promise," Julian said.

"Is that enough?" his brother demanded.

The corners of Julian's mouth quirked upward. "It's more than I hoped for. It will have to be enough. It's all I have." He did not turn cold and rigid as he had before; his pain was too deep, too raw, too new. He wondered if it would ever fade, grow old and bearable, but knew that it would not.

Colchoté stirred in his sleep and tossed aside the cedarbark blanket. He was too warm despite the chilly winter air. Perhaps it was the heat of his small wife Ki-Ki beside him, the baby curled at her breast, the boy who had known two summers pressed against her side.

Turning over, the Head Man drifted back into sleep and the dream came to him, quietly, as a hunter approaches his prey.

Voices called in the wind, through the clash of cedar and oak, through the rush of midnight water. Three voices, loud and insistent—calling, waiting, calling through the dark of a moonless night.

Colchoté knew he must go; the voices lured him, ordered him, cajoled him. He flew, running silent and sure, though he did not know where the voices led. He soared, feeling free, feeling strong, invincible, beyond weariness or harm. His feet easily found the old paths, unwalked in years, grown choked and unfamiliar with trailing vines and moss and gnarled roots.

But these things did not stop Colchoté. There was no fear in the darkness, just soft velvet shadows and the songs of nightbirds in the trees. He could feel the heat of the sun, the touch of its bright light, though dawn was not yet near.

Eventually, as he ran, protected by the trees that closed around him, he recognized the cry of the deer, the growl of the cougar, the roar of the grizzly. But again he felt no fear.

Then he saw them waiting. The cougar was burnished and regal in the darkness, its eyes fixed upon him, burning golden fire. The grizzly stood, white teeth bared, small black eyes unmoving, paws out in supplication, not aggression. The buck reared, magnificent antlers glowing, even without the moonlight. Its brown eyes were soft with yearning, and it spoke to him in the voice of a woman.

"I am not enough!" it cried. "I have never been enough. I am not a true shaman." It looked away to hide its pain.

The three animals, transformed by his faith into protectors and friends, waited for him on the rocks above the beach where he had gone many summers past to make a friend of Tanu.

Colchoté woke abruptly and sat up, surprised to find himself in the Longhouse with the warmth of his smoldering fire nearby. The air around him rose and fell—the breath of the spirits on his skin.

His wife opened her eyes to stare at him through the mists of sleep. "What is it, My Husband?"

"I must go," he said softly, so he would not wake the children. "My dreams call me back and I must go."

Saylah discarded her gown in the woods, along with her petticoat and drawers. She had not worn her button-top boots. Quickly, she put on the clothing of her childhood. She would live with the earth once more before she settled between walls of log and stone. She would be alone, with nothing between her skin and the water, her hands and the soil, her eyes and the sky.

Her pleasure in the sense of freedom that overwhelmed her was dimmed by her sorrow at leaving Julian behind. She had not thought it would hurt this much. She knew now that this dream for which she asked would cost her more than any in her life. And she was afraid.

"Do not fear your own spirits. They will not misguide you."

Saylah looked up, startled, to find Alida beside her. "Where have you come from?"

"I have come from my bed where my spirits sent me to you."

"I go to seek a dream."

"I know," Alida whispered. "But you are not prepared. You will need a canoe. I have brought you one."

Saylah blinked in wonder at the one-man canoe that rested on the riverbank. "I must go far to find this dream."

"Far enough that you do not hear the voices of the Strangers," the younger girl agreed. "Also, you will be cold. It is winter and the People are safely inside their Longhouses near their roaring fires. You will be alone in the woods. Take this to break the winter chill." She lifted her heavy cedarbark cape and draped it around Saylah's shoulders.

"I am grateful," Saylah murmured. "But why—"

"The People would do much for She Who Is Blessed. This is a little thing, and not worth counting."

Tears rose to Saylah's eyes. Julian had called her by that long-abandoned title, and she had wanted to shut out the sound. But the words, spoken in Salish by one of the People, moved her deeply. It would not be easy to put aside such things forever. "To me it is not little. I will think of you every day on my journey. I will ask the spirits to bless you."

Alida smiled. "They have already done so. Go now. You must return before the snowfall."

Saylah thanked her once more, slid the canoe into the water, took up her paddle, and started back, back into the world she had never really left behind. She headed north, toward Cowichan, where she had been born and blessed eighteen summers past on a night of moon and miracles.

Colchoté gathered his winter cloak and elkskin leggings, usually saved for the Winter Dances but necessary now to keep out the cold on his journey. He took dried fish and meat, camas roots and berries, in a pouch at his waist. He moved silently, for he did not wish to wake the children, who slept without worry or knowledge or fear.

He touched his son's forehead with affection, nuzzled the baby's cheek, and touched his lips to Ki-Ki's. "I will not be long, and there is no danger. Do not worry for me. I go to finish what is not complete."

Ki-Ki nodded and asked no questions. She trusted Colchoté, was awed by his wisdom and his kindness. She had been lucky that he asked for her as wife and did not wish to make him think she had no faith in his judgment. "May Raven not play his tricks to mislead you," she said.

—— 522 ——

Colchoté smiled fondly, touched her face and turned away.

In the center of the Longhouse sat the altar of sacred antlers on the ceremonial bearskin. In the flickering light of midnight fires, Shaula knelt there, praying. She had been looking well this past summer; she had finally recovered from her grief and despair. But tonight she looked pale, haggard.

Colchoté knelt and put his hand on her shoulder. Shaula looked up. "I could not find rest tonight. I dreamed again of Tanu. She was here, she had never left us. I was sorry to wake and find it was not so."

"She reached out to you also," Colchoté mused.

Shaula glanced at him in astonishment. A little of the color returned to her cheeks.

"In my dream," he explained, "the voices of her spirits called me."

Shaula noticed his heavy clothing and full pouch. "You will see her?" She could not disguise the hope in her voice.

"I do not know," the Head Man answered. "I know only that I must go."

Shaula turned back to the altar, running her finger along one graceful prong of the antlers. "I have often wondered where she is, if she survived alone in the Strangers' world."

Colchoté smiled. "Tanu could not help but survive. And she was never alone. Remember, she is blessed."

Shaula groaned. "I wish I had never doubted it. Perhaps then she would not have gone away."

"She had to go. Her world was never meant to be closed in by these four walls. Always, she was meant to see more, know more—to understand a world wider than our own."

"I woke and heard voices." Kwiaha, she who had once been Kitkuni, crouched beside her mother. She had returned with her husband, Chatik, and their three children to live in the village of her childhood. After the sickness had taken so many, the Salish had needed their youth and vitality, the promise of their children, who belonged to the future.

Kwiaha looked at Shaula's face and Colchoté's and knew what had awakened her. "You are speaking of Tanu. And you are prepared to leave us, *Siem*." There was a light in Kwiaha's eyes that flared as it had on the night of a storm long ago. She wanted to go with Colchoté to find Tanu. Kwiaha would always regret that she had not been there when the friend of her childhood needed her most. She wanted to see for herself that Tanu lived and prospered.

"I have been called," Colchoté said. He read the thoughts in Kwiaha's glowing eyes and shook his head. "Your mother needs you. She has fallen under the shadow of the past. You must bring her back into the light."

The young woman bowed her head. She would not question the man whose wisdom and compassion were the threads which bound the Salish, despite their great loss. "I will stay with her."

As Colchoté rose, Shaula grasped his hand. "Tell her for me—tell her I was wrong."

He covered her hand with his. "If I see her, I will tell her what she needs to know, what will ease her burden and her pain." Soundlessly, he went, and they were swallowed by the waiting hush that he left behind.

If she had doubted her love since she spoke the words, Saylah soon knew how real and deep were her feelings for Julian. Within two days, her loneliness had become a painful burden. She had never been lonely before, simply *alone* among trees and rocks and many flowing waters, serenaded by the birds and small animals of the forest. Always she had enjoyed her solitude, cherished it and sought it—the feeling that she was at one with the land which welcomed her, called her back each time her feet left its rich, dark soil.

Now these things, though achingly familiar, were not enough. She was lonely because Julian was not with her; she could not see his face or hear his voice or lay her hand in his.

His absence was a dull ache inside her, despite the cool winter beauty of the Island she loved. She moved her paddle by instinct, hardly aware of the direction she took. She had assumed she would make her way to the Longhouse, where her People lived in winter, but the canoe chose its own path. Saylah was stunned, one day, to find herself at the end of a narrow branch of a river which lay just within the woods.

Though fir and cedar, pine and spruce stood in her way, she knew what she would find when she followed the path that sloped sharply downward. She bent low to avoid fragrant clinging branches and stepped from the tinted light of the woods into the brilliance of sun on the sea.

Saylah walked forward slowly, stopped at the edge of the jagged rocks to look down on a small crescent of beach where the tide came rushing in. Here she had stood with Colchoté to win the first sweet secret victory that had bound her once and always to her friend.

Never before had she stopped in sunlight, beside the white-tipped waves of the sea to ask for a dream. She had sought the dark protection of the forest and a clear running stream or the oak and arbutus and pine that grew beside the silver-blue lake. She had turned to the shadows, where visions drifted, chimerical, intangible, where the light of day did not burn away the suggestive whispers of the cool green darkness.

Saylah stood with the light of the sun on her face, turned to the ocean—and knew her dream would come. Here and only here. Because of a day long past when she and Colchoté had conquered wind and sea and raging tide, and taken the first steps away from their childhood.

Saylah realized, when she had climbed over the jutting boulders and stood at last on fine crystal sand, that she had come to recapture that moment, that feeling.

She was amazed at how vividly, how painfully it came back to her. She thought of Colchoté, his square face, hawk nose, and eyes that did not shut her out. Friend, brother, Head Man, he had taught her once to long for things she could not have.

With the memory held close, she walked along the sand, huddling in the shelter of cave-like indentations when the tide rushed in. For two days, she fasted and walked and remembered. In the evening, she ran into the water and came out shivering, crouched beneath the rocks and rubbed herself with hemlock boughs that made her tingle and warmed away the chill.

Finally, she stretched out on a narrow strip of beach where the water could not reach. Light-headed with hunger, unaccustomed to the rough sand on her skin, she lay awake while images whirled about her. She tried to catch them, read them, understand, but they flew by too fast, too brightly.

At last, at the break of the fourth dawn, she fell asleep. She fell first into darkness and the memory of pain as her dream returned her to the Longhouse, where her mother and the father of her heart had died. She hovered outside but could not see in.

She felt a pressure on her chest that was more than pain, and the walls grew tall and clear. She saw the village going about their morning tasks. She saw Shaula and Alteo, huddled over their blazing fire. She saw Enis, with several children now, and Wahan, who carved a fine bowl for his son. She saw a stranger with a baby at her breast, watching a handsome young boy who would not rest, but asked endless questions and attempted endless tasks that were beyond his strength and age.

In her dream, Saylah smiled. Then she saw Kitkuni and her family grouped around their fire. Kitkuni, who had laughed into the storm and called the world her own and stood without protest while they took away her name and her past.

The young woman smiled at her daughter, cupping her face tenderly, meeting her husband's eyes over the child's head. There was understanding in that glance exchanged in secret, and contentment, if not passion. Kwiaha had survived and prospered.

But where was Colchoté?

Chapter
76

Colchoté journeyed quickly to the little beach where he and Tanu had been captured by the tide. He had gone there often since she went away, hoping someday she too would come and he would learn where she had gone and if her broken heart had healed.

When he arrived, the sun was low, obscured by clouds, but the sand was oddly warm against his feet. He raised his face to the sky and prayed to the spirits and the Changer for guidance and wisdom which would overcome temptation. His heart had beat wildly since he began this journey, and he no longer knew what the end would bring. When he thought of Tanu, the old pain came back, and with it the love he had borne her many years before.

Having once loved She Who Is Blessed, a man could never be the same. The emptiness she had left behind, the cold bleakness that had awakened him that night had never left him. He had merely taught himself to go on.

Then he had seen Ki-Ki and made her his wife. He had never been alone since the day of their marriage. She did not fill the space Tanu had carved inside him, but made a place of her own that obscured the other's face until it faded and grew dim. Ki-Ki cared for him deeply, and more than that, she needed him—to protect her, comfort her, guide her. Tanu had never needed him, except once, when tragedy sapped her will. She was strong, unbending, wise. She needed only herself and the spirits who had touched her and made her theirs.

The image of her face rose before him, wavered, grew bright, and he knew she was near. He turned from the contemplation of sky and drifting clouds and coming rain to survey the beach, his pulse thrumming loudly in his head.

He saw her at once, curved against a wall of rock, wrapped in a cedarbark cloak, her loosely braided hair lying across her body, bare feet buried in the sand. For a long time, Colchoté stood, unable to move, unwilling to see what he must see and learn what he must learn. His breathing was painful. He had to fight for each gust of chilly air. But he was strong; he too had survived. Slowly, one step at a time, he moved forward.

In spite of his determination, he gasped when he stood beside her. She had changed in the four summers of their parting. She had grown taller, more slender, her body more graceful. And her face, always delicately shaped, had softened, yet grown harder, more firm with pain and knowledge. He crouched to look at her more closely, was surprised to see that she wore Salish clothes and slept on the sand. He had expected her to come as a Stranger, though he could not say why.

He guessed that she had gone to live among the Whites when she left the Salish. He would have heard soon enough if she had chosen to hide with another village. He had spent many moons searching, not in order to bring her back, but to discover if she was safe and happy. He, who could track a deer from sun to sun over tangled forest paths and across swift-flowing streams, had found no trace of Tanu.

That was why he stood for so long looking into her sleeping face, seeking signs of what had happened to her since she disappeared. He saw at once that she was not pale and ill, though that was how he had imagined her—fading into a ghost bound by the unfamiliar confines of the white world. Her face had filled out, and her cheeks were nut-brown stained with red from the cool sea air. Her hair had grown longer, her hands were worn with work, as they always had been, yet graceful still.

He rocked on his heels, heart pounding, waiting for his turmoil to subside, for the joy he had felt at the sight of her to fade into a quiet ache. And so it did.

Then her face, in sleep, began to change. Her brow was furrowed with worry, her lips open in a silent question, her hands groping for something to hold on to. Colchoté offered his hands, and though she did not wake, she took them and held them.

"Perhaps you wish to know of your People," he said to the woman sleeping in the shade of a carved and aged rock. Once he had known her, but she had grown away from the child who had turned too soon into a woman. "We are well, each in his own way, and we prosper as we did before the Red Sweating Sickness took our strength and hope." Though it was difficult to think at all while she clasped his hands, he tried to remember why he had come. Colchoté spoke carefully, enunciating each word, hoping to reach her through her dreams.

"You are mourned among the Salish," he continued, closing his eyes against the awful certainty that she was very far away. "You are missed. We have not forgotten what you gave us. We will not forget. Through our voices, the voices of our children and their children's voices, your name will be spoken and honored, not only for your magic, or even your wisdom, but for the love you bore us and the love we—each of us—bear for you."

She did not stir, but he knew she had heard. The worry left her brow, her lips relaxed and curved upward, just a little. Colchoté knew with a sinking of regret that half his task was over. Now he must simply wait and watch.

Saylah heard a voice above the sounds of her People working and knew it was Colchoté. She felt his warmth come close, enfold her, then recede. He was at peace. Her People were at peace and Kitkuni once more among them. This she had come to discover. This she had had to know.

Now, with the knowledge inside her like a coal that warms but does not burn, she slept more deeply, through soundless black and gray and silver, sinking into the water, where she stood unmoving. Through the leaves, stars fell onto the undulating surface and she touched them with her outspread palms so their light danced on her warm brown skin.

She closed her eyes, and the water that was neither sea nor lake nor forest stream lapped around her, lulling her into forgetfulness. Until she heard the voice rippling through the trees on the back of the wind. The voice that called a name she could not understand.

She turned her head, listening, and heard another sound, another voice. This one she knew and welcomed. Julian called to her; his voice rose and fell in the breeze until it melded with the whispered name she could not hear and the two voices became indistinguishable.

Then he was beside her. He lifted her gently from the water, cradling her in his arms. She lay naked against him, her head on his shoulder, and for the first time in many years, she felt safe.

The fear that had taken root inside her when she lay beside the lake and dreamed—the haunting visage of what had been, the faceless dread of what might come to be—fell away with the water that streamed from her body. The starlight rose from the surface of the pond, danced over her dark skin, beaded with tiny drops that caught the light and held it fast.

Julian stood calmly while the moisture dripped from her thick black hair and starlight caressed her skin. Patiently, as if he would wait forever, he held her until the water dried and the chill left her body.

He held her until the sun began to rise from behind the splendid trees. Then they sat together and watched the dawn paint the sky and the clouds and the water at their feet.

Colchoté saw the changes in the girl's face. He did not know what she was called, only that it was no longer Queen. She had returned the gift of her name, given by the Salish as a sign of their faith, just as she had given up her People. Tanu was no more. She had become a stranger to him. It was time to let her go.

Colchoté knew the transformation had not come easily or without anguish. As he sat beside her, through her hands, clasped in his, he had felt fragments of her pain and knew none but the child of miracles could survive such grief and dare to dream again. She had fought a long and draining battle, and it was not over yet. He knew it in his heart. The spirits had given him one last gift, one glimpse inside her, one more memory, one more bead on the string he had held sacred since she was a child and he a child beside her.

He remembered the anguished cry of the deer in his dream. *I am not a true shaman!* "There is something I must tell you," he whispered, "and you must believe. Long ago you earned the right and the burden to call yourself shaman. Since you were very young, you knew how to take flight, how to soar among the clouds." He paused long and thoughtfully. "But now, at last, I think perhaps you have found a place to rest. I wish you peace."

He wanted to wish her more, but could not do it. He was, after all, a man who had lost her, not once, but three times. Two times too many.

Colchoté saw her sink deeper into sleep, saw her face change when the dream began, saw, in the end, how she smiled, and her smile was more than a curve of lips or a sigh of contentment; it was the first smile of real happiness he had ever seen on Tanu's face.

Except that Tanu had gone, grown into her sorrow and sought new dreams, born, not of the People and their rituals, but of her own strong heart. He had seen that she was healthy; now he knew she would be happy. It was what he had come to learn. Gently, he reached out to touch her lips, her eyelids, the fall of loosely woven hair.

He rose and left her sleeping, smiling the smile which had burned itself into his memory, the enchanting smile which would never leave hime, but rather serve to fill the emptiness she had left in him four summers past.

He was empty no more, Colchoté realized, though his sorrow had not passed. He turned away, knowing that she lay at peace, her face turned toward the foam-tipped waves of the endless cerulean sea.

Chapter

77

"Mr. Palmer's in the parlor. He's brought the post."

Paul leapt up from the sofa. "We'll get it! Won't we, Theron?"

The younger boy had little choice, since Paul had grasped his hand and was dragging him toward the door.

Sophia, who was sitting at her Chinese desk going over menus, barely glanced up. It had finally snowed last night, and the boys, cooped up in the house because of the storm, were restless. The school in Victoria was not yet in session, and so they were still at home. She hoped they would find something to amuse them soon. This was Theron's first visit since Jamie had returned from Seattle with Edward nearly a year and a half before.

Recently, with Saylah away, Flora had confided to Sophia that Theron was making her daft. Asking endless questions she could not answer, staring at Julian as if he could conjure Saylah with a wave of his hand, running to the window at every little sound and peering out hopefully until long after it was obvious no one was coming. "And when he's no' doin' that," Flora had explained, "he stays alone in his room, bein' altogether too quiet for my peace of mind."

When Sophia had invited Theron, offering to come in the carriage to pick him up, Flora and Julian had agreed willingly. A distraction and a change of scene would do the boy good.

"Hey! Don't pull so hard. I'm coming," Theron said to Paul's back.

Sophia smiled to herself. Paul was as restless as his friend, and did not hesitate to use his two years advantage in age—or brute force—to encourage Theron to do what he wished.

Theron blinked wide blue eyes at his friend's auburn head. Paul was acting very strange; his eyes were burning, actually burning, like the fire did when the flames turned golden. But he was grinning too. It was odd, but odd was better than boring.

Mr. Palmer was wrapped from head to toe in coat, mufflers, gloves and heavy boots. "I got caught in Victoria by the storm, or I wouldn't be out today," he was telling Clara, tapping the letters against his open palm.

Paul came skidding to a halt in front of the shortsighted neighbor. Mr. Palmer blinked at him, trying to think what the boy might want.

"You brought the post," Paul suggested. "Mama's waiting for a letter and she sent me to get it."

"The post!" Mr. Palmer slapped himself in the head with the letters. The sight of Clara had made him forget his errand.

"But she didn't—" Theron objected.

When Paul elbowed him sharply, the younger boy gasped and closed his mouth. "It was very kind of you to come so far," Paul said, smiling unabashedly. "Mama will be grateful, I'm sure."

Theron peered at his friend in amazement. He was talking like a stranger. Then Paul glanced down at the letters and the color left his face.

"You don't look very good," Theron offered tentatively. He did not want Paul to start swinging his elbow again.

"There's a letter from Boston," Paul whispered, holding it by the corner as if it had a bad smell.

"So?" Theron demanded. "Why do you look sick?"

Paul did not hear him. "With my grandfather's seal."

Theron opened his mouth, closed it abruptly. He remembered a day long ago in the cave when they had composed a letter of their own. So much had happened since that he'd forgotten all about it. Now he gazed at the thick envelope, the smear of red wax, and his stomach felt queasy.

Paul had recovered himself enough to steer them back toward the parlor, so Clara and Mr. Palmer wouldn't hear any more. Once they were alone, Theron clutched his arm.

"What're you going to do?"

Paul scratched his cheek nervously. "Give it to Mama." His voice was thin and he sounded more and more like he might be ill.

"Maybe your grandfather liked your letter," Theron said. But he sounded doubtful.

Paul sighed. "Maybe. I was only trying to help."

The younger boy nodded emphatically. "Then it'll be all right."

Paul, who had been optimistic until he actually held the letter in his hand, cleared his throat. "We might as well go see." He straightened his shoulders and marched toward the parlor, for all the world like a man about to be fed poison mushrooms.

Theron followed, wild with curiosity.

Paul went right up to his mother and laid the three letters on the desk. "There's one from Grandfather," he pointed out, in case she had not noticed the postmark or the distinctive seal.

Sophia pursed her lips. "Oh," she said. Glancing over her shoulder at Theron, she added, "How delightful." Her voice was less than enthusiastic. She turned back to her menus.

"Don't you want to read it now?" Paul asked unwisely.

Sophia frowned. "I'd probably rather not read it at all. But I suppose I must." She picked up the packet, balanced it in her hand, wondering if its weight was any indication of the bitterness inside. Sighing, she broke the seal, removed the closely written pages and turned toward the light.

The boys huddled on the settee, leaning forward eagerly, watching every expression that crossed Sophia's face.

My dear Sophia,

I have, as you know, been profoundly concerned about your safety in that wilderness of savages and pioneers. But not until I received your last letter had I any idea of how utterly beyond help you really were. I am shuddering still at the memory of the horrors described on those pages.

Since you appear to be stubbornly set on achieving your own destruction, whether at the hands of wild Indians with guns or at the tables of common merchants and sheepherders from Scotland, I find that I must be the one to act. Before you are swallowed inexorably by the darkness of that godforsaken island, I shall put aside my anger, deny my first instinct, which is to watch you wallow in the muck of your own making, and dredge up those fond memories of your youth which alone could compel me to come to your aid.

Accordingly, I have made arrangements to come to Vancouver Island at once and see for myself these horrors and aberrations, and, need I add, to bring you home.

Sophia blinked, reread the last line again, and then once more. Her vision blurred as she dropped the letter from nerveless fingers. "Oh, dear Lord, *what* have I done?" Her face was so pale that the vein down the middle of her forehead was visible, and her hands shook so much that she clasped them together to hold them still.

Paul was at her side in an instant. "Mama! What is it?"

"He's coming," she said in despair. "Here!" she added, in case he didn't understand.

Paul's eyes widened, and though he opened his mouth several times, no sound came out.

Theron sat where Paul had left him, arms crossed tightly over his chest. He had the strongest urge to giggle uncontrollably. There were Paul and his mother, acting like the earth had fallen in around them, their faces gray with horror. They clutched each other, swaying, unable to let go.

When Theron had fought back the laughter that kept rising inside him like bubbles that would *not* burst, he said, "I'd *love* my grandfather to come for a visit. Maybe yours'll like it here. It's very pretty." When neither Paul nor Sophia responded, he shrugged. "Well, *I* think it is."

"It's winter. Maybe there'll be no ship to bring him until spring. Perhaps by then he will have forgotten," Sophia said hopefully.

Paul looked skeptical and Theron frankly disbelieving.

"What will I tell Edward?" Sophia moaned. "It's all my fault. I shouldn't have written that letter."

"Maybe it *isn't* your fault," Paul said, desperate to ease her distress. "Maybe it's mine."

Sophia stared. "How could it possibly be yours?"

Theron decided it was time to intervene. "There are lots more pages," he said, coming over and tapping them repeatedly. "You should read those too." He glared at Paul, eyes narrowed.

Shaking her head, Sophia gripped the remaining pages. What more could he have to say? And what did it matter anyway? She envisioned Edward and her father facing each other in fury across the living room—or, more likely, a misty clearing, guns drawn.

Paul, who had been on the brink of making a confession, decided, prudently, to wait. "Do you want me to read the rest to you?" he asked kindly, suppressing the guilt that made his hand tremble as he touched his mother's arm.

"No, thank you, dear. I am not so feeble that I cannot face my father's wrath unassisted." Stacking the pages neatly, with grim determination, she began to read once more.

I have just been discussing arrangements with Mary (You remember her—the housekeeper whose lips are perpetually drawn into a thin line that reminds me of the untidy seams you used to make when she tried to teach you to sew. She has not, I need hardly add, grown soft with age). She has reminded me, rather stiffly, that it is winter, and that already I have accepted several engagements for the long, chilly season. I have, in fact, agreed to sponsor more than one event here in my own house.

Under these circumstances, I can hardly leave for an extended trip. As Mary has told me repeatedly, I should return to nothing but icy stares and cold shoulders. And that, as you can imagine (even adrift as you are in such uncivilized social surroundings) I simply could not endure.

Sophia gave a shout of laughter, then covered her mouth with her hand. Surely her father did not intend to amuse her. And yet—the tone of the letter had unquestionably changed from the first page to the second. A niggling doubt took shape in her mind, and she turned back to the letter.

My first inclination was to send Mary in my stead, since I cannot ignore your pleas for help which, though not expressed in those terms, were nevertheless pathetically evident to my discerning eye. What kind of father would I be if I refused to take notice of such silent desperation and went on about my business with no further thought of your tragedy?

As I said, my first thought was to send Mary, until I recalled the unfortunate incident when you tied her to the rocking chair so she could not hinder you from ice skating with your friends (I need hardly add that she heartily disapproved of such frivolous activities, as did I, though one puzzles over why, at this late date, one felt so strongly). I concluded from this, as well as Mary's gray, stricken face when I mentioned the possibility, that such a solution would not suffice.

This time Sophia did not bother to stifle her laughter. She leaned back in the chair and giggled at the ceiling. The niggling doubt became a certainty. Her father had decided his rapid-fire questions were not achieving their desired end. Now he was going to play her game. She suspected he would be very good at it.

"Mama!" Paul said accusingly. "You're laughing!"

"Your grandfather's letter has struck me as amusing. It seems he can't come after all." She smiled at her son, who had been wringing his hands until the fingers were red and the knuckles white. "I rather think he never intended to make this particular trip."

Paul watched suspiciously for signs that his grandfather had betrayed him, but Sophia's grin revealed no anger at her son. There was a strange glint in her eye as she took up the last pages of the letter.

I am left with the weighty question of what is to be done with regard to your questionable future. The only answer that provides

—— 535 ——

itself is to leave that unknown quantity to your discretion (not that you have shown much inclination toward discretion, even in your youth). I am forced to admit that your spirit has not yet been crushed by circumstances (though one wonders often if there is, perhaps, a little more spirit than is absolutely necessary in all situations), and your sense of humor (though frequently misdirected and not altogether kind) has in no way suffered from your exile. One might almost say that both characteristics have been sharpened (to the fine-honed edge that might easily puncture, if not actual veins, then certainly illusions) by experience.

Sophia bit her lip, gazing pensively out the window at the white drifting snow. Her father's voice came through as strongly as ever, and his opinions, though somewhat less violently expressed, had not changed. But his approach was unquestionably different—a direct response to her own letter, which she now realized was more foolish than cruel. Douglas Charles was not a man to be taken in by his daughter's dramatic attempts to frighten him. Her overly sweet greeting alone would have told him something was greatly amiss.

She smiled. She had forgotten, in the avalanche of his anger, how bright he was. And she had to admit that she admired his sense of humor. Eagerly, she picked up the final page.

I am also forced to recognize that you appear to be happy in your marriage (though how this could have happened is beyond my comprehension, since you have always had me before you as a model of deportment, success and fine upstanding manhood). Naturally, I should have preferred that you marry among the chosen friends I had evaluated, studied and confirmed as worthy, but my taste, it seems, is irrelevant.

In any event, there you are with a fine, intelligent son, who would no doubt do great things if once exposed to my intellectual affiliations. I could only have wished that you had not crept away without a word of farewell, ignored my advice, and established a life contrary to all my expectations. But then, your pride, far too similar to my own, I fear, and learned from many years of the most burdensome education, is as vital as your humor, and would not, in any circumstances, have allowed you to follow my dictates concerning your future. This unfortunate fact has caused our estrangement, as well as my frequent tirades on the foolishness of females in general and my daughter in particular.

Suffice it to say that, in future, I shall express myself less fervently and less frequently on the subject. But I shall not, in any sense, ever, miss you less than on the day you left me.

—— 536 ——

I remain your intransigent, if somewhat more cognizant,

Papa

Paul watched his mother closely as she folded the pages with great care and gazed blindly out the window. He waited, heart pounding, for as long as he could bear it. Then Theron poked him in the side, and he could hold his questions in no longer.

"What did he say? Are you angry? What was so funny? Why aren't you laughing now? Are you going to cry?"

"Of course not."

"But your eyes look funny," Theron interjected. "Did he say something mean?"

Sophia smiled, still uncertain, still trying to absorb the enormity of the letter in her hand. "No, my dears," she murmured softly. "It's just, you see, that he signed it 'Papa.'"

Chapter
78

Julian paced the main room, oblivious to the heat of the fires and the brilliant light that leapt over his rigid body.

His stepmother watched with compassion. "She's been away a long time." Only Flora dared to speak her thoughts. Julian was afraid to say such things aloud.

If I say the words, it will be true. Julian swung away from the heat toward the chill that radiated inward from the frosted window. "Even if she's on her way, how could she survive in this snow?" He stared moodily at the gentle slopes of white, darkened by the shadows of drifting clouds. Pure and untouched, the landscape lay like a beautiful but dangerous warning. Yet when the sun blazed for an instant and the ground turned to glittering powdered crystal, Julian was mesmerized by the seductive sight.

"I think ye must be forgettin' 'tis Saylah ye're talkin' about. If she wants to get back to us, she'll find a way."

Julian rested his forehead on the cold glass. The thought had occurred to him more than once. The longer she was gone, the more often the doubt crept into his mind and the more unbearable the waiting became. He knew the depth of Saylah's strength and determination, knew too the strange hold of her Indian past, which would not release her. It had been ten days since she left, ten days without a word or a sign.

"I told you she's never coming back!" Theron shouted unexpectedly. "I told you!"

Covering his ears so he wouldn't have to listen to any more soothing lies, the boy slipped into his room. He went at once to the hidden cupboard near the floor, where the magic chest lay hidden.

Making certain the door was closed, he took out the chest and lifted the lid. The scent of fir drifted toward him. On top of Simone's diary and Jamie's photograph lay a piece of bough taken from Saylah's bed and a shell she had given him while he recovered from his cougar wound. He had placed these things there the day after she left, when he'd known in his heart she would not return. Like his father, she had left him.

Theron picked up the bit of fir and sniffed it. The fragrance had drowned out the scent of roses, but that didn't matter. Even the mysterious Simone did not interest him today. Tears came to his eyes but he blinked them back. He would be strong like Julian so no one could ever hurt him again.

He heard a shout, dropped the piece of fir and jumped to his feet. He started for the door, then remembered his secret. Quickly, he replaced the precious objects, closed the lid and hid the chest away. Then he ran into the main room.

Julian stood looking out the window, hands pressed to the heavy glass. "I thought I saw her—something out there," he said when Theron tugged imperiously on his trouser leg.

"Where?" The little boy squeezed in to peer out at the white landscape. "I don't see anything."

Julian tried to calm the frantic beat of his heart and think clearly. Had the motion he'd seen been a gust of wind, or a person shrouded in white and struggling in the snow?

"Julian!" Theron cried. "Where?"

"There," his half-brother said, "by the deer. I'm going to go see."

Sitting placidly in her rocking chair, working on a new apron, Flora stuck the threaded needle in and plucked it out, smiled and nodded. "I think that'd be best, *mo-run.*"

Julian did not hear her. Picking up his greatcoat, he flung open the door. Unaware that he left it hanging open so the biting cold rushed in, he began to run.

Saylah was very weary, yet oddly contented. She had paddled slowly back along the waterways from the beach where she had dreamed her dream, noticing every needle of fir and spruce, every gnarled branch of oak, every clump of bracken and veil of trailing moss. Even in winter the Island was tinted in shades of green and silver-gray. The varied patterns of bare branches were beautiful in their bent and twisted outlines against the thickening clouds.

She was cloaked in a fine light mist of her own creation, haunted by a sense of unreality that subtly altered the world around her. Each motion of her hand, each breath, each heartbeat, slowed and extended by the haze through which she moved, enthralled her. She watched from a distance, warily, as the sense of anticipation, the joy spread through her veins like warm, dark wine, dulling the ache of loss, the glimmering spun-glass thread of fear that had not yet snapped. She could not quite make herself believe that she would see Julian again. That he would be waiting.

She knew she must hurry, that her body, which had become used to thick walls and blazing fires, was not as strong as it once had been. But the fog that swirled around her made her move drowsily, sluggishly; she could not grip the paddle tighter or push it faster through the rushing winter river. The snow fell on her hair, her shoulders, melted and dripped off her cloak. She began to shiver, but clenched her teeth resolutely and guided the tiny boat away from a crescent of sunlit beach toward the clearing shaped by Julian's hands and his unbending will.

Through the blurred vision of trees and overgrown banks, she remembered his face and smiled. There was time. All else had changed but he would not. Soon, she would see him, touch him, know him. Soon.

When she reached the river in the woods near the ranch, she found Alida waiting with her other clothes. The girl had kept them warm by hiding them under her cloak and pressing them to her body. "I have come every day, hoping you would return," Alida said.

In the falling snow, Saylah removed her cedarbark clothing and slipped back into her heavy wool gown. For once, she was grateful for the weight and style, which covered her chilled body from neck to foot.

"I can never give you thanks enough for what you have done," she told Alida.

"I have done what I was called to do. It is the way of our People. So it has been and so it will be."

Saylah felt a twinge of regret at the familiar words, spoken in Salish. Such things, such fragments of her other life, would never cease to move her, to touch a quiet yearning that would not disappear.

"Go," Alida said firmly. "You are chilled and will be ill. Your body and heart have won too many battles in the past two moons. You may find that you are weaker than you think, now that there is nothing left to fight for."

Saylah did not pause to ask what the girl meant. Alida was right; she must hurry. Her hands were blue with cold and she was shivering violently. With a last cry of thanks, she moved off into the trees.

When they opened before her and she saw the carved deer rising from the snow-touched clearing, she paused while a rush of warmth enveloped her. She was home.

Tears came to her eyes and her throat ached. The doe with antlers beckoned and she stumbled forward, smiling. She had found her home at last.

She had nearly reached the deer when she fell and could not rise. Her legs were too weak, her teeth chattering.

She heard a voice and far above her she saw Julian's face. He gaped as if she were an apparition born of his hope, then leaned down to lift her in his arms. "I thought you weren't coming back."

Somehow Saylah found the strength to raise her hand and press it to his chest above his heart. "I gave you my promise."

Julian shifted the weight in his arms to make certain she was real, then leaned down to kiss her. Though her lips were tinged blue with cold, her face was flushed and her eyes gleamed with fever. "Dear God, you're ill."

Saylah wanted to protest that she was never ill, but she had no energy. In a blur, she heard Julian speak, but could only burrow deeper into his arms, seeking the heat of his body. In a blur, she heard Theron's voice, hoarse with tears, saw Flora's face, creased with worry.

Julian went white when he saw the glazed expression in Saylah's eyes, felt the heavy, frigid weight of her body in his arms.

"'Twas too late to make a journey. Ye should no' have let her go."

They hurried toward the house together. Theron jumped and wept, ran ahead and nearly tripped them. "I want to see her face. I want to see it's really her," he insisted. No one listened.

"I couldn't have stopped her. You know that."

"I'd no be seein' why," Flora grumbled.

"Because, as you once told me, she's Saylah."

Flora fell silent when she realized she was speaking out of fear. The girl looked so ill that she was deeply frightened.

Vaguely, Saylah became aware that the cold all around her had gone, though the cold inside grew and spread. They had taken her into the house and closed the door on glittering white winter. It came to her in a flash of horror that Julian was right. She was ill.

She felt a wild flutter of fear. She had been fighting so hard to remain strong in order to help the others, to hold back the waves of weariness that sometimes beset her. Now that there was nothing left to fight, not even herself, she realized the struggle had drained her dry. She had no strength left with which to conquer this illness that made her shake with waves of fever and cold. The world began to reel, spinning into beckoning blackness which she had no will to resist.

"Ye'd best keep her here where 'tis warm 'til the stove takes the chill from the loft," Flora said, rolling up her sleeves. "We'll need to be gettin' her into bed quickly."

"What's wrong with her?" Theron asked, alarmed by her pallid skin.

While Julian wrapped Saylah in his greatcoat and carried her to a bench by the fire, Flora knelt beside her son. "She's no' feelin' well. 'Twas too cold outside in the snow."

"Why didn't she come in sooner?" he demanded in a quavering voice.

Gently, Flora brushed the tumbled hair off her son's forehead. "I'm guessin' she believed she was doin' what she had to do. There's no use weepin' over what's already done. Now we must make her well."

"Can I help?" Theron asked shakily.

"Aye. I'll need Julian to carry the wood and build the fire. Stay beside her and rub her cold hands and feet while we make her bed ready. Do ye think ye can do that for me?"

Theron straightened his shoulders. "For Saylah," he said.

Julian was reluctant to leave her, but his stepmother insisted. "Take the wood up and get her stove blazin' while I heat some water and brew some of her herbs for the fever." Her tone did not allow for argument.

Cupping Saylah's burning cheeks in his hands, Julian felt her trembling through his whole body. He bent to kiss her, then swung away to stack wood in his arms and take it up to the loft. He needed to be moving, to give himself time to unsnarl the tumult of joy and terror, tenderness and pain inside his head.

Theron sat beside the bench, rubbing Saylah's cold hands furiously, glancing surreptitiously at her face to reassure himself that she was there. But when she moaned and turned her head frantically from side to side, he forgot what he was doing.

Flora came from the kitchen with bowls and cups balanced on a tray. She glanced at Saylah and knew she had slipped into delirium. Theron was frozen in place, so frightened that his normally rosy face was white.

"I've got the medicines," she said to Julian, who had reappeared at the foot of the stairs. "Ye can take her up now if ye think 'tis warm enough."

Julian did not bother to answer, but lifted Saylah and started back toward the loft. Theron stayed where he was, blue eyes wide, hands shaking.

"The coat'll keep her for a while," Flora told her son as calmly as she could. "But ye know she's got that bed of fir boughs, and I'm thinkin' 'twill no' be enough to warm her. Could ye go get the quilt from my room, Theron? The big fat soft one my mother made, and a pillow to rest her head on?"

The boy looked up, dazed, realized what she'd said, and leapt to his feet. "I will!" he shouted, too suddenly freed from his glazed terror and glad of something useful to do.

"Be still as ye can, *mo-ghraid*. She needs to rest."

Theron nodded wordlessly while Flora climbed the stairs after Julian. Setting her lips firmly, she stepped up into the loft and looked around.

Saylah lay on the low bed of boughs, shivering, moving her head wildly from side to side. Julian held her hands, but the pressure of his fingers did not keep her still. The fire in the potbellied stove was roaring; the room was warmer than it had been in years.

"I've sent Theron for real covers. Now ye find a nightgown in the chest while I get some liquid down her."

When she knelt beside Saylah, Flora fought back tears. "Poor bairn," she whispered, "poor little bairn."

"She's very ill," Julian said in a dull monotone that did not disguise his fear.

"Well, then we'd best start carin' for her. Get the nightgown and hold it by the fire a bit. I'll give her somethin' for the fever." She lifted Saylah's head and tried to get her to swallow, managing with difficulty to spill some of the drink down her throat.

Listening intently to each sound Flora made, Julian went to the chest. His hand closed over a long flannel gown, but he paused when he noticed the drum and rattles, and the necklace of animal teeth. He closed his eyes and forced himself to breathe deeply. When he rose, he saw the sacred stones and bent to touch the pink streaked with gray Saylah had found the day they'd laughed like children. It seemed a very long time ago.

"Will ye be takin' all day and half the night, do ye think?" Flora asked sharply.

Julian knew she worried and ignored her tone. His stepmother was rubbing Saylah's hands and feet, trying to break the chill. Julian tossed her the gown, then helped remove the greatcoat and wool dress. Together, they managed to pull the flannel over her head. Saylah groaned and flung her arm out, reaching for some phantom in her fevered dream.

Julian took her hand and began to knead it, more and more frightened by the way the color came and went in her face, the gray cast of her lips.

Flora pressed cool cloths to her forehead and tried to force infusions down her throat while Julian worked at the girl's hands and feet. He looked up when he heard a loud thumping on the stairs. At the top he met Theron, swathed in his mother's quilt, his face half hidden, a long train dangling down the narrow steps behind him. He clutched a pillow in his teeth and stumbled with each step he took.

Julian smiled for the first time as he took the pillow. "You should've told me. I would have carried it for you."

Theron stuck out his lower lip belligerently. "I wanted to help Saylah myself."

Julian nodded in understanding. The last week had been hard enough on the boy. And now that Saylah was back, she was not really here at all. Theron was very young to have known so much uncertainty and pain. As unobtrusively as possible, Julian picked up the trailing end of the quilt and helped his half-brother to the top of the stairs.

"Come hold her while I make the bed," Flora called.

Julian knelt while Theron untwisted the quilt, then he lifted Saylah gently, rocking her, dismayed by how chilled her body remained. When the quilt was spread to Flora's satisfaction, he lowered Saylah into the nest of down and muslin.

Theron promptly sat on the floor and started rubbing Saylah's hands. His own kept slipping, and he rubbed the dirt from his grimy fingers into her skin, but no one stopped him. He bit his lip and peered at her face, intent on his task, watching for some sign that he was helping.

Julian worked at her feet while Flora rinsed out rags and tried to break the fever, replacing one cloth after another as each grew warm from the heat of Saylah's skin.

While her fever raged, Julian and Theron worked doggedly to massage the chill from Saylah's hands and feet. When the color began to return and the bluish tinge to disappear, Flora declared that feet and hands should go inside the quilt.

Reluctantly, Theron gave up the fingers he held between his. He sat staring, lips pursed, a question in his eyes.

When his little brother did move, Julian asked, "What is it?"

Theron glanced up sharply, looked away. He chewed on his lip, toyed with the heavy quilt, swallowed noisily before he said, "God wouldn't be mean enough—" He stopped, licked his lips, and murmured, "He wouldn't bring her back to us and then—" He glared at his dirty fingernails. He couldn't say it after all.

Julian shook his head. "He wouldn't be that cruel." He realized with a jolt that he believed it. He had to believe or there was nothing left, now that Saylah had become necessary to his life and breath and happiness. "We'll take care of her and she'll recover."

There was a suspicious moisture in Theron's eyes, so he kept his head down.

Flora touched her son's shoulder. "Come, *mo-run*, we've done what we can for now. Julian can stay with her. Ye and I'd best be off to the kitchen to start a good thick broth. I expect she'll be needin' it when she wakes, to warm her insides."

Theron shuffled his feet and looked enviously at his half-brother. "Okay," he muttered, heaving a big sigh.

Julian settled away from the fire so he would not block the heat. Like Flora, he wrung out cloths and put them on Saylah's forehead, drawing one down her neck, over her shoulders in an attempt to cool her burning body.

For a day and a half, she slipped in and out of consciousness, slept a little, tossed and turned and moaned, eyes closed or staring sightlessly, seeing no one and nothing. But slowly, with the constant care of Theron and Flora and Julian, the fever broke. Then she began to cough and ache, rubbing her arms without knowing, trying to break the hold of the cold that had taken her in its grip.

At last, while Julian sat with her hands in his, she slept normally, breathing evenly, her face slightly flushed. The blue tinge was gone and she no longer shuddered and shivered. She was very still, gathering the strength that had seeped away since the night of Jamie's death. Along with the air, she breathed in energy and vitality, and the rasp in her throat disappeared.

When he could stay awake no longer, Julian stretched out with his head beside hers on the pillow. "You're all right now," he whispered. "I know you're all right." He felt a rush of elation just before he closed his eyes and drifted into sleep.

Saylah stirred, aching in every limb, but unaccountably warm and safe. The last thing she remembered was being very cold in the snow and the glittering ice. Perplexed, she ran her hand over the heavy quilt she had seen often in Flora's room. She was wearing her long flannel nightgown, which she had not put on since she arrived at the Ivys'.

Despite her aching arms and legs, she felt rested, but distinctly anxious. How had she come to be here? She remembered flashes of fevered dreams, her burning body, a racking cough. She sat up abruptly. She had been ill.

"Saylah."

The single word full of joy, the sound of that beloved and familiar voice, sent chills down her back. She was home. She turned to see Julian kneeling beside her and the pain in her head splintered and disintegrated. Blindly, she reached for him; tightly, she held him, breathing in the smell of his hair, his skin, the herbs that had stained his fingers.

Saylah stiffened and drew away. "How—" She struggled to find her long-unused voice, to form the words she must say, the doubts that tormented her, threatening her happiness. "How did I come to be here?"

Julian's stained fingers spoke for themselves, as well as the fire that burned in the stove, the quilt and soft pillow, the tray of bowls and cups beside the bed.

"I brought you up and Flora mixed the medicine and Theron and I rubbed your hands. You were very ill." His eyes glowed with pleasure at the sight of her face, paler than usual, but no longer red with fever or pallid with cold.

Saylah felt a whirling in her stomach that terrified her. "But this cannot be. It is I who came to care for you."

Julian gazed at her, confused by her vehemence, the wild look in her eyes, the turbulence that turned emerald to turquoise, then deep, shadowed green, like the forest when the sun does not shine. Now, more than when she lay ill, she looked helpless, like a wounded animal.

He was trying to understand her distress. "But you were sick. We had to make you well."

She shook her head. "It is not right," she whispered.

"What did ye expect us to do, then?" Flora said, appearing at the top of the stairs with a bowl of broth in her hands. "Let ye die because ye could no' heal yourself?"

It's harder to learn to think of yourself when all your life you've thought only of others. Jamie's voice echoed, pulsed through the room. Saylah tried to hear and understand, but her turmoil did not abate.

Startled, Julian glanced at his stepmother. She was right, but he did not think Saylah would agree. She was talking madness. Perhaps she was still delirious. "Is that what you wanted?" he asked. "For us to let you die?"

It's time for you to learn. Promise me, Saylah. It's all I ask. That promise she had not kept. She did not know how. "You must think me a fool," she muttered.

Julian took her hand, steady now and strong again. Too strong. "Did you think less of me because I accepted your help when I couldn't bear my own grief?"

She stared at him, trying to make sense of the fear, the safety, the joy she sensed was just within her grasp. "No," she said. "It was my choice to give."

"Don't I have a right to make the same choice?" Julian demanded. "To love you and care for you as you've loved and cared for us?"

Saylah sighed. It would be a great relief, a blessing she had never thought to feel to give herself willingly into Julian's care. To give the responsibility to someone else for the first time in her life. She felt a stirring of something infinitely fragile, infinitely precious, but not yet fully formed. To let go of everything she had clung to for so long, though it weighed her down and caused her pain—could she do such a thing? Could she really be free? *When I return, I will come to you unburdened by the pieces of my past. I will come to you as myself.*

"Saylah! You're awake!" Theron launched himself at her from across the room and threw his arms around her neck, tangling himself hopelessly in the covers. "I waited and waited and prayed and prayed and *here you are!*"

Saylah laughed and held him close. "I am here and I am safe. You have done your job well."

She heard a sigh of relief and realized Flora had been holding her breath. "Well, 'tis glad I am to hear that," Flora said, setting the tray on the cedar chest. "And glad to see ye've chased the foolishness from your head. Eat now, 'twill make ye strong. Ye'll have to let go of her, Theron, or she'll have broth all over ye and the quilt and her one good nightgown. Besides, she's only just awake and needs time to catch her breath. Let's leave her in peace for a bit."

Surprisingly, the boy released her at once. "So long as you promise to be here when I come back."

Saylah smiled as deep affection welled in her, blocking her throat. "I promise."

When the boy nodded, satisfied, Saylah turned to Flora. "I wanted to thank you for—"

Flora brushed her gratitude away. "Ye'd have done the same for me. To know that is enough. Besides, it does my heart good to see ye comin' back to yerself. I'll take Theron and let ye rest."

The two had reached the stairs when Theron spun on his heel. "I always knew you'd come back. Always. I knew you wouldn't leave us."

"Aye," Flora added, eyes misty. "And 'tis glad we are that ye did. 'Twould no' be a home here without ye now." Before her tears spilled over, embarrassing everyone, she was gone, Theron in tow, chattering all the way down the stairs.

Saylah watched them for a long time, frightened of turning back to Julian, afraid of letting go, of admitting, at last, what her mother had always known. *You can never be simply Tanu, because Tanu is Queen.*

"I love you, Saylah," Julian murmured when she finally met his gaze. "I *want* to help you. Have you any idea how much it means to give back some of the gifts you've given me? It makes me happy. Can you understand that?''

What was it she had told Theron once? *You must learn always to take a gift that is offered, for it is unkind to refuse.* "I understand." She looked into his hazel eyes and traced the shape of his parted lips. "I have never learned to take.''

Julian's pulse raced at her feather-light touch, but he did not pull her close. There was more that they must say. "Then it's time you did. You have a rare and wonderful gift—the power to see and understand and heal. But you've made it a burden and a responsibility. Put it down for a little while, Saylah. It's time to rest.''

"When you have carried something so heavy for so long, it is not easy simply to toss it aside.''

He frowned and she added, "It does not mean I will not keep trying. I have survived much harder tests." But that was not really true. It was hardest of all to let go, to stop waiting and watching for pain that she must ease. Harder yet to admit that sometimes she would fail.

Julian swallowed and tried to speak calmly. "When are you going to learn that you can't heal the whole world? When are you going to understand it's not your responsibility? Look at yourself—we love you just as you are. Don't you have any idea how good you are, deep down? Jamie knew it, even Theron knows it. You're the only one who doesn't.''

I don't need a shaman who knows how to make miracles.

He took her hands. "I've seen inside you, remember? I've seen your sorrow and your need which you fight so hard to hide." When she trembled, he thought he understood. "That frightens you, doesn't it?''

"A little." *I have been so long alone, inside myself, where no one else can go.* But Julian would not hurt her, because she had also known his weakness and his joy and the pleasure of his body. Somehow she must find a way to tell him. *We must not doubt each other if we are to last.*

It came to her then that Tanu had not died after all, not in the Longhouse full of death or the missionary school or even on a small crescent of beach where the dream had come. She Who Is Blessed had lingered until this moment, when Saylah learned, finally and for always, how to set her free.

A mysterious lassitude invaded her body as Julian drew her into his arms. "Julian," she said softly, speaking words she had never spoken to another and would never speak again, "I need you." It had been so easy after all. Her head felt light, her body unrestrained and warm so close to his.

"I'm here," he whispered, stroking her hair, feeling the soft, fine texture of her cheek pressed to his. "I'm here.''

—— 548 ——

All I need—no, all I want, he had told her as they stood by the gray winter lake, with past and future an impenetrable meshwork barrier between them, *is that you be Saylah and that you love me.* But that was not all he wanted. It was not all he deserved. She reached up to touch his face with an unsteady hand. "I am Saylah," she said, "and I trust you."